ROCHESTER: THE COMPLETE WORKS

JOHN WILMOT, 2ND EARL OF ROCHESTER (1647–80) has been called one of the last Metaphysical poets and one of the first of the Augustans. Lyric poet, satirist, dramatist and a leading member of the 'merry gang' surrounding Charles II, he was born at Ditchley in Oxfordshire, succeeding his father when he was eleven. He was educated at Wadham College, Oxford, and on the Grand Tour of France and Italy (1661–64). At the age of eighteen he abducted the heiress Elizabeth Malet and, despite the resistance of her family and a delay of eighteen months during which Rochester fought in the naval wars against the Dutch, she married him. Subsequently his time was divided between periods of domesticity with Lady Elizabeth and his four children in Oxfordshire and fashionable life in London with, among other mistresses, the actress Elizabeth Barry, and his riotous male friends, who included the Duke of Buckingham, the Earl of Dorset and Sir Charles Sedley. The best of his poetry is satire: *Artemisa to Chloe* (a satire on love), *A Satyr against Mankind* and *An Allusion to Horace* (a satire on Dryden). He also wrote more frankly about sex than anyone in English before the twentieth century. Marvell admired him, Dryden, Swift and Pope were influenced by him and he continues to make an impression on poets today.

FRANK H. ELLIS is Mary Augusta Jordan Professor Emeritus at Smith College in Northampton, Massachusetts. His books include *Swift's Discourse* (1967), *Twentieth Century Interpretations of Robinson Crusoe* (1969), *Poems on Affairs of State, 1697–1714* (2 vols. 1970 and 1975), *Swift vs. Mainwaring* (1985) and *Sentimental Comedy: Theory and Practice* (1990).

1 John Wilmot, Second Earl of Rochester, a drawing by David Loggan

John Wilmot, Earl of Rochester

The Complete Works

EDITED BY FRANK H. ELLIS

PENGUIN BOOKS

PENGUIN BOOKS

Published by the Penguin Group
Penguin Books Ltd, 27 Wrights Lane, London W8 5TZ, England
Penguin Books USA Inc., 375 Hudson Street, New York, New York 10014, USA
Penguin Books Australia Ltd, Ringwood, Victoria, Australia
Penguin Books Canada Ltd, 10 Alcorn Avenue, Toronto, Ontario, Canada M4V 3B2
Penguin Books (NZ) Ltd, 182–190 Wairau Road, Auckland 10, New Zealand

Penguin Books Ltd, Registered Offices: Harmondsworth, Middlesex, England

First published 1994
10 9 8 7 6 5 4 3 2 1

Typeset by Datix International Limited, Bungay, Suffolk
Printed in England by Clays Ltd, St Ives plc

No Text hath any more than one determinate Sense, otherwise it could have no sense at all.

Robert Ferguson,
The Interest of Reason in Religion (1675), 308.

Contents

List of Illustrations xi
Introduction xiii
Table of Dates xviii
Further Reading xxii

To His Sacred Majesty 1
In Obitum Serenissimae Mariae Principis Arausionensis 1
To Her Sacred Majesty, the Queen Mother, on the Death of Mary, Princess of Orange 3
The Wish 4
['Twas a dispute 'twixt heaven and earth] 5
Two Fragments 5
To his Mistress 6
On Rome's Pardons 8
A Song (Insulting beauty, you misspend) 8
A Song (My dear mistress has a heart) 9
Song (While on those lovely looks I gaze) 9
Another Song in Imitation of Sir John Eaton's Songs (Too late, alas, I must confess) 10
Song (At last you'll force me to confess) 10
Woman's Honour 11
The Submission 11
Verses put into a Lady's Prayer-book 12
Rhyme to Lisbon 13
To Celia 13
Song (Give me leave to rail at you) 15
From Mistress Price, Maid of Honour to Her Majesty, who sent [Lord Chesterfield] a Pair of Italian Gloves 16
Under King Charles II's Picture 17
To his more than Meritorious Wife 17
Rochester Extempore 17

My Lord Rochester attempting to Kiss the Duchess of Cleveland as she was stepping out of her Chariot at Whitehall Gate, she threw him on his Back, and before he rose he spoke the following Lines 18
Impromptu on Louis XIV 18
Spoken Extempore to a Country Clerk after having heard him Sing Psalms 18
A Rodomontade on his Cruel Mistress 18
The Advice 19
The Platonic Lady 20
Song (As Cloris full of harmless thought) 21
Song to Cloris (Fair Cloris in a pigsty lay) 22
To Corinna 23
Song (Phillis, be gentler, I advise) 23
[Could I but make my wishes insolent] 24
Sab: lost 25
[Great mother of Aeneas and of Love] 25
[The gods by right of nature must possess] 26
To Love 26
The Imperfect Enjoyment 28
On King Charles 30
A Ramble in St James's Park 31
Satire 35
The Second Prologue at Court to *The Empress of Morocco* 36
Song (Love a woman? You're an ass) 37
Upon his Drinking a Bowl 38
Epigram 39
Seneca's *Troas*, Act 2. Chorus 39
Grecian Kindness 39
Signior Dildo 40
Tunbridge Wells 43
Artemisa to Chloe. A Letter from a Lady in the Town to a Lady in the Country concerning the Loves of the Town 49
Timon. A Satyr 56
Upon his Leaving his Mistress 61
A Pastoral Dialogue between Alexis and Strephon 62
A Dialogue between Strephon and Daphne 65
The Fall 68
The Mistress 68

A Song (Absent from thee I languish still) 70
A Song of a Young Lady. To her Ancient Lover 71
A Satyr against Mankind 72
Plain Dealing's Downfall 78
[What vain, unnecessary things are men!] 78
Consideratus, Considerandus 81
Scene i. Mr Dainty's Chamber 82
Mistress Knight's Advice to the Duchess of Cleveland in Distress for a Prick 83
[Out of mere love and arrant devotion] 83
Epilogue to *Love in the Dark*, as it was spoken by Mr Haines 85
The Maimed Debauchee 87
A Very Heroical Epistle from My Lord All-Pride to Doll-Common 89
To all Gentlemen, Ladies, and Others, whether of City, Town, or Country, Alexander Bendo wisheth all Health and Prosperity 91
An Allusion to Horace. *The 10th Satire of the 1st Book* 98
Dialogue 101
Valentinian. A Tragedy 102
A Song (Injurious charmer of my vanquished heart) 143
[Here's Monmouth the witty and Lauderdale the pretty] 184
A Scene of Sir Robert Howard's Play 184
Song (How happy, Cloris, were they free) 191
Song (How perfect, Cloris, and how free) 192
Song (Such perfect bliss, fair Cloris, we) 193
[Leave this gaudy, gilded stage] 194
Against Constancy 195
To the Postboy 195
On the Supposed Author of a Late Poem in Defence of Satire 196
[God bless our good and gracious King] 197
Love and Life 197
Upon Carey Fraser 198
The Epilogue to *Circe* 198
The Mock Song 199
On Mistress Willis 199
Song (By all love's soft yet mighty powers) 200
On Poet Ninny 200

Upon Nothing 201
My Lord All-Pride 204
The Earl of Rochester's Answer to a Paper of Verses sent him by L[ady] B[etty] Felton and taken out of the Translation of Ovid's *Epistles*, 1680 205
[To form a plot] 205
An Epistolary Essay from M.G. to O.B. upon their Mutual Poems 206

Abbreviations and Short Titles of Works Frequently Cited 209
Biographical Dictionary 225
Glossary 282
Notes 298
Index of Titles and First Lines 410
Index of Proper Names 415

Illustrations

1 John Wilmot, Second Earl of Rochester, a drawing by David Loggan. (Courtesy of the Trustees of the British Museum.) Frontispiece
2 Princess Mary of Orange, an engraving by William Faithorne from a portrait after Sir Anthony Van Dyck. (Courtesy of the Trustees of the British Museum.) page 2
3 Catherine of Bragança, the Queen Consort, an etching by Wenceslaus Hollar. (Courtesy of the Trustees of the British Museum.) page 14
4 A bird's-eye view of Tunbridge Wells by A. M. Broadley (Lewis Melville, *Society at Royal Tunbridge Wells* (1912), opp. p. 58). (Courtesy of the Trustees of the British Museum.) page 44
5 Elizabeth, Lady Cullen, as Venus (complete with doves), a portrait by Sir Peter Lely in a private collection. (Photograph courtesy of the National Portrait Gallery.) page 59
6 Shepherds conversing, an etching by François Boucher. (Courtesy of Christopher Mendez, 58 Jermyn Street, London.) page 63
7 Adam and Eve, a drawing by Michiel Coxie in black chalk. (Courtesy of the Trustees of the British Museum.) page 69
8 Thomas Lanfiere, *A Discription of Plain-dealing, Time, and Death* (1674–9). (B.L. 22.f.6(3); courtesy of the Trustees of the British Museum.) page 78
9 Lt. Col. John Churchill's hasty retreat, a detail from William Hogarth, *Marriage-à-la-Mode* (1745), Plate V. (Courtesy of the Trustees of the British Museum.) page 84
10 An English man-o'-war with guns firing, seen from St Catherine's Point, Fowey, Cornwall, a drawing by Willem Schellincks. (Photograph courtesy of The Walpole Society). page 88
11 Mountebank, an engraving by Pierce Tempest or John Savage after a drawing by Marcellus Laroon, in *The Cryes of the City of London*, 3rd edn (1689). (B.L. 97.h.7; courtesy of the Trustees of the British Museum.) page 92

12 *Much A-do about Nothing: A Song made of Nothing* [1660]. (Bodl. Wood 401, ff. 169–70; courtesy of the Bodleian Library.) page 202

13 Posture 15, an engraving by Marcantonio Raimondi after a drawing by Giulio Romano, reprinted in *I Modi*, ed. Lynne Lawner (1988), opp. p. 88. (Photograph courtesy of Northwestern University Press.) page 351

Introduction

The reader of Rochester today needs a lot of '*Negative Capability*', or willingness to sit down 'in uncertainties, mysteries, doubts, without any irritable reaching after fact and reason'.* Rochester is an ironist and irony makes a writer say more than he may be aware of saying. One of his contemporary readers complained that 'although [Rochester] does not say a single word of what he actually thinks, he compels you to believe every word he says' (Hamilton 1930, 235). And she may have been right, for Rochester is also an illusionist. 'He took pleasure to disguise himself . . . meerly for diversion, he would go about in odd shapes, in which he acted his part so naturally, that even those who were on the secret . . . could perceive nothing by which he might be discovered' (Burnet 1680, 27–8). So except in his letters and in his *causeries* with Burnet, 'fact and reason' may be in short supply, but Rochester's literary remains, collected in the present edition, deserve to be read as free-standing works of art, not as autobiography. 'Not . . . *a single word* of what he actually thinks' is an obvious exaggeration, but Rochester's verse does not take us very far into the 'mysteries' of his psyche.

Rochester's verse also deserves to be heard. Alliteration, assonance, functional dissonance, comic rhyme, obviously delight him and the sound component of his verse will delight any reader attending to it. Rochester's verse will also reward a microscopic reading. When I finally figured out how to scan ''cause 'tis the very WORST thing they can do' (49.29),† or when I finally got the point of the stanzas' tumescence in *A Song of a Young Lady. To her Ancient Lover* (71–2), or when the full glory of Charles Stuart's foreign policy: 'Peace is his aim' (30.8) – dramatized by one of Charles's casual mistresses playing the part of Peace in a court performance of

* John Keats, *Letters*, ed. Maurice Buxton Forman (1935), 72.

†Two sets of figures, in parentheses, separated by a point, represent page and line numbers in this edition; one set represents page numbers only.

John Crowne's *Calisto* – finally burst upon me, I could almost feel Rochester's hand reaching down from heaven and patting the monkey on the head. 'There is nothing as good as Rochester, even when he is not writing lyrics, until . . .? (Let the student determine when)' (Pound 1934, 145).

Rochester himself was not a closet Puritan, as some of his biographers have made out. He was an atheist; he tried to 'fortifie his Mind . . . by dispossessing it all he could of the belief or apprehensions of Religion' (Burnet 1680, 15). And he was an equally uncompromising hedonist: 'No glory's vain which does from pleasure spring' (111.338). He celebrated pleasure, by which he meant 'the free use of Wine and Women' (Burnet 1680, 38–9). He not only practised debauchery, he advocated debauchery, 'framing Arguments for Sin, making Proselytes to it, and writing Panegyricks upon Vice' (Parsons 1680, 9). Some readers may come away with the feeling that Rochester has gone far beyond decorum, even beyond cynicism, into a frightening vision of things exactly as they are. ''Tis your choice', he warns, 'whether you'll read or no' (207.34).

CANON The canon of Rochester's work cannot be definitively established today. Not even the ten works preserved in Nottingham MS. Portland PwV 31, ff. 1–11, in his own hand can be attributed to Rochester with absolute certainty. John Oldham copied into his commonplace book (Bodl. MS. Rawl. Poet. 123, p. 116) Rochester's 'Artemisa to Chloe', but Oldham did not write it. The attribution to Rochester is certain because it is attributed to him in two independent textual traditions (345). The inferred attribution of the ten works in Rochester's hand is not *confirmed by external evidence*. On this criterion only forty-two of the ninety-five works in the present edition can be attributed to Rochester with certainty. In my opinion all the works in this edition are Rochester's; the *dubia* have been excluded. But opinion is not evidence.

If it is true that he left instructions to '*burn all his profane and lewd Writings*' upon his death (Parsons 1680, 28), the ninety-five works in this edition can be only a fraction of what Rochester wrote during his lifetime. He is said on good authority to have been 'prolific of catches, with [Goditha Price's] name as the burden and her conduct as the subject' (Hamilton 1930, 220), but not a single catch survives.

TEXT What is presented here is a clear-text edition – 'pages of text entirely free of editorial apparatus' (Tanselle 1987, 27) – of ninety-one of Rochester's panegyrics, translations, epigrams, songs, and satires, plus a tragedy in verse, one scene of another tragedy in verse, a fragment of prose comedy, and a mock-mountebank's bill in prose. The copy-texts for all these have been chosen according to principles elaborated by W. W. Greg and Fredson Bowers and magisterially summarized in Tanselle 1987. Substantive emendation of the copy-text and the source of the emendations are recorded in the textual apparatus. The accidentals of the copy-text (spelling, punctuation, type font, etc.) have been silently modernized.

Tanselle is very hard on modernizing accidentals, calling it unscholarly and insulting to the reader. But he also concedes that 'Modernized texts . . . are attempts at elucidation', and this is a point that I should like very briefly to elaborate, even though Tanselle opines that 'Arguments for modernizing are always doomed to failure' (Tanselle 1987, 134, 134n.). But Rochester is a very special case. The pointing of the ten works that survive in his hand is very light. Several of the poems, including 'Leave this gaudy, gilded stage' (194), have no punctuation at all. But this is not surprising, since Rochester was not thinking of publication when he made those copies. There is no evidence that Rochester intended to publish anything. But twenty-three of his poems, through manuscript copies circulated from hand to hand, found their way into print, by accident as it were, during his lifetime.

Only two of the ten works in Rochester's hand were published during his lifetime. For an old-spelling text, the accidentals of the remaining eight works would have to be inferred from Rochester's practice. But for the other eighty-five works in this edition, an old-spelling text could only reproduce the house style of dozens of print shops from the piratical press that produced the 'Antwerp' edition (Rochester 1680) to the elegant Nonesuch Press edition (Rochester 1926). None of these, of course, represents Rochester's intentions and none of them is likely to recommend itself to readers today. Here are two samples from the 'Antwerp' edition:

> Head long, I'm hurl'd, like *Horse-men*, who in vain,
>
> Small Bear, becomes our drink, and Wine, our Meat.
>
> (Rochester 1680, 31, 108)

'The comma', it is said, 'offers the most difficulty' (*Webster's Third International Dictionary* (1986), 46a).

It is obvious that the modernized text:

> Headlong I'm hurled like horsemen who in vain (27.33)
>
> Small beer becomes our drink and wine our meat (58.90)

is closer to Rochester's practice. Old-spelling texts, marking rhetorical and elocutionary pauses, conceal one of the most remarkable features of Rochester's verse, its surging, tumbling, run-on cadence and syntax. Modernized punctuation, in passage after passage, uncovers meaning that is covered up by the accidentals of the copy-text. In the 1685 copy-text of *Valentinian*, Chylax's speech at II ii 20–31, recording the reaction of a professional pimp when confronted by Lucina's chastity, appears as follows:

> CHYLAX I confess it freely
> I never saw her Fellow, nor ever shall:
> For all our *Graecian* Dames as I have try'd
> And sure I have try'd a hundred – if I say Two
> I speak within my Compass: All these beauties
> And all the Constancy of all these Faces,
> Maids, Widdows, Wives, of what Degree or Calling
> So they be Greeks and fat: for there's my Cunning
> I would undertake, and not sweat for't: *Proculus*,
> Were they to try again, say twice as many
> Under a Thousand pound to lay them flat:
> But this Wench staggers me.
>
> (*Valentinian* (1685), 15)

'Let the student determine' whether the 'attempt at elucidation' in the modernized text (121.20–31) is successful.

In preparing this edition I have followed the example of 'the great and learned *Hafen Slawkenbergius* . . . collating, collecting and compiling, – begging, borrowing, and stealing, as he went along' (Sterne 1940, 225, 232). An undertaking of this kind, as I have said before, becomes almost a group activity (*POAS*, Yale, VII vii), and it is a pleasure at last to be able to name those from whom I have begged, borrowed, and stolen.

My first obligation is to the editors of *The Oxford English Dictionary* from James A. H. Murray to R. W. Burchfield. It is impossible to read Rochester microscopically without the second edition of the *OED*. Almost all the definitions in the Glossary below are from this work.

My second obligation is to the distinguished scholars and editors who have preceded me in the field of Rochester studies, particularly David M. Vieth, Jeremy Treglown, and Keith Walker, who are cited below on more occasions than I care to count.

Others who have helped in ways too various to mention are John Bidwell, John Burgass, Evelyn B. Cannon, Blanche Cooney, Teodoro Gelabert, John G. Graiff, Sara S. Hodson, Steven C. Jones, Alan Jutzi, John J. Morrison, Paul W. Nash, Stephen Parks, Douglas L. Patey, Philip K. Peake, Elizabeth P. Richardson, Bruce Sajdak, Harold Skulsky, and Emily C. Walhout, each of whom I can at last thank publicly. That Reginald Williams's name does not appear on the title page as Art Editor is an effect only of his own modesty.

Christopher Ricks, General Editor of the Penguin English Poets series, and Maximillian E. Novak, co-editor of the California Dryden, have most generously read the entire book in typescript. Although they have provided invaluable new insights and corrections of recalcitrant old errors, the remaining clinkers are all my own. If readers would point these out to me, I should be much obliged.

F.H.E.

Smith College
Northampton MA 01063
USA

Table of Dates

10 April 1647	John Wilmot born in his mother's house at Ditchley, Oxfordshire, the son of Henry Wilmot, Baron Wilmot of Adderley, Oxfordshire (created Earl of Rochester in December 1652 at St Germain), and Anne St John, daughter of Sir John St John, great-great-grandfather of Henry St John, Viscount Bolingbroke.
February 1658	Succeeds as 2nd Earl of Rochester upon his father's death in Ghent.
January 1660–September 1661	Attends Wadham College, Oxford, graduating M.A.
February 1661	Awarded a pension of £500 a year by Charles II.
1661–4	Travels on the Continent with a tutor appointed by Charles II, Dr Andrew Balfour, a distinguished botanist.
1 October 1664	Sighted in Venice.
26 October 1664	Signs guest-book at the University of Padua.
25 December 1664	Received by Charles II at Whitehall bearing a letter from Charles's sister, Henrietta Anne, Duchess of Orléans.
26 May 1665	Fails to abduct Elizabeth Malet, the 'melancholy heiress' who wrote verse; imprisoned in the Tower for three weeks.
July 1665–6	Volunteers for active sea duty in the second Dutch War; distinguishes himself at Solebay (September 1665) and in St James's Fight (July 1666).
21 March 1666	Appointed gentleman of the bedchamber to Charles II with a pension of £1,000 a year for life and lodgings in Whitehall Palace.

July 1666	Commissioned captain of horse (Dalton 1960, I 76).
29 January 1667	Marries Elizabeth Malet, who is appointed groom of the stole to Anne Hyde, Duchess of York, and occupies Adderbury, the Wilmot estate near Banbury, Oxfordshire.
29 July 1667	Summoned to Parliament by royal writ, although a minor.
28 February 1668	Appointed gamekeeper for Oxfordshire (*CSPD 1667–1668*, 253, 343).
16 February 1669	Boxes Thomas Killigrew's ears in the King's presence; pardoned (Pepys, 17 February 1669).
March 1669	Goes to Paris with a letter from Charles II to Henrietta Anne, Duchess of Orléans; remains in Paris until July 1669.
30 April 1669	First child, Anne Wilmot, baptized.
22 November 1669	Forced by illness to decline a duel with John Sheffield, Earl of Mulgrave.
January 1671	Charles Wilmot baptized.
27 May–13 July 1671	Meets John Dryden at Windsor, reads and amends *Marriage à la Mode* (produced December 1671), accepts Dryden's dedication of the published play in June 1673.
30 October 1672	Appointed deputy lieutenant of Somerset (*CSPD 1672*, 101).
1673	Trains Elizabeth Barry, 'unquestionably the most important actress of her time' (Downes 1987, 116), for the stage.
13 July 1674	Elizabeth Wilmot baptized.
4 January 1675	Charles II approves construction of 'a small building in his Majesties Privie Garden [i.e. between the Stone Gallery and the Privy Garden] for the Right honorable the Earl of Rochester' (*Survey of London*, XIII 87–8).
24 January 1675	Appointed master, surveyor, and keeper of the King's hawks (*CTB 1672–1675*, 655, 688).
February 1675	Produces John Crowne's *Calisto; or, The Chaste Nymph* at court.

27 February 1675	Appointed Ranger of Woodstock Park, Oxfordshire, and in May 1675 occupies the High Lodge (*CSPD 1673–1675*, 182, 238).
25 June 1675	Smashes the King's pyramidal chronometer in the Privy Garden.
Autumn 1675–Spring 1676	Living at Adderbury.
January 1676	Malet Wilmot baptized.
February 1676	Serious illness; reported dead and buried.
March 1676	George Etherege's *The Man of Mode, or Sir Fopling Flutter* (in which Thomas Betterton created the role of Dorimant and Elizabeth Barry the role of Mrs Loveit) opens at Dorset Garden.
June 1676	Goes into hiding after a brawl at Epsom, in the London suburbs.
late 1676(?)	Banished from court.
13 April 1677	Petitions Charles II for grants of various estates in Ireland (*CSPD 1677–1678*, 89).
August 1677	Charles II and the Duke of Buckingham 'very merry one night at Lord Rochester's lodgings' in Whitehall (HMC *Seventh Report*, 469).
October 1677	Duke of Buckingham visits Rochester at the High Lodge in Woodstock Park.
November 1677	Elected alderman of Taunton, Somerset, near his wife's estate at Enmore.
December 1677	Elizabeth Clerke, Rochester's daughter by Elizabeth Barry, born; she is left £40 a year in Rochester's will (*Wills from Doctors' Commons* (1863), 140).
early 1678	'very ill and very penitent' (HMC *Seventh Report*, 470).
October 1679	Conversations with Gilbert Burnet begin.
March 1680	Accepts a challenge from Edward Seymour, privy councillor and late speaker of the House of Commons, who fails to appear on the appointed ground (HMC *Hastings MSS.*, II 390–91).

June 1680	Reconciliation with the Church of England (?).
26 July 1680	Dies at High Lodge, Woodstock Park.
1680	Aphra Behn's 'On the Death of the late Earl of Rochester' circulates in manuscript; published in *Poems on Several Occasions*, 1685.
November 1680	£5 reward offered for discovering the printer of the unauthorized Rochester in 1680, allegedly 'Printed in Antwerp' (*London Gazette*, 22–25 November 1680).
1681	John Oldham publishes 'Bion, A Pastoral, in Imitation of the Greek of Moschus, bewailing the Death of the Earl of Rochester' in *Some New Pieces Never before Published*.
c. December 1682	Nathaniel Lee's *The Princess of Cleves* opens at Dorset Garden, in which Rochester is elegized as Count Rosidore: 'He was the Spirit of Wit – and had such an art in guilding his Failures, that it was hard not to love his faults' (Lee 1954–5, II 162).
11 February 1684	*Valentinian: A Tragedy* produced at court.

Further Reading

Editions

Rochester's Poems on Several Occasions, ed. James Thorpe, Princeton, 1950. A facsimile edition of the Huntington Library copy of Rochester 1680.

Valentinian: A Tragedy. As 'tis Alter'd by the late Earl of Rochester, and Acted at the Theatre-Royal, London, 1685.

Poems, &c. on Several Occasions: with Valentinian a Tragedy written by the Right Honourable John Late Earl of Rochester [ed. Thomas Rymer], London, 1691.

Remains of the Right Honourable John, Earl of Rochester, London, 1718.

Collected Works of John Wilmot Earl of Rochester, ed. John Hayward, London, 1926.

Poems by John Wilmot Earl of Rochester, ed. Vivian de S. Pinto, London, 1953, rev. ed. 1964.

The Gyldenstolpe Manuscript Miscellany of Poems by John Wilmot, Earl of Rochester, and other Restoration Authors, ed. Bror Danielsson and David M. Vieth, Stockholm, 1967.

The Complete Poems of John Wilmot, Earl of Rochester, ed. David M. Vieth, New Haven and London, 1968.

John Wilmot, Earl of Rochester Selected Poems, ed. Paul Hammond, Bristol, 1980.

The Poems of John Wilmot, Earl of Rochester, ed. Keith Walker, Oxford, 1984.

Rochester Complete Poems and Plays, ed. Paddy Lyons, London, 1993.

Bibliography

Johannes Prinz, *John Wilmot Earl of Rochester His Life and Writings*, Leipzig, 1927.

Curt A. Zimansky, in *The New Cambridge Bibliography of English Literature*, ed. George Watson, Cambridge, 1971, II 463–4.

David M. Vieth, *Rochester Studies, 1925–1982*, New York and London, 1984.

George Wasserman, *Samuel Butler and the Earl of Rochester. A Reference Guide*, Boston, 1986.

Biography

Robert Parsons, *A Sermon Preached at the Funeral of the Rt Honorable John Earl of Rochester*, Oxford, 1680.

Gilbert Burnet, *Some Passages of the Life and Death of the Right Honourable John Earl of Rochester*, London, 1680.

Vivian de S. Pinto, *Rochester: Portrait of a Restoration Poet*, London, 1935, rptd. as *Enthusiast in Wit. A Portrait of John Wilmot Earl of Rochester 1647–1680*, Lincoln, Nebraska, 1962. The standard biography.

Graham Greene, *Lord Rochester's Monkey*, New York, 1974. Written in 1930 and published without substantial revision.

Jeremy Lamb, *So Idle a Rogue: the Life and Death of Lord Rochester*, London, 1993.

Commentary

David M. Vieth, *Attribution in Restoration Poetry. A Study of Rochester's Poems of 1680*, New Haven and London, 1963.

Anne Righter (later Barton), 'John Wilmot, Earl of Rochester', Chatterton Lecture, *Proceedings of the British Academy* 53 (1968), 47–69.

Rochester. The Critical Heritage, ed. David Farley-Hills, New York, 1972.

Dustin H. Griffin, *Satires against Man. The Poems of Rochester*, Berkeley, Los Angeles, London, 1973.

David Farley-Hills, *Rochester's Poetry*, Totowa, New Jersey, 1978.

Spirit of Wit. Reconsiderations of Rochester, ed. Jeremy Treglown, Hamden, Connecticut, 1982.

John Wilmot, Earl of Rochester: Critical Essays, ed. David M. Vieth, New York, 1988.

Marianne Thormählen, *Rochester: The Poems in Context*, Cambridge, 1993.

To His Sacred Majesty

Virtue's triumphant shrine, who dost engage
At once three kingdoms in a pilgrimage,
Which in ecstatic duty strive to come
Out of themselves as well as from their home,
5 Whilst England grows one camp and London is
Itself the nation, not metropolis,
And loyal Kent renews her arts again,
Fencing her ways with moving groves of men,
Forgive this distant homage, which doth meet
10 Your blest approach on sedentary feet.
And though my youth, not patient yet to bear
The weight of arms, denies me to appear
In steel before you, yet, Great Sir, approve
My manly wishes and more vigourous love
15 In whom a cold respect were treason to
A father's ashes, greater than to you;
Whose one ambition 'tis for to be known
By daring loyalty your Wilmot's son.

In Obitum Serenissimae Mariae Principis Arausionensis

Impia blasphemi sileant convitia vulgi:
Absolvo medicos, innocuamque manum.
Curassent alios facili medicamine morbos:
Ulcera cum veniunt, Ars nihil ipsa valet.
5 Vultu foemineo quaevis vel pustula vulnus
Lethale est; pulchras certior ense necat.
Mollia vel temeret si quando mitior ora,
Evadat forsan foemina, Diva nequit.
Cui par est animae Corpus, quae tota venustas,
10 Formae qui potis est haec superesse suae?

(Let the impious carpings of the blasphemous mob be silent: I acquit the physicians and their harmless intervention. They could have cured other diseases with easy remedies; when pustules break out, Science herself is of no avail. Any pimple on

2 Princess Mary of Orange, an engraving by William Faithorne from a portrait after Sir Anthony Van Dyck.

a woman's face is a mortal wound, slays the fair one more surely than a sword. Once even a minor blemish sullies her delicate face, perhaps a woman may escape, a goddess cannot. A being whose body matches her soul, she who is all loveliness, how can she survive her own beauty? – *translated by Harold Skulsky*.)

To Her Sacred Majesty, the Queen Mother, on the Death of Mary, Princess of Orange

Respite, great Queen, your just and hasty fears,
There's no infection lodges in our tears.
Though our unhappy air be armed with death,
Yet sighs have an untainted, guiltless breath.
5 Oh, stay awhile and teach your equal skill
To understand and to support our ill.
You that in mighty wrongs an age have spent,
And seem to have outlived ev'n banishment,
Whom traitorous mischief sought its earliest prey,
10 When unto sacred blood it made its way
And thereby did its black design impart
To take his head, that wounded first his heart;
You that unmoved great Charles his ruin stood,
When that three nations sunk beneath the load;
15 Then a young daughter lost, yet balsam found
To stanch that new and freshly bleeding wound,
And after this with fixed and steady eyes
Beheld your noble Gloucester's obsequies,
And then sustained the royal princess' fall;
20 You only can lament her funeral.
But you will hence remove and leave behind
Our sad complaints lost in the empty wind,
Those winds that bid you stay and loudly roar
Destruction and drive back unto the shore,
25 Shipwreck to safety and the envy fly
Of sharing in this scene of tragedy,
Whilst sickness, from whose rage you post away,
Relents and only now contrives your stay.

The lately fatal and infectious ill
30 Courts the fair princess and forgets to kill.
In vain on fevers curses we dispense
And vent our passions' angry eloquence.
In vain we blast the ministers of fate
And the forlorn physicians imprecate,
35 Say they to death new poisons add and fire,
Murder securely for reward and hire,
Art's basilisks, that kill whome'er they see,
And truly write bills of mortality,
Who, lest the bleeding corpse should them betray,
40 First drain those vital speaking streams away.
And will you by your flight take part with these,
Become yourself a third and new disease?
If they have caused our loss, then so have you,
Who take yourself and the fair princess too.
45 For we, deprived, an equal damage have
When France doth ravish hence as when the grave,
But that your choice th'unkindness doth improve
And dereliction adds unto remove.

The Wish

Oh, that I could by any chemic art
To sperm convert my spirit and my heart,
That at one thrust I might my soul translate
And in the womb myself regenerate!
5 There steeped in lust nine months I would remain,
Then boldly fuck my passage back again.

[*’Twas a dispute ’twixt heaven and earth*]

’Twas a dispute ’twixt heaven and earth
Which had produced the nobler birth.
For heaven appeared Cynthia with all her train,
Till you came forth
5 More glorious and more worth
Than she with all those trembling imps of light
With which this envious queen of night
Had proudly decked her conquered self in vain.

I must have perished in that first surprise
10 Had I beheld your eyes.
Love, like Apollo when he would inspire
Some holy breast, laid all his glories by:
Else the god, clothed in his heavenly fire,
Would have possessed too pow’rfully
15 And making of his priest a sacrifice
Had so returned unhallowed to the skies.

Two Fragments

Custom does often reason overrule
And only serves for reason to the fool.

Wit like tierce claret, when’t begins to pall,
Neglected lies and’s of no use at all,
But in its full perfection of decay
Turns vinegar and comes again in play.

To his Mistress

I

Why dost thou shade thy lovely face? Oh, why
Does that eclipsing hand of thine deny
The sunshine of the sun's enlivening eye?

II

Without thy light, what light remains in me?
5 Thou art my life, my way; my light's in thee;
I live, I move, and by thy beams I see.

III

Thou art my life; if thou but turn away,
My life's a thousand deaths; thou art my way;
Without thee, love, I travel not but stray.

IV

10 My light thou art; without thy glorious sight
My eyes are darkened with eternal night.
My love, thou art my way, my life, my sight.

V

Thou art my way; I wander if thou fly;
Thou art my light; if hid, how blind am I.
15 Thou art my Life; if thou withdraw'st, I die.

VI

My eyes are dark and blind, I cannot see;
To whom or whither should my darkness flee
But to that light? And who's that light but thee?

VII

If that be all, shine forth and draw thee nigher;
20 Let me be bold and die for my desire:
A phoenix likes to perish in the fire.

VIII

If my puffed light be out, give leave to tine
My flameless snuff at the bright lamp of thine;
Ah! What's thy light the less for lighting mine?

IX

25 If I have lost my path, dear lover, say,
Shall I still wander in a doubtful way?
Love, shall a lamb of Israel's sheepfold stray?

X

My path is lost; my wandering step does stray;
I cannot go nor safely stay;
30 Whom should I seek but thee, my path, my way?

XI

And yet thou turn'st thy face away and fliest me,
And yet I sue for grace, and thou deniest me;
Speak, art thou angry, love, or triest me?

XII

Display those heavenly lamps or tell me why
35 Thou shad'st thy face; perhaps no eye
Can view their flames and not drop down and die.

XIII

Thou art the pilgrim's path and blind man's eye,
The dead man's life; on thee my hopes rely;
If I but them remove, I err, I die.

XIV

40 Dissolve thy sunbeams; close thy wings and stay;
See, see how I am blind and dead and stray;
Oh, thou that art my life, my light, my way.

XV

Then work thy will; if passion bid me flee,
My reason shall obey; my wings shall be
45 Stretched out no further than from me to thee.

On Rome's Pardons

If Rome can pardon sins, as Romans hold,
And if those pardons can be bought and sold,
It were no sin t'adore and worship gold.

If they can purchase pardons with a sum
5 For sins they may commit in time to come
And for sins past, 'tis very well for Rome.

At this rate they are happiest that have most;
They'll purchase heaven at their own proper cost.
Alas! the poor! All that are so are lost.

10 Whence came this knack, or when did it begin?
What author have they, or who brought it in?
Did Christ e'er keep a custom-house for sin?

Some subtle Jesuit without more ado
Did certainly this sly invention brew
15 To gull 'em of their souls and money too.

A Song

Insulting beauty, you misspend
  Those frowns upon your slave;
Your scorn against such rebels bend
Who dare with confidence pretend
5 That other eyes their hearts defend
  From all the charms you have.

Your conquering eyes so partial are,
  Or mankind is so dull,
That while I languish in despair,
10 Many proud, senseless hearts declare
They find you not so killing fair
  To wish you merciful.

They an inglorious freedom boast;
I triumph in my chain;
15 Nor am I unrevenged, though lost,
Nor you unpunished, though unjust,
When I alone, who love you most,
Am killed with your disdain.

A Song

My dear mistress has a heart
Soft as those kind looks she gave me,
When with Love's resistless art
And her eyes she did enslave me.
5 But her constancy's so weak,
She's so wild and apt to wander,
That my jealous heart would break,
Should we live one day asunder.

Melting joys about her move,
10 Killing pleasures, wounding blisses.
She can dress her eyes in love,
And her lips can arm with kisses.
Angels listen when she speaks,
She's my delight, all mankind's wonder;
15 But my jealous heart would break,
Should we live one day asunder.

Song

While on those lovely looks I gaze,
You see a wretch pursuing
In raptures of a sweet amaze
A pleasing, happy ruin.

5 'Tis not for pity that I move,
His fate is too aspiring
Whose heart broke with a load of love
Dies wishing and admiring.

But if this murder you'd forgo,
10 Your slave from death removing,
Let me your art of charming know,
Or learn you mine of loving.
Thus whether life or death betide,
In love 'tis equal measure:
15 The victor lives with empty pride,
The vanquished dies with pleasure.

Another Song in Imitation of Sir John Eaton's Songs

Too late, alas, I must confess
You need no arts to move me:
Such charms by nature you possess,
'Twere madness not to love you.

5 Then spare a heart you may surprise
And give my tongue the glory
To boast, though my unfaithful eyes
Betray a kinder story.

Song

At last you'll force me to confess
You need no arts to vanquish:
Such charms from nature you possess,
'Twere dullness not to languish.

5 Yet spare a heart you may surprise
And give my tongue the glory
To scorn, while my unfaithful eyes
Betray a kinder story.

Woman's Honour

Love bade me hope, and I obeyed;
Phillis continued still unkind.
'Then you may ev'n despair,' he said,
'In vain I strive to change her mind.

5 'Honour's got in and keeps her heart;
Durst he but venture once abroad,
In my own right I'd take your part
And show myself the mightier god.

'This huffing Honour domineers
10 In breasts alone where he has place,
But if true gen'rous Love appears,
The hector dares not show his face.'

Let me still languish and complain,
Be most unhumanly denied.
15 I have some pleasure in my pain;
She can have none with all her pride.

I fall a sacrifice to Love,
She lives a wretch for Honour's sake:
Whose tyrant does most cruel prove,
20 The diff'rence is not hard to make.

Consider real honour then,
You'll find hers cannot be the same:
'Tis noble confidence in men,
In women, mean distrustful shame.

The Submission

To this moment a rebel I throw down my arms,
Great Love, at first sight of Olinda's bright charms.
Made proud and secure by such forces as these,
You may now play the tyrant as soon as you please.

5 When innocence, beauty, and wit do conspire
To betray and engage and inflame my desire,
Why should I decline what I cannot avoid
And let pleasing hope by base fear be destroyed?

Her innocence cannot contrive to undo me,
10 Her beauty's inclined, or why should it pursue me?
And wit has to pleasure been ever a friend,
Then what room for despair, since delight is love's end?

There can be no danger in sweetness and youth,
Where love is secured by good nature and truth.
15 On her beauty I'll gaze and of pleasure complain,
While every kind look adds a link to my chain.

'Tis more to maintain than it was to surprise,
But her wit leads in triumph the slave of her eyes.
I beheld with the loss of my freedom before,
20 But hearing, forever must serve and adore.

Too bright is my goddess, her temple too weak.
Retire, divine image, I feel my heart break.
Help, Love! I dissolve in a rapture of charms
At the thought of those joys I should meet in her arms.

Verses put into a Lady's Prayer-book

Fling this useless book away
And presume no more to pray;
Heaven is just and can bestow
Mercy on none but those that mercy show.
5 With a proud heart maliciously inclined
Not to increase, but to subdue mankind,
In vain you vex the gods with your petition;
Without repentance and sincere contrition
You're in a reprobate condition.
10 Phillis, to calm the angry powers
And save my soul as well as yours,

Relieve poor mortals from despair
And justify the gods that made you fair;
And in those bright and charming eyes
15 Let pity first appear, then love,
That we by easy steps may rise
Through all the joys on earth to those above.

Rhyme to Lisbon

(14)

Here's a health to Kate, our sovereign's mate,
Of the royal house of Lisbon,
But the Devil take Hyde and the bishop beside,
That made her bone of his bone.

To Celia

Celia, the faithful servant you disown
Would in obedience keep his love unknown,
But bright ideas such as you inspire
We can no more conceal than not admire.
5 My heart at home in my own breast did dwell
Like humble hermit in a peaceful cell,
Unknown and undisturbed it rested there,
Stranger alike to hope and to despair,
But Love's tumultuous train does now invade
10 The sacred quiet of this hallowed shade;
His fatal flames shine out to every eye
Like blazing comets in a winter's sky.
Fair and severe like heaven you enjoin
Commands that seem cross to your own design,
15 Forbidding what yourself inclines us to.
Since if from heavenly powers you will allow
That all our faculties proceed, 'tis plain
Whate'er we will is what the gods ordain;

3 Catherine of Bragança, the Queen Consort, an etching by Wenceslaus Hollar

But they and you rights without limit have
20 Over your creatures and (more yours) your slave.
And I am one, born only to admire,
Too humble e'er to hope, scarce to desire,
A thing whose bliss depends upon your will,
Who would be proud you'd deign to use him ill.
25 How can my passion merit your offence
That challenges so little recompence?
Let me but ever love and ever be
The example of your power and cruelty.
Since so much scorn does in your breast reside,
30 Be more indulgent to its mother, pride.
Kill all you strike and trample on their graves,
But own the fates of your neglected slaves:
When in the crowd yours undistinguished lies,
You give away the triumph of your eyes.
35 Permit me then to glory in my chains,
My fruitless sighs, and my unpitied pains.
Perhaps obtaining this you'll think I find
More mercy than your anger has designed.
But Love has carefully contrived for me
40 The last perfection of misery,
For to my state those hopes of common peace
Which death affords to every wretch, must cease;
My worst of fates attends me in my grave,
Since, dying, I must be no more your slave.

Song

Give me leave to rail at you,
I ask nothing but my due,
To call you false and then to say
You shall not keep my heart a day.
5 But alas, against my will
I must be your captive still.
Ah! be kinder then, for I
Cannot change and would not die.

Kindness has resistless charms,
10 All things else but weakly move,
Fiercest anger it disarms
And clips the wings of flying Love.
Beauty does the heart invade,
Kindness only can persuade;
15 It gilds the lover's servile chain
And makes the slave grow pleased again.

From Mistress Price, Maid of Honour to Her Majesty, who sent [*Lord Chesterfield*] *a Pair of Italian Gloves*

My Lord,
These are the gloves that I did mention
Last night, and 'twas with the intention
That you should give me thanks and wear them,
For I most willingly can spare them.
5 When you this packet first do see,
'Damn me,' cry you, 'she has writ to me;
I had better be at Bretby still
Than troubled with love against my will;
Besides, this is not all my sorrow:
10 She writ today, she'll come tomorrow.'
Then you consider the adventure
And think you never shall content her.
But when you do the inside see,
You'll find things are but as they should be,
15 And that 'tis neither love nor passion,
But only for your recreation.

Under King Charles II's Picture

I, John Roberts, writ this same,
I pasted it and plastered it and put it in a frame
In honour of my master's master, King Charles the Second by
name.

To his more than Meritorious Wife

I am by fate slave to your will
And shall be most obedient still;
To show my love I will compose ye
For your fair finger's ring a posy,
5 In which shall be expressed my duty,
And how I'll be forever true t'ye;
With low-made legs and sugared speeches,
Yielding to your fair bum the breeches,
I'll show myself, in all I can,
Your faithful, humble servant,

10 Jan.

Rochester Extempore

And after singing Psalm the 12th
He laid his book upon the shelf.
And looked much simply like himself;
With eyes turned up, as white as ghost,
5 He cried, 'Ah Lard, ah Lard of Hosts!
I am a rascal, that thou know'st.'

My Lord Rochester attempting to Kiss the Duchess of Cleveland as she was stepping out of her Chariot at Whitehall Gate, she threw him on his Back, and before he rose he spoke the following Lines

By Heavens, 'twas bravely done,
First to attempt the chariot of the sun
And then to fall like Phaeton.

Impromptu on Louis XIV

Lorraine you stole; by fraud you got Burgundy;
Flanders you bought; but, Gad! you'll pay for't one day.

Spoken Extempore to a Country Clerk after having heard him Sing Psalms

Sternhold and Hopkins had great qualms
When they translated David's psalms,
  To make the heart full glad,
But had it been poor David's fate
5 To hear thee sing, and them translate,
  By God! 'twould have made him mad.

A Rodomontade on his Cruel Mistress

Seek not to know a woman, for she's worse
Than all ingredients crammed into a curse.
Were she but ugly, peevish, proud, a whore,
Perjured or painted, so she were no more,

5 I could forgive her and connive at this,
Alleging still she but a woman is:
But she is worse and may in time forestall
The Devil and be the damning of us all.

The Advice

All things submit themselves to your command,
Fair Celia, when it does not Love withstand;
The power it borrows from your eyes alone,
All but the god must yield to, who has none;
5 Were he not blind, such are the charms you have,
He'd quit his godhead to become your slave,
Be proud to act a mortal hero's part
And throw himself for fame on his own dart.
But fate hath otherwise disposed of things,
10 In different bonds subjecting slaves and kings:
Fettered in forms of royal state are they,
While we enjoy the freedom to obey.
That fate (like you resistless) does ordain
That Love alone should over beauty reign.
15 By harmony the universe does move:
And what is harmony but mutual love?
See gentle brooks, how quietly they glide,
Kissing the rugged banks on either side,
Whilst in their crystal stream at once they show
20 And with them feed the flowers which they bestow;
Though rudely thronged by a too near embrace,
In gentle murmurs they keep on their pace
To their loved sea, for ev'n streams have desires;
Cool as they are, they feel love's powerful fires,
25 And with such passion that if any force
Stop or molest them in their am'rous course,
They swell with rage, break down and ravage o'er
The banks they kissed, the flowers they fed before.
Who would resist an empire so divine
30 Which universal nature does enjoin?

Submit then, Celia, ere you be reduced,
For rebels vanquished once are vilely used.
And such are you, whene'er you dare obey
Another passion and your love betray.
35 You are Love's citadel, by you he reigns
And his proud empire o'er the world maintains;
He trusts you with his stratagems and arms,
His frowns, his smiles, and all his conquering charms.
Beauty's no more but the dead soil which Love
40 Manures and does by wise commerce improve,
Sailing by sighs through seas of tears he sends
Courtship from foreign hearts for your own ends.
Cherish the trade, for as with Indians we
Get gold and jewels for our trumpery,
45 So to each other for their useless toys
Lovers afford whole magazines of joys.
But if you're fond of baubles, be, and starve;
Your gewgaw reputation preserve,
Live upon modesty and empty fame,
50 Forgoing sense for a fantastic name.

The Platonic Lady

I could love thee till I die,
Wouldst thou love me modestly
And ne'er press, whilst I live,
For more than willingly I'd give,
5 Which should sufficient be to prove
I'd understand the art of love.
I hate the thing is called enjoyment.
Besides, it is a dull employment,
It cuts off all that's life and fire
10 From that which may be termed desire,
Just like the bee whose sting is gone
Converts the owner to a drone.
I love a youth should give me leave
His body in my arms to wreathe,

15 To press him gently and to kiss,
To sigh and look with eyes that wish
For what, if I could once obtain,
I would neglect with flat disdain.
I'd give him liberty to toy
20 And play with me and count it joy.
Our freedom should be full complete,
And nothing wanting but the feat.
Let's practise then and we shall prove
These are the only sweets of love.

Song

As Cloris full of harmless thought
Beneath the willows lay,
Kind Love a comely shepherd brought
To pass the time away.
5 She blushed to be encountered so
And chid the amorous swain,
But as she strove to rise and go,
He pulled her down again.

A sudden passion seized her heart
10 In spite of her disdain,
She found a pulse in every part
And love in every vein.
'Ah, youth,' quoth she, 'what charms are these
That conquer and surprise?
15 Ah, let me, for unless you please,
I have no power to rise.'

She faintly spoke and trembling lay
For fear he should comply,
But virgins' eyes their hearts betray
20 And give their tongues the lie.
Thus she, who princes had denied
With all their pompous train,
Was in the lucky minute tried
And yielded to a swain.

Song to Cloris

Fair Cloris in a pigsty lay,
  Her tender herd lay by her.
She slept; in murmuring gruntlings they,
Complaining of the scorching day,
5 Her slumbers thus inspire.

She dreamt, while she with careful pains
  Her snowy arms employed
In ivory pails to fill out grains,
One of her love-convicted swains
10 Thus hasting to her cried:

'Fly, nymph! Oh fly! ere 'tis too late
  A dear loved life to save,
Rescue your bosom pig from fate,
Who now expires, hung in the gate
15 That leads to Flora's cave.

'Myself had tried to set him free
  Rather than brought the news,
But I am so abhorred by thee
That ev'n thy darling's life from me
20 I know thou wouldst refuse.'

Struck with the news, as quick she flies
  As blushes to her face;
Not the bright lightning from the skies
Nor love, shot from her brighter eyes,
25 Move half so swift a pace.

This plot, it seems, the lustful slave
  Had laid against her honour,
Which not one god took care to save,
For he pursues her to the cave
30 And throws himself upon her.

Now piercèd is her virgin zone,
  She feels the foe within it;
She hears a broken, amorous groan,
The panting lover's fainting moan,
35 Just in the happy minute.

Frighted she wakes and waking frigs.
 Nature thus kindly eased
In dreams raised by her murmuring pigs
And her own thumb between her legs,
40 She's innocent and pleased.

To Corinna

What cruel pains Corinna takes
 To force that harmless frown:
When not one charm her face forsakes,
 Love cannot lose his own.

5 So sweet a face, so soft a heart,
 Such eyes so very kind,
Betray, alas, the silly art
 Virtue had ill designed.

Poor feeble tyrant, who in vain
10 Would proudly take upon her,
Against kind Nature to maintain
 Affected rules of honour.

The scorn she bears, so helpless proves
 When I plead passion to her,
15 That much she fears, but more she loves,
 Her vassal should undo her.

Song

Phillis, be gentler, I advise,
 Make up for time misspent.
When beauty on its deathbed lies,
 'Tis high time to repent.

5 Such is the malice of your fate,
 That makes you old so soon,
Your pleasure ever comes too late,
 How early e'er begun.

Think what a wretched thing is she
10 Whose stars contrive in spite,
The morning of her love should be
Her fading beauty's night.

Then if to make your ruin more,
You'll peevishly be coy,
15 Die with the scandal of a whore,
And never know the joy.

May transports that can give new fire
To stay the flying soul,
Ne'er answer you in your desire,
20 But make you yet more dull.

May raptures that can move each part
To taste the joys above,
In all their height improved by art,
Still fly you when you love.

[*Could I but make my wishes insolent*]

Could I but make my wishes insolent
And force some image of a false content!
But they, like me, bashful and humble grown,
Hover at distance about beauty's throne,
5 There worship and admire, and then they die,
Daring no more lay hold of her than I.
Reason to worth bears a submissive spirit,
But fools can be familiar with merit.
Who but that blundering blockhead Phaëton
10 Could e'er have thought to drive about the sun?
Just such another durst make love to you
Whom not ambition led, but dullness drew.
No amorous thought could his dull heart incline
But he would have a passion, for 'twas fine!
15 That, a new suit, and what he next must say
Runs in his idle head the livelong day.

Hard-hearted saint, since 'tis your will to be
So unrelenting pitiless to me
Regardless of a love so many years
20 Preserved 'twixt lingering hopes and awful fears
(Such fears in lovers' breasts high value claims
And such expiring martyrs feel in flames.
My hopes yourself contrived with cruel care
Through gentle smiles to lead me to despair),
25 'Tis some relief in my extreme distress
My rival is below your power to bless.

Sab: lost

She yields, she yields, pale Envy said amen,
The first of women to the last of men.
Just so those frailer beings, angels, fell.
There's no midway (it seems) 'twixt heaven and hell.
5 Was it your end in making her, to show
Things must be raised so high to fall so low?
Since her nor angels their own worth secures,
Look to it, gods! the next turn must be yours.
You who in careless scorn laughed at the ways
10 Of humble love and called 'em rude essays,
Could you submit to let this heavy thing,
Artless and witless, no way meriting

[*Great mother of Aeneas and of Love*]

Great mother of Aeneas and of Love,
Delight of mankind and the powers above,
Who all beneath those sprinkled drops of light
Which slide upon the face of gloomy night
5 Whither vast regions of that liquid world
Where groves of ships on watery hills are hurled
Or fruitful earth, dost bless, since 'tis by thee
That all things live which the bright sun does see.

[*The gods by right of nature must possess*]

The gods by right of nature must possess
An everlasting age of perfect peace:
Far off removed from us and our affairs,
Neither approached by dangers or by cares,
5 Rich in themselves, to whom we cannot add,
Not pleased by good deeds nor provoked by bad.

To Love

O! numquam pro me satis indignate Cupido

O Love! how cold and slow to take my part,
Thou idle wanderer about my heart.
Why thy old faithful soldier wilt thou see
Oppressed in my own tents? They murder me;
5 Thy flames consume, thy arrows pierce thy friends.
Rather on foes pursue more noble ends.
Achilles' sword would generously bestow
A cure as certain, as it gave the blow.
Hunters who follow flying game give o'er
10 When the prey's caught; hope still leads on before.
We thine own slaves feel thy tyrannic blows,
Whilst thy tame hand's unmoved against thy foes.
On men disarmed how can you gallant prove,
And I was long ago disarmed by Love.
15 Millions of dull men live, and scornful maids:
We'll own Love valiant when he these invades.
Rome from each corner of the wide world snatched
A laurel, or't had been to this day thatched.
But the old soldier has his resting place,
20 And the good battered horse is turned to grass.
The harassed whore, who lived a wretch to please,
Has leave to be a bawd and take her ease.
For me then, who have freely spent my blood,
Love, in thy service and so boldly stood

25 In Celia's trenches, were't not wisely done
Ev'n to retire and live at peace at home?
No! Might I gain a godhead to disclaim
My glorious title to my endless flame,
Divinity with scorn I would forswear,
30 Such sweet, dear, tempting devils women are.
Whene'er those flames grow faint, I quickly find
A fierce, black storm pour down upon my mind.
Headlong I'm hurled like horsemen who in vain
Their fury-foaming coursers would restrain,
35 As ships, just when the harbour they attain,
Are snatched by sudden blasts to sea again,
So Love's fantastic storms reduce my heart,
Half-rescued, and the god resumes his dart.
Strike here, this undefended bosom wound,
40 And for so brave a conquest be renowned.
Shafts fly so fast to me from every part,
You'll scarce discern your quiver from my heart.
What wretch can bear a livelong night's dull rest
Or think himself in lazy slumbers blest?
45 Fool! Is not sleep the image of pale death?
There's time for rest when fate has stopped your breath.
Me may my soft-deluding dear deceive;
I'm happy in my hopes whilst I believe.
Now let her flatter, then as fondly chide.
50 Often may I enjoy, oft be denied.
With doubtful steps the god of war does move
By thy example led, ambiguous Love.
Blown to and fro like down from thy own wing,
Who knows when joy or anguish thou wilt bring?
55 Yet at thy mother's and thy slave's request,
Fix an eternal empire in my breast,
  And let th'inconstant charming sex,
  Whose wilful scorn does lovers vex,
  Submit their hearts before thy throne,
60 The vassal world is then thy own.

The Imperfect Enjoyment

Naked she lay, clasped in my longing arms,
I filled with love, and she all over charms,
Both equally inspired with eager fire,
Melting through kindness, flaming in desire;
5 With arms, legs, lips, close clinging to embrace,
She clips me to her breast and sucks me to her face.
Her nimble tongue (Love's lesser lightning) played
Within my mouth and to my thoughts conveyed
Swift orders that I should prepare to throw
10 The all-dissolving thunderbolt below.
My fluttering soul, sprung with a pointed kiss,
Hangs hovering o'er her balmy brinks of bliss,
But whilst her busy hand would guide that part
Which should convey my soul up to her heart,
15 In liquid raptures I dissolve all o'er,
Melt into sperm and spend at every pore.
A touch from any part of her had done't,
Her hand, her foot, her very look's a cunt.
Smiling, she chides in a kind, murmuring noise,
20 And from her body wipes the clammy joys,
When with a thousand kisses wandering o'er
My panting bosom, 'Is there then no more?'
She cries, 'All this to love and rapture's due,
Must we not pay a debt to pleasure too?'
25 But I, the most forlorn, lost man alive,
To show my wished obedience vainly strive,
I sigh, alas, and kiss, but cannot swive.
Eager desires confound my first intent,
Succeeding shame does more success prevent,
30 And rage at last confirms me impotent.
Ev'n her fair hand, which might bid heat return
To frozen age and make cold hermits burn,
Applied to my dead cinder warms no more
Than fire to ashes could past flames restore.
35 Trembling, confused, despairing, limber, dry,
A wishing, weak, unmoving lump I lie.

This dart of Love, whose piercing point oft tried,
With virgin blood ten thousand maids has dyed,
Which nature still directed with such art
40 That it through every cunt reached every heart;
Stiffly resolved, 'twould carelessly invade
Woman or boy, nor ought its fury stayed;
Where'er it pierced, a cunt it found or made,
Now languid lies in this unhappy hour,
45 Shrunk up and sapless like a withered flower.
Thou treacherous, base deserter of my flame,
False to my passion, fatal to my fame,
By what mistaken magic dost thou prove
So true to lewdness, so untrue to Love?
50 What oyster, cinder, beggar, common whore
Didst thou e'er fail in all thy life before?
When vice, disease, and scandal lead the way,
With what officious haste dost thou obey?
Like a rude, roaring hector in the streets
55 That scuffles, cuffs, and justles all he meets,
But if his king or country claim his aid,
The rakehell villain shrinks and hides his head;
Ev'n so thy brutal valor is displayed,
Breaks every stew, does each small whore invade,
60 But if great Love the onset does command,
Base recreant to thy prince, thou dar'st not stand.
Worst part of me and henceforth hated most,
Through all the town the common fucking post
On whom each whore relieves her tingling cunt,
65 As hogs on gates do rub themselves and grunt,
May'st thou to ravenous chancres be a prey,
Or in consuming weepings waste away.
May strangury and stone thy days attend;
May'st thou ne'er piss who didst refuse to spend
70 When all my joys did on false thee depend.
And may ten thousand abler pricks agree
To do the wronged Corinna right for thee.

On King Charles

In the isle of Great Britain long since famous grown
For breeding the best cunts in Christendom,
There reigns, and oh, long may he reign and thrive,
The easiest prince and best-bred man alive.
5 Him no ambition moves to seek renown
Like the French fool, to wander up and down
Starving his subjects, hazarding his crown.
Peace is his aim, his gentleness is such,
And love he loves, for he loves fucking much.
10 Nor are his high desires above his strength,
His sceptre and his prick are of a length;
And she that plays with one may sway the other
And make him little wiser than his brother.
I hate all monarchs and the thrones they sit on,
15 From the hector of France to the cully of Britain.
Poor prince, thy prick, like thy buffoons at court,
It governs thee, because it makes thee sport.
'Tis sure the sauciest prick that e'er did swive,
The proudest, peremptoriest prick alive.
20 Though safety, law, religion, life lay on't,
'Twould break through all to make its way to cunt.
Restless he rolls about from whore to whore,
A merry monarch, scandalous and poor.
To Carwell, the most dear of all his dears,
25 The sure relief of his declining years,
Oft he bewails his fortune and her fate:
To love so well, and to be loved so late.
For when in her he settles well his tarse,
Yet his dull, graceless ballocks hang an arse.
30 This you'd believe, had I but time to tell y'
The pain it costs to poor, laborious Nelly,
While she employs hands, fingers, lips, and thighs,
Ere she can raise the member she enjoys.

A Ramble in St James's Park

Much wine had passed with grave discourse
Of who fucks who and who does worse,
Such as you usually do hear
From them that diet at the Bear,
5 When I, who still take care to see
Drunkenness relieved by lechery,
Went out into St James's Park
To cool my head and fire my heart.
But though St James has the honour on't,
10 'Tis consecrate to prick and cunt.
There by a most incestuous birth
Strange woods spring from the teeming earth,
For they relate how heretofore,
When ancient Pict began to whore,
15 Deluded of his assignation
(Jilting it seems was then in fashion),
Poor pensive lover in this place
Would frig upon his mother's face,
Whence rows of mandrakes tall did rise
20 Whose lewd tops fucked the very skies.
Each imitative branch does twine
In some loved fold of Aretine.
And nightly now beneath their shade
Are buggeries, rapes, and incests made.
25 Unto this all-sin-sheltering grove
Whores of the bulk and the alcove,
Great ladies, chambermaids, and drudges,
The rag-picker and heiress trudges.
Carmen, divines, great lords, and tailors,
30 'Prentices, pimps, poets, and jailers,
Footmen, fine fops do here arrive,
And here promiscuously they swive.
  Along these hallowed walks it was
That I beheld Corinna pass.
35 Whoever had been by to see
The proud disdain she cast on me

Through charming eyes, he would have swore
She dropped from heav'n that very hour,
Forsaking the divine abode
40 In scorn of some despairing god.
But mark what creatures women are,
So infinitely vile, when fair.
    Three knights of th'elbow and the slur
With wriggling tails made up to her.
45 The first was of your Whitehall blades,
Near kin to th'Mother of the Maids,
Graced by whose favour he was able
To bring a friend to th'waiters' table,
Where he had heard Sir Edward Sutton
50 Say how the King loved Banstead mutton;
Since when he'd ne'er be brought to eat
By's good will any other meat.
In this, as well as all the rest,
He ventures to do like the best,
55 But wanting common sense, th'ingredient
In choosing well not least expedient,
Converts abortive imitation
To universal affectation.
So he not only eats and talks,
60 But feels and smells, sits down and walks,
Nay, looks and lives and loves by rote
In an old tawdry birthday coat.
    The second was a Gray's Inn wit,
A great inhabiter of the pit,
65 Where critic-like he sits and squints,
Steals pocket handkerchiefs and hints
From's neighbour and the comedy,
To court and pay his landlady.
    The third, a lady's eldest son
70 Within few years of twenty-one,
Who hopes from his propitious fate
Against he comes to his estate,
By these two worthies to be made
A most accomplished, tearing blade.

75 One in a strain 'twixt tune and nonsense
Cries, 'Madam, I have loved you long since,
Permit me your fair hand to kiss';
When at her mouth her cunt says, 'Yes'.
 In short, without much more ado,
80 Joyful and pleased away she flew
And with these three confounded asses
From park to hackney coach she passes;
So a proud bitch does lead about
Of humble curs the amorous rout,
85 Who most obsequiously do hunt
The savory scent of salt-swol'n cunt.
Some power more patient now relate
The sense of this surprising fate,
Gads! that a thing admired by me
90 Should fall to so much infamy.
Had she picked out to rub her arse on
Some stiff-pricked clown or well-hung parson,
Each job of whose spermatic sluice
Had filled her cunt with wholesome juice,
95 I the proceeding should have praised
In hope she'd quenched a fire I raised.
Such natural freedoms are but just:
There's something generous in mere lust.
But to turn damned abandoned jade
100 When neither head nor tail persuade,
To be a whore in understanding,
A passive pot for fools to spend in –
The devil played booty, sure, with thee
To bring a blot on infamy.
105 But why am I of all mankind
To so severe a fate designed?
Ungrateful! why this treachery
To humble, fond, believing me,
Who gave you privileges above
110 The nice allowances of love?
Did ever I refuse to bear
The meanest part your lust could spare?

When your lewd cunt came spewing home
Drenched with the seed of half the town,
115 My dram of sperm was supped up after
For the digestive surfeit water.
Full gorgèd at another time
With a vast meal of nasty slime
Which your devouring cunt had drawn
120 From porters' backs and footmen's brawn,
I was content to serve you up
My ballock-full for your grace cup;
Nor ever thought it an abuse,
While you had pleasure for excuse.
125 You that could make my heart away
For noise and colour and betray
The secrets of my tender hours
To such knight-errant paramours,
When leaning on your faithless breast,
130 Wrapped in security and rest,
Soft kindness all my powers did move,
And reason lay dissolved in love.
May stinking vapours choke your womb,
Such as the men you dote upon.
135 May your depravèd appetite,
That could in whiffling fools delight,
Beget such frenzies in your mind
You may go mad for the north wind
And fixing all your hopes upon't
140 To have him bluster in your cunt
Turn up your longing arse to th'air
And perish in a wild despair.
But cowards shall forget to rant,
Schoolboys to frig, old whores to paint;
145 The Jesuits' fraternity
Shall leave the use of buggery;
Crab-louse, inspired with grace divine,
From earthly cod to heaven shall climb;
Physicians shall believe in Jesus,
150 And disobedience cease to please us,
Ere I desist with all my power
To plague this woman and undo her.

But my revenge will best be timed
When she is married that is limed.
155 In that most lamentable state
I'll make her feel my scorn and hate,
Pelt her with scandals, truth, or lies,
And her poor cur with jealousies,
Till I have torn him from her breech,
160 While she whines like a dog-drawn bitch,
Loathed and despised, kicked out of town
Into some dirty hole alone,
To chew the cud of misery
And know she owes it all to me.
165 And may no woman better thrive
Who dares profane the cunt I swive.

Satire

Too long the wise Commons have been in debate
About money and conscience, those trifles of state,
While dangerous grievances daily increase,
And the subject can't riot in safety and peace,
5 Unless, as against Irish cattle before,
You now make an act to forbid Irish whore.

The Cootes black and white, Clanbrassil and Fox,
Invade us with impudence, beauty, and pox:
Each carries a fate which no man can oppose
10 Without loss of his heart and the fall of his nose.
Should we dully resist, yet would each take upon her
To beseech us to do it and engage us in honour.

O, ye powers above who of mortals take care,
Make the women more modest, more sound, or less fair.
15 Is it just that with Love cruel Death should conspire,
And our tarses be burnt by our hearts taking fire?
There's an end of communion, if humble believers
Must be damned in the cup like unworthy receivers.

The Second Prologue at Court to The Empress of Morocco *Spoken by the Lady Elizabeth Howard*

Wit has of late took up a trick t'appear
Unmannerly, or at the best severe.
And poets share the fate by which we fall
When kindly we attempt to please you all.
5 'Tis hard your scorn should against such prevail
Whose ends are to divert you, though they fail
You men would think it an ill-natured jest,
Should we laugh at you when you did your best.
Then rail not here, though you see reason for't.
10 If wit can find itself no better sport,
Wit is a very foolish thing at court.
Wit's business is to please and not to fright.
'Tis no wit to be always in the right:
You'll find it none, who dare be so tonight.
15 Few so ill-bred will venture to a play
To spy out faults in what we women say.
For us no matter what we speak, but how:
How kindly can we say, 'I hate you now.'
And for the men, if you'll laugh at 'em, do:
20 They mind themselves so much, they'll ne'er mind you.
But why do I descend to lose a prayer
On those small saints in wit? The god sits there.
[*To the King.*]
To you, great sir, my message hither tends
From youth and beauty, your allies and friends.
25 See my credentials written in my face,
They challenge your protection in this place
And hither come with such a force of charms
As may give check ev'n to your prosperous arms.
Millions of cupids hovering in the rear,
30 Like eagles following fatal troops appear,
All waiting for the slaughter which draws nigh
Of those bold gazers who this night must die.
Nor can you 'scape our soft captivity
From which old age alone must set you free.

35 Then tremble at the fatal consequence,
Since 'tis well known for your own part, great prince,
'Gainst us you still have made a weak defence.
Be generous and wise and take our part;
Remember we have eyes, and you a heart.
40 Else you may find, too late, that we are things
Born to kill vassals and to conquer kings.
But oh! to what vain conquest I pretend,
Whilst Love is our commander and your friend.
Our victory your empire more assures,
45 For Love will ever make the triumph yours.

Song

Love a woman? You're an ass.
'Tis a most insipid passion
To choose out for your happiness
The idlest part of God's creation.

5 Let the porter and the groom,
Things designed for dirty slaves,
Drudge in fair Aurelia's womb
To get supplies for age and graves.

Farewell, woman! I intend
10 Henceforth every night to sit
With my lewd, well-natured friend,
Drinking to engender wit.

Then give me health, wealth, mirth, and wine,
And if busy Love intrenches,
15 There's a sweet, soft page of mine
Does the trick worth forty wenches.

Upon his Drinking a Bowl

Vulcan, contrive me such a cup
As Nestor used of old;
Show all thy skill to trim it up,
Damask it round with gold.

5 Make it so large that, filled with sack
Up to the swelling brim,
Vast toasts on the delicious lake
Like ships at sea may swim.

Engrave not battle on its cheek:
10 With war I've nought to do;
I'm none of those that took Maastricht,
Nor Yarmouth leaguer knew.

Let it no name of planets tell,
Fixed stars, or constellations;
15 For I am no Sir Sidrophel,
Nor none of his relations.

But carve thereon a spreading vine,
Then add two lovely boys;
Their limbs in amorous folds intwine,
20 The type of future joys.

Cupid and Bacchus my saints are,
May drink and love still reign,
With wine I wash away my cares
And then to cunt again.

Epigram

Poet, whoe'er thou art, I say God damn thee;
Take my advice and burn thy *Mariamne*.

Seneca's Troas, *Act 2. Chorus*

After death nothing is, and nothing, death,
The utmost limit of a gasp of breath.
Let the ambitious zealot lay aside
His hopes of heaven, whose faith is but his pride;
5 Let slavish souls lay by their fear
Nor be concerned which way nor where
After this life they shall be hurled.
Dead, we become the lumber of the world,
And to that mass of matter shall be swept
10 Where things destroyed with things unborn are kept.
Devouring time swallows us whole.
Impartial death confounds body and soul.
For Hell and the foul fiend that rules
God's everlasting fiery jails
15 (Devised by rogues, dreaded by fools),
With his grim, grisly dog that keeps the door,
Are senseless stories, idle tales,
Dreams, whimseys, and no more.

Grecian Kindness

The utmost grace the Greeks could show,
When to the Trojans they grew kind,
Was with their arms to let them go
And leave their lingering wives behind.
5 They beat the men and burnt the town,
Then all the baggage was their own.

There the kind deity of wine
Kissed the soft wanton god of love;
This clapped his wings, that pressed his vine,
10 And their best powers united move,
While each brave Greek embraced his punk,
Lulled her asleep, and then grew drunk.

Signior Dildo

You ladies all of merry England
Who have been to kiss the Duchess's hand,
Pray, did you not lately observe in the show
A noble Italian called Signior Dildo?

5 This signior was one of the Duchess's train
And helped to conduct her over the main;
But now she cries out, 'To the Duke I will go,
I have no more need for Signior Dildo.'

At the Sign of the Cross in St James's Street,
10 When next you go thither to make yourselves sweet
By buying of powder, gloves, essence, or so,
You may chance to get a sight of Signior Dildo.

You would take him at first for no person of note,
Because he appears in a plain leather coat,
15 But when you his virtuous abilities know,
You'll fall down and worship Signior Dildo.

My Lady Southesk, heaven prosper her for't,
First clothed him in satin, then brought him to court;
But his head in the circle he scarcely durst show,
20 So modest a youth was Signior Dildo.

The good Lady Suffolk, thinking no harm,
Had got this poor stranger hid under her arm.
Lady Betty by chance came the secret to know
And from her own mother stole Signior Dildo.

25 The Countess of Falmouth, of whom people tell
Her footmen wear shirts of a guinea an ell,
Might save that expense, if she did but know
How lusty a swinger is Signior Dildo.

By the help of this gallant the Countess of Rafe
30 Against the fierce Harris preserved herself safe;
She stifled him almost beneath her pillow,
So closely she embraced Signior Dildo.

The pattern of virtue, Her Grace of Cleveland,
Has swallowed more pricks than the ocean has sand;
35 But by rubbing and scrubbing so wide it does grow,
It is fit for just nothing but Signior Dildo.

Our dainty fine duchesses have got a trick
To dote on a fool for the sake of his prick,
The fops were undone did their graces but know
40 The discretion and vigour of Signior Dildo.

The Duchess of Modena, though she looks so high,
With such a gallant is content to lie,
And for fear that the English her secrets should know,
For her gentleman usher took Signior Dildo.

45 The Countess o'th' Cockpit (who knows not her name?
She's famous in story for a killing dame),
When all her old lovers forsake her, I trow,
She'll then be contented with Signior Dildo.

Red Howard, red Sheldon, and Temple so tall
50 Complain of his absence so long from Whitehall.
Signior Barnard has promised a journey to go
And bring back his countryman, Signior Dildo.

Doll Howard no longer with His Highness must range,
And therefore is proferred this civil exchange:
55 Her teeth being rotten, she smells best below,
And needs must be fitted for Signior Dildo.

St Albans with wrinkles and smiles in his face,
Whose kindness to strangers becomes his high place,
In his coach and six horses is gone to Bergo
60 To take the fresh air with Signior Dildo.

Were this signior but known to the citizen fops,
He'd keep their fine wives from the foremen o'their shops;
But the rascals deserve their horns should still grow
For burning the Pope and his nephew, Dildo.

65 Tom Killigrew's wife, that Holland fine flower,
At the sight of this signior did fart and belch sour,
And her Dutch breeding the further to show,
Says, 'Welcome to England, Mynheer Van Dildo.'

He civilly came to the Cockpit one night,
70 And proferred his service to fair Madam Knight.
Quoth she, 'I intrigue with Captain Cazzo;
Your nose in mine arse, good Signior Dildo.'

This signior is sound, safe, ready, and dumb
As ever was candle, carrot, or thumb;
75 Then away with these nasty devices, and show
How you rate the just merit of Signior Dildo.

Count Cazzo, who carries his nose very high,
In passion he swore his rival should die;
Then shut himself up to let the world know
80 Flesh and blood could not bear it from Signior Dildo.

A rabble of pricks who were welcome before,
Now finding the porter denied them the door,
Maliciously waited his coming below
And inhumanly fell on Signior Dildo.

85 Nigh wearied out, the poor stranger did fly,
And along the Pall Mall they followed full cry;
The women concernèd from every window
Cried, 'For heaven's sake, save Signior Dildo.'

The good Lady Sandys burst into a laughter
90 To see how the ballocks came wobbling after,
And had not their weight retarded the foe,
Indeed 't had gone hard with Signior Dildo.

Tunbridge Wells

At five this morn when Phoebus raised his head
From Thetis' lap, I raised myself from bed
And mounting steed, I trotted to the waters,
The rendezvous of feigned or sickly praters,
5 Cuckolds, whores, citizens, their wives and daughters.
My squeamish stomach I with wine had bribed
To undertake the dose it was prescribed,
But turning head, a sudden noisome view
That innocent provision overthrew
10 And without drinking made me purge and spew.
Looking on t'other side, a thing I saw
Who some men said could handle sword and law.
It stalked, it stared, and up and down did strut,
And seemed as furious as a stag at rut.
15 As wise as calf it looked, as big as bully,
But handled, proved a mere Sir Nicholas Cully,
A bawling fop, a natural Nokes, and yet
He dared to censure as if he had wit.
To make him more ridiculous, in spite
20 Nature contrived the fool should be a knight.
Grant ye lucky stars this o'ergrown boy
To purchase some inspiring pretty toy
That may his want of sense and wit supply,
As buxom crab-fish do his lechery.
25 Though he alone were dismal sight enough,
His train contributed to set him off,
All of his shape, all of the self-same stuff.
In short, no malice need on him be thrown,
Nature has done the business of lampoon,
30 And in his looks his character hath shown.
Endeavouring this irksome sight to balk,
And a more irksome noise, his silly talk,
I silently slunk down to th' Lower Walk.
But often when one would Charybdis shun,
35 Down upon Scylla 'tis one's fate to run;

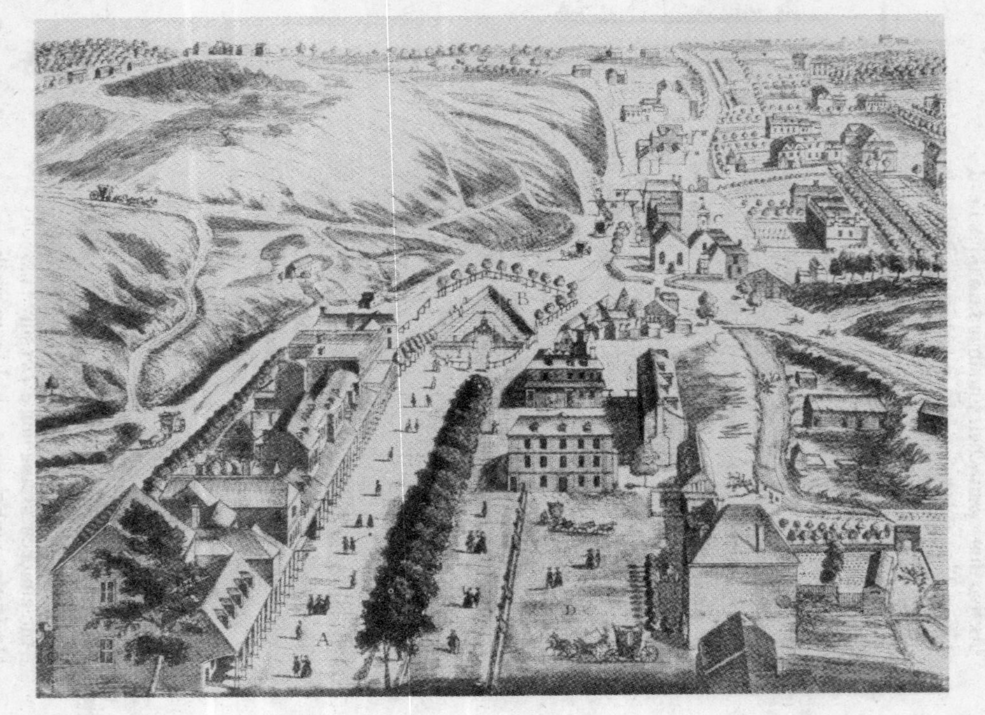

4 A bird's-eye view of Tunbridge Wells by A. M. Broadley

So here it was my cursèd fate to find
As great a fop, though of another kind,
A tall, stiff fool who walked in Spanish guise;
The buckram puppet never stirred its eyes,
40 But grave as owl it looked, as woodcock wise.
He scorned the empty talking of this mad age
And spoke all proverbs, sentences, and adage,
Can with as much solemnity buy eggs
As a cabal can talk of their intrigues,
45 A man of parts, and yet he can dispense
With the formality of speaking sense.
From hence into the upper end I ran,
Where a new scene of foppery began
Among the serious and fanatic elves,
50 Fit company for none besides themselves.
Assembled thus, each his distemper told:
Scurvy, stone, strangury. Some were so bold
To charge the spleen to be their misery,
And on the wise disease bring infamy.
55 But none were half so modest to complain
Their want of learning, honesty, and brain,
The general diseases of that train.
These call themselves ambassadors of Heaven
And saucily pretend commissions given,
60 But should an Indian king, whose small command
Seldom extends above ten miles of land,
Send forth such wretched fools in an embassage,
He'd find but small effects of such a message.
Listening, I found the cob of all this rabble,
65 Pert Bayes, with his importance comfortable.
He, being raised to an archdeaconry
By trampling on religious liberty,
Was grown too great and looked too fat and jolly
To be disturbed with care or melancholy,
70 Though Marvell has enough exposed his folly.
He drank to carry off some old remains
His lazy dull distemper left in's veins.
Let him drink on, but 'tis not a whole flood
Can give sufficient sweetness to his blood

75 To make his nature or his manners good.
Importance drank too, though she'd been no sinner,
To wash away some dregs he had spewed in her.
Next after these a foolish whining crew
Of sisters frail were offered to my view.
80 The things did talk, but th' hearing what they said
I did myself the kindness to evade.
Looking about, I saw some gypsies too
(Faith, brethren, they can cant as well as you).
Nature hath placed these wretches beneath scorn;
85 They can't be called so vile as they are born.
Amidst the crowd next I myself conveyed,
For now were come, whitewash and paint being laid,
Mother and daughters, mistress and the maid,
And squire with wig and pantaloons displayed.
90 But ne'er could conventicle, play, or fair
For a true medley with this herd compare.
Here squires, ladies, and some say countesses,
Chandlers, egg-wives, bacon-women, seamstresses
Were mixed together, nor did they agree
95 More in their humours than their quality.
Here waiting for gallant, young damsel stood,
Leaning on cane and muffled up in hood.
The would-be wit, whose business was to woo,
With hat removed and solemn scrape of shoe
100 Advanceth bowing, then genteelly shrugs
And ruffled foretop into order tugs,
And thus accosts her, 'Madam, methinks the weather
Is grown much more serene since you came hither.
You influence the heavens; and should the sun
105 Withdraw himself to see his rays outdone,
Your brighter eyes could then supply the morn
And make a day before a day be born.'
With mouth screwed up, conceited winking eyes,
And breasts thrust forwards, 'Lord, sir,' she replies,
110 'It is your goodness, and not my deserts,
Which makes you show this learning, wit, and parts.'
He, puzzled, bites his nail, both to display
The sparkling ring and think what next to say,

And thus breaks forth afresh, 'Madam, egad,
115 Your luck at cards last night was very bad.
At cribbage fifty-nine, and the next show
To make the game, and yet to want those two.
God damn me, madam, I'm the son of a whore
If in my life I saw the like before.'
120 To pedlar's stall he drags her, and her breast
With hearts and such-like foolish toys he dressed;
And then more smartly to expound the riddle
Of all his prattle, gives her a Scotch fiddle.
Tired with this dismal stuff, away I ran
125 Where were two wives with girl just fit for man,
Short-breathed, with pallid lips, and visage wan.
Some curtsies passed, and the old compliment
Of being glad to see each other, spent,
With hand in hand they lovingly did walk,
130 And one began thus to renew the talk.
'I pray, good madam, if it may be thought
No rudeness, what cause was it hither brought
Your ladyship?' She soon replying, smiled,
'We have a good estate, but have no child,
135 And I'm informed these wells will make a barren
Woman as fruitful as a cony warren.'
The first returned, 'For this cause I am come,
For I can have no quietness at home.
My husband grumbles, though we have got one,
140 This poor girl, and mutters for a son.
And this is grieved with headache pangs and throes,
Is full sixteen and never yet had those.'
She soon replied, 'Get her a husband, madam.
I married at that age and ne'er had had 'em,
145 Was just like her. Steel waters let alone,
A back of steel will bring 'em better down.'
And ten to one but they themselves will try
The same means to increase their family.
Poor foolish fribbles, who by subtlety
150 Of midwife, truest friend to lechery,
Persuaded are to be at pains and charge
To give their wives occasion to enlarge

Their silly heads. For here walk Cuff and Kick
With brawny back and legs and potent prick,
155 Who more substantially will cure thy wife,
And on her half-dead womb bestow new life.
From these the waters got the reputation
Of good assistants unto generation.
Now warlike men were got into the throng,
160 With hair tied back, singing a bawdy song.
Not much afraid, I got a nearer view,
And 'twas my chance to know the dreadful crew.
They were cadets, that seldom can appear,
Damned to the stint of thirty pound a year.
165 With hawk on fist or greyhound led in hand,
The dogs and footboys sometimes they command.
And having trimmed a cast-off spavined horse,
With three hard-pinched-for guineas in the purse,
Two rusty pistols, scarf about the arse,
170 Coat lined with red, they here presume to swell;
This goes for captain, that for colonel.
So the Bear Garden ape on his steed mounted,
No longer is a jackanapes accounted,
But is by virtue of his trumpery then
175 Called by the name of the young gentleman.
Bless me, thought I, what thing is man, that thus
In all his shapes he is ridiculous?
Ourselves with noise of reason we do please
In vain: humanity's our worst disease.
180 Thrice happy beasts are, who, because they be
Of reason void, are so of foppery.
Troth, I was so ashamed that with remorse
I used the insolence to mount my horse;
For he, doing only things fit for his nature,
185 Did seem to me (by much) the wiser creature.

Artemisa to Chloe.
A Letter from a Lady in the Town to a Lady in the Country concerning the Loves of the Town

Chloe,
In verse by your command I write,
Shortly you'll bid me ride astride and fight;
Such talents better with our sex agree
Than lofty flights of dangerous poetry.
5 Amongst the men, I mean the men of wit
(At least they passed for such before they writ),
How many bold adventurers for the bays,
Proudly designing large returns of praise,
Who durst that stormy, pathless world explore,
10 Were soon dashed back and wrecked on the dull shore,
Broke of that little stock they had before?
How would a woman's tottering bark be tossed
Where stoutest ships, the men of wit, are lost.
When I reflect on this, I straight grow wise,
15 And my own self thus gravely I advise:
Dear Artemisa, poetry's a snare;
Bedlam has many mansions, have a care:
Your muse diverts you, makes your reader sad;
You fancy you're inspired, he thinks you mad.
20 Consider too 'twill be discreetly done
To make yourself the fiddle of the town,
To find th'ill-humoured pleasure at their need,
Scorned if you fail and cursed if you succeed.
Yet like an arrant woman as I am,
25 No sooner well convinced writing's a shame,
That whore is scarce a more reproachful name
Than poetess –
As men that marry or as maids that woo
'Cause 'tis the very worst thing they can do,
30 Pleased with the contradiction and the sin,
Methinks I stand on thorns till I begin.
You expect to hear at least what loves have passed
In this lewd town since you and I met last,

What change hath happened of intrigues, and whether
35 The old ones last, and who and who's together.
But how, my dearest Chloe, shall I set
My pen to write what I would fain forget
Or name that lost thing, love, without a tear,
Since so debauched by ill-bred customs here?
40 Love, the most generous passion of the mind,
The softest refuge innocence can find,
The safe director of unguided youth,
Fraught with kind wishes and secured by truth,
That cordial drop heaven in our cup has thrown
45 To make the nauseous draught of life go down;
On which one only blessing God might raise
In lands of atheists subsidies of praise,
For none did e'er so dull and stupid prove
But felt a god and blest his power in love.
50 This only joy for which poor we were made
Is grown, like play, to be an arrant trade:
The rooks creep in, and it has got of late
As many little cheats and tricks as that.
But what yet more a woman's heart would vex,
55 'Tis chiefly carried on by our own sex,
Our silly sex, who born like monarchs, free,
Turn gypsies for a meaner liberty
And hate restraint, though but from infamy.
They call whatever is not common, nice,
60 And deaf to nature's rules and love's advice,
Forsake the pleasures to pursue the vice.
To an exact perfection they have wrought
The action, love; the passion is forgot.
'Tis below wit, they'll tell you, to admire,
65 And ev'n without approving, they desire.
Their private wish obeys the public voice;
'Twixt good and bad, whimsey decides, not choice.
Fashions grow up for taste, at forms they strike,
They know what they would have, not what they like.
70 Bovey is a beauty, if some few agree
To call him so; the rest to that degree
Affected are, that with their ears they see.

Where I was visiting the other night
Comes a fine lady with her humble knight,
75 Who had prevailed on her by her own skill
At his request though much against his will
To come to London.
As the coach stopped, we heard her voice, more loud
Than a great-bellied woman's in a crowd,
80 Telling her knight that her affairs require
He for some hours obsequiously retire.
I think she was ashamed to have him seen
(Hard fate of husbands): the gallant had been,
Though a diseased, hard-favoured fool, brought in.
85 'Dispatch,' says she, 'that business you pretend,
That beastly visit to your drunken friend.
A bottle ever makes you look so fine,
Methinks I long to smell you stink of wine.
Your country drinking breath's enough to kill,
90 Sour ale corrected with a lemon peel.
Prithee, farewell, we'll meet again anon.'
The necessary thing bows and is gone.
She flies upstairs, and all the haste does show
That fifty antic postures will allow,
95 And then bursts out, 'Dear madam, am not I
The altered'st creature breathing, let me die;
I find myself ridiculously grown
Embarrassée with being out of town,
Rude and untaught like any Indian queen,
100 My country nakedness is strangely seen.
How is love governed, love that rules the state,
And pray, who are the men most worn of late?
When I was married, fools were *à la mode*,
The men of wit were then held *incommode*,
105 Slow of belief and fickle in desire,
Who, ere they'll be persuaded, must inquire
As if they came to spy, not to admire.
With searching wisdom, fatal to their ease,
They'll still find out why what may, should not please,
110 Nay, take themselves for injured if we dare
Make them think better of us than we are,

And if we hide our frailties from their sights,
Call us deceitful jilts and hypocrites.
They little guess, who at our arts are grieved,
115 The perfect joy of being well deceived,
Inquisitive as jealous cuckolds grow;
Rather than not be knowing, they will know
What being known creates their certain woe.
Women should these of all mankind avoid,
120 For wonder by clear knowledge is destroyed.
Woman, who is an arrant bird of night,
Bold in the dusk before a fool's dull sight,
Should fly when reason brings the glaring light.
But the kind, easy fool, apt to admire
125 Himself, trusts us; his follies all conspire
To flatter his and favour our desire.
Vain of his proper merit, he with ease
Believes we love him best who best can please.
On him our common, gross, dull flatteries pass,
130 Ever most joyful when most made an ass:
Heavy to apprehend, though all mankind
Perceive us false, the fop concerned is blind,
Who doting on himself,
Thinks everyone that sees him of his mind.
135 These are true women's men.' Here forced to cease
For want of breath, not will to hold her peace,
She to the window runs, where she had spied
Her much esteemed dear friend, the monkey, tied.
With forty smiles, as many antic bows
140 As if 't had been the lady of the house,
The dirty, chattering monster she embraced,
And made it this fine tender speech at last:
'Kiss me, thou curious miniature of man,
How odd thou art, how pretty, how japan!
145 Oh, I could live and die with thee.' Then on
For half an hour in compliment she run.
I took this time to think what nature meant
When this mixed thing into the world she sent,
So very wise, yet so impertinent:

150 One who knew everything, who 'twas thought fit
Should be a fool through choice, not want of wit,
Whose foppery without the help of sense
Could ne'er have rose to such an excellence.
Nature's as lame in making a true fop
155 As a philosopher; the very top
And dignity of folly we attain
By curious search and labour of the brain,
By observation, counsel, and deep thought:
God never made a coxcomb worth a groat;
160 We owe that name to industry and arts,
An eminent fool must be a fool of parts.
And such a one was she, who had turned o'er
As many books as men, loved much, read more,
Had a discerning wit; to her was known
165 Everyone's fault and merit but her own.
All the good qualities that ever blest
A woman so distinguished from the rest,
Except discretion only, she possessed.
And now, 'Monsieur dear Pug,' she cries, 'adieu',
170 And the discourse broke off, does thus renew:
'You smile to see me, whom the world perchance
Mistakes to have some wit, so far advance
The interest of fools that I approve
Their merit more than men's of wit, in love.
175 But in our sex too many proofs there are
Of such whom wits undo and fools repair.
This in my time was so received a rule
Hardly a wench in town but had her fool;
The meanest common slut, who long was grown
180 The jest and scorn of every pit buffoon,
Had yet left charms enough to have subdued
Some fop or other fond to be thought lewd.
Foster could make an Irish lord a Nokes,
And Betty Morris had her City cokes.
185 A woman's ne'er so ruined but she can
Be still revenged on her undoer, man:
How lost soe'er, she'll find some lover more
A lewd, abandoned fool than she's a whore.

'That wretched thing, Corinna, who had run
190 Through all the several ways of being undone,
Cozened at first by love, and living then
By turning the too dear-bought trick on men:
Gay were the hours and winged with joy they flew,
When first the town her early beauty knew;
195 Courted, admired, and loved, with presents fed
Youth in her looks and pleasure in her bed,
Till fate or her ill angel thought it fit
To make her dote upon a man of wit,
Who found 'twas dull to love above a day,
200 Made his ill-natured jest, and went away.
Now scorned by all, forsaken, and oppressed,
She's a *memento mori* to the rest,
Diseased, decayed, to take up half a crown
Must mortgage her long scarf and manteau gown.
205 Poor creature, who unheard of as a fly
In some dark hole must all the winter lie,
And want and dirt endure a whole half year
That for one month she tawdry may appear.
In Easter term she gets her a new gown,
210 When my young master's worship comes to town,
From pedagogue and mother just set free,
The heir and hopes of a great family,
Who with strong ale and beef the country rules,
And ever since the Conquest have been fools.
215 And now with careful prospect to maintain
This character, lest crossing of the strain
Should mend the booby breed, his friends provide
A cousin of his own for his fair bride.
And thus set out
220 With an estate, no wit, and a young wife,
The solid comforts of a coxcomb's life,
Dunghill and pease forsook, he comes to town,
Turns spark, learns to be lewd, and is undone.
Nothing suits worse with vice than want of sense:
225 Fools are still wicked at their own expense.
This o'ergrown schoolboy lost Corinna wins
And at first dash to make an ass begins,

Pretends to like a man who has not known
The vanities nor vices of the town.
230 Fresh in his youth and faithful in his love,
Eager of joys which he does seldom prove;
Healthful and strong, he does no pains endure
But what the fair one he adores can cure;
Grateful for favours, does the sex esteem,
235 And libels none for being kind to him;
Then of the lewdness of the town complains,
Rails at the wits and atheists, and maintains
'Tis better than good sense, than power, than wealth
To have a love untainted, youth, and health.
240 The unbred puppy, who had never seen
A creature look so gay or talk so fine,
Believes, then falls in love, and then in debt,
Mortgages all, ev'n to the ancient seat,
To buy his mistress a new house for life,
245 To give her plate and jewels, robs his wife;
And when to th' height of fondness he is grown,
'Tis time to poison him, and all's her own.
Thus meeting in her common arms his fate,
He leaves her bastard heir to his estate,
250 And, as the race of such an owl deserves,
His own dull lawful progeny he starves.
Nature who never made a thing in vain,
But does each insect to some end ordain,
Wisely contrived kind keeping fools, no doubt,
255 To patch up vices men of wit wear out.'
Thus she ran on two hours, some grains of sense
Mixed with whole volleys of impertinence.
But now 'tis time I should some pity show
To Chloe, since I cannot choose but know
260 Readers must reap the dullness writers sow.
By the next post such stories I will tell
As joined with these, shall to a volume swell,
As true as heaven, more infamous than hell;
But now you're tired, and so am I.
Farewell.

Timon. A Satyr

A. What, Timon, does old age begin t'approach
That thus thou droop'st under a night's debauch?
Hast thou lost deep to needy rogues on tick
Who ne'er could pay, and must be paid next week?
5 TIMON Neither, alas, but a dull dining sot
Seized me i'th' Mall, who just my name had got;
He runs upon me, cries, 'Dear rogue, I'm thine,
With me some wits of thy acquaintance dine.'
I tell him I'm engaged, but as a whore
10 With modesty enslaves her spark the more,
The longer I denied, the more he pressed.
At last I ev'n consent to be his guest.
He takes me in his coach and, as we go,
Pulls out a libel of a sheet or two,
15 Insipid as the praise of pious queens
Or Shadwell's unassisted former scenes,
Which he admired and praised at every line.
At last it was so sharp it must be mine.
I vowed I was no more a wit than he,
20 Unpractised and unblessed in poetry.
A song to Phillis I perhaps might make,
But never rhymed but for my pintle's sake.
I envied no man's fortune nor his fame,
Nor ever thought of a revenge so tame.
25 He knew my style, he swore, and 'twas in vain
Thus to deny the issue of my brain.
Choked with his flattery, I no answer make,
But silent, leave him to his dear mistake,
Which he by this had spread o'er the whole town
30 And me with an officious lie undone.
Of a well-meaning fool I'm most afraid,
Who sillily repeats what was well said.
But this was not the worst. When he came home,
He asked, 'Are Sedley, Buckhurst, Savile come?'
35 No, but there were above Halfwit and Huff,
Kickum and Dingboy. 'Oh, 'tis well enough.

They're all brave fellows,' cries mine host, 'Let's dine,
I long to have my belly full of wine.
They will both write and fight, I dare assure you,
40 They're men *tam Marte quam Mercurio.*'
I saw my error, but 'twas now too late:
No means nor hopes appear of a retreat.
Well, we salute, and each man takes his seat.
'Boy,' says my sot, 'is my wife ready yet?'
45 A wife, good gods! a fop and bullies too!
For one poor meal what must I undergo?
In comes my lady straight; she had been fair,
Fit to give love and to prevent despair,
But age, beauty's incurable disease,
50 Had left her more desire than power to please.
As cocks will strike although their spurs be gone,
She with her old blear eyes to smite begun.
Though nothing else, she (in despite of time)
Preserved the affectation of her prime:
55 However you begun, she brought in love
And hardly from that subject would remove.
We chanced to speak of the French king's success;
My lady wondered much how heaven could bless
A man that loved two women at one time,
60 But more how he to them excused his crime.
She asked Huff if love's flame he never felt.
He answered bluntly, 'Do you think I'm gelt?'
She at his plainness smiled, then turned to me,
'Love in young minds precedes ev'n poetry.
65 You to that passion can no stranger be,
But wits are given to inconstancy.'
She had run on, I think, till now, but meat
Came up, and suddenly she took her seat.
I thought the dinner would make some amends,
70 When my good host cries out, 'You're all my friends,
Our own plain fare and the best tierce the Bull
Affords I'll give you and your bellies full.
As for French kickshaws, sillery, and champagne,
Ragouts and fricassees, in troth, we've none.'

75 'Here's a good dinner towards,' thought I, when straight
Up comes a piece of beef, full horseman's weight,
Hard as the arse of Moseley, under which
The coachman sweats as ridden by a witch,
A dish of carrots, each of them as long
80 As tool that to fair countess did belong,
Which her small pillow could not so well hide
But visitors his flaming head espied.
Pig, goose, and capon followed in the rear,
With all that country bumpkins call good cheer,
85 Served up with sauces, all of 'eighty-eight,
When our tough youth wrestled and threw the weight.
And now the bottle briskly flies about,
Instead of ice, wrapped up in a wet clout.
A brimmer follows the third bit we eat,
90 Small beer becomes our drink and wine our meat.
The table was so large that in less space
A man might, safe, six old Italians place:
Each man had as much room as Porter, Blunt,
Or Harris had in Cullen's bushel cunt.
95 And now the wine began to work. Mine host
Had been a colonel; we must hear him boast,
Not of towns won, but an estate he lost
For the King's service, which indeed he spent
Whoring and drinking, but with good intent.
100 He talked much of a plot, and money lent
The King in Cromwell's time. My lady, she
Complained our love was coarse, our poetry
Unfit for modest ears; small whores and players
Were of our hare-brained youth the only cares,
105 Who were too wild for any virtuous league,
Too rotten to consummate the intrigue.
Falkland she praised, and Suckling's easy pen,
And seemed to taste their former parts again.
Mine host drinks to the best in Christendom,
110 And decently my lady quits the room.
Left to ourselves, of several things we prate,
Some regulate the stage and some the state.

5 Elizabeth, Lady Cullen, as Venus (complete with doves), a portrait by Sir Peter Lely

Halfwit cries up my lord of Orrery,
'Ah, how well Mustapha and Zanger die!
115 His sense so little forced that by one line
You may the other easily divine:
And which is worse, if any worse can be,
He never said one word of it to me.
There's fine poetry! You'd swear 'twere prose,
120 So little on the sense the rhymes impose.'
'Damn me!' says Dingboy, 'In my mind, God's wounds,
Etherege writes airy songs and soft lampoons
The best of any man; as for your nouns,
Grammar, and rules of art, he knows 'em not,
125 Yet writ two talking plays without one plot.'
Huff was for Settle, and *Morocco* praised,
Said rumbling words, like drums, his courage raised:
Whose broad-built bulks the boist'rous billows bear,
Safi and Salé, Mogador, Oran,
130 *The famed Arzile, Alcazar, Tetuan.*
'Was ever braver language writ by man?'
Kickum for Crowne declared, said in romance
He had outdone the very wits of France:
'Witness *Pandion* and his *Charles the Eight*,
135 Where a young monarch, careless of his fate,
Though foreign troops and rebels shock his state,
Complains another sight afflicts him more,
Viz.
The queen's galleys rowing from the shore,
Fitting their oars and tackling to be gone,
140 *Whilst sporting waves smiled on the rising sun.*
"Waves smiling on the sun!" I'm sure that's new,
And 'twas well thought on, give the Devil his due.'
Mine host, who had said nothing in an hour,
Rose up and praised *The Indian Emperour*:
145 *As if our old world modestly withdrew,*
And here in private had brought forth a new.
'There are two *lines*! Who but he durst presume
To make th' old world a new withdrawing room,
Where of another world she's brought to bed!
150 What a brave midwife is a laureate's head!

But pox of all these scribblers. What d'you think,
Will Souches this year any champagne drink?
Will Turenne fight him?' 'Without doubt,' says Huff,
'When they two meet, their meeting will be rough.'
155 'Damn me!' says Dingboy, 'The French cowards are;
They pay, but th' English, Scots, and Swiss make war.
In gaudy troops at a review they shine,
But dare not with the Germans battle join.
What now appears like courage, is not so;
160 'Tis a short pride which from success does grow.
On their first blow they'll shrink into those fears
They showed at Crécy, Agincourt, Poitiers.
Their loss was infamous; honour so stained
Is by a nation not to be regained.'
165 'What they were then, I know not, now they're brave.
He that denies it lies and is a slave,'
Says Huff and frowned. Says Dingboy, 'That do I!'
And at that word at t'other's head let fly
A greasy plate, when suddenly they all
170 Together by the ears in parties fall.
Halfwit with Dingboy joins, Kickum with Huff.
Their swords were safe, and so we let them cuff
Till they, mine host, and I had all enough.
Their rage once over, they begin to treat,
175 And six fresh bottles must the peace complete.
I ran downstairs with a vow nevermore
To drink beer-glass and hear the hectors roar.

Upon his Leaving his Mistress

'Tis not that I am weary grown
Of being yours, and yours alone;
But with what face can I incline
To damn you to be only mine,
5 You, whom some kinder power did fashion,
By merit and by inclination,
The joy at least of one whole nation.

Let meaner spirits of your sex
With humbler aims their thoughts perplex
10 And boast if by their arts they can
Contrive to make one happy man;
Whilst, moved by an impartial sense,
Favours like nature you dispense
With universal influence.

15 See, the kind seed-receiving earth
To every grain affords a birth;
On her no showers unwelcome fall,
Her willing womb retains 'em all;
And shall my Celia be confined?
20 No! Live up to thy mighty mind,
And be the mistress of mankind.

A Pastoral Dialogue between Alexis and Strephon

ALEXIS There sighs not on the plain
So lost a swain as I;
Scorched up with love, frozen with disdain,
Of killing sweetness I complain.
5 STREPHON If 'tis Corinna, die.

Since first my dazzled eyes were thrown
On that bewitching face,
Like ruined birds robbed of their young,
Lamenting, frighted, and alone,
10 I fly from place to place.

Framed by some cruel powers above,
So nice she is and fair,
None from undoing can remove,
Since all who are not blind must love,
15 Who are not vain, despair.

6 Shepherds conversing, an etching by François Boucher

ALEXIS The gods no sooner give a grace,
But, fond of their own art,
Severely jealous, ever place,
To guard the glories of a face,
20 A dragon in the heart.

Proud and ill-natured powers they are,
Who, peevish to mankind,
For their own honour's sake, with care
Make a sweet form divinely fair
25 And add a cruel mind.

STREPHON Since she's insensible of love,
By honour taught to hate,
If we, forced by decrees above,
Must sensible to beauty prove,
30 How tyrannous is fate!

ALEXIS I to the nymph have never named
The cause of all my pain.
STREPHON Such bashfulness may well be blamed,
For since to serve we're not ashamed,
35 Why should she blush to reign?

ALEXIS But if her haughty heart despise
My humble proffered one,
The just compassion she denies,
I may obtain from others' eyes;
40 Hers are not fair alone.

Devouring flames require new food;
My heart's consumed almost.
New fires must kindle in her blood,
Or mine go out, and that's as good.
45 STREPHON Wouldst live when love is lost,

Be dead before thy passion dies?
For if thou shouldst survive,
What anguish would the heart surprize
To see her flames begin to rise
50 And thine no more alive.

ALEXIS Rather, what pleasure should I meet
In my triumphant scorn,
To see my tyrant at my feet,
Whilst, taught by her, unmoved I sit,
55 A tyrant in my turn.

STREPHON Ungentle shepherd, cease for shame!
Which way can you pretend
To merit so divine a flame,
Who to dull life make a mean claim,
60 When love is at an end?

As trees are by their bark embraced,
Love to my soul doth cling;
When torn by the herd's greedy taste,
The injured plants feel they're defaced,
65 They wither in the spring.

My rifled love would soon retire,
Dissolving into air,
Should I that nymph cease to admire,
Blest in whose arms I will expire,
70 Or at her feet despair.

A Dialogue between Strephon and Daphne

STREPHON Prithee now, fond fool, give o'er;
Since my heart is gone before,
To what purpose should I stay?
Love commands another way.

5 DAPHNE Perjured swain, I knew the time
When dissembling was your crime.
In pity now employ that art
Which first betrayed, to ease my heart.

STREPHON Women can with pleasure feign;
10 Men dissemble still with pain.
What advantage will it prove
If I lie, who cannot love?

DAPHNE Tell me then the reason why
Love from hearts in love does fly;
15 Why the bird will build a nest
Where he ne'er intends to rest?

STREPHON Love, like other little boys,
Cries for hearts, as they for toys,
Which, when gained, in childish play
20 Wantonly are thrown away.

DAPHNE Still on wing, or on his knees,
Love does nothing by degrees:
Basely flying when most prized,
Meanly fawning when despised,

25 Flattering or insulting ever,
Generous and grateful never:
All his joys are fleeting dreams,
All his woes severe extremes.

STREPHON Nymph, unjustly you inveigh;
30 Love, like us, must fate obey.
Since 'tis Nature's law to change,
Constancy alone is strange.

See the heavens in lightnings break,
Next in storms of thunder speak,
35 Till a kind rain from above
Makes a calm – so 'tis in love.

Flames begin our first address,
Like meeting thunder we embrace;
Then you know the showers that fall
40 Quench the fire, and quiet all.

DAPHNE How should I these showers forget,
'Twas so pleasant to be wet;
They killed love, I knew it well,
I died all the while they fell.

45 Say at least what nymph it is
Robs my breast of so much bliss?
If she's fair, I shall be eased;
Through my ruin you'll be pleased.

STREPHON Daphne never was so fair,
50 Strephon scarcely so sincere.
Gentle, innocent, and free,
Ever pleased with only me.

Many charms my heart enthrall,
But there's one above them all:
55 With aversion she does fly
Tedious, trading, constancy.

DAPHNE Cruel shepherd! I submit;
Do what Love and you think fit.
Change is fate, and not design;
60 Say you would have still been mine.

STREPHON Nymph, I cannot; 'tis too true,
Change has greater charms than you.
Be, by my example, wise;
Faith to pleasure sacrifice.

65 DAPHNE Silly swain, I'll have you know,
'Twas my practice long ago:
Whilst you vainly thought me true,
I was false in scorn of you.

By my tears, my heart's disguise,
70 I thy love and thee despise.
Womankind more joy discovers
Making fools than keeping lovers.

The Fall

How blest was the created state
Of man and woman ere they fell,
Compared to our unhappy fate;
We need not fear another hell.

5 Naked beneath cool shades they lay;
Enjoyment waited on desire.
Each member did their wills obey,
Nor could a wish set pleasure higher.

But we poor slaves to hope and fear
10 Are never of our joys secure;
They lessen still as they draw near,
And none but dull delights endure.

Then, Cloris, while I duty pay
The nobler tribute of a heart,
15 Be not you so severe to say
You love me for a frailer part.

The Mistress

An age in her embraces passed
Would seem a winter's day
Where life and light with envious haste
Are torn and snatched away.

5 But oh, how slowly minutes roll
When absent from her eyes
That feed my love, which is my soul,
It languishes and dies.

For then no more a soul but shade,
10 It mournfully does move
And haunts my breast, by absence made
The living tomb of love.

7 Adam and Eve, a drawing by Michiel Coxie in black chalk

You wiser men, despise me not,
  Whose lovesick fancy raves
15 On shades of souls and heaven knows what:
  Short ages live in graves.

Whene'er those wounding eyes so full
  Of sweetness you did see,
Had you not been profoundly dull,
20 You had gone mad like me.

Nor censure us, you who perceive
  My best beloved and me
Sigh and lament, complain and grieve,
  You think we disagree.

25 Alas! 'tis sacred jealousy,
  Love raised to an extreme,
The only proof 'twixt her and me
  We love and do not dream.

Fantastic fancies fondly move
30 And in frail joys believe,
Taking false pleasure for true love,
  But pain can ne'er deceive.

Kind jealous doubts, tormenting fears,
  And anxious cares, when past,
35 Prove our hearts' treasure fixed and dear,
  And make us blest at last.

A Song

Absent from thee I languish still;
Then ask me not when I return.
The straying fool 'twill plainly kill
To wish all day, all night to mourn.

5 Dear, from thine arms then let me fly,
That my fantastic mind may prove
The torments it deserves to try
That tears my fixed heart from my love.

When wearied with a world of woe
10 To thy safe bosom I retire
Where love and peace and truth does flow,
May I contented there expire,

Lest, once more wandering from that heaven,
I fall on some base heart unblest,
15 Faithless to thee, false, unforgiven,
And lose my everlasting rest.

A Song of a Young Lady. To her Ancient Lover

Ancient person, for whom I
All the flattering youth defy,
Long be it ere thou grow old,
Aching, shaking, crazy, cold.
5 But still continue as thou art,
Ancient person of my heart.

On thy withered lips and dry,
Which like barren furrows lie,
Brooding kisses I will pour
10 Shall thy youthful heat restore,
Such kind showers in autumn fall
And a second spring recall,
Nor from thee will ever part,
Ancient person of my heart.

15 Thy nobler part, which but to name
In our sex would be counted shame,
By Age's frozen grasp possessed,
From his ice shall be released,
And, soothed by my reviving hand,
20 In former warmth and vigour stand.
All a lover's wish can reach,
For thy joy my love shall teach.

And for thy pleasure shall improve
All that art can add to love.
25 Yet still I love thee without art,
Ancient person of my heart.

A Satyr against Mankind

Were I (who to my cost already am)
One of those strange, prodigious creatures, man
A spirit free to choose for my own share
What case of flesh and blood I pleased to wear,
5 I'd be a dog, a monkey, or a bear,
Or anything but that vain animal
Who is so proud of being rational.
The senses are too gross, and he'll contrive
A sixth to contradict the other five,
10 And before certain instinct, will prefer
Reason, which fifty times for one does err;
Reason, an *ignis fatuus* in the mind,
Which leaves the light of nature, sense, behind,
Pathless and dangerous wandering ways it takes
15 Through error's fenny bogs and thorny brakes,
Whilst the misguided follower climbs with pain
Mountains of whimseys heaped in his own brain;
Tumbling from thought to thought, falls headlong down
Into doubt's boundless sea, where, like to drown,
20 Books bear him up awhile and make him try
To swim with bladders of philosophy.
In hope still to o'ertake th'escaping light,
The vapour dances in his dazzled sight
Till spent, it leaves him to eternal night.
25 Then Old Age and Experience, hand in hand,
Lead him to death and make him understand,
After a search so painful and so long,
That all his life he has been in the wrong.
Huddled in dirt, the reasoning engine lies,
30 Who was so proud, so witty, and so wise.

Pride drew him in, as cheats their bubbles catch,
And made him venture to be made a wretch.
His wisdom did his happiness destroy,
Aiming to know that world he should enjoy.
35 And wit was his vain, frivolous pretense
Of pleasing others at his own expense.
For wits are treated just like common whores;
First they're enjoyed and then kicked out of doors.
The pleasure past, a threatening doubt remains
40 That frights th'enjoyer with succeeding pains.
Women and men of wit are dangerous tools
And ever fatal to admiring fools.
Pleasure allures, and when the fops escape,
'Tis not that they're belov'd but fortunate,
45 And therefore what they fear, at heart they hate.
But now methinks some formal band and beard
Takes me to task. Come on, sir, I'm prepared.
'Then, by your favour, anything that's writ
Against this gibing, jingling knack called wit
50 Likes me abundantly, but you'll take care
Upon this point, not to be too severe.
Perhaps my muse were fitter for this part,
For I profess I can be very smart
On wit, which I abhor with all my heart.
55 I long to lash it in some sharp essay,
But your grand indiscretion bids me stay
And turns my tide of ink another way.
What rage ferments in your degenerate mind
To make you rail at reason and mankind?
60 Blest, glorious man, to whom alone kind heaven
An everlasting soul hath freely given,
Whom his great maker took such care to make
That from himself he did the image take
And this fair frame in shining reason dressed
65 To dignify his nature above beast;
Reason, by whose aspiring influence
We take a flight beyond material sense,
Dive into mysteries, then soaring pierce
The flaming limits of the universe,

70 Search heaven and hell, find out what's acted there,
And give the world true grounds of hope and fear!'
'Hold, mighty man,' I cry, 'all this we know
From the pathetic pen of Ingelo,
From Patrick's *Pilgrim*, Stillingfleet's replies,
75 And 'tis this very reason I despise
This supernatural gift that makes a mite
Think he's the image of the infinite,
Comparing his short life, void of all rest,
To the eternal and the ever blest,
80 This busy, puzzling stirrer up of doubt
That frames deep myst'ries and then finds them out,
Filling with frantic crowds of thinking fools
Those reverend bedlams, colleges and schools,
Borne on whose wings, each heavy sot can pierce
85 The limits of the boundless universe;
So charming ointments make an old witch fly
And bear a crippled carcass through the sky.
'Tis this exalted power, whose business lies
In nonsense and impossibilities,
90 This made a whimsical philosopher
Before the spacious world his tub prefer,
And we have modern, cloistered coxcombs who
Retire to think, 'cause they have nought to do.
But thoughts were given for action's government;
95 Where action ceases, thought's impertinent.
Our sphere of action is life's happiness,
And he who thinks beyond thinks like an ass.
Thus, whilst against false reasoning I inveigh,
I own right reason, which I would obey,
100 That reason which distinguishes by sense
And gives us rules of good and ill from thence,
That bounds desires with a reforming will
To keep them more in vigour, not to kill.
Your reason hinders, mine helps to enjoy,
105 Renewing appetites yours would destroy.
My reason is my friend, yours is a cheat:
Hunger calls out, my reason bids me eat,
Perversely, yours your appetite does mock;

This asks for food, that answers, "What's o'clock?"
110 This plain distinction, sir, your doubt secures:
'Tis not true reason I despise, but yours.'

Thus I think reason righted, but for man
I'll ne'er recant; defend him if you can.
For all his pride and his philosophy,
115 'Tis evident beasts are in their degree
As wise at least and better far than he.
Those creatures are the wisest who attain
By surest means the ends at which they aim.
If therefore Jowler finds and kills his hares
120 Better than Meres supplies committee chairs,
Though one's a statesman, t'other but a hound,
Jowler in justice would be wiser found.

You see how far man's wisdom here extends,
Look next if human nature makes amends.
125 Whose principles most gen'rous are and just,
And to whose morals you would sooner trust,
Be judge yourself, I'll bring it to the test
Which is the basest creature, man or beast?
Birds feed on birds, beasts on each other prey,
130 But savage man alone does man betray.
Pressed by necessity, they kill for food;
Man undoes man to do himself no good.
With teeth and claws by nature armed, they hunt
Nature's allowance to supply their want,
135 But man with smiles, embraces, friendship, praise,
Most humanly his fellow's life betrays,
With voluntary pains works his distress,
Not through necessity but wantonness.
For hunger or for love they bite and tear,
140 Whilst wretched man is still in arms for fear.
For fear he arms and is of arms afraid,
From fear to fear successively betrayed,
Base fear, the source whence his best actions came,
His boasted honour and his dear-bought fame,
145 The lust of power to which he's such a slave
And for the which alone he dares be brave,
To which his various projects are designed,

Which makes him generous, affable, and kind,
For which he takes such pains to be thought wise,
150 And screws his actions in a forced disguise,
Leads a most tedious life in misery
Under laborious, mean hypocrisy.
Look to the bottom of this vast design,
Wherein man's wisdom, power, and glory join:
155 The good he acts, the ill he does endure,
'Tis all from fear, to make himself secure.
Merely for safety, after fame they thirst,
For all men would be cowards if they durst,
And honesty's against all common sense:
160 Men must be knaves, 'tis in their own defence.
Mankind's dishonest; if you think it fair
Amongst known cheats to play upon the square,
You'll be undone.
Nor can weak truth your reputation save:
165 The knaves will all agree to call you knave.
Wronged shall he live, insulted o'er, oppressed,
Who dares be less a villain than the rest.
Thus here you see what human nature craves:
Most men are cowards, all men should be knaves.
170 The difference lies, as far as I can see,
Not in the thing itself, but the degree,
And all the subject matter of debate
Is only, Who's a knave of the first rate?
All this with indignation have I hurled
175 At the pretending part of the proud world,
Who, swollen with selfish vanity, devise
False freedoms, holy cheats, and formal lies
Over their fellow slaves to tyrannize.
But if in court so just a man there be
180 (In court, a just man, yet unknown to me)
Who does his needful flattery direct,
Not to oppress and ruin, but protect;
Since flattery, which way soever laid,
Is still a tax on that unhappy trade,
185 If so upright a statesman you can find,
Whose passions bend to his unbiased mind,

Who does his arts and policies apply
To raise his country, not his family,
Nor while his pride owned avarice withstands,
190 Receives close bribes from friends' corrupted hands;
Is there a churchman who on God relies,
Whose life, his faith and doctrine justifies;
Not one blown up with vain, prelatic pride,
Who for reproof of sins does man deride;
195 Whose envious heart makes preaching a pretense,
With his obstreperous, saucy eloquence,
Dares chide at kings and rail at men of sense;
Who from his pulpit vents more peevish lies,
More bitter railings, scandals, calumnies,
200 Than at a gossiping are thrown about
When the good wives get drunk and then fall out;
None of that sensual tribe whose talents lie
In avarice, pride, sloth, and gluttony,
Who hunt good livings but abhor good lives,
205 Whose lust exalted to that height arrives
They act adultery with their own wives,
And ere a score of years completed be,
Can from the lofty pulpit proudly see
Half a large parish their own progeny;
210 Nor doting bishop who would be adored
For domineering at the council board,
A greater fop in business at fourscore,
Fonder of serious toys, affected more
Than the gay, glittering fool at twenty proves
215 With all his noise, his tawdry clothes, and loves;
But a meek, humble man of modest sense,
Who, preaching peace, does practise continence,
Whose pious life's a proof he does believe
Mysterious truths which no man can conceive;
220 If upon earth there dwell such God-like men,
I'll here recant my paradox to them,
Adore those shrines of virtue, homage pay,
And with the rabble world their laws obey.
If such there are, yet grant me this at least,
225 Man differs more from man than man from beast.

Plain Dealing's Downfall

Long time Plain Dealing in the haughty town,
Wand'ring about, though in a threadbare gown,
At last unanimously was cried down.

When almost starved, she to the country fled
5 In hopes though meanly she should there be fed
And tumble nightly on a pea-straw bed.

But Knavery, knowing her intent, took post
And rumoured her approach through every coast,
Vowing his ruin that should be her host.

10 Frighted at this, each rustic shut his door,
Bid her be gone and trouble him no more,
For he that entertained her must be poor.

At this, grief seized her, grief too great to tell,
When weeping, sighing, fainting, down she fell,
15 Whilst Knavery, laughing, rung her passing bell.

[*What vain, unnecessary things are men!*]

What vain, unnecessary things are men!
How well we do without 'em! Tell me then
Whence comes that mean submissiveness we find
This ill-bred age has wrought on womankind?
5 Fall'n from the rights their sex and beauties gave
To make men wish, despair, and humbly crave,
Now 'twill suffice if they vouchsafe to have.
To the Pall Mall, playhouse, and the drawing room,
Their women fairs, these women coursers come
10 To chaffer, choose, and ride their bargains home.
At the appearance of an unknown face
Up steps the arrogant, pretending ass,
Pulling by th'elbow his companion, Huff,
Cries, 'Look, by God that wench is well enough,

A Discription of *Plain-dealing*, *Time*, and *Death*,
Which all Men ought to mind whilst they do live on earth.
Abuse not *Plain-dealing*, but keep your Conscience clear;
Spend well your Time also, then Death you need not fear.

Plain-dealing *is grown out of Date*
Because he is poor, many him hate:
Conscience *likewise is laid aside,*
'Cause he base Actions can't abide.

To the Tune of, *A Letter for a Christian Family.* Written by *Thomas Lanfire.*

Time it doth pass away full fast,
Yet many doth spend Time in waste:
When Time is gone then cometh Death,
And puts a stop to Mortal Breath.

Plain-dealing loves Honesty,
Conscience hates Knavery.

Time doth stay for none. *Death* Cuts down every one.

Plain-Dealing.

I Am Plain-dealing which all men ought to use,
But many now a days doth me abuse:
Dissemulation is esteemed best,
Poor Plain-dealing is grown out of request.

In City, Town, and likewise in Country,
They say plain-dealing will a Beggar Dye:
Gallants they at me do both mock and flout,
Because that I go in a Thread-bare Coat.

The reason that so many doth me slight,
Is because I am Honest and Downright:
I use no Deceit, Fraud, nor Flattery,
But does to all men as I'de be done by.

I am not Covetous nor Worldly wise,
I crave no more then what will me suffice:
I hate vain Pride which now too much doth reign,
Therefore plain dealing they'l not entertain.

In Days of Old I was a welcome Guest,
And had good entertainment with the best:
I was esteemed amongst Rich and Poor,
But now plain-dealing is turn'd out of Door.

For now Dissemulation hath got the Day,
And in this Nation bears a mighty sway:
plain-dealing is held in scorn and disgrace,
Alack, when shall I find a resting-place.

Conscience.

My Name is Conscience, poor plain-dealing's mate
Although like him, I'm Old and out of date:
Many with their whole hearts doth me defie,
'Cause Conscience can't agree with Knavery.

But if I within their Bosoms once do creep,
With their bad actions I prick their hearts deep:
I mind them of their Covetousness and Pride,
Therefore poor Conscience they cannot abide.

The Lawyer and Usurer hath forgot me,
They Gripe poor Men Unconscionably:
They study only how to keep up Gold,
Conscience and plain-dealing they quite have sold.

And many others in these times there are,
That of their Conscience do not take no care:
They pawn their Conscience for Lucre of gain,
Which Conscience will to them at last make plain.

So many are inclin'd to Cruelty,
And doth Conscience and plain-dealing defie:
Tell them of Conscience they'l count you their foe,
Quoth they Conscience was Hang'd long time ago.

But I wish such men they folly would refuse,
Lest Conscience at the last should them accuse:
In a good Conscience a man may put trust,
Then see you keep your Conscience right and just.

TIME.

I Am the antient standard of great fame,
Which all men ought to prize, Time is my name:
But this vain world doth now so many blind,
So that I am almost grown out of mind.

For why, I am slighted by many a one,
Who ne'r thinks on me till i'm past and gone:
And then too late they do mourn and complain,
Wishing they could recall back Time again.

Some spendeth their whole Time most wickedly,
In Drunkenness, Whoredom, and Blasphemy:
And some again sets their delight in Pride,
Not thinking how their precious Time doth slide.

Time is a stately jewel of great gain,
If it be well priz'd and not spent in vain:
Those that their time bestows in doing well,
In happiness no doubt but they shall dwell.

And those that spends their time in Idleness,
Shall one day want it in their great distress:
The whole world can't lost time restore,
Yesterday's gone and will ne'r return more.

Time's last Speech to the World.

Like to an Arrow shot out of a Bow,
Like to the Tide the which doth Ebb and Flow:
Like to a Bird full swift I flye away,
For Rich nor Poor i'le not make any stay.

DEATH.

I am the chief Commander Captain Death,
I Fight against all Mortals upon Earth:
When I amongst them chance to have a care,
I Conquer all, none dare with me hold War.

I fear not the bravest Champions that be,
Though they are stout, yet they can't Conquer me:
'Tis not Manhood nor Valour can them save,
I make them stoop and yield unto the Grave.

The chiefest Prince that in the world doth Live,
When I him strike, he up the Ghost must give:
His whole Kingdom can't him from me retain,
From Dust he came, and shall to Dust again,

Of Rich mens Power I do not stand in fear,
Nor for their loftiness I do not care:
Their Pride and Honour in the Earth I lay,
When their Glass is out, with me they must away,

Thus Rich and Poor, with Old and Young also,
Both Wise and Simple to the Grave must go:
There's no respect of Persons, worst or best,
All must at last by me lye *Mortuus est*.

When I on Mortals lay my fatal stroke,
They can't in no wise slip out of my Yoak:
I come suddenly and unawares to all,
Then see you are prepar'd when Death doth call.

FINIS.

Printed for *F. Coles*, *T. Vere*, *J. Wright*, and *J. Clarke*.

8 Thomas Lanfiere, *A Discription of Plain-dealing, Time, and Death*

15 Fair and well-shaped, good lips and teeth, 'twill do;
She shall be tawdry for a month or two
At my expense, be rude and take upon her,
Show her contempt of quality and honour,
And with the general fate of errant woman
20 Be very proud awhile, then very common.'
Ere bear this scorn, I'd be shut up at home,
Content with humouring myself alone,
Force back the humble love of former days
In pensive madrigals and ends of plays,
25 When, if my lady frowned, th'unhappy knight
Was fain to fast and lie alone that night.
But whilst th'insulting wife the breeches wore,
The husband took her clothes to give his whore,
Who now maintains it with a gentler art;
30 Thus tyrannies to commonwealths convert.
Then after all, you find, whate'er we say,
Things must go on in their lewd, natural way.
Besides, the beastly men we daily see
Can please themselves alone as well as we.
35 Therefore, kind ladies of the town, to you
For our stol'n, ravished men we hereby sue.
By this time you have found out, we suppose,
That they're as arrant tinsel as their clothes,
Poor broken properties that cannot serve
40 To treat such persons so as they deserve.
Mistake us not, we do not here pretend
That like young sparks you can condescend
To love a beastly playhouse creature. Foh!
We dare not think so meanly of you. No,
45 'Tis not the player pleases but the part;
She may like Rollo who despises Hart.
To theatres, as temples, you are brought
Where Love is worshipped and his precepts taught.
You must go home and practise, for 'tis here,
50 Just as in other preaching places, where
Great eloquence is shown 'gainst sin and papists
By men who live idolators and atheists.

These two were dainty trades indeed, could each
Live up to half the miracles they teach;
55 Both are a

Consideratus, Considerandus

What pleasures can the gaudy world afford?
What true delights does teeming nature hoard
In her great store-house where she lays her treasure?
Alas, 'tis all the shadow of a pleasure;
5 No true content in all her works are found,
No solid joys in all earth's spacious round
For labouring man, who toils himself in vain,
Eagerly grasping what creates his pain.
How false and feeble, nay scarce worth a name
10 Are riches, honour, power, and babbling fame.
Yet 'tis, for these men wade through seas of blood,
And bold in mischief, storm to be withstood,
Which when obtained breed but stupendous fear,
Strife, jealousies, and sleep-disturbing care.
15 No beam of comfort, not a ray of light
Shines thence, to guide us through fate's gloomy night,
But lost in devious darkness, there we stay,
Bereft of reason in an endless way.
Virtue's the solid good, if any be;
20 'Tis that creates our true felicity,
Though we despise, contemn, and cast it by
As worthless or our fatal'st enemy
Because our darling lusts it dare control
And bound the rovings of the madding soul.
25 Therefore in garments poor, it still appears
And sometimes naked, it no garments wears,
Shunned by the great and worthless thought by most,
Urged to be gone or wished for ever lost.
Yet it is loath to leave our wretched coast,
30 But in disguise does here and there intrude,
Striving to conquer base ingratitude,

And boldly ventures now and then to shine,
So to make known it is of birth divine,
But clouded oft, it like the lightning plays,
35 Loosing as soon as seen its pointed rays.
Which scarceness makes those that are weak in wit
For virtue's self admire its counterfeit,
With which damned hypocrites the world delude
As we on Indians glass for gems intrude.

Scene i. Mr Dainty's Chamber

Enter Dainty in his nightgown, singing.

DAINTY *J'ai l'amour dans le cœur et la rage dans les os.* I am confident I shall never sleep again. And t'were no great matter, if it did not make me look thin. For naturally I hate to be so long absent from myself, as one is in a manner
5 those seven dull hours he snores away. And yet methinks not to sleep till the sun rise is an odd effect of my disease and makes the night tedious without a woman. Reading would relieve me, but books treat of other men's affairs,
10 and to me that's tiresome. Besides, I seldom have candle. But I am resolved to write some love passages of my own life. They will make a pretty novel. And when my boy buys a link, it shall burn by me when I go to bed, while I divert myself with reading my own story, which will be pleasant
15 enough. Boy!

Enter Boy.

BOY Sir?

DAINTY Who knocked at door just now? Was it some woman?

BOY Mistress Manners's maid, sir, with a posset for you.

DAINTY And you never brought her up, you rascal? How can
20 you be so ill-bred and belong to me? See who knocks there. Some other woman? *Exit Boy*
Mistress Manners's fondness for me is very useful, for besides the good things she always sends me, and money I borrow of her sometimes, I have a further prospect. Sir Lionel's
25 daughters, which are in her charge, both like me, but the youngest I pitch upon. And because I can't marry 'em

both, my young nobility, Mr Squab, shall have the other sister. But I'll bubble him afterwards. Thus I'll raise my fortune, which is all I want, for I am an agreeable man and
30 everybody likes me.

Enter Boy.

BOY 'Tis Mr Squab, sir.

DAINTY Call him up, but comb your periwig first. Let me comb it. You are the laziest sloven!

Mistress Knight's Advice to the Duchess of Cleveland in Distress for a Prick

Quoth the Duchess of Cleveland to councillor Knight,
'I'd fain have a prick, knew I how to come by't.
I desire you'll be secret and give your advice,
Though cunt be not coy, reputation is nice.'

5 'To some cellar in Sodom Your Grace must retire,
Where porters with black pots sit round a coal fire;
There open your case, and Your Grace cannot fail
Of a dozen of pricks for a dozen of ale.'

'Is it so?' quoth the Duchess. 'Aye, by God,' quoth the whore,
10 'Then give me the key that unlocks the back door,
For I'd rather be fucked by porters and carmen
Than thus be abused by Churchill and Jermyn.' (84)

[*Out of mere love and arrant devotion*]

Out of mere love and arrant devotion,
Of marriage I'll give you this galloping notion:
It's the bane of all business, the end of all pleasure,
The consumption of wit, youth, virtue, and treasure;
5 It's the rack of our thoughts, the nightmare of sleep,
It sets us to work before the day peep;
It makes us make brick without stubble or straw,
And a cunt has no sense of conscience or law.

9 Lt. Col. John Churchill's hasty retreat, a detail from William Hogarth, *Marriage-à-la-Mode* (1745), Plate V

If you needs must have flesh, take the way that is noble:
10 In a generous wench there is nothing of trouble,
You come on, you come off, you do what you please,
And the worst you can fear is but a disease.
And diseases, you know, will admit of a cure,
But the hell-fire of marriage none can endure.

Epilogue to Love in the Dark, *as it was spoken by Mr Haines*

As charms are nonsense, nonsense seems a charm
Which hearers of all judgement does disarm;
For songs and scenes a double audience bring,
And doggerel takes which smiths in satin sing.
5 Now to machines and a dull masque you run,
We find that wit's the monster you would shun,
And by my troth 'tis most discreetly done.
For since with vice and folly wit is fed,
Through mercy 'tis most of you are not dead.
10 Players turn puppets now at your desire,
In their mouths nonsense, in their tails a wire,
They fly through clouds of clouts and showers of fire.
A kind of losing loadum is their game,
Where the worst writer has the greatest fame.
15 To get vile plays like theirs shall be our care,
But of such awkward actors we despair.
False taught at first,
Like bowls ill-biased, still the more they run
They're further off than when they first begun.
20 In comedy their unweighed action mark,
There's one is such a dear, familiar spark;
He yawns as if he were but half awake
And fribbling for free speaking does mistake.
False accent and neglectful action too
25 They have both so nigh good, yet neither true,
That both together, like an ape's mock face,
By near resembling man do man disgrace.

Thorough-paced ill actors may perhaps be cured;
Half-players like half-wits can't be endured.
30 Yet these are they who durst expose the age
Of the great wonder of our English stage,
Whom nature seemed to form for your delight,
And bid him speak as she bid Shakespeare write.
Those blades indeed are cripples in their art,
35 Mimic his foot, but not his speaking part;
Let them the Traitor or Volpone try.
Could they
Rage like Cethegus or like Cassius die,
They ne'er had sent to Paris for such fancies
40 As monsters' heads and Merry Andrew's dances.
Withered perhaps, not perished we appear,
But they were blighted and ne'er came to bear.
Th'old poets dressed your mistress wit before,
These draw you on with an old painted whore
45 And sell like bawds patched plays for maids twice o'er.
Yet they may scorn our house and actors too,
Since they have swelled so high to hector you.
They cry, 'Pox o' these Covent Garden men,
Damn 'em, not one of them but keeps out ten.
50 Were they once gone, we for those thundering blades
Should have an audience of substantial trades,
Who love our muzzled boys and tearing fellows,
My Lord great Neptune *and great Nephew* Eolus.
Oh how the merry citizen's in love
55 With
Psyche, *the goddess of each field and grove.*
He cries, "I' faith, methinks 'tis well enough",
But you roar out and cry, "'Tis all damned stuff."'
So to their house the graver fops repair,
60 While men of wit find one another here.

The Maimed Debauchee

As some brave admiral, in former war
Deprived of force but pressed with courage still,
Two rival fleets appearing from afar, (88)
Crawls to the top of an adjacent hill,

5 From whence (with thoughts full of concern) he views
The wise and daring conduct of the fight,
And each bold action to his mind renews
His present glory and his past delight;

From his fierce eyes flashes of rage he throws,
10 As from black clouds when lightning breaks away,
Transported, thinks himself amidst his foes,
And absent, yet enjoys the bloody day;

So when my days of impotence approach,
And I'm by pox and wine's unlucky chance
15 Forced from the pleasing billows of debauch
On the dull shore of lazy temperance,

My pains at least some respite shall afford,
Whilst I behold the battles they maintain
When fleets of glasses sail about the board,
20 From whose broadsides volleys of wit shall rain;

Nor shall the sight of honourable scars,
Which my too forward valour did procure,
Frighten new-listed soldiers from the wars:
Past joys have more than paid what I endure.

25 Should any youth (worth being drunk) prove nice
And from his fair inviter meanly shrink,
'Twould please the ghost of my departed Vice
If at my counsel he repent and drink.

Or should some cold-complexioned sot forbid,
30 With his dull morals, our bold night alarms,
I'll fire his blood by telling what I did
When I was strong and able to bear arms.

10 An English man-o'-war with guns firing, seen from St Catherine's Point, Fowey, Cornwall, a drawing by Willem Schellincks

I'll tell of whores attacked (their lords at home),
Bawds' quarters beaten up and fortress won,
35 Windows demolished, watches overcome,
And handsome ills by my contrivance done.

Nor shall our love-fits, Cloris, be forgot,
When each the well-looked linkboy strove t'enjoy,
And the best kiss was the deciding lot
40 Whether the boy fucked you, or I the boy.

With tales like these I will such heat inspire
As to important mischief shall incline;
I'll make him long some ancient church to fire
And fear no lewdness he's called to by wine.

45 Thus statesmanlike I'll saucily impose
And safe from action valiantly advise,
Sheltered in impotence urge you to blows,
And being good for nothing else, be wise.

A Very Heroical Epistle from My Lord All-Pride to Doll-Common

The Argument: *Doll-Common being forsaken by My Lord All-Pride and having written him a most lamentable Letter, his Lordship sends her the following Answer.*

Madam,
  If you're deceived, it is not by my cheat,
For all disguises are below the great.
What man or woman upon earth can say
I ever used 'em well above a day?
5 How is it then that I inconstant am?
He changes not who always is the same.
In my dear self I centre everything,
My servants, friends, my mistress, and my King,
Nay, heaven and earth to that one point I bring.
10 Well-mannered, honest, generous, and stout
(Names by dull fools to plague mankind found out),

Should I regard, I must myself constrain,
And 'tis my maxim to avoid all pain.
You fondly look for what none e'er could find,
15 Deceive yourself, and then call me unkind,
And by false reasons would my falsehood prove,
For 'tis as natural to change as love.
You may as justly at the sun repine
Because alike it does not always shine.
20 No glorious thing was ever made to stay;
My blazing star but visits and away.
As fatal too it shines as those i'th' skies;
'Tis never seen but some great lady dies.
The boasted favour you so precious hold
25 To me's no more than changing of my gold.
Whate'er you gave, I paid you back in bliss,
Then where's the obligation, pray, of this?
If heretofore you found grace in my eyes,
Be thankful for it and let that suffice.
30 But women, beggar-like, still haunt the door
Where they've received a charity before.
O happy sultan, whom we barbarous call,
How much refined art thou above us all!
Who envies not the joys of thy serail?
35 Thee, like some god, the trembling crowd adore,
Each man's thy slave and womankind thy whore.
Methinks I see thee underneath the shade
Of golden canopies supinely laid,
Thy crouching slaves all silent as the night,
40 But at thy nod all active as the light.
Secure in solid sloth thou there dost reign
And feel'st the joys of love without the pain.
Each female courts thee with a wishing eye,
While thou with awful pride walk'st careless by,
45 Till thy kind pledge at last marks out the dame
Thou fanciest most to quench thy present flame.
Then from thy bed submissive she retires
And thankful for thy grace no more requires.
No loud reproach nor fond unwelcome sound
50 Of women's tongues thy sacred ear dares wound.

If any do, a nimble mute straight ties
The true-love knot and stops her foolish cries.
Thou fear'st no injured kinsman's threatening blade
Nor midnight ambushes by rivals laid;
55 While here with aching hearts our joys we taste
Disturbed by swords like Damocles's feast.

To all Gentlemen, Ladies, and Others, whether of City, Town, or Country, Alexander Bendo wisheth all Health and Prosperity

Whereas this famous metropolis of England (and were the endeavours of its worthy inhabitants equal to their power, merit, and virtue, I should not stick to denounce it in a short time the metropolis of the whole world), whereas, I say, this
5 city (as most great ones are) has ever been infested with a numerous company of such whose arrogant confidence, backed with their ignorance, has enabled them to impose upon the people, either by premeditated cheats or at best the palpable, dull, and empty mistakes of their self-deluded imaginations in
10 physic, chemical and Galenic, in astrology, physiognomy, palmistry, mathematics, alchemy, and even in government itself: the last of which I will not propose to discourse of or meddle at all in, since it no ways belongs to my trade or vocation, as the rest do, which (thanks to my God) I find much more safe,
15 I think, equally honest, and therefore more profitable. But as to all the former, they have been so erroneously practised by many unlearned wretches whom poverty and neediness for the most part (if not the restless itch of deceiving) has forced to straggle and wander in unknown paths, that even the profes-
20 sions themselves, though originally the products of the most learned and wise men's laborious studies and experiences and by them left a wealthy and glorious inheritance for ages to come, seem by this bastard race of quacks and cheats to have been run out of all wisdom, learning, perspicuousness, and
25 truth with which they were so plentifully stocked and now run into a repute of mere mists, imaginations, errors, and deceits

11 Mountebank, an engraving by Pierce Tempest or John Savage after a drawing by Marcellus Laroon, in *The Cryes of the City of London*, 3rd edn (1689)

such as, in the management of these idle professors, indeed they were.

You will therefore (I hope) gentlemen, ladies, and others 30 deem it but just that I, who for some years have with all faithfulness and assiduity courted these arts and received such signal favours from them that have admitted me to the happy and full enjoyment of themselves and trusted me with their greatest secrets, should with an earnestness and concern more 35 than ordinary, take their parts against these impudent fops whose saucy, impertinent addresses and pretensions have brought such scandal upon their most immaculate honours and reputations.

Besides, I hope you will not think I could be so impudent 40 that, if I had intended any such foul play myself, I would have given you so fair warning by my severe observations upon others. *Qui alterum incusat probri, ipsum se intueri oportet.* PLAUTUS. However, Gentlemen, in a world like this, where virtue is so exactly counterfeited and hypocrisy so generally 45 taken notice of that everyone (armed with suspicion) stands upon his guard against it, 'twill be very hard, for a stranger especially, to escape censure. All I shall say for myself on this score is this: if I appear to anyone like a counterfeit, even for the sake of that chiefly ought I to be construed a true man. 50 Who is the counterfeit's example, his original, and that which he employs his industry and pains to imitate and copy? Is it therefore my fault if the cheat by his wits and endeavours makes himself so like me that consequently I cannot avoid resembling of him? Consider, pray, the valiant and the coward, 55 the wealthy merchant and the bankrupt, the politician and the fool; they are the same in many things and differ but in one alone. The valiant man holds up his head, looks confidently round about him, wears a sword, courts a lord's wife and owns it. So does the coward. One only point of honour, and that's 60 courage which like false metal one only trial can discover, makes the distinction. The bankrupt walks the Exchange, buys bargains, draws bills and accepts them with the richest whilst paper and credit are current coin. That which makes the difference is real cash, a great defect indeed, and yet but 65 one, and that the last found out, and still 'till then the least perceived. Now for the politician. He is a grave, deliberating, close, prying man. Pray, are there not grave, deliberating, close, prying fools?

70 If then the difference betwixt all these (though infinite in effect) be so nice in all appearance, will you expect it should be otherwise betwixt the false physician, astrologer, &c. and the true? The first calls himself learned doctor, sends forth his bills, gives physic and counsel, tells and foretells. The other is 75 bound to do just as much. 'Tis only your experience must distinguish betwixt them, to which I willingly submit myself. I'll only say something to the honour of the mountebank, in case you discover me to be one.

Reflect a little what kind of creature 'tis. He is one then 80 who is fain to supply some higher ability he pretends to with craft; he draws great companies to him by undertaking strange things which can never be effected. The politician (by his example no doubt) finding how the people are taken with specious miraculous impossibilities, plays the same game, pro- 85 tests, declares, promises I know not what things which he is sure can never be brought about. The people believe, are deluded, and pleased. The expectation of a future good, which shall never befall them, draws their eyes off a present evil. Thus are *they* kept and established in subjection, peace, and 90 obedience, *he* in greatness, wealth, and power. So you see the politician is and must be a mountebank in state affairs; and the mountebank no doubt, if he thrives, is an arrant politician in physic. But that I may not prove too tedious, I will proceed faithfully to inform you what are the things in which I pretend 95 chiefly at this time to serve my country.

First, I will (by leave of God) perfectly cure that *labes Britannica* or grand English disease, the scurvy, and that with such ease to my patient that he shall not be sensible of the least inconvenience whilst I steal his distemper from him. I 100 know there are many who treat this disease with mercury, antimony, and salts, being dangerous remedies in which I shall meddle very little and with great caution, but, by more secure, gentle, and less fallible medicines together with the observation of some few rules in diet, perfectly cure the patient, having 105 freed him from all the symptoms, as looseness of the teeth,

scorbutic spots, want of appetite, pains and lassitude in the limbs and joints, especially the legs. And to say true, there are few distempers in this nation that are not, or at least proceed not originally from, the scurvy, which were it well rooted out
110 (as I make no question to do it from all those who shall come into my hands), there would not be heard of so many gouts, aches, dropsies, and consumptions; nay, even those thick and slimy humours which generate stones in the kidneys and bladder are for the most part offsprings of the scurvy. It would
115 prove tedious to set down all its malignant race, but those who address themselves here shall be still informed by me of the nature of their distempers and the grounds I proceed upon to their cure. So will all reasonable people be satisfied that I treat them with care, honesty, and understanding, for I am not of
120 their opinion who endeavour to render their vocations rather mysterious than useful and satisfactory.

I will not here make a catalogue of diseases and distempers. It behooves a physician, I am sure, to understand them all, but if any one come to me (as I think there are very few that have
125 escaped my practice), I shall not be ashamed to own to my patient where I find myself to seek and at least he shall be secure with me from having experiments tried upon him, a privilege he can never hope to enjoy, either in the hands of the grand doctors of the court and town or in those of the lesser
130 quacks and mountebanks.

It is thought fit that I assure you of great secrecy as well as care in diseases where it is requisite, whether venereal or other, as some peculiar to women, the green-sickness, weaknesses, inflammations or obstructions in the stomach, reins, liver,
135 spleen, &c., for I would put no word in my bill that bears any unclean sound; it is enough that I make myself understood. I have seen physician's bills as bawdy as Aretine's *Dialogues*, which no man that walks warily before God can approve of. But I cure all suffocations in those parts producing fits of the
140 mother, convulsions, nocturnal inquietudes, and other strange accidents not fit to be set down here, persuading young women very often that their hearts are like to break for love, when God knows the distemper lies far enough from that place.

I have likewise got the knowledge of a great secret to

145 cure barrenness (proceeding from any accidental cause, as it often falls out, and no natural defect, for nature is easily assisted, difficultly restored, but impossible to be made more perfect by man than God himself had at first created and bestowed it), which I have made use of for many years with 150 great success, especially this last year wherein I have cured one woman that had been married twenty years, and another that had been married one and twenty years, and two women that had been three times married, as I can make appear by the testimony of several persons in London, Westminster, and 155 other places thereabouts. The medicines I use cleanse and strengthen the womb and are all to be taken in the space of seven days. And because I do not intend to deceive any person, upon discourse with them I will tell them whether I am like to do them any good. My usual contract is to receive 160 one half of what is agreed upon when the party shall be quick with child, the other half when she is brought to bed.

Cures of this kind I have done signal and many, for the which I doubt not but I have the good wishes and hearty prayer of many families who had else pined out their days 165 under the deplorable and reproachful misfortunes of barren wombs, leaving plentiful estates and possessions to be inherited by strangers.

As to astrological predictions, physiognomy, divination by dreams and otherwise (palmistry I have no faith in because 170 there can be no reason alleged for it), my own experience has convinced me more of their considerable effects and marvellous operations, chiefly in the directions of future proceedings to the avoiding of dangers that threaten and laying hold of advantages that might offer themselves.

175 I say, my own practice has convinced me more than all the sage and wise writings extant of these matters. For I might say this for myself (did it not look like ostentation) that I have very seldom failed in my predictions and often been very serviceable in my advice. How far I am capable in this way, I 180 am sure is not fit to be delivered in print. Those who have no opinion of the truth of this art will not, I suppose, come to me about it; such as have, I make no question of giving them ample satisfaction.

Nor will I be ashamed to set down here my willingness to
185 practise rare secrets (though somewhat collateral to my profession) for the help, conservation, and augmentation of beauty and comeliness, a thing created at first by God chiefly for the glory of his own name and then for the better establishment of mutual love between man and woman. For when God had
190 bestowed on man the power of strength and wisdom and thereby rendered woman liable to the subjection of his absolute will, it seemed but requisite that she should be endued likewise, in recompense, with some quality that might beget in him admiration of her and so enforce his tenderness and love.

195 The knowledge of these secrets I gathered in my travels abroad (where I have spent my time ever since I was fifteen years old to this my nine and twentieth year) in France and Italy. Those that have travelled in Italy will tell you to what a miracle art does there assist nature in the preservation of
200 beauty, how women of forty bear the same countenance with those of fifteen, that ages are no ways distinguished by faces. Whereas here in England, look a horse in the mouth and a woman in the face, you presently know both their ages to a year. I will therefore give you such remedies that without
205 destroying your complexion (as most of your paints and daubings do) shall render them purely fair, clearing and preserving them from all spots, freckles, heats, pimples, and marks of the smallpox, or any other accidental ones, so the face be not seamed or scarred.

210 I will also cleanse and preserve your teeth white and round as pearls, fastening them that are loose. Your gums shall be kept entire, as red as coral, your lips of the same colour and soft as you could wish your lawful kisses.

I will likewise administer that which shall cure the worst of
215 breaths, provided the lungs be not totally perished and imposthumated, as also certain and infallible remedies for those whose breaths are yet untainted, so that nothing but either a very long sickness or old age itself shall ever be able to spoil them.

220 I will besides (if it be desired) take away from their fatness who have overmuch, and add flesh to those that want it, without the least detriment to the constitution.

Now should Galen himself look out of his grave and tell me these were baubles below the profession of a physician, I
225 would boldly answer him that I take more glory in preserving God's image in its unblemished beauty upon one good face than I should do in patching up all the decayed carcasses in the world.

They that will do me the favour to come to me shall be
230 sure from three of the clock in the afternoon till eight at night at my lodgings in Tower street, next door to the sign of the Black Swan at a goldsmith's house, to find

Their humble servant,
Alexander Bendo.

An Allusion to Horace. The 10th Satire of the 1st Book

Nempe incomposito Dixi pede &c.

Well sir, 'tis granted I said Dryden's rhymes
Were stol'n, unequal, nay dull many times.
What foolish patron is there found of his
So blindly partial to deny me this?
5 But that his plays, embroidered up and down
With wit and learning, justly pleased the town
In the same paper I as freely own.
Yet having this allowed, the heavy mass
That stuffs up his loose volumes must not pass:
10 For by that rule I might as well admit
Crowne's tedious scenes for poetry and wit.
'Tis therefore not enough when your false sense
Hits the false judgement of an audience
Of clapping fools, assembling a vast crowd
15 Till the thronged playhouse crack with the dull load;
Though ev'n that talent merits in some sort
That can divert the rabble and the court,
Which blundering Settle never could attain,
And puzzling Otway labours at in vain.
20 But within due proportions circumscribe
Whate'er you write, that with a flowing tide

The style may rise, yet in its rise forbear
With useless words t'oppress the wearied ear.
Here be your language lofty, there more light,
25 Your rhetoric with your poetry unite.
For elegance' sake sometimes allay the force
Of epithets; 'twill soften the discourse.
A jest in scorn points out and hits the thing
More home than the morosest satire's sting.
30 Shakespeare and Jonson did herein excel
And might in this be imitated well;
Whom refined Etherege copies not at all,
But is himself a sheer original;
Nor that slow drudge in swift Pindaric strains,
35 Flatman, who Cowley imitates with pains,
And rides a jaded muse, whipped with loose reins.
When Lee makes temperate Scipio fret and rave,
And Hannibal a whining amorous slave,
I laugh and wish the hot-brained fustian fool
40 In Busby's hands to be well lashed at school.
Of all our modern wits, none seems to me
Once to have touched upon true comedy
But hasty Shadwell and slow Wycherley.
Shadwell's unfinished works do yet impart
45 Great proofs of force of nature, none of art;
With just, bold strokes he dashes here and there,
Showing great mastery with little care,
And scorns to varnish his good touches o'er
To make the fools and women praise 'em more.
50 But Wycherley earns hard whate'er he gains;
He wants no judgement, nor he spares no pains.
He frequently excels, and at the least
Makes fewer faults than any of the best.
Waller, by nature for the bays designed,
55 With force and fire and fancy unconfined,
In panegyrics does excel mankind.
He best can turn, enforce, and soften things
To praise great conquerors or to flatter kings.
For pointed satires I would Buckhurst choose,
60 The best good man with the worst-natured muse,

For songs and verses mannerly obscene,
That can stir nature up by springs unseen,
And without forcing blushes, warm the Queen.
  Sedley has that prevailing, gentle art,
65 That can with a resistless charm impart
The loosest wishes to the chastest heart,
Raise such a conflict, kindle such a fire,
Betwixt declining virtue and desire,
Till the poor vanquished maid dissolves away
70 In dreams all night, in sighs and tears all day.
  Dryden in vain tried this nice way of wit,
For he to be a tearing blade thought fit.
But when he would be sharp, he still was blunt;
To frisk his frolic fancy, he'd cry, 'Cunt',
75 Would give the ladies a dry bawdy bob,
And thus he got the name of Poet Squab.
But, to be just, 'twill to his praise be found
His excellencies more than faults abound;
Nor dare I from his sacred temples tear
80 That laurel which he best deserves to wear.
But does not Dryden find ev'n Jonson dull;
Fletcher and Beaumont uncorrect and full
Of lewd lines, as he calls 'em; Shakespeare's style
Stiff and affected; to his own the while
85 Allowing all the justness that his pride
So arrogantly had to these denied?
And may not I have leave impartially
To search and censure Dryden's works and try
If those gross faults his choice pen does commit
90 Proceed from want of judgement or of wit;
Or if his lumpish fancy does refuse
Spirit and grace to his loose slattern muse?
Five hundred verses every morning writ
Proves you no more a poet than a wit.
95 Such scribbling authors have been seen before;
Mustapha, *The English Princess*, forty more
Were things perhaps composed in half an hour.
To write what may securely stand the test
Of being well read over, thrice at least,

100 Compare each phrase, examine every line,
Weigh every word, and every thought refine,
Scorn all applause the vile rout can bestow
And be content to please those few who know.
Canst thou be such a vain, mistaken thing
105 To wish thy works might make a playhouse ring
With the unthinking laughter and poor praise
Of fops and ladies, factious for thy plays?
Then send a cunning friend to learn thy doom
From the shrewd judges of the drawing room.
110 I've no ambition on that idle score,
But say with Betty Morris heretofore
When a court lady called her Buckhurst's whore,
'I please one man of wit, am proud on't too;
Let all the coxcombs dance to bed to you.'
115 Should I be troubled when the purblind knight,
Who squints more in his judgement than his sight,
Picks silly faults, and censures what I write;
Or when the poor-fed poets of the town
For scraps and coach-room cry my verses down?
120 I loathe the rabble, 'tis enough for me
If Sedley, Shadwell, Sheppard, Wycherley,
Godolphin, Butler, Buckhurst, Buckingham,
And some few more, whom I omit to name,
Approve my sense: I count their censure fame.

Dialogue

NELL When to the King I bid good morrow
With tongue in mouth and hand on tarse,
Portsmouth may rend her cunt for sorrow
And Mazarin may kiss mine arse.

5 PORTSMOUTH When England's monarch's on my belly
With prick in cunt, though double crammed,
Fart of mine arse for small whore Nelly,
And great whore Mazarin be damned.

KING When on Portsmouth's lap I lay my head,
10 And Knight does sing her bawdy song,
I envy not George Porter's bed,
Nor the delights of Madam Long.

PEOPLE Now heaven preserve our faith's defender
From Paris plot and Roman cunt,
15 From Mazarin, that new pretender,
And from that *politique* Gramont.

Valentinian. A Tragedy

Act I. Scene i

The curtain flies up with the music of trumpets and kettledrums and discovers the Emperor passing through to the garden, attended with a great court. Æcius and Maximus stay behind.

MAXIMUS Great is the honour which our Emperor
Does by his frequent visits throw on Maximus.
Not less than thrice this week has his gay court
With all its splendour shined within my walls.
5 Nor does this glorious sun bestow his beams
Upon a barren soil; my happy wife,
Fruitful in charms for Valentinian's heart,
Crowns the soft moments of each welcome hour
With such variety of successive joys
10 That lost in love, when the long day is done,
He willingly would give his empire up
For the enjoyment of a minute more.
While I,
Made glorious through the merit of my wife,
15 Am at the court adored as much as she,
As if the vast dominion of his world
He had exchanged with me for my Lucina.
ÆCIUS I rather wish he would exchange his passions,

Give you his thirst of love for yours of honour,
20 And leaving you the due possession
Of your just wishes in Lucina's arms,
Think how he might by force of worth and virtue,
Maintain the right of his imperial crown
Which he neglects for garlands made of roses;
25 Whilst in disdain of his ill-guided youth
Whole provinces fall off and scorn to have
Him for their prince who is his pleasures' slave.

MAXIMUS I cannot blame the nations, noble friend,
For falling off so fast from this wild man,
30 When (under our allegiance be it spoken
And the most happy tie of our affections)
The whole world groans beneath him. By the gods
I'd rather be a bondslave to his panders,
Constrained by power to serve their vicious wills,
35 Than bear the infamy of being held
A favourite of this fool-flattered tyrant.
Where lives virtue,
Honour, discretion, wisdom? Who are called
And chosen to the steering of his empire
40 But traitors, bawds, and wenches? Oh my Æcius,
The glory of a soldier and the truth
Of men made up for goodness' sake, like shells,
Grow to the ragged walls for want of action.
Only your happy self and that I love you,
45 Which is a larger means to me than favour –

ÆCIUS No more, my worthy friend! Though these be truths,
And though these truths would ask a reformation,
At least a little mending, yet remember
We are but subjects, Maximus. Obedience
50 To what is done and grief for what's ill done
Is all we can call ours. The hearts of princes
Are like the temples of the gods; pure incense
(Till some unhallowed hands defile their offerings)
Burns ever there. We must not put them out
55 Because the priests who touch those sweets are wicked.
We dare not, dearest friend. Nay more, we cannot,
While we consider whose we are, and how,

To what laws bound, much more to what lawgiver,
While majesty is made to be obeyed
60 And not enquired into, whilst gods and angels
Make but a rule, as we do (though stricter),
Like desperate and unseasoned fools let fly
Our killing angers and forsake our honours.

MAXIMUS Thou best of friends and men, whose wise instructions
65 Are not less charitable, weigh but thus much,
Nor think I speak it with ambition,
For by the gods I do not. Why, my Æcius,
Why are we thus, or how became thus wretched?

ÆCIUS You'll fall again into your fit.

MAXIMUS I will not.
70 Or are we now no more the sons of Romans,
No more the fellows of their mighty fortunes,
But conquered Gauls or quivers for the Parthians?
Why is this Emperor, this man we honour,
This god that ought to be –

ÆCIUS You are too curious.

75 MAXIMUS Give me leave. Why is this author of us –

ÆCIUS I dare not hear you speak thus.

MAXIMUS (I'll be modest) –
Thus led away, thus vainly led away,
And we beholders? Misconceive me not;
I sow no danger in my words. But wherefore
80 And to what end are we the sons of fathers
Famous and fast to Rome? Why are their virtues
Stamped in the dangers of a thousand battles,
For goodness' sake their honours Time outdaring?
I think for our example.

ÆCIUS You speak well.

85 MAXIMUS Why are we seeds of those, then, to shake hands
With bawds and base informers, kiss Discredit
And court her like a mistress? Pray, your leave yet.
You'll say th'Emperor's young and apt to take
Impression from his pleasures.
90 Yet even his errors have their good effects,
For the same gentle temper which inclines

His mind to softness does his heart defend
From savage thoughts of cruelty and blood,
Which through the streets of Rome in streams did flow
95 From hearts of senators under the reigns
Of our severer, warlike emperors.
While under this scarcely one criminal
Meets the hard sentence of the dooming law,
And the whole world dissolved into a peace
100 Owes its security to this man's pleasures.
But Æcius, be sincere. Do not defend
Actions and principles your soul abhors.
You know this virtue is his greatest vice.
Impunity is the highest tyranny.
105 And what the fawning court miscalls his pleasures
Exceeds the moderation of a man.
Nay, to say justly, friend, they are loath'd vices
And such as shake our worths with foreign nations.
ÆCIUS You search the sore too deep. And let me tell you,
110 In any other man this had been treason,
And so rewarded. Pray depress your spirit,
For though I constantly believe you honest
(You were no friend for me else), and what now
You freely speak but good you owe to th'empire,
115 Yet take heed, worthy Maximus, all ears
Hear not with that distinction mine do. Few you'll find
Admonishers, but urgers of your actions,
And to the heaviest, friend. And pray consider
We are but shadows; motions others give us.
120 And though our pities may become the times,
Our powers cannot. Nor may we justify
Our private jealousies by open force.
Wife or what else, to me it matters not.
I am your friend, but durst my own soul urge me
125 (And by that soul I speak my just affections)
To turn my hand from truth, which is obedience,
And give the helm my virtue holds to anger,
Though I had both the blessings of the Bruti
And both their instigations, though my cause
130 Carried a face of justice beyond theirs,

And as I am a servant to my fortunes,
That daring soul that first taught disobedience
Should feel the first example.

MAXIMUS Mistake me not, my dearest Æcius,
135 Do not believe that through mean jealousy
(How far th'Emperor's passion may prevail
On my Lucina's thoughts to our dishonour),
That I abhor the person of my prince.
Alas, that honour were a trivial loss
140 Which she and I want merit to preserve.
Virtue and Maximus are placed too near
Lucina's heart to leave him such a fear.
No private loss or wrong inflames my spirits.
The Roman glory, Æcius, languishes;
145 I am concerned for Rome and for the world.
And when th'Emperor pleases to afford
Time from his pleasures to take care of those,
I am his slave and have a sword and life
Still ready for his service.

ÆCIUS Now you are brave
150 And like a Roman justly are concerned.
But say he be to blame. Are therefore we
Fit fires to purge him? No, my dearest friend,
The elephant is never won with anger.
Nor must that man who would reclaim a lion
155 Take him by the teeth.
Our honest actions and the truth that breaks
Like morning from our service, chaste and blushing,
Is that that pulls a prince back. Then he sees
And not till then truly repents his errors.

160 MAXIMUS My heart agrees with yours; I'll take your counsel.
The Emperor appears. Let us withdraw.
And as we both do love him, may he flourish. *Exeunt.*

Enter Valentinian and Lucina.

VALENTINIAN Which way, Lucina, hope you to escape
The censures both of tyrannous and proud,
165 While your admirers languish by your eyes
And at your feet an Emperor despairs?
Gods! Why was I marked out of all your brood
To suffer tamely under mortal hate?

Is it not that I do protect your shrines,
170 Am author of your sacrifice and prayers?
Forced by whose great commands the knowing world
Submits to own your beings and your power.
And must I feel the torments of neglect,
Betrayed by love to be the slave of scorn?
175 But 'tis not you, poor harmless deities,
That can make Valentinian sigh and mourn.
Alas, all power is in Lucina's eyes.
How soon could I shake off this heavy earth,
Which makes me little lower than yourselves,
180 And sit in heaven as equal with the first,
But Love bids me pursue a nobler aim:
Continue mortal and Lucina's slave.
From whose fair eyes, would Pity take my part
And bend her will to save a bleeding heart,
185 I in her arms such blessings should obtain
For which th'unenvied gods might wish in vain.

LUCINA Ah, cease to tempt those gods and virtue too.
Great Emperor of the world and lord of me,
Heaven has my life submitted to your will.
190 My honour's heaven's, which will preserve its own.
How vile a thing am I when that is gone!
When of my honour you have rifled me,
What other merit have I to be yours?
With my fair fame let me your subject live
195 And save that humbleness you smile upon.
Those gracious looks whose brightness should rejoice,
Make your poor handmaid tremble when she thinks
That they appear like lightning's fatal flash,
Which by destructive thunder is pursued,
200 Blasting those fields on which it shined before.
And should the gods abandon worthless me
A sacrifice to shame and to dishonour,
A plague to Rome and blot to Caesar's fame,
For what crime yet unknown shall Maximus
205 By me and Caesar be made infamous?
The faithful'st servant and the kindest lord,

So true, so brave, so gen'rous, and so just,
Who ne'er knew fault, why should he fall to shame?

VALENTINIAN Sweet innocence! Alas, your Maximus
210 (Who I like you esteem) is in no danger,
If duty and allegiance be no shame.
Have I not praetors through the spacious earth
Who in my name do mighty nations sway,
Enjoying rich dominions in my right?
215 Their temporary governments I change,
Divide, or take away as I see good,
And this they think no injury nor shame.
Can you believe your husband's right to you
Other than what from me he does derive,
220 Who justly may recall my own at pleasure?
Am I not Emperor, this world my own,
Given me without a partner by the gods?
Each man, each beast, even to the smallest fly
No mortal creature dare call his but I.
225 And shall these gods who gave me all allow
That one less than myself should have a claim
To you, the pride and glory of the whole,
You, without whom the rest is worthless dross,
Life a base slavery, empire but a mock,
230 And love, the soul of all, a bitter curse?
No, only blessing! Maximus and I
Must change our provinces. The world shall bow
Beneath my sceptre grasped in his strong hand,
Whose valour may reduce rebellious slaves
235 And wise integrity secure the rest
In all those rights the gods to me have given.
While I from tedious toils of empire free
The servile pride of government despise,
Find peace and joy and love and heaven in thee,
240 And seek for all my glory in those eyes.

LUCINA Had heaven designed me for so great a fate
As Caesar's love, I should have been preserved
By careful providence for him alone,
Not offered up at first to Maximus.
245 For princes should not mingle with their slaves

Nor seek to quench their thirst in troubled streams.
Nor am I framed with thoughts fit for a throne.
To be commanded still has been my joy,
And to obey the height of my ambition.
250 When young in anxious cares I spent the day,
Trembling for fear lest each unguided step
Should tread the paths of error and of blame,
Till heaven in gentle pity sent my lord
In whose commands my wishes meet their end.
255 Pleased and secure while following his will,
Whether to live or die I cannot err.
You like the sun, great sir, are placed above,
I, a low myrtle in the humble vale,
May flourish by your distant influence,
260 But should you bend your glories nearer me,
Such fatal favour withers me to dust.
Or I in foolish gratitude desire
To kiss your feet, by whom we live and grow.
To such a height I should in vain aspire
265 Who am already rooted here below;
Fixed in my Maximus's breast I lie;
Torn from that bed, like withered flowers I die.

VALENTINIAN Cease to oppress me with a thousand charms;
There need no succours to prevailing arms.
270 Your beauty had subdued my heart before;
Such virtue could alone enslave me more.
If you love Maximus to this degree,
How would you be in love did you love me?
In her who to a husband is so kind,
275 What raptures might a lover look to find?
I burn, Lucina, like a field of corn
By flowing streams of kindled flames o'erborne
When north winds drive the torrent with a storm.
These fires into my bosom you have thrown
280 And must in pity quench them in your own.
Heav'n, when it gave your eyes th'inflaming pow'r
Which was ordained to cast an Emperor
Into love's fever, kindly did impart
That sea of milk to bathe his burning heart.

Through all those joys –

285 LUCINA Hold, sir, for mercy's sake!

Lays hold on her.

Love will abhor whatever force can take.
I may perhaps persuade myself in time
That this is duty which now seems a crime.
I'll to the gods and beg they will inspire
290 My breast or yours with what it should desire.

VALENTINIAN Fly to their altars straight and let them know
Now is their time to make me friend or foe,
If to my wishes they your heart incline
Or they're no longer favourites of mine. *Exit Lucina.*
295 None in my world shall dare to own a power
That can't or will not help their Emperor.
Incense no longer to those gods shall burn
Unless they strive to serve me in their turn.
Ho, Chylax! Proculus!

Enter Chylax, Proculus, Balbus, and Lycinius.

300 As ever you do hope to be by me
Protected in your boundless infamy,
For dissoluteness cherished, loved, and praised
On pyramids of your own vices raised
Above the reach of law, reproof, or shame,
305 Assist me now to quench my raging flame.
'Tis not as heretofore a lambent fire
Raised by some common beauty in my breast,
Vapours from idleness or loose desire
By each new motion easily suppressed,
310 But a fixed heat that robs me of all rest.
Before my dazzled eyes could you now place
A thousand willing beauties to allure
And give me lust for every loose embrace,
Lucina's love my virtue would secure.
315 From the contagious charm in vain I fly;
'T has seized upon my heart and may defy
That great preservative variety.
Go call your wives to council and prepare
To tempt, dissemble, promise, fawn, and swear.
320 To make faith look like folly use your skill,
Virtue an ill-bred crossness in the will,

Fame the loose breathings of a clamorous crowd;
Ever in lies most confident and loud,
Honour a notion, piety a cheat.
325 And if you prove successful bawds, be great.
CHYLAX All hind'rance to your hopes we'll soon remove
And clear the way to your triumphant love.
BALBUS Lucina for your wishes we'll prepare
And show we know to merit what we are. *Exeunt.*
330 VALENTINIAN Once more the pow'r of vows and tears I'll prove;
These may perhaps her gentle nature move
To pity first, by consequence to love.
Poor are the brutal conquests we obtain
O'er barbarous nations by the force of arms,
335 But when with humble love a heart we gain
And plant our trophies on our conqueror's charms,
Enter Æcius.
Such triumphs ev'n to us may honour bring.
No glory's vain which does from pleasure spring.
How now, Æcius, are the soldiers quiet?
340 ÆCIUS Better, I hope, sir, than they were.
VALENTINIAN They're pleased, I hear, to censure me extremely
For my pleasures. Shortly they'll fight against me.
ÆCIUS Gods defend, sir. And for their censures, they are
Such shrewd judges
345 A donative of ten sesterces
I'll undertake shall make them ring your praises
More than they sung your pleasures.
VALENTINIAN I believe thee.
Art thou in love, Æcius, yet?
ÆCIUS Oh no, sir,
I am too coarse for ladies. My embraces,
350 That only am acquainted with alarms,
Would break their tender bodies.
VALENTINIAN Never fear it. They are stronger than you think.
The Empress swears thou art a lusty soldier;
A good one I believe thee.
355 ÆCIUS All that goodness is but your creature, sir.

VALENTINIAN But tell me truly, for thou dar'st tell me.
ÆCIUS Anything concerns you
That's fit for me to speak or you to pardon.
VALENTINIAN What say the soldiers of me? And the same words,
360 Mince them not, good Æcius, but deliver
The very forms and tongues they talk withal.
ÆCIUS I'll tell you, sir, but with this caution
You be not stirred. For should the gods live with us,
Even those we certainly think are righteous,
Give them but drink, they'd censure them too.
365 VALENTINIAN Forward!
ÆCIUS Then to begin, they say you sleep too much,
By which they judge you, sir, too sensual,
Apt to decline your strength to ease and pleasure.
And when you do not sleep, you drink too much,
370 From which they fear suspicions first, then ruin.
And when you neither drink nor sleep, you guess, sir,
Which they affirm first breaks your understanding,
Then dulls the edge of honour, makes them seem,
That are the ribs and rampires of the empire,
375 Fencers and beaten fools, and so regarded.
But I believe them not, for were these truths,
Your virtue can correct them.
VALENTINIAN They speak plainly.
ÆCIUS They say, moreover, sir, since you will have it,
For they will take their freedoms though the sword
380 Were at their throats, that of late times like Nero
And with the same forgetfulness of glory,
You have got a vein of fiddling, so they term it.
VALENTINIAN Some drunken dreamers, Æcius.
ÆCIUS I hope so, sir.
They say besides you nourish strange devourers,
385 Fed with the fat of empire, they call bawds,
Lazy and lustful creatures that abuse you.
VALENTINIAN What sin's next?
For I perceive they have no mind to spare me.
ÆCIUS Nor hurt you, on my soul, sir. But such people
390 (Nor can the pow'r of man restrain it)

When they are full of meat and ease must prate.
VALENTINIAN Forward!
ÆCIUS I have spoken too much, sir.
VALENTINIAN I'll have all.
ÆCIUS It is not fit
Your ears should hear their vanities. No profit
395 Can justly arise to you from their behaviour,
Unless you were guilty of these crimes.
VALENTINIAN It may be I am so. Therefore, forward!
ÆCIUS I have ever learned to obey –
VALENTINIAN No more apologies!
400 ÆCIUS They grieve besides, sir,
To see the nations whom our ancient virtue
With many a weary march and hunger conquered,
With loss of many a daring life subdued,
Fall from their fair obedience, and even murmur
To see the warlike eagles mew their honours.
405 In obscure towns, that used to prey on princes,
They cry for enemies and tell the captain
The fruits of Italy are luscious, give us Egypt
Or sandy Affrick to display our valours,
There, where our swords may get us meat and dangers,
410 Digest our well-got food, for here our weapons
And bodies that were made for shining brass
Are both unedged and old with ease and women.
And then they cry again, 'Where are the Germans,
Lined with hot Spain or Gallia? Bring 'em on
415 And let the son of war, steeled Mithridates,
Pour on us his wing'd Parthians like a storm,
Hiding the face of heaven with showers of arrows.
Yet we dare fight like Romans.' Then as soldiers
Tired with a weary march, they tell their wounds,
420 Ev'n weeping ripe they were no more nor deeper,
And glory in those scars that make 'em lovely,
And sitting where a camp was, like sad pilgrims
They reckon up the times and loving labours
Of Julius or Germanicus, and wonder
425 That Rome, whose turrets once were topped with honour,
Can now forget the custom of her conquests.

And then they blame you, sir, and say, 'Who leads us?
Shall we stand here like statues? Were our fathers
The sons of lazy Moors, our princes Persians,
430 Nothing but silk and softness? Curses on 'em
That first taught Nero wantonness and blood,
Tiberius doubts, Caligula all vices,
For from the spring of these succeeding princes –'
Thus they talk, sir.

VALENTINIAN Well, why do you hear these things?

435 ÆCIUS Why do you do them?
I take the gods to witness, with more sorrow
And more vexation hear I these reproaches
Than were my life dropped from me through an hourglass.

VALENTINIAN 'Tis like then you believe them or at least
440 Are glad they should be so. Take heed! You were better
Build your own tomb and run into it living
Than dare a prince's anger.

ÆCIUS I am old, sir,
And ten years more addition is but nothing;
Now if my life be pleasing to you, take it.
445 Upon my knees, if ever any service
(As let me brag, some have been worthy notice),
If ever any worth or trust you gave me,
Deserved a favour, sir, if all my actions,
The hazards of my youth, colds, burnings, wants
450 For you and for the empire, be not vices,
By the style you have stamped upon me, soldier,
Let me not fall into the hands of wretches.

VALENTINIAN I understand you not.

ÆCIUS Let not this body
That has looked bravely in his blood for Caesar
455 And covetous of wounds and for your safety,
After the 'scape of swords, spears, slings, and arrows
'Gainst which my beaten body was my armour
Through seas and thirsty deserts, now be purchase
For slaves and base informers. I see anger
And death look through your eyes. I'm marked for
460 slaughter
And know the telling of this truth has made me

A man clean lost to this world. I embrace it,
Only my last petition, sacred Caesar,
Is I may die a Roman.

VALENTINIAN Rise, my friend still

465 And worthy of my love. Reclaim the soldiers.
I'll study to do so upon myself.
Go, keep your command and prosper.

ÆCIUS Life to Caesar! *Exit.*

VALENTINIAN The honesty of this Æcius,
Who is indeed the bulwark of my empire,
470 Is to be cherished for the good it brings,
Not valued as a merit in the owner.
All princes are slaves bound up by gratitude,
And duty has no claim beyond acknowledgement,
Which I'll pay Æcius, whom I still have found
475 Dull, faithful, humble, vigilant, and brave,
Talents as I could wish them for my slave.
But oh this woman!
Is it a sin to love this lovely woman?
No! She is such a pleasure, being good,
480 That though I were a god, she'd fire my blood. *Exit.*

Act II. Scene i

A Garden. Enter Lucina, Ardelia, and Phorba.

ARDELIA You still insist upon that idol, honour.
Can it renew your youth? Can it add wealth
Or take off wrinkles? Can it draw men's eyes
To gaze upon you in your age? Can honour,
5 That truly is a saint to none but soldiers,
And, looked into, bears no reward but danger,
Leave you the most respected woman living?
Or can the common kisses of a husband
(Which to a sprightly lady is a labour)
10 Make you almost immortal? You are cozened.
The honour of a woman is her praises,
The way to get these, to be seen and sought too,

And not to buy such a happy sweetness
Under a smoky roof.

LUCINA I'll hear no more.

15 PHORBA That white and red and all that blessed beauty,
Kept from the eyes that make it so, is nothing.
Then you are truly fair when men proclaim it.
The phoenix that was never seen is doubted,
But when the virtue's known, the honour's doubled.
20 Virtue is either lame or not at all,
And love is a sacrilege and not a saint
When it bars up the way to men's petitions.

ARDELIA Nay, you shall love your husband too. We come not
To make a monster of you.

LUCINA Are you women?

25 ARDELIA You'll find us so. And women you shall thank, too,
If you have but grace to make your use.

LUCINA Fie on you!

PHORBA Alas, poor bashful lady, by my soul
Had you no other virtue but your blushes,
30 And I a man, I should run mad for those.
How prettily they set her off, how sweetly.

ARDELIA Come, goddess, come, you move too near the earth.
It must not be; a better orb stays for you.

LUCINA Pray leave me.

35 PHORBA That were a sin, sweet madam, and a way
To make us guilty of your melancholy.
You must not be alone. In conversation
Doubts are resolved, and what sticks near the conscience
Made easy and allowable.

40 LUCINA Ye are devils –

ARDELIA That you may one day bless for your damnation.

LUCINA I charge you in the name of chastity,
Tempt me no more. How ugly you seem to me.
There is no wonder men defame our sex
45 And lay the vices of all ages on us,
When such as you shall bear the name of women.
If you had eyes to see yourselves, or sense,
Above the base rewards you earn with shame,
If ever in your lives you heard of goodness,

50 Though many regions off, as men hear thunder,
If ever you had fathers, and they souls,
Or ever mothers, and not such as you are,
If ever anything were constant in you
Besides your sins,
55 If ever any of your ancestors
Died worth a noble deed that would be cherished,
Soul-frighted with this black infection
You would run from one another's repentance
And from your guilty eyes drops out those sins
That made you blind and beasts.
60 PHORBA You speak well, madam,
A sign of fruitful education,
If your religious zeal had wisdom in it.
ARDELIA This lady was ordained to bless the empire,
And we may all give thanks for't.
PHORBA I believe you.
65 ARDELIA If anything redeem the Emperor
From his wild, flying courses, this is she.
She can instruct him; if you mark, she's wise too.
PHORBA Exceeding wise, which is a wonder in her,
And so religious that I well believe
Though she would sin, she cannot.
70 ARDELIA And besides
She has the empire's cause in hand, not love's.
There lies the main consideration
For which she is chiefly born.
PHORBA She finds that point
Stronger than we can tell her, and (believe it)
75 I look by her means for a reformation,
And such a one and such a rare way carried!
ARDELIA I never thought the Emperor had wisdom,
Pity, or fair affection to his country,
Till he professed his love. Gods give them children
80 Such as her virtues merit and his zeal.
I look to see a Numa from this lady
Or greater than Octavius.
PHORBA Do you mark too
(Which is a noble virtue) how she blushes,

And what flowing modesty runs through her,
When we but name the Emperor.

85 ARDELIA But mark it,
Yes, and admire it too. For she considers
Though she be fair as heaven and virtuous
As holy truth, yet to the Emperor
She is a kind of nothing but her service,
90 Which she is bound to offer, and she'll do it.
And when her country's cause commands affection,
She knows obedience is the key of virtues.
Then fly the blushes out like Cupid's arrows,
And though the tie of marriage to her lord
95 Would fain cry, 'Stay, Lucina', yet the cause
And general wisdom of the prince's love
Makes her find surer ends and happier;
And if the first were chaste, this is twice doubled.

PHORBA Her tartness unto us too.

ARDELIA That's a wise one.

100 PHORBA I rarely like it. It shows a rising wisdom
That chides all common fools who dare enquire
What princes would have private.

ARDELIA What a lady shall we be blest to serve!

LUCINA Go, get you from me.
105 You are your purses' agents, not the prince's.
Is this the virtuous love you trained me out to?
Am I a woman fit to imp your vices?
But that I had a mother, and a woman
Whose ever-living fame turns all it touches
110 Into the good itself was, I should now
Ev'n doubt myself, I have been searched so near
The very soul of honour. Why should you two,
That happily have been as chaste as I am,
Fairer, I think, by much (for yet your faces,
115 Like ancient, well-built piles, show worthy ruins),
After that angel age turn mortal devils?
For shame, for womanhood, for what you have been
(For rotten cedars have borne goodly branches),
If you have any hope of any heaven but court,
120 Which like a dream you'll find hereafter vanish,

Or at the best but subject to repentance,
Study no more to be ill spoken of.
Let women live themselves; if they must fail,
Their own destruction find them.

125 ARDELIA Madam, you are so excellent in all
That I must tell it you with admiration.
So true a joy you have, so sweet a fear,
And when you come to anger, 'tis so noble
That for my own part I could still offend
130 To hear you angry. Women that want that
And your way guided (else I count it nothing)
Are either fools or fearful.

PHORBA She were no mistress for the world's great lord
Could she not frown a ravished kiss from anger,
135 And such an anger as this lady shows us,
Stuck with such pleasing dangers (gods, I ask ye),
Which of you all could hold from?

LUCINA I perceive you.
Your own dark sins dwell with you, and that price
You sell the chastity of modest wives at
140 Runs to diseases with you. I despise you.
And all the nets you have pitched to catch my virtue
Like spider webs I sweep away before me.
Go, tell th'Emperor you have met a woman
That neither his own person (which is godlike),
145 The world he rules, nor what that world can purchase,
Nor all the glories subject to a Caesar,
The honours that he offers for my honour,
The hopes, the gifts, and everlasting flatteries,
Nor anything that's his and apt to tempt,
150 No, not to be the mother of the empire
And queen of all the holy fires he worships,
Can make a whore of.

ARDELIA You mistake us, madam.

LUCINA Yet tell him this: he's thus much weakened me
That I have heard his slaves and you his matrons,
155 Fit nurses for his sins, which gods forgive me,
But ever to be leaning to his folly
Or to be brought to love his vice, assure him,

And from her mouth whose life can make it certain,
I never can. I have a noble husband,
160 Pray tell him that too, yet a noble name,
A noble family, and last a conscience.
Thus much by way of answer. For yourselves,
You have lived the shame of women, die the better.
Exit Lucina.

PHORBA What's now to do?
ARDELIA Even as she said, to die.
165 For there's no living here, and women thus,
I am sure for us two.
PHORBA Nothing stick upon her?
ARDELIA We have lost a mass of money. Well, Dame Virtue,
Yet you may halt, if good luck serve.
PHORBA Worms take her!
ARDELIA So godly! This is ill-breeding, Phorba.
170 PHORBA If the women
Should have a longing now to see this monster,
And she convert them all.
ARDELIA That may be, Phorba.
But if it be, I'll have the young men gelded.
Come, let's go think. She must not 'scape us thus.

Act II. Scene ii

Enter Balbus, Proculus, Chylax, Lycinius.

BALBUS I never saw the like. She's no more stirred,
No more another woman, no more altered
With any hopes or promises laid to her,
Let them be ne'er so weighty, ne'er so winning,
5 Than I am with the motion of my own legs.
PROCULUS Chylax, you are a stranger yet in these designs,
At least in Rome. Tell me and tell me truth,
Did you e'er know in all your course of practice,
In all the ways of women you have run through,
10 For I presume you have been brought up, Chylax,
As we, to fetch and carry.
CHYLAX True, I have so.

PROCULUS Did you, I say again, in all this progress
Ever discover such a piece of beauty,
Ever so rare a creature, and no doubt
15 One that must know her worth too and affect it,
Aye, and be flattered, else 'tis none, and honest,
Honest against the tide of all temptations,
Honest to one man, to her husband only,
And yet not eighteen, not of age to know
Why she is honest.
20 CHYLAX I confess it freely,
I never saw her fellow nor e'er shall.
For all our Grecian dames as I have tried
(And sure I have tried a hundred – if I say two
I speak within my compass), all these beauties,
25 And all the constancy of all these faces,
Maids, widows, wives, of what degree or calling,
So they be Greeks and fat (for there's my cunning),
I would undertake, and not sweat for't, Proculus
(Were they to try again, say twice as many),
30 Under a thousand pound to lay 'em flat.
But this wench staggers me.
LYCINIUS Do you see these jewels?
You would think these pretty baits now. I'll assure you
Here's half the wealth of Asia.
BALBUS These are nothing
To the full honours I propounded to her.
35 I bid her think and be, and presently,
Whatever her ambition, what the counsel
Of others would add to her, what her dreams
Could more enlarge, what say precedent
Of any woman rising up to glory
40 And standing certain there and in the highest
Could give her more, nay to be Empress.
PROCULUS And cold at all these offers?
BALBUS Cold as crystal,
Never to be thawed.
CHYLAX I tried her further,
And so far that I think she is no woman,
At least as women go now.

45 LYCINIUS Why, what did you?
CHYLAX I offered that, that had she been but mistress
Of as much spleen as doves have, I had reached her:
A safe revenge of all that ever hate her,
The crying down for ever of all beauties
That may be thought come near her.
50 PROCULUS That was pretty.
CHYLAX I never knew that way fail. Yet I tell you
I offered her a gift beyond all yours
That, that had made a saint start, well-considered:
The law to be her creature; she to make it;
55 Her mouth to give it; everything alive
From her aspect to draw their good or evil,
Fixed in them spite of fortune; a new nature
She should be called and mother of all ages;
Time should be hers; what she did, flattering virtues,
60 Should bless to all posterities; her air
Should give us life, her earth and water feed us,
And last to none but to the Emperor.
And then, but when she pleased to have it so,
She should be held for mortal.
LYCINIUS And she heard you?
65 CHYLAX Yes, as a sick man hears a noise, or he
That stands condemned his judgement. Let me perish,
But if there can be virtue, if that name
Be anything but name and empty title,
If it be so as fools are pleased to feign it,
70 A power that can preserve us after ashes
And make the names of men outreckon ages,
This woman has a god of virtue in her.
BALBUS I would the Emperor were that god.
CHYLAX She has in her
75 All the contempt of glory and vain-seeming
Of all the Stoics, all the truth of Christians
And all their constancy. Modesty was made
When she was first intended. When she blushes,
It is the holiest thing to look upon,
80 The purest temple of her sect that ever
Made nature a blest founder.

If she were fat or any way inclining
To ease or pleasure or affected glory,
Proud to be seen or worshipped, 'twere a venture,
85 But on my soul she is chaster than cold camphire.
BALBUS I think so too, for all the ways of woman
Like a full sail she bears against. I asked her,
After my many offers, walking with her,
And her many down denials, how
90 If the Emperor grown mad with love should force her?
She pointed to a Lucrece that hung by
And with an angry look that from her eyes
Shot vestal fire against me, she departed.
PROCULUS This is the first woman I was ever posed in,
95 Yet I have brought young loving things together
This two and thirty year.
CHYLAX I find by this fair lady
The calling of a bawd to be a strange,
A wise, and subtle calling, and for none
100 But staid, discreet, and understanding people.
And as the tutor to great Alexander
Would say, A young man should not dare to read
His moral books till after five and twenty;
So must that he or she that will be bawdy
105 (I mean discreetly bawdy and be trusted),
If they will rise and gain experience,
Well-steeped in years and discipline, begin it;
I take it 'tis no boys' play.
BALBUS Well, what's thought of?
PROCULUS The Emperor must know it.
110 LYCINIUS If the women should chance to fail too –
CHYLAX As 'tis ten to one.
PROCULUS Why, what remains but new nets for the purchase?
The Emperor!

Enter Valentinian.

VALENTINIAN What! Have you brought her?
CHYLAX Brought her, sir, alas,
115 What would you do with such a cake of ice
Whom all the love i'th'empire cannot thaw,
A dull, cross thing, insensible of glory,

Deaf to all promises, dead to desire,
A tedious stickler for her husband's right,
120 Who like a beggar's cur has brought her up
To fawn on him and bark at all besides,
True to the budget, beyond all temptation.

VALENTINIAN Lewd and ill-mannered fool, wer't not for fear
To do thee good by mending of thy manners,
125 I'd have thee whipped. Is this th'account you bring
To ease the torments of my restless mind?

BALBUS (*kneeling*) Caesar, in vain your vassals have endeavoured,
By promises, persuasions, reasons, wealth,
All that can make the firmest virtue bend,
130 To alter her. Our arguments, like darts
Shot in the bosom of the boundless air,
Are lost and do not leave the least impression.
Forgive us if we failed to overcome
Virtue that could resist the Emperor.

135 VALENTINIAN You impotent provokers to my lust,
Who can incite and have no power to help,
How dare you be alive and I unsatisfied,
Who to your beings have no other title
Nor least hopes to preserve them but my smiles;
140 Who play like poisonous insects all the day
In the warm sunshine of me, your vital sun,
And when night comes, must perish;
Wretches whose vicious lives, when I withdraw
The absolute protection of my favour,
145 Will drag you into all the miseries
That your own terrors, universal hate,
And law with whips and jails can bring upon you.
As you have failed to satisfy my wishes,
Perdition is the least you can expect,
150 Who durst to undertake and not perform.
Slaves! Was it fit I should be disappointed?
Yet live,
Continue infamous a little longer.
You have deserved to end, but for this once
155 I'll not tread out your nasty snuff of life.

But had your poisonous flatteries prevailed
Upon her chastity I so admire,
Which adds this flaming fury to my fire,
Dogs had devoured ere this your carcasses.
160 Is that an object fit for my desires
Which lies within the reach of your persuasion?
Had you by your infectious industry
Showed my Lucina frail to that degree,
You had been damned for undeceiving me.
165 But to possess her chaste and uncorrupted,
There lies the joy and glory of my love,
A passion too refined for your dull souls
And such a blessing as I scorn to owe
The gaining of to any but myself.
170 Haste straight to Maximus and let him know
He must come instantly and speak with me.
The rest of you wait here; I'll play tonight.
(*To Chylax*) You, saucy fool, send privately away
For Lycias hither by the garden gate,
175 That sweet-faced eunuch that sung
In Maximus's grove the other day,
And in my closet keep him till I come. *Exit Valentinian.*

CHYLAX I shall, sir. 'Tis a soft rogue, this Lycias.
And rightly understood,
180 He's worth a thousand women's nicenesses.
The love of women moves even with their lust,
Who therefore still are fond, but seldom just.
Their love is usury, while they pretend
To gain the pleasure double which they lend.
185 But a dear boy's disinterested flame
Gives pleasure, and for mere love gathers pain;
In him alone fondness sincere does prove,
And the kind, tender, naked boy is Love. *Exit.*

Act III. Scene i

A grove and forest. Enter Lucina.

LUCINA Dear solitary groves, where peace does dwell,

Sweet harbours of pure love and innocence,
How willingly could I forever stay
Beneath the shade of your embracing greens,
5 List'ning to harmony of warbling birds,
Tuned with the gentle murmurs of the streams
Upon whose banks in various livery
The fragrant offspring of the early year,
Their heads like graceful swans bent proudly down,
10 See their own beauties in the crystal flood.
Of these I could mysterious chaplets weave,
Expressing some kind, innocent design
To show my Maximus at his return
And fondly chiding, make his heart confess
15 How far my busy idleness excels
The idle business he pursues all day
At the contentious court or clamorous camp,
Robbing my eyes of what they love to see,
My ears of his dear words they wish to hear,
20 My longing arms of the embrace they covet.
Forgive me, heav'n, if when I these enjoy,
So perfect is the happiness I find
That my soul satisfied feels no ambition
To change these humble roofs and sit above.

Enter Lycias.

25 LYCIAS Madam, my lord just now alighted here
Was by an order from the Emperor
Called back to court.
This he commanded me to let you know,
And that he would make haste in his return.

30 LUCINA The Emperor!
Unwonted horror seizes me all o'er
When I but hear him named. Sure 'tis not hate,
For though his impious love with scorn I heard
And fled with terror from his threat'ning force,
35 Duty commands me humbly to forgive
And bless the lord to whom my lord does bow.
Nay more, methinks he is the gracefulest man,
His words so framed to tempt, himself to please,
That 'tis my wonder how the pow'rs above,

40 Those wise and careful guardians of the good,
Have trusted such a force of tempting charms
To enemies declared of innocence.
'Tis then some strange prophetic fear I feel
That seems to warn me of approaching ills.
45 Lycias, go fetch your lute and sing that song
My lord calls his. I'll try to wear away
The melancholy thoughts his absence breeds.
Come gentle slumbers, in your flattering arms
I'll bury these disquiets of my mind
50 Till Maximus returns. For when he's here,
My heart is raised above the reach of fear.

Lycias sings.

Where would coy Aminta run
From a despairing lover's story?
When her eyes have conquests won,
55 *Why should her ear refuse the glory?*
Shall a slave whom racks constrain
Be forbidden to complain?
Let her scorn me, let her fly me,
Let her looks her life deny me.
60 *Ne'er can my heart change for relief,*
Or my tongue cease to tell my grief.
Much to love and much to pray
Is to heaven the only way.

LYCIAS She sleeps.

Here begins the dance of satyrs, which is to represent a frightful dream to Lucina. Lycias continues.

65 Now to the flattering prospect of my hopes.
The messenger that came to fetch my lord
Has brought me here a note from Chylax.
Let's read a little.

Reads.

Lycias, thou art the most fortunate of men.
70 *Riches and honours come upon thee full sail.*
What can determine thy glory and greatness?
The Emperor loves thee, longs for thy company,
Will delight in thee and trust thee. What an
Opportunity hast thou to destroy thy enemies,
75 *Delude thy friends, enrich thyself,*

Enslave the world, raise thy kindred,
Humble thy master, and govern him. He expects
Thee about the evening in his closet. Fail not
And remember poor Chylax who always loved
80 *And honoured thee, though till this hour it was*
His misfortune never to let thee know it.
Farewell.
This is a summons to prosperity,
And if I stop or falter at the means,
85 Or think they can be vile and infamous,
Be what they will, that may my fortunes raise,
On vestal's altar for some lamb or calf
May I be burnt a senseless sacrifice.
Time hurries on. Lest therefore dull delay
90 Should blast my springing hopes, I'll haste away. *Exit.*

Act III. Scene ii

The scene opens and discovers the Emperor at dice. Maximus, Lycinius, Proculus, and Chylax.

VALENTINIAN Nay, set my hand out. 'Tis not just I should neglect my luck when 'tis so prosperous.

CHYLAX If I have anything to set you, sir, but clothes and good conditions, let me perish. You have all my
5 money.

PROCULUS And mine.

LYCINIUS And mine too.

MAXIMUS You may trust us sure, sir, till tomorrow. Or if you please, I'll send home for money presently.

10 VALENTINIAN 'Tis already morning, and staying will be tedious. Besides, my luck will vanish before your money comes.

CHYLAX Shall we redeem 'em if we set our houses? For by heaven, sir, no tavern will receive us.

15 VALENTINIAN Yes, fairly.

CHYLAX Then at my villa!

VALENTINIAN At it. (*Throws dice.*) 'Tis mine.

CHYLAX Then farewell, fig trees, for I can ne'er redeem 'em.

VALENTINIAN Who sets? Set anything.

20 LYCINIUS At my horse!
VALENTINIAN The dapple Spaniard?
LYCINIUS He.
VALENTINIAN (*Throws dice.*) He's mine!
LYCINIUS He is so.
25 VALENTINIAN Hah?
LYCINIUS Nothing, my lord, but pox on my damned fortune.
VALENTINIAN Come, Maximus, you were not wont to flinch.
MAXIMUS By heaven, sir, I have not a penny.
VALENTINIAN Then that ring.
30 MAXIMUS Oh, good sir, this was not given to lose.
VALENTINIAN Some love token. Set it, I say.
MAXIMUS I beg you, sir.
VALENTINIAN How silly and how fond you're grown of toys.
MAXIMUS Shall I redeem it?
35 VALENTINIAN When you please, tomorrow or next day, as you will. I do not care; only for luck sake.
MAXIMUS There, sir. Will you throw?
VALENTINIAN Why then have at it fairly. The last stake. (*Throws dice.*) 'Tis mine.
40 MAXIMUS You're ever fortunate. Tomorrow I'll bring you what you please to think it worth.
VALENTINIAN Then your Arabian horse. But for this night I'll wear it as my victory.

Enter Balbus.

BALBUS From the camp
45 Æcius in haste has sent these letters, sir.
It seems the cohorts mutiny for pay.
VALENTINIAN Maximus, this is ill news. Next week they are to march.
You must away immediately. No stay,
No, not so much as to take leave at home.
50 This careful haste may probably appease them.
Send word what are their numbers,
And money shall be sent to pay them all,
Besides something by way of donative.
MAXIMUS I'll not delay a moment, sir.
55 The gods preserve you in this mind for ever.
VALENTINIAN I'll see them march myself.

MAXIMUS Gods ever keep you.

Exeunt Maximus and Balbus.

VALENTINIAN To what and how d'you think this ring shall
serve?
For you are the dullest and the veriest rogues,
Fellows that know only by rote, as birds
Whistle and sing.

60 CHYLAX Why, sir, 'tis for the lady.

VALENTINIAN The lady, blockhead, which end of the lady,
Her nose?

CHYLAX Faith, sir, that I know not.

VALENTINIAN Then pray for him that does.
Fetch in the eunuch. *Exit Chylax.*
65 You. See the apartment made very fine
That lies upon the garden, masques and music,
With the best speed you can. And all your arts
Serve to the highest, for my masterpiece
Is now on foot.

PROCULUS Sir, we shall have a care,

70 VALENTINIAN I'll sleep a hour or two. And let the women
Put on a graver show of welcome.
Your wives, they are such haggard bawds,
A thought too eager.

Enter Chylax and Lycias.

CHYLAX Here's Lycias, sir.

LYCIAS Long life to mighty Caesar.

75 VALENTINIAN Fortune to thee, for I must use thee, Lycias.

LYCIAS I am the humble slave of Caesar's will,
By my ambition bound to his commands
As by my duty.

VALENTINIAN Follow me.

LYCIAS With joy. *Exeunt.*

Act III. Scene iii

Enter Claudia and Marcellina to Lucina.

CLAUDIA Prithee, what ails my lady that of late
She never cares for company?

MARCELLINA I know not,
Unless it be that company causes cuckolds.
CLAUDIA Ridiculous! That were a childish fear.
5 'Tis opportunity does cause 'em rather,
When two made one are glad to be alone.
MARCELLINA But Claudia, why this sitting up all night
In groves by purling streams? This argues heat,
Great heat and vapours, which are main corrupters.
10 Mark when you will, your ladies that have vapours,
They are not flinchers. That insulting spleen
Is the artillery of powerful Lust
Discharged upon weak Honour, which stands out
Two fits of the headache at the most, then yields.
15 CLAUDIA Thou art the frailest creature, Marcellina,
And think'st all women's honour like thine own,
So thin a cobweb that each blast of passion
Can blow away. But for my own part, girl,
I think I may be well-styled Honour's martyr.
20 With firmest constancy I have endured
The raging heats of passionate desire.
While flaming love and boiling nature both
Were poured upon my soul with equal torture,
I, armed with resolution, stood it out
And kept my honour safe.
25 MARCELLINA Thy glory's great!
But, Claudia, thanks to heaven that I am made
The weakest of all women, framed so frail
That Honour ne'er thought fit to choose me out
His champion against Pleasure. My poor heart,
30 For divers years still tossed from flame to flame,
Is now burnt up to tinder. Every spark
Dropped from kind eyes sets it on fire afresh.
Pressed by a gentle hand I melt away;
One sigh's a storm that blows me all along.
35 Pity a wretch who has no charm at all
Against th'impetuous tide of flowing pleasure,
Who wants both force and courage to maintain
The glorious war made upon flesh and blood,
But is a sacrifice to every wish

40 And has no power left to resist a joy.
CLAUDIA Poor girl! How strange a riddle virtue is.
They never miss it who possess it not,
And they who have it ever find a want.
With what tranquillity and peace thou liv'st!
45 For stripped of shame thou hast no cause to fear,
While I, the slave of virtue, am afraid
Of everything I see, and think the world
A dreadful wilderness of savage beasts.
Every man I meet I fancy will devour me,
50 And swayed by rules not natural but affected,
I hate mankind for fear of being loved.
MARCELLINA 'Tis nothing less than witchcraft can constrain
Still to persist in errors we perceive.
Prithee reform! What nature prompts us to
55 And reason seconds, why should we avoid?
This Honour is the veriest mountebank;
It fills our fancies with affected tricks
And makes us freakish. What a cheat must that be
Which robs our lives of all the softer hours.
60 Beauty, our only treasure, it lays waste,
Hurries us over our neglected youth
To the detested state of age and ugliness,
Tearing our dearest heart's desires from us.
Then in reward of what it took away,
65 Our joys, our hopes, our wishes, and delights,
It bountifully pays us all in pride.
Poor shifts! Still to be proud and never pleased,
Yet this is all your honour can do for you.
CLAUDIA Concluded like thyself; for sure thou art
70 The most corrupt corrupting thing alive.
Yet glory not too much in cheating wit;
'Tis but false wisdom, and its property
Has ever been to take the part of vice,
Which though the fancy with vain shows it pleases,
75 Yet wants a power to satisfy the mind.
Lucina wakes.
But see, my lady wakes and comes this way.
Bless me, how pale and how confused she looks.

LUCINA In what fantastic new world have I been,
What horrors passed, what threatening visions seen?
80 Rapt as I lay in my amazing trance,
The host of heaven and hell did round me dance.
Debates arose betwixt the pow'rs above
And these below. Methought they talked of love
And named me often, but it could not be
85 Of any love that had to do with me.
For all the while they talked and argued thus,
I never heard one word of Maximus.
Discourteous nymphs who own these murmuring floods
And you unkind divinities o'th' woods,
90 When to your banks and bowers I came distressed,
Half-dead through absence, seeking peace and rest,
Why would you not protect by these your streams
A sleeping wretch from such wild, dismal dreams?
Misshapen monsters round in measures went,
95 Horrid in form with gestures insolent,
Grinning through goatish beards, with half-closed eyes
They looked me in the face. Frighted to rise,
In vain I did attempt. Methought no ground
Was, to support my sinking footsteps, found.
100 In clammy fogs like one half-choked I lay;
Crying for help, my voice was snatched away,
And when I would have fled,
My limbs benumbed or dead,
Could not my will, with terror winged, obey.
105 Upon my absent lord for help I cried,
But in that moment when I must have died
With anguish of my fear's confusing pains,
Relenting sleep loosed his tyrannic chains.
CLAUDIA Madam, alas, such accidents as these
110 Are not of value to disturb your peace.
The cold, damp dews of night have mixed and wrought
With the dark melancholy of your thought
And through your fancy these illusions brought.
I still have marked your fondness will afford
115 No hour of joy in th'absence of my lord.
Enter Lycias.
LUCINA Absent all night and never send me word?

LYCIAS Madam, while sleeping by these banks you lay,
One from my lord commanded me away.
In all obedient haste I went to court,
120 Where busy crowds confus'dly did resort.
News from the camp, it seems, was then arrived
Of tumults raised and civil wars contrived.
The Emperor frighted from his bed does call
Grave senators to council in the hall.
125 Throngs of ill-favoured faces filled with scars,
Wait for employments, praying hard for wars,
At council door attend with fair pretence,
In knavish decency and reverence.
Bankers, who with officious diligence
130 Lend money to supply the present need
At treble use that greater may succeed
(So public wants will private plenty breed),
Whispering in every corner you might see.

LUCINA But what's all this to Maximus and me?
135 Where is my lord? What message has he sent?
Is he in health? What fatal accident
Does all this while his wished return prevent?

LYCIAS Whene'er the gods that happy hour decree,
May he appear safe and with victory.
140 Of many heroes who stood candidate
To be the arbiters 'twixt Rome and fate,
To quell rebellion and protect the throne,
A choice was made of Maximus alone.
The people, soldiers, senate, Emperor
145 For Maximus with one assent concur.
Their new-born hopes now hurry him away;
Nor will their fears admit one moment's stay.
Trembling through terror lest he come too late,
They huddle his dispatch, while at the gate
150 The Emperor's chariots to conduct him wait.

LUCINA These fatal honours my dire dream foretold.
Why should the kind be ruined by the bold?
He ne'er reflects upon my destiny,
So careless of himself, undoing me.
155 Ah, Claudia, in my visions so unskilled

He'll to the army go and there be killed.
Forgetful of my love, he'll not afford
The easy favour of a parting word.
Of all my wishes he's alone the scope,
160 And he's the only end of all my hope,
My fill of joy, and what is yet above
Joys, hopes, and wishes, he is all my love.
Mysterious Honour, tell me what thou art
That takes up different forms in every heart,
165 And dost to diverse ends and interests move.
Conquest is his, my honour is my love.
Both these do paths so oppositely choose
By following one, you must the other lose.
So two straight lines from the same point begun
170 Can never meet, though without end they run.
Alas, I rave.

LYCIAS Look on thy glory, Love, and smile to see
Two faithful hearts at strife for victory,
Who blazing in thy sacred fires contend,
175 While both their equal flames to heaven ascend.
The god that dwells in eyes light on my tongue,
Lest in my message I his passion wrong.
You'll better guess the anguish of his heart
From what you feel than what I can impart.
180 But, madam, know the moment I was come
His watchful eye perceived me in the room,
When with a quick, precipitated haste
From Caesar's bosom where he stood embraced,
Piercing the busy crowd, to me he passed.
185 Tears in his eyes, his orders in his hand,
He scarce had breath to give this short command,
'With thy best speed to my Lucina fly.
If I must part unseen by her, I die.
Decrees inevitable from above
190 And fate which takes too little care of love
Force me away. Tell her 'tis my request,
By those kind fires she kindled in my breast,
Our future hopes, and all that we hold dear,
She instantly would come and see me here,

195 That parting griefs to her I may reveal
And on her lips propitious omens seal.
Affairs that press in this short space of time
Afford no other place without a crime.
And that thou may'st not fail of wished-for ends
200 In a success whereon my life depends,
Give her this ring.'
Looks on the ring.

LUCINA How strange soever these commands appear,
Love awes my reason and controls my fear.
But how couldst thou employ thy lavish tongue
205 So idly to be telling this so long,
When ev'ry moment thou hast spent in vain
Was half the life that did to me remain.
Flatter me, hope, and on my wishes smile,
And make me happy yet a little while.
210 If through my fears I can such sorrow show
As to convince I perish if he go,
Pity perhaps his gen'rous heart may move
To sacrifice his glory to his love.
I'll not despair.
215 Who knows how eloquent these eyes may prove,
Begging in floods of tears and flames of love. *Exit Lucina.*

LYCIAS Thanks to the devil, my friend, now all's our own.
How easily this mighty work was done.
Well, first or last all women must be won;
220 It is their fate and cannot be withstood.
The wise do still comply with flesh and blood;
Or if through peevish honour nature fail,
They do but lose their thanks; art will prevail.

Act IV. Scene i

Enter Æcius pursuing Pontius and Maximus following.

MAXIMUS Temper yourself, Æcius.
PONTIUS Hold, my lord, I am a soldier and a Roman.
MAXIMUS Pray sir!
ÆCIUS Thou art a lying villain and a traitor.

5 Give me myself or by the gods, my friend,
You'll make me dangerous. How dar'st thou pluck
The soldiers to sedition and I living,
And sow seeds of rank rebellion even then
When I am drawing out to action?

PONTIUS Hear me.

MAXIMUS Are you a man?

10 ÆCIUS I am true-hearted, Maximus,
And if the villain live, we are dishonoured.

MAXIMUS But hear him what he can say.

ÆCIUS That's the way
To pardon him. I am so easy-natured
That if he speak but humbly, I forgive him.

15 PONTIUS I do beseech you, worthy general.

ÆCIUS H'as found the way already. Give me room.
One stroke and if he 'scape me then, h'as mercy.

PONTIUS I do not call you worthy that I fear you.
I never cared for death. If you will kill me,
20 Consider first for what, not what you *can* do.
'Tis true I know you are my general,
And by that great prerogative may kill.

ÆCIUS He argues with me.
By heaven a made-up, finished rebel!

25 MAXIMUS Pray consider what certain ground you have.

ÆCIUS What grounds?
Did I not take him preaching to the soldiers
How lazily they lived, and what dishonour
It was to serve a prince so full of softness?
These were his very words, sir.

30 MAXIMUS These, Æcius,
Though they were rashly spoken (which was an error,
A great one, Pontius) yet from him that hungers
For war and brave employment might be pardoned.
The heart and harboured thoughts of ill makes traitors,
Not spleeny speeches.

35 ÆCIUS Why should you protect him?
Go to, it scarce shows honest.

MAXIMUS Taint me not,
For that shows worse, Æcius. All your friendship

And that pretended love you lay upon me
(Hold back my honesty) is like a favour
40 You do your slave today, tomorrow hang him.
Was I your bosom friend for this?

ÆCIUS Forgive me.
So zealous is my duty for my prince
That oft it makes me to forget myself.
And though I strive to be without my passion,
45 I am no god, sir. For you whose infection
Has spread itself like poison through the army
And cast a killing fog on fair allegiance,
First thank this noble gentleman; you had died else.
Next from your place and honour of a soldier
I here seclude you.

PONTIUS May I speak yet?

50 MAXIMUS Hear him.

ÆCIUS And while Æcius holds a reputation,
At least command, you bear no arms for Rome, sir.

PONTIUS Against her, I shall never. The condemned man
Has yet the privilege to speak, my lord;
Law were not equal else.

55 MAXIMUS Pray hear, Æcius,
For happily the fault he has committed,
Though I believe it mighty, yet considered,
If mercy may be thought upon, will prove
Rather a hasty sin than heinous.

ÆCIUS Speak.

60 PONTIUS 'Tis true, my lord, you took me tired with peace,
My words as rough and ragged as my fortune,
Telling the soldiers what a man we serve,
Led from us by the flourishes of fencers.
I blamed him too for softness.

ÆCIUS To the rest, sir.

65 PONTIUS And like enough I blessed him then, as soldiers
Will do sometimes. 'Tis true I told them too
We lay at home to show our country
We durst go naked, durst want meat and money,
And when the slave drinks wine, we durst be thirsty.
70 I told this too, that the trees and roots

Were our best paymasters, the charity
Of longing women (who had bought our bodies)
Our beds, fires, tailors, nurses.
'Tis likely too I counselled them to turn
75 Their warlike pikes to ploughshares, their sure targets
And swords, hatched with the blood of many nations,
To spades and pruning-knives, their warlike eagles
Into daws and starlings,
To give a hail to Caesar as he passes
80 And be rewarded with a thousand drachmas.
For thus we got only old age and roots.

ÆCIUS What think you?
Were these words to be spoken by a captain,
One that should give example?

MAXIMUS That was too much.

85 PONTIUS My lord, I did not woo them from the empire
Nor bid them turn their daring steel against Caesar.
The gods forever hate me if that motion
Were part of me. Give me but employment
And a way to live, and where you hold me vicious,
90 Bred up to mutiny, my sword shall tell you,
And (if you please) that place I held maintain it
'Gainst the most daring foes of Rome, I'm honest,
A lover of my country, one that holds
His life no longer his than kept for Caesar.
95 Weigh not (I thus low on my knee beseech you)
What my rude tongue discovered was my want,
No other part of Pontius. You have seen me
(And you, my lord) do something for my country.
And both the wounds I gave and took,
Not like a backward traitor –

100 ÆCIUS All your language
Makes but against you, Pontius. You are cast,
And by my honour and my love to Caesar
By me shall never be restored in my camp.
I will not have a tongue, though to himself,
105 Dare talk but near sedition. As I govern
All shall obey. And when they want, their duty
And ready service shall redress their needs,

Not prating what they would be.

PONTIUS Thus I leave you.
Yet shall my prayers, although my wretched fortune
110 Must follow you no more, be still about you.
Gods give you where you fight the victory!
You cannot cast my wishes.

ÆCIUS Come, my lord,
Now to the field again.

MAXIMUS Alas, poor Pontius.

Act IV. Scene ii

Enter Chylax at one door, Lycinius and Balbus at another.

LYCINIUS How now!

CHYLAX She's come.

BALBUS Then I'll to the Emperor.

Exit Balbus.

CHYLAX Is the music placed well?

LYCINIUS Excellent.

CHYLAX Lycinius, you and Proculus receive 'em
In the great chamber at her entrance.

LYCINIUS Let us alone.

5 CHYLAX And do you here, Lycinius.
Pray let the women ply her farther off
And with much more discretion. One word more;
Are all the masquers ready?

LYCINIUS Take no care, man.

Exit Lycinius.

CHYLAX I am all over in a sweat with pimping.
10 'Tis a laborious, moiling trade this.

Enter Valentinian, Balbus, and Proculus.

VALENTINIAN Is she come?

CHYLAX She is, sir, but 'twere best
That you were last seen to her.

VALENTINIAN So I mean.
Keep your court empty, Proculus.

PROCULUS 'Tis done, sir.

VALENTINIAN Be not too suddenly to her.

CHYLAX Good, sweet sir,
15 Retire and man yourself. Let us alone.
We are no children this way. One thing, sir,
'Tis necessary that her she-companions
Be cut off in the lobby by the women;
They'd break the business else.
VALENTINIAN 'Tis true. They shall.
20 CHYLAX Remember your place, Proculus.
PROCULUS I warrant you.
Exeunt Valentinian, Balbus, and Proculus.
Enter Lucina, Claudia, Marcellina, and Lycias.
CHYLAX She enters. Who waits there? The Emperor
Calls for his chariots. He will take the air.
LUCINA I am glad I came in such a happy hour
When he'll be absent. This removes all fears.
25 But, Lycias, lead me to my lord.
Heaven grant he be not gone.
LYCIAS Faith, madam, that's uncertain.
I'll run and see. But if you miss my lord
And find a better to supply his room,
30 A change so happy will not discontent you. *Exit Lycias.*
LUCINA What means the unwonted insolence of this slave?
I now begin to fear again. O Honour,
If ever thou hadst temple in weak woman
And sacrifice of modesty offered to thee,
35 Hold me fast now and I'll be safe forever.
CHYLAX The fair Lucina here. Nay then, I find
Our slandered court has not sinned up so high
To fright all the good angels from its care,
Since they have sent so great a blessing hither.
40 Madam, I beg the advantage of my fortune,
Who as I am the first have met you here,
May humbly hope to be made proud and happy
With the honour of your first command and service.
LUCINA I am so far from knowing how to merit
45 Your service that your compliment's too much,
And I return it you with all my heart.
You'll want it, sir, for those who know you better.
CHYLAX Madam, I have the honour to be owned

By Maximus for his most humble servant,
50 Which gives me confidence.
MARCELLINA Now, Claudia, for a wager,
What thing is this that cringes to my lady?
CLAUDIA Why some grave statesman, by his looks a courtier.
MARCELLINA Claudia, a bawd! By all my hopes a bawd.
55 What use can reverend gravity be of here
To any but a trusty bawd?
Statesmen are marked for fops by it. Besides
Nothing but sin and laziness could make him
So very fat and look so fleshy on't.
60 CLAUDIA You think great blessings attend on sin?
MARCELLINA The soft sins of the flesh give good content,
And that's a blessing in my poor opinion.
Of other kind of sins I have little use
And therefore I abhor them.
65 CLAUDIA A hopeful girl. I would my lady heard you.
LUCINA But is my lord not gone yet, do you say, sir?
CHYLAX He is not, madam, and must take this kindly,
Exceeding kindly of you, wondrous kindly,
You come so far to visit him. I'll guide you.
70 LUCINA Whither?
CHYLAX Why, to my lord.
LUCINA Is it impossible
To find him in this place without a guide?
For I would willingly not trouble you.
CHYLAX My only trouble, madam, is my fear
75 I'm too unworthy of so great an honour.
But here you're in the public gallery
Where th'Emperor must pass, unless you'd see him.
LUCINA Bless me, sir, no. Pray lead me any whither.
My lord cannot be long before he find me. *Exeunt.*

Enter Lycinius, Proculus, and Balbus. Music.

80 LYCINIUS She's coming up the stairs. Now the music.
And as that softens, her love will grow warm
Till she melts down. Then Caesar lays his stamp.
Burn those perfumes there.
PROCULUS Peace, no noise without.

A Song

NYMPH

Injurious charmer of my vanquished heart,
85 *Canst thou feel love and yet no pity know?*
Since of myself from thee I cannot part,
Invent some gentle way to let me go.
For what with joy thou didst obtain,
And I with more did give,
90 *In time will make thee false and vain*
And me unfit to live.

SHEPHERD

Frail angel, that wouldst leave a heart forlorn
(With vain pretense falsehood therein might lie),
Seek not to cast wild shadows o'er your scorn;
95 *You cannot sooner change than I can die.*
To tedious life I'll never fall,
Thrown from my dear loved breast;
He merits not to live at all
Who cares to live unblest.

CHORUS

100 *Then let our flaming hearts be joined,*
While in that sacred fire
(Ere thou prove false or I unkind)
Together both expire.

Enter Chylax, Lucina, Claudia, Marcellina.

LUCINA Where is this wretch, this villain, Lycias?
105 Pray heav'n my lord be here, for now I fear it.
I am certainly betrayed. This cursed ring
Is either counterfeit or stolen.
CLAUDIA Your fear
Does but disarm your resolution,
Which may defend you in the worst extremes.
110 Or if that fail, are there not gods and angels?
LUCINA None in this place, I fear, but evil ones.
Heav'n pity me.
CHYLAX But tell me, dearest madam,
How do you like the song?

LUCINA Sir, I am no judge
Of music, and the words, I thank my gods,
I did not understand.

115 CHYLAX The Emperor
Has the best talent at expounding 'em.
You'll ne'er forget a lesson of his teaching.

LUCINA Are you the worthy friend of Maximus
Would lead me to him? He shall thank you, sir,
As you deserve.

120 CHYLAX Madam, he shall not need.
I have a master will reward my service,
When you have made him happy with your love,
For which he hourly languishes. (*Whispers*) Be kind.

LUCINA The gods shall kill me first.

CHYLAX Think better on't.
125 'Tis sweeter dying in the Emperor's arms.

Enter Phorba and Ardelia.

But here are ladies come to see you, madam.
They'll entertain you better; I but tire you.
Therefore I'll leave you for a while and bring
Your much-loved lord unto you. *Exit Chylax.*

LUCINA Then I'll thank you.
130 (*Aside*) I am betrayed for certain.

PHORBA You are a welcome woman.

ARDELIA Bless me heaven,
How did you find your way to court?

LUCINA I know not. Would I had never trod it.

Enter Emperor behind.

PHORBA Prithee tell me.
135 Good pretty lady and dear sweet heart, love us,
For we love thee extremely. Is not this place
A paradise to live in?

LUCINA Yes, to you
Who know no paradise but guilty pleasure.

ARDELIA Heard you the music yet?

LUCINA 'Twas none to me.

140 PHORBA You must not be thus froward. Well, this gown
Is one o'th' prettiest, by my troth, Ardelia,
I ever saw yet. 'Twas not to frown in, madam,

You put this gown on when you came.
ARDELIA How do you?
(*Aside*) Alas, poor wretch, how cold it is.
LUCINA Content you,
145 I am as well as may be and as temperate,
So you will let me be so. Where's my lord?
For that's the business I come for hither.
PHORBA We'll lead you to him. He's in the gallery.
ARDELIA We'll show you all the court too.
LUCINA Show me him
And you have showed me all I come to look on.
150 PHORBA Come on, we'll be your guides. And as you go,
We have some pretty tales to tell you, madam,
Shall make you merry too. You come not hither
To be sad, Lucina.
LUCINA Would I might not.
Exeunt Lucina, Claudia, Marcellina, and Phorba.
Enter Chylax and Balbus in haste.
CHYLAX Now see all ready.
BALBUS I fly, boy. *Exit Balbus.*
155 CHYLAX The women by this time are warming of her.
If she holds out them, the Emperor
Takes her to task. He has her. Hark, I hear 'em.
Enter Valentinian drawing in Lucina.
VALENTINIAN Would you have run away so slyly, madam?
LUCINA I beseech you, sir,
Consider what I am, and whose.
160 VALENTINIAN I do so.
For what you are, I am filled with such amaze,
So far transported with desire and love,
My slippery soul flows to you while I speak.
And whose you were, I care not, for now you are mine
165 Who love you and will dote on you more
Than you do on your virtue.
LUCINA (*kneeling*) Sacred Caesar –
VALENTINIAN You shall not kneel to me. Rise!
LUCINA Look upon me,
And if you be so cruel to abuse me,
Think how the gods will take it. Does this face

170 Afflict your soul? I'll hide it from you ever.
Nay more, I will become so leprous
That you shall curse me from you. My dear lord
Has ever served you truly, fought your battles
As if he daily longed to die for Caesar,
175 Was never traitor, sir, nor never tainted
In all the actions of his life.

VALENTINIAN (*aside*) How high does this fantastic virtue swell?
She thinks it infamy to please too well.
(*To her*) I know it.

LUCINA His merits and his fame have grown together,
Together flourished like two spreading cedars
Over the Roman diadem. Oh let not
(As you have a heart that's human in you)
The having of an honest wife decline him.
185 Let not my virtue be a wedge to break him,
Much less my shame his undeserved dishonour.
I do not think you are so bad a man.
I know report belies you. You are Caesar,
Which is the father of the empire's glory.
190 You are too near the nature of the gods
To wrong the weakest of all creatures, woman.

VALENTINIAN (*aside*) I dare not do it here. (*To her*) Rise, fair Lucina.
When you believe me worthy, make me happy.
Chylax, wait on her to her lord within.
Wipe your fair eyes. *Exeunt Lucina and Chylax.*
195 Ah Love, ah cursed boy,
Where art thou that torments me thus unseen
And ragest with thy fires within my breast?
With idle purpose to inflame her heart,
Which is as inaccessible and cold
200 As the proud tops of these aspiring hills
Whose heads are wrapped in everlasting snow,
Though the hot sun roll o'er them every day,
And as his beams, which only shine above,
Scorch and consume in regions round below,
205 Soft Love, which throws such brightness through her eyes,

Leaves her heart cold and burns me at her feet.
My tyrant – but her flattering slave thou art,
A glory round her lovely face, a fire within my heart.
Who waits without? Lycinius?

Enter Lycinius.

LYCINIUS My lord.

210 VALENTINIAN Where are the masquers that should dance tonight?

LYCINIUS In the old hall, sir, going now to practise.

VALENTINIAN About it straight. 'Twill serve to draw away
Those list'ning fools who trace it in the gallery.
And if by chance odd noises should be heard,
215 As women's shrieks or so, say 'tis a play
Is practising within.

LYCINIUS *The Rape of Lucrece*,
Or some such merry prank. It shall be done, sir.

Exit Lycinius.

VALENTINIAN 'Tis nobler like a lion to invade
Where appetite directs and seize my prey
220 Than to wait tamely like a begging dog
Till dull consent throws out the scraps of love.
I scorn those gods who seek to cross my wishes
And will in spite of them be happy. Force,
Of all powers, is the most generous.
225 For what that gives, it freely does bestow
Without the after-bribe of gratitude.
I'll plunge into a sea of my desires
And quench my fever, though I drown my fame,
And tear up pleasure by the roots. No matter
230 Though it never grow again. What shall ensue
Let gods and fate look to it; it's their business.

Act IV. Scene iii

The scene opens and discovers five or six dancing-masters practising.

FIRST DANCER That is the damned'st shuffling step. Pox on't.

SECOND DANCER I shall never hit it. Thou hast naturally

All the neat motions of a merry tailor,
Ten thousand wriggles. With thy toes inward,
5 Cut clear and strong. Let thy limbs play about thee.
Keep time and hold thy back upright and firm.
It may prefer thee to a waiting-woman.

FIRST DANCER Or to her lady, which is worse.

They dance. Enter Lycinius.

LYCINIUS Bless me, the loud shrieks and horrid outcries
10 Of the poor lady! Ravishing d'you call it?
She roars as if she were upon the rack.
'Tis strange there should be such a difference
Betwixt half-ravishing, which most women love,
And thorough force, which takes away all blame
15 And should be therefore welcome to the virtuous.
These tumbling rogues, I fear, have overheard 'em,
But their ears with their brains are in their heels.
Good morrow, gentlemen.
What, is all perfect? I have taken care
20 Your habits shall be rich and glorious.

THIRD DANCER That will set off. Pray sit down and see
How the last entry I have made will please you.

Second dance.

LYCINIUS 'Tis very fine indeed.

SECOND DANCER I hope so, sir. *Exeunt dancers.*

Enter Chylax, Proculus, and Lycias.

PROCULUS 'Tis done, Lycinius.

LYCINIUS How?

PROCULUS I blush to tell it.
25 If there be any justice, we are villains
And must be so rewarded.

LYCIAS Since 'tis done,
I take it 'tis not time now to repent it.
Let's make the best o'th' trade.

CHYLAX Now vengeance take it,
Why should not he have settled on a beauty
30 Whose modesty's stuck in a piece of tissue,
Or one a ring might rule, or such a one
That had a husband itching to be honourable,
And ground to get it? If he must have women

(And no allay without 'em), why not those
35 That know the mystery and are best able
To play a game with judgement, such as she is?
Grant they be won with long siege, endless travail,
And brought to opportunities with millions,
Yet when they come to motion, their cold virtue
40 Keeps 'em like beds of snow. I'll melt a diamond
And make a dead flint fire himself ere they
Give greater heat than new-departing embers
Afford old men that watch 'em.

LYCINIUS A good whore
Had saved all this, and happily as wholesome,
45 Ay, and (the thing once done) as well thought of too.
But this same chastity, forsooth –

CHYLAX A pox on't.
Why should not women be as free as we are?
They are, but will not own it, and far freer,
And the more bold you bear yourself, more welcome.
50 And there is nothing you dare say but truth,
But they dare hear it.

PROCULUS No doubt of it. Away!
Let them who can repent go home and pray. *Exeunt.*

Scene opens, discovers the Emperor's chamber. Lucina newly unbound by the Emperor.

VALENTINIAN. Your only virtue now is patience.
Be wise and save your honour. If you talk –

55 LUCINA As long as there is life in this body
And breath to give me words, I'll cry for justice.

VALENTINIAN Justice will never hear you. I am justice.

LUCINA Wilt thou not kill me, monster, ravisher?
Thou bitter bane o'th' empire, look upon me,
60 And if thy guilty eyes dare see the ruins
Thy wild lust hath laid level with dishonour,
The sacrilegious razing of that temple
The tempter to thy black sins would have blushed at,
Behold and curse thyself! The gods will find thee
65 (That's all my refuge now), for they are righteous.
Vengeance and horror circle thee! The empire,
In which thou liv'st a strong continued surfeit,

Like poison will disgorge thee; good men raze thee
From ever being read again;
70 Chaste wives and fearful maids make vows against thee.
Thy worst slaves, when they hear of this, shall hate thee,
And those thou hast corrupted, first fall from thee,
And if thou let'st me live, the soldier,
Tired with thy tyrannies, break through obedience
And shake his strong steel at thee.
75 VALENTINIAN This prevails not,
Nor any agony you utter, madam.
If I have done a sin, curse her that drew me.
Curse the first cause, the witchcraft that abused me.
Curse your fair eyes, and curse that heavenly beauty,
And curse your being good too.
80 LUCINA Glorious thief,
What restitution canst thou make to save me?
VALENTINIAN I'll ever love and ever honour you.
LUCINA Thou canst not.
For that which was my honour thou hast murdered.
85 And can there be a love in violence?
VALENTINIAN You shall be only mine.
LUCINA Yet I like better
Thy villainy than flattery; that's thy own,
The other basely counterfeit. Fly from me,
Or for thy safety's sake and wisdom, kill me.
90 For I am worse than thou art: thou may'st pray
And so recover grace; I am lost for ever,
And if thou let'st me live, thou'rt lost thyself too.
VALENTINIAN I fear no loss but love. I stand above it.
LUCINA Gods, what a wretched thing has this man made me?
95 For I am now no wife for Maximus,
No company for women that are virtuous,
No family I now can claim or country,
Nor name but Caesar's whore. O sacred Caesar
(For that should be your title), was your empire,
100 Your rods and axes that are types of justice,
Those fires that ever burn to beg you blessings,
The people's adoration, fear of nations,
What victory can bring you home, what

Else the useful elements can make your servants,
105 Ev'n light itself and sun of light, truth, justice,
Mercy, and starlike piety, sent to you,
And from the gods themselves – to ravish women?
The curses that I owe to enemies,
Ev'n those the Sabines sent, when Romulus
110 (As thou hast me) ravished their noble maids,
Made more and heavier, light on thee.

VALENTINIAN This helps not.

LUCINA The sins of Tarquin be remembered in thee.
And where there has a chaste wife been abused,
Let it be thine, the shame thine, thine the slaughter,
115 And last, forever thine the feared example.
Where shall poor virtue live now I am fallen?
What can your honours now and empire make me
But a more glorious whore?

VALENTINIAN A better woman.
If you be blind and scorn it, who can help it?
120 Come leave these lamentations. You do nothing
But make a noise. I am the same man still.
Were it to do again (therefore be wiser), by all
This holy light I would attempt it.
You are so excellent and made to ravish,
There were no pleasure in you else.

125 LUCINA O villain!

VALENTINIAN So bred for man's amazement that my reason
And every help to hold me right has left me.
The god of love himself had been before me,
Had he but eyes to see you. Tell me justly
130 How should I choose but err. Then, if you will,
Be mine and only mine, for you are so precious
I envy any other should enjoy you,
Almost look on you. And your daring husband
Shall know he has kept an off'ring from the Emperor
135 Too holy for his altars. Be the greatest;
More than myself I'll make you. If you will not,
Sit down with this and silence; for which wisdom
You shall have use of me. If you divulge it,
Know I am far above the faults I do.

140 And those I do, I am able to forgive.
And where your credit in the telling of it
May be with gloss enough suspected, mine
Is as my own command shall make it. Princes,
Though they be sometimes subject to loose whispers,
145 Yet wear they two-edged swords for open censures.
Your husband cannot help you, nor the soldiers;
Your husband is my creature, they my weapons
And only where I bid them strike. I feed them.
Nor can the gods be angry at this action,
150 Who, as they made me greatest, meant me happiest,
Which I had never been without this pleasure.
Consider, and farewell. You'll find your women
Waiting without. They have been diverted too,
But are more thankful for't. *Exit Valentinian.*

LUCINA Destruction find thee!
155 Now which way shall I go? My honest house
Will shake to shelter me, my husband fly me,
My family,
Because they're honest and desire to remain so,
Must not endure me, not a neighbour know me.
160 What woman now dare see me without blushes,
And pointing as I pass, 'There, there behold her.
Look on her, little children, that is she.
The ravished woman mark.' Oh my sad fortune,
Is this the end of goodness, this the prize
165 Of all my early prayers to protect me?
Why then I see there is no god but power,
Nor virtue now alive that cares for us
But what is either lame or sensual.
How had I been thus wretched else?

Enter Maximus and Æcius.

ÆCIUS Let Titus
170 Command the company that Pontius lost.

MAXIMUS How now, sweet heart. What makes you here and thus?

ÆCIUS Lucina weeping? This is some strange offence.

MAXIMUS Look up and tell me
Why thou art thus. My ring! Oh friend, I've found it.

175 You are at court then?
LUCINA This and that vile wretch, Lycias, brought me hither.
MAXIMUS Rise and go home. I have my fears, Æcius.
Oh my best friend, I am ruined. Go, Lucina.
Already in thy tears I've read thy wrongs,
180 Already found a Caesar. Go, thou lily,
Thou sweetly drooping flower. Be gone, I say
And (if thou dar'st) outlive this wrong.
LUCINA I dare not.
ÆCIUS Is that the ring you lost?
MAXIMUS That, that, Æcius,
That cursed ring myself and all my fortunes have undone.
185 'T has pleased the Emperor, my noble master,
For all my services and dangers for him,
To make me my own pander. Was this justice?
Oh my Æcius, have I lived to bear this?
LUCINA Farewell forever, sir.
MAXIMUS That's a sad saying,
190 But such a one becomes you well, Lucina.
And yet methinks we should not part so slightly.
Our loves have been of longer growth, more rooted
Than the sharp blast of one farewell can scatter.
Kiss me. I find no Caesar here. These lips
195 Taste not of ravisher in my opinion.
Was it not so?
LUCINA Oh yes.
MAXIMUS I dare believe you.
I know him and thy truth too well to doubt it.
Oh my most dear Lucina! Oh my comfort,
Thou blessing of my youth, life of my life!
200 ÆCIUS I have seen enough to stagger my obedience.
Hold me, ye equal gods. This is too sinful.
MAXIMUS Why wert thou chosen out to make a whore of,
Thou only one 'mongst millions of thy sex
Unfeignedly virtuous? Fall, fall, crystal fountains,
205 And ever feed your streams, you rising sorrows,
Till you have wept your mistress into marble.
Now go forever from me.
LUCINA Long farewell, sir.

As I have been faithful, gods, think on me.
ÆCIUS Madam, farewell. Since you resolve to die,
210 Which well considered,
If you can cease awhile from these strange thoughts,
I wish were rather altered.
LUCINA No.
ÆCIUS Mistake not.
I would not stain your virtue for the empire,
Nor any way decline you to dishonour;
215 It is not my profession but a villain's.
I find and feel your loss as deep as you do,
And still am the same Æcius, still as honest,
The same life I have still for Maximus,
The same sword wear for you where justice bids me,
220 And 'tis no dull one. Therefore misconceive me not.
Only I'd have you live a little longer,
But a short year.
LUCINA Alas, sir, why so long?
Am I not wretched enough already with grief?
ÆCIUS To draw from that wild man a sweet repentance,
And goodness in his days to come.
225 MAXIMUS They are so,
And will be ever becoming, my Æcius.
ÆCIUS. For who knows but the sight of you, presenting
His swollen sins at the full and your wronged virtue,
May like a fearful vision fright his follies
230 And once more bend him right again, which blessing,
If your dark wrong would give you leave to read,
Is more than death, and the reward more glorious.
Death only eases you, this the whole empire
Besides, compelled and forced by violence
235 To what was done. The deed was none of yours.
For should th'eternal gods desire to perish
Because we daily violate their truth,
Which is the chastity of heaven? No, madam –
LUCINA The tongues of angels cannot alter me.
240 For could the world again restore my honour,
As fair and absolute as e'er I bred it,
That world I should not trust. Again, the Emperor

Can by my life get nothing but my story,
Which whilst I breathe must be his infamy.
245 And where you counsel me to live that Caesar
May see his errors and repent, I'll tell you
His penitence is but increase of pleasure;
His prayers are never said but to deceive us,
And when he weeps (as you think, for his vices),
250 'Tis but as killing drops from baleful yew trees
That rot his harmless neighbours. If he can grieve
As one that yet desires his free conversion,
I'll leave him robes to mourn in – my sad ashes.

ÆCIUS The farewells then of happy souls be with thee,
255 And to thy memory be ever sung
The praises of a just and constant woman.
This sad day, whilst I live, a soldier's tears
I'll offer on thy monument.

MAXIMUS All that is chaste upon thy tomb shall flourish;
260 All living epitaphs be thine. Time's story,
And what is left behind to piece our lives,
Shall be no more abused with tales and trifles,
But full of thee stand to eternity.

ÆCIUS Once more, farewell. Go find Elysium,
265 There where deserving souls are crowned with blessings.

MAXIMUS There where no vicious tyrants come. Truth, honour,
Are keepers of that blessed place. Go thither. *Exit Lucina.*

ÆCIUS Gods give thee justice.
(*Aside*) His thoughts begin to work. I fear him yet.
270 He ever was a worthy Roman, but
I know not what to think on't. He has suffered
Beyond a man, if he stand this.

MAXIMUS Æcius,
Am I alive or has a dead sleep seized me?
It was my wife the Emperor abused thus.
275 And I must say I'm glad I had her for him,
Must I not, Æcius?

ÆCIUS I am stricken
With such a stiff amazement that no answer
Can readily come from me nor no comfort.

Will you go home, or to my house?

MAXIMUS Neither.

280 I have no home, and you are mad, Æcius,
To keep me company. I am a fellow
My own sword would forsake, not tied to me.
A pander is a prince to what I'm fallen to.
By heav'n I dare do nothing.

ÆCIUS You do better.

285 MAXIMUS I'm made a branded slave, Æcius,
Yet I must bless the maker.
Death on my soul! Shall I endure this tamely?
Must Maximus be mentioned for his wrongs?
I am a child too; what do I railing?
290 I cannot mend myself. 'Twas Caesar did it,
And what am I to him?

ÆCIUS 'Tis well remembered.
However you are tainted, be no traitor.

MAXIMUS Oh would to god you were not living and my friend!

ÆCIUS I'll bear a wary eye upon your actions.
295 I fear you, Maximus, nor can I blame you
If you break out. For by the gods your wrong
Deserves a general ruin. Do you love me?

MAXIMUS That's all I have to live on.

ÆCIUS Then go with me.
You shall not to your own house.

MAXIMUS Nor to any.
300 My griefs are greater far than walls can compass.
And yet I wonder how it happens with me.
I am not dangerous and in my conscience
Should I now see the Emperor i'th' heat on't,
I should scarce blame him for't. An awe runs through me
305 (I feel it sensibly) that binds me to it.
'Tis at my heart now. There it sits and rules,
And methinks it is a pleasure to obey it.

ÆCIUS This is a mask to cozen me. I know you
And how far you dare do, no Roman farther
310 Nor with more fearless valour, and I'll watch you.

MAXIMUS Is a wife's loss

(For her abuse much good may do his heart;
I'll make as bold with his wife if I can)
More than the fading of a few fresh colours?

315 ÆCIUS No more, Maximus, to one that truly lives.

MAXIMUS Why then I care not. I can live well enough, Æcius.
For look you, friend, for virtue and those trifles,
They may be bought, they say.

ÆCIUS (*aside*) He's crazed a little.
His grief has made him talk things from his nature.
(*To him*) Will you go any ways?

320 MAXIMUS I'll tell thee, friend,
If my wife for all this should be a whore now,
A kind of kicker out of sheets, 'twould vex me.
For I'm not angry yet. The Emperor
Is young and handsome, and the woman, flesh.
325 And may not these two couple without scratching?

ÆCIUS Alas, my Maximus.

MAXIMUS Alas not me,
I'm not wretched. For there's no man miserable
But he that makes himself so.

ÆCIUS Will you walk yet?

MAXIMUS Come, come, she dares not die, friend. That's the
truth on't.
330 She knows the enticing sweets and delicacies
Of a young prince's pleasure, and I thank her.
She has made way for Maximus to rise by.
Will't not become me bravely?

ÆCIUS Dearest friend,
These wild words show your violated mind,
335 Urged with the last extremity of grief,
Which since I cannot like a man redress
With tears, I must lament it like a child.
For when Caesar does the injury,
Sorrow is all the remedy I know.

340 MAXIMUS 'Tis then a certain truth that I am wronged,
Wronged in that barb'rous manner I imagined.
Alas, I was in hopes I had been mad,
And that these horrors which invade my heart
Were but distracted, melancholy whimsies.

345 But they are real truths (it seems) and I
The last of men and vilest of all beings.

Bear me, cold earth, who am too weak to move
Beneath my load of shame and misery.
Wronged by my lawful prince, robbed of my love,
350 Branded with everlasting infamy.
Take pity, fate, and give me leave to die.

Gods, would you be adored for being good,
Or only feared for proving mischievous?
How would you have your mercy understood,
355 Who could create a wretch like Maximus,
Ordained though guiltless to be infamous?

Supreme first causes, you whence all things flow,
Whose infiniteness does each little fill,
You who decree each seeming chance below
360 (So great in power), were you as good in will,
How could you ever have produced such ill?

Had your eternal minds been bent to good,
Could human happiness have proved so lame,
Rapine, revenge, injustice, thirst of blood,
365 Grief, anguish, horror, want, despair, and shame
Had never found a being nor a name.

'Tis therefore less impiety to say
Evil with you has coeternity
Than blindly taking it the other way,
370 That merciful and of election free
You did create the mischiefs you foresee.

Wretch that I am 'gainst heav'n to exclaim,
When this poor, tributary worm below,
More than myself in nothing but in name,
375 Who durst invade me with this fatal blow,
I dare not crush in the revenge I owe,

Base notion which my just resentment clogs
With the fantastic awe of prince and slave.
I'll rip him up and throw his heart t'th' dogs.
380 Not all his power shall the wild monster save;
Him and my shame I'll tread into one grave.

ÆCIUS (*aside*) Does he but seem so,
Or is he mad indeed? Now to reprove him
Were counsel lost. But something must be done
385 With speed and care which may prevent that fate
Which threatens this unhappy Emperor.

MAXIMUS O gods, my heart, would it would fairly break.
Methinks I am somewhat wilder than I was,
And yet I thank the gods I know my duty.

Enter Claudia.

390 CLAUDIA Forgive me my sad tidings, sir. She's dead.

MAXIMUS
Why so it should be. (*He rises*) How?

CLAUDIA When first she entered
Into the house, after a world of weeping
And blushing like the sunset as we see her,
'Dare I', said she, 'defile my husband's house
395 Wherein his spotless family has flourished?'
At this she fell, choked with a thousand sighs.
And now the pleased, expiring saint,
Her dying looks, where new-born beauty shines,
Oppressed with blushes, modestly declines,
400 While Death approaches with a majestic grace,
Proud to look lovely once in such a face.
Her arms spread to receive her welcome guest,
With a glad sigh she drew into her breast.
Her eyes then languishing towards heaven she cast
405 To thank the powers that Death has come at last.
And at the approach of the cold, silent god,
Ten thousand hidden glories rushed abroad.
Nature in the last minute seemed undone,
And beauty's magazine blown up and gone,
410 Such brightness did through dying features dash
Like burning ships extinguished in a flash. *Exit Claudia.*

MAXIMUS No more of this. Begone. Now, my Æcius,
If thou wilt do me pleasure, weep a little.

Act V. Scene i

Æcius solus with a letter.

ÆCIUS Look down, ye equal gods, and guide my heart,
Or it will throw upon my hands an act
Which after ages shall record with horror.
As well might I kill my offended friend
5 As think to punish my offending prince.
The laws of friendship we ourselves create,
And 'tis but simple villainy to break them,
But faith to princes broke is sacrilege,
An injury to the gods. And that lost wretch
10 Whose breast is poisoned with so vile a purpose
Tears thunder down from heaven on his own head
And leaves a curse to his posterity.
Judge him yourselves, ye mighty gods, who know
Why you permit sometimes that honour bleed,
15 That faith be broke, and innocence oppressed.
My duty's my religion. And howe'er
The great account may rise 'twixt him and you,
Through all his crimes I see your image on him
And must protect it no way then but this:
20 To draw far off the injured Maximus
And keep him there fast prisoner to my friendship.
Revenge shall thus be flattered or destroyed,
And my bad master, whom I blush to serve,
Shall by my means at least be safe. This letter
25 Informs him I am gone to Egypt, there
I shall live secure and innocent.
His sins shall ne'er o'ertake me, nor his fears.

Enter Proculus.

Here comes one for my purpose. Proculus,
Well met. I have a courtesy to ask of you.
30 PROCULUS Of me, my lord? Is there a house on fire?
Or is some knotty point now in debate
Betwixt your lordship and the scavengers?
For you have such a popular and public spirit
As in dull times of peace will not disdain
35 The meanest opportunity to serve your country.

ÆCIUS You witty fools are apt to get your heads broke.
This is no season for buffooning, sirrah.
Though heretofore I tamely have endured
Before the Emperor your ridiculous mirth,
40 Think not you have a title to be saucy.
When monkeys grow mischievous, they are whipped,
Chained up and whipped. There has been mischief done,
And you (I hear) a wretched instrument.
Look to't. Whene'er I draw this sword to punish,
45 You and your grinning crew will tremble, slaves.
Nor shall the ruined world afford a corner
To shelter you nor that poor prince's bosom
You have envenomed and polluted so
As if the gods were willing it should be
50 A dungeon for such toads to crawl and croak in.
PROCULUS All this in earnest to your humblest creature?
Nay then, my lord, I must no more pretend
With my poor talent to divert your ears,
Since my well-meaning mirth is grown offensive.
55 Though heaven can tell
There's not so low an act of servile duty
I would not with more pride throw myself on
For great Æcius's sake than gain a province
Or share with Valentinian in his empire.
60 ÆCIUS Thou art so fawning and so mean a villain
That I disdain to hate, though I despise thee.
Whene'er thou art not fearful, thou art saucy.
Be so again (my pardon gives thee leave),
And to deserve it, carry this my letter
65 To th'Emperor. Tell him I am gone for Egypt,
And with me Maximus. 'Twas scarce fit we two
Should take our leaves of him. Pray use your interest
He may forgive us. 'Twill concern your much.
For when we are gone, to be base, vicious villains
70 Will prove less dang'rous. *Exit Æcius.*
PROCULUS What the devil possesses
This rusty back and breast without a headpiece?
Villains and vicious? Maximus and Egypt?
This may be treason, or I'll make it so.

75 The Emperor's apt enough to fears and jealousies
Since his late rape. I must blow up the fire
And aggravate this doting hero's notions,
Till they such terrors in the prince have bred
May cost the fool his worst part. That's his head. *Exit.*

Act V. Scene ii

Enter Valentinian, Lycinius, Chylax, and Balbus.

VALENTINIAN Dead?
BALBUS 'Tis too certain.
VALENTINIAN How?
LYCINIUS Grief and disgrace,
As people say.
VALENTINIAN No more. I have too much on't,
Too much by you, you whetters of my follies,
Ye angel formers of my sins but devils.
5 Where is your cunning now? You would work wonders;
There was no chastity above your practice.
You'd undertake to make her love her wrongs
And dote upon her rape. Mark what I tell you:
If she be dead –
CHYLAX Alas, sir.
VALENTINIAN Hang you rascals!
10 Ye blasters of my youth, if she be gone,
'Twere better ye had been your father's camels,
Groaned under weight of wood and water –
Am I not Caesar?
LYCINIUS Mighty and our maker –
VALENTINIAN Than thus have given my pleasures to destruction.
Look she be living, slaves.
15 CHYLAX We are no gods, sir,
If she be dead, to make her live again.
VALENTINIAN She cannot die, she must not die. Are those
I plant my love upon but common livers,
Their hours told out to them? Can they be ashes?
20 Why do you flatter a belief in me

That I am all that is, the world my creature;
The trees bring forth their fruit when I say 'Summer';
The wind that knows no limits but its wildness,
At my command moves not a leaf; the sea,
25 With his proud mountain-waters envying heav'n,
When I say 'Still', runs into crystal mirrors.
Can I do this, and she die? Why, ye bubbles
That with my least breath break, no more remembered,
Ye moths that fly about my flames and perish,
30 Why do ye make me god, that can do nothing?
Is she not dead?

CHYLAX All women are not dead with her.

VALENTINIAN A common whore serves you, and far above you.
The pleasures of a body lamed with lewdness,
A mere perpetual motion makes you happy.
35 Am I a man to traffic with diseases?
You think, because ye have bred me up to pleasures
And almost run me over all the rare ones,
Your wives will serve the turn. I care not for them.
Your wives are fencers' whores and shall be footmen's.
40 Though sometimes my fantastic lust or scorn
Has made you cuckolds for variety,
I would not have ye hope or dream, ye poor ones,
Always so great a blessing from me. Go,
Get your own infamy hereafter, rascals.
45 I have done too nobly for ye. Ye enjoy
Each one an heir, the royal seed of Caesar,
And I may curse ye for it. Thou, Lycinius,
Hast such a Messalina, such a Laïs,
The backs of bulls cannot content, nor stallions;
50 The sweat of fifty men a night does nothing.

LYCINIUS I hope, sir, you know better things of her.

VALENTINIAN 'Tis oracle.
The city can bear witness thine's a fool, Chylax.
Yet she can tell her twenty and all lovers,
55 All have lain with her too, and all as she is,
Rotten and ready for a hospital.
Yours is a holy whore, friend Balbus.

BALBUS Well, sir.

VALENTINIAN One that can pray away the sin she suffers,
But not the punishment. She has had ten bastards
60 (Five of them now are lictors), yet she prays.
She has been the song of Rome and common pasquil.
Since I durst see a wench, she was camp-mistress
And mustered all the cohorts, paid them too
(They have it yet to show), yet she prays.
65 She is now to enter old men turned children
That have forgot their rudiments. And am I
Left for these withered vices? And was there but one,
But one of all the world that could content me,
And snatched away in showing. If your wives
70 Be not yet witches, or yourselves, now be so
And save your lives. Raise me the dearest beauty,
As when I forced her, full of chastity,
Or by the gods –

LYCINIUS Most sacred Caesar!

VALENTINIAN Slaves.

Enter Proculus.

PROCULUS Hail Caesar. Tidings of concern and danger
75 My message does contain in furious manner.
With oaths and threat'nings stern Æcius
Enjoined me on the peril of my life
To give this letter into Caesar's hands.
Armed at all points, prepared to march he stands
80 With crowds of mutinous officers about him.
Among these, full of anguish and despair
Like pale Tisiphone along hell brinks,
Plotting revenge and ruin, Maximus
With ominous aspect walks in silent horror.
85 In threat'ning murmurs and harsh, broken speeches
They talk of Egypt and their provinces,
Of cohorts ready with their lives to serve them.
And then with bitter curses they named you.

VALENTINIAN Go tell thy fears to thy companions, slave.
90 For 'tis a language princes understand not.
Be gone and leave me to myself. *Exeunt all but Valentinian.*
The names of this Æcius and of Maximus

Run through me like a fever, shake, and burn me.
But to my slaves I must not show my poorness.
95 They know me vicious; should they find me base
How would the villains scorn me and insult.
Reads the letter.
Sir,
Would some god inspire me with another way to serve you, I would not thus fly from you without leave. But Maximus his
100 *wrongs have touched too many, and should his presence here encourage them, dangers to you might follow. In Egypt he will be more forgot, and you safe by his absence.*

VALENTINIAN A plot, by heav'n, a plot laid for my life.
This is too subtle for my dull friend, Æcius.
105 Heav'n give you, sir, a better servant to guard you;
A faithfuller you'll never find than Æcius.
Since he resents his friend's wrongs, he'll revenge them.
I know the soldiers love him more than heav'n.
Me they hate more than peace. What this may breed
110 If dull security and confidence
Let him grow up, a fool may find and laugh at.
Who waits there? Proculus!
Enter Proculus.
Well, hast thou observed
The growing pow'r and pride of this Æcius?
He writes to me with terms of insolence,
115 And shortly will rebel if not prevented.
But in my base, lewd herd of vicious slaves
There's not a man that dares stand up to strike
At my command and kill this rising traitor.

PROCULUS The gods forbid Caesar should be thus served.
120 The earth would swallow him did you command it.
But I have studied a safe, sure way
How he shall die and your will ne'er suspected.
A soldier waits without whom he has wronged,
Cashiered, disgraced, and turned to beg or starve.
125 This fellow for revenge would kiss the devil.
Encouragement of pardon and reward,
Which in your name I'll give him instantly,
Will make him fly more swiftly on the murder

Than longing lovers to their first appointment.
130 VALENTINIAN Thou art the wisest, watchful, wary villain
And shall partake the secrets of my soul
And ever feel my favour and my bounty.
Tell the poor soldier he shall be a general,
Æcius once dead.
PROCULUS Ay, there you've found the point, sir,
135 If he can be so brutish to believe it.
VALENTINIAN Oh never fear, urge it with confidence.
What will not flattered, angry fools believe?
Minutes are precious; lose not one.
PROCULUS I fly, sir. *Exit Proculus.*
VALENTINIAN What an infected conscience do I live with,
140 And what a beast I've grown. When lust has gained
An uncontrolled dominion in man's heart,
Then fears succeed with horror and amazement
Which wrack the wretch and tyrannize by turns.
But hold.
145 Shall I grow then so poor as to repent?
Though Æcius, mankind, and the gods forsake me,
I'll never alter and forsake myself.
Can I forget the late discourse he held,
As if he had intent to make me odious
150 To my own face, and by a way of terror
What vices I was grounded in, and almost
Proclaimed the soldiers' hate against me? Is not
The name and dignity of Caesar sacred?
Were this Æcius more than man sufficient
155 To shake off all his honesty? He is dangerous,
Though he is good, and though a friend, a feared one,
And such I must not sleep by. As for Maximus,
I'll find a time when Æcius is dispatched.
I do believe this Proculus and I thank him.
160 'Twas time to look about. If I must perish,
Yet shall my fears go foremost. That's determined. *Exit.*

Act V. Scene iii

Enter Proculus and Pontius.

PROCULUS Besides this, if you do it, you enjoy
The noble name of patrician. More than that too,
The friend of Caesar you're styled. There's nothing
Within the hopes of Rome or present being,
But you may safely say is yours.

5 PONTIUS Pray stay, sir.
What has Æcius done to be destroyed?
At least I would have a colour.

PROCULUS You have more.
Nay, all that can be given: he is a traitor,
One any man would strike that were a subject.

PONTIUS Is he so foul?

10 PROCULUS Yes, a most fearful traitor.

PONTIUS (*aside*) A fearful plague upon thee, for thou liest.
(*To him*) I ever thought the soldiers would undo him
With their too much affection.

PROCULUS You have hit it.
They have brought him to ambition.

PONTIUS Then he's gone.

15 PROCULUS The Emperor out of a foolish pity
Would save him yet.

PONTIUS Is he so mad?

PROCULUS He's madder,
Would go to the army to him.

PONTIUS Would he so?

PROCULUS Yes, Pontius, but we consider –

PONTIUS Wisely.

PROCULUS (How else, man?) – that the state lies in it.

PONTIUS And your lives too.

PROCULUS And every man's.

Enter Aretus behind.

20 PONTIUS He did me
All the disgrace he could.

PROCULUS And scurvily.

PONTIUS Out of a mischief merely. Did you mark it?

PROCULUS Yes, well enough. Now you have means to quit it.
The deed done, take his place.

PONTIUS Pray let me think on't.

'Tis ten to one I do it.

25 PROCULUS Do and be happy. *Exit Proculus.*

PONTIUS This Emperor is made of nought but mischief;
Sure Murder was his mother. None to lop
But the main link he had? Upon my conscience
The man is truly honest, and that kills him.
30 For to live here and study to be true
Is all one as to be traitor. Why should *he* die?
Have they not slaves and rascals for their offerings
In full abundance, bawds more than beasts for slaughter?
Have they not singing whores enough and knaves besides
35 And millions of such martyrs to sink Charon
But the best sons of Rome must fall too? I'll show him
(Since he must die) a way to do it truly.
And though he bears me hard, yet shall he know
I'm born to make him bless me for a blow.

Act V. Scene iv

Enter Phidias, Aretus, and Æcius.

ARETUS The treason is too certain. Fly, my lord.
I heard that villain Proculus instruct
The desperate Pontius to dispatch you here,
Here in the antechamber.

PHIDIAS Curst wretches!
5 Yet you may escape to the camp. We'll hazard with you.

ARETUS Lose not your life so basely, sir. You are armed,
And many when they see your sword out and know why
Must follow your adventure.

ÆCIUS Get ye from me.
Is not the doom of Caesar on this body?
10 Do I not bear my last hour here now sent me?
Am I not old Æcius ever dying?
You think this tenderness and love you bring me;
'Tis treason and the strength of disobedience.
And if ye tempt me further, ye shall feel it.
15 I seek the camp for safety, when my death,
Ten times more glorious than my life and lasting,

Bids me be happy. Let fools fear to die,
Or he that weds a woman for his honour,
Dreaming no other life to come but kisses.
20 Æcius is not now to learn to suffer.
If ye dare show a just affection, kill me;
I stay but those that must. Why do ye weep?
Am I so wretched as to deserve men's pities?
Go, give your tears to those that lose their worths;
25 Bewail their miseries. For me wear garlands,
Drink wine, and much. Sing paeans to my praise.
I am to triumph, friends, and more than Caesar,
For Caesar fears to die. I love to die.

PHIDIAS Oh my dear lord.

ÆCIUS No more. Go, go, I say.
30 Show me not signs of sorrow. I deserve none.
Dare any man lament I should die nobly?
When I am dead, speak honourably of me,
That is, preserve my memory from dying.
There, if you needs must weep your ruined master,
35 A tear or two will seem well. This I charge you
(Because ye say ye yet love old Æcius):
See my poor body burnt, and some to sing
About my pile what I have done and suffered,
If Caesar kill not that too. At your banquets
40 When I am gone, if any chance to number
The times that have been sad and dangerous,
Say how I fell, and 'tis sufficient.
No more, I say. He that laments my end,
By all the gods, dishonours me. Be gone,
45 And suddenly and wisely from my dangers.
My death is catching else.

PHIDIAS We fear not dying.

ÆCIUS Yet fear a wilful death, the just gods hate it.
I need no company to that. That children
Dare do alone, and slaves are proud to purchase.
50 Live till your honesties, as mine have done,
Make this corrupted age sick of your virtues.
Then die a sacrifice. And then you'll know
The noble use of dying well and Romans.

ARETUS And must we leave you, sir?
ÆCIUS We must all die,
55 All leave ourselves. It matters not where, when,
Nor how, so we die well. And can that man does so
Need lamentation for him? Children weep
Because they have offended, or for fear;
Women for want of will and anger. Is there
60 In noble man, that truly feels both poises
Of life and death, so much of this wet weakness
To drown a glorious death in child and woman?
I am ashamed to see you, yet you move me.
And were it not my manhood would accuse me
65 For covetous to live, I should weep with you.
PHIDIAS Oh shall we never see you more?
ÆCIUS 'Tis true.
Nor I the miseries that Rome shall suffer,
Which is a benefit life cannot reckon.
But what I have been, which is just and faithful,
70 One that grew old for Rome, when Rome forgot him,
And for he was an honest man durst die,
Ye shall have daily with you. Could that die too
And I return no traffic of my travels,
No annals of old Æcius, but he lived.
75 My friends, ye had cause to weep (and bitterly)
The common overflows of tender women
And children new-born. Crying were too little
To show me then most wretched. If tears must be,
I should in justice weep them, and for you.
80 You are to live and yet behold those slaughters
The dry and withered bones of death would bleed at.
But sooner than I have time to think what must be,
I fear you'll find what shall be. If you love me,
Let that word serve for all. Be gone and leave me.
85 I have some little practice with my soul
And then the sharpest sword is welcom'st. Go,
Pray be gone. Ye have obeyed me living,
Be not for shame now stubborn. So I thank ye,
And fare you well. A better fortune guide ye.
90 PHIDIAS (*aside*) What shall we do to save our best-loved master?

ARETUS (*aside*) I'll to Affranius, who with half a legion
Lies in the old Subura. All will rise
For the brave Æcius.
PHIDIAS (*aside*) I'll to Maximus
And lead him hither to prevent this murder,
95 Or help in the revenge, which I'll make sure of.
Exeunt Phidias and Aretus.
ÆCIUS. I hear them come. Who strikes first? I stay for you.
Enter Balbus, Chylax, Lycinius.
Yet will I die a soldier, my sword drawn,
But against none. Why do you fear? Come forward.
BALBUS You were a soldier, Chylax.
CHYLAX Yes, I mustered,
But never saw the enemy.
100 LYCINIUS He's armed.
By heav'n I dare not do it.
ÆCIUS Why do you tremble?
I am to die. Come ye not from Caesar
To that end? Speak.
BALBUS We do and we must kill you.
'Tis Caesar's will.
CHYLAX I charge you put your sword up
That we may do it handsomely.
105 ÆCIUS Ha, ha, ha!
My sword up, handsomely! Where were you bred?
You are the merriest murderers, my masters,
I ever met withal. Come forward, fools.
Why do you stare? Upon my honour, bawds,
I will not strike you.
LYCINIUS I'll not be first.
BALBUS Nor I
110 CHYLAX You had best die quietly. The Emperor
Sees how you bear yourself.
ÆCIUS I would die, rascals,
If you would kill me quietly.
BALBUS Plague on Proculus,
115 He promised us to bring a captain hither
That had been used to kill.
ÆCIUS I'll call the guard,

Unless you kill me quickly, and proclaim
What beastly, base, and cowardly companions
The Emperor has trusted with his safety.
120 Nay, I'll give out you fell on my side, villains.
Strike home, you bawdy slaves.

CHYLAX He will kill us.
I marked his hand. He waits but time to reach us.
Now do you offer?

ÆCIUS If you do mangle me
And kill me not at two blows or at three,
125 Or not so stagger me my senses fail me,
Look to yourselves.

CHYLAX I told ye.

ÆCIUS Strike me manly.
And take a thousand strokes.

Enter Pontius.

BALBUS Here's Pontius.

Lycinius runs away.

PONTIUS Not killed him yet?
Is this the love you bear the Emperor?
130 Nay, then I see you are traitors. Have at ye.

CHYLAX Oh, I am hurt.

Exeunt Chylax and Balbus.

BALBUS And I am killed.

PONTIUS Die, bawds,
As you have lived and flourished.

ÆCIUS Wretched fellow,
What hast thou done?

PONTIUS Killed them that durst not kill,
And you are next.

ÆCIUS Art thou not Pontius?

135 PONTIUS I am the same you cast, Æcius,
And in the face of all the camp disgraced.

ÆCIUS Then so much nobler, as thou wert a soldier,
Shall my death be. Is it revenge provoked thee,
Or art thou hired to kill me?

PONTIUS Both.

ÆCIUS Then do it.

PONTIUS Is that all?
ÆCIUS Yes.
PONTIUS Would you not live?
140 ÆCIUS Why should I?
To thank thee for my life?
PONTIUS Yes, if I spare it.
ÆCIUS Be not deceived, I was not made to thank
(For any courtesy but killing me)
A fellow of thy fortune. Do thy duty.
PONTIUS Do you not fear me?
ÆCIUS No.
145 PONTIUS Nor love me for it?
ÆCIUS That's as thou dost thy business.
PONTIUS When you are dead, your place is mine, Æcius.
ÆCIUS Now I fear thee,
And not alone thee, Pontius, but the empire.
PONTIUS Why? I can govern, sir.
150 ÆCIUS I would thou could'st,
And first thyself. Thou canst fight well and bravely.
Thou canst endure all dangers, heats, colds, hungers.
Heav'n's angry flashes are not suddener
Than I have seen thee execute, nor more mortal.
155 The wingèd feet of flying enemies
I have stood and seen thee mow away like rushes,
And still kill the killer. Were thy mind
But half so sweet in peace as rough in dangers,
I died to leave a happy heir behind me.
Come strike and be a general.
160 PONTIUS Prepare then,
And for I see your honour cannot lessen,
And 'twere a shame for me to strike a dead man,
Fight your short span out.
ÆCIUS No. Thou know'st I must not.
I dare not give thee such advantage of me
As disobedience.
165 PONTIUS Dare you not defend you
Against your enemy?
ÆCIUS Not sent from Caesar.
I have no power to make such enemies,

For as I am condemned, my naked sword
Stands but a hatchment by me, only held
170 To show I was a soldier. Had not Caesar
Chained all defence in this doom, let him die
(Old as I am and quenched with scars and sorrows),
Yet would I make this withered arm do wonders
And open in an enemy such wounds
Mercy would weep to look on.

175 PONTIUS Then have at you,
And look upon me and be sure you fear not.
Remember who you are and why you live,
And what I have been to you. Cry not hold
Nor think it base injustice I should kill thee.

ÆCIUS I am prepared for all.

180 PONTIUS For now, Æcius,
Thou shalt behold and find I was no traitor.
Pontius kills himself.
And as I do it, bless me. Die as I do.

ÆCIUS Thou hast deceived me, Pontius, and I thank thee.
By all my hopes in heav'n thou art a Roman.

185 PONTIUS To show you what you ought to do this is not.
But, noble sir, you have been jealous of me
And held me in the rank of dangerous persons.
And I must, dying, say it was but justice
You cast me from my credit. Yet believe me,
190 For there is nothing now but truth to save me
And your forgiveness, though you hold me heinous
And of a troubled spirit that like fire
Turns all to flames it meets with, you mistook me.
If I were foe to anything, 'twas ease,
195 Want of the soldier's due, the enemy;
To the nakedness we found at home, and scorn
Of children of peace and pleasures, no regard
Nor comfort for our scars nor how we got them;
To rusty time that eats our bodies up
200 And ev'n began to prey upon our honours;
To wants at home and more than wants, abuses;
To them that when the enemy invaded
Made us their saints, but now the sores of Rome;

To silken flattery and pride planed over,
205 Forgetting with what wind their fathers sailed
And under whose protection their soft pleasures
Grow full and numberless; to this I am foe,
Not to the state or any point of duty
(And let me speak but what a soldier may),
210 Truly I ought to be so. Yet I erred,
Because a far more noble sufferer
Showed me the way to patience, yet I lost it.
This is the end I die for. To live basely,
And not the follower of him that bred me
215 In full account and virtue, Pontius dares not,
Much less to outlive what is good and flatter.

ÆCIUS I want a name to give thy virtue, soldier,
For only 'good' is far below thee, Pontius.
The gods shall find thee one. Thou hast fashioned death
220 In such an excellent and beauteous manner
I wonder men can live. Canst thou speak one word more?
For thy words are such harmony a soul
Would choose to fly to heav'n in.

PONTIUS A farewell,
Good noble general, your hand. Forgive me
225 And think whatever was displeasing to you
Was none of mine. You cannot live.

ÆCIUS I will not.
Yet one word more.

PONTIUS Die nobly. Rome farewell,
And Valentinian fall.
In joy you have given me a quiet death.
230 I would strike more wounds, if I had more breath. *Dies.*

ÆCIUS Is there an hour of goodness beyond this,
Or any man that would outlive such dying?
Would Caesar double all my honours on me
And stick me o'er with favours like a mistress,
235 Yet would I grow to this man. I have loved,
But never doted on a face till now.
Oh death, thou art more than beauty, and thy pleasures
Beyond posterity. Come friends and kill me.
Caesar, be kind and send a thousand swords;

240 The more the greater is my fall. Why stay you?
Come and I'll kiss your weapons. Fear me not.
By all the gods I'll honour ye for killing.
Appear, or through the court and world I'll search ye.
I'll follow ye and ere I die proclaim ye
245 The weeds of Italy, the dross of nature.
Where are ye villains, traitors, slaves.

Act V. Scene v

Valentinian and Lycias discovered on a couch.

VALENTINIAN Oh let me press these balmy lips all day
And bathe my love-scorched soul in thy moist kisses.
Now by my joys thou art all sweet and soft.
And thou shalt be the altar of my love;
5 Upon thy beauties hourly will I offer
And pour out pleasure and blest sacrifice
To the dear memory of my Lucina.
No god nor goddess ever was adored
With such religion as my love shall be.
10 For in these charming raptures of my soul,
Clasped in thy arms, I'll waste myself away
And rob the ruined world of their great lord,
While to the honour of Lucina's name
I leave mankind to mourn the loss for ever.

A Song

15 *Kindness hath resistless charms,*
All things else but weakly move,
Fiercest anger it disarms
And clips the wings of flying Love.

Beauty does the heart invade,
20 *Kindness only can persuade;*
It gilds the lover's servile chain
And makes the slave grow pleased again.

Enter Æcius with two swords.

VALENTINIAN Ha!
What desperate madman, weary of his being,
25 Presumes to press upon my happy moments?
Æcius? And armed? Whence comes this impious boldness?
Did not my will, the world's most sacred law,
Doom thee to die?
And dar'st thou in rebellion be alive?
30 Is death more frightful grown than disobedience?

ÆCIUS Not for a hated life condemned by you,
Which in your service has been still exposed
To pain and labours, famine, slaughter, fire,
And all the dreadful toils of horrid war.
35 Am I thus lowly laid before your feet?
For what mean wretch, who has his duty done,
Would care to live when you declare him worthless?
If I must fall, which your severe disfavour
Hath made the easier and the nobler choice,
40 Yield me not up a wretched sacrifice
To the poor spleen of a base favourite.
Let not vile instruments destroy the man
Whom once you loved, but let your hand bestow
That welcome death your anger has decreed.

Lays his sword at his feet.

45 VALENTINIAN Go seek the common executioner,
Old man, through vanity and years grown mad.
Or to reprieve thee from the hangman's stroke,
Go use thy military interest
To beg a milder death among the guards
50 And tempt my kindled wrath no more with folly.

ÆCIUS Ill-counselled, thankless prince, you did indeed
Bestow that office on a soldier,
But in the army could you hope to find,
With all your bribes, a murderer of Æcius,
55 Whom they so long have followed, known, and owned
Their god in war and thy good genius ever?
Speechless and cold without, upon the ground
The soldier lies whose generous death will teach
Posterity true gratitude and honour

60 And press as heavily upon thy soul,
Lost Valentinian, as thy barb'rous rape,
For which, since heav'n alone must punish thee,
I'll do heav'n's justice on thy base assister.
Runs at Lycias.

LYCIAS Save me, my lord.

VALENTINIAN Hold, honest Æcius, hold.

65 I was too rash. Oh spare the gentle boy,
And I'll forgive thee all.

LYCIAS. Furies and death! *Dies.*

VALENTINIAN He bleeds. Mourn, ye inhabitants of heav'n,
For sure my lovely boy was one of you.
But he is dead, and now ye may rejoice
70 For ye have stol'n him from me, spiteful powers.
Empire and life I ever have despised,
The vanity of pride, of hope, and fear.
In love alone my soul found real joys.
And still ye tyrannize and cross my love.
75 Oh that I had a sword
To drive this raving fool headlong to hell
And pacify the ghost of my dear boy.
Æcius throws him a sword.

ÆCIUS Take your desire and try if lawless lust
Can stand against truth, honesty, and justice.
80 I have my wish. Gods give you true repentance
And bless you still. Beware of Maximus.
They fight. Æcius runs on Valentinian's sword and falls.
Dies.

VALENTINIAN Farewell, dull honesty, which, though despised,
Canst make thy owner run on certain ruin.
Old Æcius, where is now thy name in war,
85 Thy interest with so many conquered nations,
The soldiers' reverence and the people's love,
Thy mighty fame and popularity
With which thou kept'st me still in certain fear,
Depending on thee for uncertain safety?
90 Ah, what a lamentable wretch is he
Who, urged by fear or sloth, yields up his pow'r

To hope protection from his favourite,
Wallowing in ease and vice, feels no contempt,
But wears the empty name of prince with scorn
95 And lives a poor, led pageant to his slave!
Such have I been to thee, honest Æcius;
Thy pow'r kept me in awe, thy pride in pain.
Till now I lived, but since thou'rt dead, I'll reign.

Enter Phidias with Maximus.

PHIDIAS Behold, my lord, the cruel Emperor
100 By whose tyrannic doom the noble Æcius
Was doomed to die.

VALENTINIAN He was so, saucy slave,
Struck by this hand. Here, grovelling at my feet,
The traitor lies, as thou shalt do, bold villain.
Go to the furies, carry my defiance,
And tell them Caesar fears nor earth nor hell. *Strikes Phidias.*

106 PHIDIAS Stay, Æcius, and I'll wait thy mightier ghost.
O Maximus, through the long vault of death
I hear thy wife cry out, 'Revenge me,
Revenge me on the ravisher.' No more.
110 Aretus comes to aid thee. Oh, farewell. *Dies.*

VALENTINIAN Ha! What? Speak not yet, thou whose wrongs are greatest?
Or do the horrors that we have been doing
Amaze thy feeble soul? If thou art a Roman,
Answer the Emperor. Caesar bids thee speak!

115 MAXIMUS A Roman? Ha! And Caesar bids thee speak,
Pronounce thy wrongs, and tell them o'er in groans.
But, oh, the story is ineffable.
Caesar's commands, backed with the eloquence
Of all the inspiring gods, cannot declare it.
120 O Emperor, thou picture of a glory,
Thou mangled figure of a ruined greatness.
'Speak', say'st thou, speak of the wrongs of Maximus?
Yes, I will speak. Imperial murderer!
Ravisher! Oh thou royal villainy
125 In purple dipped to give a gloss to mischief.
Yet ere thy death enriches my revenge
And swells the book of fate, you statelier madman,

Placed by the gods upon a precipice
To make thy fall more dreadful. Why hast thou slain
130 Thy friend, thy only stay for sinking greatness?
What frenzy, what blind fury did possess thee
To cut off thy right hand and fling it from thee?
For such was Æcius.

VALENTINIAN Yes, and such art thou,
Joint traitors to my empire and my glory.
135 Put up thy sword. Be gone for ever; leave me.
Though traitor, yet because I once did wrong thee,
Live like a vagrant slave. I banish thee.

MAXIMUS Hold me, ye gods, and judge our passions rightly
Lest I should kill him, kill this luxurious worm
140 Ere yet a thought of danger has awaked him,
End him even in the midst of night debauches,
Mounted upon a tripos, drinking healths
With shallow rascals, pimps, buffoons, and bawds
Who with vile laughter take him in their arms
145 And bear the drunken Caesar to his bed,
Where to the scandal of all majesty
At every grasp he belches provinces,
Kisses off fame, and at the empire's ruin
Enjoys his costly whore.

VALENTINIAN Peace, traitor, or thou diest.
150 Though pale Lucina should direct thy sword,
I would assault thee if thou offer more.

MAXIMUS More? By the immortal gods I will awake thee;
I'll rouse thee, Caesar, if strong reason can,
If thou hadst ever sense of Roman honour,
155 Or th'imperial genius ever warmed thee.
Why hast thou used me thus, for all my service,
My toils, my frights, my wounds in horrid war?
Why didst thou tear the only garland from me
That could make proud my conquests? O ye gods,
160 If there be no such thing as right or wrong,
But force alone must swallow all possession,
Then to what purpose for so long descents
Were Roman laws observed and heav'n obeyed?
If still the great for ease and vice were formed,

165 Why did our first kings toil? Why was the plough
Advanced to be the pillar of the state?
Why was the lustful Tarquin with his house
Expelled, but for the rape of bleeding Lucrece?

VALENTINIAN I cannot bear thy words, vexed wretch. No more!
170 He shocks me. Prithee, Maximus, no more.
Reason no more; thou troublest me with reason.

MAXIMUS What servile rascal, what most abject slave
That licked the dust where'er his master trod,
Bounded not from the earth upon his feet
175 And shook his chain that heard of Brutus' vengeance?
Who that e'er heard the cause applauded not
That Roman spirit for his great revenge?
Yet mine is more and touches me far nearer:
Lucrece was not his wife, as thou art mine,
180 Forever ravished, ever lost Lucina!

VALENTINIAN Ah, name her not. That name, thy face, and reason
Are the three things on earth I would avoid.
Let me forget her, I'll forgive thee all
And give thee half the empire to be gone.

185 MAXIMUS Thus steeled with such a cause, what soul but mine
Had not upon the instant ended thee,
Sworn in that moment, 'Caesar is no more'?
And so I had. But I will tell thee, tyrant,
To make thee hate thy guilt and curse thy fears,
190 Æcius, whom thou hast slain, prevented me.
Æcius, who on this bloody spot lies murdered
By barb'rous Caesar, watched my vowed revenge
And from my sword preserved ungrateful Caesar.

VALENTINIAN How then dar'st thou, viewing this great example,
195 With impious arms assault thy Emperor?

MAXIMUS Because I have more wit than honesty,
More of thyself, more villainy than virtue,
More passion, more revenge, and more ambition
Than foolish honour and fantastic glory.
200 What? Share your empire? Suffer you to live,

After the impious wrongs I have received?
Could'st thou thus lull me, thou might'st laugh indeed.
VALENTINIAN I'm satisfied that thou didst ever hate me.
Thy wife's rape therefore was but an act of justice,
205 And so far thou hast eased my tender conscience.
Therefore to hope a friendship from thee now
Were vain to me, as is the world's continuance
Where solid pains succeed our senseless joys
And short-lived pleasures fleet like passing dreams.
210 Æcius, I mourn thy fate as much as man
Can do in my condition, that am going,
And therefore should be busy with myself.
Yet to thy memory I will allow
Some grains of time and drop some sorrowing tears.
O Æcius, O!
215 MAXIMUS Why this is right, my lord.
And if these drops are orient, you will set
True Caesar, glorious in your going down,
Though all the journey of your life was cloudy.
Allow at least a possibility,
220 Where thought is lost, and think there may be gods,
An unknown country after you are dead,
As well as there was one ere you were born.
VALENTINIAN I've thought enough and with that thought resolve
To mount imperial from the burning pile.
225 I grieve for Æcius. Yes, I mourn him, gods,
As if I had met my father in the dark
And striving for the way, had murdered him.
Oh such a faithful friend that when he knew
I hated him and had contrived his death,
230 Yet then he ran his heart upon my sword
And gave a fatal proof of dying love.
MAXIMUS 'Tis now fit time. I've wrought you to my purpose.
Else at my entrance with a brutal blow,
I'd felled you like a victim for the altar,
235 Not warned you thus and armed you for your hour,
As if whene'er fate called a Caesar home,
The judging gods looked down to mark his dying.

VALENTINIAN Oh subtle traitor! How he dallies with me.
Think not, thou saucy counsellor, my slave,
240 Though at this moment I should feel thy foot
Upon my neck and sword within my bowels,
That I would ask a life from thee. No, villain,
When once the Emperor is at thy command,
Power, life, and glory must take leave for ever.
245 Therefore prepare the utmost of thy malice,
But to torment thee more and show how little
All thy revenge can do, appears to Caesar,
Would the gods raise Lucina from the grave
And fetter thee but while I might enjoy her,
250 Before thy face I'd ravish her again.
MAXIMUS Hark, hark, Aretus and the legions come.
VALENTINIAN Come all! Aretus and the rebel legions!
Let Æcius too start from the jail of death
And run the flying race of life again.
255 I'll be the foremost still and snatch fresh glory
To my last gasp from the contending world.
Garlands and crowns too shall attend my dying;
Statues and temples, altars shall be raised
To my great name, while your more vile inscriptions
260 Time rots, and mould'ring clay is all your portion.
Enter Aretus and soldiers. They kill Valentinian.
MAXIMUS Lead me to death or empire, which you please,
For both are equal to a ruined man.
But fellow soldiers, if you are my friends,
Bring me to death that I may there find peace,
265 Since empire is too poor to make amends
For half the losses I have undergone:
A true friend and a tender, faithful wife,
The two blest miracles of human life.
Go now and seek new worlds to add to this;
270 Search heav'n for blessings to enrich the gift;
Bring power and pleasure on the wings of fame
And heap this treasure upon Maximus.
You'll make a great man, not a happy one.
Sorrows so just as mine must never end,
275 For my love ravished and my murdered friend. *Exeunt omnes.*

[*Here's Monmouth the witty and Lauderdale the pretty*]

Here's Monmouth the witty and Lauderdale the pretty
  And Fraser, that learned physician,
But above all the rest here's the Duke for a jest
  And the King for a grand politician.

A Scene of Sir Robert Howard's Play, written by the Earl of Rochester

The army appears drawn up in three battalions, the Empress leading the main body, on the right hand Hyachian, on the left Lycungus.

EMPRESS Lead faster on! Why creep you thus to fight?
  Faintly to charge is shamefuller than flight.
  Your Emperor deified hovers in the air,
  Commands revenge, and does rewards prepare:
5 For the brave, glory; for the base, despair.
  Perhaps they think, or would persuade the foe,
  War led by women must be cold or slow.
  This day I'll prove the injustice of that scorn
  Men treat our sex withal. Woman is born
10 With equal thirst of honour and of fame,
  But treacherous man misguides her in her aim,
  Makes her believe that all her glories lie
  In dull obedience, truth, and modesty,
  That to be beautiful is to be brave,
15 And calls her conqueror when she's most his slave,
  Forbidding her those noble paths to tread
  Which through bold daring deeds to glory lead,
  With the poor hypocritical pretence
  That women's merit is her innocence.
20 Who treacherously advised retaining thus
  The sole ambition to be virtuous
  Thinks 'tis enough if she's not infamous.

On these false grounds is man's stol'n triumph laid,
Through crafts alone the nobler creature made.
25 Woman henceforth by my example taught
To vaster heights of virtue shall be wrought,
Trained up in war and arms she shall despise
The mean pretended conquests of her eyes,
Nor be contented with the low applause
30 Left to her sex by man's tyrannic laws.
Glory was never got by sitting still,
The lazy merits of not doing ill.
Whoe'er aspires to reach a glorious name
By acting greatly must lay in their claim,
35 Storm, tear, and fight with all the world for fame.

HYACHIAN Now all the powers of war and victory
Forever to your arms propitious be,
And may that fame they for your sword reserve
Equal the glory we obtain to serve.

40 LYCUNGUS I will not mingle wishes with the crowd,
Nor, till my service pleases you, be proud,
But if revenge through conquest you design,
For that depend on this sole arm of mine,
Guarded by this, danger you may despise
45 And find your sword as powerful as your eyes,
Whose brightness should the god of battle see,
As full of charms as they appear to me,
He'd think his Venus were grown young again,
Leap down from heaven and resume his chain,
50 Nor (though a god) should he your fetters wear
Without the hazard of a rival here.

EMPRESS That prince who to my aid his army brings
I do expect shall fight, not say fine things.
If his presuming vanity be such,
55 Let him take care his courage be as much,
And with his daring hand build a pretense
To be forgiv'n his tongue's impertinence.

LYCUNGUS Pride and contempt that often blind the fair
Make them least pertinent when most severe.
60 From unaffected truths no errors flow:
I think you lovely and I hold you so.

What of myself I said, I shall make good
And when I fight, be better understood.
EMPRESS Fighting indeed your riddle will explain,
65 Distinguishing the valiant from the vain.
HYACHIAN And that distinction quickly will be made.
For I perceive from yonder gloomy shade
Which those tall woods do o'er the valleys throw,
Like swelling tides the numerous Tartars flow.
70 Their glittering helmets force a brighter day,
And moving shields
Like dancing billows in the sunbeams play.
EMPRESS They meet my just revenge and their own fate.
And have the manners not to make me wait. (*To Hyachian*)
75 But you, brave prince, whose deeds advance your name
Ev'n with the foremost in the mouth of Fame,
Who wheresoe'er you come bring victory,
Blush not this day to leave a part to me.
I to your conduct will the trust afford
80 Of the first blooming honour of my sword;
All here to your unequalled worth must yield.
This day I make you general of the field.
HYACHIAN Few conquests yet my feeble hand has wrought,
But were my deeds as humble as my thought,
85 Ranked with the meanest slave that does pursue
The matchless glory here to fight for you,
Since on my arm you place such confidence
To think it worthy of your fame's defence,
The sole ambition not to prove unjust
90 May raise my merit equal to my trust.
EMPRESS My judgement I but weakly should express
To value you so much and trust you less.
But in what order will you now bestow
The bold Chineses to receive the foe,
95 Whose discipline as well as ours you know?
HYACHIAN Fiercely the Tartars with confusion charge
In broken order here and there at large.
With wide excursions to and fro they bound,
And if not well observ'd, will charge you round.

100 But a large front shall hinder that design.
Half the first legion draw into a line;
Let the other half the two extremes enforce,
And let the point be winged with all the horse.
I'th' middle, which the greatest shock must prove,
105 Let the main body of the army move.

EMPRESS Myself and guards will at the head be placed.

HYACHIAN My force may follow next.

EMPRESS Lycungus last.
Now, father, draw thy veiling cloud and see
Thy vowed revenge thy daughter pays for thee,
110 While from the walls each gazing slave admires
Thy daring glory this revenge inspires.

Exeunt Empress and Hyachian.

LYCUNGUS Lycungus last! Empress, I thank your care.
'Tis for Hyachian then that we make war.
You who create, what difference can you see
115 'Twixt this admired Hyachian and me?
Woman, ah worthless woman, erring still
In the wild maze of thy fantastic will,
Equally shared betwixt thy pride and lust,
Averse to all that's good and blind to all that's just.
120 Forever is the man of worth undone
When Fate into thy barb'rous power has thrown,
Who in the dumb greensickness of her mind
Still hungers for the trash of all mankind.
Not an insipid fop on earth does move
125 For whom some woman does not die in love.

Enter an Officer.

OFFICER Both armies, sir, by this time are so near
They'll be engaged ere you can reach the rear.

LYCUNGUS Bid my advancing troops with speed be gone.
Bid 'em stand still, be quiet, and look on. *Exit Officer.*
130 Eternal gods! But sure there can be none
To see injustice and look idly on,
But if there be,
Which of you all, below or in the skies,
Is not in debt to me for sacrifice?

135 To the bright, shining god some prayers I make,
Some to the hurtful, grim, bloodthirsty black;
Where either hope or fear points out the way
With equal zeal I sacrifice and pray.
If all my prayers cannot these blessings raise,
140 Have you the conscience to expect my praise?
Though hitherto
My innocent desires success do want,
But I'll ask favours you'll not stick to grant.
When we for blessings sue, you stop your ears,
145 But if we curse, there's not one god but hears.
Assist me then to bring full ruin down
On this insulting woman and her crown.
Are you not scorned, blasphemed, denied each day
For letting chance in mortal actions sway?
150 You'll mend the matter well if you permit
The rule of things to woman's will or wit.
Woman, of all the creatures you did make
The only sign and proof you could mistake,
That heap of contradictions, mass of lies,
155 Snare of our wishes, bane of all our joys.
If for a blessing they were sent us, why
Have you not given them one good quality?
If for a curse, how are you just or wise
To lend 'em your own form for a disguise?

Enter a Soldier.

160 SOLDIER The overpowered Chineses give ground.
The Empress with her guards encompassed round,
The Prince Hyachian's to her rescue fled,
And both by this time taken or else dead.
The wings retire, the main battalion's broke.
165 LYCUNGUS No matter, see my men fight not a stroke.

Exit Soldier.

Before the sun dip in the azure wave,
She shall be Death's, the Tartars', or my slave.
My slave? My wife,
My hated wife! Now my revenge grows strong,
170 And may this way be equal to my wrong.
Thanks to your powers who marriage have allowed
To make those wretched whom you first made proud.

But first Hyachian must in dust be laid;
The army next deserted or betrayed.
175 'Tis worth the blackest mischief I can do
To be revenged and get an empire too.
If on the Tartars' side the day be lost,
I'll take th'advantage of my noble post,
When the pursuit most eager does appear,
180 I'll fall on the Chineses in the rear.
If they are put to flight, my forces lie
Nearest the town, and thither first I'll fly.
And if my beaten Empress 'scape the rout,
I'll let her in but shut the army out.
185 Then shall she from the walls a prospect take
Of the free massacre the Tartars make.
If after she'll consent to marry me,
When she's my slave I'll set her empire free,
From my own province call a fresh supply
190 And beat Syunges home with infamy.
If the proud wretch my proffered hand disdain,
Instead of me ruin and death shall reign.
With desolation I'll the city fill,
And my fierce troops shall plunder, fire, and kill.
195 When in their blood the murdered people swim,
And flames for want of more supply grow dim,
I'll ravish her and call the Tartars in.

Enter an Officer.

OFFICER The China army, sir, has lost the day
And driven by conquering Tartars fly this way.
200 Your forces unengaged your orders wait.
LYCUNGUS Bid 'em retire and seize the city gate.
You with some chosen horse must stay behind
And if the false Hyachian you can find
Among the scattered runaways of the field,
205 Be it your business, sir, to see him killed. *Exit Officer.*
Go on, Lycungus, murder and betray,
All acts that lead to thy designs obey.
No mischief is so black, no crime so high,
But to the world success will justify.
210 And you pale deadly demons of the night
Whom altars bathed in human gore delight,

Assist my plots to make my conquests good,
And when I reign you shall not want for food. *Exit Lycungus.*
A noise of fighting and running. Enter Hyachian, bloody, with his sword drawn, stopping some who fly.

HYACHIAN Stay, ye base wretches, whither would you fly?
215 Is it a race for chains and infamy?
Are you such cowards to hide yourselves in graves,
Or have ye hopes to be the Tartars' slaves?
In shameful flight what safety does appear,
Can ye escape a greater hell than fear?
Enter an Officer.

220 OFFICER Ah my dear lord, are you alive and free?

HYACHIAN Yes, and ashamed to see your infamy.
How durst you be my friend and run away?

OFFICER Where torrents drive, what single force can stay?
North winds broke loose you might as soon recall,
225 Fix scattered leaves that in the autumn fall,
Resist the rapid motion of the sphere,
As stop the flowing tide of panic fear.
Through every rank a swift report was spread
That you were taken and the Empress dead.
230 At which they (flying) cried,
After such losses 'twas not worth their pains
To fight for conquest or decline their chains.

HYACHIAN The Empress, by rash honour driven on
Into the thickest of the foe, was flown.
235 I to her rescue ran midst showers of darts,
Cutting my bloody way through Tartars' hearts.
On foot I found her, for her horse was killed,
Strewing with gasping carcasses the field.
Some drops of blood,
240 Which from her wounds on her fair neck did flow,
Like rubies set in rocks of silver show.
Alone she fought, exposed to vulgar blows,
Like a maimed eagle in a flock of crows.
While I sought death with her I could not save,
245 One more than all the rest generous and brave

Presses in through the assassinating crowd
And with a voice of terror cries aloud,
'Desist for shame, ye feeble murderers;
Stain not with woman's blood your scimitars,
250 I'll lead you on to nobler victories.'
The men obey him and away he flies.
Thus got we time our army to regain.
But where's Lycungus? Taken, fled, or slain?

OFFICER Lycungus, sir, has never charged at all
255 And now stands gazing o'er the city wall.

HYACHIAN In him the stupid rage of envy see;
Though brave, turns coward to be revenged on me.

Enter an Officer.

OFFICER The scattered troops
At Amacoa's presence stay their flight
260 And led by her renew a bloody fight.

HYACHIAN No more shall nations in distress and thrall
On helpless man for aid in battles call;
This woman's valour is above us all.
Where'er she fights beauty and ruin join,
265 Rage on her arms, while in her eyes they shine.
With story and with death the field she fills,
So thunder led by lightning shines and kills.

Song

How happy, Cloris, were they free,
Might our enjoyments prove,
But you with formal jealousy
Are still tormenting love.

5 Let us, since wit instructs us how,
Raise pleasure to the top:
If rival bottle you'll allow,
I'll suffer rival fop.

There's not a brisk, insipid spark
10 That flutters in the town
But with your wanton eyes you mark
The coxcomb for your own.

You never think it worth your care
How empty nor how dull
15 The heads of your admirers are
So that their cods be full.

All this you freely may confess,
Yet we'll not disagree,
For did you love your pleasure less,
20 You were not fit for me.

While I, my passion to pursue,
Am whole nights taking in
The lusty juice of grapes, take you
The lusty juice of men.

Song

How perfect, Cloris, and how free
Would these enjoyments prove,
But you with formal jealousy
Are still tormenting love.

5 Let us, since wit instructs us how,
Raise pleasure to the top:
If rival bottle you'll allow,
I'll suffer rival fop.

Upbraid me not that I design
10 Tricks to delude your charms,
When running after mirth and wine
I leave your longing arms.

For wine, whose power alone can raise
Our thoughts so far above,
15 Affords ideas fit to praise
What we think fit to love.

There's not a brisk, insipid spark
That flutters in the town
But with your wanton eyes you mark
20 Him out to be your own.

You never think it worth your care
How empty nor how dull
The heads of your admirers are
So that their backs/purse be full.

25 All this you freely may confess,
Yet we'll not disagree,
For did you love your pleasures less,
You were not fit for me.

Whilst I my passion to pursue,
30 Am whole nights taking in
The lusty juice of grapes, take you
The juice of lusty men.

Song

Such perfect bliss, fair Cloris, we
In our enjoyments prove,
'Tis pity restless jealousy
Should mingle with our love.

5 Let us, since wit has taught us how,
Raise pleasure to the top:
You rival bottle must allow,
I suffer rival fop.

Think not in this that I design
10 Treason against love's charms,
When, following the god of wine,
I leave my Cloris' arms,

Since you have that, for all your haste
(At which I'll ne'er repine),
15 Will take its liquor off as fast
As I do take off mine.

There's not a brisk, insipid spark
That flutters in the town
But with your wanton eyes you mark
20 Him out to be your own.

Nor do you think it worth your care
How empty and how dull
The heads of your admirers are
So that their bags be full.

25 All this you freely may confess,
Yet we'd ne'er disagree,
For did you love your pleasure less,
You were no mate for me.

Whilst I, my pleasures to pursue,
30 Whole nights am taking in
The lusty juice of grapes, take you
The juice of lusty men.

[*Leave this gaudy, gilded stage*]

Leave this gaudy, gilded stage,
From custom more than use frequented,
Where fools of either sex and age
Crowd to see themselves presented.
5 To love's theatre, the bed,
Youth and beauty fly together
And act so well it may be said
The laurel there was due to either.
'Twixt strifes of love and war the difference lies in this:
10 When neither overcomes, love's triumph greater is.

Against Constancy

Tell me no more of constancy,
The frivolous pretense
Of cold age, narrow jealousy,
Disease, and want of sense.

5 Let duller fools on whom kind chance
Some easy heart has thrown,
Despairing higher to advance,
Be kind to one alone.

Old men and weak, whose idle flame
10 Their own defects discovers,
Since changing can but spread their shame,
Ought to be constant lovers,

But we, whose hearts do justly swell
With no vainglorious pride,
15 Who know how we in love excel,
Long to be often tried.

Then bring my bath and strew my bed,
As each kind night returns:
I'll change a mistress till I'm dead,
20 And fate change me for worms.

To the Postboy

ROCHESTER Son of a whore, God damn you, can you tell
A peerless peer the readiest way to Hell?
I've outswilled Bacchus, sworn of my own make
Oaths would fright Furies and make Pluto quake.
5 I've swived more whores more ways than Sodom's walls
E'er knew, or the college of Rome's cardinals.
Witness heroic scars, look here, ne'er go,
Cerecloths and ulcers from top to toe.
Frighted at my own mischiefs I have fled
10 And bravely left my life's defender dead,

Broke houses to break chastity, and dyed
That floor with murder which my lust denied.
Pox on't, why do I speak of these poor things?
I have blasphemed my God and libelled kings.
15 The readiest way to Hell? Come quick, ne'er stir.
BOY The readiest way, my lord, 's by Rochester.

On the Supposed Author of a Late Poem in Defence of Satire

To rack and torture thy unmeaning brain
In satire's praise, to a low, untuned strain,
In thee was most impertinent and vain,
When in thy person we more clearly see
5 That satire's of divine authority,
For God made one on man when he made thee.
To show there are some men, as there are apes,
Framed for mere sport, who differ but in shapes.
In thee are all those contradictions joined
10 That make an ass prodigious and refined.
A lump deformed and shapeless wert thou born,
Begot in love's despite and nature's scorn,
And art grown up the most ungraceful wight,
Harsh to the ear and hideous to the sight,
15 Yet love's thy business, beauty thy delight.
Curse on that silly hour that first inspired
Thy madness to pretend to be admired,
To paint thy grisly face, to dance, to dress,
And all those awkward follies that express
20 Thy loathsome love and filthy daintiness,
Who needs will be an ugly *beau garçon*,
Spit at and shunned by every girl in town,
Where, dreadfully, love's scarecrow thou art placed
To fright the tender flock that long to taste,
25 While every coming maid, when you appear,
Stands back for shame and straight turns chaste for fear;

For none so poor or prostitute have proved,
Where you made love, t'endure to be beloved.
'Twere labour lost, or else I would advise,
30 But thy half wit will ne'er let thee be wise.
Half witty and half mad and scarce half brave,
Half honest (which is very much a knave),
Made up of all these halfs, thou canst not pass
For anything entirely but an ass.

[*God bless our good and gracious King*]

God bless our good and gracious King,
Whose promise none relies on,
Who never said a foolish thing,
Nor ever did a wise one.

Love and Life

All my past life is mine no more;
The flying hours are gone
Like transitory dreams given o'er,
Whose images are kept in store
5 By memory alone.

Whatever is to come is not;
How can it then be mine?
The present moment's all my lot
And that, as fast as it is got,
10 Phillis, is wholly thine.

Then talk not of inconstancy,
False hearts, and broken vows,
If I by miracle can be
This livelong minute true to thee,
15 'Tis all that heaven allows.

Upon Carey Fraser

Her father gave her dildoes six;
Her mother made 'em up a score,
But she loves nought but living pricks
And swears by God she'll frig no more.

The Epilogue to Circe

Some few from wit have this true maxim got
That 'tis still better to be pleased than not
And therefore never their own torment plot,
While the malicious critics still agree
5 To loathe each play they come and pay to see;
The first know 'tis a meaner part of sense
To find a fault than taste an excellence,
Therefore they praise and strive to like, while these
Are dully vain of being hard to please.
10 Poets and women have an equal right
To hate the dull, who dead to all delight
Feel pain alone and have no joy but spite.
'Twas impotence did first this vice begin,
Fools censure wit as old men rail of sin,
15 Who envy pleasure which they cannot taste,
And good for nothing would be wise at last.
Since therefore to the women it appears
That all these enemies of wit are theirs,
Our poet the dull herd no longer fears.
20 Whate'er his fate may prove, 'twill be his pride
To stand or fall with beauty on his side.

The Mock Song

'I swive as well as others do,
I'm young, not yet deformed.
My tender heart, sincere and true,
Deserves not to be scorned.
5 Why, Phillis, then, why will you swive
With forty lovers more?'
'Can I,' said she, 'with Nature strive?
Alas I am, alas I am a whore.

'Were all my body larded o'er
10 With darts of love so thick
That you might find in every pore
A well-stuck, standing prick,
Whilst yet my eyes alone were free,
My heart would never doubt,
15 In amorous rage and ecstasy,
To wish those eyes, to wish those eyes fucked out.'

On Mistress Willis

Against the charms our ballocks have,
How weak all human skill is,
Since they can make a man a slave
To such a bitch as Willis.

5 Whom that I may describe throughout,
Assist me, bawdy powers;
I'll write upon a double clout
And dip my pen in flowers.

Her look's demurely impudent,
10 Ungainly beautiful,
Her modesty is insolent,
Her mirth is pert and dull.

A prostitute to all the town
    And yet with no man friends,
15 She rails and scolds when she lies down
    And curses when she spends.

Bawdy in thoughts, precise in words,
    Ill-natured though a whore,
Her belly is a bag of turds,
20 And her cunt a common shore.

Song

By all love's soft yet mighty powers,
    It is a thing unfit
That men should fuck in time of flowers
    Or when the smock's beshit.

5 Fair nasty nymph, be clean and kind
    And all my joys restore
By using paper still behind
    And sponges for before.

My spotless flames can ne'er decay
10 If after every close
My smoking prick escape the fray
    Without a bloody nose.

If thou wouldst have me true, be wise
    And take to cleanly sinning;
15 None but fresh lovers' pricks can rise
    At Phillis in foul linen.

On Poet Ninny

Crushed by that just contempt his follies bring
On his crazed head, the vermin fain would sting,
But never satire did so softly bite,
Or gentle George himself more gently write.

5 Born to no other but thy own disgrace,
Thou art a thing so wretched and so base
Thou canst not ev'n offend, but with thy face,
And dost at once a sad example prove
Of harmless malice and of hopeless love.
10 All pride and ugliness! Oh how we loathe
A nauseous creature so composed of both!
How oft have we thy capering person seen,
With dismal look and melancholy mien,
The just reverse of Nokes when he would be
15 Some mighty hero and makes love like thee.
Thou art below being laughed at, out of spite
Men gaze upon thee as a hideous sight
And cry, 'There goes the Melancholy Knight.'
There are some modish fools we daily see,
20 Modest and dull: why they are wits to thee!
For of all folly sure the very top
Is a conceited ninny and a fop.
With face of farce joined to a head romancy,
There's no such coxcomb as your fool of fancy.
25 But 'tis too much on so despised a theme,
No man would dabble in a dirty stream;
The worst that I could write would be no more
Than what thy very friends have said before.

Upon Nothing

Nothing, thou elder brother even to Shade,
Thou hadst a being ere the world was made,
And (well fixed) art alone of ending not afraid.

Ere time and place were, Time and Place were not,
5 When primitive Nothing, Something straight begot;
Then all proceeded from the great united what.

Something, the general attribute of all,
Severed from thee, its sole original,
Into thy boundless self must undistinguished fall.

Much A-do, about Nothing:

A Song made of *Nothing*, the newest in Print; He that seriously minds it, shall find *All-things* in't.

To the Tune of, *Which no body can deny.*

I'le sing you a Sonnet, that ne're was in Print,
'Tis truly and newly come out of the Mint,
But I'l tell you before hand you'l find Nothing in't;
  That any man can deny.

On Nothing I think, on Nothing I Write,
'Tis Nothing I Covet, yet Nothing I slight,
And I care not a Pin, if I get Nothing by't,
  'Tis all one to me, cry I.

Fire, Air, Earth and Water, Beast, Birds, Fish and Men,
Did start out of Nothing a Chaos, a Den:
And all things shall turn into Nothing agen:
  Which no body can deny.

'Tis Nothing somtimes that makes many things hit,
As when a Fool amongst Wise-men doth silently sit,
A Fool that says nothing may pass for a Wit:
  Wise *Solomon* found it so.

That one Man doth love, is another Man's loathing,
This Blade loves a quick thing, & that loves a slow thing
And both in the very coclusion loves Nothing:
  So fickle are Humours now.

Your Lad that makes love to a very fine smooth-thing,
And thinks to obtain her with sighing and sothing,
Doth frequently make much a-do about Nothing:
  Experience finds it true.

At last, when his Patience and Purse is decay'd,
He may to the Bed of a Whore be betray'd;
But she that hath nothing must needs be a Maid,
  For she can have Nothing to do.

Your Slashing and Clashing, and Flashing of Wit,
Doth start out of Nothing, but Fancy and Fit;
'Tis little or Nothing to what hath been Writ,
  There's Nothing invented new.

When we first together by the Ears did fall,
Then Somthing got Nothing, and Nothing got All,
From Nothing it came, unto Nothing it shall:
  This Kingdom hath found it true.

That party that Sealed to a Covenant in hast,
Who made King and Kingdom, and Churches lie wast,
Their Project and All came to Nothing at last:
  'Tis well we have found it so.

They raised an Army of Horse and of Foot,
To tumble down Monarchy, Branch and Root
They Thundred and Plunder'd, but nothing would do't,
  And *vive le Roy*, cry I.

The Organ and Alter, and Ministers Cloathing,
In Presbiter-Jack did beget such a loathing,
That he must needs set up a Petty-new-Nothing:
  Which Loyalty did deny.

And when he had rob'd us in Sanctified Clothing,
And Perjur'd the People, by Faithing and Trothing,
At last he was Catch'd and all came to Nothing:
  I wish they had had their due.

In several Factions we Quarrel and Brawl,
Dispute and contend, and to fighting we fall,
But I'l lay All to Nothing, that Nothing wins All,
  Conclusion will make it true.

When War and Rebellion, and Plundering grows,
The Mendicant-man is the freest from Foes,
For he is most happy hath Nothing to lose:
  We frequently find it true.

Brave Cæsar, and Pompey, and Great Alexander,
Whom Armies did follow as Goose follows Gander,
Have Nothing to say to an Action of Slander:
  Which no-body can indure.

The wisest great Prince, were he never so stout,
Could he conquer the World, and give Mankind a Rout,
Did bring Nothing in, nor shall carry Nothing out,
  There's Nothing that can be truer.

Old Nol that did Rise up to High-thing, from Low-thing
By Brewing Rebellion, and Nicking and Frothing,
In seven Years distance, was All-things and Nothing:
  Which every Man doth know.

Dick, (Olivers Heir) that pittiful Slow-thing,
Who once was Invested with Purple Clothing,
Now stands for a Cipher, and a Cipher is Nothing;
  King *Dick* he hath Nothing to do.

If King-killers are Excluded from Bliss,
Old Bradshaw (that feels the Reward on't by this)
Had better been Nothing, than what now he is:
  The Devil will have his due.

Blind Colonel Hewson, that lately did Crawl,
To a lofty Degree, from a low Coblers-Stall,
Did bring Awl to Nothing, when Awl came to All,
  With *Oakey* and *Baxter* too.

Your Gallant, that lives by fine Meat, Drink, & Clothing
Who was, th'other day a pittiful Low-thing,
Pays Butcher, and Baker, and Draper with Nothing,
  The City doth find it true.

The nimble tongu'd Lawyer that Pleads for his Pay,
When Death doth Arrest him and Carry him away,
At the General Bar, will have Nothing to say;
  To you, nor you, nor you.

If any here Tax me with weakness of Wit,
And say, That on Nothing, I Nothing have Writ;
I shall answer, Ex nihilo, nihil fit,
  Of Nothing, comes Nothing, ye know.

Yet let his Discretion be never so tall,
This very word Nothing, that give it a fall,
For in Writing of Nothing, I Comprehend All,
  That is in Creation made.

Let every Man give the Poet his Due,
'Cause then 'twas with him, as now it's with you;
He Studied it, when he had Nothing to do:
  For Nothing was then his Trade.

This very Word Nothing, if took the right way,
May prove Advantagious; For, What would you say,
If the Vinter should tell you, There's Nothing to Pay:
  As good as if all were Paid.

London, Printed for T. Vere, at the sign of the Cock in St. *Johns-street.* 1660

12 *Much A-do about Nothing: A Song made of Nothing* [1660].

10 Yet Something did thy mighty power command
And from thy fruitful Emptiness's hand
Snatched men, beasts, birds, fire, water, air, and land.

Matter, the wicked'st offspring of thy race,
By Form assisted, flew from thy embrace,
15 And rebel Light obscured thy reverend dusky face.

With Form and Matter, Time and Place did join;
Body, thy foe, with these did leagues combine
To spoil thy peaceful reign and ruin all thy line.

But turncoat Time assists the foe in vain
20 And bribed by thee destroys their short-lived reign
And to thy hungry womb drives back the slaves again.

Thy mysteries are hid from laic eyes,
And the divine alone by warrant pries
Into thy bosom, where the truth in private lies.

25 Yet this of thee the wise may truly say,
Thou from the virtuous nothing tak'st away,
And to be part of thee the wicked wisely pray.

Great Negative, how vainly would the wise
Inquire, define, distinguish, teach, devise
30 Didst thou not stand to point their dull philosophies.

Is or Is Not, the two great ends of Fate,
And True or False, the subject of debate
That perfects or destroys the vast designs of state,

When they have racked the politician's breast,
35 Within thy bosom most securely rest
And when reduced to thee are least unsafe and best.

But Nothing, why does Something still permit
That sacred monarchs should at council sit
With persons thought, at best, for nothing fit,

40 While weighty Something modestly abstains
From princes' coffers and from statesman's brains;
And nothing there like stately Nothing reigns.

Nothing, that dwells with fools in grave disguise,
For whom they reverend forms and shapes devise,
45 Lawn sleeves, and furs, and gowns, when they like thee look
wise.

French truth, Dutch prowess, British policy,
Hibernian learning, Scotch civility,
Spaniards' dispatch, Danes' wit are mainly seen in thee.

The great man's gratitude to his best friend,
50 Kings' promises, whores' vows, to thee they bend,
Flow swiftly into thee and in thee ever end.

My Lord All-Pride

Bursting with pride the loathed impostume swells,
Prick him, he sheds his venom straight and smells,
But 'tis so lewd a scribbler that he writes
With as much force to nature as he fights.
5 Hardened in shame, 'tis such a baffled fop
That every schoolboy whips him like a top.
And with his arm and heart his brain's so weak
That his starved fancy is compelled to rake
Among the excrements of others' wit
10 To make a stinking meal of what they shit;
So swine for nasty meat to dunghills run
And toss their gruntling snouts up when they've done.
Against his stars the coxcomb ever strives
And to be something they forbid, contrives.
15 With a red nose, splay foot, and goggle eye,
A ploughman's looby mien, face all awry,
A filthy breath, and every loathsome mark,
The Punchinello sets up for a spark.
With equal self-conceit he takes up arms,
20 But with such vile success his part performs
That he burlesques the trade, and what is best
In others, turns like Harlequin to jest;

So have I seen at Smithfield's wondrous fair
(When all his brother monsters flourish there)
25 A lubbard elephant divert the town
With making legs and shooting off a gun.
Go where he will, he never finds a friend,
Shame and derision all his steps attend,
Alike abroad, at home, i'th' camp and court,
30 This Knight o'th' Burning Pestle makes us sport.

The Earl of Rochester's Answer to a Paper of Verses sent him by L[ady] B[etty] Felton and taken out of the Translation of Ovid's Epistles, *1680*

What strange surprise to meet such words as these,
Such terms of horror were ne'er chose to please,
To meet, midst pleasures of a jovial night,
Words that can only give amaze and fright,
5 No gentler thought that does to love invite.
Were it not better far your arms t'employ
Grasping a lover in pursuit of joy
Than handling sword and pen, weapons unfit?
Your sex gains conquest by their charms and wit.
10 Of writers slain I could with pleasure hear,
Approve of fights, o'erjoyed to cause a tear;
So slain, I mean, that she should soon revive,
Pleased in my arms to find herself alive.

[*To form a plot*]

To form a plot
The blustering bard whose rough, unruly rhyme
Gives Plutarch's *Lives* the lie in every line,
Who rapture before nature does prefer,
5 And now himself turned his own imager,
Defaceth God's in every character.

An Epistolary Essay from M.G. to O.B. upon their Mutual Poems

Dear friend,
I hear this town doth so abound
With saucy censurers that faults are found
With what of late we, in poetic rage
Bestowing, threw away on the dull age;
5 But howsoe'er envy their spleen may raise
To rob my brow of the deservèd bays,
Their thanks at least I merit, since through me
They are partakers of your poetry.
And this is all I'll say in my defence:
10 T'obtain one line of your well-worded sense,
I'd be content t'have writ *The British Prince*.
I'm none of those who think themselves inspired
Nor write with the vain hope to be admired,
But from a rule I have (upon long trial)
15 T'avoid with care all sort of self-denial,
Which way soe'er desire and fancy lead
(Contemning fame) that path I boldly tread.
And if exposing what I take for wit,
To my dear self a pleasure I beget,
20 No matter though the censuring critics fret.
These whom my muse displeases are at strife
With equal spleen against my course of life,
The least delight of which I'll not forgo
For all the flattering praise man can bestow.
25 If I designed to please, the way were then
To mend my manners rather than my pen:
The first's unnatural, therefore unfit,
And for the second, I despair of it,
Since grace is not so hard to get as wit.
30 Perhaps ill verses ought to be confined
In mere good breeding, like unsavory wind.
Were reading forced, I should be apt to think
Men might no more write scurvily than stink.

But 'tis your choice whether you'll read or no;
35 If likewise of your smelling it were so,
I'd fart just as I write for my own ease,
Nor should you be concerned unless you please.
I'll own that you write better than I do,
But I have as much need to write as you.
40 What though the excrement of my dull brain
Runs in a costive and insipid strain,
Whilst your rich head eases itself of wit.
Must none but civet cats have leave to shit?
In all I write, should sense and wit and rhyme
45 Fail me at once, yet something so sublime
Shall stamp my poem that the world may see
It could have been produced by none but me;
And that's my end, for man can wish no more
Than so to write as none e'er writ before.
50 Yet why am I no poet of the times?
I have allusions, similes, and rhymes,
And wit – or else 'tis hard that I alone
Of the whole race of mankind should have none.
Unequally the partial hand of heaven
55 Has all but this one only blessing given.
The world appears like a great family
Whose lord, oppressed with pride and poverty
(That to a few great bounty he may show)
Is fain to starve the numerous train below;
60 Just so seems providence as poor and vain,
Keeping more creatures than it can maintain;
Here 'tis profuse and there it meanly saves,
And for one prince it makes ten thousand slaves.
In wit alone 't has been magnificent,
65 Of which so just a share to each is sent
That the most avaricious are content.
For none e'er thought (the due division's such)
His own too little or his friend's too much.
Yet most men show or find great want of wit,
70 Writing themselves or judging what is writ.
But I, who am of sprightly vigour full,
Look on mankind as envious and dull.

Born to myself, myself I like alone
And must conclude my judgement good or none.
75 For should my sense be nought, how could I know
Whether another man's were good or no?
Thus I resolve of my own poetry
That 'tis the best, and there's a fame for me.
If then I'm happy, what does it advance
80 Whether to merit due or arrogance?
'Oh! but the world will take offence thereby.'
Why then the world shall suffer for't, not I.
Did e'er this saucy world and I agree
To let it have its beastly will of me?
85 Why should my prostituted sense be drawn
To every rule their musty customs spawn?
'But men will censure you.' 'Tis two to one,
Whene'er they censure, they'll be in the wrong.
There's not a thing on earth that I can name
90 So foolish and so false as common fame.
It calls the courtier knave, the plain man rude,
Haughty the grave, and the delightful lewd,
Impertinent the brisk, morose the sad,
Mean the familiar, the reserved one mad.
95 Poor helpless woman is not favoured more,
She's a sly hypocrite or public whore.
Then who the devil would give this – to be free
From th'innocent reproach of infamy?
These things considered, make me (in despite
100 Of idle rumour) keep at home and write.

Abbreviations and Short Titles of Works Frequently Cited

AND	B. E., *A New Dictionary of the Terms Ancient and Modern of the Canting Crew* . . . (1699).
Aubrey 1898	John Aubrey, *Brief Lives*, ed. Andrew Clark, 2 vols. (1898).
Barton	See Righter.
BDAA	*A Biographical Dictionary of Actors, Actresses* . . ., ed. Philip H. Highfill, Jr., *et al.*, 12 vols. to date, Illinois University Press (1973–).
Beaumont and Fletcher	*The Works of Francis Beaumont and John Fletcher*, ed. Arnold Glover, 10 vols. (1905–12).
Biographia Britannica 1747–66	*Biographia Britannica: or, The Lives of the Most Eminent Persons*, ed. William Oldys *et al.*, 6 vols. in 7 (1747–66).
B.L.	The British Library, London.
Blake 1957	*The Complete Writings of William Blake*, ed. Geoffrey Keynes (1957).
Blount 1680	Charles Blount, *The Two First Books of Philostratus, concerning the Life of Apollonius Tyaneus* (1680).
Bodl.	The Bodleian Library, Oxford.
Boswell 1932	Eleanor Boswell, *The Restoration Court Stage (1660–1702)* (1932).
Browne 1685	Edward Browne, *A Brief Account of some Travels in divers Parts of Europe*, 2nd ed. (1685).
Browning 1951	Andrew Browning, *Thomas Osborne, Earl of Danby and Duke of Leeds 1632–1712*, 2 vols. (1951).

Buckingham 1723	*The Works of John Sheffield, Earl of Mulgrave, Marquis of Normanby, and Duke of Buckingham*, 2 vols. (1723).
Bulstrode 1721	Sir Richard Bulstrode, *Memoirs and Reflections upon the Reign and Government of King Charles the 1st, and K. Charles the IId.* (1721).
Burnet 1680	Gilbert Burnet, *Some Passages of the Life and Death of the Right Honourable John Earl of Rochester* (1680).
Burnet 1724–34	Gilbert Burnet, *History of His Own Time*, 2 vols. (1724–34).
Butler 1928	Samuel Butler, *Satires and Miscellaneous Poetry and Prose*, ed. René Lamar (1928).
Butler 1967	Samuel Butler, *Hudibras*, ed. John Wilders (1967).
Case	Arthur E. Case, *A Bibliography of English Poetical Miscellanies 1521–1750* (1935 for 1929).
Chamberlayne	Edward Chamberlayne, *Angliae Notitia; or, the Present State of England*, 21 vols. (1669–1707).
Cibber 1740	Colley Cibber, *An Apology for the Life of Mr Colley Cibber, Comedian and Late Patentee of the Theatre-Royal* (1740).
CJ	*Journals of the House of Commons*, 51 vols. (1803).
Clarendon 1707	Edward Hyde, Earl of Clarendon, *The History of the Rebellion and Civil Wars in England*, 2nd ed., 3 vols. (1707).
Clarendon 1759	Edward Hyde, Earl of Clarendon, *The Life* (1759).
Congreve 1967	*The Complete Plays of William Congreve*, ed. Herbert Davis (1967).
Conway Letters 1930	*Conway Letters. The Correspondence of Anne, Viscountess Conway, Henry More, and their Friends, 1642–1684*, ed. Marjorie H. Nicolson (1930).

Cowley 1905	Abraham Cowley, *Poems*, ed. A. R. Waller (1905).
Crocker 1937	S. F. Crocker, *West Virginia University Studies, III. Philological Papers* 2 (May 1937), 57–73.
CSPD	*Calendar of State Papers, Domestic Series, 1660–1704*, ed. Mary Anne E. Greene *et al.*, 44 vols. (1860–1972).
CTB	*Calendar of Treasury Books, 1660–1704*, ed. William A. Shaw, 19 vols. in 35, H. M. Stationery Office (1904–38).
Culpeper 1652	Nicholas Culpeper, *The English Physician: Or, An Astrologo-Physical Discourse of the Vulgar Herbs of this Nation* . . . (1652).
Dalton 1960	*English Army Lists and Commission Registers, 1661–1714*, ed. Charles Dalton, 4 vols. (1960).
Davies 1969	Paul C. Davies, *Comparative Literature* 21 (1969), 348–55.
Dennis 1939–43	*The Critical Works of John Dennis*, ed. Edward N. Hooker, 2 vols. (1939–43).
DNB	*The Dictionary of National Biography*, ed. Sir Leslie Stephen and Sir Sidney Lee, 22 vols. (1949–50).
Donne 1912	*The Poems of John Donne*, ed. Herbert J. C. Grierson, 2 vols. (1912).
Dorset 1979	*The Poems of Charles Sackville, Sixth Earl of Dorset*, ed. Brice Harris (1979).
Downes 1987	John Downes, *Roscius Anglicanus* [*1708*], ed. Judith Milhous and Robert D. Hume (1987).
Dryden 1882–93	*The Works of John Dryden*, ed. Sir Walter Scott and George Saintsbury, 18 vols. (1882–93).
Dryden 1956–	*The Works of John Dryden*, ed. Edward N. Hooker, H. T. Swedenberg *et al.* (1956–).

Eachard 1672	[John Eachard], *Mr Hobb's State of Nature Considered; in a Dialogue between Philautus and Timothy*, 2nd ed. (1672).
ECS	*Eighteenth-Century Studies*, 1967– .
EHR	*English Historical Review*, 1886– .
Ellis 1951	Frank H. Ellis, *PMLA* 66 (1951), 971–1008.
ELN	*English Language Notes*, 1962– .
Essex Papers 1890	*Essex Papers. Volume I. 1672–1679*, ed. Osmund Airy (1890).
Etherege 1927	*The Works of Sir George Etherege*, ed. H. F. B. Brett-Smith, 2 vols. (1927).
Etherege 1963	*The Poems of Sir George Etherege*, ed. James Thorpe (1963).
Etherege 1974	*Letters of Sir George Etherege*, ed. Frederick Bracher (1974).
Evelyn	*The Diary of John Evelyn*, ed. E. S. de Beer, 5 vols. (1955).
Fabricant 1969	Carole Fabricant, *JEGP* 68 (1969), 701–8.
Farley-Hills 1978	David Farley-Hills, *Rochester's Poetry* (1978).
Forneron 1897	Henri Forneron, *The Court of Charles II 1649–1734*, 5th ed. (1897).
Foxon 1964	David F. Foxon, *Libertine Literature in England 1660–1745* (1964).
Fraser 1979	Antonia Fraser, *Royal Charles: Charles II and the Restoration* (1979).
GEC	George E. Cokayne, *The Complete Peerage*, 2nd ed., ed. Vicary Gibbs, 13 vols. in 14 (1910–39).
GEC, *Baronetage*	George E. Cokayne, *Complete Baronetage*, 6 vols. (1900–1909).
Gramont	See Hamilton.
Granger 1769	James Granger, *A Biographical History of England*, 2 vols. in 4 (1769).
Griffin 1973	Dustin H. Griffin, *Satires against Man. The Poems of Rochester* (1973).

Grove 1980	*The New Grove Dictionary of Music and Musicians*, ed. Stanley Sadie, 20 vols. (1980).
Halifax 1912	*The Complete Works of George Savile First Marquess of Halifax*, ed. Walter Raleigh (1912).
Hamilton 1930	Anthony Hamilton, *Memoirs of the Comte de Gramont*, tr. Peter Quennell (1930).
Harris 1940	Brice Harris, *Charles Sackville, Sixth Earl of Dorset, Patron and Poet of the Restoration* (1940).
Hartmann 1926	Cyril H. Hartmann, *The Vagabond Duchess. The Life of Hortense Mancini, Duchess Mazarin* (1926).
Hatton Correspondence	*Correspondence of the Family of Hatton*, ed. Edward M. Thompson, 2 vols. (1878).
Hearne 1884–1918	*Remarks and Collections of Thomas Hearne*, ed. C. E. Doble, 11 vols. (1884–1918).
HMC	Historical Manuscripts Commission, London.
HMC *Bath MSS.*	*Calendar of the Manuscripts of the Marquis of Bath Preserved at Longleat, Wiltshire*, 4 vols. (1904–68).
HMC *Hastings MSS.*	*Report of the Manuscripts of the late Reginald Rawdon Hastings, Esq.*, 4 vols. (1928–47).
HMC *Lords MSS.*	*The Manuscripts of the House of Lords, 1678–1714*, 4 vols., and new series, 10 vols. (1887–1953).
HMC *Ormonde MSS.*	*The Manuscripts of the Marquis of Ormonde*, 2 vols., and new series, 8 vols. (1893–1920).
HMC *Portland MSS.*	*The Manuscripts of His Grace the Duke of Portland*, 10 vols. (1891–1931).
HMC *Rutland MSS.*	*Twelfth Report, Appendix, Part IV, The Manuscripts of His Grace the Duke*

	of Rutland, G.C.B., Preserved at Belvoir Castle, 4 vols. (1888–1905).
HMC *Seventh Report*	*Seventh Report of the Royal Commission on Historical Manuscripts*, Part I. Appendix (1879).
HMC *Sixth Report*	*Sixth Report of the Royal Commission on Historical Manuscripts*, Part I. Report and Appendix (1877).
HMC *Various Collections*	*Historical Manuscripts Commission Report on Manuscripts in Various Collections, Vol. VIII, The Manuscripts of the Hon. Frederick Lindley Wood et al.* (1913).
Hobbes 1935	Thomas Hobbes, *The Leviathan, or The Matter, Forme & Power of a Commonwealth, Ecclesiasticall and Civill*, ed. A. R. Waller (1935).
HoP 1660–1690	*The History of Parliament. The House of Commons 1660–1690*, ed. Basil Duke Henning, 3 vols. (1983).
Huntington	The Huntington Library, Art Collections, and Botanical Gardens, San Marino, California.
Hutton 1989	Ronald Hutton, *Charles the Second, King of England, Scotland, and Ireland* (1989).
I Modi 1988	*I Modi, The Sixteen Pleasures . . . Giulio Romano, Marcantonio Raimondi, Pietro Aretino, and Count Jean-Frédéric-Maximilien de Waldeck*, ed. Lynne Lawner (1988).
JEGP	*Journal of English and Germanic Philology*, 1903– .
Jesse 1857	John H. Jesse, *Memoirs of the Court of England during the Reign of the Stuarts*, 3 vols. (1857).
Johnson 1755	*A Dictionary of the English Language*, ed. Samuel Johnson, 2 vols. (1755).
Johnson 1779–81	Samuel Johnson, *Prefaces, Biographical*

	and Critical, to the Works of the English Poets, 10 vols. (1779–81).
Jonson 1925–52	*Ben Jonson*, ed. C. H. Herford *et al.*, 11 vols. (1925–52).
Langbaine 1691	Gerard Langbaine, *An Account of the English Dramatick Poets* (1691).
Lee 1954	*The Works of Nathaniel Lee*, ed. Thomas B. Stroup *et al.*, 2 vols. (1954).
Leneve 1873	Peter Leneve, *Leneve's Pedigrees of the Knights*, ed. George W. Marshall (1873).
LJ	*Journals of the House of Lords. 1509–1857*, 89 vols. (n.d.).
London Stage	*The London Stage 1660–1800*, ed. William Van Lennep *et al.*, 5 vols. in 11 (1960–68).
Love 1972	Harold Love, in *Restoration Literature. Critical Approaches* (1972).
Love 1981	Harold Love, in *Poetry and Drama 1570–1700*, ed. Antony Coleman *et al.* (1981).
Luttrell	Narcissus Luttrell, *A Brief Historical Relation of State Affairs from September 1678 to April 1714*, 6 vols. (1857).
Macdonald 1939	Hugh Macdonald, *John Dryden. A Bibliography of Early Editions and of Drydeniana* (1939).
Machiavelli 1977	Niccolò Machiavelli, *Il Principe* (1532), tr. Robert M. Adams (1977).
Macky 1733	*Memoirs of the Secret Services of John Macky*, ed. Spring Macky, 2nd ed. (1733).
Madan 1895–1931	Falconer Madan, *Oxford Books: A Bibliography of Printed Books relating to the University and City of Oxford or printed and published there*, 3 vols. (1895–1931).
Manning 1986	Gillian Manning, *N&Q* 231 (1986), 38–40.

Marvell(?) 1677	[Andrew Marvell(?)], *A Seasonable Argument to Perswade all the Grand Juries in England to Petition for a New Parliament* (1677).
Marvell 1927	*The Poems and Letters of Andrew Marvell*, ed. H. M. Margoliouth, 2 vols. (1927).
Milton 1931–8	*The Works of John Milton*, ed. Frank A. Patterson *et al.*, 18 vols. in 20 (1931–8).
MLN	*Modern Language Notes*, 1886– .
MLQ	*Modern Language Quarterly*, 1940– .
MLR	*Modern Language Review*, 1905– .
Montaigne 1700	*Essays of Michael Seigneur de Montaigne*, tr. Charles Cotton, 3 vols. (1700).
Moskovit 1968	Leonard A. Moskovit, *SEL* 8 (1968), 451–3.
Motif-Index	*Motif-Index of Folk-Literature*, ed. Stith Thompson, 2nd ed., 6 vols. (1955). Folklore motifs are cited by the letter-and-number system of this work.
N&Q	*Notes and Queries; for Readers and Writers*, 1849– .
Needham 1934	Francis Needham, *A Collection of Poems by Several Hands*, Welbeck Miscellany No. 2 (1934).
Nichols 1780	John Nichols, *A Select Collection of Poems*, 3 vols. (1780).
Novak 1968	Settle, Dryden, Shadwell, Crowne, Duffet. The Empress of Morocco *and its Critics*, ed. Maximillian E. Novak (1968).
NUC	*The National Union Catalog* [*sic*] *Pre-1956 Imprints, with Supplement*, 754 vols. (1968–81).
OED	*The Oxford English Dictionary*, ed. James A. H. Murray *et al.*, 2nd ed., 20 vols. (1989).

Ogg 1956	David Ogg, *England in the Reign of Charles II*, 2nd ed., 2 vols. (1956).
Oldham 1987	*The Poems of John Oldham*, ed. Harold F. Brooks *et al.* (1987).
Oliver 1963	H. J. Oliver, *Sir Robert Howard, 1626–1698* (1963).
Otway 1926	*The Complete Works of Thomas Otway*, ed. Montague Summers, 3 vols. (1926).
Otway 1932	*The Works of Thomas Otway*, ed. J. C. Ghosh, 2 vols. (1932).
Parsons 1680	Robert Parsons, *A Sermon Preached at the Funeral of the Rt Honorable John Earl of Rochester* (1680).
Partridge 1951	Eric Partridge, *A Dictionary of Slang and Unconventional English* (1951).
Paulson 1972	Kristoffer F. Paulson, *Satire Newsletter* 10 (1972), 28–9.
Pepys	*The Diary of Samuel Pepys*, ed. Robert Latham *et al.*, 11 vols. (1970–83).
Pinto 1927	Vivian de S. Pinto, *Sir Charles Sedley 1639–1701* (1927).
Pinto 1935	Vivian de S. Pinto, *Rochester: Portrait of a Restoration Poet* (1935, rptd. 1971).
Pinto 1962	Vivian de S. Pinto, *Enthusiast in Wit. A Portrait of John Wilmot Earl of Rochester 1647–1680* (1962).
PLL	*Papers on Language and Literature*, 1965– .
PMLA	*Publications of the Modern Language Association of America*, 1884– .
POAS 1697–1707	*Poems on Affairs of State, From the Year 1640, to the Year 1704*, 4 vols. (1697–1707) (Case 211).
POAS 1698	*Poems on Affairs of State, From Oliver Cromwell to this present Time* (1698) (Case 215).
POAS, Yale	*Poems on Affairs of State*, ed. George deF. Lord *et al.*, 7 vols. (1963–75).

Pope 1939–67	*The Twickenham Edition of the Poems of Alexander Pope*, ed. John Butt *et al.*, 10 vols. in 11 (1939–67).
Pound 1934	Ezra Pound, *ABC of Reading* (1934).
PQ	*Philological Quarterly*, 1922–
Reliquiae Hearnianae	Thomas Hearne, *Reliquiae Hearnianae*, ed. Philip Bliss, 2nd ed., 3 vols. (1869).
Remarques 1673	*Remarques on the Humours and Conversations of the Town. Written in a Letter to Sir T.L.* (1673).
Reresby 1936	Sir John Reresby, *Memoirs*, ed. Andrew Browning (1936).
RES	*Review of English Studies*, 1925–50, n.s., 1950–
Review	*Defoe's Review*, ed. Arthur W. Secord, 9 vols. in 22 and index vol. by William Payne (1938–48).
Righter 1968	Anne Righter, Chatterton Lecture, *Proceedings of the British Academy* 53 (1968), 47–69.
Rochester 1680$^{1\,2\,3}$	*Poems on Several Occasions by the Right Honourable, the E. of R—* (1680). Rochester 1680 falls into three parts: 1680^{1} (pp. 3–54) includes 15 satires and translations of which 11 are Rochester's; 1680^{2} (pp. 54–75) includes 23 songs of which 20 are Rochester's; 1680^{3} (pp. 76–151) includes 34 poems of which 6 are Rochester's (Vieth 1963, 93–100).
Rochester 1680 (Pforzheimer)	The Britwell copy now in the Harry Ransom Humanities Research Center, University of Texas, Austin, Texas, is an editorial revision of Rochester 1680 with 34 unique readings (Rochester 1950, xv–xvi).
Rochester 1685	*Poems on Several Occasions, Written by a late Person of Honour*, London: for

	A. Thorncome (1685). The Thorncome edition of Rochester 1680 adds five new poems, two by Thomas Randolph and three included in the present volume.
Rochester 1691	*Poems on Several Occasions: with Valentinian, A Tragedy. Written by the Right Honourable John Late Earl of Rochester* [ed. Thomas Rymer], London: for Jacob Tonson (1691).
Rochester 1707 (Bragge)	*The Miscellaneous Works of the Right Honourable the Late Earls of Rochester and Roscommon. With the Memoirs of the Life and Character of the late Earl of Rochester, in a Letter to the Dutchess of Mazarine. By Mons. St. Evremont*, London: sold by B. Bragge (1691) (Case 242). This is the first edition to include the memoir of Rochester by Pseudo-St Evremond.
Rochester 1709 (Booksellers)	*The Works of the Right Honourable the Earls of Rochester and Roscommon*, 3rd ed. (1709). This may be a Henry Hills piracy of Rochester 1709 (Curll).
Rochester 1709 (Curll)	*The Works of the Right Honourable the Earls of Rochester and Roscommon*, 3rd ed., London: for E. Curll (1709).
Rochester 1714 (Curll)[1]	*The Works of the Earls of Rochester, Roscommon, Dorset, &c.*, 4th ed., 2 vols., London: for E. Curll (1714).
Rochester 1714 (Curll)[2]	*Poems on Several Occasions. By the Earls of Roscommon and Dorset, &c.*, London: for E. Curll (1714).
Rochester 1714 (Tonson)	*The Works of John Earl of Rochester*, London: for Jacob Tonson (1714).
Rochester 1718	*Remains of the Right Honourable John, Earl of Rochester*, London: for Tho. Dryar, sold by T. Harbin and W. Chetwood (1718).

Rochester 1926	*Collected Works of John Wilmot Earl of Rochester*, ed. John Hayward, London: Nonesuch (1926).
Rochester 1950	*Rochester's Poems on Several Occasions*, ed. James Thorpe (1950). Thorpe sorted out ten editions and two hypothetical editions of Rochester 1680. Rochester 1950 is a facsimile edition of the Huntington copy of Rochester 1680.
Rochester 1953	*Poems by John Wilmot Earl of Rochester*, ed. Vivian de S. Pinto (1953, 2nd ed. 1964).
Rochester 1961	Rochester, *Dr Alexander Bendo's Bill*, transcribed by Thomas Alcock, ed. Vivian de S. Pinto (1961).
Rochester 1968	*The Complete Poems of John Wilmot, Earl of Rochester*, ed. David M. Vieth (1968).
Rochester 1980	*Rochester Selected Satires and Other Poems*, ed. David Brooks (1980).
Rochester 1982	*John Wilmot, Earl of Rochester, Selected Poems*, ed. Paul Hammond (1982).
Rochester 1984	*The Poems of John Wilmot Earl of Rochester*, ed. Keith Walker (1984).
Rochester *Letters* 1980	*The Letters of John Wilmot Earl of Rochester*, ed. Jeremy Treglown (1980).
Rowzee 1671	Lodwick Rowzee, *The Queens Wells. That is, A Treatise of the nature and vertues of the Tunbridge Water* (1671, 1st ed. 1632).
Roxburghe Ballads	*The Roxburghe Ballads*, ed. William Chappell and Joseph W. Ebsworth, 9 vols. (1871–97).
Savile Correspondence	*Savile Correspondence. Letters to and from Henry Savile, Esq., Envoy at Paris, and Vice-Chamberlain to Charles II and James II*, ed. William D. Cooper (1858).

Secret History 1690	*The Secret History of the Reigns of K. Charles II and K. James II* (1690).
Sedley 1928	*The Poetical and Dramatic Works of Sir Charles Sedley*, ed. Vivian de S. Pinto, 2 vols. (1928).
SEL	*Studies in English Literature 1500–1900*, 1960– .
Seymour 1752	[John Seymour], *Memoirs of the Life of Eleanor Gwinn, a Celebrated Courtesan in the Reign of King Charles II, and Mistress to that Monarch* (1752).
Shadwell 1927	*The Complete Works of Thomas Shadwell*, ed. Montagu Summers, 5 vols. (1927).
Shaw 1971	William A. Shaw, *The Knights of England*, 2 vols. (1971).
Sidney 1912–26	Sir Philip Sidney, *The Complete Works*, ed. Albert Feuillerat, 2 vols. (1912–26).
Simpson 1966	Claude M. Simpson, *The British Broadside Ballad and its Music* (1966).
Sitter 1976	John E. Sitter, *PLL* 12 (1976), 285–98.
Spence 1966	Joseph Spence, *Observations, Anecdotes, and Characters of Books and Men Collected from Conversation*, ed. James M. Osborn, 2 vols. (1966).
Steinman 1871	G[eorge] Steinman, *A Memoir of Barbara, Duchess of Cleveland* (1871).
Sterne 1928	Laurence Sterne, *A Sentimental Journey through France and Italy* (1928).
Sterne 1940	Laurence Sterne, *The Life and Opinions of Tristram Shandy, Gentleman*, ed. James A. Work (1940).
Stillingfleet 1675	Edward Stillingfleet, *A Sermon Preach'd before the King Feb. 24, 1674/5* (1675).
Suckling 1971	*The Works of Sir John Suckling*, ed. Thomas Clayton *et al.*, 2 vols. (1971).

Survey of London	*Survey of London*, 42 vols. to 1986 (1900–).
Swift 1937	*The Poems of Jonathan Swift*, ed. Harold Williams, 1 vol. in 3 (1937).
Swift 1939–68	*The Prose Writings of Jonathan Swift*, ed. Herbert Davis *et al.*, 14 vols. (1939–68).
Tanselle 1987	G. Thomas Tanselle, *Textual Criticism. A Chronicle, 1950–1985* (1987).
T.C.	*The Term Catalogues 1668–1709 A.D.*, ed. Edward Arber, 3 vols. (1903).
Thompson 1979	Roger Thompson, *Unfit for Modest Ears* (1979).
Thormählen 1988	Marianne Thormählen, *English Studies* 69 (1988), 396–409.
Tibullus 1971	*Albii Tibulli Aliorumque Carminum Libri Tres*, ed. Fridericus W. Lenz *et al.* (1971).
Tilley	Morris P. Tilley, *A Dictionary of the Proverbs in England in the Sixteenth and Seventeenth Centuries* (1950).
TLS	[*The London*] *Times Literary Supplement*, 1902– .
Treglown 1973	Jeremy Treglown, *RES* n.s. 24 (1973), 42–8.
Treglown 1976	Jeremy Treglown, *N&Q* 221 (1976), 554–9.
Treglown 1980	Jeremy Treglown, *MLR* 75 (1980), 18–47.
Treglown 1982	*Spirit of Wit: Reconsiderations of Rochester*, ed. Jeremy Treglown (1982).
Trevelyan 1938	George M. Trevelyan, *England under the Stuarts*, 17th ed. (1938).
UTQ	*The University of Toronto Quarterly*, 1931– .
Venn	*Alumni Cantabrigiensis, Part I, From the Earliest Times to 1751*, ed. John Venn and J. A. Venn, 4 vols. (1922–7).

Vieth 1963	David M. Vieth, *Attribution in Restoration Poetry* (1963).
Vieth and Griffin 1988	David M. Vieth and Dustin Griffin, *Rochester and Court Poetry* (1988).
Waller 1893	*The Poems of Edmund Waller*, ed. G. Thorn Drury (1893).
Wentworth Papers	*The Wentworth Papers 1705–1739 Selected from the Private and Family Correspondence of Thomas Wentworth, Lord Raby, created in 1711 Earl of Strafford*, ed. James J. Cartwright (1883).
Westminster Abbey Registers	*The Marriage, Baptismal, and Burial Registers of the Collegiate Church or Abbey of St. Peter, Westminster*, ed. Joseph L. Chester (1876).
Whincop 1747	Thomas Whincop, *Scanderbeg: or Love and Liberty. A Tragedy. To which are added a List of all the Dramatic Authors, with some Account of their Lives* (1747).
Wilcoxon 1979	Reba Wilcoxon, *Studies in Eighteenth-Century Culture* 8 (1979), 137–49.
Wilson 1952	John H. Wilson, *Nell Gwyn Royal Mistress* (1952).
Wilson 1976	John H. Wilson, *Court Satires of the Restoration* (1976).
Wing	*Short Title Catalogue of Books Printed in England, Scotland, Ireland, Wales, and British America . . . 1641–1700*, ed. Donald Wing, 2nd ed., 3 vols. (1972–88).
Winn	James A. Winn, *John Dryden and His World* (1987).
Wood 1813–20	Anthony à Wood, *Athenae Oxoniensis. An Exact History of all the Writers and Bishops who have had their Education in the University of Oxford*, 3rd ed., ed.

	Philip Bliss, 4 vols. (1813–20, rptd. 1967).
Wood 1891–1900	*The Life and Times of Anthony Wood*, ed. Andrew Clark, 5 vols. (1891–1900).
Wycherley 1979	*The Plays of William Wycherley*, ed. Arthur Friedman (1979).

Biographical Dictionary

Two sets of figures, in parentheses, separated by a point, represent page and line numbers in this edition; one set represents page numbers only. Two dates in parentheses after the titles of plays are the date of first performance and the date of publication.

Bagot, see **Falmouth**

James **Barnardi** or Bernardi (*fl.* 1673–96), of the parish of St Margaret's Westminster, was an Italian painter and dealer in erotica at the sign of the Cross in St James's Street (40.^{2}9). In 1684 he was prosecuted for vending and uttering a pack of playing cards 'on which are represented divers obscene postures and figures not fit to be expressed among Christians'. In 1696 a whole cartload of his obscene books and prints was burnt near the Gatehouse in Westminster (*Middlesex County Records*, IV 239; Foxon 1964, 11–12; Thompson 1979, 179). Thompson suggests that Barnardi may have executed the 'severall lascivious pictures' at the Ranger's Lodge in Woodstock Park, Rochester's principal residence after 1675 (Aubrey 1898, II 304; Thompson 1979, 188); cf. Suetonius, *Vitae*, III 43.

Thomas **Betterton** (1635–1710), the son of an under-cook to Charles I and 'the greatest English actor between Burbage and Garrick' (*BDAA*, II 73), was born in Westminster and apprenticed to a London bookseller. He began his theatrical career just before the Restoration in John Rhodes's Company playing at the Cockpit in Drury Lane. When the two patent houses were franchised, Betterton bought a share in Sir William Davenant's Duke's Company, where he remained for twenty-two years as actor, director, manager, and playwright. His first listed role is that of De Flores in a revival of *The Changeling* in February 1661. In June 1661 he created the role of Solyman in Davenant's *The Siege of Rhodes* at the opening of the converted tennis court in Lincoln's Inn Fields. His Hamlet was 'beyond imagination' (Pepys, 24 August 1661). In the winter of 1661–2 the King sent him abroad to observe the French theatre of Molière, Corneille, and Racine. In April 1668 upon Davenant's death Betterton and Henry Harris were made co-managers of the Duke's Company and Betterton was one of the principals in the construction of the elegant new theatre at Dorset Garden. About the same time Betterton began to adapt old plays for the Restoration stage. The most successful of these, in which he may have collaborated with Aphra Behn, was *The Amorous Widow* (November 1670; 1706), based on Molière's *Georges Dandin* (July 1668). Betterton played Lovemore. Betterton was sent abroad again, this time in the company of Joseph Haines, a comedian in the King's Company. In January 1671 they saw the Lully-Molière-Corneille production of the tragedy-ballet *Psyché* at the Salle des Machines in the Tuileries with an orchestra of 300 pieces to accompany some seventy dancers. 'The acoustics were appalling' (Grove 1980, IV 781). From December 1674 to February 1675 Betterton and his wife, Mary Saunderson, coached the royal and aristocratic performers for the last great court masque, John Crowne's *Calisto* (February 1675; 1675). Betterton also commissioned Thomas Shadwell to adapt *Psyché* for performance at Dorset Garden. Betterton created the role of Dorimant in Etherege's *The Man of Mode* (March 1676; 1676).

Sir Ralph **Bovey** (?–1679), the son of a London merchant, was educated at St Catharine's College, Cambridge, and Gray's Inn, and admitted to practice in the court of common pleas. In August 1660 he was created a baronet and subsequently acquired two estates, Long Stow in Cambridgeshire and Warden Abbey, Bedfordshire. In a by-election for Agmondesham, Buckinghamshire, in November 1669, he spent £40 a day treating the electors, but he lost the election. By his wife, Mary Maynard, he had no children, but by Elizabeth Symonds he had an illegitimate son *c.* 1676. He died in October 1679 (Venn, I 189; *HoP 1660–90*, I 137; GEC, *Baronetage*, III 117–18).

Charles Sackville, Lord **Buckhurst**, later Earl of Middlesex and Dorset (1643–1706) was the eldest son of Richard Sackville, 5th Earl of Dorset. He attended Westminster School under Richard Busby and then 'saunter'd Europe round' with a tutor in the classical fashion of *The Dunciad*. From 1661 to 1675 he sat in the Cavalier Parliament as a member for East Grinstead, Sussex, but his only recorded speech, on 13 January 1674, was against a motion to remove the Duke of Buckingham, his cousin (*HoP 1660–1690*, III 376). As a favourite of Charles II he became 'the finest gentleman' at court (GEC, IV 426n.). His frolics included 'that notorious business in the balcony' at Oxford Kate's, for which Sir Charles Sedley was fined £500 for gross indecency (Pepys, 1 July 1663; Wood 1891–1900, I 476–7) and the fathering of two illegitimate daughters, born 1663 and 1675. He was both a poet and a patron of poets (Dryden, Etherege, Wycherley, Otway, Prior), but like Rochester he published nothing. Like Rochester he volunteered for sea duty in the second Dutch War (1665–7), but his famous song, 'To all you ladies now at land', long associated with that occasion, seems to have been written the year before (Dorset 1979, 65). In 1668 he was appointed a gentleman of the bedchamber, allegedly for surrendering to Charles II 'his playwench', Nell Gwyn. In June 1674 he secretly married as his first wife the infamous Mary Bagot, widow of Charles Berkeley, Earl of Falmouth. He was styled Buckhurst until 4 April 1675, when he succeeded his maternal uncle as 4th Earl of Middlesex. On 27 August 1677 he succeeded his father as 6th Earl of Dorset. Even Burnet agreed that he was 'extremely witty'.

George Villiers, 2nd Duke of **Buckingham** (1628–87), succeeded to his title at the age of seven months, when his father was assassinated by Captain John Felton at Portsmouth. He grew up in Whitehall along with the children of Charles I and was educated at Trinity College, Cambridge, where he met Abraham Cowley. In the Civil War he survived an ambush at St Neots in July 1648 and escaped in disguise to Holland. Charles II conferred upon him the Order of the Garter in September 1649 and admitted him to the privy council in April 1650. He commanded a regiment of horse at Worcester (September 1651) and again escaped in disguise to Holland. Without Cromwell's permission, Buckingham returned to England in 1657 to marry Mary Fairfax and thereby regain some of his sequestered estates; Cowley wrote an epithalamium for the occasion. Upon the Restoration Buckingham became a gentleman of the bedchamber, a privy councillor (April 1662), and the most prominent figure at court. 'When he came into the presence chamber 'twas impossible for you not to follow him with your eye as he went along – he moved so gracefully' (Spence 1966, I 276). He served at sea in the second Dutch War (1665–7) and entertained the King with his imitations of Clarendon, using the fire shovel and bellows for the chancellor's mace and great seal. For his opposition to Clarendon's government, however, Charles sent him to the Tower and removed him from all his offices. After Clarendon's fall in August 1667, Buckingham was (erroneously) regarded as the King's first minister (Pepys, 27 November 1667, 30 December 1667; Hutton 1989, 259) even though he held no public office. Buckingham's 'shameless cohabiting' with the Countess of Shrewsbury was made no less shameful when Buckingham killed Francis Talbot, 11th Earl of Shrewsbury, in a duel on 16 January 1668. In the 1670s Buckingham began to lose influence. Thus the two Catholic members of the ruling Cabal, Sir Thomas Clifford and Henry Bennet, Earl of Arlington, signed the secret Treaty of Dover on 22 May 1670, while Buckingham, who was of no religion, was sent to Dunkirk to negotiate the *traité simulé* by which the French and English agreed to attack the United Provinces in the hapless third Dutch War (1672–4). In 1671 Buckingham was disappointed to learn that James Scott, Duke of Monmouth, was to command the English volunteers in the French army. In 1674 when Parliament attacked him for the French alliance and for advocating arbitrary government, Charles was glad to remove Buckingham from his presence and councils for ever. As a self-proclaimed 'patriot', Buckingham was welcomed by the country party as one of their leaders. He began to be seen at church with the long-suffering Mary Fairfax and he began to pay his bills. In April 1675 he was replaced as master of the horse to the King by the Duke of Monmouth. When Parliament reconvened in February 1677 after a prorogation of fifteen months, Buckingham argued that by two unrepealed statutes of Edward III a prorogation of this length required a new election. Shaftesbury, Wharton, and Salisbury supported Buckingham, but all four lords were committed to the Tower for refusing to ask pardon of the House. As soon as he was released, he moved into Rochester's lodgings in Whitehall (Marvell 1927, II 329) and entered into treasonable engagements with Paul Barillon, the French ambassador. When the Popish Plot broke in September 1678, Buckingham was equally aggressive in finding and fabricating evidence against Papists. But he failed to become leader of the opposition, declared himself an enemy of Monmouth, and let it be known that his descent from the Plantagenets gave him a claim to the throne himself. Buckingham was not a poet of sufficient importance to be noticed by Samuel Johnson, but seven editions of *The Rehearsal* (December 1671; 1672), his burlesque of rhymed heroic plays, were published between 1672 and 1693, and six editions of his collected works were published between 1704 and 1775. Buckingham also wished to be a patron of the arts and he was able to secure Wycherley a commission in his regiment (1672) and Cowley a funeral monument in Westminster Abbey, but his inveterate extravagance prevented him from keeping his promises to Samuel Butler and Nathaniel Lee. As the historian Sir Charles Firth has said, Dryden's Zimri is not a caricature but 'a faithful likeness' (*DNB*, XX 344).

Richard **Busby** (1606–95), educated at Westminster School and Christ Church, Oxford, became a distinguished churchman, prebendary of Westminster and canon of Wells, and the headmaster of Westminster School from 1640 until his death. In this latter capacity he appears in *The Dunciad* (1742) as the Spectre Schoolmaster: 'Words we teach alone' (Pope 1939–67, V 355–8). He was notorious for application of the birchen rod and his victims included Francis Atterbury, John Locke, Robert South, John Dryden, and Elkanah Settle but not Nathaniel Lee.

Samuel **Butler** (1613–80), the fifth son of a Worcestershire farmer, was educated at King's School, Worcester. From 1628 to 1662 he served as clerk or secretary to a succession of county families. With the publication of the first part of his mock epic *Hudibras* in November 1662, Butler became famous. Lord Buckhurst brought a copy of *Hudibras* to court and it became one of the King's favourite books: 'He never ate nor drank nor slept, / But "Hudibras" still near him kept.' Nine editions were required in 1663, including four piracies. The second part, published in 1664, required two editions and the third part five editions in 1678–80. Butler failed, however, to obtain the preferment for which he hoped and relapsed into obscurity. In his latter years he lived in Rose Alley. He died in September 1680 and was buried in St Paul's, Covent Garden, John Aubrey and Thomas Shadwell being among his pallbearers. He was credited with 'a severe and sound judgement: a good fellowe' (Aubrey 1898, I 136).

Carwell, see **Portsmouth**.

Catherine of Bragança (1638–1705) was the eldest daughter of João, Duke of Bragança (who became João IV of Portugal after a revolution in 1640), by his wife Luise de Guzman, eldest daughter of Caspar Alfonso Guzman, Duke of Medina Sidonia. Her father proposed her as a bride for Charles Stuart, Prince of Wales, as early as 1645. In

July 1660 Francisco de Mello, the Portuguese envoy, offered Charles II Catherine and 'the richest dowry brought by any Queen of England': Bombay, Tangiers, trading privileges throughout the Portuguese empire, and 2,000,000 cruzados (about £330,000) (Hutton 1989, 158). The Spanish ambassador warned that the infanta was sterile. In May 1662 Charles and Catherine, who had a bad cold, were married first in a secret Catholic ceremony and then in a 'mutilated' public ceremony performed by Gilbert Sheldon, Archbishop of Canterbury. At this time Catherine was twenty-three; Barbara Palmer was nineteen and at the height of her power over the King. Catherine was short, plain, and childishly pious; her teeth stuck out but she loved dancing. Reared in a convent, she spoke neither French nor English. In the beginning she and Charles had to converse in Spanish, which both of them spoke badly. The King amused himself by teaching her English and laughing at her mistakes. But after eighteen months, when she still spoke broken English and had proved 'incapable of children', Charles began to lose interest (Pepys, 22 February 1664). His appalling cruelty to her in the first years of their marriage did not continue, but the claim that 'henceforth Catherine received with kindness and forbearance the long series of her husband's mistresses' is not borne out by the facts (*DNB*, III 1224; Hutton 1989, 417).

Philip Stanhope, 2nd Earl of **Chesterfield** (1633–1713), whose father died in 1635, was raised at the court of the Princess Royal, Princess Mary of Orange, in The Hague and at the court of Queen Henrietta Maria in Paris. He was educated at the universities of Leyden and Breda and by travel in Italy. He succeeded to his title upon the death of his grandfather in September 1656. Upon his return to England, £10,000 in debt, he soon became notorious for duelling, drinking, gaming, 'exceeding wildness', and for love affairs with Barbara Villiers, afterwards the Duchess of Cleveland, and Lady Elizabeth Howard, who subsequently married John Dryden. (Dryden's biographer doubts that Lady Elizabeth had an affair with Chesterfield, but does not consider the evidence of Chesterfield's letter cited by Sir Charles Firth (Winn 1987, 125; *DNB*, XVIII 910). In 1660 Chesterfield married as his second wife Lady Elizabeth Butler, eldest daughter of James Butler, 1st Duke of Ormonde. He was appointed chamberlain to Queen Catherine (1662–5) and raised a regiment of foot in the second Dutch War (1665–7) (Dalton 1960, I 79). In November 1679 he was constituted warden of all the King's forests on this side of Trent in place of the Duke of Monmouth.

John **Churchill** (1650–1722), the future Duke of Marlborough, was the son of Sir Winston Churchill. He was educated at the Dublin Free Grammar School and St Paul's School in London. 'The Duke of *York*'s Love for his Sister [Arabella] (by whom he had the Duke of Berwick, and other Children) first brought him to Court [as a page]; and the Beauty of his own Person . . . so gained on the Dutchess of *Cleveland* . . . that she effectually established him there' (Macky 1733, 4). In September the Duke of York secured him a commission as ensign in the first company of foot guards, but it was after service as a gentleman volunteer in Tangiers (1668–70) that Churchill became the Duchess of Cleveland's lover (Plate 9). Her daughter Barbara, born 16 July 1672, is the only one of her six children not acknowledged by Charles II, and Churchill's father mentions 'the King's displeasure' in a letter of 25 October 1672 (GEC, VIII 491). In the third Dutch War Churchill saw action in all the most dangerous posts: the first company of foot guards survived the battle of Solebay (May 1672) aboard the Duke of York's flagship (after which Churchill received a double promotion to captain), and as a gentleman volunteer Churchill was at the Duke of Monmouth's side in the desperate and successful assault upon Maastricht in June 1673 (for which he was publicly thanked by Louis XIV and promoted lieutenant-colonel). In the same year he was appointed gentleman of the bedchamber to the Duke of York, a post that he held until he deserted James II in November 1688. In April 1674 he was given command of one of the English regiments under Turenne and promoted colonel in the French army. The Duchess of Cleveland 'effectually established' Churchill in 1674 when she gave him £4,500 to buy a life annuity of £500 a year. 'That Marlborough in early life was . . . [not] wanting in an eye for the main chance may be taken as proved' (*DNB*, IV 316). In the autumn of 1675 he met fifteen-year-old Sarah Jennings, a maid of honour to Maria Beatrice of Modena, the new Duchess of York. The Duchess of Cleveland retired to Paris and Churchill married Sarah Jennings in October 1678.

Lady Alice Moore (?–1677), daughter of Henry Moore, 1st Earl of Drogheda, married Henry Hamilton, 2nd Earl of **Clanbrassil**, in

May 1677. 'The wicked Lady Alice', as she came to be known, was a candidate for the King's affection in June 1671: 'my Lady Clanbra[ssil] . . . thinks to trip up Nell Guin's heels, and you cannot imagine how highly my Lord Arran [Richard Butler, 5th son of James Butler, 1st Duke of Ormonde] and many others do value themselves upon the account of managing Lady Clanbra[ssil] in this affair' (Helen Selina Sheridan Blackwood, Baroness Dufferin, *Songs, Poems, & Verses*, ed. Frederick Hamilton-Temple-Blackwood, Marquess of Dufferin and Ava (1894), 44; *Conway Letters* (1930), 339) (Rochester 1968, 46n.). She became *The Antiquated Coquet* of Dorset's satire: 'Ere we can ask, she cries consent' (Dorset 1979, 33).

Edward Hyde, 1st Earl of **Clarendon** (1609–74), the son of Henry Hyde of Dinton, Wiltshire, by Mary Langford, daughter of Edward Langford of Trowbridge, Wiltshire, was educated at Magdalen Hall, Oxford, and the Middle Temple. In his early years his friends included Ben Jonson, Edmund Waller, and Lucius Cary, Lord Falkland. By the time he was sent to Bristol in March 1645 as a member of the council appointed to advise the Prince of Wales, Hyde was chancellor of the exchequer and a privy councillor; Charles Stuart was a boy of fifteen. Hyde followed Charles Stuart into exile a year later and for fourteen years shared with him the poverty and frustration of a government in exile. After his father's execution in January 1649, Charles II retained Hyde in all his offices and in January 1658 appointed him lord chancellor as well. Hyde rode into London with Charles II on 29 May 1660 and became Charles's first minister *de facto*. In July 1660 Charles informed Hyde of the advantageous marriage contract that had been offered him by the Portuguese ambassador and Hyde acquiesced in the terms. When offered £10,000 to promote a French marriage, Hyde refused the bribe even after Charles urged him to take it (Burnet 1724–34, I 167). The secret marriage of his pregnant daughter to the Duke of York threatened to wreck his career and Hyde reacted badly, urging Charles to punish Anne 'with the utmost Severity' (Clarendon 1759, ²28). Charles responded by creating him Earl of Clarendon in November 1660 and giving him £20,000 to support his new dignity. But the King found his self-righteous moralizing increasingly tedious. His intransigence cost him any influence with Parliament. And at court the Duke of Buckingham and 'the Lady', as the Countess of

Castlemaine was called, started rumours designed to get rid of him: he was said to have promoted the marriage to Catherine of Bragança, whom he knew to be sterile – 'she haveing a continuall flux of blood in her secret parts' – so that his granddaughters, the issue of Anne Hyde and the Duke of York, could succeed to the throne (which of course they did) (Reresby 1936, 204, 41). While the Dutch were setting fire to English warships in the Medway in June 1667 and the London mob was breaking Clarendon's windows, these verses were tacked to his front door: 'Three sights to be seen: / Dunkirk, Tangier and a barren Queen' (Trevelyan 1938, 362). Charles demanded his retirement on 30 August 1667 and with charges of high treason pending against him, Clarendon fled to France in November. 'But when, again in exile, he was thrown back on the resources of his own virtue and intellect, and again set himself, an old and broken man, to complete the great literary work of his life [*The History of the Rebellion and Civil Wars in England, Begun in the Year 1641*], he seemed once more to enter the pure presence of the friend who had deserted him on the field of Newbury [Lucius Cary, Lord Falkland, q.v.], of whose love he had once been worthy and was again worthy at the end' (Trevelyan 1938, 363).

Barbara Villiers, Duchess of **Cleveland** (1641–1709), 'the finest woeman of her age', so beautiful that Pepys could forgive her anything (Reresby 1936, 41; Pepys, 16 July 1662), was the only child of William Villiers, 2nd Viscount Grandison, by Mary Bayning, third daughter of Paul Bayning, 1st Viscount Bayning. Her first known lover was Philip Stanhope, 2nd Earl of Chesterfield (q.v.), 'the greatest knave in Engl[an]d' (Swift 1939–68, V 259). In April 1659 she married Roger Palmer, a student at the Inner Temple who was converted to Roman Catholicism in 1661. On the night of Charles II's return to London on his thirtieth birthday, 29 May 1660, he went to bed with Barbara Palmer, or in other words 'the restored wanderer showed his gratitude to heaven by taking Barbara Villiers for the ruler of himself and his Court' (Trevelyan 1938, 350). Her daughter Anne, born 25 February 1661, almost certainly the child of Charles II, was acknowledged by Roger Palmer. Charles rewarded him by making him Earl of Castlemaine in the Irish peerage (December 1661) and her by making her a lady of the bedchamber over the hysterical protests of the newly wed Queen Catherine of Bragança

(August 1662). 'The insatiable Countess carried on intrigues (at the same time as with the King) with [Charles] Hart and [Cardell] Goodman, the actors, with Jacob Hall, the rope dancer, with "the invincible" Henry Jermyn, with [John] Churchill (afterwards the great Duke), with [William] Wycherley, the dramatist, &c.' (GEC, III 281). The 'cetera' include, in alphabetical order, Sir Charles Berkeley, John Ellis, Colonel James Hamilton, Thomas Killigrew, and Ralph Montagu. In April 1663 it was reported that she 'is removed, as to her bed', from Roger Palmer's house in King street 'to a chamber . . . next to [actually above] the King's owne' (Pepys, 25 April 1663). Her children (except one) were acknowledged by the King and duly raised to the peerage. But 'her principal business', as Clarendon saw, 'was to get an estate for herself and her children' and in this business she was enormously successful. The only thing that Charles is known to have refused her was Phoenix Park in Dublin. In April 1668 she was removed from Whitehall to Berkshire House, across the street from St James's Palace, for which Charles paid £4,000 (Pepys, 8 May 1668). As a further consolation she was created Duchess of Cleveland (August 1669). Pepys liked to think that she practised 'all the tricks of Aretin', the sixteen 'postures' engraved by Marcantonio Raimondi after drawings by Giulio Romano (Pepys, 15 May 1663) (Plate 13), and by 1672 her infamy had passed into proverb: 'Thou talkest just as if thou camest reeking hot from Barbara —' (Eachard 1672, 111). The Test Act of March 1673 required her to resign as lady of the bedchamber, for she had become a convert to Roman Catholicism in 1663. In April 1677 she received her last grant from the crown, the office of Ranger of Hampton Court and Keeper of the Chace, with residence in the Lodge at Bushey Park (Steinman 1871, 152). The same year she withdrew to Paris, where she entertained herself by an affair with the English ambassador to Versailles, Ralph Montagu. Thereafter she visited England only occasionally.

Lady Jane and Lady Dorothy **Coote** (1652–77) were the daughters of Sir Charles Coote, Bart. of Castle Coote, county Roscommon, and 1st Earl of Mountrath, by his second wife, Jane Hannay, daughter of Sir Robert Hannay, Bart. of Mochrum, county Kirkcudbright. Lady Jane died unmarried. Lady Dorothy married the Rev. Moses Viredett, minister of the French Church in Dublin.

Abraham **Cowley** (1618–67), Rochester's 'favourite English author'

(Rochester *Letters* 1980, 15–16), was the seventh and posthumous child of a London stationer and grocer. Three editions of his first volume of poems, *Poeticall Blossoms* (1633, 1636, 1637) were published while Cowley was still a student at Westminster School. He proceeded to Trinity College, Cambridge, in 1637. In March 1641 Prince Charles was entertained at the university by a production of *The Guardian*, a comedy hastily put together by Cowley for the occasion. Rewritten in 1658, it was produced by Sir William Davenant at Lincoln's Inn Fields as *The Cutter of Coleman Street* (December 1661; 1663) with the Bettertons and James Nokes in the leading roles. Despite making fun of 'Cavalier Indigent Officers', 'it was perform'd a whole Week with a full Audience' (Downes 1987, 57). In 1644 Cowley followed the royal family into exile and for eleven years served as cipher clerk, diplomatic courier, and intelligence agent for Henry Jermyn, Lord Jermyn. *The Mistress, or Several Copies of Love Verses* was published in London in 1647 and became 'the favourite love poems of the age' (*DNB*, IV 1305). Samuel Johnson observes that they 'might have been written . . . for hire by a philosophical rhymer who had only heard of another sex' (Johnson 1779–81, I [1]106). In April 1655 on a clandestine mission in support of an insurrection in which both the Duke of Buckingham and the 1st Earl of Rochester were engaged, Cowley was arrested in London. Under direct interrogation by Cromwell he capitulated and remained on bail until the Restoration, writing pindaric odes celebrating the Lord Protector as 'God-like *Brutus*'. His next volume, *Poems* (1656), includes the Anacreontiques admired by Johnson, the Pindarique Odes, and *Davideis*, an unfinished epic in decasyllabic couplets, all of which provided models for the next generation of poets. In December 1667 Cowley was created M.D. at Oxford; he was also one of the first members of the Royal Society. In January 1662 Henry Jermyn, now Earl of St Albans, obtained a pension for him from the Dowager Queen that enabled him to retire to the country. He was buried with full poetic honours in Westminster Abbey.

John **Crowne** (*c.* 1640–1712) was the son of William Crowne, one of Cromwell's colonels who invested his war-time profits in the joint proprietorship of the province of Nova Scotia, a huge tract of land between the Penobscot and Machias rivers and extending 300 miles inland in what is now the state of Maine. John Crowne accompanied his father to the Massachusetts Bay Colony and entered Harvard University in September 1657. He boarded with John Norton, minister of the First Church of Boston, but left without taking a degree in December 1660 when his father returned to England to defend (unsuccessfully) his claims in court. Reduced to 'Gentleman-Usher to an old Independant Lady' (Dennis 1939–43, II 404), Crowne began writing to support himself. His first work was *Pandion and Amphigenia* (1665), a prose romance that has apparently never been reprinted. His first play, *Juliana, or The Princess of Poland*, a tragicomedy in prose, blank verse, and rhyme, was produced by the Duke's Company in June 1671, 'when the Dog-star was near his Reign' (sig. A4r) and the court was at Windsor. Crowne had better luck with his second play, *The History of Charles the Eighth of France*, a rhymed heroic play that Betterton chose as the second new play to be acted at Dorset Garden. It opened in November 1671, played six nights, and was published the next year with a dedication to Crowne's new patron, Lord Rochester. In 1675, allegedly 'to mortify Mr *Dryden*', Rochester secured for Crowne the commission to write, in little more than a month, a masque with parts for the Princesses Mary and Anne (aged twelve and ten) and five other court ladies, two of whom – Lady Henrietta Wentworth and Sarah Jennings – were to play 'in Mens Habits' (Dennis 1939–43, II 405; *Calisto: or The Chaste Nymph* (1675, sig. a1v). The result, partly in pindarics and partly in heroics, Crowne, with disarming candour, called 'a weak, lean, ricketty, deformed piece' (sig. a2r). But it was played at least three times in February 1675 to the great satisfaction of the court. The Duke of Monmouth danced and two of the royal mistresses, Moll Davis and Mary Knight, represented the Thames and Peace, respectively. Dryden *may* have written an epilogue that Rochester *may* have contrived to omit (Macdonald 1939, 69n., 210n.; Winn 1987, 271). Two of Crowne's next plays, *The Country Wit; or Sir Mannerly Shallow* (April 1675?; 1675), a comedy in prose, and *The Destruction of Jerusalem by Titus Vespasian* (January 1677; 1677), a rhymed heroic play, were highly successful. Pseudo-St Evremond reports that after the 'wild and unaccountable Success' of the latter, Rochester withdrew his patronage of Crowne 'as if he would be still in Contradiction to the Town' (Rochester 1707 (Bragge), sig. b8r). Crowne's best plays, *The City Politiques* (January 1683; 1683) and

Sir Courtly Nice (May 1685; 1685), were written after Rochester's death.

Elizabeth Trentham (1640–1713), the daughter of Francis Trentham of Rocester Priory, Staffordshire, married Brien Cokayne, 2nd Viscount **Cullen** in the Irish peerage, sometime before 1 April 1657. Known as 'the beautiful Lady Cullen' (Plate 5) and an heiress worth £6,000 a year, she was appointed lady of the bedchamber to Queen Catherine. She was so extravagant that her husband had to secure a private act of Parliament in 1676 to enable him to pay her debts and raise portions out of his entailed estate for their younger children (GEC, III 563).

Sir Francis **Dayrell** (1646–75), son and heir of Sir Thomas Dayrell, Kt, of Lillingstone Dayrell, Buckinghamshire, and Castle Camps, Cambridge, was educated at Emmanuel College, Cambridge, and Lincoln's Inn. He married Elizabeth, daughter of Edward Lewis of The Venn, Glamorganshire, and was knighted on 29 February 1672 (Shaw 1971, II 247).

Dorset, see **Buckhurst**.

John **Dryden** (1631–1700) was born at Aldwinkle All Saints, Northamptonshire, where his maternal grandfather was rector of the parish church. Dryden's paternal grandfather was Sir Erasmus Dryden of Canons Ashby, 1st Baronet, the sheriff of Northamptonshire in the reigns of Elizabeth I and James I. The two sides of Dryden's family therefore represent the establishment in church and state but were strongly puritanical. The first Royalist whom Dryden encountered may have been Richard Busby, the headmaster of Westminster School. While still a schoolboy Dryden published 'Upon the Death of Lord Hastings' in a volume of elegies entitled *Lachrymae Musarum, the Tears of the Muses* (1649), to which Andrew Marvell contributed an equally bad exercise in the same decadent metaphysical style. Dryden graduated B.A. from Trinity College, Cambridge, in January 1654 and proceeded to London, presumably to study law. Upon the reopening of the theatres, he contracted with Sir William Davenant, patentee of the King's Company, to write three plays a year for a ten per cent interest in the company and soon became the most popular playwright in London, producing about twenty plays between 1663 and 1680. In December 1663 he married Lady

Elizabeth Howard, the daughter of Thomas Howard, 1st Earl of Berkshire, an inconsequential Royalist peer. Like Rochester, he took his mistress, Anne Reeves, from the stage. His comedies, beginning with *Secret Love, or The Maiden Queen* (*c.* February 1667; 1668), and his 'heroic tragedies', as he called them, *Tyrannic Love, or The Royal Martyr* (June 1669; 1670) and the two parts of *The Conquest of Granada* (December 1670 and January 1671; 1672), were supported by the acting of Nell Gwyn. But Sir Leslie Stephen complains that Dryden adopted 'other not very creditable devices to catch the public taste' (*DNB*, VI 67). In 1668 Dryden was created M.A. by the Archbishop of Canterbury and in August 1670 he succeeded Sir William Davenant as poet laureate and James Howell as historiographer royal at a combined salary of £200 a year, which was regularly in arrears. Dryden acquired his nickname Bayes not directly from the laureateship but from the character (played by John Lacy) who impersonated him in Buckingham's *The Rehearsal* (December 1671; 1672). It is Mr Bayes's 'new way of writing' that is parodied in Buckingham's farce, in which lines from *Tyrannic Love* and *The Conquest of Granada* are quoted. By 1675 Dryden tired of writing plays and longed to write an epic poem (Dryden 1882–93, V 195–6). He even solicited an academic appointment so that he could retire to Oxford (Winn 1987, 270). But he kept on writing plays. In 1676, however, he wrote *MacFlecknoe*, the first of the great satires which, together with his translations and critical essays, form the basis of his reputation today.

George **Etherege** (1636?–91), the son of Captain George Etherege, was apprenticed to an attorney in Beaconsfield, Buckinghamshire, and proceeded to London in February 1659 to study law at Clement's Inn. His three comedies were all produced by the Duke's Company. The first, *The Comical Revenge, or Love in a Tub* (March? 1664; 1664) 'got the Company more Reputation and Profit than any preceding Comedy' (Downes 1987, 57). The second, *She Would if She Could* (February 1668; 1668), was called 'the best Comedy that has been written since the Restauration of the Stage' (Shadwell 1927, I 183). In that same year he was appointed a gentleman of the privy chamber to Charles II and joined 'the merry gang' at court. His poems, never collected by himself, are scattered in the miscellanies. His first diplomatic post was at Istanbul (1668–71), where he was secretary to the ambassador. In his third play, the paradigmatic Restoration comedy of manners, *The Man of Mode, or Sir Fopling Flutter* (March 1676; 1676), Elizabeth Barry may have played Loveit, the cast mistress (Downes 1987, 76n.), Betterton mimicked Rochester in the role of Dorimant, and Dryden wrote the epilogue. Etherege was knighted in 1679 and, like his friend Rochester, acknowledged paternity of a child by Elizabeth Barry (*Biographia Britannica* 1747–66, III 1844).

Lucius Cary, 2nd Viscount **Falkland** (1610?–43) was the son of Sir Henry Cary, Viscount Falkland in the Scottish peerage, lord deputy of Ireland from 1622 to 1629. Lucius Cary was educated at Trinity College, Dublin, and St John's College, Cambridge. In 1629 he inherited from his maternal grandfather estates at Great Tew and Burford, Oxfordshire, where he became a neighbour of Rochester's father at Adderbury. He surrounded himself with poets from London (Ben Jonson, Sir John Suckling, Edmund Waller) and divines from Oxford (William Chillingworth, Gilbert Sheldon, George Morley) and devoted himself to study. 'His whole Conversation,' it was said, 'was one continued *Convivium Philosophicum*, or *Convivium Theologicum*' (Clarendon 1759, [1]22). In 1630 he married Lettice Morison, daughter of Sir Richard Morison 'of noe meanes' (GEC, V 240), and succeeded his father as 2nd Viscount Falkland in 1633. In that year he was also appointed a gentleman of the privy chamber to Charles I. He sat in Parliament as a member for Newport, Isle of Wight, and was made secretary of state and a privy councillor in 1642. But the Civil War broke his heart (Clarendon 1707, II 276). He was with the King at Edgehill Fight and in the siege of Gloucester but was killed in the first battle of Newbury in 'a death which is scarcely distinguishable from suicide' (*DNB*, III 1160).

Mary Bagot, (1645–79), the daughter of Colonel Harvey Bagot of Pipe Hall, Warwickshire, had large red ears and flat feet (Hamilton 1930, 232). When she was appointed maid of honour to the Duchess of York, she 'blushed at everything' (ibid., 223), but after she married Charles Berkeley in December 1664, she blushed at nothing. Berkeley, who was raised to the peerage as Viscount Fitzharding in the Irish peerage in July 1663 and then created Earl of **Falmouth** in March 1664, was 'a Fellow of great Wickedness' – Pepys called him a pimp (Clarendon 1759, [2]34; Pepys, 15 December 1662). The countess was widowed when Falmouth was killed on 3 June 1665 at the side of the Duke of York aboard the *Royal Charles* in the battle of Lowestoft in the second Dutch War, when his shattered head 'gave the last-first proof that he had brains' (*POAS*, Yale, I 44). The Countess of Falmouth secretly married Charles Sackville, Lord Buckhurst, in June 1674 and died without issue five years later, 'A teeming Widow, but a barren Wife' (Buckingham 1723, I 122).

Felton, see **Howard**.

Thomas **Flatman** (1637–88) was born within sound of Bow Bells, the son of a clerk in chancery. He was educated at Winchester School and New College, Oxford, and called to the bar in May 1662 from the Inner Temple. He was created M.A. at Cambridge by royal letter in December 1666 and elected a Fellow of the Royal Society in April 1668. Flatman was both a poet and a miniaturist, but it was said that 'one of his heads is worth a ream of his Pindarics' (Granger 1769, II ii 390). Twenty-three of his pindarics were published in *Poems and Songs* (1674), which achieved a fourth edition in 1686.

Foster, a woman of whom nothing is known but what is included in the following letter of September 1671 from John Muddiman to Rochester: 'Now my lord as to a concerne of your owne: Fate has taken care to vindicate your proceeding with Foster; whoe is discoverd to bee a damsell of low degre, and very fit for the latter part of your treatment: noe northerne lass but a mere dresser at Hazards scoole: her uncle a wyght that wields the puissant spiggot at Kensington: debaucht by Mr Buttler a gentleman of the cloak and gallow shoe [i.e. dressed like a Puritan] – an order of knighthood, very fatall to maydenhead' (Rochester *Letters* 1980, 70–71) (Rochester 1968, 110n.).

Fox: this pocky Irish beauty remains unidentified, but in February 1688 Sir George Etherege reminds Charles Middleton, 2nd Earl of Middleton, 'you can never be more happy than you were in Mrs Fox's days' (Etherege 1974, 182).

Sir Alexander **Fraser** (*c.* 1607–81) of Dores, county Kincardine, was educated at Aberdeen and Leyden and graduated M.D. at Montpellier in October 1635. He was elected a fellow of the Royal College of Physicians in London in November 1641 and was successively physician-in-ordinary to Charles I and Charles II, whom he followed into exile (Browne 1685, 115). At the Restoration he bought a house in Scotland Yard and married as his second wife Mary Carey, fourth daughter of Sir Ferdinando Carey, who was appointed one of the dressers of Queen Catherine. According to backstairs gossip, Fraser was 'great with my lady Castlemaine . . . and all the ladies at court' as purveyor-in-ordinary of abortifacients (Pepys, 19 September 1664). He was created baronet in August 1673.

Carey **Fraser** (*c.* 1658–1709) was the only daughter of Sir Alexander Fraser, Charles II's principal physician, and Mary Carey. She was 'Sent over to Paris while very Young under the Tuition of a very wise and prudent Gentlewoman'. At the age of sixteen she was presented at court, where 'her face and shape' were widely approved, and appointed a maid of honour to Queen Catherine (Walter Macfarlane, *Genealogical Collections concerning Families in Scotland*, 2 vols. (1900), II 329; HMC *Rutland MSS.*, II 32). She was ostentatiously courted by Sir Carr Scrope in 1676, but her attire for the Queen's birthday (15 November), 'ermine upon velvet imbroidered with gold and lined with cloth of gold', frightened him 'from marying her, saying his estate will scarce maintaine her in clothes' (HMC *Rutland MSS.*, II 31). John Sheffield, Earl of Mulgrave, was not so cautious: 'He got the better of Sir Carr, / Although his love was not so true' (B.L. MS. Add. 34362, f. 118, quoted in Wilson 1976, 240). During the Duchess of Portsmouth's illness in 1677 it was rumoured that Carey Fraser aspired to replace her in the King's affections: 'In stepped stately Carey Frazier, . . . / She vowed the King . . . must take 'er / Rowley replied he was retrenching / And would no more of costly wenching' (Wilson 1976, 26–7). So instead she became the mistress of Charles Mordaunt, 2nd Viscount Mordaunt. When she was 'discovered to be with child' in May 1680, it was supposed that a 'marriage . . . will now be speedily consummated' (HMC *Ormonde MSS.*, n.s., V 325). But it was not until December 1681 that 'My Lord Mordaunt . . . brought out as well as owned his lady' (HMC *Rutland MSS.*, II 62).

Sidney **Godolphin** (1645–1712), the third son of Francis Godolphin, governor of the Scilly Isles during the Civil War, and Dorothy, daughter of Sir Henry Berkeley of Yarlington, Somersetshire, was raised in the household of Charles II. He was appointed a page of honour (September 1662–8), groom of the bedchamber (1670–78), and master of the robes (July 1678–9). In Parliament, where he represented the Cornish boroughs of Helston (October 1668–70) and St Mawes (1679–81), he voted with the court and was put down as 'doubly vile' by Shaftesbury, but he served on few committees and made no recorded speeches (*HoP 1660–1690*, II 405). He escorted Henrietta Anne, Duchess of Orléans, to Dover for the secret treaty against the Dutch in May 1670. In May 1675 he married Margaret Blagge, daughter of Thomas Blagge of Horningsheath, Suffolk, a maïd of honour to the Queen and a *dévote* who is designated by the pentacle in Evelyn's diary (Evelyn, 16 October 1672). She died in childbirth in September 1677 and Godolphin never remarried. Godolphin, found his real career in March 1679 when he was appointed one of the lords of the treasury. In November 1679 Godolphin, Laurence Hyde, and Robert Spencer, Earl of Sunderland, known derisively as the Chits, succeeded Danby at the head of the government. 'Godly Godolphin' was laughed at by 'the merry gang' at court but 'allowed [to be] a very cunning man' (*HoP 1660–1690*, II 405; Marvell 1927, II 329; *Wentworth Papers*, 131). Except for one act that he contributed to the 'confederate' translation of Corneille for Edmund Waller's *Pompey the Great* (January 1664; 1664), Godolphin's cunning was exercised in managing the Treasury.

Philibert, comte de **Gramont** (1624–1707), a younger son of Antoine de Gramont, viceroy of Navarre, was educated in the Jesuit college at Paris. At the age of fourteen he was tonsured and beneficed *in commendam* with the abbacy of Lahonce in the diocese of Bayonne. But Gramont's career was to be amatory and military, not ecclesiastical. As a volunteer he served three campaigns under Turenne and three campaigns under Condé. But when he paid court to Anne Lucie de la Mothe, one of Louis XIV's mistresses, he was banished and made his way to England. He arrived at Whitehall in the midst of the festivities celebrating the King's marriage to Catherine of Bragança and was delighted by the opportunities of the English court. In December 1663 'the doubtful *Monsieur*' married Elizabeth, 'La belle Hamilton', daughter of Sir George Hamilton and first cousin of James Butler, Duke of Ormonde, under circumstances which, according to stage tradition, furnished Molière with the plot of *Le Mariage forcé* (February 1664). After November 1664 the couple lived mainly in Paris. In 1670 Gramont came to Dover in the train of Henrietta Anne, Duchess of Orléans, on the occasion of the signing of the secret treaty against the Netherlands. In the subsequent wars Gramont saw action at Maastricht (1673), Cambrai (1677), and Namur (1678). He was promoted lieutenant-general of Béarn in 1679. His brother-in-law, Anthony Hamilton, wrote the famous *Mémoires de la Vie du Comte de Grammont* in 1704–5, partly from the count's dictation. But Bernard de Fontenelle refused to license the book for publication in France and it was finally published in Cologne in 1713. An English translation by Abel Boyer appeared the next year and in 1817 the book was added to the Index Librorum Prohibitorum.

Neither the identity of her parents nor the time and place of the birth of Eleanor **Gwyn** (1650?–87) is known, but she told Elias Ashmole (for the purpose of casting her horoscope) that she was born at 6 a.m. on Saturday, 2 February 1650. No one disputes her claim that she was brought up in a bawdy house, or the tradition that she sold oranges at the Theatre Royal in Bridges Street, Drury Lane, when it opened in May 1663 (Pepys, 26 October 1667; Seymour 1752, 9). Nor is it certain who was her first lover, but she herself called Charles Hart (q.v.) her Charles the First. She probably began acting during the 1663–4 season, for a year later she was well enough known to be recognized as 'pretty witty Nell' in the audience at the Lincoln's Inn Fields theatre (Pepys, 3 April 1665). With the King in the audience she played Florimell, a breeches part, in Dryden's new play, *Secret Love, or The Maiden Queen* (*c.* February 1667; 1668), opposite Charles Hart. She was playing opposite Hart again in James Howard's masterpiece, *All Mistaken, or The Mad Couple* (September 1667; 1672), when she attracted the attention of her Charles the Second, Charles Sackville, Lord Buckhurst (q.v.). Her part in Dryden's *Tyrannic Love, or The Royal Martyr* (June 1669; 1670) required her to die on stage in the last scene and then 'to rise again and speak the Epilogue'. It was after this performance that Charles II became her Charles the Third. What the satirist said in scorn, 'And Rowley's soul she did ensnare' (*POAS*, Yale, II 243), is literally true. Her first son by Charles II, Charles Beauclerk, was born in May 1670 and created Duke of St Albans in January 1684. After her performance in the two parts of *The Conquest of Granada* (December 1670 and January 1671; 1672) – she played the lead opposite Charles

Hart and spoke the prologue in a broad-brimmed hat having the circumference of a cartwheel and a waist-belt, in mockery of the short laced coat and broad waist-belt in which James Nokes played at Dover (Downes 1987, 64) – Nell Gwyn left the stage. The King bought her a house on the site of 79 Pall Mall that conveniently backed onto the Royal Garden in St James's Park, where John Evelyn was shocked at the familiarity with which she addressed the King (Evelyn, 1 March 1671). Her second son, James Beauclerk, was born on 25 December 1671. Sir Peter Lely painted her full-length nude portrait, with Charles Beauclerk as Cupid, in 1672. Burnet called her 'the indiscreetest and wildest creature that ever was in a Court' but unlike her rivals, the Duchess of Cleveland ('the prerogative Whore') and the Duchess of Portsmouth ('*Me no Whore*'), Nell Gwyn did not try to wield the prerogative (Burnet 1724–34, I 263; *BDAA*, VI 462; *The Secret History*, 1690, 23). She was appointed lady of the Queen's privy chamber in 1675. Rochester must have been well known to her for she appointed him trustee of some disputed properties of hers in Ireland. She left an estate of about £1,000,000 when she died in 1687 (*BDAA*, VI 469).

Joseph **Haines** (?–1701) was educated at St Martin's School in London and in May 1659 matriculated at Queen's College, Oxford, where the infamous Joseph Williamson was a Fellow. Haines may have been Williamson's 'private Clerk' when Williamson invaded Roger L'Estrange's monopoly on government news and began publication in November 1665, during the plague in London, of the first true newspaper, the *Oxford Gazette* (renamed the *London Gazette* in February 1666 and still published). Haines migrated to Cambridge for an M.A. but threw over an academic career to join John Coysh's company of strolling actors. By the time it was discovered that Haines was an 'incomparable dancer' (Pepys, 7 May 1668), he had trained at the Hatton Garden Nursery and joined the King's Company at the Bridges Street theatre. In July 1670 Haines went to France in the train of the Duke of Buckingham (q.v.) and danced at the opening of Molière's *Le Bourgeois Gentilhomme* before Louis XIV on 14 October 1670. The next year he returned to Paris with Betterton (q.v.). When he was dismissed from the King's Company, allegedly for mimicking the manager, Charles Hart, Haines played the Dancing Master in *The Citizen Turn'd Gentleman*, Edward

Ravenscroft's adaptation of *Le Bourgeois Gentilhomme*, which opened at the Duke's Company's new Dorset Garden theatre in July 1672. The next year, however, he rejoined the King's Company and played Benito in Dryden's *The Assignation, or Love in a Nunnery* (November 1672; 1673), a role that required him to sing and play the guitar. Haines is said to have arranged the dances for Shadwell's multimedia production of *The Tempest* that opened at Dorset Garden on 30 April 1674 and he certainly spoke the introduction and prologue to Thomas Duffet's *The Mock-Tempest* (November 1674; 1675) that was intended to 'draw the Town from the Duke's Theatre'. In the early months of 1675 Haines played Sparkish in Wycherley's *The Country Wife*, Rodrigo in *Othello*, and a Swordsman in John Fletcher's *A King and No King* in the King's Company's new theatre in Drury Lane. In Sir Francis Fane's *Love in the Dark* (May 1675; 1675), Haines played Visconti, one of the three gentlemen of Milano, and spoke Rochester's epilogue. Haines was in frequent legal difficulties, both with his creditors and with the theatre management. During summer seasons in Oxford he augmented his salary by playing the famous Italian mountebank Signor Salmatius and telling fortunes. In June 1677 he was apprehended 'for reciteinge . . . [an undetermined] Scurrilous & obscoene Epilogue' (*BDAA*, VII 11) and in April 1679, with others of the King's Company, he absconded and joined Thomas Sydserf's company in Edinburgh. Here Elizabeth Knepp, Pepys's 'mad-humoured' inamorata, became his mistress and died in childbirth (Pepys, 6 December 1665; *BDAA*, IX 57–8).

Nothing is known of the origins or education of Henry **Harris** (*c.* 1634–1704). He first appears as a party of the first part to the contract establishing Sir William Davenant's Duke's Company in November 1660. He was a singer admired by Pepys, a dancer (he could 'handle [a pike] in a dance to admiration' (Pepys, 25 February 1669)), an actor (he played Horatio to Betterton's Hamlet), and a minor court official (yeoman of the revels and chief engraver of seals) with quarters in the Cockpit at Whitehall. In April 1668 upon the death of Sir William Davenant, Harris became co-patentee with Betterton of the Duke's Company. The next month he created the role of Sir Positive At-All in Shadwell's *The Sullen Lovers* (2 May 1667; 1668), mimicking Sir Robert Howard. In that same month he explained to Pepys the activities of the Ballers, in whose company

Rochester enjoyed 'dancing naked' with the 'ladies' of Mother Bennett's bordello (Rochester *Letters* 1980, 63; Pepys, 30 May 1668). In December 1663, in a highly successful revival of *Henry VIII*, Hart played Cardinal Wolsey, in which role John Greenhill painted his portrait. By the 1670s Harris's financial interest in the Duke's Company was about eighteen per cent and he moved into an apartment in the front of the building that housed the Dorset Garden playhouse. He married Anne Sears (?) in January 1672 and was sued for non-support in January 1676 (*BDAA*, VII 129–30). Harris created the role of Medley in Etherege's *The Man of Mode* mimicking the dress and mannerisms of Sir Charles Sedley. In 1678 Nell Gwyn complained that Lord Dorset spent 'all day long' drinking ale with Harris and Shadwell 'at the Dukes House' and in April 1681 Harris retired from the stage (*BDAA*, VII 130).

Charles **Hart** (*c.* 1630–83) began his career before the Civil War, playing women's parts at the Blackfriars theatre. When the theatres were closed in 1642, he enlisted in the royalist army and rose to the rank of lieutenant in Prince Rupert's regiment of cavalry. After the defeat at Worcester in September 1651, Hart returned to London and began playing in clandestine productions at the Cockpit in Drury Lane. In November 1660 he joined the King's Company, of which Thomas Killigrew was the patentee. He was not only one of the company's leading actors and active shareholders, but some time after 1663 he also became co-manager with Michael Mohun and John Lacy. He specialized in playing royalty and was so successful that it was said at court that '*Hart* might Teach any King on Earth how to Comport himself' (Downes 1987, 41). But he also played Mosca in *Volpone* (January 1665), Hotspur in *1 Henry IV* (November 1667), and Ranger in Wycherley's *Love in a Wood* (March 1671; 1672). The lover of Nell Gwyn and Lady Castlemaine – 'by this means [Lady Castlemaine] is even with the Kings love to [Moll] Davis' (Pepys, 7 April 1668) – was typecast as Horner in Etherege's *The Country Wife* (January 1675). No portrait of this kingly lover is known to exist, and he never married.

The Honourable Edward **Howard** (1624–*c.* 1700), the fifth son of Thomas Howard, 1st Earl of Berkshire, by Elizabeth Cecil, daughter of William Cecil, 2nd Earl of Exeter, seems to have attended neither Oxford nor Cambridge. But he became 'addicted . . . to the Study of

Dramatick Poetry' (Langbaine 1691, 274) none the less. His first effort, *The Usurpers, a Tragedy* (January 1664; 1668) was said to be 'no good play' (Pepys, 2 January 1664) and was revived only once. *The Brittish Princes: an Heroick Poem* (1669), 'this worthless poem' (*DNB*, X 12), was published with commendatory verses by Roger Boyle, Earl of Orrery, author of *Parthenissa* (two editions: 1654, 1665), and by Sir John Denham but never reprinted. Howard's fourth play, *The Six Days Adventure, or The New Utopia* (March 1671; 1671) suffered 'a Miscarriage . . . in Acting' and was not revived. Buckhurst's reputation as a satirist is based on *To Mr. Edward Howard, on his Incomparable, Incomprehensible Poem called The British Princes* (1669) and *On Mr. Edward Howard upon his 'New Utopia'* (1671), and Howard's 'language . . . at the rehearsal of his Plays' is mocked in Buckingham's *The Rehearsal* (December 1671; 1672). But Howard survived these attacks to publish a second epic poem, *Caroloiades, or The Rebellion of Forty One*, which achieved two editions (1689, 1695).

Lady Elizabeth **Howard** (1656–81), the second daughter and co-heir of James Howard, 3rd Earl of Suffolk, by his second wife Barbara Villiers, daughter of Sir Edward Villiers, 'dont la beauté & la jeunesse avoient quelque chose d'éblouïssant, était aimée de tous ceux qui la voyoient' (whose youth and beauty were so dazzling that everyone who saw her fell in love with her) (Marie Catherine Jumelle de Berneville, comtesse d'Aulnoy, *Mémoires de la cour d'Angleterre*, 2 vols. (1695), I 277). Her father was, like Rochester, a gentleman of the bedchamber and her mother was groom of the stole to Queen Catherine. It seems unlikely that she stole a dildo from her mother (40.24), but it is a matter of stage history that she spoke Rochester's prologue in the production at court of Settle's *The Empress of Morocco c.* May 1673 (Boswell 1932, 131–4). Much against her parents' wishes she eloped with Thomas Felton of Playford, 'a harmless little man and an excellent jockey' (Wilson 1976, 239), who was a groom of the King's bedchamber, and comptroller of the household to Queen Catherine. Whatever her behaviour, her reputation was uniformly bad (ibid., 38, 47, 57, 82; *POAS*, Yale, II 224). 'Son humeur enjoüée ne la mettoit pas en état de jetter des pierres à ses Amans' (her playful manner did not dispose her to scare off lovers) (d'Aulnoy, I 277), who were said to include the Duke of Monmouth, William Cavendish, the future Duke of Devonshire, and 'bold' Frank Newport.

Sir Robert **Howard** (1626–98) was the sixth son of Thomas Howard, 1st Earl of Berkshire, by Elizabeth Cecil, daughter of William Cecil, 2nd Earl of Exeter. His stage career probably began in 1634 when a 'Mr. Robert Howard' played in a production at court of Thomas Carew's masque, *Coelum Britannicum.* The basis for Howard's later friendship with Rochester (Rochester *Letters* 1980, 78, 115) may lie in the fact that in June 1644 he was knighted on the battlefield for his heroism in rescuing Lord Wilmot of Adderbury who was wounded in a skirmish on the Cherwell. In Parliament, where he sat for Stockbridge, Hampshire (1661–79) and Castle Rising, Norfolk (1679–98), he was a very active but irresolute member: he was listed as a court dependant in 1664, went into opposition in the session of 1666–7, and was one of the five 'recanters' who deserted the country party in 1669; Shaftesbury put him down as 'vile' in 1679 (*HoP 1660–1690*, II 595–600). On one occasion he entertained the House by 'maintain[ing] a contradiction *in terminis*, in the face of three hundred persons' (Dryden 1956– , IX 5). His career as a playwright began successfully with *The Committee* (November 1662; 1665), 'one of the most popular of all Restoration comedies', and with the play that introduced 'Caterwalling in the Modern Heroic Way', *The Indian Queen* (January 1664; 1665), written in collaboration with his brother-in-law, John Dryden (Oliver 1963, 50; Butler 1928, 135). But it also included a tedious dispute with Dryden over rhyme in stage plays and *The Surprisal* (April 1662; 1665), a comedy in blank verse so ragged that the compositor set the first four pages as prose (Oliver 1963, 47). Before Dryden succeeded to the role, Howard was the original Mr Bayes in Buckingham's *The Rehearsal* (December 1671; 1672). He was also immortalized in Shadwell's *The Sullen Lovers* (May 1668; 1668) as Sir Positive At-All, 'so foolishly Positive, that he will never be convinced of an Error, though never so grosse' (Shadwell 1927, I 14). After collaborating with Buckingham in *The Country Gentleman*, which was prohibited from the stage and never printed (Pepys, 6 March 1669), Howard wrote no more plays. His career in the marriage market was equally unsuccessful. In February 1645 he married Anne Kingsmill, but the love poems in his *Poems* (1660) were, he said, 'unassisted by the influence of a mistress'. In

August 1665 he married Lady Honora, daughter of Henry O'Brien, 6th Earl of Thomond, and the widow of Sir Francis Englefield, 3rd Baronet, who was at least ten years older than he was but worth £2,000 a year. The marriage was a failure and Howard's 'W[hore Mary] *Uphill*', it was said, 'spends all, and . . . refuses to marry him' (Marvell(?) 1677, 9). Howard made a fortune, however, in buying and selling court offices, post-fines, and country estates. His plum was his post as auditor of receipts in the Exchequer, worth £3,000 a year, which he held from 1673 to 1698. In November 1677, charged with embezzlement, he defended himself successfully before the privy council, but his retention in office is regarded today as 'little short of a major disaster' for the Exchequer (*HoP 1660–1690*, II 603).

Hyde, see **Clarendon**.

Henry **Jermyn** (1636–1708), the future Baron Dover of Dover, was the second son of Thomas Jermyn of Rushbroke, Suffolk, the younger brother of Thomas Jermyn, 2nd Baron Jermyn, and a nephew of Henry Jermyn, 1st Earl of St Albans. Despite his small size, 'big head and spindle-shanks', 'to get what he wanted' from women, 'he had only to open his mouth' (Hamilton 1930, 101). During the Interregnum he went into exile with the household of the Duke of York and gained the reputation of a liaison with Mary Stuart, the widowed Princess of Orange and sister of Charles II (Pepys, 21 December 1660). A Roman Catholic, Jermyn was promoted master of the horse to the Duke of York in 1660. In England his most distinguished intrigues were with Anne Maria Brudenell, Countess of Shrewsbury, and with Barbara Villiers, Countess of Castlemaine: 'young Jermin . . . hath of late lain with her oftener then the King . . . . The King . . . is mad at her entertaining Jermin, and she is mad at Jermin's going to marry from her' (Pepys, 29 July 1667). Not until April 1675 did Jermyn marry Judith Poley, daughter of Sir Edmund Poley of Badley, Suffolk, and 'a conceited country wench' (Hamilton 1930, 323).

Jermyn, see **St Albans**.

Thomas **Killigrew**, the dramatist and favourite of Charles II, married as his second wife Charlotte de Hesse (1629–?) at The Hague in January 1655. Killigrew was bankrupt and his wife, seventeen years his junior, was heiress to a fortune of £10,000. Upon the Restoration she was appointed to positions in the Queen's household and became *ex officio* 'Lady Killigrew' but in the verses *On the Court Ladyes* (1664) she is said to be 'whore enough' (Elmer L. Brooks, *ELN* 10 (March 1973), 204). Killigrew was appointed a gentleman of the bedchamber and the first patentee of the King's Company of Players. When he rallied Rochester for keeping his wife in the country, Rochester struck Killigrew in the King's presence. Charles ignored the attack, forcing Killigrew to pocket the insult, but Rochester asked 'pardon of Harry Killigrew for the affront he offered his father' (HMC *Seventh Report*, 531). Edward Montagu, Earl of Sandwich, heard that Rochester was banished from the court, but Pepys saw him walking with Charles the next morning 'as free as ever' (Pepys, 17 February 1669).

Mary or Mall **Kirke** (?–1711), the second daughter of George Kirke by his second wife, Mary Townshend, and the sister of Percy Kirke, was appointed a maid of honour to Mary of Modena, Duchess of York, in 1674. She was consecutively or simultaneously mistress to the Duke of York, the Duke of Monmouth, and the Earl of Mulgrave. After the scandal culminating in her brother's duel with Mulgrave in July 1675 (91.53), she was turned out of St James's Palace (*Savile Correspondence*, 39) and retired to a convent in Paris. There she became first the mistress and, after his wife's death in 1676, the second wife of Sir Thomas Vernon of Hodnet, Shropshire, a teller of the Exchequer (Wilson 1976, 259).

Mary or Moll Birkhead (1631–after 1696), the daughter of a London tavern-keeper in the parish of St Gregory and the sister of Henry Birkhead the poet, apparently studied music with Henry Lawes: some commendatory verses by her are prefixed to Lawes's *Second Book of Ayres* (1655). She became estranged from her husband, Henry Geery, whom she had married in July 1649. Ten years later she had become 'the famous Singer Mrs **Knight**' (Evelyn, 19 May 1659). By 1671 she had become a mistress of Charles II, a confidante of Nell Gwyn – whom traditionally she introduced to the King – and a neighbour of the Duchess of Cleveland in Berkshire House. In February 1675 in the production at court of Crowne's *Calisto, or The Chaste Nymph* she played the parts of Peace in a costume 'of silver tabby covered all over with silver and gold lace' and Daphne the shepherdess in 'a white straw hat and with a crook' (Boswell, 1932, 306, 328). In a will dated 1693, by which he left her five shillings, her brother funded the Oxford Chair of Poetry 'as far as it can be for ever' and appointed 'Mrs. Mary Knight *alias* Geery my sister' an executor of the trust. Mrs Knight declined the honour (J. W. Mackail, *Henry Birkhead and the Foundation of the Oxford Chair of Poetry* (1908), 6–7).

John Maitland, 2nd Earl of **Lauderdale** (1616–82), was the eldest surviving son of John Maitland, 1st Earl of Lauderdale, by Isobel, daughter of Alexander Seton, Earl of Dunfermline, lord high chancellor of Scotland. He first met Charles Stuart in August 1648 aboard ship in the Downs where he presented an invitation to the Prince of Wales to join the Scots army in an invasion of England (which Cromwell terminated a week later at Preston). He joined Charles II in Holland and was with the King (and the Duke of Buckingham and Henry Wilmot, Viscount Wilmot of Athlone) when the King vanished through the north gate of Worcester after the débâcle of 3 September 1651. Lauderdale was captured and imprisoned until General Monk's entry into London in March 1660. He then rejoined Charles II at Breda and accompanied him back to Whitehall, where he was installed in lodgings between the Stone Gallery and the Privy Gardens (*English Illustrated Magazine*, 1 (1883), 79). As 'the only Scot Charles actually liked' (Fraser 1979, 60), Lauderdale served as secretary of state for Scotland from January 1661 to October 1680 and lord high commissioner for Parliament from 1669 until he was replaced by the Duke of York in 1679. He ruled Scotland for Charles II 'more like the vizier of an oriental sovereign than the servant of a constitutional king' (*DNB*, XII 809). He provided the 'l' for the Cabal ministry of 1667–73. Something of his political orientation and his 'northern tone' are preserved in *A Dream of the Cabal*: 'De'il hoop his lugs [Devil box his ears] that loves a parliament! / Twa houses, aw my saul are twa too mickle. / They'll gar the laird shall ne'er have more a prickle [Parliament will emasculate the King], / Na siller get to gie the bonny lass' (*POAS*, Yale, I 193–4). In May and June 1672 Lauderdale was elevated to a dukedom and nominated Knight of the Garter. In 1679 he was made a privy councillor. In the same year Shaftesbury found it convenient to attack the King through the sides of Lauderdale. In May 1678 an address to remove Lauderdale was lost by only one vote in the House of Commons and in 1680 he was deprived of all his offices. 'Hating Lautherdale' (Rochester *Letters* 1980, 193) was a popular pastime. 'He made a very ill appearance: He was very big: His hair red, hanging odly about him: His tongue was too big for his mouth, which made him bedew all that he talked to: And his whole manner was rough and boisterous, and very unfit for a Court' (Burnet 1724–34, I 101).

Nathaniel **Lee** (1648?–92), 'except for Dryden . . . the most popular and successful dramatist of his day', was the son of an Anglican churchman who made public confession of his multiple apostasies during the Interregnum and was rewarded by appointment as a chaplain in ordinary to Charles II (Lee 1954, I 1–2, 10). Lee was educated at Charterhouse and Trinity College, Cambridge, whence he graduated B.A. in 1669. According to tradition he was brought up to London by George Villiers, Duke of Buckingham, chancellor of Cambridge University, and abandoned. Like Otway, he turned to playwrighting when he failed as an actor (Downes 1987, 72–3). His first play, *The Tragedy of Nero, Emperour of Rome* (May 1674; 1675), mostly in rhyme, was also a failure and was not revived. In the dedication to Rochester, Lee remarked drily that the play had been 'sufficiently censur'd' (Lee 1954, I 24). Lee's second play, *Sophonisba, or Hannibal's Overthrow* (May 1675; 1676), achieved the success he sought. With Elizabeth Cox in the title role and Michael Mohun playing Hannibal, it 'receiv'd some applause upon the stage', as Lee allows in his dedication to Louise de Kéroualle, Duchess of Portsmouth, and reigning mistress at court. Rochester may have known that shortly after the production of Lee's third play, *Gloriana, or The Court of Augustus Caesar* (February 1676; 1676), Lee 'joined the circle of the Earl of Mulgrave, Rochester's chief enemy, a group in which John Dryden was the leading figure' (Lee 1954, I 81, 12). Thereafter, with Dryden's generous encouragement and collaboration, Lee wrote four successful plays that were repeatedly revived into the nineteenth century: *The Rival Queens, or The Death of Alexander the Great* (March 1677; 1677), *Mithridates, King of Pontus* (February 1678; 1679), *Oedipus* (September 1678; 1679), and *Theodosius, or The Force of Love* (September 1680; 1682), for which Henry Purcell wrote his first music for the stage (Downes 1987, 80). Lee's last words on Rochester, spoken by Duke Nemours in *The Princess of Cleve* (1680–82?; 1689), are reproduced on p. xxi above. Montague Summers and Robert D. Hume argue that Nemours himself, 'a Ruffian reeking' from the stews, represents Rochester (Montague Summers, *The Playhouse of Pepys* (1935), 301; Robert D. Hume, *JEGP* 75 (1976), 117–38; Lee 1954, II 162, 153). But the evidence is equivocal: Nemours is 'black sanguine Brawny' (Lee 1954, II 159) whereas Rochester's portraits show a slight, fair, almost girlish figure.

Aside from the record of her supporting roles in the productions of the Duke's Company – she created the part of Mrs Rich in Etherege's *The Comical Revenge, or Love in a Tub* (March 1664; 1664) – there are few traces of Jane **Long** (*fl.* 1661–78). She was the mistress of Charles Stuart, 3rd Duke of Richmond, who died in December 1672. The next year, after playing Lady Macduff in a revival of Sir William Davenant's adaptation of *Macbeth* (February 1673; 1673), Long left the stage to become the mistress of a much older man, George Porter, a groom of the bedchamber to Charles II. Leaving his wife in London, Porter retired to Berkshire, and his visit to London in December 1677 is recounted in Henry Savile's letter to Rochester: 'the rogue is grown soe ravenous that now hee surfeits of everything hee sees but Mrs. Long and his [dissolute] sonn Nobbs' (Rochester *Letters* 1980, 175).

Hortense Mancini, known as the Duchess of **Mazarin** in England (1646–99), was born in Rome, the youngest child of Michele Lorenzo Mancini and Girolama Mazzarino, the sister of Cardinal Mazarin, first minister of France from December 1647 to March 1661. She was brought to Paris in March 1653 with her older sister Maria, for whom the young Louis XIV had conceived a violent passion. In the Convent of the Visitation in the Faubourg St Jacques she developed into the most beautiful of Mazarin's five nieces. Her portrait by Sir Peter Lely is the original of Sophia Western's dark eyes, black hair, and perfect Roman nose (*Tom Jones* (1749), IV ii). From among her numerous suitors, including Charles Stuart of England during his *Wanderjahre* (Hartmann 1926, 41–2), Mancini chose as her husband Armand-Charles de la Porte, marquis de la Meilleraye, for whom Mazarin provided a dowry of 28,000,000 livres, making him 'the Richest subject in Europ' (Evelyn, 15 June 1699), with a new title, duc Mazarin. The couple were married in February 1661 but the duke was a *dévot* who believed himself inspired – the original (according to stage tradition) of Orgon in Molière's *Tartuffe* (February 1669) – and the marriage was not happy. The duchess sued for separate maintenance in 1666 and retired to a convent. In June 1668, however, she fled to Switzerland in the company of the notorious Louis, Prince de Rohan-Gueménée and began the *Wanderjahre* that made her famous. While she was living in the palace of Chambéry as a guest of the Duke of Savoy, her favourite nightingale was eaten by rats (Hartmann 1926, 138). In November 1675 she reached London and was seen at court on 8 December. Charles II set her up in an apartment in St James's Palace – an awkward arrangement that required him to retire in the bedchamber, rise, dress, and slip across St James's Park – and gave her a pension of £3,000 a year, 'another French whore', as the anonymous satirist quickly and not wholly accurately observed (*POAS*, Yale, I 279). Like Nell Gwyn she seems to have had little political ambition, but her *avant garde* salon, featuring Isaak Vossius and Charles de Marguetel de Saint-Evremond, attracted the best minds and greatest wits in London. Mazarin amused herself with what the scientists now call extra-pair copulation, with gambling for high stakes, and with her aviary, which boasted a white sparrow and a talking starling named Jacob. That her favourite game was blindman's buff may not be without historical significance (Hartmann 1926, 237–8, 142). Saint-Evremond called her 'la plus belle femme du monde' and a few weeks before his death the King was observed 'toying with his Concubines Portsmouth, Cleaveland, & Mazarine' while a French boy sang love songs (Evelyn, 6 February 1685).

Sir Thomas **Meres** (1634–1715) was educated at Sidney Sussex College, Cambridge, and the Middle Temple. He was elected to Parliament in April, called to the bar in May, and knighted in June 1660. 'In the Cavalier Parliament [where he sat for Lincoln] Meres was distinguished by the sheer volume of his activity. He was named to 686 committees, delivered well over 500 reported speeches and 109 reports.' In February 1673 he was rebuked by Henry Coventry because he 'laboured to make a distinction in the House between the country gentlemen and the courtiers . . . and often used the words "of this side of that House, and that side", which were not parliamentary' (*HoP 1660–1690*, III 49, 52). Despite his opposition to the court, he became Charles's candidate for speaker in March 1679 when Sir Charles Seymour was again elected (*CSPD 1679–80*, 98) and the Whigs believed that 'turncoat Meres' had been bought by the court (*POAS*, Yale, II 295).

Laura Martinozzi, Duchess of **Modena** (?–1687) was another niece of Cardinal Mazarin and a sister of Anna Maria Martinozzi, princesse de Conti. Upon the death of her husband, Alphonso IV, Duke of Modena, in July 1662, she succeeded as regent and went to war with Mantua over some islands in the Po that separated the two dukedoms. Cardinal Mazarin, who ruled France during the minority of Louis XIV, urged her to propose her daughter, Maria Beatrice d'Este, as a second wife for the Duke of York upon the death of Anne Hyde in March 1671. She came to England in November 1673 in the wedding party and returned to Modena in January 1674. Upon the succession of her son, Francesco II, in 1676, she retired to Rome.

Maria Beatrice d'Este, called Mary of **Modena** in England (1658–1718), was the only daughter of Alphonso IV of Modena and Laura Martinozzi. Upon the death of her father in July 1662, her mother assumed the government of the duchy as regent for her son. Maria Beatrice's wish was to enter the Convent of the Visitation that her mother had founded in Modena. Until she was proposed at the age of thirteen as the Duke of York's second wife, she had never heard of England or the Duke of York. The Duke on the other hand regarded her as the illegitimate daughter of Louis XIV, who provided a dowry of 400,000 crowns (Ogg 1956, I 378). She married the Duke in Modena on 30 September 1673 with Henry Mordaunt, Earl of Peterborough, as proxy and again at Dover on 21 November 1673. Upon her first sight of the Duke, who was forty, she burst into tears.

Michael **Mohun** (1620–84) began his career as a boy actor, probably in Queen Henrietta's Company. When the theatres were closed in 1642, he enlisted in the royalist army, was wounded at the siege of Dublin (1646), and spent thirteen months as a prisoner of war. When released, he joined the regiment of William Cavendish, Earl of Newcastle, in Dixmüde and rose to the rank of major. In February 1658, in an entertainment given by Newcastle in Antwerp for the royal family, Mohun appeared in a black satin robe and a garland of bays to recite Newcastle's verses prophesying the restoration of Charles II (*CSPD 1657–8*, 296, 311). Even before the Restoration Mohun returned to London and formed a company to play at the Red Bull, an open-air theatre in St John's Street, Clerkenwell. When Sir William Davenant and Thomas Killigrew were able to enforce their exclusive patents from Charles II, Mohun joined the King's Company under Killigrew. In November 1660, in the converted tennis court in Vere Street by Clare Market, he revived a role that he had played before the wars, Bellamente in James Shirley's *Loves Cruelty* (1631) (James Wright, *Historia Histrionica* (1699), 3). In the role of Goswin in Fletcher and Massinger's *The Beggar's Bush*, he was 'said to be the best actor in the world' (Pepys, 20 November 1660). In May 1663 he played Leontius in John Fletcher's *The Humourous Lieutenant* (*c.* 1620) at the opening of the new Theatre Royal in Bridges Street. About the same time he married Ann Bird, the daughter of Theophilus Bird with whom he had played before the Civil War. The Bridges Street theatre was destroyed by fire in January 1672, but a month later the King's Company reopened in the Lincoln's Inn Fields playhouse recently vacated by the Duke's Company, with Mohun playing Valentine in John Fletcher's *Wit without Money* (*c.* 1614) before Charles II. He also spoke Dryden's prologue addressed to the King. In 1672–3 Mohun played roles in three of Dryden's new plays: Rhodophil in *Marriage à la Mode*, the Duke of Mantona in *The Assignation, or Love in a Nunnery*, and Mr Beamont in *Amboyna*. On 26 March 1674, Christopher Wren's new Theatre Royal off Drury Lane opened with another revival of *The Beggar's Bush*. Mohun read Dryden's prologue apologizing for the plainness of the new house with its 'mean ungilded stage' (in contrast to the magnificence of the Dorset Garden theatre) and warning 'That as a Fire the former house o'erthrew, / Machines and Tempests will destroy the new', with its pointed reference to the Duke's Company's spectacular production of Shadwell's semi-opera, *The Tempest* (April 1674; 1674) (Dryden 1882–93, X 318–29). Although a Roman Catholic, Mohun is buried in the Church of St Giles-in-the-Fields.

James Scott, Duke of **Monmouth** (1649–85), the eldest of the fourteen acknowledged bastards of Charles II (GEC, VI 706–8), was born in Rotterdam. In 1657 he was taken from his mother, Lucy Walter, and placed in the Collège de Notre Dame de Verluz at Colombes near Paris. William Crofts, whose name he took, was appointed his governor and raised to the peerage as Baron Crofts of Saxham. When he was brought to England in July 1662 by Henrietta Maria, the Queen Mother, Pepys saw that he was 'a most pretty sparke of about 15 year old' and began hearing rumours that Charles had married his mother (Pepys, 27 October 1662). Marriage with a twelve-year-old heiress, Anne Scott, Countess of Buccleuch in her own right, was soon arranged and solemnized in April 1663. Besides a bride, James got a new name, Scott. His father's love for him is shown not only in the large sums of money lavished on him (GEC, IX 61, note b), but also in the titles and honours heaped upon him: Duke of Monmouth and Buccleuch, Earl of Doncaster and Dalkeith, Lord Scott of Tynedale, Whichester, and Eskdale, lord great chamberlain of Scotland, lord-lieutenant of the East Riding of Yorkshire, governor of Kingston-upon-Hull, chief justice in Eyre of all His Majesty's forests, chases, parks, and warrens on the south side of Trent, lord general of all His Majesty's land forces, captain of His Majesty's Life Guards of Horse, chancellor of the University of Cambridge, master of horse to the King, one of the lords of the privy council, and Knight of the Order of the Garter (Dryden 1882–93, IX 222n.). Pepys further noticed that 'the Duke of Monmouth is the most skittish, leaping gallant that ever I saw, always in action, vaulting or leaping or clambering' (Pepys, 26 July 1665). Besides six children by his wife, Monmouth had four more by his mistress, Eleanor Needham. In January 1668 he acted in a revival at court of Dryden's *The Indian Emperor* (April 1665; 1667). In May 1670, during negotiation of the secret treaty of Dover (to which he was not privy), Monmouth entertained the court at a command performance of John Caryll's *Sir Salomon, or The Cautious Coxcomb* by giving the comedian James Nokes his sword and sword-belt and buckling it on himself 'on purpose to Ape the *French*' (Downes 1987, 64). In February 1675 he danced in the performance at court of Crowne's *Calisto*. In March 1671 Monmouth was involved in a brawl in Whetstone Park in which a parish officer was killed (*CSPD 1671*, 183). Monmouth first saw military action in the second Dutch War aboard the Duke of York's flagship in the battle of Lowestoft (3 June 1665). Thereafter he served with distinction in four campaigns on the Continent – three in the French army (the failed march on Amsterdam in 1672, the siege of Maastricht in 1673, the capture of Valenciennes, Cambrai, and St Omer in 1677) and one with William of Orange (St Denis in 1678) – and one in Scotland (Bothwell Bridge in 1679). By September 1679, however, Monmouth had so completely identified himself with Shaftesbury, the Green Ribbon Club, and the country opposition that Charles dismissed him as lord general of the army and ordered him to The Hague. Two months later Monmouth returned to London to the wild acclamation of the people. When he refused the King's orders to return to The Hague, he became technically an outlaw. On 24 July 1680, two days before Rochester's death, Paul de Barillon told Louis XIV that the Duke of Monmouth as he left London to begin his western progress (Dryden 1956– , II 25–8), 'is now more considerable than anybody else' (Forneron, 1897, 238).

Elizabeth Wriothesley, Countess of Northumberland, later Lady **Montagu** (*c.* 1646–90), was the sixth and youngest daughter of Thomas Wriothesley, Earl of Southampton, lord high treasurer (1660–67), by his second wife, Elizabeth Leigh, daughter of Francis Leigh, 1st Earl of Chichester. One of the great beauties of her day, she married in December 1662 Joceline Percy, who succeeded as 11th and last Earl of Northumberland in 1668. In September 1669 Lord and Lady Northumberland, accompanied by John Locke, newly elected Fellow of the Royal Society, as their personal physician, left England for Italy. Lord Northumberland died in Turin in May 1670, leaving only a daughter, Lady Elizabeth Percy. Back in England the nineteen-year-old William Seymour, 3rd Duke of Somerset, is said to have died for love of the young widow in December 1671, but she failed to become the second Duchess of York. So in September 1672 Lady Northumberland settled in Paris. There she encountered Ralph Montagu, the past and future British ambassador, who had conducted 'the disgraceful negotiations' leading to the secret Treaty of Dover in 1670 (GEC, IX 107, note b). Montagu was 'a person not at all formidable as far as his face was concerned', but 'witty . . . and passably malicious' (Hamilton 1930, 115, 284). His gallantry to Lady Northumberland aroused the jealousy of Maria Madeleine Pioche de la Vergne, comtesse de La Fayette, the novelist whose salon he frequented. In August 1673 the Countess of Northumberland became 'the countess of Rafe' (40.29) by marrying Ralph Montagu, who did not succeed as Earl of Montagu until 1689.

Betty **Morris** (or Morrice) (*fl.* 1667–73) was a popular prostitute celebrated as 'bonny Black Bess' who 'knows how . . . / To kill us by looking as if she would die' in Buckhurst's song *Methinks the poor town has been troubled too long* and a bawd whose establishment may have been 'in Brick-Court against the dead wall in Westminster', convenient to the Houses of Parliament (Dorset 1979, 90).

That Mother **Moseley** (*fl.* 1673–89) was a bawd is attested by two independent sources and a third claims that Anthony Ashley Cooper, 1st Earl of Shaftesbury, frequented her establishment (Thomas Duffet, *The Empress of Morocco. A Farce* (1674), 34; *POAS*, Yale, II 106; Wilson 1976, 218, 220), but little more is known.

John Sheffield (1648–1721) was the only son of Edmund Sheffield, 2nd Earl of Mulgrave, by Elizabeth Cranfield, daughter of Lionel Cranfield, 1st Earl of Middlesex. He succeeded as 3rd Earl of **Mulgrave** in 1658. Like Rochester, Mulgrave volunteered for sea duty in the second Dutch War and saw action off Lowestoft (June 1665). In June 1667 he was commissioned captain in the army, but unsuccessfully opposed Monmouth for captaincy of the King's Own Troop of Horse Guards. After an illness forced Rochester to decline a duel with him for an insult that not even Mulgrave believed that Rochester had delivered, Mulgrave felt obliged to ruin Rochester's 'reputation as to courage' (Buckingham 1723, II 8, 10). Mulgrave volunteered again for sea duty in the third Dutch War and saw action at Solebay (May 1672). In January 1673 he was promoted colonel and his Old Holland regiment served one campaign on the Continent under Turenne (Dalton 1960, I 76, 136, 163). In 1682 at the age of thirty-four he was deprived of all offices and banished from the court for making love to Princess Anne (aged seventeen). But he succeeded in marrying into the royal family in March 1706 when he took the Lady Katherine Darnley, illegitimate daughter of James, Duke of York, and the mad Atossa (Pope 1939–67, III ii 57–8), to live with him as his third wife in the original of Buckingham Palace, which he built in 1703.

Little is known of the origins or early life of James **Nokes** (?–1696). Like Thomas Betterton he began his career before the

Restoration playing women's parts in John Rhodes's company at the Cockpit in Drury Lane and joined Sir William Davenant's Duke's Company at the Salisbury Court theatre in November 1660. He specialized in comic roles and soon attracted the attention of Charles II. He created the role of Puny in Cowley's *The Cutter of Coleman Street* (December 1661; 1663), played the Nurse in *Romeo and Juliet* (March 1662), and created the role of Poet Ninny in Shadwell's *The Sullen Lovers* (May 1668; 1668). In May 1670 in a command performance of John Caryll's *Sir Salomon, or The Cautious Coxcomb* to entertain the King's sister, Henrietta Anne, Duchess of Orléans, Nokes played Sir Arthur Addle: 'The *French* Court wearing then Excessive short Lac'd Coats . . . with Broad wa[i]st Belts; Mr. *Nokes* having . . . one shorter than the *French* Fashion . . . lookt more like a Drest up Ape, than a Sir *Arthur*: Which upon his first Entrance on the Stage, put the King and Court to an Excessive Laughter; at which the *French* look'd very Shaggrin, to see themselves Ap'd by such a Buffoon' (Downes 1987, 64). Colley Cibber thought that Nokes's best roles were Sir Nicholas Cully in Etherege's *The Comical Revenge* (March 1664; 1664), the title role in Dryden's *Sir Martin Mar-all* (August 1667; 1668) written 'purposely' to be played by Nokes (Downes 1987, 62), and Barnaby Brittle in Thomas Betterton's *The Amorous Widow* (*c.* 1669; 1706) (Cibber 1740, 85). But the role that pleased the King 'above all Plays' was that of Mr Jorden in Edward Ravenscroft's adaptation of Molière's *Le Bourgeois Gentilhomme* (October 1670), entitled *The Citizen Turn'd Gentleman* (July 1672; 1672) (Downes 1987, 69–70). By 1674, when he had acquired one and a half shares in the Duke's Company, Nokes had only to walk on stage to arouse laughter and 'involuntary Applause'. His name became a common noun (see Glossary) and his acting established a powerful tradition on the English stage. 'I have still', Cibber wrote, 'the Sound of every Line he spoke, in my Ear' (Cibber 1740, 85–6).

Roger Boyle, Earl of **Orrery** (1621–79), was the third son of Richard Boyle, 1st Earl of Cork, by his second wife, Catherine Fenton, daughter of Sir Geoffrey Fenton of Dublin. At his father's request he was created 1st Baron of Broghill in April 1628. He was educated at Trinity College, Dublin, at Gray's Inn, and in travel abroad (1636–9). In September 1640 he carried £1,000 in gold from his father to Charles I in Westminster. Upon the occasion of his marriage to Margaret Howard, daughter of Theophilus Howard, 2nd Earl of Suffolk, Sir John Suckling wrote *Ballad upon a Wedding*, a 'masterpiece of sportive gaiety' (*DNB*, XIX 144). Broghill began the Civil War as a captain of cavalry and distinguished himself in putting down the Irish Rebellion of 1641–3, but after his defection to Parliament in July 1644 he became general of the horse in Munster, master of ordnance, and one of Cromwell's principal advisers. He was one of three genuine peers who sat in Cromwell's 'Other House' in January 1658 and it was Broghill who urged Cromwell to assume the crown. In January 1660 he defected again and seized Dublin Castle for Charles II. Charles II knew him to be 'a rogue' (HMC *Ormonde MSS*., n.s. IV 243) but allowed him to remain in Dublin as one of the governors of Ireland (January 1660–February 1662) and made him Earl of Orrery in September 1660. In Parliament Orrery sat for Arundel, Chichester (1660–79), as a court dependant whom Shaftesbury put down as 'doubly vile' in 1677 (*HoP 1660–1690*, I 703). In the seven theatrical seasons from 1663–4 to 1669–70 seven of Orrery's plays were produced by the Duke's Company, two comedies in prose and five rhymed heroic plays with 'the very same design and words and sense and plot as every one of his plays have' (Pepys, 8 December 1668). A successful, but deceitful, soldier and courtier, Orrery 'never made a bad figure but as an author' (Horace Walpole, *A Catalogue of the Royal and Noble Authors of England, Scotland, and Ireland*, ed. Thomas Park, 5 vols. (1806), V 191).

Thomas **Otway** (1652–85), the 'gentlest *Otway*' of William Collins's *Ode to Pity* (1747), is an important figure in the history of sentimental drama and the 'egotistical sublime'. He was born in a village in Sussex, the only child of the curate of Trotton, where the river Arun may have blended its murmurs with his nurse's song (cf. Wordsworth, *The Prelude*, I 271). He was educated at Winchester School and Christ Church, Oxford, but following the death of his father in February 1671 he left the university seven months later without taking a degree. In July 1671, however, the first play of another undergraduate, Elkanah Settle's *Cambyses, King of Persia*, was acted at the New Tennis Court in Oxford (Wood 1891–1900, II 226). In London in great financial straits Otway secured a few parts as an actor, but this career was 'dasht' by stage fright (Otway 1932, I 12n.; Downes 1987, 72). When he was trying to decipher 'puzzling Otway' (98.19), Rochester may have known no more of him than his poverty, his acquaintance with Aphra Behn and Thomas Shadwell, and the failure of his play *Alcibiades* (October 1675; 1675), worked up from Cornelius Nepos and Plutarch, very much in the manner of Elkanah Settle, including stage directions like 'A glorious Temple appears in the Ayr, where the Spirits of the happy are seated ... The whole body of the Temple moves downward ... They all vanish, and the SCENE changes again to the Tent' (Otway 1932, I 158–9). Although *Alcibiades*, in which seventeen-year-old Elizabeth Barry, Rochester's protégée, played her first part, was an embarrassment, it gained Otway the patronage of Rochester and the good opinion of the King and the Duke of York. Otway's second play, *Don Carlos King of Spain* (June 1676; 1676), dedicated to the Duke of York, played ten nights and 'got more Money than any preceding Modern Tragedy' (Downes 1987, 76). Otway's third play, *Titus and Berenice* (November 1676; 1677), adapted from Racine and dedicated to Rochester, was 'perfectly well Acted' by Betterton and Elizabeth Barry and had 'good Success' (Downes 1987, 79). In February 1678, however, Otway enlisted in the army, was commissioned an ensign in the Duke of Monmouth's regiment, and was sent to Holland. Promoted lieutenant in November 1678, he nevertheless returned to London early in 1679, 'a poor Disbanded Souldier' (Dalton 1960, I 208, 222; Otway 1932, I 520). In June 1679 he fought a duel with Colonel John Churchill. Most of Otway's later successes, including the two tragedies on which his historical importance is based, *The Orphan* (*c.* February 1680; 1680) with Barry as Monimia, *The Soldier's Fortune* (June 1680; 1681) with Barry as Lady Dunce, and *Venice Preserv'd* (February 1682; 1682), came during or after Rochester's final illness.

Samuel **Parker** (1640–88) was born in Northampton, where his father, John Parker, was a judge. He was 'puritanically educated' at Northampton grammar school and at Wadham College, Oxford, whence he graduated B.A. in February 1660, the month after Rochester's arrival there. Upon the Restoration Parker was reconciled to the Church of England and ordained a priest in 1664. His career as an Anglican apologist began in 1665 with the publication of

Tentamina physico-theologica de Deo, dedicated to Gilbert Sheldon, Archbishop of Canterbury. Parker was 'a Violent, passionate haughty man' who believed that the best body of divinity is 'that which would help a Man to keep a Coach and Six Horses' (Evelyn, 23 March 1688; *Somers Tracts*, 16 vols. (1748–95), II 509). 'It is not the Roman Clergy only that pretends the Kingdome of God to be of this world', Hobbes observed (Hobbes 1935, 518). Not surprisingly Parker rose rapidly in the church: chaplain to Archbishop Sheldon (1667), rector of Chartham, Kent (1667), archdeacon of Canterbury (1670), D.D., Cambridge, *per litteras regias* (1671) . . ., bishop of Oxford (1686), and James II's candidate for president of Magdalen College, Oxford (1687). He was dubbed 'Bayes', after the scapegoat dramatist in Buckingham's farce *The Rehearsal* (December 1671; 1672), by Andrew Marvell in *The Rehearsal Transpros'd* (1672), a reply to Parker's scurrilous preface to *Bishop Bramhall's Vindication of Himself and the Episcopal Clergy from the Presbyterian Charge of Popery* (1672). Parker responded with *A Reproof to the Rehearsal Transpos'd* (1673), but he did not reply to Marvell's counter-attack, *The Rehearsall Transpros'd: The Second Part* (1673), for 'the odds and victory lay on Marvell's side' (Wood 1813–20, IV 231).

Samuel **Pordage** (1633–91?), the son of John Pordage the astrologer and mystic by his first wife, Mary Lane, was educated at the Merchant Taylors' school and Lincoln's Inn. His first published work, *Poems upon Several Occasions* (1660), includes an adaptation of Seneca's *Troades* which seems never to have been produced. But compelled by the 'fantastical necessity imposed by fashion on a Gentleman', Pordage wrote a second play, *Herod and Mariamne*, about 1661 (*Remarques* 1673, 108; Langbaine 1691, 406). It was not produced, however, until Elkanah Settle took it in hand and secured a production at Lincoln's Inn Fields by the supporting players in the Duke's Company *c.* August 1673. Pordage's third and last play, *The Siege of Babylon* (*c.* September 1677; 1678), was produced in the sumptuous new Dorset Garden playhouse with Thomas Betterton and Henry Harris in leading roles. But it was never revived. By 1679 Pordage had become one of Shaftesbury's hacks and wrote 'a stupid poem', *Azaria and Hushai* (January 1682), in supposed reply to Dryden's *Absalom and Achitophel* (November 1681) and 'a very stupid poem', *The Medal Revers'd* (31 March 1682), in supposed reply to Dryden's *The Medal* (16 March 1682) (Dryden 1882–93, IX 353–4).

George **Porter** (1622?–83) was the eldest son of Endymion Porter, the poet, diplomat, and art collector, by Olivia Boteler. He began his career as a soldier and by the time of the battle of Marston Moor (July 1644), where he was wounded, he held the rank of major general of foot. But his real career was debauchery, and his brother-in-law, George Goring, Lord Goring, called him 'the best Company, but the worst Officer, that ever served the king' (Bulstrode 1721, 137). By his wife, Diana Goring, daughter of George Goring, 1st Earl of Norwich, he had three sons and five daughters. He defected to Parliament in November 1645 but involved himself in plots to restore Charles II in time to be appointed a gentleman of the privy chamber to Queen Catherine in 1662. Although commissioned major in the Duke of Buckingham's regiment of foot in June 1672, he left his wife and children the next year and retired into Berkshire (Dalton 1960, I 120; Rochester *Letters* 1980, 172). At the same time Jane Long (q.v.) retired from the stage.

Louise Renée de Penancoët de Kéroualle (anglicized to Carwell), Duchess of **Portsmouth** (1649–1734) was born at Kéroualle, near Brest, into a Breton family that was considered ancient in the fourteenth century. In 1668 she was appointed a maid of honour to Henrietta Anne, Duchess of Orléans, Louis XIV's sister-in-law and Charles II's youngest sister. In May 1670 she accompanied her mistress to Dover, where her dark hair, baby face, and sad, reproachful eyes captivated Charles II. She returned to St Cloud when the secret Treaty of Dover had been signed, but when her mistress died on 30 June 1670, she was sent back to England. Buckingham escorted her as far as Dieppe, where he abandoned her to pursue some other project, but she finally reached England on a royal yacht (Burnet 1724–34, I 337). After some kind of mock marriage at Catholic Lord Arlington's 'palace' at Euston during the race season at Newmarket and in the presence of the French ambassador, Charles Colbert, marquis de Croissy, Kéroualle was installed in sumptuous apartments off the Stone Gallery in Whitehall as *maîtresse en titre* (Evelyn, 9 October 1671, 10 September 1675). The English declaration of war against the United Provinces, that Louis XIV demanded, followed in March 1672. In July 1672 was born Kéroualle's only child by Charles II, Charles Lennox, created Duke of Richmond in August 1675. Although naturalized as an English subject in August 1673 on Louis XIV's orders, Kéroualle remained a loyal French subject and one of Louis XIV's best sources of information in Whitehall. Also in August 1673 she was created Duchess of Portsmouth and sworn lady of the bedchamber to Queen Catherine. Louis XIV rewarded her in December 1673 with the rich fief of Aubigny-sur-Nievre. Of all Charles II's mistresses she was 'the most absolute', the most rapacious – in 1681 alone she received £22,952 from the privy purse – and the most political, 'Her Chamber was the true Cabinet Council' (GEC, X 608, [2]130; Halifax 1912, 195). Buckingham's disgrace in November 1674 was attributed to her and when Rochester crossed her in 1676, he was exiled (Reresby 1936, 93; Rochester *Letters* 1980, 124). Nathaniel Lee dedicated to her two of his early plays, *Sophonisba, or Hannibal's Overthrow* (April 1675; 1676) and *Gloriane* (January 1676; 1676). And despite a serious illness in 1677, the constant jealousy of Queen Catherine, the Duchess of Cleveland, and (after 1675) the Duchess Mazarin, and the frights of the Popish Plot (1678–81), Portsmouth remained the King's mistress until his death (Evelyn, 6 February 1685).

Henrietta Maria **Price** (?–1678) was a daughter of Colonel Sir Herbert Price of the Priory, Brecon, 1st Baronet, and a sister of Goditha 'fat Price', who was maid of honour to the Duchess of York, mistress to the Duke, and whose name provided the burden for many of Rochester's catches that have not survived (Hamilton 1930, 220, 243). Sir Herbert, a confidant of Rochester's father (Clarendon 1707, III 440) and master of the household, first for Queen Henrietta Maria and then for Charles II, sat in Parliament for Breconshire (1640–43, 1661–January 1679). Henrietta Maria Price was a maid of honour in the first household of Queen Catherine (1662), but resigned her post in December 1673 to marry (as his second wife) Alexander Stanhope of the Inner Temple, a cousin of Philip Stanhope, 2nd Earl of Chesterfield, to whom she had given a pair of gloves in 1665 or 1666 (Steinman 1871, 73).

Alexander **Radcliffe** (*fl.* 1669–99), born in Hampstead, Middlesex, was admitted to Gray's Inn in November 1669. In March 1672 upon Charles II's declaration of war upon the United Provinces, he was commissioned captain in Colonel John Fitzgerald's regiment of foot (Dalton 1960, I 119). Some of Radcliffe's best poems, for example *A Satyr upon Love and Women* (Rylands MS. Eng. 521, p. 20), remain unpublished. Three poems in the first edition of Rochester's verse are Radcliffe's (Rochester 1680, 35, 131, 146). One of these, *The Argument* ('Say *Heav'n-born Muse*, for only thou canst tell'), a feckless attack on Rochester, Gilbert Burnet, and Lady Bridget Sanderson (q.v.), the mother of the maids, affords an unexpected glimpse of Rochester's 'spiney' silhouette. Rochester is also one of the 'Damn'd' poets in Radcliffe's *News from Hell*, 'Damn'd only by the ignorant' (Nichols 1780, I 143, 146). There is no record that Radcliffe was called to the bar, but he continued to live in Gray's Inn as one of the 'sharpers about town' in Tom Brown's circle. His most popular work is *Ovid Travestie, a Burlesque upon Several of Ovid's Epistles*, of which four editions were published between 1680 and 1705. In 1699 he was implored to 'print dull songs no more'.

Henry Wilmot, 1st Earl of **Rochester** (1613–58), was the son of Charles Wilmot, 1st Viscount Wilmot of Athlone in the Irish peerage, by his first wife, Sarah Anderson, daughter of Sir Henry Anderson, sheriff of London in 1601–2. A hard-drinking cavalry officer who 'lov'd Debauchery' (Clarendon 1707, II 396, 427), Wilmot was wounded at Breda (1635), at Worcester (September 1642), and at Cropredy Bridge (June 1644). He was a popular and successful military commander, whose greatest success came in July 1643 at Roundway Down, near Devizes, where he routed the Parliamentary army commanded by Sir William Waller, the poet's cousin. But like so many successful military commanders, he was a failure as a politician (Clarendon 1707, II 396–8). In June 1643 he was created Baron Wilmot of Adderbury, Oxfordshire, and before April 1644 he succeeded as 2nd Viscount Wilmot of Athlone. In the same year he married as his second wife Anne St John, daughter of Sir John St John, 1st Baronet of Lydiard Tregoze, Wiltshire, and widow of Sir Francis Henry Lee, 2nd Baronet of Ditchley, Oxfordshire, where John Wilmot, the poet, was born in April 1647. In August 1644, 'sacrificed to some Faction and Intrigue', he was deprived of his command of the royalist cavalry and allowed to retire to France (Clarendon 1707, II 398). At the court of Charles II in exile he was made a gentleman of the bedchamber (April 1649) and privy councillor (1650). He fought again at Worcester in September 1651 and accompanied the King in his escape from Worcester to Boscobel to Lyme and finally to Brighton, where he was able to secure shipping for both of them to Fécamp. In December 1652, he was created Earl of Rochester. After a series of diplomatic assignments on the Continent, he returned to England clandestinely in February 1655 in a futile effort to coordinate the efforts of scattered royalist groups who had determined upon a general insurrection. It was on this occasion that he might have seen his son, aged eight. Although Wilmot adopted a whole series of disguises – a Frenchman in a little yellow periwig, a fat grazier with a basket-hilted sword at his back – he was said to be 'the least wary in making his Journies in safe hours, so he departed very unwillingly from all places where there was good eating and drinking' (Clarendon 1707, III 436), but somehow he made his way from Dunkirk to Margate, to London, to Yorkshire, and back to the English court at Cologne, in four months. In this same operation the poet Abraham Cowley failed to return. Rochester's widow testified after the Restoration that he had once been arrested by Cromwell's agents but that Colonel John Hutchinson, the regicide, had allowed him to escape (Clarendon 1707, III 436; *EHR* 4 (1889), 330 n.72). In 1656 he was commissioned colonel of the King's Regiment of Guards, one of the four regiments that became the nucleus of Charles II's army. He died in Ghent, was buried at Sluys, and reinterred at Spelsbury, Oxfordshire.

Sackville, see **Buckhurst**.

Henry Jermyn, Earl of **St Albans** (*c*. 1604–84), was the second son of Sir Thomas Jermyn, comptroller of the household, and Catherine Killigrew, the daughter of Sir William Killigrew. In Parliament he sat for Bodmin, Cornwall (1625–6), Liverpool (1628–9), and Corfe Castle (1640). As vice-chamberlain (1639) and chamberlain (1645) to Queen Henrietta Maria, he handled the Queen's finances during her lifetime. In September 1643 he was created Baron Jermyn of St Edmundsbury. He repeatedly served as ambassador to France (1644, 1660, 1667, 1669) and in his last tour of duty adjusted the preliminaries to the secret Treaty of Dover. Charles II, who called him 'more a Frenchman than an Englishman' (*DNB*, X 780), created him Earl of St Albans (April 1660) and made him a privy councillor (1660), lord chamberlain of the household (1671–4), and K.G. (1672). At court he remained 'a loathsome monument of decayed debauchery' (GEC, VII 86).

St André (*fl.* 1671–96), first name unknown, choreographed and danced in the spectacular production of the Lully–Molière–Corneille tragedy-ballet, *Psyché*, at the Tuileries in January 1671. The next year he danced in Lully's *Les Fêtes de l'Amour et de Bacchus* in which the Duke of Monmouth also danced. Through Monmouth's effort St André was brought to England as 'master of the compositions for ballet' to arrange the dances for the production of Shadwell's *Psyche* at the Dorset Garden theatre in February 1675. In the same month he danced in the amateur production at court of Crowne's *Calisto*. Etherege's reference to him in *The Man of Mode* (March 1676; 1676) suggests that he was also teaching dancing. 'St André's feet' achieved a kind of immortality in Dryden's *MacFlecknoe* (1682). By 1696 he had returned to Paris.

Bridget Tyrrell (*c.* 1592–1682), was the daughter of Sir Edward Tyrrell, Baronet, of Thornton, Buckinghamshire. About 1626 she married William **Sanderson**, the historian of the early Stuart kings. He was an officer in the footguards who was knighted and made a gentleman of the privy chamber by Charles II. From 1662 Lady Bridget was mother of the maids, or governess of the maids of honour at the court of Queen Catherine. She is leagued with Rochester in Alexander Radcliffe's poem, *The Argument*, published in Rochester 1680 but which Rochester did not write. Her post at court was a perennial object of humour: in 1663 she is made to instruct her charges to fall 'To none . . . / but Caesar and his brother' and in 1672 John Eachard asks, 'What do I care if *Plato* calls memory the *Mother* of the *Maids?*' (Wilson 1976, 4; Eachard 1672, 203). The post was abolished in 1689.

Lady Lucy Hamilton **Sandys** (*fl.* 1675–87) is said to have been a daughter of George Kirke, gentleman of the robes to Charles I and groom of the bedchamber to Charles II, by his first wife, Anne Killigrew, who died in 1641 (*Westminster Abbey Registers*, 218). If so, she would have been a niece of Thomas Killigrew (q.v.). She is known to have appeared at court in the company of Nell Gwyn, but she is not mentioned in Nell Gwyn's will. Her name as well as her title may have been assumed.

The life of Henry **Savile** (*c.* 1642–87), Rochester's closest friend, not surprisingly parallels that of Rochester in several passages. As the youngest child of Sir William Savile and Lady Anne Coventry, he was the younger brother of Sir George Savile, Marquis of Halifax. He was educated at Christ Church, Oxford, and in travel abroad (1661–5). Upon his return to England he was appointed a groom of the bedchamber to the Duke of York, and the Duchess was said to be in love with him (Pepys, 17 November 1665). He volunteered for sea duty in the second Dutch War and saw action aboard the Duke of York's flagship in the St James's Fight (July 1666). Before he received his first diplomatic appointment, he was constantly in trouble: when he carried a challenge from his uncle, Sir William Coventry, to the Duke of Buckingham (March 1669), he was confined in the Gatehouse and forbidden to attend the Duke of York (March 1669); during a house-party at Althorp he broke into the bedroom of another house guest, Lady Northumberland, the rich young widow of Joceline Percy, 11th Earl of Northumberland, and the host, Robert Spencer, 2nd Earl of Sunderland, chased him all the way back to London (Rochester *Letters* 1980, 68–70). Savile's regular mistress was another widow, Lady Scrope, widow of Sir Adrian Scrope and mother of Sir Carr Scrope. He served again with the Duke of York in the third Dutch War and published *A True Relation of the Engagement of His Majesties Fleet under the Command of His Royal Highness, with the Dutch Fleet, May 28, 1672* (1672), an account of the battle of Solebay in which Pepys's Edward Montagu, 1st Earl of Sandwich, died a hero's death. Thereafter his career advanced rapidly: he was appointed an envoy extraordinary to France (September 1672), elected member of Parliament for Newark, Nottinghamshire (May 1677), and finally succeeded Sunderland in Paris, but with only the title of envoy (1679). But during these same years he succeeded in 'mocking [the Duke of York's] bigotry and militarism to his face' and voting for the dismissal of Lauderdale in May 1678, the only household servant to do so. He 'deserves to be remembered for a degree of independence probably unsurpassed by any of his fellow placemen' in Parliament (*HoP 1660–1690*, III 398, 399) or by Rochester in his verse.

Sir Carr **Scrope** (1649–80) was the eldest son of Sir Adrian Scrope of Cockerington, Lincolnshire, a royalist army officer who was created Knight of the Bath at the coronation of Charles II, by Mary Carr, daughter of Sir Robert Carr of Sleaford, Lincolnshire. He was educated at Wadham College, Oxford (August 1664–6), created first baronet in January 1667 and M.A. the following month. Despite his small size, literary ability and fashionable dress enabled him to cut a considerable figure at court. He courted (but declined to marry) Carey Fraser (q.v.) and publicly quarrelled with witty Catherine Sedley. He wrote a prologue and a song for Etherege's *The Man of Mode* (April 1676; 1676), a prologue for Lee's *The Rival Queens* (March 1677; 1677), and a song, 'Myrtillo's sad Despair', for Lee's *Mithridates* (*c.* February 1678; 1678). Some of the verse which Scrope wrote in his paper war with Rochester was first published as Rochester's (Rochester 1680, 45, 50, 74).

Sir Charles **Sedley** (1639–1701) was born in London, the youngest and posthumous son of Sir John Sedley of Aylesford, Kent, 2nd Baronet, by Elizabeth Savile, daughter of Sir Henry Savile, provost of Eton. He succeeded as 5th Baronet in April 1656. He spent a year at Wadham College (1656–7) while the Royal Society was taking shape in the Lodge of the Warden, John Wilkins. In February 1657 he married Lady Catherine Savage, daughter of John Savage, 2nd Earl Rivers, and a Roman Catholic, by whom he had one daughter. Upon the Restoration he 'lived mostly in the great city, became a debauchee, set up for a satyrical wit, a comedian, poet, and courtier of ladies' (Wood 1891–1900, IV 731). By 1667 Sedley had become a legend: 'worse than Sir Charles Sedley' is John Gregory's comparative for 'one of the lewdest fellows of the age' (Pepys, 16 November 1667). In May 1668 he was elected to Parliament from New Romney, Kent, which he represented (with intervals) until his death. Initially he voted with Buckingham and the court party, but he was an inactive member. His real interests were poetry and debauchery, including indecent exposure (Wood 1891–1900, IV 732; Pepys, 1 July 1663, 23 October 1668), mayhem (Pinto 1927, 111–12; Pepys, 2 February 1669), and getting bastards (Pinto 1927, 130). 'Little Sid', as he was known at court, is Lisideius in Dryden's *Of Dramatic Poesy, an Essay* (1668) and Medley in Etherege's *The Man of Mode* (April 1676; 1676) (E. D. Forgues, *Revue des deux mondes*, 2nd series, 27 (August 1857), 844). Dryden's assessment of his friend's poetry is for once not extravagant. He calls Sedley 'a more Elegant

Tibullus' (Dryden 1956– , XI 320), which is an interesting parallel: Tibullus was called the most correct of the Roman poets, and no less a critic than Charles II predicted that '*Sedley*'s Stile, either in Writing, or Discourse, would be the Standard of the *English* Tongue' (*The Works of the Honourable Sir Charles Sedley, Bart.*, 2 vols. (1722), I ^{1}5). Pepys was disappointed that the 'long expected' first play of 'so reputed a wit', *The Mulberry Garden* (May 1668; 1668), 'had nothing extraordinary in it at all, neither of language nor design', but he went back to see a second performance and took his wife to see a third (Pepys, 18 May, 20 May, 29 June 1668). Sedley accompanied Buckingham to France in 1670 to conclude the *traité simulé* or public version of the secret Treaty of Dover. Following a bigamous marriage to Ann Ayscough in April 1672 he underwent some kind of religious conversion: he was reconciled to the Church of England, left the court, followed Buckingham into opposition to Charles II, and was found 'doubly worthy' by Shaftesbury (*HoP 1660–1690*, III 409). All this happened before his daughter was seduced by the Duke of York. His complete works, edited by Vivian de S. Pinto in 1927, include four plays and 136 occasional poems, among which are some of the best songs of the period. He was falsely reported to be killed when the roof of a tennis court in Peters Street collapsed (*The True Domestic Intelligence*, 16 January 1680).

Elkanah **Settle** (1649–1724), the eldest son of Josias Settle, a barber-surgeon and innkeeper in Dunstable, Bedfordshire, was educated at Westminster School and Trinity College, Oxford. While still an undergraduate he wrote his first play, *Cambyses, King of Persia*, a rhymed tragedy, produced by the Duke's Company both in London and Oxford in 1670–71 (Downes 1987, 59–60). Settle left Oxford without a degree and hastened to London to write two more plays. *The Conquest of China* was rejected for presentation at court, but possibly through Rochester's influence Settle received an appointment as one of the poets in the King's Company (Boswell 1932, 134). *The Empress of Morocco*, a tragedy in heroic couplets with a delightful 'Masque for Orpheus', set by Matthew Locke, was played twice at court and twice at the Duke's Company's new theatre at Dorset Garden and published 'with Sculptures [engraved illustrations]' in 1673. This spectacular success produced an equally extravagant reaction. Thomas Duffet's *The Empress of Morocco. A Farce* was rushed into production (December 1673; 1674) by the King's Company, and Crowne, Dryden, and Shadwell collaborated in *Notes and Observations on The Empress of Morocco, or, Some few Erratas to be Printed instead of the Sculptures with the Second Edition of that Play* (1674), attacking Settle's 'blundering, hobling Verse' (sig. a1r). Literary squabbles, however, were already turning political. *Notes and Observations* also condemns Settle as a Whig *avant la lettre*, a 'great Authour amongst Town Fools and City Wits' (sig. A3v), five years before he was employed by Shaftesbury to produce pope-burning processions and seventeen years before he was appointed City Poet (Whincop 1747, 282). Settle's reply, *Notes and Observations on The Empress of Morocco Revised* (1674), is generally conceded to have turned the tables on his tormentors (Novak 1968, xiv). Settle 'Spurr'd boldly on' as Dryden's 'rival poet' but none of his seven succeeding productions was as successful as *The Empress of Morocco*, and three of them, *Love and Revenge* (November 1674; 1675), *The Conquest of China* (May 1675; 1676), and *Fatal Love* (*c.* October 1680; 1680), were failures.

Thomas **Shadwell** (*c.* 1641–92) was the son of John Shadwell, a justice of the peace in the parish of Broomhall, Norfolk, and later the recorder of Galway (which provides his son's Irish connection). In December 1655 he was admitted to Caius College, Cambridge, but left without a degree to study law at the Middle Temple. His first play, *The Sullen Lovers* (May 1668; 1668), adapted from Molière's comedy-ballet, *Les Facheux* (1663), was produced by the Duke's Company at Lincoln's Inn Fields with James Nokes and Shadwell's wife, Anne Gibbs, in leading roles. It was a 'wonderful Success', being acted twelve days and revived at Dover before the court in May 1670 (Downes 1987, 64). In the preface Shadwell acknowledged or boasted that the play was 'wrote in haste'. In the next eight years Shadwell turned out eight plays: five comedies, a tragedy, and two semi-operas, all but one of them for the Duke's Company. Three of these he wrote in haste (Shadwell 1927, I 12), 'which in the best Interpretation must render an Author Lazy ... Or else proves himself a Blockhead' (Elkanah Settle, *Love and Revenge* (1673), [84]). If he had had the choice, Shadwell would have preferred to think himself lazy (Shadwell 1927, II 16). He was also an accomplished lutanist – 'The Lute still trembling underneath thy nail' (Dryden

1956– , II 55) – and at least five songs by him are preserved in contemporary songbooks and mss. (Grove 1980, XVII 212). As Dryden did for *An Allusion to Horace* (98–101), Shadwell set himself up for satiric reduction in *MacFlecknoe* (1676; 1682): 'the higher sort of Rabble', he said, 'are more pleased with the extravagant and unnatural actions, the trifles and fripperies of a Play, or the trappings and ornaments of Nonsense, than with all the wit in the world' (Shadwell 1927, I 185) and in 1689 he succeeded, not Richard Flecknoe as emperor of nonsense, but John Dryden as poet laureate of Great Britain.

Gilbert **Sheldon** (1598–1677), the son of Roger Sheldon, a 'menial servant' of Gilbert Talbot, 7th Earl of Shrewsbury, graduated B.A. from Trinity College, Oxford, in November 1617 and D.D. from All Souls College in June 1634. Warden of All Souls from March 1626 until he was ejected in March 1648, a close friend of Edward Hyde, and a member of Lord Falkland's circle of poets and divines at Great Tew, he was appointed a royal chaplain in 1646. He was with Charles I on the Isle of Wight in 1648 but remained in England during the Interregnum. At the Restoration he met Charles II in Canterbury and was made dean of the royal chapel, bishop of London (October 1660), master of the Savoy, a privy councillor (1663), and Archbishop of Canterbury (June 1663). In May 1662 he married Charles II and Catherine of Bragança in the Great Chamber of the house of the governor of Portsmouth (Fraser 1979, 206). Sheldon became one of Charles's principal ecclesiastical advisers and manager of the episcopal bench in Parliament. Much more than Clarendon, he was responsible for the so-called Clarendon Code and the form of the re-established church. Samuel Parker (q.v.) was his chaplain. When Charles dismissed Clarendon in August 1667 he sent for Sheldon and told him what he had done. Sheldon 'answered nothing. When the King insisted to oblige him to declare himself, he said, *Sir, I wish you would put away this woman that you keep* . . . [and] from that day forward *Sheldon* could never recover the King's confidence' (Burnet 1724–34, I 252–3). Whether Sheldon spoke out of loyalty to Clarendon or concern for Charles's soul may never be known. But Pepys was astonished to learn from his cousin Roger Pepys, a member of Parliament opposed to the court, that Sheldon 'doth keep a wench, and that he is as very a wencher as can be. And . . . that Sir Ch. Sidly [Sedley] hath got away one of the Archbishop's wenches from him' (Pepys, 29 July 1667). Andrew Marvell names two of the archbishop's wenches: Catherine Boynton, one of the four original maids of honour to Queen Catherine, who 'affected to be languishing, to speak husky and low, and to be capable of feeling faint two or three times every day', and 'this worthless little slut of a Middleton [Jane, the wife of Charles Middleton], all white and golden', whose other lovers were said to include the Duke of York; William Russell, Lord Russell; Richard Jones, the future Earl of Ranelagh; Edmund Waller the poet; and Ralph Montagu the ambassador (Marvell 1927, I 160, 177; Hamilton 1930, 249, 153, 109, 355). Charles was amused when his pet crow hopped up on Sheldon's shoulder and croaked, 'Wilt thou have a whore, thou lascivious dog?' and Burnet wondered whether Sheldon had 'any [sense of religion] at all' (Hutton 1989, 338; Burnet 1724–34, I 177). At this distance it may be impossible to know whether Sheldon was the perfect Medicean archbishop for the Restoration court, with his patronage of Anthony à Wood and Christopher Wren (£25,000 for the Sheldonian Theatre and £4,000 towards the rebuilding of St Paul's), and his 'mistresses with great smooth marbly limbs' (in Browning's phrase), or whether he was a victim of the Restoration preoccupation with scandal.

Fleetwood **Sheppard** (1634–98) was the second son of William Sheppard of Great Rollright, Oxfordshire, by Mary Dormer of Grange, Buckinghamshire, a cousin of Lady Elizabeth Dormer, third wife of Philip Stanhope, 2nd Earl of Chesterfield (q.v.). He entered Magdalen Hall, Oxford, in November 1650 but soon after migrated to Christ Church, whence he graduated B.A. in 1654. In October 1657 he was entered at Gray's Inn but apparently remained in Oxford. Upon the Restoration he is said to have 'retir'd to London, hang'd on the court, became a debauchee and atheist, a grand companion with Charles [Sackville] lord Buckhurst, afterwards Earl of Dorset and Middlesex, Henry Savile, and others'. The 'others' included Nell Gwyn, Buckingham, and Rochester, 'the King's companions at most suppers in the week, an[no] 1676, 77, *&c.*' (Wood 1813–20, IV 627). 'Inspired by wine' Sheppard and Buckhurst played opposite Rochester in the sundial caper in the Privy Garden (*POAS*, Yale, I 271). At the birth of Nell Gwyn's first child by Charles II, Sheppard was appointed her steward and managed her growing fortune with much success. Sheppard's satires and facetiae in the manner of Boccalini have never been collected but gained him considerable reputation as a critic. Some of them are reprinted in *POAS*, Yale, V 55, 223, 402–3. Thomas Rymer's *The Tragedies of the Last Age Consider'd and Examin'd by the Practice of the Ancients* (1678 for 1677), for which Dryden wrote 'Heads of an Answer to Rymer', is addressed to Sheppard in the form of a letter. Like his friend Henry Savile, Sheppard never married.

Anne Maria Brudenell (1642–1702), the daughter of Robert Brudenell, Earl of Cardigan, by his second wife, Anne Savage, daughter of Thomas Savage, 1st Viscount Savage, was born in Paris and in January 1659 married, as his second wife, Francis Talbot, 11th Earl of **Shrewsbury**, she being sixteen and he about thirty-six years old. The Earl of Gramont called her 'prodigieuse' and her early lovers were said to include Richard Butler, Earl of Arran, Colonel Thomas Howard, and Henry Killigrew, eldest son of Thomas Killigrew (Hamilton 1930, 113, 189, 300). Howard and Henry Jermyn fought a duel over her in which Jermyn's second, Giles Rawlins, was killed (ibid., 115). Her liaison with Colonel Howard's brother-in-law, George Villiers, Duke of Buckingham, began in 1666. The Earl of Shrewsbury, who never boggled at his wife's earlier infidelities, unaccountably took exception to this one. In a duel at Barn Elms on 16 January 1668 Buckingham's second, Captain William Jenkins, an officer in the Horse Guards, was killed on the spot and Shrewsbury died two months later (Pepys, 17 January 1668; HMC *Seventh Report*, 486). Charles's grant of pardon for Shrewsbury's murder was issued to Buckingham on 19 May 1668 (GEC, XI 719). Thereafter the lovers lived in open and flagrant adultery (Pepys, 15 May 1668) until February 1673, when the House of Lords ordered them to separate and to post bonds of £10,000 each for their security (*LJ*, XII 628). The Countess of Shrewsbury retired to France but returned and married George Rodney-Bridges in 1677.

Lady Anne Hamilton (?–1695) was the eldest daughter and co-heir of William Hamilton, 2nd Duke of Hamilton, by Elizabeth Maxwell, daughter and co-heir of James Maxwell, Earl of Dirletoun. She had already 'passed through the hands of [Philip Stanhope, 2nd Earl of Chesterfield, and] several other gentlemen' (Hamilton 1930, 164) in

1660 when she married Robert Carnegie, Lord Carnegie, only son and heir of James Carnegie, 2nd Earl of **Southesk**, whom he succeeded in January 1669. In 1662 she became the mistress of James, Duke of York. The story that Carnegie, a cavalry officer, deliberately contracted syphilis in order to infect the Duke of York was widely believed (Pepys, 6 April 1668; Burnet 1724–34, I 227–8; Hamilton 1930, 167) but vigorously denied by Southesk. When seen in public she was 'most devilishly painted' (Pepys, 3 December 1668). By 1671 she had been legally separated from her husband and because she was a Roman Catholic her children were removed from her care. After October 1675 she lived largely on the Continent (GEC, XIIi 143–4).

Sir John **Suckling** (1609–41?) was the eldest son of Sir John Suckling, a member of Parliament for Dunwich and Reigate who was knighted by James I in 1616 and appointed comptroller of the royal household in 1622. Suckling was educated at Trinity College, Cambridge, and Gray's Inn. Upon his father's death in 1627 he inherited estates in Suffolk, Lincolnshire, and Middlesex and a house in London. He was knighted by Charles I at Theobalds in September 1630 and became 'the greatest gallant of his time, and the greatest gamester, both for bowling and cards', improving the odds by playing with marked cards (Aubrey 1898, II 240–41, 245). His courtship of Anne Willoughby was terminated in November 1634 when he was cudgelled 'almost to an handfull' by her accepted suitor Sir John Digby, 'never offering to draw his sword'. In a second confrontation with Digby, 'the best swordman of his time', Suckling ran away and one of his seconds was killed (Suckling 1971, I xxxvi–xxxvii; Aubrey 1898, II 241). He wrote his first play, *Aglaura*, in 1637 and his deist tract, *An Account of Religion by Reason* in August–September 1637; by the end of 1637 *The Wits*, the first satire in the sessions-of-the-poets subgenre, was circulating in manuscript. In November 1638 Suckling was appointed a gentleman of the privy chamber and next year, when Charles I raised an army to march into Scotland, Suckling at his own expense recruited and outfitted ('in white doubletts and scarlett breeches, and scarlet coates, hatts, and . . . feathers') a cavalry troop that participated in the general retreat from Maxwellheugh in June 1639 (Aubrey 1898, II 242). In 1640 he was commissioned captain of a troop of carabineers that was routed by the Scots cavalry at Newburn Ford, near Newcastle. In March 1641, like Rochester's father, Suckling was involved in the First Army Plot to support Charles I against Parliament. In May, with Strafford in the Tower, Suckling was examined by Parliament to determine why he had mustered his troop of carabineers nearby at the White Horse tavern in Bread Street. When summoned to reappear, Suckling took ship for Dieppe. He was found guilty of treason *in absentia* and probably *post mortem* in August 1641. By this time he had completely wasted his vast fortune and 'reflecting on the miserable and despicable condition he should be reduced to, having nothing left to maintaine him, he (having a convenience for that purpose, lyeing at an apothecarie's house, in Paris) tooke poyson, which killed him miserably' (Aubrey 1898, II 242). The four plays and seventy-five poems of 'Natural, easie *Suckling*', as Millamant calls him, were published posthumously in *Fragmenta Aurea* (1646) and *The Last Remains* (1659). Three of the plays, *Aglaura, Brenoralt, or The Contented Colonel*, and *The Goblins*, were repeatedly played on the Restoration stage, but not apparently after 1674 (*London Stage*, I cclxxix).

Barbara Villiers (1622–81) was the daughter of Sir Edward Villiers by Barbara St John, and the sister of William Villiers, 2nd Viscount Grandison, the father of Barbara Villiers, Duchess of Cleveland. Her first husband was Richard Wenman, the son and heir of Thomas Wenman, 2nd Viscount Wenman of Tuam. When he died in 1646, she married in February 1651, as his second wife, James Howard, 3rd Earl of **Suffolk**. While her husband played tennis with the King, she served Queen Catherine as first lady of the bedchamber, groom of the stole, and keeper of the privy purse (1662–81). For a performance at court of John Crowne's *Calisto*, she let Margaret Blagge, who played Diana, wear her jewels worth nearly £20,000 (Evelyn, 22 December 1674). Her opposition to the marriage of her daughter Lady Elizabeth Howard (q.v.) to Thomas Felton of Playford in July 1675 (*Savile Correspondence*, 39) probably did not cause the apoplexy that carried off mother and daughter within days of each other in December 1681. Their coffins were carried through the streets together 'in great state, with severall of his majesties coaches' and interred together in Saffron Walden, Essex (Luttrell, I 150–51, 153–4).

Sir Edward **Sutton** (?–1695), of Irish origin, was knighted by

Charles II at Whitehall in June 1660. In 1667 he was appointed one of the gentlemen of the privy chamber – 'when the King eats in the Privy Chamber, they wait at the Table and bring in his Meat' (Chamberlayne 1670, 264) – which explains why Sir Edward is so knowledgeable about the King's taste in mutton (32.50). A guest for dinner at the groom porter's lodgings in Whitehall heard Sutton 'play excellently on the Irish harp' (Evelyn, 14 November 1668). He married Anne Byron, daughter of Sir John Byron, Kt, and widow of Sir Thomas Lucas, Kt., who died about 1650. When he died in July 1695 he was said to be nearly a hundred years old (Luttrell, III 506). In his will he styles himself baronet, 'but no evidence has been discovered that he was ever created a baronet' (*Westminster Abbey Registers*, 237).

Villiers, Barbara, see **Suffolk**.

Villiers, Barbara, see **Cleveland**.

Villiers, George, see **Buckingham**.

Edmund **Waller** (1606–87) was born in Coleshill, Hertfordshire, the eldest son of Robert Waller, but grew up and died in the manor house of Beaconsfield, Buckinghamshire. His mother, Anne Hampden, was a cousin of John Hampden, 'the zealot of rebellion' (Johnson 1779–81, I [2]1). Sir William Waller, the parliamentary general, and Sir Hardress Waller, the regicide, were his third cousins. He was educated at Eton, King's College, Cambridge (which he left without a degree), and Lincoln's Inn. Before the Civil War he sat in Parliament for four boroughs (*c*. February 1624–July 1643). In July 1631 he married Anne Bancks, heiress of a rich City mercer, and became, in George Thorn Drury's phrase, 'the richest poet known to English literature' (*DNB*, XX 580). But even before his election to the Long Parliament, his reputation as a poet had been established by his Sacharissa poems, addressed to Dorothy Sidney, Countess of Sunderland, eldest daughter of the 2nd Earl of Leicester. Upon the outbreak of the rebellion, Waller was involved in a royalist plot but saved his life in the classic fashion by disbursing large bribes and giving evidence against his co-conspirators, who were hanged. Waller was fined and banished. During his exile three editions of his *Poems* were published in London in 1645. In 1651 he was pardoned by the Rump and awarded a seat on Cromwell's committee of trade. After the Restoration he represented Hastings in the Cavalier Parliament (1661–78) and Saltash in the Parliament of James II (1685). He was one of the most active members of the Cavalier Parliament, 'the delight of the House . . . being a vain and empty, tho' a witty, man' (Burnet 1724–34, I 388), but he was also genuinely tolerant, opposing persecution of papists and non-conformists alike (*HoP 1660–1690*, III 654). Waller's presence at court was most evident during the period of the Cabal (1670–73), when he enjoyed a seat on the plantations committee at £500 a year and leaked or sold privileged information to the French ambassador. When the plantations committee was dissolved, he was thought to be 'no longer a courtier' and was rated 'Worthy' by Shaftesbury (*HoP 1660–1690*, III 655, 656). By the ladies he was rated a dangerous old lecher (Rochester *Letters* 1980, 71). Waller had dealt in panegyric (99.54–6) from his first published work, *To the King on his Return*, in *Rex Redux* (1633), celebrating Charles I, Cromwell, and Charles II impartially. 'The general character of his poetry', Johnson concludes, 'is elegance and gaiety. He is never pathetick, and very rarely sublime' (Johnson 1779–81, I [2]117). Rochester's 'agreeable Manner of . . . repeating, on every Occasion, the Verses of *Waller*' is one of his singularities that Etherege captures in Dorimant.

Susan **Willis** aka Weldon aka Laycock (?–1720?), about whose origin nothing is known, is said to have begun her career in Mother Moseley's bawdy house and to have progressed to the stage (Wilson 1976, 218); but there is no record of her acting. In the late 1660s or early 1670s she had two daughters by 'a goatish peer', Thomas Colepeper, 2nd Baron Colepeper of Thoresby, one of whom married Sir Charles Englefield of Englefield, Berkshire, 5th Baronet, in February 1686 (GEC, *Baronetage*, I 92). Colepeper, the son of a distinguished favourite of Charles I and Charles II, was governor of the Isle of Wight (1661–7) and governor of Virginia (1675–82). 'He spent most of the revenue of his estate upon [Susan Willis], which expense amounted to at least 60,000*l*' (HMC *Lords MSS.*, [II] 434). In June 1673 he was reported to have 'returned from Paris with Mrs. Willis, whom he carry'd thither to buy whatsoever pleased her there and this nation could not afford' (*Savile Correspondence*, 62). From 1675 to 1683 she kept her own bawdy house in Whetstone Park at the sign of the two white balls (HMC *Seventh Report*, 477).

In a letter of 22 May 1687 the English ambassador to the Imperial Diet at Regensburg sent her his 'kindest compliments' (Etherege 1974, 118). Lord Colepeper died in January 1689 and within months Willis was said to be mistress to Willem Bentinck, the recently widowed favourite of William III, raised to the peerage as Earl of Portland (April 1689) (Wilson 1976, 294). When Colepeper's will was read, it was found that 'a great part of his estate is by pretence disposed of to [Susan Willis] and her children, and no provision is made for the payment of his debts, which are great, and contracted for the buying of rich household stuff, plate, jewels, etc. for the said Susan, which she possesses to a great value, pretending them to be the said Lord Culpeper's gift'. Lady Colepeper brought a bill in the House of Lords to set aside the will, but on 15 January 1690 it was defeated 36 to 35, even without the vote of the Earl of Portland, who was absent (HMC *Lords MSS*., [II] 434–5; *LJ*, XIV 414).

Wilmot, see **Rochester**.

William **Wycherley** (1641–1716) was born in Clive Hall in the village of Clive, Shropshire, the eldest son of Daniel Wycherley, a real estate speculator and estate manager for John Paulet, Marquis of Winchester. His early education was completed in France, presumably at a Jesuit college near Angoulême, whence he proceeded to Queen's College, Oxford, in July 1660, and the Middle Temple without taking a degree or being called to the bar. His first choice of career may have been the military. One of his early poems, *On a Sea Fight, which the Author was in, Betwixt the English and the Dutch*, probably describes the engagement off Lowestoft on 3 June 1665, in which Buckingham, Mulgrave, Rochester, Roger Palmer, *et al.* saw the action celebrated by Waller in *Instructions to a Painter* (1665) and turned into farce by Marvell in *The Second Advice to a Painter* (1666). Wycherley's first published poem is *Hero and Leander in Burlesque* (1669), mocking Marlowe in the manner of Samuel Butler. Thereafter Wycherley wrote four plays in four years: *Love in a Wood, or St. James's Park* (*c.* March 1671; 1672), *The Gentleman Dancing-Master* (February 1672; 1673), *The Country-Wife* (*c.* January 1675; 1675), and *The Plain-Dealer* (December 1676; 1677). And then he wrote no more plays. All these with the exception of the second were produced by the King's Company with Charles Hart playing the leading roles opposite Elizabeth Cox and Elizabeth Boutell. *Love* *in a Wood*, dedicated to the Duchess of Cleveland, ran only a few nights but gained £500 for the company and for Wycherley the patronage and something more of the Duchess of Cleveland (Dennis 1939–43, II 409–10). The Duchess, in a perfect Restoration pastoral, 'used to visit Wycherley at his chambers in the Temple, dressed like a country maid in a straw hat, with pattens on, a basket . . . in her hand' (Wilson 1976, 21–2). The Duchess's cousin, George Villiers, Duke of Buckingham, made Wycherley a captain-lieutenant in his regiment of foot, but Wycherley resigned his commission after only a week (Dalton 1960, I 120, 170). *The Gentleman Dancing-Master*, Wycherley's second play, was 'like't but indifferently' (Downes 1987, 70). The only contemporary criticism of Wycherley's most brilliant play, *The Country-Wife*, seems to be in Act II of *The Plain-Dealer*: 'OLIVIA. O, believe me, 'tis a filthy Play, and . . . the lewdest, filthiest thing, is his *China*' (Wycherley 1979, 411). Of Wycherley's last play, however, there is considerable evidence of its success: three editions were required in 1677 and two more in 1678 and 1681. When on the opening night 'the Town . . . appeard Doubtfull what Judgment to Form of it, the foremention'd gentlemen [Villiers] Duke of Buckingham, Wilmot Earl of Rochester, [Charles Sackville] the late Earl of Dorsett, the Earl of Mulgrave . . . Mr. [Henry] Savil, Mr. Buckley, Sir John Denham [who died in 1669!], Mr. Waller &c. by their loud aprobation of it, gave it both a sudden and a lasting reputation' (Dennis 1939–43, II 277). Two months later John Dryden sealed its success by proclaiming it 'one of the most bold, most general, and most useful satires, which has ever been presented on the English theatre [i.e. stage]' (Dryden 1882–93, V 115). In the eighteenth century Voltaire called the Widow Blackacre 'la plus plaisante créature et le meilleur caractère qui soit au théâtre' (the most comical character that was ever brought upon the stage) (*Letters concerning the English Nation* (1733), 185).

Glossary

Unless otherwise stated the definitions are adapted from the second edition of the *Oxford English Dictionary* (1989).

action (85.20): mode of acting; gesture, oratorical management of the body and features in harmony with the subject described. Betterton's 'action' in Philip Massinger's *The Bondman* was said to be pleasing (Pepys, 19 March 1661).

advance (208.79): make progress; put in a better position.

alarm (87.30): a call to arms, a signal calling upon men to arm.

alcove (31.26): a vaulted recess in which is placed a bed of state: 'in the close Alcove, /... *Keppell* and He are *Ganymede* and *Jove*' (*POAS*, Yale, VI 18).

allay (149.34): alloy; admixture [of gold] with a base metal (*OED* cites Durfey, *Wit and Mirth: or Pills to Purge Melancholy* (1719), II 306: 'No Gold will Coyn without allay').

amaze (9.^{2}3): bewilderment.

antic (51.94): absurd from fantastic incongruity, grotesque, bizarre, uncouthly ludicrous.

appear (5.^{1}3): present oneself as legal representative of another.

arrant (80.38): a variant of 'errant', 'wandering, vagrant, vagabond', which from its frequent use in such expressions as *arrant thief*, became an intensive, 'thorough, notorious, downright'.

aspiring (10.^{1}6, 73.66): desirous of advancement, ambitious.

baggage (39.^{2}6): *OED* cites William Robertson, *Phraseologia Generalis* (1681), 197: 'A baggage, or Souldier's Punk, *Scortum Castrense*'.

balk (43.31): to pass over, overlook, refrain from noticing.

balsam (3.15): an aromatic oily or resinous medicinal preparation usually for external application, for healing wounds.

band (73.46): a falling collar, a pair of strips hanging down in front as part of a conventional dress, clerical, legal, or academic, resembling those worn by the Swiss Calvinist clergy.

basilisk (4.37): a fabulous reptile; its breath, and even its look, was fatal.
bay (49.7): usually in plural: leaves or sprigs of bay-tree or laurel woven into a wreath or garland to reward a poet.
beau garçon (196.21): a handsome fellow, an exquisite, a fop.
Bedlam (49.17): the Hospital of St Mary of Bethlehem, used as an asylum for mentally deranged persons; originally situated in Bishopsgate, in 1676 rebuilt near London Wall.
beer-glass (61.177): a glass holding half a pint.
before (65.2): in time previous to a time in question; already.
bend (204.50): bow in submission or reverence.
birthday coat (32.62): worn on the king's birthday.
black pot (83.^{1}6): a tarred beer-mug.
blade (32.74): a gallant, attentive to women.
blot (33.104): a disgrace, fault, blemish.
board (87.19): a table (*obsolete*).
bowl (38.title): a drinking vessel (*OED* cites John Heywood, *Woorkes* (1562), sig. U1r: 'Drownd theyr soules in ale boules').
brisk (192.^{1}9): aggressive (*OED* cites Etherege, *The Man of Mode* (1676), I i 387: 'He has been, as the sparkish word is, Brisk upon the Ladies already').
broke (49.11): penniless.
bubble (73.31): one that is cheated (*AND*).
buggery (34.146): unnatural intercourse of men with one another.
bulk (31.26): a framework projecting from the front of a shop.

cadet (48.163): a younger son or brother, traditionally impoverished.
camphire (123.85): camphor, formerly in repute as an aphrodisiac.
carman (31.29): a carter, carrier.
case (83.^{1}7): the state of facts juridically considered; a thing to contain or enclose something else.
cast (139.101): dismissed, cashiered.
cerecloth (195.^{2}8): cloth impregnated with wax, used as a plaster in surgery in the treatment of venereal disease; cf. Sir Carr Scrope is 'lapt in sear cloth'; Sir Alexander Fraser 'may cure his pox' (HMC *Rutland MSS.*, II 37; Wilson 1976, 240).
chaffer (78.^{2}10) bargain, haggle about terms or price.
challenge (15.26): assert one's title to, lay claim to, demand as a right (*obsolete*).

charm (85.1): the chanting or recitation of a verse supposed to possess magic power or occult influence.

charming (74.86): exercising magic power.

City (53.184): that part of London situated within the ancient boundaries which is under the jurisdiction of the Lord Mayor and Corporation; more particularly, the business part of this, in the neighbourhood of the Royal Exchange, the centre of financial and commercial activity.

civet (207.43): a yellowish or brownish oily substance, having a strong musky smell, obtained from glands in the anal pouch of several animals of the civet genus, especially of the African civet cat, and used as a stabilizer in perfume-making; it is King Lear who requires 'an Ounce of Civet . . . to sweeten [his] imagination' (IV vi 132).

civility (204.47): freedom from barbarity; the state of being civilized (Johnson 1755).

clip (28.6): clasp with the arms, embrace, hug.

close (200.10): sexual encounter.

clout (85.^{2}12) a piece of cloth, especially a small or worthless piece or one put to mean uses; slang for what is now called a sanitary towel (Rochester 1980, 110).

clown (33.92): a countryman; one very ill-bred or unmannerly (*AND*).

coast (78.^{1}8): quarter, part (*obsolete*).

cob (45.64): leader.

cod (192.16): codpiece, a bagged appendage to the front of the close-fitting breeches worn by men from the 15th to the 17th century, often conspicuous and ornamented.

cokes (53.184): a silly fellow, simpleton, one easily taken in. Bartholomew Cokes is the comic victim in Ben Jonson's *Bartholomew Fair* (1614).

colour (34.126): outward appearance, show.

combine (203.17): band together, confederate, or league.

comfortable (45.65): cf. 'importance'.

common (55.248): free to be used by everyone; low-class, vulgar, unrefined.

complexioned (87.29): having a specified mental constitution, disposition, or temperament (*obsolete*).

conceited (46.108): having an overweening opinion of oneself (*OED*); wise in his own opinion (*AND*).

control (136.203): overpower, overmaster (*obsolete*).

conventicle (46.90): a meeting of nonconformists, or dissenters from the Church of England, for religious worship during the period when such meetings were prohibited by law.

cony (47.136): a rabbit.

councillor (83.[1]1): counsellor-at-law; one whose profession is to give legal advice to clients and conduct their cases in court.

coxcomb (53.159): a fool, simpleton (*obsolete*).

creature (32.41): a human being, a term of reprobation or contempt; cf. 'a thing' (33.89).

cully (30.15): a fool or silly creature that is easily drawn in and cheated by whores or rogues (*AND*).

dainty (41.37): possessing delicate taste, fastidious; (81.53): valuable, fine, choice, excellent.

damask (38.4): ornament with designs incised in the surface and filled in with gold or silver.

dazzled (72.[2]23): having lost the faculty of distinct and steady vision, especially from gazing at too bright light.

die (10.16): have an orgasm; cf. '*Benedick* [to Beatrice]. I will . . . die in thy lap' (*Much Ado about Nothing*, V ii 99).

diet (31.4): take one's ordinary meals.

dildo (40.title): a penis substitute made of glass, wax, horn, leather, etc., used for female gratification. While *Signior Dildo* was circulating in manuscript, dildoes were called 'Signior' (Wilson 1976, 14).

Dingboy (56.36): a rogue, hector, bully, sharper (*AND*).

discreetly (49.20): with self-regarding prudence.

discretion (41.40): prudence, sagacity, circumspection, sound judgement.

dissolve (12.23): have an orgasm; cf. 28.15.

do the trick (37.16): accomplish one's purpose, do what is wanted.

drawing room (78.[2]8): shortened from withdrawing-room, a private chamber attached to a more public room.

drudge (37.7): toil at laborious and distasteful work.

dry (28.35): feeling no emotion.

dry-bob (100.75): coition without spending (Partridge 1951).

elf (45.49): in a depreciatory sense, 'a poor creature'.

endure (85.[1]14): undergo without succumbing or giving way.
engine (72.29): a mechanical contrivance, machine.
enjoin (19.30): impose a duty, or obligation, prescribe authoritatively.
enter (164.65): give a person initiatory information or instruction.
entry (148.22): a dance introduced between the parts of an entertainment; cf. *entrée de ballet*.
errant (80.19): straying from the proper course.
experience (91.21): experiments (*obsolete*).
expire (65.69): to have an orgasm; cf. 71.[1]12.

face (61.3): command of countenance, especially with reference to freedom from indications of shame.
faculty (13.[2]17): one of the several 'powers' of the mind. *OED* cites Locke, *An Essay concerning Human Understanding* (1695), II xxi: 'The Understanding and Will are two Faculties of the Mind'.
fall (36.3): surrender one's chastity; cf. 201.[2]9.
fantastic (70.6): having a lively imagination; fanciful, impulsive, capricious.
fatal (37.35): doomed.
fiddle (49.21): one to whose music others dance; hence, a mirth-maker, jester.
fill out (22.8): pour out.
first rate (76.173): of the first rate (said of vessels, especially of the old three-deckers carrying 74–120 guns, such as *The Triumph* on which Rochester served in the second Dutch War); hence of the highest class or degree of excellence.
flatter (160.22): beguile, charm away.
flowers (199.[2]8): menstrual discharge.
fold (31.22): posture adopted during sexual intercourse.
fond (64.17): having strong affection for; (65.1): eager, desirous.
fop (57.45): a fool (*obsolete*); (191.8): a conceited person, a pretender to wit, wisdom, or accomplishments (*obsolete*).
foppery (45.48): foolishness, imbecility, stupidity, folly (*obsolete*).
force (204.4): violence or coercion.
form (19.11): a set, customary, or prescribed way of doing anything; (203.14): in the scholastic philosophy, the essential determinant principle of a thing, that which makes anything (matter) a determinate species or kind of being.

formal (191.3): merely in outward form or appearance (*obsolete*).
framed (62.^{2}11): made. *OED* cites *Paradise Lost* (1667, 1674), IV 691: '[God] fram'd / All things to man's delightful use'.
free speaking (85.23): freedom from internal constraints; unimpeded, articulate.
fribble *sb.* (47.149): a trifling, frivolous fellow, easily beguiled, like Messer Nicia in Machiavelli's *Mandragola* (1520) or Mr Fribble in Shadwell's *Epsom-Wells* (1673).
fribble *v.* (85.23): to falter, stammer.
frig (23.36): to masturbate.

gewgaw (20.48): splendidly trifling; showy without value (Johnson 1755).
give away (15.34): give up, resign, surrender (*rare*).
give over (197.^{2}3): desist, leave off.
glory (10.^{2}6): the disposition to claim honour for oneself, boastful spirit; (76.154): praise, honour, or admiration accorded by common consent to a person; (87.8): a state of exaltation.
go for (48.171): pass as.
gossiping (77.200): a meeting of friends and acquaintances, especially at the birth of a child.
grace cup (34.122): the last cup of liquor drunk before retiring, a parting draught.
grasp (180.147): embrace.
green-sickness (95.133): an anaemic disease, often characterized by morbid appetite for chalk, coal, etc., which affects young women about the age of puberty.
groat (53.159): a coin (1351–1662) worth four old pence.
gruntling (22.3): a low grunt.

handled (43.16): taken hold of (figuratively), examined, sized up.
hard-favoured (51.84): having an aspect harsh or unpleasant (*OED*); ugly (*AND*).
hard-pinched-for (48.168): stolen with difficulty (apparently Rochester's coinage); cf. *OED*, **Pinch**, *v.* 15a.
heart (47.121): a jewel or ornament in the shape of a heart.
heats (97.207): a redness or eruption on the skin, accompanied by a sensation of heat.

hector (11.12): a braggart blusterer, bully (*OED*); a vaporing, swaggering coward (*AND*).
heretofore (101.111): in time past.
high (41.41): high-class.
horseman's weight (58.76): the weight of a jockey in stones (14 lb = 1 stone).
huff (56.35): one puffed up with conceit of his own importance, valour, etc.; one who blusters or swaggers, a hector, a bully (*obsolete*).
huffing (11.9): blustering, hectoring, bullying.

idle (24.[2]16): empty, vacant.
ignis fatuus (72.12): 'A phosphorescent light seen hovering or flitting over marshy ground ... called Will-o'-the-wisp.... When approached, the *ignis fatuus* appears to recede, and finally to vanish, sometimes reappearing in another direction. This led to the notion that it was the work of a mischievous sprite intentionally leading benighted travellers astray' (*OED*).
imp (5.6): offspring, child (*obsolete* since 17th century).
impertinent (74.95): irrelevant; (52.149): not consonant with reason; absurd, idle, trivial, silly.
importance comfortable (45.65): a wife (*AND*).
impostume (204.1): a purulent swelling or cyst, an abscess.
inclined (12.[1]10): bent towards a particular object.
incommode (51.104): inconvenient, troublesome.
infamy (50.58): public reproach, shame, or disgrace; the loss of all or certain of the rights of a citizen.
insolent (24.1): offensively familiar.
insult on (313.5): manifest arrogant or scornful delight over, upon, or on an object of scorn (*obsolete*).
intrench (37.14): encroach or trespass upon.

jade (33.99): a term of reprobation applied to a woman.
japan (52.144): of, belonging to, native to, or produced in Japan; fashionable, exotic, 'whatever is not common' (50.59).
jingling (73.49): playing with words for the sake of sound.
job (33.93): a portion of some substance.
Jowler (75.122): here the name of a dog, but a jowler is a breed of heavy-jawed dogs, like basset hounds and mastiffs.

kickshaw (57.73): (a corruption of the French *quelque chose*) a fancy, insubstantial French dish.
kindly (23.37): in an easy, natural way; (36.4): with natural affection, lovingly.
kindness (16.[1]9): kind feeling; a feeling of tenderness or fondness; affection, love.
knack (73.49): a trick; a device, artifice; formerly often a deceitful or crafty device; a mean or underhand trick.
knight of the elbow (32.43): a gambler.

ladies of the town (80.35): prostitutes.
lawn sleeves (204.45): sleeves of fine linen, part of the episcopal dress.
leaguer (38.12): (Dutch *leger*), a military camp.
leg (17.7): an obeisance made by drawing back one leg and bending the other.
lewd (204.3): unlearned, unlettered, untaught (*obsolete*).
libel (56.14): a verse satire.
limber (28.35): limp.
lime (35.154): impregnate a bitch; copulate with.
lined (113.414): reinforced (*obsolete*).
linkboy (89.38): a boy employed to carry a torch made of tow and pitch to light passengers along the streets.
livelong (197.14): an emotional intensive of *long*, used of periods of time.
looby (204.16): lazy, hulking; awkward, stupid, clownish.
loose (98.9): free from moral restraint; lax in principle, conduct, or speech; immoral; (99.36): not tightly drawn, slack.
love-convicted (22.9): overcome with love.
lubbard (205.25): big, clumsy, stupid.
lumpish (100.91): stupidly dull, heavy, or lethargic.

machine (85.5): a contrivance for the production of stage-effects.
magazine (20.46): a place where goods are laid up; a storehouse (now *rare*).
magnificent (207.64): characterized by munificence on a grand scale (*OED* cites *Paradise Lost* (1667, 1674), IX 153: 'Man he made, and for him built / Magnificent this World').
make (195.[2]3): making or manufacture.

make a leg (205.26): bow by drawing back one leg and bending the other.
make away (34.125): destroy, dispose of, get rid of.
mark (204.17): a visible trace diversifying a surface, as a spot, stain, discoloration, scar; cf. birth-mark.
matter (203.13): physical or corporeal substance, contradistinguished from immaterial or incorporeal substance (spirit, soul, mind).
measure (10.14): a quantity, degree, or proportion of something, especially as granted to or bestowed upon a person.
memento mori (54.202): (Latin) remember that you have to die; a warning of death.
mere (33.98): pure, unmixed (*obsolete*).
mew (113.404): moult, shed.
motion (110.309; 139.87): a desire or inclination; an emotion (*obsolete*); (149.39): the action of moving, prompting, or urging a person to do something (*obsolete*).
move (10.[1]5): apply to or solicit a person for something.
mutton (32.50): a woman (*AND*).

nice (62.[2]12): difficult to please; (33.110): precise, strict, careful; (83.[1]4): coy, shy, affectedly modest (*obsolete*); (50.59): strange, rare, uncommon (*obsolete*); (87.25): reluctant, unwilling (*obsolete*); (100.71): refined, cultured. 'In many examples from the 16th and 17th centuries it is difficult to say in what particular sense the writer intended the word to be taken' (*OED*).
ninny (200.title): a simpleton, a fool.
noise (48.178): reputation (*obsolete*).
nokes (43.17): a ninny or fool.

onset (29.60): attacking an enemy.
open your case (83.[1]7): state your case to the court.
owl (45.40): 'Applied to a person in allusion to . . . appearance of gravity and wisdom (often with implication of underlying stupidity)' (*OED*).
own (15.32): acknowledge something in its relation to oneself; acknowledge a thing to be what is claimed.
owned (77.189): acknowledged.

parts (58.108): abilities, capacities, talents; also *absolutely*, high intellectual ability, cleverness, talent; a euphemism for genitals.
patched (86.45): put together hastily or insecurely.
pathetic (74.73): producing an effect upon the emotions. 'The sense of "miserably inadequate" is not recorded before 1937' (*OED*).
pea-straw (78.6): the stalks and leaves of the pea-plant.
peevish (64.22): spiteful, malignant.
pintle (56.22): penis.
pit (32.64): the floor of a theatre; the theatre audience. 'The Pit . . . is fill'd with Benches without Backboards, and adorn'd and cover'd with green Cloth. Men of Quality, particularly the younger Sort, some ladies of Reputation and Vertue, and abundance of Damsels that hunt for Prey, sit all together in this place, Higgledy-piggledy' (Henri Misson, *M. Misson's Memoirs and Observations in his Travels over England* (1719), 219).
place (11.10): high rank.
planed over (175.204): smoothed over.
play (50.51): gambling.
play booty (33.103): join with confederates in order to victimize another player; play or act falsely so as to gain a desired object; (*proverbial*) (Tilley B539).
plead (23.14): urge as a plea.
pledge (90.45): something given as a sign or token of favour or as an earnest of something to come.
point (203.30): give point to; give force to; lend prominence to; the wing (flank) of an army (*obsolete*).
poise (170.60): load, burden (*obsolete*).
policy (206.46): political sagacity; skill in the conduct of public affairs.
politician (184.[1]4): a shrewd schemer, a crafty plotter or intriguer.
politique (102.[1]16): 'politic' in the sense of 'scheming, crafty, cunning'.
pore (199.[1]11): any opening, sinus, or hollow in the human body including (in Rochester's surreal image) the eye-sockets of the skull.
pose (123.94): place in a difficulty with a question or problem.
posy (17.[1]4): 'A syncopated form of *Poesy*, a short motto, originally a

line or verse of poetry inscribed within a ring' (*OED* cites *Hamlet* (1603), II ii 162: 'Is this . . . the Poesie of a Ring?').

precise (200.17): strict or scrupulous in religious observance; in the 16th and 17th centuries, 'puritanical' (*OED*); foolishly scrupulous (*AND*).

presently (396.10n.): without any delay, at once, immediately.

pretending (76.175): professing falsely, feigning.

primitive (201.^{2}5): original, as opposed to derivative.

prodigious (72.2): unnatural, abnormal, monstrous.

proper (52.127): belonging to oneself, own (*archaic*).

prove (64.29): turn out to be; (20.5): show to be such as is asserted or claimed; (21.23): find out or learn, or know by experience; have experience of.

provision (43.9): something provided or arranged in advance.

puffed (6.22): blown out, extinguished with a puff.

Pug (53.169): here the name of a monkey, but 'pug' is a colloquial term for 'monkey'.

Punchinello (204.18): name of the principal character in a puppet show of Italian origin, the prototype of Punch (*OED* cites Disraeli, *Vivian Gray* (1826–7), V iv: 'A long grinning wooden figure, with great staring eyes, and the parrot nose of a pulcinello').

punk (40.11): prostitute.

purely (97.206): without blemish, corruption, or uncleanness; faultlessly, guilelessly, innocently.

puzzling (74.80): (*transitive*) laboriously trying to puzzle something out; (*intransitive*) bewildering, confusing (*OED* cites Thomas Sherlock, *Several Discourses Preached at the Temple Church* (1734), 42: 'Mysteries . . . to puzzle the Minds of Men').

qualm (18.^{3}1): a fit of sickening fear, misgiving, or depression.

rack (196.1): an instrument of torture consisting of a frame having a roller at each end; the victim was fastened to these by the wrists and ankles and had the joints of his limbs stretched by their rotation.

ramble (31.title): a walk in search of sexual partners; cf. 'Take you your Ramble, Madam, and I'll take mine' (Lee, 1954, II 2).

rampires (112.374): ramparts.

raze (150.68): erase by scraping (*obsolete*).

recreation (16.^{2}16): comfort produced by something affecting the senses or body (*obsolete*).
reduce (20.31): compel to submit or surrender.
refined (90.33): characterized by the possession of refinement in manners, action, or feeling; (99.32): having a high degree of subtlety, nicety, or precision.
reforming (74.102): forming a second time.
remove (62.^{2}13): free one from some condition, etc., especially one of a bad or detrimental kind. *OED* cites *Paradise Lost* (1667, 1674), XII 29: 'Law can discover sin, but not remove'.
rifled (65.66): despoiled or stripped bare of something. *OED* cites Shakespeare, *The Rape of Lucrece* (1593), 692: 'Pure Chastity is rifled of her store'.
rigour (313.14): puritanic severity or strictness.
romancy (201.23): romantic (*obsolete*).
rook (50.52): a cheat, swindler, or sharper, especially in gaming.

sack (38.5): dry white wines formerly imported from Spain and the Canaries.
sad (49.18): sorrowful, mournful; (208.93): grave, serious (*obsolete*).
salt-swol'n (33.86): in heat.
saucy (77.196): insolent towards superiors, presumptuous.
scarf (48.169): a broad band of silk worn by military officers across the body from one shoulder to the opposite hip.
scorbutic spots (95.106): ulcerations of the skin symptomatic of scurvy (vitamin C deficiency); 'by how much they encline to blackness, so much the worse' (Everard Maynwaring, *Morbus Polyrhizos* (1669), 51).
screw (76.150): to force or strain, as by means of a screw.
secure (25.^{1}7): to insure (Johnson 1755); (75.110): to make free from care or apprehension; to free from doubt; to make one feel secure of or against some contingency (*obsolete*).
sense (62.^{1}12): the recognition of a duty, virtue, etc., as incumbent upon one, or as a motive or standard for one's own conduct; (53.152): intelligence, especially as bearing on action or behaviour.
serail (90.34): seraglio, apartments reserved for wives and concubines.
set (128.1): put a sum down as a stake; cover the roller's bet in a dice game.

severe (36.2): rigorous in one's treatment of or attitude towards offenders.

shade (13.10): partial or comparative darkness; (68.^{2}9): the visible but impalpable form of a dead person; (201.1): the total darkness before God said, 'Let there be light' (Genesis 1.3).

shadow (143.94): unreal appearance; delusive semblance or image. 'To cast wild shadows o'er' presumably means to conceal.

shipwreck (3.25): cause a person to suffer shipwreck.

shore (200.20): sewer.

shrug (46.100): move the body from side to side as a gesture of joy or self-satisfaction; fidget about.

sillery (57.73): a high-class wine produced in and around the village of Sillery in Champagne.

slur (32.43): the sliding of a die out of the box so that it does not turn (*obsolete*) (*OED*); a cheat at dice (*AND*).

snuff (6.23): that portion of a wick, etc., which is partly consumed in the course of burning.

Sodom (83.^{1}5): an extremely wicked or corrupt place.

sot (56.5): a foolish or stupid person (*obsolete*).

spark (192.^{1}9): a young man of an elegant or foppish character; one who affects smartness or display in dress and manners. Chiefly depreciatory.

spend (28.16): to ejaculate; to have an orgasm.

sponge (200.8): various species of porifers used in bathing.

sprittle staff (396.10n.): properly a spittle-staff or mattock, 'A staff of wood four or five feet long, shod at the lower end with a wedge-like piece of iron, to *stub* thistles with' (James O. Halliwell, *A Dictionary of Archaic and Provincial Words*, 2 vols. (1847), II 785).

sprung (28.11): of game birds: made to fly up.

squab (100.76): a raw, inexperienced person (*obsolete*); short, fat person.

on the **square** (76.162): in a fair, honest, or straightforward manner; without artifice, deceit, fraud, or trickery.

stand (29.61): take up an offensive or defensive position; to await an onset; of the penis: to become erect; (131.13, 24): remain steadfast; hold out.

start (122.53): to swerve from a principle (*obsolete*); (183.253): come suddenly from a place of concealment.

stew (29.59): brothel.
still (66.10): continually, constantly, always.
stint (48.164): allotted amount, allowance.
stir (196.[1]15): make any movement, move at all or in the least.
stone (29.68): a morbid concretion in the bladder, etc.
stout (89.10): valiant, brave, undaunted.
strangury (29.68): a disease of the urinary organs characterized by slow and painful urination (*OED*); 'pissing by drops' (Culpeper 1652, 49).
strike (15.31): cause a person to be overwhelmed or seized with terror, amazement, grief, or, rarely, love.
sublime (207.45): standing high above others by reason of nobility or grandeur of nature or character; expressing lofty ideas in a grand and elevated manner.
such (34.134): as much.
surfeit water (34.116): a medicinal drink for the cure of surfeit, a 17th-century Bromo-Seltzer.
surprise (10.[2]5): overcome (the mind, will, heart); captivate (*obsolete*).
swain (21.[2]24): a man of low degree, a farm labourer, a countryman, a rustic (*archaic*).
swinger (41.28): a vigorous performer (*obsolete*); a person who is sexually promiscuous.
swive (28.27): copulate with.

take (85.4): take the fancy, win favour, gain acceptance, become popular.
take up (36.1): adopt.
take upon (80.17): put on airs.
take upon oneself (23.10): behave presumptuously or haughtily, assume airs (*obsolete*).
tarse (35.16): penis.
tawdry (32.62): dressed in cheap and pretentious finery (*OED*); 'gawdy, with lace or mismatched and staring colours' (*AND*).
tearing (32.74): violent, headstrong.
thorough-paced (86.28): of a horse: thoroughly trained, having all his paces.
thronged (19.21): crowded. *OED* cites William Browne, *Britannia's Pastorals* (1616), II 115: 'the thronged Creeke / Ran lessened up'.

on **tick** (56.3): on credit.
tierce (57.71): a third of a pipe, or 14 gallons (of French claret in this case). 'Tierce claret' may be a phrase like 'draught beer'.
tine (6.22): a variant of 'tind' (*obsolete*), kindle.
toast (38.7): bread browned at the fire and put in wine.
top (204.6): the common top is kept spinning by lashing it with a whip.
trade (50.51): the practice of some occupation, business, or profession habitually carried on, especially when practised as a means of livelihood or gain, frequently in a depreciatory sense.
trades (86.51): tradesmen.
trading (67.56): tradesmanlike, perhaps 'With sinister implication: [driving] a trade in something which should not be bought or sold' (*OED*).
traffic (170.73): recórd; communication (*rare*).
train (5.[1]3): a body of persons, animals, vehicles, etc., travelling together.
translate (4.3): to remove from one place or condition to another.
treat (61.174): carry on negotiations with a view to settling terms.
trim (48.167): cheat a person out of money, in this case by selling a spavined horse.
true-love knot (91.52): a kind of knot of a complicated and ornamental form (usually either a double-looped bow or a knot formed of two loops intertwined), used as a symbol of true love.
truth (204.46): faithfulness, fidelity (now *rare* or *archaic*).
try (70.7): have the experience of; undergo, go through (*obsolete*).
twat (201.[2]6): the female pudendum.

unblest (71.14): sexually unsatisfied; cf. 'the blest Lover' (Pope 1939–67, II 205).
undo (23.16): unfasten the clothing of; (53.176): ruin by seducing.
unmeaning (196.1): vacant, possibly a Rochester coinage; the earliest example in *OED* is 1704.
unweighed (85.20): hasty, inconsiderate.
use (194.2): utility, advantage, benefit.

vassal (27.60): subject, subordinate.
virtuous (40.15): distinguished by manly qualities (*obsolete*).

whiffling (34.136): trifling, insignificant.
whimsey (72.17): a fantastic or freakish idea; (39.18): a capricious notion or fancy.
whitewash (46.87): a cosmetic wash used for imparting a light colour to the skin (*obsolete*).
winged (187.103): reinforced with additional troops on the wings (flanks) (*OED* cites *Richard III*, V iii 300: 'well-winged with our cheefest Horse').
withal (184.9): with; cf. 'a potsherd to scrape himself withal' (Job 2.8).
withdrawing room (60.148): a private chamber attached to a more public room.
women coursers (78.[2]9): dealers in women (*OED* cites Beaumont and Fletcher, *The Captain* (1613), V i: 'I am no Bawd, nor Cheater, nor a Courser / Of broken-winded women').
women fairs (78.[2]9): places for the sale (*lit.* or *fig.*) of women.
worn (51.102): in fashion.
worth (5.5): of account or importance; entitled to respect or honour; worthy (*obsolete*).

Notes

The Bible is quoted in the authorized King James version, the classics in the Loeb Classical Library (Harvard University Press and Heinemann), and Shakespeare in *The Norton Facsimile* [*of*] *The First Folio*, ed. Charlton Hinman (1968).

To His Sacred Majesty (Virtue's triumphant shrine, who dost engage)

Britannia Rediviva is a volume of poems in Latin, Greek, Hebrew, Arabic, French, and English published by Oxford University to celebrate the Restoration of Charles II. Rochester's contribution, the first among the English poems in the volume, affords a striking example of how much meaning typography can add to a poem. Rochester's poem is the only English poem to be illustrated by an ornamental headpiece, a factotum initial, and a row of type ornaments. The only other poem to be so honoured is the vice-chancellor's Latin poem, the first in the volume. Rochester's poem and the next English poem, by Sir William Portman, 6th Baronet, of All Souls College, are the only contributions to be set in italic type. The names of the vice-chancellor, the senior proctor of the University, Rochester, and Portman are the only ones to be set in upper-case type. The names of the others, John Freke, who later wrote *The History of Insipids* (1674), Ambrose Phillips, Robert South, and John Locke, are printed in lower-case type. The typography of *Britannia Rediviva* says unequivocally that *To His Sacred Majesty* is an important poem. It is one of Ezra Pound's 'exhibits' in *ABC of Reading*, where it is quoted in full (Pound 1934, 134).

ATTRIBUTION Anthony à Wood attributes the poem to Robert Whitehall, a fellow of Merton College (Wood 1813–20, III 1232). Confirmatory external evidence for the attribution to Rochester in the copy-text is lacking. There is only one textual tradition, the other witness to the text of this and the two following examples of Rochester's juvenilia, Rochester 1691, 121–7, being set up from the 1660 texts. But internal evidence strongly suggests that Rochester wrote the verses. The evidence includes two characteristic Rochesterian puns (ll. 3,10), a characteristic comic rhyme (ll. 5–6, cf. 13.2, 4), and some characteristic imperfect rhymes (ll. 3–4, cf. 78.^{2}9–10, 89.33, 35; ll. 11–12, cf. 86.41–2, 198.17–18; ll. 13–14, cf. 26.13–14, 53.173–4).

Whitehall may have 'pretended to instruct [Rochester] . . . in the art of poetry' (ibid.), but it is not likely that he wrote these verses. Whitehall's ability is demonstrated in his New Year's letter to Rochester in 1667:

> My Lord,
> Our picture we have sent,
> An Embleme of approaching Lent:

But that redd letter in each cheeke
Speaks Holyday, not Ember-weeke:
So incorporeall, so aery
This Christmas 'twill be ta'ne for Fairy.
(Needham 1934, 44)

and by some verses he wrote to celebrate the inauguration of the Sheldonian Theatre in 1669:

. . . the Lion, Bull, and savage Beare
Contended in [Augustus Caesar's] Amphitheater
With Bore, Rhinoceros and Elephant,
That did at once Spectators please, and daunt.
(Bodl. MS. Wood 423, f. 42)

In *Britannia Rediviva* Rochester's contribution occupies the place of honour; Robert Whitehall's is last, coming after that of John Locke, who wrote adulatory verses to Oliver Cromwell. Rochester's friend, Sir Francis Fane, was aware that 'already in [his] tender age [Rochester] set out . . . new and glorious Lights in Poetry . . . Orthodox and Unquestionable' (*Love in the Dark: or The Man of Business* (1675), sig. A2v).

DATE The Thomason copy of the copy-text in the British Library is dated 7 July [1660] (Madan 1895–1913, III 112).

COPY-TEXT *Britannia Rediviva*, Oxford, 1660, sig. Aa1.

ANNOTATION
2 *pilgrimage*: to Dover to greet the fleet bringing Charles II back to England: 'it being endlesse to reckon or number those that are gone, who are the flower of the Gentry of *England*, all striving to exceed each other in costliness of their Furniture and Equipage' (*The Publick Intelligencer*, 21–28 May 1660).
3 *ecstatic*: punning on two meanings of the word: the etymological sense of 'out of place', 'Out of themselves' (l. 4) and the lexical sense of 'intensely pleasurable' (*OED*) (Rochester 1984, 229).
5 *one camp*: the Lord General George Monck ordered the Parliamentary army, that defeated Charles II at Worcester in 1651, to march out of London on 23 May 1660 and to encamp at Blackheath, beyond Greenwich in Kent. 'At Black Heath the Army was drawn up where His Majesty viewed them, giving out many expressions of His Gracious favor to the Army, which were received by loud shoutings and rejoycings' (*The Parliamentary Intelligencer*, 28 May–4 June 1660).
7 *loyal Kent*: in 1648 a widespread insurrection in Kent on behalf of Charles I was savagely suppressed by Fairfax.
8 *Fencing her ways*: on Tuesday 29 May 1660 'His Majesty took his journey from Rochester betwixt four and five in the morning, the Military forces of Kent lining the wayes, and maidens strewing herbs and flowers, and the several towns hanging out white sheets' (*Mercurius Publicus*, 24–31 May 1660); *moving groves*: '2 or 300 Maids of the Town [Pursely, Kent] . . . marched in Rank and File, each carrying a green Beechen bough, with Drums and Trumpets, up to Stinchcomb Hill, where . . . they drank the Kings Health upon their Knees' (ibid.); cf. *Macbeth*, V v 38: 'MESSENGER: . . . may you see it comming. / I say, a moving Grove'.
10 *sedentary feet*: punning on two meanings of the phrase: 'idle feet' and 'halting verse' (Rochester 1984, 229).

11 *youth*: Rochester was thirteen on 10 April 1660; *not patient*: impatient, 'Restlessly desirous, eagerly longing' (*OED*).
16 *father's ashes*: Henry Wilmot, 1st Earl of Rochester, died on 19 February 1658 at Ghent. He was buried first in Sluys, in the Netherlands, and was reinterred at Spelsbury, Oxfordshire.

In Obitum Serenissimae Mariae Principis Arausionensis (Impia blasphemi sileant convitia vulgi)

Mary Stuart, Princess Royal of England and Princess of Orange (Plate 2), was widowed in November 1650 at the age of nineteen and died of smallpox on 24 December 1660 during a state visit to England. The court physicians could not agree whether the Princess's illness was measles, spotted fever, or smallpox, and Dr Alexander Fraser, who attended her, came under criticism (Marvell 1927, II 13; Pepys, 26 December 1660). In Oxford University's collection of elegies, *Epicedia Academiae Oxoniensis, in Obitum Serenissimae Mariae Principis Arausionensis* (1660), Rochester's contribution again occupies a place of honour. Set in italic type it immediately follows the first poem, by Paul Hood the 76-year-old rector of Lincoln College and vice-chancellor of the University, and immediately precedes the contribution of Edward Hyde, chancellor of the Exchequer and chancellor of the University, soon to be created Earl of Clarendon. It was Clarendon who planted a paternal kiss upon Rochester's cheek when he was created M.A. in September 1661 at the age of fifteen. Robert Whitehall's contribution is the last among the poems in classical languages.

ATTRIBUTION This is another poem that Anthony à Wood attributes to Whitehall (Wood 1813–20, III 1232) despite the fact that it is published over Rochester's name. Yet even in this mechanical exercise there is some slight evidence of Rochester's style. The assonance in ll. 4–6, 'Ulcera . . . / Vultu . . . pustula vulnus / . . . pulchras', is characteristic of Rochester's later practice, e.g. 'quietly . . . glide, / . . . either side' (19.17–18).

DATE 'early in the year 1661' (Madan 1895–1931, III 143).

COPY-TEXT *Epicedia Academiae Oxoniensis, in Obitum Serenissimae Mariae Principis Arausionensis*, Oxford: 1660, sig. A2v.

EMENDATION OF COPY-TEXT Roman and italic type reversed.

To Her Sacred Majesty, the Queen Mother, on the Death of Mary, Princess of Orange (Respite, great Queen, your just and hasty fears)

ATTRIBUTION Contingencies in the royal family kept Rochester busy during his twenty months at Wadham College. This is the third of his juvenilia that is attributed to Robert Whitehall, that 'useless member' of Merton College (Wood 1813–20, III 1232, IV 178). The internal evidence again may suggest that Rochester wrote the verses printed over his name. The evidence includes a characteristic paradox or oxymoron, 'Shipwreck to safety' (l. 25), functional dissonance (l. 36), word play (l. 38), and imperfect rhymes that recur in Rochester's later verse (ll. 13–14, cf. 78.[2]8–10; ll. 15–16, cf. 27.39–40, 90.49–50; ll. 45–6, cf. 78.[2]5–7, 199.[2]1,3). Since internal evidence convinces no one but the deponent, and without confirmation by external evidence, the attribution stands unproven. Rochester's contribution again occupies a place of honour: the first of the elegies in English. Whitehall's is the last elegy in Latin. Like Milton's *Lycidas* (1638) Rochester's elegy soon turns to satire – on the court physicians who attended the Princess of Orange (ll. 33–40).

COPY-TEXT *Epicedia Academiae Oxoniensis, in Obitum Serenissimae Mariae Principis Arausionensis*, Oxford: 1660, sig. G1.

DATE After the 'great wind' of 18 January 1661 (l. 23) and before the news of the Queen Mother's sailing on 25 January 1661 (l. 21) reached Oxford.

EMENDATION OF COPY-TEXT Roman and italic reversed; 31 curses] cures
Corrected in Rochester 1691, 126.

ANNOTATION
7 *wrongs*: on 23 May 1643 the Commons voted unanimously to charge the Queen with high treason for waging war against the Parliament (*CJ*, III 98) (Rochester 1968, 157).
8 *banishment*: when Charles I marched out of Oxford to take the field for the campaign of 1644, Henrietta Maria was sent to Exeter where she gave birth to her seventh and last child, Henrietta Anne, in April. When refused a safe conduct to Bath, she made her way to Falmouth and took shipping for Brest on 14 July. She did not return to England until October 1660, 'a very little plain old woman' (Pepys, 22 November 1660). She arrived a month after the death of her youngest son, Henry Duke of Gloucester, and two months before the death of her eldest daughter, the Princess of Orange.
12 *head*: Charles I was beheaded on 30 January 1649 on a scaffold erected outside the Banqueting House, Whitehall Palace.
15 *young daughter lost*: fifteen-year-old Princess Elizabeth, Henrietta Maria's second daughter, died at Carisbroke Castle on 8 September 1650 while Henrietta Maria was living in exile in the Louvre.
18 *noble Gloucester's obsequies*: Henry, Duke of Gloucester, died of smallpox in London on 13 September 1660 at the age of twenty. None of the elegies in *Epicedia Academiae Oxoniensis, in Obitum Celsissimi Principis Henrici Ducis Glocestrensis* (1660) is attributed to Rochester but it may be surmised that he wrote one.
19 *fall*: the death of the Princess Royal of England and Princess of Orange on 24 December 1660.
20 *funeral*: Rochester could have read about Princess Mary's funeral in *The Kingdomes Intelligencer* (31 December 1660–7 January 1661): at 9 p.m. on 29 December 1660 the cortège left Denmark House 'through a Lane of Guards of the Duke of Albemarl's Regiment . . . the Pall being supported by six Earles . . . His Highness the Duke of York following the Corps with an Herald before him, and divers Persons of Quality bearing his Train . . . [and] proceeded till they came to King *Henry* the sevenths Chappel'.
21 *remove*: Pepys heard in November 1660 that Henrietta Maria intended to leave London 'within five or six days' (Pepys, 25 November 1660). The Queen Mother was to escort Princess Henrietta Anne, aged sixteen, to France for her marriage to Philippe, duc d'Anjou (later Orléans), younger brother of Louis XIV. Bad weather and the Princess's illness delayed their departure until 25 January 1661 (*CSPD 1660–61*, 487–8).
23 *winds*: Pepys mentions 'a great wind' on 18 January 1661.
25 *Shipwreck to safety*: because shipwreck before Portsmouth would prevent the Queen Mother from taking Princess Henrietta Anne to France (?).

30 *the fair princess*: 'the Princesse Henriette is fallen sick of the meazells on board the *London*, after the Queen [Mother] and she were under sail – and so was forced to come back again into Portsmouth harbour . . . The Queene and she continue aboard, and do not entend to come on shore till she sees what will become of the young Princesse. This newes doth make people think something endeed; that three of them [the Duke of Gloucester, Princess Mary, and Princess Henrietta Anne] should fall sick of the same disease one after another' (Pepys, 11 January 1661).
35 *new poisons*: Philippus Aureolus Theophrastus Bombastus von Hohenheim (1493–1541), or Paracelsus, as he called himself, founded a new chemical or spagyric school of medical practice, introducing a number of new poisons, including lead, sulphur, iron, arsenic, and copper sulphate, into the pharmacopoeia; *fire*: open wounds were treated by cauterization (with chemicals or red-hot iron), and gunshot wounds with boiling oil.
36 *Murder*: the faltering of the insistent iambic beat – only four feet in the poem are *not* iambic – calls attention to the failure of the court physicians to save the lives of Henry, Duke of Gloucester, and Princess Mary.
38 *write bills*: punning on two meanings of 'bills': medical prescriptions written by a physician and weekly reports of the number and causes of deaths in the 109 parishes of London, called bills of mortality, that the Company of Parish Clerks began to publish in 1592.
39 *bleeding corpse*: corpses traditionally bleed in the presence of the murderer (*Motif-Index* D1318.5.2), as in the ballad *Young Hunting*.
40 *drain*: the discovery by another court physician, William Harvey, of the circulation of the blood (1628) had the unfortunate consequence that phlebotomy became specific for almost every known disease.
42 *third . . . disease*: assuming that Princess Elizabeth died of a fever and the Duke of Gloucester and Princess Mary of smallpox, the Queen Mother herself becomes the third fatal disease to strike the royal family, for taking the Princess Henrietta Anne to live in France is a form of killing. This far-fetched metaphysical conceit may be compared to the conceit of the seventeen-year-old Dryden in *Upon the Death of the Lord Hastings* (1649), in which the suppuration of the smallpox pustules is imagined to be tears weeping for Hastings: 'Each little Pimple had a Tear in it, / To wail the fault its rising did commit'.

The Wish (Oh, that I could by any chemic art)

ATTRIBUTION This squib is attributed to Rochester in Harvard MS. Eng. 636F, p. 75, Princeton MS. Taylor 3, p. 254, University of Illinois MS. [The Commonplace book. Poems], f. 16v, and Rochester 1714 (Curll)[1], 112, representing at least two independent textual traditions. James Thorpe finds it 'incredible that [Rochester] composed this mature piece at such an age that it could find its way into print in a drollery by the time he was barely fourteen' (*MLN* 62 (1947), 268). But Rochester was an undergraduate at the time and another critic observes that 'this seems exactly the kind of verse he might have written at that . . . sexually precocious age' (Fabricant 1969, 705).

COPY-TEXT *The Second Part of Merry Drollery* [1661?], 31.

EMENDATION OF COPY-TEXT Title: the verses are entitled *Insatiate Desire* in the copy-text, but some variant of *The Wish* is found in three manuscript copies (Harvard, Princeton, and University of Illinois) and in Rochester 1714 (Curll)[1] and printed copies derived from it, including Rochester 1926, 120. In two other manuscript copies the squib is called *Votum* (Edinburgh MS. Dc.1.3, p. 78, and Yale) MS. Osborn b.105, p. 397). 4 the] her regenerate!] degenerate; 6 *fuck*] ---- The substantive emendations are supplied from Yale MS. Osborn b.105, p. 397, and Illinois MS. [The Commonplace book. Poems], f. 16v.

ANNOTATION
3 *translate*: traduction is the belief that the soul is not pre-existent but conveyed by the sperm in the act of reproduction; cf. Dryden 1956– , III 110.

'Twas a dispute 'twixt heaven and earth

David Vieth observes that this lyric, 'almost unique among Rochester's poems in its use of . . . hyperbolic compliment', is 'reminiscent of Ben Jonson's lyrics' (Vieth 1963, 221; Rochester 1968, 171). One of Jonson's exercises in 'hyperbolic compliment', *How he saw her*, combines the mistress's 'glorie', Cupid's surrender, and fatal eyes. Another one, *Her Triumph*, introduces a 'Chariot of Love' (Jonson 1925–52, VIII 132, 134), but the similarities are neither verbal nor striking. They are those of two poets working in the same tradition.

The two stanza forms of this 'subtle metrical experiment' (Anne Barton, *English Studies* 52 (1971), 556), $A^4A^4B^5C^2C^3D^5D^4B^5$ and $A^5A^3B^5C^5B^5C^4A^5A^5$, are hybrids, variants of the octave stanza, $A^5B^5A^5B^5C^5D^5C^5D^5$, with the irregular line-lengths and irregular rhyme schemes of the Pindaric ode. The metre seems equally experimental: 'Else the GOD' (l. 13) is an anapaestic substitution in the iambic pattern; in order to scan and to rhyme with 'GLO-ries BY' (l. 12), 'POW'R-ful-LY' (l. 14) must receive emphasis on the last syllable, like wrenched accent in the ballad tradition.

ATTRIBUTION Although not confirmed by external evidence, the attribution to Rochester (Needham 1934, 51) is as certain as the nature of the case permits: the unique witness to the text of the poem is a copy in Rochester's hand with corrections in Rochester's hand.

COPY-TEXT Nottingham MS. Portland Pw V 31, f. 2.

ANNOTATION
3 *For*: on behalf of; *Cynthia*: the name given to Diana, the chaste goddess of hunting, from Mount Cynthus in Delos, where she and her brother, Apollo, were born, the offspring of Jupiter and Latona.
6 *imps of light*: Diana's attendant nymphs, like herself, abjured concourse with men.
7 *envious*: after Diana admitted Orion to her train, Aurora fell in love with him and spirited him away to Delos, where Diana tracked him down and killed him with her arrows; *queen of night*: Diana was Triformis, and in one manifestation was Luna, the moon, represented pictorially by a crescent moon on her head.
8 *conquered*: by the celebrated giant Orion, of whom Diana became enamoured.
12 *glories*: Apollo's nimbus, or circle of radiant light.
13 *the god*: Cupid, the son of Venus and Mars.
15 *making of his priest a sacrifice*: cf. 'Each one, his owne Priest, and owne Sacrifice' (Donne 1912, I 178).
16 *unhallowed*: unblest, in Pope's sense of 'the blest Lover' (Pope 1939–67, II 205); cf. 65.69.

Two Fragments (Custom does often reason overrule) (Wit like tierce claret, when't begins to pall)

ATTRIBUTION As well as *Song* (Give me leave to rail at you), *The Agreeable Variety* (1717), 148 includes two more fragments 'From the Lord Rochester', but there is no other evidence that Rochester wrote them.

To his Mistress (Why dost thou shade thy lovely face? Oh, why)

ATTRIBUTION This parody of Francis Quarles, *Emblemes* (1635), 149–50, 170, is attributed to Rochester only in the copy-text. The attribution is confirmed by no other evidence and must remain 'in a doubtful way' (l. 26). But the whole enterprise seems sufficiently Rochesterian to warrant inclusion here. By changing the order of the stanzas and a few words and phrases – 'My love' for 'My God' – Quarles's passionate poem of sacred love is turned into an equally passionate poem of profane love.

DATE Unknown but the nature of the exercise and the grammatical errors (l. 28) may suggest early work.

COPY-TEXT Rochester 1707 (Bragge), [1]32.

EMENDATION OF QUARLES, EMBLEMES, III vii AND xii **2** of thine] so long **3** the sun's] thy soule **4** thy] that **5** light's] *Light*: **9** love] Lord **11** eternal] perpetuall **12** love] God **15** withdraw'st] withdraw **16** dark and blind] blind and darke **18** to that] to the **20** be bold] behold **21** A phoenix likes] is *Phoenix*-like the] that **24** Ah!] O **25** dear lover] great Shepheard **27** Love] Lord **28** does] do **29** go] safely go **31** thy face away] away thy face **33** love] Lord triest] onely try'st **34** Display] Unskreene **35** perhaps no] Perhaps, thou think'st, no **36** their] those **37** and] the **39** I but them] thou err, I] erre; I grope; I **40** Dissolve] Disclose **42** life, my light] *Light*, my *Life* **45** me] Thee

ANNOTATION

19–21 'Stanza xi of Quarles's *Emblemes*, III vii reads as follows: "If that be all, shine forth and draw thee nigher; / Let me behold, and die, for my desire / Is phoenix-like, to perish in that fire." In Rochester, this becomes: "If that be all Shine forth and draw thou nigher. / Let me be bold and Dye for my Desire. / A *Phenix* likes to perish in the Fire." There are only two verbal substitutions here of any consequence: . . . "behold" into "be bold", and the most striking introduction of the word "likes" in Rochester's versions of the third line. Otherwise, the transformation has been effected by means which are not properly linguistic: by end-stopping the second line where Quarles had permitted an enjambment and by a change in punctuation and accentual stress which suddenly throws the erotic connotations of the word "die" . . . into relief. . . . The lines are the same and not the same; another voice is speaking Quarles's words, from another point of view' (Righter 1968, 58).

23 *flameless*: the copy-text reads 'shameless', but the context requires Quarles's word.

27 *lamb . . . stray*: cf. 'it is not the will of your Father which is in heaven, that one of these little ones should perish' (Matthew 18.14).

35 *thy*: the copy-text reads 'my', but the context requires Quarles's word; cf. line 1.
36 *die*: cf. 'the LORD . . . said, Thou canst not see my face: for there shall no man see me, and live' (Exodus 33.20).
43 *thy*: the copy-text reads 'my', but the context requires Quarles's word.

On Rome's Pardons (If Rome can pardon sins, as Romans hold)

In these verses Rochester undertakes another variation on a theme by Quarles in iambic pentameter triplets. Quarles's verses are these:

> If Rome could *pardon* sins, as Romans hold,
> And if such *Pardons* might be bought for *Gold*,
> An easie Judgement might determine which
> To choose; To be *religious*, or else *rich*;
> Nay Rome does *pardon*: *Pardons* may be sold;
> Wee'l search no Scriptures; But the *Mines*, for Gold.
>
> (Francis Quarles, *Divine Fancies: Digested into Epigrammes, Meditations, and Observations* (1632), 156)

An early reader recalls 'a Copy of Verses written by the Earl of Rochester (who had . . . seen all the Fopperies and Idolatries of the Church of Rome, as they are practis'd abroad)'. 'I thinke they are very pathetick', he adds (Harvard MS. Eng. 586, p. 188).

ATTRIBUTION The verses are attributed to Rochester in eight ms. copies (Bodl. MS. Add. B.106, f. 33v; Bodl. MS. Sancroft 53, p. 69; Harvard MS. Eng. 586, p. 188; Harvard MS. Eng. 606, p. 8; Yale MS. Osborn fb 142, p. 25; Yale MS. Osborn C 188, p. 68; Yale MS. Osborn Poetry Box, IV/9; Folger MS. M.a.187, f. 165r) and the copy-text, representing at least two independent textual traditions. Vieth's argument (that Rochester could not have written this anti-Catholic squib because Stephen College is alleged to have said that Rochester procured the conversion to Roman Catholicism of Lady Rochester in 1667) lacks conviction (Vieth 1963, 359–62).

COPY-TEXT Rochester 1680^3, 151.

EMENDATION OF COPY-TEXT 13 Jesuit] *Devil*
The emendation, actually 'Jesuist', an obsolete variant of 'Jesuit', is preserved in B.L. MS. Sloane 1731A, f. 171.

ANNOTATION
8 *at their own proper cost*: at their own expense. The archaic meaning of 'proper', 'belonging to oneself' (*OED*), recurs in *A Letter from Artemisa to Chloe* (52.127).
10 *knack*: in the original, pejorative sense of 'a mean or underhand trick' (*OED*), the word also occurs in *A Satyr against Mankind* (73.49).

A Song (Insulting beauty, you misspend)

The unusual stanza form, $A^4B^4A^4A^4A^4B^3$, may be a variant of tail rhyme, $A^4A^4B^3A^4A^4B^3$, which Chaucer parodies in *The Tale of Sir Thopas*. The complaint motif can be 'traced ultimately to Ovid's *Amores*, II ix' (Mario Praz, *English Studies* 10 (1928), 49), which Rochester translated (26.7).

ATTRIBUTION Since the attribution to Rochester in the copy-text is not confirmed by external evidence, it must have been internal evidence that caused Hayward, Pinto, Vieth, and Walker to include the poem in their editions. The attribution to Rochester of another poem in *Examen Poeticum* (1693), 'Too late, alas! I must confess' (10), *is* confirmed by external evidence; a version of it in Rochester's hand is preserved in Nottingham MS. Portland Pw V 31, f. 3r. On this evidence Vieth concludes that 'the general reliability of Tonson's volume seems sufficient to warrant the retention of this poem ['Insulting beauty . . .'] in the Rochester canon' (*N&Q* 201 (1956), 338–9). But the same volume attributes to 'My Lord R.' *A Paean, or Song of Triumph, on the Translation and Apotheosis of King Charles the Second* ('O Muse, to whom the Glory does belong'), *not* accepted by Hayward, Pinto, Vieth, or Walker and in fact written by Edward Radclyffe, 2nd Earl of Derwentwater (David Vieth, *PMLA* 72 (1957), 612–14).

The internal evidence is slight. It includes a characteristic teasing paradox: 'inglorious freedom' (l. 13; cf. 'freedom to obey' (19.12), and a few imperfect rhymes that recur in Rochester's later work (ll. 2, 6, cf. 78.^{2}5, 7, 199.^{2}1, 3, 198.15–16; ll. 13, 15, cf. 197.2–5, 8.^{1}7–9). On the other hand the complaint motif, the repetitive structure, and the diction: 'charms . . . conquering eyes . . . killing fair' are so implacably conventional that they could have been tacked together by a dozen poets in the period. Nor is there any evidence that this is a parody of an absent poem, or an answer to Elizabeth Malet's *Song* ('Nothing adds to love's fond fire'), or a poetic response to a biographical contretemps. What is missing is the biographical accident or the literary object to which this poem could be a response, an imitation, or a parody. So the attribution to Rochester awaits confirming evidence.

COPY-TEXT *Examen Poeticum: Being the Third Part of Miscellany Poems*, London: by R. E. for Jacob Tonson, 1693, ^{1}381.

A Song (My dear mistress has a heart)

In this experimental form Rochester creates a double heptasyllabic ballad stanza with a two-line refrain, $A^4B^4A^4B^4C^4D^4C^{4R}D^{4R}$, a variation of the heptasyllabic stanza that he used in 'Give me leave to rail at you' (15), $A^4B^4B^4B^4C^4C^4D^4D^4$. As a further embellishment the even-numbered lines have double rhymes. 'The result of this delicately asymmetrical scansion is that every line ends with what sounds like an unexplained falter, the odd lines because they have one syllable too few, the even because they have one too many. With a striking technical mastery, this effect of varying but inevitable falter, like a flaw in nature or an irony in the mind . . . is repeated conclusively in the structure of the whole [stanza] . . . the repetition at the end of the second verse of the last two lines of the first, a *reprise* like a stammer that turns the whole poem into an echo of its sustaining and yet faltering pairs of line' (Barbara Everett in Treglown 1982, 16–17). Nathaniel Lee records Rochester's 'Hesitation in his Speech' (Lee 1954, II 162).

ATTRIBUTION The attribution to Rochester in the copy-text is not confirmed by external evidence, since Rochester 1691, 64, where the poem is also attributed to Rochester, almost certainly derives from the copy-text. But the fact that the editor of the copy-text, Aphra Behn, knew Rochester and wrote an elegy on his death makes the attribution probable.

COPY-TEXT *Miscellany, Being a Collection of Poems by Several Hands*, London: for J. Hindmarsh, 1685, 43.

EMENDATION OF COPY-TEXT 9 move,] moves
The emendation is preserved in Rochester 1691, 64.

ANNOTATION
11 *dress*: Although the basic meaning of the verb is 'to array, make ready ... to adorn' (*OED*), the parallel construction, 'dress her eyes' and 'arm her lips', suggests a military context for 'dress', equivalent perhaps to 'deploy'.

Song (While on those lovely looks I gaze)

This exercise in double common ballad stanza, $A^4B^3A^4B^3C^4D^3C^4D^3$ (with double rhyme in the short lines, like 'My dear mistress has a heart' (9)) can be sung to the tune of 'When love with unconfined wings' (Simpson 1966, 761–2).

ATTRIBUTION This song is attributed to Rochester in two ms. copies (B.L. MS. Add. 27408, f. 11r, and Harvard MS. Eng. 636F, pp. 67–8) and two printed copies (Rochester 1680[2], 71, and Rochester 1691, 43), representing two independent textual traditions.

COPY-TEXT *A New collection of the Choicest Songs* (1676), sig. A8r.

EMENDATION OF COPY-TEXT 15 victor lives with] victors love in 16 dies] dye
The emendation of l. 15 is preserved in Rochester 1680[2], 71.

ANNOTATION
16 *dies*: Vieth prints 'die', the reading of the copy-text and four other witnesses, perhaps not aware that in l. 8 the rejected lover imagines that he 'Dies wishing' while in l. 16 he imagines that his disdainful mistress dies in orgasm, illustrating Rochester's paradox that in love, life and death are equivalent (l. 14). So 'dies', the reading of Nottingham MS. Portland Pw V 40, p. 64, two other mss. (Rochester 1984, 166), and B.L. MS. 27408, f. 11r, which Walker does not collate, may be what Rochester wrote, *pleasure*: it has been observed that in Rochester's amatory verse getting into bed is never far from the speaker's mind (354.69n.).

Another Song in Imitation of Sir John Eaton's Songs (Too late, alas, I must confess)

Sir John Eaton or Ayton, K.G., whom Etherege called a bully (Rochester *Letters* 1980, 89), was first gentleman usher to Charles II and *ex officio* gentleman usher of the Black Rod, which required him to attend the House of Lords every day during the sitting of Parliament. He was also usher of the Honourable Order of the Garter (Chamberlayne 1670, 265).

Rochester's exercise in common ballad stanza with double rhyme in the short lines, like 'While on those lovely looks I gaze' (9–10), is called an 'Imitation', but the imitation is limited to two sets of rhymes and the verses may be read as parody:

A Song by Sir John Eaton

Tell me not I my time mispend,
'Tis time lost to reprove me;
Persue thou thine, I have my end
So *Chloris* only love me.

Tell me not others Flocks are full,
Mine poor, let them despise me
Who more abound with Milk and Wool,
So *Chloris* only prize me.

Tire others easier Ears with these
  Unappertaining Stories;
He never felt the World's Disease
  Who car'd not for its Glories.

For pity Thou that wiser art,
  Whose thoughts lie wide of mine;
Let me alone with my own Heart,
  And I'le ne're envy thine.

Nor blame him who e're blames my Wit,
  That seeks no higher Prize,
Than in unenvy'd Shades to sit,
  And sing of *Chloris* Eyes.

ATTRIBUTION The attribution to Rochester in the copy-text is confirmed by a copy of another (later?) version of the poem in Rochester's hand with a correction in Rochester's hand (Nottingham MS. Portland Pw V 31, f. 3r).

COPY-TEXT *Examen Poeticum: Being the Third Part of Miscellany Poems* (1693), [1]424.

ANNOTATION
7 *boast*: presumably that the speaker is mad enough *not* to love Chloris; *unfaithful*: the ambiguity leaves a slight smudge on Sir John Eaton's impeccable verses.

Song (At last you'll force me to confess)

This exercise in double common ballad stanza, $A^4B^3A^4B^3C^4D^3C^4D^3$, with double rhyme in the short lines like 'My dear mistress has a heart' (9), appears to be a revised version of 'Too late, alas! I must confess' (10) made before 28 April 1676 when the volume in which it appeared was licensed.

ATTRIBUTION A copy of the poem in Rochester's hand with an emendation in Rochester's hand (Nottingham MS. Portland Pw V 31, f. 3r) confirms the attribution to Rochester of an earlier(?) version of the poem in *Examen Poeticum: Being the Third Part of Miscellany Poems* (1693), [1]424. The poem was restored to the Rochester canon by Pinto in 1953 (Rochester 1953, 38).

COPY-TEXT *A New Collection of the Choicest Songs* (1676), sig. A8r, printed as third stanza of *Song* (While on those lovely looks I gaze).

Woman's Honour (Love bade me hope, and I obeyed)

ATTRIBUTION In addition to the eight copies collated by Walker (Rochester 1984, 155) there are witnesses to the text of this poem in *Female Poems on Several Occasions*, 2nd ed. (1682), 166–7, Rochester 1685, 56–7, and Rochester 1691, 22–3. The verses are attributed to Rochester in Harvard MS. Eng. 636F, pp. 65–6, Rochester 1680[2], 66–7, Rochester 1685, 56–7, and Rochester 1691, 22–3, but there is not sufficient evidence that these witnesses represent more than one textual tradition. Vieth calls it 'Probably Rochester' (Vieth 1963, 421).

COPY-TEXT Rochester 1680[2], 66–7.

ANNOTATION
1 *Love bade me hope*: Treglown cites George Herbert, 'Love III', *The Temple* (1633), 183: 'Love bade me welcome' (Treglown 1973, 43), but the parallel stops there.
5 *keeps*: holds 'as a captive or prisoner' (*OED*). The guard–prisoner image is continued in the next line; cf. 307.11n.
19 *Whose*: whosesoever, the genitive of whosoever, with ellipsis of the antecedent (*archaic*) (*OED*), i.e. whoever's tyrant, the speaker's (Love) or the woman's (Honour), is the more cruel, it is not difficult to distinguish between them.
20 *diff'rence . . . to make*: 'to . . . treat differently' (*OED*). In the next stanza Rochester distinguishes between 'real honour' and 'Woman's Honour'.

The Submission (To this moment a rebel I throw down my arms)

For an experiment in anapaestic metre Rochester chooses a common broadside ballad stanza, $A^4A^4B^4B^4$, for which there seems to be no name, but which can be sung to the tune of 'Packington's Pound' (Simpson 1966, 564) or 'The Blind Beggar of Bednall-Green'. If sung to these tunes, the gaiety of the music would moderate the misery of unrequited love.

ATTRIBUTION Since the poem is attributed to Rochester only in the copy-text and derivative texts, the attribution stands unproven; see 310.5n.

COPY-TEXT Rochester 1680^2, 67–8.

EMENDATION OF COPY-TEXT The title is supplied from Nottingham MS. Portland Pw V 40, p. 57; in the copy-text it is *Song*.

ANNOTATION
1 *arms*: cf. military images at 9.12, 10.15–16.
5 *innocence, beauty, and wit*: the following lines provide a good example of repetitive structure, 'innocence (l. 9) . . . beauty (l. 10) . . . wit (l. 11) . . . sweetness and youth (l. 13) . . . beauty (l. 15) . . . wit' (l. 18), which F. W. Bateson calls typical of Elizabethan verse (*English Poetry and the English Language* (1934), 31–3, 63).
10 *inclined*: i.e. 'maliciously inclined' ($12.{}^{2}5$).
16 *adds a link*: playing on the ambiguity between 'fastens more firmly' and 'gives some rope'.

Verses put into a Lady's Prayer-Book (Fling this useless book away)

This poem was found attributed to Rochester in the copy-text by J. H. Wilson (*N&Q* 187 (12 August 1944), 79). As Wilson points out, it is an adaptation of two poems of Malherbe:

Pour mettre devant des heures

Tant que vous serez sans amour
Calliste priez nuict & iour
Vous n'aurez point misericorde:
Ce n'est pas que Dieu ne soit doux:
Mais pensez vous qu'il vous accorde
Ce qu'on ne peut avoir de vous?

Autre sur le mesme subject

Prier Dieu qu'il vous soit propice
Tant que vous me tourmenterez:
C'est le prier d'un iniustice,
Faites moy grace & vous l'aurez.
(*Les Deliçes de la poesie françoise*, 2 vols. (1615–20), I 415–16)

Wilson also points out that the first of these is translated by Charles Cotton:

Writ in Calista's Prayer-Book. An Epigram of Monsieur de Malherbe

Whilst you are deaf to love, you may,
Fairest *Calista*, weep and pray,
And yet, alas! no mercy find;
Not but God's mercifull, 'tis true,
But can you think he'll grant to you
What you deny to all mankind?
(Charles Cotton, *Poems on Several Occasions* (1689), 51)

The second is translated by George Granville, Lord Lansdowne:

Written in Clarinda's Prayer-Book

In vain, *Clarinda*, Night and Day
For Mercy to the Gods you Pray:
What Arrogance on Heav'n to call
For that, which you deny to All!
(George Granville, Lord Lansdowne, *Poems upon Several Occasions* (1712), 124)

Another example of the verses-in-prayer-book sub-genre is Fleetwood Sheppard's 'The Preface to a Common Pray'r Book' (O all ye People of this Land) (Nottingham MS. Portland Pw V 47, p. 164).

ATTRIBUTION Since Thomas Brown's attribution of the verses to Rochester is not confirmed by external evidence, it must stand unproven. Brown himself, writing seventeen years after Rochester's death, is surprised that the verses 'could be continued in private hands all this while, since the great care that has been taken to Print every Line of his Lordship's Writing', and 'cannot swear to their being genuine'. Some slight internal evidence is included below (ll. 5n., 10–11n., 17n.).

COPY-TEXT *Familiar Letters: Written by the Right Honourable John late Earl of Rochester, and several other Persons of Honour and Quality*, 2 vols. (1697), I 173.

EMENDATION OF COPY-TEXT The title is supplied from *A Collection of Miscellany Poems, Letters, &c. by Mr. Brown, &c.* (1699), 85 (Rochester 1984, 156); it is omitted in the copy-text.

ANNOTATION

5 *maliciously inclined*: the fact that this phrase interprets 'Her beauty's inclined' (12.[1]10) may suggest common authorship of the two poems.

8 *Without repentance*: cf. 'O God . . . Restore thou them that are penitent' (*The Book of Common Prayer* (1683), sig. B1r).

10–11 *powers* . . . *yours*: similar imperfect rhymes with similar comic effects occur at 34.151–2, 49.20–21, 54.222–3.
16 *easy steps*: 'There is no source in Malherbe for Rochester's ideas of a sensual *gradus ad Parnassum*. . . . The metaphor was probably familiar to Rochester from Socrates' speech in the *Symposium* but in the anti-religious context of the poem it is made to provide an ironic commentary on its Christian application, exemplified in Crashaw's title *Steps to the Temple* and in Adam's words to Raphael in *Paradise Lost*, Book V, "In contemplation of created things / By steps we may ascend to God"' (Treglown 1973, 45–6).
17 *joys* . . . *above*: the phrase recurs in a poem of which the attribution to Rochester is confirmed (24.22).

Rhyme to Lisbon (Here's a health to Kate, our sovereign's mate)

'The . . . E. of Roch[ester] coming in . . . when the K. Charles was drinking Lisbon ["A white wine produced in the province of Estremadura in Portugal" (*OED*)], They had bin trying to make a Rhime to Lisbon, Now saies the K. here's one will do it. Rochester takes a glass, and saies A health to Kate! . . .' (B.L. MS. Add. 29921, f. 3v). For these extemporaneous verses Rochester employed a common ballad stanza, $A^4B^3A^4B^3$, with double rhyme in the short line. It can be sung to the tune of 'Chevy Chase' (Simpson 1966, 96).

ATTRIBUTION The verses are attributed to Rochester in the copy-text, B.L. MS. Add. 29921, f. 3v, and *The Agreeable Companion; or An Universal Medley of Wit and Good-Humour* (1745), 341–2, but there is not sufficient evidence that these witnesses represent more than one textual tradition.

DATE After 21 May 1662, when Charles II and Catherine of Bragança were married, and before 20 August 1667, when Clarendon was dismissed.

COPY-TEXT *A Choice Collection of Poetry, by the Most Ingenious Men of the Age*, ed. Joseph Yarrow, 2 vols., York: 1738, I 61.

EMENDATION OF COPY-TEXT Printed in ballad stanza format] lines 1, 3 printed as half lines 3 But the] The 4 of his] his
The emendations are supplied in *The Agreeable Companion* (1745).

ANNOTATION
1 *Kate*: Biographical Dictionary, s.v. Catherine of Bragança.
3 *Hyde*: Edward Hyde, Earl of Clarendon, was blamed for negotiating Charles's marriage to 'a barren Queen' (Biographical Dictionary, s.v. Hyde); *bishop*: Gilbert Sheldon, Archbishop of Canterbury, married Charles and Catherine of Bragança at Portsmouth on 21 May 1662 (Biographical Dictionary, s.v. Sheldon).
4 *of his bone*: cf. the solemnization of matrimony: 'we are members of [the Lord's] body, of his flesh, and of his bones. For this cause . . . they two shall be one flesh. This is a great mystery' (*The Book of Common Prayer* (1683), sig. K12r).

To Celia (Celia, the faithful servant you disown)

In this exercise, apparently neither an adaptation nor a parody of an earlier work, Rochester grafts the Petrarchan idiom onto the decasyllabic couplets of heroic drama.

ATTRIBUTION Since the attribution to Rochester in Rochester 1691, 19–21 is not confirmed by external evidence, it stands unproven.

DATE After 25 December 1664 (l. 12n.) and before 28 October 1671 when the copy-text was entered in the Stationers' Register.

COPY-TEXT *A Collection of Poems, Written upon several Occasions, by several Persons* (1672), ²57–9.

EMENDATION OF COPY-TEXT **10** hallowed] Hollowed **15** yourself inclines] your selves incline **17** faculties] faculty **31** you] they
Lines 10 and 31 are corrected from Rochester 1691, 19–21. Lines 13–20 are omitted in Rochester 1691, apparently to satisfy Mrs Grundy. Lines 15 and 17 are emended by the present editor.

ANNOTATION
9 *But*: the poem moves forward by turning backward: 'But (9) . . . But (19) . . . But (32) . . . But (39)' and the last reversal makes the discovery that ceasing to love Celia is a fate worse than death.
12 *blazing comets in a winter's sky*: the great comet of 1664–5 was first observed on 7 November 1664 in Spain. Pepys saw it on 24 November 1664 (Pepys, 15 December 1664). It was discussed at the Royal Society and Robert Hooke read a paper on his observations of the comet before Gresham College (Evelyn, 14 December 1664–1 February 1665; Pepys, 1 March 1665). In the midst of all this excitement Rochester returned to England from his Grand Tour and was received at court on 25 December 1664. Since later comets (April 1665, August 1665, May 1668) did not appear in winter, this line provides a *terminus a quo* for composition of the poem.
16–17 *from heavenly powers . . . all our faculties proceed*: cf. 'superorum numine . . . inde genus' (Ovid, *Metamorphoses*, I 411–14), 'By . . . power divine . . . we derive our nature' in Dryden's translation (Dryden 1882–93, XII 87).
19 *rights without limit*: according to what Pepys heard, Lauderdale and Buckingham were telling Charles II 'how neither privileges of Parliament nor City is anything; but his will is all' (Pepys, 22 February 1664); cf. 318.29n.
33 *in the crowd . . . lies*: cf. 'Forgotten in the crowd I wisht to lye' (Sir Charles Sedley, *The Platonick*, in *A Collection of Poems, Written upon several Occasions, by several Persons* (1672), ²5).
40 *perfection*: the metre requires four syllables, 'per-FEC-ti-ON', stretching out the word and prolonging the speaker's 'misery'; cf. 318.48n.

Song (Give me leave to rail at you)

Rochester's experiments in heptasyllabic couplets (15–16, 37, 71–2), like Thomas Gray's, have precedents in Sidney's *Astrophel and Stella* (1591) and the witches' pudder in *Macbeth* (*c.* 1606): 'Double, double, toile and trouble; / Fire burne, and cauldron bubble' (IV i 10–11). They can be sung to the tune of the Old Hundred, 'Gaudeamus igitur'. Pope called this 'the Infantine style'. More pertinent are these lines from *Ninth Song* in *Astrophel and Stella*, 'Why (alas) then doth she sweare /

That she loveth me so deerly; / Seeing me so long to beare / Coales of love that burne so cleerly' (Sidney 1912–26, II 297).

ATTRIBUTION The poem is attributed to Rochester in the British Library copy of *Songs for 1 2 & 3 Voyces Composed by Henry Bowman* [1677], 31–2; Rochester 1680², 63; *Valentinian: A Tragedy* (1685), 75; Rochester 1691, 55; and *The Agreeable Variety* (1717), 148, representing at least two independent textual traditions.

DATE The verses may reflect Rochester's attempted abduction of Elizabeth Malet in May 1665, for which he was sent to the Tower. Lines 1–8 were published in *Songs for 1 2 & 3 Voyces Composed by Henry Bowman* [1677], 31. Lines 1–16 were first published in Rochester 1680², 63. Lines 9–16 were included in Rochester's adaptation of *Valentinian: A Tragedy* (1685), 75.

COPY-TEXT Rochester 1680², 63.

EMENDATION OF COPY-TEXT **10** things else] besides
The phrase 'things else' is preserved in *The Agreeable Variety* (1717), 148.

ANSWER A reply to Rochester's verses, in Elizabeth Malet's hand with corrections in her hand, is preserved in Nottingham MS. Portland Pw V 31, f. 12r:

Song

Nothing adds to love's fond fire
More than scorn and cold disdain.
I to cherish your desire
Kindness used, but 'twas in vain.
5 You insulted on your slave;
To be mine you soon refused.
Hope not then the power to have
Which ingloriously you used.

Think not, Thyrsis, I will e'er
10 By my love my empire lose.
You grow constant through despair,
Kindness you would soon abuse.
Though you still possess my heart,
Scorn and rigor I must feign.
15 There remains no other art
Your love, fond fugitive, to gain.

You that cou'd my *Heart* subdue,
To new *Conquests* ne're pretend,
Let your example make me true,
20 And of a Conquer'd *Foe*, a *Friend*:
Then if e're I shou'd complain,
Of your *Empire*, or my *Chain*,
Summon all your pow'rful *Charmes*,
And sell the *Rebel* in your *Armes*.

A third stanza is added in Rochester 1680², 64:

ANNOTATION OF ANSWER

2 *scorn and . . . disdain*: cf. 'LADY WISHFORT: . . . a little Disdain is not amiss; a little Scorn is alluring' (Congreve, *The Way of the World* (1700), III 164–5).

9–10 *love . . . empire*: the speaker refuses to cast herself as heroine in a Restoration heroic drama; cf. 'ZEMPOALLA: Were but this stranger kind, I'd . . . give my Empire where I gave my heart' (Sir Robert Howard and John Dryden, *The Indian Queen. A Tragedy* (1664), IV i 55–6). Since Elizabeth Malet was an heiress, 'worth . . . 2500*l.* per annum' (Pepys, 28 May 1665), her 'empire' was no fiction.

24 *sell*: Walker emends 'sell' to 'fell' (Rochester 1984, 22); 'quell' may be the word intended; cf. quell a rebellion.

From Mistress Price, Maid of Honour to Her Majesty, who sent [*Lord Chesterfield*] *a Pair of Italian Gloves* (My Lord, These are the gloves that I did mention)

Nicholas Fisher points out that the poem adopts the three-part structure and dramatic situation of Ovid's *Heroides* (375), but unexpectedly puts the woman in complete control of the situation (*Classical and Modern Literature* 11 (1991), 341–3).

ATTRIBUTION The unique witness to the text of these verses is the copy-text, the letterbook of Philip Stanhope, 2nd Earl of Chesterfield, which was published in London in 1829. Chesterfield docketed the letter, 'From Mrs. [Henrietta Maria] Prise [i.e. Price], Maid of Honour to her Majesty, who sent me a pair of Italian Gloves'. The verse letter begins with a salutation, 'My Lord', and ends with a prose coda, 'I had a mind you should see these enclosed papers, which were writ by the Lord Rochester, and that hath occationed you this trouble from Your humble servant'; it is unsigned and undated (136–7). Since the attribution is unconfirmed by external evidence, it must stand unproven.

DATE 1665–6 (Steinman 1871, 73n.).

COPY-TEXT B.L. MS. Add. 19253, f. 38r.

ANNOTATION

7 *Bretby*: Bretby Park was the Chesterfield estate in Derbyshire.

Under King Charles II's Picture (I, John Roberts, writ this same)

ATTRIBUTION The unique witness to the text of this squib was reported by David Vieth in 1954 (Rochester 1953, xlv n.). Without confirmatory external evidence, however, the attribution must remain uncertain. Vieth's plea – 'The virtual certainty that the first six poems in Harleian MS. 7316 derive from an authoritative source [Nottingham MS. Portland Pw V 31] argues that the seventh poem of the group is probably genuine Rochester' (Vieth 1963, 229) – will not stand up in court. The squib is *not* in Nottingham MS. Portland Pw V 31 and a penny coming up heads six times in a row does not increase the odds that it will come up heads a seventh time.

COPY-TEXT B.L. MS. Harl. 7316, f. 23v.

ANNOTATION

1 *writ*: in the obsolete sense of 'draw the figure of (something)' (*OED*).

3 *by name*: Rochester may be mimicking Roberts's actual speech or mocking the

traditional English carol: 'That there was born in Bethlehem, / The Son of God by name'; 'born of a virgin, / Blessed Mary by name' (*Oxford Book of Carols*, ed. Percy Dearmer *et al.* (1928), 25, 62).

To his more than Meritorious Wife (I am by fate slave to your will)

According to an anonymous source, these lines were written 'extempore to his Lady, who sent a servant on purpose desiring to hear from him being very uneasy at his long Silence' (*The Literary Magazine: or, Universal Review* January–August 1758, 24).

ATTRIBUTION The verses are attributed to Rochester in B.L. MS. Harl. 7316, f. 12r, in the copy-text, and in *The Literary Magazine: or, Universal Review* January–August 1758, 24, representing at least two different textual traditions.

DATE Written after Rochester's marriage on 29 January 1667.

COPY-TEXT *The Museum: or, The Literary and Historical Register* 3 (23 May 1747), 156.

EMENDATION OF COPY-TEXT **Title** his] My **3** ye] you **6** t'ye] t'you **10** Jan] John
The copy-text is corrected from the other witnesses.

ANNOTATION
1–2 *I am by fate slave to your will / And shall be most obedient still*: the 'hyperbolic compliment' (303) of the first two lines is undercut by the comic double rhymes, 'compose ye . . . a posy', 'duty . . . true t'ye', and 'speeches . . . breeches' (pronounced 'britches'), that follow.
8 *Yielding . . . the breeches*: surrendering the authority of a husband (Tilley B645).
10 *Jan*: Rochester's surviving letters to his wife are signed 'Your humble servant Rochester' or 'R'.

Rochester Extempore (And after singing Psalm the 12th)

ATTRIBUTION The attribution to Rochester in the copy-text is confirmed by Defoe (*Review*, 14 February 1713).

DATE The squib is dated 1670 in the copy-text. It was first published by David M. Vieth in Rochester 1968, 22.

COPY-TEXT Yale MS. Osborn b.54, p. 1200.

ANNOTATION
1 *Psalm the 12th*: Psalm 12, signed T[homas] S[ternhold] begins: 'Help, Lord, for good and godly men / do perish and decay: / And faith and truth from worldly men / is parted clean away' (Sternhold and Hopkins, *The Whole Book of Psalms, Collected into English Metre* (1703), sig. A4r).
6 *I am a rascal, that thou know'st*: Defoe quotes this line in the *Review* of 14 February 1713, attributing it to 'Lord Rochester's Confession to his Penitentials'; *rascal*: this ancestor of Robert Burns's Holy Willie is equally 'fash'd wi' fleshly lust'.

My Lord Rochester attempting to Kiss the Duchess of Cleveland as she was stepping out of her Chariot at Whitehall Gate, she threw him on his Back, and before he rose he spoke the following Lines (By Heavens, 'twas bravely done)

ATTRIBUTION Since these lines, the title of which requires more words than the text, are attributed to Rochester only in the copy-text, the attribution stands unproven.

The third part of Rochester 1707 (Bragge), a poetical miscellany (Case 242), attributes to Rochester poems that are not his, but also includes the sole witness to the text of *To his Mistress* (Why dost thou shade thy lovely face? Oh, why).

DATE After 3 August 1670 when Barbara Villiers was created Duchess of Cleveland.

COPY-TEXT Rochester 1707 (Bragge), [3]135.

Impromptu on Louis XIV (Lorraine you stole; by fraud you got Burgundy)

The copy-text provides the occasion for these verses: 'The *French* Tyrant, in a vain-glorious Boast, caus'd the following Verses to be inscrib'd on a Marble Pillar at *Versailles*, to tell the Greatness of his Actions to future Ages, *viz*.

> *Una Dies* Lotheros, Burgundos *Hebdomas una*.
> *Una domat* Batavos *Luna; Quid Annus aget*?

In *English* thus:

> Lorain *a Day, a Week* Burgundy *won*,
> Flanders *a Month; what would a Year have done*?

Which being seen by the Lord *Wilmot*, the late ingenious Earl of *Rochester*, he presently writ underneath [the distich in the text]'. In Princeton MS. AM 14401, p. 354, these lines are followed by another distich entitled *Resp*[*onsus*]:

> In Lotheros raptu Burgundos fraude petisti
> In Batavos emptu fur cito lusor agit.

which are the lines that Rochester translates (A. S. G. Edwards, *N&Q* 219 (November 1974), 419).

ATTRIBUTION The translation is attributed to Rochester in three ms. copies (Bodl. MS. Sancroft 53, p. 39, Bodl. MS. Tanner 89, f. 261r, Folger MS. W.a.135, f. 6r) and the copy-text, but there is evidence of only one textual tradition. The internal evidence includes a characteristic comic double rhyme, 'Bur-*gun*-dy . . . for't *one* day'.

DATE After August 1670, when Louis XIV occupied Lorraine.

COPY-TEXT *The Agreeable Companion; or, An Universal Medley of Wit and Good-Humour* (1745), 344.

ANNOTATION
1 *Lorraine*: Louis XIV occupied Lorraine in August 1670.
2 *Flanders*: by the treaty of Aix-la-Chapelle in April 1668 Louis XIV acquired Lille, Douai, Charleroi, and other fortified towns in the Spanish Netherlands (Ogg 1956, I 335).

Spoken Extempore to a Country Clerk after having heard him Sing Psalms (Sternhold and Hopkins had great qualms)

It is said to be 'at Bodicot (a chapelry to Adderbury) that Rochester made his extempore lines addressed to the psalm-singing clerk' (Alfred Beesley, *The History of Banbury* [1841], 488) (Rochester 1968, 22).

ATTRIBUTION The verses are attributed to Rochester in two ms. copies (B.L. MS. Harl. 7316, f. 18r and Bodl. MS. B.105, f. 32r) and two printed copies (the copy-text and *A Choice Collection of Poetry*, 2 vols. (1738), I 61), representing at least two independent textual traditions.

COPY-TEXT Rochester 1709 (Curll), [3]5.

ANNOTATION

1 *Sternhold and Hopkins*: Thomas Sternhold (d. 1549) and John Hopkins (d. 1570) collaborated to produce a metrical version of the Psalms (*c.* 1549) which survived in the next age as the standard for bad poetry (Thomas Brown, *The Works* (1711), IV 163–5).

A Rodomontade on his Cruel Mistress (Seek not to know a woman, for she's worse)

These verses are an adaptation of lines 15–24 of Ben Jonson's *A Satyricall Shrub* in *Underwoods* (1640), 190:

> Knew I this Woman? yes; And you doe see,
> How penitent I am, or I should be!
> Doe not you aske to know her, she is worse
> Then all Ingredients made into one curse,
> And that pour'd out upon Man-kind can be!
> Thinke but the Sin of all her sex, 'tis she!
> I could forgive her being proud! a whore!
> Perjur'd! and painted! if she were no more –,
> But she is such, as she might, yet, forestall
> The Divell; and be the damning of us all.
>
> (Jonson 1925–52, VIII 172) (Harold F. Brooks, *TLS* (11 December 1969), 1426)

ATTRIBUTION The copy in B.L. MS. Add. 18220, f. 103r is entitled 'Ld Buckhurst's Rodomondado upon his Mistris' and subscribed 'Communic: à Mrs. Sam: Naylour Aug: 14. 1672'. The copy in Merton College MS. D.1.2, f. 1v has no title and is subscribed 'Rochester'. The internal evidence is equivocal: 'crammed', 'peevish', 'but a woman' suggest Rochester, but 'connive', 'Alleging', 'forestall' appear nowhere in his work. The harsh, uncompromising tone and the similarity to his other works, 'Love a woman, you're an ass' (37) and 'What vain, unnecessary things are men' (78) may tip the balance in favour of Rochester, but Vieth and Brice Harris, Dorset's editor, are doubtful (Dorset 1979, 177).

DATE Before 30 May 1671 when the copy-text was advertised in the Term Catalogue.

COPY-TEXT *Westminster-Drollery* (1672), 14.

ANNOTATION

1 *Seek not to know a*: Merton College MS. D.1.2, f. 1v reads 'Trust not that thing call'd', which Vieth adopts (Rochester 1968, 159), but the equivalent line in Jonson's poem is 'Doe not you aske to know her'; *know*: punning on the biblical sense: 'Adam knew Eve . . . and she conceived' (Genesis 4.1).

4 *Perjured or painted*: Merton College MS. D.1.2, f. 1v reads 'Poxt, painted, perjured', but Jonson reads 'Perjur'd! and painted!'.

The Advice (All things submit themselves to your command)

In a second complaint to Celia, Rochester again grafts Petrarchan sentiments onto decasyllabic couplets, but the tone shifts from 'hyperbolic compliment' (303) to barely concealed threat.

ATTRIBUTION Since the attribution to Rochester in Rochester 1691, 16–18 is not confirmed by external evidence, it stands unproven. Covert allusions to Charles II (ll. 10–11), puns (ll. 31, 42), and pronunciation comically stretched out to accommodate the metre (318.48n.) may suggest Rochester's hand to some readers.

DATE Before 28 October 1671 when the copy-text was entered in the Stationers' Register.

COPY-TEXT *A Collection of Poems, Written upon several Occasions, by several Persons* (1672), ²60–63.

EMENDATION OF COPY-TEXT **3** borrows] borrowed **4** the god must] himself would **21** rudely thronged] prest upon a] their near] rude **35** citadel] Citadels **43** the] a **46** whole magazines of] Inestimable **47** baubles] Trifles
Except for l. 35, the copy-text is emended from Rochester 1691, 16–18, which seems to represent an authorial revision, but which omits ll. 32–8. Line 35 is '*an apparent misprint*' in the copy-text (Rochester 1968, 177).

ANNOTATION
4 *none*: Love is blind (Tilley, L506).
21 The copy-text reads 'Though prest upon by their too rude embrace', but the reading of Rochester 1691, 17 is adopted as the *lectio difficilior* of authorial revision, particularly since 'thronged' is supported by a line in William Browne's *Britannia's Pastorals* (1613–16); see Glossary, s.v. 'thronged'.
29 *empire*: *OED* cites 'Love is an Empire only of two Persons' (*The Accomplish'd Woman*, trans. Walter Montague (1656), 124); *divine*: Charles II was being urged to claim that his rule was *iure divino*; cf. 312.19n.
31 *reduced*: i.e. taken, like a city, with a possible pun on 'seduced'.
42 *foreign hearts*: a play on 'foreign parts' is possible; *OED* cites an example from *c.* 1674.
46 *magazines*: 'A place where goods are laid up; a storehouse' (*OED*). 'The "magazine of joys" . . . which are seen . . . as the reward of sexual activity being urged on Celia, derive from the language of courtly adoration repeatedly employed in the poem [ll. 1–4, 9–12] to disguise an aggressive assertion of male superiority' (Treglown 1973, 45).
48 *gewgaw*: cf. 'quaint Honour' (Marvell 1927, I 26); *reputation*: the metre stretches out pronunciation to five full syllables, 'RE-pu-TA-ti-ON', to prolong the speaker's scorn for Celia's 'long preserv'd Virginity' (ibid.). Assuming a four-syllable pronunciation, 'RE-pu-TA-tion', Rochester 1691, 18 adds a redundant 'still' to preserve the metre; cf. 312.40n.

The Platonic Lady (I could love thee till I die)

This exercise in octosyllabic couplets is an adaptation of some verses attributed to Petronius (Oldham 1987, 462):

> Foeda est in coitu et brevis voluptas
> Et taedet Veneris statim peractae.
> Non ergo ut pecudes libidinosae
> Caeci protinus irruamus illuc
> (Nam languescit amor peritque flamma);
> Sed sic sic sine fine feriati

Et tecum iaceamus osculantes.
Hic nullus labor est ruborque nullus:
Hoc iuvit, iuvat et diu iuvabit;
Hoc non deficit incipitque semper.

(From *Poetae Latini Minores*, ed. E. Baehrens (1882), IV 99), which are translated by Ben Jonson in *Underwoods* (1640):

A Fragment from Petronius Translated

Doing, a filthy pleasure is, and short;
And done, we straight repent us of the sport:
Let us not then rush blindly on unto it,
Like lustfull beasts, that onely know to doe it:
For lust will languish, and that heat decay.
But thus, thus, keeping endlesse Holy-day,
Let us together closely lie, and kisse,
There is no labour, nor no shame in this;
This hath pleas'd, doth please, and long will please; never
Can this decay, but is beginning ever.

(Jonson 1925–52, VIII 294)

The title is ironical. What the lady advocates is not platonic love, 'free from sensual desire' (*OED*), but *coitus reservatus* (Sanskrit *karezza*), in which 'by a technique of deliberate control [i.e. 'the art of love' (l. 6)] . . . orgasm is avoided and copulation thereby prolonged' (*OED*, s.v. **coitus**). Walker observes that 'The theme was popular in the seventeenth century, e.g. Henry King's "Paradox. That Fruition destroyes Love" [and] Sir John Suckling's "Against Fruition"' (Rochester 1984, 236). But neither of these poems is about *coitus reservatus*. Nor is Rochester's poem related to Davenant's *The Platonick Lovers. A Tragæ Comedy* (1665) or two poems entitled 'Platonick Love' by Edward Lord Herbert of Cherbury and Abraham Cowley.

ATTRIBUTION Since the attribution to Rochester in the copy-text is not confirmed by external evidence, it must stand unproven.

DATE First published by John Hayward (Rochester 1926, 142).

COPY-TEXT Bodl. MS. Add. A.301, pp. 24–5.

EMENDATION OF COPY-TEXT 13 should] ~~will~~ sho'd

ANNOTATION

7 *enjoyment*: ejaculation, which 'Converts the owner to a drone' (l. 12).
11–12 *sting . . . gone . . . drone*: cf. 'If once he lose his *sting*, he grows a *Drone*' (Cowley, *Against Fruition* (1668), 32).
17 *what*: penis.
23–4 *Let's practise then and we shall prove / These are the only sweets of love*: Possibly a parody of Marlowe's 'Come live with mee and be my love, / And we will all the pleasures prove' (*The Passionate Pilgrim* (1599), sig. D5) (Rochester 1953, 228).

Song (As Cloris full of harmless thought)

Corydon and Cloris or, The Wanton Sheepherdess (n.d.), a broadside ballad based on Rochester's verses in eight-line ballad metre stanzas, was set to 'a pleasant Play-house new tune' by Nicholas Staggins called 'Amoret and Phillis'. The tune takes its name from the opening line of a song written by Sir Carr Scrope for Etherege's *The Man of Mode* (March 1676; 1676), V ii, *As Amoret with Phillis sat*. Rochester's song in turn was set by James Hart in *New Ayres and Dialogues* (1678), 14–15 and by an anonymous composer in *Choyce Ayres & Songs* (1679), 8 (Simpson 1966, 19, 105–7, 812).

ATTRIBUTION Since the three copies that attribute the poem to Rochester (Bodl. MS. Rawl. Poet. 173, f. 71v, Rochester 1680², 58, and Rochester 1691, 53–4) represent the same textual tradition, the attribution stands unproven.

COPY-TEXT *The Wits Academy or, The Muses Delight* (1677), ²115.

ANNOTATION
23 *the lucky minute*: cf. 'Twelve is my appointed lucky Minute, when all the Blessings that my Soul could wish Shall be resign'd to me' (Aphra Behn, *The Lucky Chance* (1686?; 1687), 58); 'Lovers that . . . in the lucky Minute want the Pow'r' (Samuel Garth, *The Dispensary* (1699), *POAS*, Yale, VI 735). Treglown isolates a lucky Minute/happy Time/Shepherd's Hour sub-genre of seventeenth-century erotic lyric and cites examples including Sir Carr Scrope's song in *The Man of Mode* (1676) (cf. headnote above), John Glanvill's *The Shepherd's Hour* (1686), and Dryden's song in *Amphitryon* (1690), IV i: *A Pastoral Dialogue betwixt Thyrsis and Iris* (Treglown 1982, 86–7). 'The Lucky Minute' also became a popular tune title (Simpson 1966, 106).

Song to Cloris (Fair Cloris in a pigsty lay)

This unusual stanza, $A^4B^3A^4A^4B^3$, is an extended form of common metre ballad stanza, $A^4B^3A^4B^3$; cf. 353, 398.

ATTRIBUTION The poem is attributed to Rochester in Harvard MS. Eng. 636F, pp. 77–9, Rochester 1680², 61–2, Rochester 1691, 59–61, and Rochester 1718, 70–73, representing three different textual traditions.

COPY-TEXT Rochester 1680², 61–2.

EMENDATION OF COPY-TEXT 15 Flora's] yonder   21 she] the
The copy-text is corrected from Nottingham MS. Portland Pw V 40, pp. 60–62.

ANNOTATION
8 *ivory pails*: the rarity and expensiveness of ivory (£167 per hundredweight in 1905) makes these ivory swill buckets a refinement of mock-epic proportions, like the ivory gate through which Cloris's false dream reaches her (*Odyssey*, XIX 562; *Aeneid*, VI 895).
15 *Flora's cave*: the cave in which the Greek nymph Chloris is raped by Zephyrus, the west wind, and from which she emerges as Flora, the Roman goddess of flowers and spring (Ovid, *Fasti*, V 195). The cave is Ovid's and the hymeneal gate may be Shakespeare's (*The Winter's Tale* (1609–10; 1623), I ii 196–8), but the phallic pig appears to be Rochester's.
31 *piercèd*: one reader wishes that this dream of rape had been a real rape 'perhaps' (Felicity Nussbaum, *The Brink of All We Hate* (1972), 62); *zone*: literally 'any encircling band' (*OED*, citing Francis Quarles, *Emblemes* (1635), 274: 'untie / The sacred Zone of thy Virginity'), cf. Aphrodite's zone which creates 'the lucky minute'

(21.[2]23) for anyone wearing it (*Iliad*, XIV 214–16, trans. Richmond Lattimore, 'the elaborate, pattern-pieced / zone . . . [the] passion of sex is there'); figuratively that part of the body around which a girdle is fastened; cf. pelvic girdle.
39 *legs*: the moral disorder is reflected in a rhyming disorder, 'frigs . . . pigs . . . legs', that is unique in the poem.
40 *innocent and pleased*: *virgo intacta* and sexually satisfied.

To Corinna (What cruel pains Corinna takes)

ATTRIBUTION These verses in common ballad metre, $A^4B^3A^4B^3$, are attributed to Rochester in Bodl. MS. Rawl. Poet. 173, f. 71v, Rochester 1680², 65–6, *The Theatre of Music: Or, A Choice Collection of the Newest and Best Songs Sung at the Court, and Public Theatres* (1685), 57, and Rochester 1691, 30–31, representing at least two independent textual traditions. Whereas Rochester 1680 is clearly a pirated edition, Rochester 1691, in some still to be determined fashion, is authoritative; cf. 354.

COPY-TEXT Rochester 1691, 30–31.

ANNOTATION
7 *the silly art*: coyness, 'Affected rules of honour' (l. 12).
9 *tyrant*: virtue.
12 *honour*: cf. 11.5–10.
13 *she*: Corinna.
16 *undo her*: cf. 307.16n.

Song (Phillis, be gentler, I advise)

ATTRIBUTION These lines in common ballad measure are attributed to Rochester in two ms. copies (Edinburgh MS. DC.1.3, p. 67, Harvard MS. Eng. 636F, pp. 64–5) and two printed copies (Rochester 1680², 65, Rochester 1691, 34–5), representing two independent textual traditions.

COPY-TEXT Lines 1–16, Rochester 1680², 65; ll. 17–24, *The Triumph of Wit, or Ingenuity Display'd in its Perfection* (1688), 165–6.

EMENDATION OF COPY-TEXT Harvard MS. Eng. 636F, pp. 64–5 and *Female Poems*, 2nd ed. (1682), 168–9 read 'ill spent' for 'misspent' in l. 2, a reading that may be authorial.

ANNOTATION
2 *Make . . . time*: 'The poem is identical in form, length and, it at first seems, subject matter to the famous lyric recalled by the second line, Herrick's "To the Virgins, to make much of Time" . . . Yet there could not be a greater difference between them in substance or in tone . . .; while Herrick's poem is rooted in the present . . . Rochester's cruelly anticipates what is in store in the future: faded beauty, scandal, ruin, and death' (Treglown 1980, 24).
4 *time to repent*: Rochester's alleged deathbed repentance is described in Parsons 1680, 1–37.
15–16 *Die with the scandal of a whore, / And never know the joy*: quoted in Defoe, *An Elegy on the Author of the True-Born-English-Man* (1704), 32.
20 *dull*: cf. 'dull . . . dead to all delight' (198.11).

22–3 *joys . . . improved by art*: cf. 311.16n. and 'All that art can add to love' (72.[1]24).

Could I but make my wishes insolent

Although the poem has been called an epistle, it is not an epistle. Lines 1–6 address a reader about 'her' (l. 6) in the third person. Lines 7–26 address her in the first person, 'you . . . your' (ll. 11, 17, 26). Lines 1–6 are a kind of proem to the dramatic monologue that follows. After ll. 14–16 the switching of skirts can be heard.

ATTRIBUTION Although not confirmed by external evidence, the attribution to Rochester (Needham 1934, 52) seems as certain as the nature of the case permits. The unique witness to the text of the poem is a copy in Rochester's hand with corrections in Rochester's hand (recorded in Rochester 1984, 151). The internal evidence includes a striking parallel to *Tunbridge Wells* (322.15n.) and several salient features of Rochester's style: comical allusions to the Bible and the classics (322.6n., 9n.), imperfect rhyme, and metre comically stretching out pronunciation (322.7–8n.), high-frequency words like 'humble . . . dull' (ll. 3, 13), imperfect grammatical agreement (l. 21), and oxymoron, 'cruel care' (l. 23).

COPY-TEXT Nottingham MS. Portland Pw V 31, f. 7.

ANNOTATION
6 *lay hold of her*: cf. 'lay hold on her, and lie with her' (Deuteronomy 22.28).
7–8 *spirit . . . merit*: imperfect rhyme and the unique double rhyme make this couplet outstanding in the poem. The metre, stretching out 'fa-MIL-i-AR' over two full iambs, makes this the outstanding word in the couplet. 'Familiar' is what the speaker designs to be.
9 *blundering . . . Phaëton*: the son of Helios (the sun) and Klymene, 'foolish Phaëton . . . doest desire . . . A greater charge than any God coulde ever have' (Ovid, *Metamorphoses* (1567), f. 15), namely, to drive the chariot of the sun. The horses bolted and Phaëton was destroyed.
15 *what he next must say*: cf. 'think what next to say' (46.113).
19 *Regardless of a love so many years*: Rochester originally wrote, 'That not the humble Love of many years'. Then he wrote 'Regardless of my Love soe many yeares'. Finally he struck out 'my' and added 'A' (Nottingham MS. Portland Pw V 31, f. 7v).

Sab: lost (She yields, she yields, pale Envy said amen)

It was supposed that this fragment in heroic couplets which breaks off in mid-sentence is 'a reversal of Milton's *Comus*' (Treglown 1982, 78–9). But the verdict must be 'Not proven', for (1) there is no evidence that 'Sab' expands to 'Sabrina', (2) Comus cannot be 'the last of men' (l. 2) for he is 'not mortal' (*Comus*, 802), and (3) it is the Lady and not Sabrina who is tempted by Comus. Much more convincing is John A. Murphy's argument that 'Sab' expands to 'Sabinus', Ovid's friend, which may have been Sir Charles Sedley's and Alexander Radcliffe's name for Rochester. If this is true, 'The poem is self-referring, describing a love affair Rochester lost to a "heavy thing, / Artless and witless, no way meriting"' (*N&Q* 218 (May 1973), 176).

ATTRIBUTION The unique witness to the text of the fragment is a fair copy in Rochester's hand. Although the internal evidence is not so strong as it is in the case of 'Could I but make my wishes insolent' (24), it seems sufficient to establish a high degree of probability. The threat to bring down the gods in a comic Götterdämmerung (l. 8) is perhaps the most Rochesterian detail.

DATE The fragment was first attributed to Rochester and published in Pinto 1935, 49.

COPY-TEXT Nottingham MS. Portland Pw V 31, f. 6r.

ANNOTATION
6 *raised so high to fall so low*: cf. 'So *Lycidas* sunk low, but mounted high' (*Lycidas* (1634), 172).

Great mother of Aeneas and of Love

This fragment is a 'paraphrase, or translation with latitude' (Dryden 1882–93, XII 16) of part of the first sentence of Lucretius, *De rerum natura*, I 1–5:

> Aeneadum genetrix, hominum divomque voluptas,
> alma Venus, caeli subter labentia signa
> quae mare navigerum, quae terras frugiferentis
> concelebras, per te quoniam genus omne animantum
> concipitur visitque exortum lumina solis:

or in Dryden's translation, published in 1685:

> Delight of humankind, and gods above,
> Parent of Rome, propitious Queen of Love!
> Whose vital power, air, earth, and sea supplies,
> And breeds whate'er is born beneath the rolling skies;
> For every kind, by thy prolific might,
> Springs, and beholds the regions of the light.
> (Dryden 1882–93, XII 329)

ATTRIBUTION The unique witness to the text of the fragment is the copy-text in Rochester's hand with corrections by Rochester.

DATE The fragment was first attributed to Rochester and published in Rochester 1953, 50.

COPY-TEXT Nottingham MS. Portland Pw V 31, f. 5r.

ANNOTATION
5 *Whither vast regions of that liquid world*: Rochester first wrote 'Whither orbiting that liquid world', then struck out 'orbiting' and wrote 'vast regions of' above it.
6 *Where groves of ships on watery hills are hurled*: Rochester first wrote 'Where borrow'd groves', then struck out 'borrow'd' and added 'of shipps' between 'groves' and 'on'.

The gods by right of nature must possess

In the opening speech of Shadwell's *The Virtuoso* (25 May 1676; 1676) Bruce, the hero, apostrophizes 'great *Lucretius*', the patron saint of gentlemen of wit and sense like Bruce himself and Shadwell and Shadwell's friend Rochester. 'Almost alone', Bruce says, Lucretius demonstrates 'that Poetry and Good Sence may go together' (Shadwell

1927, III 105). As an example of 'Good Sence' in poetry, Bruce quotes *De rerum natura* I 44–9 (or II 646–51 in the Loeb Classical Library text):

> omnis enim per se divom natura necessest
> inmortali aevo summa cum pace fruatur
> semota ab nostris rebus seiunctaque longe;
> nam privata dolore omni, privata periclis,
> ipsa suis pollens opibus, nil indiga nostri,
> nec bene promeritis capitur neque tangitur ira.

These are the lines that Rochester translates, almost as a 'metaphrase, or turning an author . . . line by line, from one language into another' (Dryden 1882–93, XII 16).

ATTRIBUTION The attribution to Rochester in the copy-text and copies derived from it awaits confirmatory evidence.

COPY-TEXT Rochester 1691, 109.

ANNOTATION
5–6 *Rich in themselves, to whom we cannot add, / Not pleased by good deeds nor provoked by bad*: cf. 'ipsa suis pollens opibus, nil indiga nostri, / nec bene promeritis capitur neque tangitur ira' ('[divinity] . . . strong by its own strength, needing nothing from us, neither propitiated by worship nor aroused by anger') (Lucretius, *De rerum natura*, II 650–51). Rochester's translation is quoted without acknowledgement in Blount 1680, 158 (Manning 1986, 38); cf. '[Rochester] could not see that there was to be either reward or punishment' (Burnet 1680, 52); cf. 39.3–5.

To Love (O Love! how cold and slow to take my part)

The translation of Ovid's *Amores*, II ix provides a kind of bill of fare for Rochester's major love poems, which celebrate not the acts but the mishaps of love, 'Love's fantastic storms' (l. 37): premature ejaculation (28), falling in love with a whore (34.125), the fear of inadequacy (68.[1]9–10), falling in love with an old man (71). The translation, in heroic couplets, is another 'metaphrase' (324 above), almost a line-by-line rendering.

Although modern editors of *Amores*, II ix print it as two poems, ll. 1–24 and 25–54, Rochester's translation is clearly one poem. This is revealed (1) by the structure:

1–26 The speaker complains that Love attacks his own unarmed subjects and refuses to let them retire;

27–60 but the speaker scorns retirement and, still unarmed, begs to be attacked again by Love

and (2) by correspondences in the phrasing:

10 hope . . . leads on	**48** happy in my hopes
14 disarmed	**39** undefended
15 scornful maids	**57–8** th'inconstant charming sex / Whose . . . scorn
17 the wide world	**60** The vassal world

ATTRIBUTION The translation is attributed to Rochester in three manuscript copies (Cambridge MS. Add. 6339, f. 20; Harvard MS. Eng. 636F, pp. 58–61, and Yale MS. Osborn b.105, pp. 67–71) and two printed copies, the copy-text and *Miscellany Poems* (1684), [1]135–8, representing at least two independent textual traditions.

COPY-TEXT Rochester 1680[1], 30.

EMENDATION OF COPY-TEXT 4 my] thy 52 example led,] example, in
The copy-text is emended by the readings of Nottingham MS. Portland Pw V 40, pp. 53–5 (Rochester 1984, 169).

ANNOTATION
Epigraph: the first line of Ovid's *Amores*, II ix: 'O Cupid, who never can be sufficiently reviled'.
4 *my*: the copy-text reads 'thy', but Ovid's Latin reads 'in castris . . . meis' (*Amores*, II ix 4); *They*: 'the women whom the poet [i.e. the speaker] cannot help loving' (Love 1981, 142); *They murder me*: cf. 'They flee from me, that sometime did me seeke' (Sir Thomas Wyatt in *Songs and Sonnets* (1585), f. 22r.
9 *give o'er*: leave behind the birds taken and press on for more.
13–14 *disarmed . . . disarmed*: Rochester imitates the Ovidian 'turn', as Dryden called it, but not the striking Ovidian image: 'in nudis . . . / ossibus? ossa mihi nuda' (on naked bones . . . my bones naked) (*Amores*, II ix 13–14).
15 *dull*: without love; the word translates Ovid's phrase 'sine amore'; *scornful maids*: cf. 'she who scorns a Man, must die a Maid' (Pope 1939–67, II 197).
17–18 'Since *Roma* and *Amor* are palindromes, Ovid may be making the witty point that their opposite behaviour is natural' (Francis Cairns, in *Creative Imitation and Latin Literature*, ed. David West *et al.* (1979), 126).
21–2 *whore . . . to be a bawd*: '[Ovid's] images of ships laid up in dock and of a retired gladiator exchanging his sword for a practice foil are replaced by the distinctively Restoration' whore who graduates to a bawd (Love 1981, 143).
25 *in Celia's trenches*: Rochester's phrase has no counterpart in Ovid, but does occur in *Priapea*, XLVI 9: 'fossas inguinis ut teram dolemque' (labour in that ditch between your thighs); cf. 'said my uncle *Toby* – but I declare, corporal, I had rather march up to the very edge of a trench – A woman is quite a different thing – said the corporal. – I suppose so, quoth my uncle Toby' (Sterne 1940, 583).
44–50 cf. *in lazy slumbers blest / . . . happy . . . whilst I believe*:

> And slumbring, thinks himselfe much blessed by it.
> Foole, what is sleepe but image of cold death,
> Long shalt thou rest when Fates expire thy breath.
> But let me crafty damsells words deceive,
> Great joyes by hope I inly shall conceive.
> (C[hristopher] M[arlowe], *All Ovids Elegies* [*c.* 1640], sig. C5r)

52 *example led*: ten witnesses are equally divided between 'example led,' and 'example, in' (Rochester 1984, 169), but the former allows 'ambiguous Love' to be read as direct address, as in the Latin 'per te . . . Cupido . . . / et . . . exemplo . . . tuo' (*Amores*, II ix 47–8).
60 *vassal world*: Rochester (but not Ovid) closes the poem by bringing it back to Rome's 'wide world' (l. 17): if Cupid could make women love, his domination of the world of lovers would be as complete as Rome's domination of the world of nations.

The Imperfect Enjoyment (Naked she lay, clasped in my longing arms)

A poem on the premature ejaculation mishap was almost an obligatory exercise for the Restoration poet. George Etherege, Aphra Behn, William Congreve, and three anonymous poets cranked out examples, but Rochester's is the funniest. Richard E.

Quaintance and John H. O'Neill record five French and six English examples (*PQ* 42 (1963), 190–99; *PLL* 13 (Spring 1977), 197–202), and the song 'As *Amoret* and *Thyrsis*, lay' in *The Old Batchelour* (1693) (Congreve 1967, 71) may be added to the list. Ovid's *Amores*, III vii, *Priapea*, II (Quid hoc novi est? quid ira nuntiat deum?) attributed to Tibullus (Tibullus 1971, 173), and the Encolpius–Circe episode in Petronius's *Satyricon*, 127–30, generated all these examples, but none of them concludes with a malediction worthy of Ernulphus (Sterne, 1940, 170–79).

The existence of these examples emphasizes the traditional nature of Rochester's poem and shrinks the autobiographical element, if any. Rochester is no more exposing 'his personal failure' in *The Imperfect Enjoyment* (William B. Ober, *Boswell's Clap and Other Essays* (1979), 251) than Shakespeare is exposing his personal cowardice in Falstaff. *The Imperfect Enjoyment* is not the kind of love poem we encounter in Cowley or Waller, but 'denying it the status of a love poem narrows the province of art to only a portion of experience' (Charles C. Doyle, *ECS* 4 (Fall 1970), 105). It is a love poem of the sub-genre *ejaculatio praecox*, a mirror image of the lucky minute sub-class (320.23n.).

The speaker's elaborate curse upon his recreant member alludes to Encolpius's curse upon his recreant member in the *Satyricon* (Farley-Hills 1978, 113). Petronius's lines in turn parody, in coarse sotadic metre, the epic hexameters of Virgil. Two of them, in fact, 'ter corripui terribilem manu bipennem, / ter languidior coliculi repente thyrso' (Three times with razor raised I tried to lop; / three times my trembling fingers let it drop), are imitated in *The Rape of the Lock* (1714): 'thrice they twitch'd the Diamond in her Ear, / Thrice she look'd back, and thrice the Foe drew near' (Virgil, *Aeneid*, II 479; Petronius, *The Satyricon*, trans. William Arrowsmith (1959), 162; Pope 1939–67, II 175). The tone of the poem in short is mock-heroic.

ATTRIBUTION The poem is attributed to Rochester in four ms. copies (B.L. MS. Harl. 7312, pp. 85–7; Bodl. MS. Add. B.106, ff. 39–40; Harvard MS. Eng. 636F, pp. 114–17; Yale MS. Osborn b.105, p. 62) and two printed copies (the copy-text and Rochester 1714 (Curll)[1], 114), representing at least two independent textual traditions.

COPY-TEXT Rochester 1680[1], 28–30.

EMENDATION OF COPY-TEXT 7 Her] The 11 a] the 12 brinks] *Limbs* 22 bosom,] *Breast*, and 55 justles] Ruffles 57 rakehell] *Rascal* 59 stew] *Stews* 65 gates] *Goats*, 68 strangury] *Stranguries*, 69 ne'er] om.
The copy-text is corrected by readings of the ms. copies (Rochester 1984, 159–60).

ANNOTATION
1 *Naked she lay*: 'She lay all naked in her bed' was the title of a popular tune (Simpson 1966, 657).
3–4 *equally inspired . . . eager fire, / . . . kindness . . . flaming . . . desire*: heightened interest and intensity in Rochester's verse are frequently accompanied by heightened sound effects, particularly assonance ('equally . . . eager', 'inspired . . . fire . . . kindness . . . desire') and alliteration ('fire . . . flaming'); cf. 'balmy brinks of bliss' (l. 12) and 'I . . . alive . . . strive: / I sigh . . . swive' (ll. 25–7).
12 *brinks*: the copy-text reads '*Limbs*', but 'brinks', a more difficult reading, occurs in three ms. copies and 'brink' in one.
18 *Her hand, her foot, her very look's a cunt*: cf. *The Conquest of Granada I* (December 1670; 1672), III i 71: 'Her tears, her smiles, her every look's a Net' (Dryden 1956– , XI 47) (Treglown 1976, 555).

19 *Smiling*: decorum does not permit her to laugh; cf. 36.7–8.
22–3 *'Is there then no more?' / She cries*: cf. 'Why mock'st thou me she cry'd?' (C[hristopher] M[arlowe], *All Ovids Elegies* [*c.* 1640], sig. E2v).
23 *this*: foreplay.
23–4 *love . . . pleasure*: 'We'd had more pleasure had our love been less' (Etherege, 1963, 8).
27 *I sigh, alas! . . . but cannot swive*: in the Garden of Eden 'Each member did their wills obey' (68.7); cf. 'How just is Fate . . . / To make him *Love* the *Whore* he cannot *Please*' (Defoe, *The Dyet of Poland* (1705), *POAS*, Yale VII 119).
29 *shame*: cf. 'To this adde shame . . . / The second cause why vigour faild me' (Marlowe, op. cit., sig. E2r).
30 *impotent*: both rhyme scheme and metre require that the third syllable be fully accented, 'IM-PO-TENT', prolonging and emphasizing the crucial word in the poem.
31 *her fair hand*: cf. 'Her touch could have made Nestor young again' (Ovid, *Amores*, III vii 41).
45 *withered flower*: cf. 'member . . . more withered than yesterday's rose' (Ovid, *Amores*, III vii 65–6). Rochester omits Ovid's nice detail of the prostitute thoughtfully spilling water so her maid would not know of her client's failure, and substitutes the frightful curse, which is not in Ovid. When he is rescued from Orgoglio's dungeon, the Red Crosse knight is 'Decay'd, and al his flesh shronk up like withered flowres' (Spenser, *The Faerie Queene* (1590), I viii 41) (John H. O'Neill, *Tennessee Studies in Literature* 25 (1980), 63).
46 *base deserter of my flame*: cf. 'nefande destitutor inguinum' (unspeakable deserter of my loins) (Tibullus 1971, 174). The transition from history of the recreant member to apostrophe to the recreant member (ll. 46–72) may recall Marvell's *An Horatian Ode upon Cromwell's Return from Ireland* (1650; 1681) which also moves from history of a recreant Member (ll. 1–112) to apostrophe to a recreant Member (ll. 113–20).
48 *magic*: cf. 'Why would not magic arts be the cause of my malfunction?' (Ovid, *Amores*, III vii 35).
50 *oyster, cinder, beggar*: apparently shorthand for oyster-wench, cinder-woman, London beggar; cf. 'Oyster, Beggar, Cinder Whore' (Defoe, *Reformation of Manners* (1702) (*POAS*, Yale, VI 408).
54–7 *hector in the streets / . . . hides his head*: Quaintance suggests that these lines expand Remy Belleau's phrase, 'Brave sur le rempart et couard à la brèche' (Bold on the battlements, coward in the breach) (*PQ* 42 (1963), 191).
54 *hector*: in June 1675 Rochester 'in a frolick after a rant [a bombastic speech] did . . . beat downe the dyill which stood in the middle of the Privie [Gard]ing, which was esteemed the rarest in Europ' (Davies 1969, 351). Whereupon John Oldham wrote *A Satyr against Vertue* 'Suppos'd to be spoken by a Court-Hector at Breaking of the Dial in Privy Garden' (Oldham 1987, 57–67; cf. Marvell 1927, I 310). Rochester's words on the occasion have been preserved: 'Rochester, lord Buckhurst, Fleetwood Shephard, etc. comeing in from their revells. "What!" said the earl of Rochester, "doest thou stand here to [fuck] time?" Dash they fell to worke' (Aubrey 1898, II 34).
55 *justles*: the copy-text reads '*Ruffles*' but 'justles' is preserved in two ms. copies and hectors seem more likely to justle than ruffle.
56–7 *if his king . . . claim his aid, / The . . . villain shrinks*: Rochester did not volunteer for service in the third Dutch War (1672–4); cf. 1.17–18; *rakehell*: the copy-text reads '*Rascal*' but the more difficult reading 'rakehell' is preserved in two ms. copies.

59 *stew*: the copy-text reads 'ev'ry *Stews*' but the error of agreement is corrected in four ms. copies.
62 *Worst part of me*: cf. 'pars pessima nostri' (worst part of me) (Ovid, *Amores*, III vii 69).
69 *refuse to spend*: cf. 28.27.

On King Charles (In the isle of Great Britain long since famous grown)

Although the custom of fosterage was no longer institutional at the Stuart court, Charles II gave Rochester an allowance of £500 a year while he was at Oxford, chose Dr Andrew Balfour to be his travelling governor, received Rochester at Whitehall upon his return from his travels, provided him lodgings in the palace, appointed him gentleman of the bedchamber with a pension of £1,000 a year for life, and chose for his wife a most sought-after heiress who also wrote verse. In all this the King manifestly acted as foster-father (Ronald Paulson, in *The Author in His Work*, ed. Louis L. Martz and Aubrey Williams (1978), 117). In his juvenile verse Rochester acknowledged that he owed much more than 'cold respect' (1.15) to this distant figure.

The relation between the two, therefore, is the old love–hate business of father and son. Whereas the precocious boy wanted nothing more than to throw away his life for his king (1.17–18), the disillusioned adult regarded Charles with 'a mixture of irony, contempt and genuine affection' (Pinto 1962, 75). 'The King loved his company for the diversion it afforded', Burnet says, 'And there was no love lost between them' (Burnet 1724–34, I 264), i.e. their affection was reciprocal (*OED*, Love, sb. 8d). There is indeed evidence of real affection on both sides. The powerful affect of this poem could hardly be generated by anything but real affection.

But the poem is not the sworn deposition of John Wilmot, Earl of Rochester, in the trial of Charles Stuart. It is the imagined utterance of an imagined character at the court of Charles II speaking in character. It is what 'people' are saying. The poem can be read as a warning to Charles II. Just as Marvell's envoy 'To the King' in *The Second Advice to a Painter* is a warning to Charles of the necessity to discard Clarendon (*POAS*, Yale, I 52), Rochester's *On King Charles* can be read as a warning to Charles of the necessity to discard 'the most dear of all his dears' (l. 24), the French spy, Louise de Kéroualle, newly created Duchess of Portsmouth. This is where Rochester's real affection may come in.

What the imaginary courtier saw (or imagined that he saw) was 'political power symbols and erect (or semi-erect) penises . . . fused into the vision of a cosmos all of whose functions and activities emanate from sexual impulses . . . the political arena virtually dissolve[d] into an omnipresent, all-encompassing sexuality' (Fabricant 1969, 707).

On the mistaken presentation of the verses to the King, Burnet's story is fully corroborated: 'Once being drunk', Burnet says, 'he intended to give the King a libel that he had writ on some ladies: But by a mistake he gave him one written on himself' (Burnet 1724–34, I 265). A letter of 20 January 1674 confirms the mistake: 'my Lord Rochester fled from Court some time since for delivering (by mistake) into the King's hands a terrible lampoon of his own making against the King, instead of another the King asked him for' (K. H. D. Haley, *William of Orange and the English Opposition 1672–4* (1953), 60–61).

ATTRIBUTION The poem is attributed to Rochester in ten ms. copies (Vienna MS. 14090, f. 61; Edinburgh MS. DC.1.3, pp. 71–2; B.L. MS. Add. 23722, f. 310v;

V&A MS. Dyce 43, pp. 110–12; Bodl. MS. Rawl. D.924, f. 16; Bodl. MS. Don.b.8, pp. 585–6; Harvard MS. Eng. 636F, p. 293; Princeton MS. AM 14401, pp. 319–23; Princeton MS. Taylor 3, pp. 241–2; Folger MS. W.a.135, f. 36v) and in the copy-text, representing at least two independent textual traditions.

DATE If *On King Charles* is the 'terrible lampoon' in the letter of 20 January 1674 mentioned above, then the date 1673 of Bodl. MS. Rawl. D.924, f. 310v is confirmed.

COPY-TEXT *POAS* 1697–1707, I 181.

EMENDATION OF COPY-TEXT 1 grown] known 2 cunts] C---- 3 oh,] om. 11 prick] ----- 14 thrones] thrones that 16 prick] P---- thy] the 21 'Twould] 'Twill cunt] ---- 24 his] thy 25 his] thy 28 tarse] T---- 29 ballocks] Buttocks

Except line 29 (Rochester 1968, 193), the emended readings are preserved in Bodl. MS. Rawl. D.924, f. 310v.

ANNOTATION

4 *easiest*: cf. 'This Principle of making the *love* of *Ease* exercise an entire Sovereignty in his Thoughts, would have been less censured in a private Man, than might be in a Prince' (Halifax, 1912, 204) (Rochester 1982, 86).

5 *no ambition*: cf. 'the profuseness, and inadvertency of the King hath saved *England* from falling into destruction' (*A Letter to Monsieur Van B— de M— at Amsterdam, written Anno 1676 by Denzil Lord Holles concerning the Government of England* [1676?], 5–6).

6 *the French fool*: Charles II was negotiating a separate peace with the Dutch (329.8n.), but Louis XIV carried on the war for four more years.

8 *Peace*: 'our King . . . being always most willing to hear of peace' (Roger Palmer, Earl of Castlemaine, *A Short and True Account of the Material Passages in the late War between the English and Dutch*, 2nd ed. (1672), 47), negotiations with the Dutch were opened during the winter of 1672–3 and the Treaty of Westminster was signed on 19 February 1674. The sexual pun on peace/piece could not have displeased Charles II.

11 *length*: Pepys heard about the King 'hav[ing] a large -----' (Pepys, 15 May 1663); cf. 'his *Majesty* [is] the most potent Prince in Christendom' (Carew Reynel, *The True English Interest* (1674), sig. A6r). The length of Charles's sceptre was two feet, ten and a half inches (Rochester 1982, 86).

13 *brother*: James, Duke of York.

14 *I hate all monarchs*: neither this nor its antithesis, 'I loathe the rabble' (101.120) provides evidence of Rochester's political orientation.

14–15 *I hate all monarchs . . . Britain*: Vieth (Rochester 1968, 61), Walker, and some of the ms. copies put these lines at the end of the poem, 'although this gives the poem a perhaps too defiantly republican slant' (Rochester 1984, 75, 271). But six ms. copies and the copy-text put the lines here, allowing the poem to close with the diminished sexuality of Charles II's 'declining years' (ll. 25–33). The reaction to '*all* monarchs' comes more appropriately here at the end of the contrast between Charles II and Louis XIV.

25 *declining years*: Charles was forty-three on 29 May 1673.

29 *hang an arse*: 'hold back' (*OED*).

32 *hands . . . thighs*: cf. 'my advice to [Nell Gwyn] has ever been this . . . with hand, body, head, heart and all the faculties you have, contribute to his pleasure all you can' (Rochester to Henry Savile, June 1678, Rochester *Letters* 1980, 189).

A Ramble in St James's Park (Much wine had passed with grave discourse)

The meaning of 'ramble' dilucidated below (Annotation: *Title*) is essential to understanding the dramatic situation assumed in the opening lines of the poem. There is no reason to identify the speaker with Rochester, who would be unlikely to prowl in St James's Park 'unaccompanied by . . . a purse bearer, a page, and a couple of footmen' (Love 1972, 161). The *chagrin d'amour* of this aristocratic speaker (324. Headnote) is that he has fallen in love with a whore with whom he is presently cohabiting (ll. 107–32). An historical analogue to this dilemma is provided by the cohabitation of Edward Mountagu, Earl of Sandwich, with Betty Becke, 'a common Courtizan', so damaging to Sandwich's reputation that Samuel Pepys felt compelled to write 'a great letter of reproof' to his patron and kinsman (Pepys, 22 July 1663, 18 November 1663).

Now drunk and overwhelmed with lust for his whore, Rochester's imagined speaker sallies forth in search of her, i.e. 'rambles' in St James's Park (where presumably he knows that she patrols). He catches up with her just as Corinna picks up three clients and drives off with them in a hackney coach (ll. 82), to the speaker's unspeakable frustration.

Throughout 'this unprintable poem' (Ronald Berman, *Kenyon Review* 26 (1964), 362) in Hudibrastic verse there is a surprising leitmotif of Christian imagery: 'consecrate (l. 10) . . . hallowed (l. 33) . . . heaven (ll. 38, 148) . . . fall (l. 90) . . . Jesus (l. 149)' and a remarkable concentric structure turning round an axis of 'natural freedoms' (l. 97):

1–42 Corinna is discovered in St James's Park
43–86 Corinna picks up three 'whiffling fools' (l. 136) and thereby falls into depravity
86–104 Natural lust vs. depravity
105–32 Speaker defends Corinna's natural lust for porters, footmen, etc.
133–66 For Corinna's unnatural lust for fools, the speaker damns her never to achieve satisfaction and to be banished from St James's Park

(Thomas K. Pasch, *Essays in Literature* 6 (Spring 1979), 21–8)

ATTRIBUTION The poem is attributed to Rochester in six ms. copies (B.L. MS. Harl. 6057, ff. 60–62; B.L. MS. Sloane 2332, f. 5v; Edinburgh MS. DC.1.3, pp. 90–92; Harvard MS. Eng. 636F, pp. 12–20; Yale MS. Osborn b.105, p. 34; Yale MS. Osborn fb. 140, p. [iii]) and two printed copies (the copy-text and Rochester 1680 (Pforzheimer)), representing at least two independent textual traditions.

DATE Before 20 March 1673 when the poem is mentioned in a letter from Godfrey Thacker to Theophilus Hastings, Earl of Huntingdon (Huntington MS. HA 12525).

COPY-TEXT Rochester 1680[1], 14–19.

EMENDATION OF COPY-TEXT **32** swive] strive **42** when] and **49** Sutton] *S----* **78** cunt] *C---* **90** fall to so much] taste so much of **104** on] of **126** colour] Colours, **133** vapours] *Vapour* **148** earthly] Earthy **161** despised] depriv'd
All the adopted readings are preserved in Royal Library, Stockholm MS. Vu 69, pp. 77–86.

ANNOTATION
Title *Ramble*: to go looking for a sexual partner; cf. 'RANGER. Intending a Ramble to

St. *James*'s Park to night, upon some probable hopes of some fresh Game' (Wycherley, 1979, 24) (John D. Patterson, *N&Q* 226 (1981), 209–10).
4 *the Bear*: the Bear and Harrow in Bear Yard off Drury Lane (Rochester 1984, 263) was said to be 'an excellent ordinary after the French manner' (Pepys, 18 February 1668).
7 *St James's Park*: a deer park enclosed with a brick wall, created by Henry VIII and improved by Charles II. The Mall was a wooded alley for playing a mallet game, the Canal was made by damming a tributary of the Thames, and the famous trysting place was the heavily wooded area around Rosamund's Pond in the south-west corner of the Park.
9 *James*: presumably James the son of Zebedee, the first apostle to be martyred, whose remains are venerated at Santiago de Compostela.
10 *consecrate*: cf. 'how lovingly the Trees are joyned . . . as if Nature had design'd this Walk for the private Shelter of forbidden Love' (Colley Cibber, *Love's Last Shift* (1696), III ii 2).
19 *mandrakes*: Rochester's fancy that mandrake grows up from semen spilled on the ground is a variant of the folklore motif (A2611.5) that mandrake grows up from blood spilled on the ground.
20 *fucked the very skies*: cf. 'aged trees / . . . invade the sky' (*On St. James's Park, as lately improved by his Majesty* (1661) (Waller 1893, 170); cf. 327.54n.
22 *Aretine*: About 1524 in Rome Marcantonio Raimondi published sixteen engravings after drawings by Giulio Romano of sixteen positions or 'postures' of sexual intercourse (afterwards called *I Modi*). Pope Clement VII insured that this became an extremely rare book by ordering Raimondi to be imprisoned and the plates and copies of Raimondi's book to be destroyed. After effecting Raimondi's release, Pietro Aretino (1492–1556), 'the scourge of princes', wrote sixteen *Sonetti Lussoriosi* to illustrate a second edition of Raimondi's prints (*c.* 1525) and then fled to Florence. Although Rochester may have been able to buy a copy of this book when he visited Italy (1662–4), no copy of either edition is now known. But about 1527 and probably in Venice a pirated edition of *I Modi* with Aretino's sonnets was published and of this edition one copy survives in private hands. A facsimile of this book with English translations of Aretino's sonnets was edited by Lynne Lawner and published by Northwestern University Press in 1988. Posture 15 is reproduced below (351).
23–4 *shade . . . made*: cf. 'Methinks I see the love that shall be made, / The Lovers walking in that Amorous shade' (*On St. James's Park, as lately improved by his Majesty* (1661) (Waller 1893, 168) (Rochester 1984, 263)).
26 *Whores*: of the lowest and highest class. A bulker was a streetwalker who performed on the bulkheads in front of shops. An alcove was a recess in a bedroom for a bed of state (*OED*).
33 *walks*: there were walks along Pall Mall, on both sides of the Canal, and around Rosamund's Pond.
37 *charming eyes*: cf. 'eyes, / . . . make . . . men their prize' (*On St. James's Park as lately improved by his Majesty* (1661) (Waller 1893, 169)).
44 *tails*: 'The simile comparing Corinna to a bitch in heat recurs throughout the poem' (Paulson 1972, 28).
46 *Mother of the Maids*: Biographical Dictionary, s.v. Sanderson; cf. '*Mother*, a Bawd' (*AND*).
49–50 *Sir Edward Sutton*: Biographical Dictionary. These lines may be alluded to in Dorset's *Colin* (1679): 'Chance threw on him Sir Edward Sutton, / A jolly knight that rhymes to mutton' (*POAS*, Yale, II 168); *Banstead*: Banstead Downs in Surrey, about fifteen miles south of London, was 'covered with a short grass intermixed with

thyme, and other fragrant herbs, that render the mutton of this tract . . . remarkable for its sweetness' (*London and Its Environs Described*, 6 vols. (1761), I 246); *mutton*: 'loose women' (*OED*). 'He loves laced mutton' is proverbial (Tilley M1338). This is a quibble that Shakespeare found equally irresistible: 'The Duke (I say to thee againe) would eate Mutton on Fridaies' (*Measure for Measure* (*c*. 1604; 1623), III ii 192).

67–8 *comedy . . . landlady*: the first of a series of comic rhymes: 'arse on . . . parson' (ll. 91–2), 'fraternity . . . of buggery' (ll. 145–6). The grammatical construction here is elliptical: 'from' is omitted before 'the comedy'.

77–8 *kiss . . . 'Yes'*: the dissonant rhyme reflects the 'anatomical distortion' in the couplet (Farley-Hills 1978, 111).

97 *natural freedoms*: cf. '[Rochester] thought that all pleasure, when it did not [hurt another or injure one's health], was to be indulged as the gratification of our natural Appetites. It seemed unreasonable to imagine these were put into a man only to be restrained, or curbed' (Burnet 1680, 38).

101 *a whore in understanding*: Mistress Flareit likewise comes to regard her affair with a fool, Sir Novelty Fashion, as a 'forfeiture of my Sense and Understanding' (Colley Cibber, *Love's Last Shift* (1696), IV i 52).

102 *fools*: the word receives heavy rhetorical emphasis as the first term of a crucial contrast with porters and footmen (ll. 120, cf. 83.'6). The speaker's incredulity is emphasized by an incomplete sentence.

114 *Drenched*: 'like Juvenal's Messalina' (Vieth and Griffin 1988, 60).

116 *digestive surfeit water*: the speaker's rage may be expressed by redundancy: the phrase is redundant (surfeit water is a digestive) and ll. 117–22 are redundant (they replicate ll. 113–16).

119 *devouring cunt*: cf. *Motif-Index* F547.1.1 Vagina dentata.

133–66 The pronouncement of the curse on Corinna (*Motif-Index* M410) is a specialized form of ordaining the future, a kind of malign prophecy. Satire in turn may be a specialized form of pronouncing curses, not on Corinna, of course, but on the system of which Corinna is a sympton.

136 *in . . . fools delight*: cf. 'a Woman who is not a Fool, can have but one Reason for associating with a Man that is' (Congreve 1967, 399).

138 *go mad for the north wind*: to fall in love with Boreas, whose sexual exploits include turning himself into a horse, would correspond with the speaker's mishap in falling in love with Corinna.

142 *perish*: in orgasm.

143–50 These are the impossible tasks of folklore (*Motif-Index* H1010) which add up to an emphatic 'never'.

160 *dog-drawn bitch*: When a dog and bitch are locked together in mating, the dog may throw a hind leg over the bitch's back and try to pull away, dragging the bitch behind him with great pain to both (Paulson 1972, 28–9).

165–6 *And may no woman better thrive / Who dares profane the cunt I swive*: cf. 'May no man share the blessings I enjoy without my curses' (Rochester *Letters* 1980, 123, to Elizabeth Barry).

Satire (Too long the wise Commons have been in debate)

The tenth session of the Cavalier Parliament sat from 4 February to 20 October 1673. It had been prorogued since 22 April 1671, so there was a large backlog of business and a long list of grievances. Charles opened the session by exhorting Parliament to vote the money needed to carry on the unpopular third Dutch War and the next day

Anthony Ashley Cooper, Earl of Shaftesbury, delivered his famous *delenda est Carthago* speech in the House of Lords. But the invasion army encamped at Blackheath was commanded by a foreigner, Frederick Herman Schomberg, a marshal of France, and many of the officers were Roman Catholics. The navy was commanded by the Duke of York, whom everyone knew to be a Catholic (Pepys, 15 April 1668). So Parliament began with grievances. The principal grievance was the Declaration of Indulgence that Charles had promulgated on 15 March 1672 while Parliament was prorogued. On 14 February and again on 26 February the House of Commons voted addresses affirming that the penal laws against non-conformists could be suspended only by Parliament. On 8 March Charles capitulated, breaking the seals of the Declaration with his own hands. In the meantime Parliament voted £1,238,750 in supplies to continue the war. On 29 March Charles gave his reluctant assent to the Test Act, excluding non-conformists from the political life of the nation, and prorogued Parliament (Ogg 1956, I 364–71).

As the opening lines imply, this is a political satire. The immediate occasion for the poem was the Commons' resolution on 18 March 1673, responding to 'frequent Complaints that *Ireland* was likely to be Over-run with *Popery* . . . That an Address be presented to his Majesty, representing the State and Condition of the Kingdom of *Ireland*, and the danger of the *English* Protestant Interest there' (*A Relation of the Most Material Matters Handled in Parliament: Relating to Religion, Property, and the Liberty of the Subject* (1673), 14). Whereupon Rochester wrote an address to His Majesty representing the state and condition of the court of England and the danger to the English Protestant interest there of being overrun with pocky Irish beauties.

Although political parties did not yet exist, the opposition to the court in the House of Commons was led by Sir Thomas Meres, who claimed to speak for '"a few plain, country gentlemen who, though rude and unmannerly, had as good hearts as the best of their fellow members", . . . suggesting a distinction between those who were honoured with the confidence of the Court and those who were not, a distinction at once dismissed as unparliamentary by secretary [Sir William] Coventry, who contended that there was no reason to discriminate between the loyalty of these two sections of the House' (Ogg 1956, I 366). Rochester's tactic of turning the complex Irish issue into a joke may have pleased the King, who responded to the Commons' address by observing that it 'did consist of many different Parts' (*CJ*, IX 278) and proroguing the Parliament.

These unusual six-line anapaestic tetrameter stanzas can be sung to the patriotic tune of 'Let Caesar live long' (Simpson 1966, 444n.).

ATTRIBUTION The lampoon is attributed to Rochester in two ms. copies (Bodl. MS. Don.b.8, p. 409, Huntington MS. HA 12525) and one printed copy (Rochester 1707 (Bragge), [1]10–11), representing at least two independent textual traditions.

DATE After 18 March 1673 when the House of Commons voted an address to the King on 'the Danger of the *English* Protestant Interest' in Ireland (*CJ*, IX 270) and before 20 March 1673 when a copy was sent by Godfrey Thacker to Theophilus Hastings, Earl of Huntingdon (Huntington MS. HA 12525).

COPY-TEXT *POAS* 1704, III 65.

EMENDATION OF COPY-TEXT 1 Too] Thus 6 to forbid] against 7 Cootes] *Colts* Fox] *Cox* 9 which] om. 10 and the] or 11–14] om. 17 an] no
Variant readings and the missing lines are supplied from Bodl. MS. Don.b.8, p. 409 (Rochester 1984, 178–9).

ANNOTATION
4 *safety and peace*: cf. 'the Peace and Safety of That Your Kingdom [of Ireland] . . . so much of late endangered by the Practices of the said *Irish* Papists' (*CJ*, IX 277).
5 *against Irish cattle*: Charles gave his assent to an Act prohibiting the Importation of Cattle from Ireland on 18 January 1667 (*LJ*, XII 81).
7 *The Cootes*: Biographical Dictionary.
18 *damned in the cup*: cf. 'so is the danger great, if we receive [communion] unworthily. For then . . . we eat and drink our damnation' (*The Book of Common Prayer* (1683), sig. I 1v).

The Second Prologue at Court to The Empress of Morocco *Spoken by the Lady Elizabeth Howard* (Wit has of late took up a trick t'appear)

The distinguished patronage of Anne, Duchess of Buccleuch and Monmouth, and Henry Howard, Earl of Norfolk and Earl Marshal of England, secured a performance at court of Elkanah Settle's second play, *The Empress of Morocco*. The play was an extravaganza with a prologue by John Sheffield, Earl of Mulgrave, spoken by Lady Elizabeth Howard, a masque of Orpheus and Eurydice set by Matthew Locke, and the parts acted by 'great personages of the court'. For a second performance at court Rochester (who at this time was a patron of John Dryden) wrote a second prologue, which was also spoken by Lady Elizabeth Howard.

ATTRIBUTION The attribution of the prologue to Rochester in the copy-text establishes a degree of probability just short of certainty.

DATE *The Empress of Morocco* was presented at court *c.* April 1673 (Boswell 1932, 132–3). Rochester presumably wrote his prologue during the time between the two performances.

COPY-TEXT Elkanah Settle, *The Empress of Morocco. A Tragedy* (1673), sig. A3.

EMENDATION OF COPY-TEXT Following **22** *To the King.*] om.
The omitted stage direction is supplied from Rochester 1691, 136.

ANNOTATION
8 *laugh*: cf. 327.19n.
12 *to please*: in his dedication of *Marriage à la Mode* to Rochester (written before 18 March 1673 when the play was entered in the Stationers' Register), Dryden deplored those petty courtiers who 'suffer such to be in necessity, who endeavour at least to please' (Dryden 1956– , XI 223).
17–18 *For us no matter what we speak, but how: | How kindly can we say, 'I hate you now'*: elliptical: 'For us [it is] no matter . . . [It is] How kindly can we say . . .'; *I hate you*: cf. 'Et, jusqu'à *je vous hais*, tout s'y dit tendrement' (And even *I hate you* comes out tenderly) (Boileau, *Satire* III 188).
22 *there*: in the King's chair of state.
Following **22**: the apostrophe to the King was conventional; cf. *POAS*, Yale, I 32, 52.
26 *They*: presumably 'youth and beauty' (l. 24); 'credentials' do not deploy 'a force of charms' (l. 27); *protection in this place*: 'the Kings Palace is exempt from all inferiour Temporal Jurisdiction . . . For the *Civil* Government of the Kings Court, the Chief Officer is the Lord *Steward* . . . He judgeth of all disorders committed in the Court . . . [which is] subject to a special exempted Jurisdiction depending on the Kings

Person and Great Officers. . . . Where the King was . . . Justice should be sought . . . immediately from the Kings own Officers' (Chamberlayne 1670, 234, 241–2).
28 *prosperous*: British success in the third Dutch War was on land, not at sea. The French army under Turenne with twenty-four companies of English infantry commanded by the Duke of Monmouth crossed the Rhine in May 1672 and occupied three of the seven Dutch provinces. At sea, however, on 28 May the Anglo-French fleet commanded by the Duke of York, despite a clear numerical advantage over the Dutch fleet under Michael de Ruyter, barely escaped destruction in Southwold Bay (Solebay) off the Suffolk coast. In July 1672 the Anglo-French fleet attempting to put troops ashore at Kijkduin in West Friesland was scattered by a storm.
33 *captivity*: the iambic metre requires that the word receive four full syllables, 'cap-TI-VI-TY', prolonging the King's well-known subjection to 'youth and beauty' (l. 24) into a graceful compliment.
35–7 *consequence . . . prince . . . defence*: cf. defence . . . sense . . . *Prince* (206.9–11).

Song (Love a woman? You're an ass)

ATTRIBUTION The verses are attributed to Rochester in Harvard MS. Eng. 636F, pp. 247–8, the copy-text, and Rochester 1691, 44–5, which seem to represent two independent textual traditions.

COPY-TEXT Rochester 1680^2, pp. 60–61.

ANNOTATION
3 *happiness*: an outrageous chore is emphasized by an outrageous comic rhyme with 'You're an ass' (l. 1).
4 *idlest*: Harvard MS. Eng. 636F, p. 247 and Rochester 1691, 44, derived from it, reads 'silliest', but 'idlest', the reading of the copy-text, meaning 'empty, vacant' (*OED*), enforces the geographic image of 'God's creation'.
9 *Farewell, woman!*: cf. 'Two Paradises 'twere in one / To live in Paradise alone' (Marvell, 1927, I 49). Both Marvell and Rochester are bluffing.

Upon his Drinking a Bowl (Vulcan, contrive me such a cup)

This is an adaptation of ll. 13–24 of Ronsard's *Ode à Vulcan. Pris d'Anacréon* (Odes XVII and XVIII), the lines beginning, 'Vulcan! en faveur de moi, / Je te pri, depesche toy / De me tourner une tasse / Qui de profondeur surpasse / Celle de vieillard Nestor' (Pierre de Ronsard, *Oeuvres complètes*, 2nd ed. (1924–37), V 80n. (Vulcan, for my delight I beg you, hasten to fashion me a drinking cup deeper than old Nestor's) (*The Critical Works of Thomas Rymer*, ed. Curt A. Zimansky (1956), 226) (John D. Patterson, *Restoration* 5 (1981), 10).

ATTRIBUTION The verses are attributed to Rochester in two ms. copies (Bodl. MS. Add. B.106, f. 42; Harvard MS. Eng. 636F, pp. 62–4) and the copy-text, representing two independent textual traditions. Two more printed copies (not included in the apparatus of Rochester 1984, 164), *Female Poems*, 2nd ed. (1682), 152–4, and *The Works of Anacreon, and Sappho* (1713), 17, derive from the copy-text, bowdlerized by the substitution of 'Love' in l. 24. Cf. note to ll. 21–4 below.

DATE After 26 June 1673 when news of the surrender of Maastricht reached London (*London Gazette*, 26 June 1673).

COPY-TEXT Rochester 1680², 56–7.

EMENDATION OF COPY-TEXT 9 its] his
The emended reading is preserved in Nottingham MS. Portland Pw V 40, pp. 12–13.

ANNOTATION
1–2 *such a cup* | *As Nestor used*: a two-handled golden beaker (*Iliad*, XI 631–6; *Odyssey*, III 40–62) (Rochester 1968, 52).
11 *Maastricht*: As captain-general of all the King's land forces, Monmouth commanded the English contingent that joined the French in the successful invasion of the Netherlands in 1672. In June 1673 he distinguished himself at the siege of Maastricht. On 24 June he 'led the storming party, took possession of the counterscarp, and made good his quarters against the repeated and desperate attempts of the besieged to dislodge him' (Dryden 1882–93, IX 221n.). On 30 June Maastricht surrendered (*A Narrative of the Siege and Surrender of Maestricht, to the Most Christian King* (1673), 8–12). The rhyme requires a pronunciation like 'Mas-TREEK'. The true heroism of Monmouth was soon turned into the mock heroics of a tourist attraction. A scale model of Maastricht was built in Windsor Castle at the head of the Long Terrace (*A True Description of the New-Erected Fort at Windsor . . . Being an Heroick Representation of the late Memorable Siege of Maestritch* (1674), 3). Monmouth, assisted by the Duke of York, obliged by re-enacting the siege. 'To shew their skill in *Tactics* . . . They made their approaches, opened trenches, raised batteries, [took] the Conterscarp, [and] Ravelin, after a stout Defence. Greate Gunns fir'd on both sides, Granados shot, mines Sprung . . . to the greate satisfaction of a thousand spectators' (Evelyn, 21 August 1674; cf. Swift 1939–68, XI 231; Sterne 1940, 443–9).
12 *Yarmouth*: Yarmouth was the port of embarkation for an invasion of Zeeland, which was to have been Britain's share in the partition of the Netherlands with Louis XIV. An army was assembled at Blackheath in May 1673 and marched to Yarmouth in July. Despite mass desertions and near mutiny the army was officially reported to be 'very orderly' (*London Gazette*, 11–14 August 1673), but was disbanded in September without having fired a shot.
15 *Sir Sidrophel*: 'Sidrophel the Rosy-crucian' is the astrologer in Butler's *Hudibras*, II iii, whom Hudibras consults about his prospects with the Widow.
21–4 Nathaniel Lee paraphrases these lines in *The Princess of Cleve* (*c.* December 1682; 1689), III i 130–32: 'let me Dream of nothing but dimpl'd Cheeks, and laughing Lips, and flowing Bowls, Venus be my Star, and Whoring my House, and Death I defie thee. Thus sung Rosidore in the Urn' (Lee 1954, II 188). These lines provide additional evidence that Rochester wrote *Upon his Drinking a Bowl*, for Lee knew Rochester well. The recently dead Count Rosidore is Lee's figure for the recently dead Rochester, and in his elegy for Count Rosidore (*The Princess of Cleve*, I ii 94–6) Lee alludes to three more of Rochester's poems, *A Satire against Mankind*, *Against Constancy*, and *The Advice* (Lee 1954, II 162).

Epigram (Poet, whoe'er thou art, I say God damn thee)

Samuel Pordage's failure to find a patron may explain the fact that his first play, *Herod and Mariamne. A Tragedy*, had to wait 'a dozen Years, before it was made publick' (Langbaine 1691, 406). Elkanah Settle finally secured its production about August 1673 by the Duke's Company in Lincoln's Inn Fields. For its anonymous publication the same year Settle wrote a dedication to Elizabeth Cavendish, the young 'mad Duchess' of Albemarle.

Rochester's epigram is preserved in an anonymous introduction to Elijah Fenton's *Mariamne: a Tragedy* (1723): 'There was another Tragedy likewise written upon this Story, called *Herod and Mariamne*, by Samuel Pordage, Esq. We have Reason to suspect this was of no great Reputation, because a merry Story is recorded of it. The Author, or somebody for him . . . left it to the Perusal of the witty Lord Rochester, to have the Concurrence of his Opinion in its Favour: But his Lordship was so out of Humour with it, that he return'd it with this Distich written on the Cover' (*The History of Herod and Mariamne; Collected and Compil'd from the best Historians, and serving to illustrate the Fable of Mr. Fenton's Tragedy of that Name*, 2nd ed. (1723), sig. A4).

ATTRIBUTION The epigram is attributed to Rochester in Harvard MS. Eng. 28.13F, p. 16, and the copy-text (with identical texts).

DATE Before August 1673.

COPY-TEXT *The History of Herod and Mariamne*, London: 1723, sig. A4.

Seneca's Troas, *Act 2. Chorus* (After death nothing is, and nothing, death)

This is a close translation – Dryden would have called it a metaphrase (324) – of the concluding lines (397–408) of the chorus of the second act of Seneca's *Troades* (*c.* 54 A.D.). Rochester transposes Seneca's lesser asclepiads into a mock Pindaric ode.

ATTRIBUTION The attribution to Rochester in Charles Blount's letter to Rochester of 7 February 1680 (Rochester *Letters* 1980, 234) is confirmed in Rochester 1680[1], 50–51.

DATE The poem was copied into Bodl. MS. Don.b.8, p. 498 by Sir William Haward between 11 August 1673 and February 1675 (Paul Hammond, *Bodleian Library Record* 11 (November 1982), 58–9). The verses 'seem to be echoed' in Nathaniel Lee's *The Tragedy of Nero, Emperour of Rome* (16 May 1674; 1675) (Rochester 1984, 254).

COPY-TEXT Blount 1680, 158–9.

ANNOTATION

1 *After death nothing is, and nothing, death*: Rochester translates the first line literally: 'Post mortem nihil est ipsaque mors nihil' (Seneca, *Troades*, 397); cf. 'Nil igitur mors est ad nos . . . scilicet haud nobis quicquam' (Therefore death is nothing to us . . . nothing at all will be able to happen to us) (Lucretius, *De rerum natura*, III 830, 840).

8 *become . . . lumber*: cf. 'maior enim turbae disiectus materiai / consequitur . . . materies opus est ut crescant postera saecla' (a greater dispersion of the disturbed matter takes place at death . . . matter is needed that coming generations may grow) (ibid. III 928–9, 967).

10 *Where . . . things unborn are kept*: 'quo non nata iacent' (where they lie who were never born) (Seneca, *Troades*, 408).

11 *Devouring time swallows us whole*: 'A few phrases from . . . *Troades englished*, by Samuel Pordage, published in 1660 while Rochester was still at Wadham, seem to have remained in his mind: "*Time* us, and *Chaos*, doth devour" [39.11], "*Body* and *Soul*" [39.12], and "idle tailes" [39.17]' (Rochester 1984, 255).

13–18 *Hell and the foul fiend . . . / Are senseless stories . . . / Dreams*: 'Taenara et aspero / regnum sub domino limen et obsidens / custos non facili Cerberus ostio / rumores vacui verbaque inania / et par sollicito fabula somnio' (the underworld, the savage god who rules the dead, and the dog Cerberus who guards the exit, are empty words, old wives' tales, the stuff of bad dreams) (Seneca, *Troades*, 402–6); cf. 'nil esse in morte timendum . . . nec quisquam in barathrum nec Tartara deditur atra . . . nec miser inpendens magnum timet acre saxum / Tantalus, ut famast . . . nec Tityon volucres ineunt Acherunte iacentem' (there is nothing to be feared after death . . . There is no wretched Tantalus, as the story goes, fearing the great rock that hangs over his head . . . No Tityos lying in Acheron is ravaged by winged creatures) (Lucretius, *De rerum natura*, III 866, 966, 980–81, 984); *no more*: cf. 'there is no naturall knowledge of mans estate after death; much lesse of the reward that is then to be given . . . but onely a beliefe grounded upon other mens saying' (Hobbes, 1935, 100). Rochester told Burnet that 'he could not see there was to be either reward or punishment' after death (Burnet 1680, 52).

Grecian Kindness (The utmost grace the Greeks could show)

'The shortest anti-heroic exposure of the Trojan War', as it has been called (Claude Rawson, *TLS*, 29 January 1985, 335), assumes the dramatic situation of the *Troades* of Euripides and Seneca, the women of Troy left at the mercy of the victorious Greek army, but it does not seem to allude to either play. The rape of the Trojan women is, of course, non-Homeric.

ATTRIBUTION Since the attribution in the copy-text is confirmed by no other textual tradition, it must stand unproven. The heavy irony of the title, the pun on 'baggage' (l. 6), the imperfect rhyme (ll. 5–6, cf. 50.44–5, 51.97–8, 55. 228–9), and the bacchantic tone may suggest Rochester's style to some readers.

COPY-TEXT Rochester 1691, 24.

ANNOTATION
6 *baggage*: *OED* quotes William Robertson, *Phraseologia generali* (1681), 197: 'A baggage, or *Souldiers Punk*; Scortum Castrense'.
9 *clapped his wings*: this phrase, for which there is no equivalent in Chaucer, recurs in Dryden's translation of *The Nun's Priest's Tale* (1700): 'This Chanticleer . . . / Stood high upon his toes, and clapped his wings'. (Dryden 1882–93, XI 361).

Signior Dildo (You ladies all of merry England)

This may be another poem with a latent political agenda (333). When Parliament reconvened on 27 October 1673, it immediately took up a new grievance, the marriage of the heir presumptive, James, Duke of York, to a Catholic princess, Maria Beatrice d'Este, Princess of Modena. Unaware that the marriage contract had been sealed and a marriage by proxy performed in Modena on 10 September, the House of Commons moved an address 'That the intended Marriage of his Royal Highness with the [Princess] of *Modena* be not consummated; and he may not be married to any Person but of the Protestant Religion' (*CJ*, IX 281). The address presented to Charles II on 3 November 'foreseeing the dangerous Consequences, which may follow the Marriage of his Royal Highness the Duke of *Yorke* with the Princess of *Modena*', humbly beseeched the King 'to put a Stop to the Consummation of this intended Marriage . . . to the unspeakable Joy and Comfort of all Your loyal Subjects' (*CJ*, IX 285), whereupon Rochester wrote a mock address foreseeing the solid advantage of a Catholic marriage, namely the wholesale importation of Italian dildoes to the unspeakable joy and comfort of all the ladies of merry England.

Rochester's tactic of once again turning an inflammatory political issue into a joke may not have displeased the King, who again responded by proroguing Parliament to 7 January 1674. But to cause it to be said and sung that this is all that can be said for the Italian connection begins to sound like *lèse majesté*, an attack on the court party, in short a satire. And the reader may be left in a state of delighted puzzlement.

The improvisatory nature of the verses may indicate that adding stanzas to them became something of a court game in the winter of 1673–4 (Treglown 1982, 84). Besides the twenty-three stanzas printed here, thirteen more are included in Rochester 1984, 186–8. The anapaestic tetrameter quatrains (cf. 309) can be sung to the tune of 'Peggie is over the Sea with the Souldier' (Bodl. MS. Don.b.8, p. 477; Simpson 1966, 572).

ATTRIBUTION The verses are attributed to Rochester in five ms. copies and the copy-text. Three of the manuscripts, Vienna MS. 14090, ff. 66–8, Bodl. MS. Firth c.15, pp. 10–14, and V&A MS. Dyce 43, pp. 119–24, derive from a common source, but B.L. MS. Harl. 7319, ff. 4–6, Ohio State MS. Eng. 15, pp. 10–14, and the copy-text represent at least two independent textual traditions. In Nottingham MS. Portland Pw V 42, pp. 13–20 the verses are attributed to 'Lord Dorset & Mr. Shepperd', but Brice Harris calls the poem 'almost certainly Rochester's' (Dorset 1979, 195).

DATE The verses were written between 26 November 1673 when the Duke of York's bride, Maria Beatrice, Princess of Modena, and her large Italian retinue reached London, and 26 January 1674 when 'a song of a certain senior' is mentioned in a letter (*Letters Addressed from London to Sir Joseph Williamson*, ed. W. D. Christie, 2 vols. (1874), II 132).

COPY-TEXT *POAS* 1697–1707, II 188–91.

EMENDATION OF COPY-TEXT **16** You'll] you would **17** Southesk] *Louthesk* **26** wear] wore **27** but] om. **34** pricks] P----s ocean has sand] Nation has Land **37** duchesses have] Duchess having **38** prick]----- **43** for fear that] lest **53** Doll] *Moll* **59** Bergo] pergo **72** arse] A--- **74** or thumb] or your Thumb **75** these] the **81** pricks] P----s **90** ballocks] B------ks
The emendation of all but ll. 34, 43, 59, and 90 is supplied from Ohio State MS. Eng. 15, pp. 10–14. The remainder are editorial.

ANNOTATION

1 *England*: the anaspaestic metre requires the second syllable to be accented, as in 'pil-LOW' (l. 31), 'Cleve-LAND' (l. 33), 'White-HALL' (l. 50), 'Caz-ZO' (l. 71), 'win- DOW' (l. 87), and most notably in 'Dil-DO' in the refrain, with the wrenched accent characteristic of broadside ballad. 'Dildo' was a meaningless word in ballad refrains – 'And he but a squire's son. Sing trang dil do lee' (Francis J. Child, *English and Scottish Popular Ballads*, 5 vols. (1883–98), II 459) – before it became the name of a penis substitute.

2 *kiss the Duchess's hand*: 'It being St. *Andrews* day I saw first [at St. James's Palace] the new *Dutchesse* of *York*, and the *Dutchesse* of *Modena* her mother, newly come over & married &c.' (Evelyn, 30 November 1673).

9 Biographical Dictionary, s.v. Barnardi.

19 *in the circle*: punning on court circle/female pudendum; cf. 'MERCUTIO: ... 'twould anger him / To raise a spirit in his Mistresse circle' (*Romeo and Juliet*, II i 23–4).
23 *Lady Betty*: Biographical Dictionary, s.v. Howard.
26 *shirts of a guinea an ell*: since two and a half yards (ninety inches) or two ells are needed to make a shirt and assuming the guinea at 25 shillings, these shirts cost 50*s*., more than three times what a clergyman paid for shirts, not for his servant, but for himself in 1703 (Jonathan Swift, *The Account Books*, ed. Paul V. Thompson *et al.* [*c.* 1984], 37).
29 *Countess of Rafe*: Biographical Dictionary, s.v. Montagu.
30 *Harris*: James Harris (Biographical Dictionary) was dangerous because he put out Philip Cademan's eye in a stage duel on 9 August 1673.
35 *it*: Her Grace's pudendum.
44 *gentleman usher*: whereas gentlemen of the bedchamber (of which Rochester was one) 'constitute ... the Prime Nobility of *England*' and receive £1,000 a year, gentlemen ushers, whose office is to wait in the presence chamber, were only knights or esquires of note and receive less than £100 a year (Chamberlayne 1660, 258, 265–6).
45 *countess o'th' Cockpit*: Anne Maria Brudenell, Countess of Shrewbury (Biographical Dictionary), was the mistress of George Villiers, Duke of Buckingham, who had lodgings in the Cockpit, an octagonal building across the Privy Garden from the Stone Gallery. She was literally fatal (l. 46), for three men had died for her: Giles Rawlins, William Jenkins, and Francis Talbot, 11th Earl of Shrewsbury (Wilson 1976, 19).
49 Howard: Anne (*c.* 1656–1703), the younger daughter of William, fourth son of Thomas Howard, Earl of Berkshire, Frances Sheldon, daughter of Sir Edward Sheldon, and Philippa Temple were maids of honour to Queen Catherine.
51 *Barnard*: Biographical Dictionary, s.v. Barnardi.
53 *Doll Howard*: Dorothy Howard, elder sister of Anne Howard (49n.) 'ranged' with the Duke of York when she was a maid of honour to Anne Hyde, Duchess of York, until the Duchess's death in March 1671. She was now a maid of honour to Queen Catherine.
59 *Bergo*: the variants include 'Bargo', 'Bergo', 'Borgo', 'Burgoe', and 'Pergo'. The best guess may be 'Bergo', short for Bergholt, East Suffolk, sixty-one miles from London (Wilson 1976, 19), *en route* to Rushbrooke Hall, the country estate of Henry Jermyn, Earl of St Albans.
64 *burning the Pope*: burning papier mâché figures of the Pope was a regular feature of Guy Fawkes Day, 30 November, celebrating the discovery of the Gunpowder Plot in 1605; *the Pope ... his nephew*: the Pope was Clement X (1670–76). His adopted nephew, Cardinal Paluzzi degli Albertoni, aggressively resisted Louis XIV's exercise of the *regale*, the royal right to appoint successors to (and collect the revenue of) vacant sees in France. If there was a partisan political point to this in 1673, it now seems to be lost; *burning ... Dildo*: cf. 'your Lordship has been extreamly wanting heere to make friends at the custome house where has been lately unfortunately seized a box of those leather instruments your Lordship carryed downe one of, but these barbarian Farmers [of the customs duty] prompted by the villanous instigation of theire wives voted them prohibited goods soe that they were burnt' (Henry Savile to Rochester, 26 January 1671, Rochester *Letters* 1980, 62–3).
65 *wife*: Biographical Dictionary, s.v. Killigrew.
71 *Cazzo*: *It.* prick.

76 *you*: 'ladies all of merry England' (l. 1).
89 *Lady Sandys*: Biographical Dictionary, s.v. Sandys.
90 *ballocks*: the prosopopoeia is in the style of Hieronymus Bosch (cf. 30.29).

Tunbridge Wells (At five this morn when Phoebus raised his head)

Tunbridge Wells, about thirty miles south-east of London, is the site of chalybeate springs supposed to have medicinal properties. It became a fashionable resort after visits by King Charles and Queen Catherine (Pepys, 22 July 1663) and by the Duke and Duchess of York with the Princesses Mary and Anne in 1670.

The poem seems experimental in several ways at once. It may be a parody of the Virgilian loco-descriptive poem, examples of which include *To Penshurst* (1616), with its 'walkes for health as well as sport' (Jonson 1925–52, VIII 93) and Waller's reprise, *At Penshurst* (1645) (Waller 1893, 46). But its speaker seems pointedly un-Georgic. He is 'querulous, foul-mouthed, and dyspeptic, and in no sense . . . to be identified with [Rochester]' (Love 1972, 153). He is in fact a perfect satyr, more sympathetic with the equine than with the human race (ll. 183–5).

The ramshackle structure of *Tunbridge Wells* has repeatedly been noted: 'One could shuffle the episodes with no loss of sense or satirical effect' (Earl Miner, *The Restoration Mode from Milton to Dryden*) (1974), 413). It is indeed the inorganic structure of a gallery talk, 'unrelated epigrams directed at a heterogeneous body of victims' (Love 1972, 150), like Pope's *Epistle II. To a Lady*. The imperfect macrostructure is reflected in the versification, as if Rochester were intent to try the effects of slant rhymes ('bully . . . Cully' ll. 15–16), comic rhymes ('mad age . . . adage' ll. 41–2; 'buy eggs . . . intrigues' ll. 43–4), and riddle rhymes ('embassage . . . a message' ll. 62–3). Why is an embassage like a message? Juxtaposing stage characters like Sir Nicholas Cully (l. 16) and Dorothy Fribble (343.149n) with historical figures like Sir Robert Howard (342.14n) and Samuel Parker (342.65n) creates a peculiarly unsettling effect, a kind of literary anomie.

ATTRIBUTION The poem is attributed to Rochester in four ms. copies (Bodl. MS. Douce 357, ff. 136v–138v; Harvard MS. Eng. 636F, pp. 131–40, Yale MS. Osborn b.52/2, pp. 164–7; Princeton MS. Taylor 3, pp. 213–21) and the copy-text, representing at least two independent textual traditions. Pope's doubt that Rochester wrote the poem (W. J. Cameron, *N&Q* 203 (July 1958), 294) can be ignored; Pope did not like Rochester.

DATE Before 25 March 1674 (Vieth 1963, 277–8); the poem is dated 1673 in Yale MS. Osborn b.52/2, p. 164.

COPY-TEXT Richard Head, *Proteus Redivivus: or The Art of Wheedling* (1675), 124–9.

EMENDATION OF COPY-TEXT **19–27**] om. **41** mad age] *Age* **42** proverbs, sentences,] Proverb, Sentence **43–4**] om. **64–77**] om. **67** religious] Religion **85** vile] *vil'd* **93** egg-wives] Egg seamstresses] *and* Semstresses **99** hat] *that* **120–23**] om. **125** girl] *Girls* **141–8**] Is't so (*quoth t'other*) *faith, I pity then / Your Husband much, and all such sapless Men.* **141** is grieved] griev'd **154–6**] *Who wait for Women, or lay wait to* Nick. **163**] *Who are* (*though gaudily they thus appear*) **166** sometimes they] they
The emendation in l. 93 is editorial. The emendation in ll. 141–8 is preserved in Yale MS. Osborn b.52/2, pp. 164–7, in the table of contents of which the poem is

noted as 'very witty & Satyricall'. The remaining emendations and all the lines omitted in the copy-text are supplied from Yale MS. Osborn b.105, pp. 251–63.

ANNOTATION

1 *At five*: cf. 'the morning, when the Sun is an hour more or lesse high, is the fittest time to drink the water' (Rowzee 1671, 53).

3 *trotted*: cf. 'the nearest good lodgings were at Rusthall and Southborough [Plate 4, upper left], a mile or two distant from the wells' (Rochester 1968, 73).

14 *a stag at rut*: 'the allusion is almost certainly to Sir Robert Howard, who had made himself ridiculous with his pompous poem, *The Duel of the Stags*' (1668) (Robert Jordan, *ELN* 10 (June 1973), 269). Rochester's friend Henry Savile wrote a parody of Sir Robert's poem entitled 'The Duel of the Crabs' (i.e. of the crab lice) (*The Annual Miscellany for the Year 1694: Being the Fourth Part of Miscellany Poems* (1694), 293–7).

16 *Sir Nicholas Cully*: Sir Nicholas, a booby squire, is tricked into marriage with the cast mistress of a London fop in Etherege's first comedy, *The Comical Revenge: or Love in a Tub* (1664). The role was created by James Nokes.

24 *crab-fish*: crabmeat, an aphrodisiac? cf. Tilley C785.

31 *Endeavouring*: the metre stretches out 'en-DEAV-our-ING' into four syllables as the speaker strains to avoid the two knighted fools.

33 *th'Lower Walk*: In Plate 4 the Lower Walk is to the right of the Upper Walk (A) (44).

37 *fop*: identified in three ms. copies as Sir Francis Dayrell (Biographical Dictionary).

38–9 *A tall, stiff fool . . . / The buckram puppet*: cf. 'He takes as much care and pains to *new-mold* his *Body* at the *Dancing-Schools*, as if the onely *shame* he fear'd were the retaining of that *Form* which *God* and *Nature* gave him. Sometimes he walks as if he went in a *Frame*, again as if both head and every member of him *turned* upon *Hinges*. Every step he takes presents you with a perfect Puppit-play' (Clement Ellis, *The Gentile Sinner, or, England's Brave Gentleman: Characterized* (1660), 30) (David Trotter in Treglown 1982, 125).

40 *as woodcock wise*: proverbial (Tilley W746).

44 *intrigues*: one seventeenth-century spelling, 'intregues', may indicate how the word was pronounced: 'IN-tregues'.

52 *Scurvy, stone, strangury*: Tunbridge water was supposed to be specific for genito-urinary diseases and scurvy (Rowzee 1671, 41, 42).

54 *wise*: the context requires 'wise' to mean 'fashionable'. This nonce meaning is not recorded in *OED*, but pushing words beyond the range of their current meanings is Rochester's practice, cf. 46.93; *on . . . disease bring infamy*: cf. 33.104.

58 *ambassadors*: cf. 'the mystery of the gospel, For which I am an ambassador' (Ephesians 6.19–20) (Rochester 1982, 89).

59 *pretend commissions given*: apostolic succession, 'the continued transmission of the ministerial commission, through an unbroken line of bishops from the Apostles onwards' (*OED*).

65 *Bayes*: Samuel Parker (Biographical Dictionary); *his importance comfortable*: Rochester mocks Parker's coy reference to his wedding plans as 'Matters of a closer and more comfortable importance to my self' (Parker, *Bishop Bramhall's Vindication* (1672), sig. A2r) (Rochester 1968, 75–6). Marvell wonders 'What this thing should be' and concludes that 'it must be . . . a Female' (*The Rehearsal Transpros'd* (1672), 7–8). The mockery is reinforced by the comic rhyme, 'all this rabble . . . comfortable'.

66 *archdeaconry*: Parker was appointed archdeacon of Canterbury in June 1670.
67 *trampling on religious liberty*: In *A Discourse of Ecclesiastical Polity* (1670) (and two later works) Parker assumes an extreme Erastian position, warning 'how Dangerous a thing Liberty of Conscience is' (xlvi) and arguing that the unstable nature of man made it 'absolutely necessary . . . that there be set up a more severe Government over mens Consciences and Religious perswasions, than over their Vices and Immoralities' (xliii). He concludes that 'there is not the least possibility of setling a Nation, but by Uniformity in Religious Worship' (325).
70 *Marvell*: this is Rochester's only surviving reference to the man who said that 'the earle of Rochester was the only man in England that had the true vaine of satyre' (Aubrey 1898, II 54).
72 *distemper*: Parker complains that he was 'prevented by a dull and lazy distemper' from replying sooner to *The Rehearsal Transpros'd* (*A Reproof to the Rehearsal Transpros'd* (1673), 1). Marvell assumes that the distemper was venereal (*The Rehearsal Transpros'd: The Second Part* (1673), 8–9) (Rochester 1968, 76). Tunbridge water was specific for 'running of the reines, whether it be *Gonorrhea simplex* or *Venerea* . . . nay and the Pox also' (Rowzee 1671, 46–7).
74 *sweetness*: according to the humours theory (not yet discredited in the seventeenth century), choler was bitter, melancholy sour, blood sweet, etc.; cf. Burton, *The Anatomy of Melancholy* (1621), Part I, Section 1, Member 2, Subsection 2.
76 *Importance*: presumably Parker's fiancée or wife; see l. 65n. above.
79 *sisters frail*: 'whores' (l. 5).
82 *gypsies*: 'even the late L. of *Rochester* . . . was not ashamed to keep the *Gypsies* Company' (*AND*, sig. A8v).
90 *conventicle*: pronounced 'CON-ven-TIC-le' (*OED*). Dryden rhymes 'roar and stickle . . . Conventicle' (Prologue to *The Disappointment* (1684), 71).
98 *The would-be wit*: Sir Robert Howard(?) (l. 18).
99 *scrape of shoe*: 'to avoid the horrible absurdity of setting both Feet flat on the Ground, when one should always stand tottering on the Toe, as waiting in readiness for a *Congée*' (*News from Covent Garden; or, The Town-Gallants Vindication* (1675), 6).
101 *ruffled foretop*: the hair on the crown of a wig dressed in frills.
110 *It is your goodness, and not my deserts*: cf. 'MISS: My Lord, that was more their Goodness, than my Desert' (Swift 1939–68, IV 155).
113 *think what next to say*: cf. 24.[2]15.
116 *cribbage fifty-nine*: having moved her scoring pegs through fifty-nine of the sixty holes on the cribbage board, she was unable to advance to the sixtieth and final 'game hole' (Rochester 1968, 77).
123 *a Scotch fiddle*: 'The itch' (*OED*) of sexual excitement; cf. 'a Tailor might scratch her where ere she did itch' (Shakespeare, *The Tempest* (1611; 1623), II ii 55).
135–6 *a barren / Woman . . . fruitful*: cf. 'there is nothing better against barrenness, and to make fruitful, if other good and fitting means, such as the several causes shall require, be joyned with the water' (Rowzee 1671, 48).
142 *those*: menstrual periods.
149 *fribbles*: cf. 'MRS BISKET: Ay, Mr. *Fribble* maintains his Wife like a Lady . . . and lets her take her pleasure at *Epsom* two months together. / DOROTHY FRIBBLE: Ay, that's because the Air's good to make one be with Child; and he longs mightily for a Child: and truly, Neighbour, I use all the means I can' (*Epsom Wells* (1673), II i; Shadwell 1927, II 128) (Robert L. Root, Jr., *N&Q* 221 (May–June 1976), 242–3).

152 *enlarge*: by the addition of cuckold's horns.
153 *Cuff and Kick*: 'Two cheating, sharking, cowardly Bullies' in *Epsom Wells*, which opened at Dorset Garden on 2 December 1672. In the fifth act, Doll Fribble and Molly Bisket are discovered in bed with Cuff and Kick, respectively.
157 *reputation*: Gaston Jean Baptiste, comte de Cominges, the French ambassador (1663–65), was not so gullible. The queen is still at Tunbridge, he reported to Louis XIV in July 1663, 'ou les eaux n'ont rien produit ce qu'il l'en avait espère. On peut les nommer les eaux de scandale, puisqu'elles, on pense, ruinent les femmes et les filles de reputation' (where the waters have done nothing of what was expected of them. Well may they be called the waters of scandal, for they nearly ruined the good names of the maids of honour and of the married women who were there without their husbands) (J. J. Jusserand, *A French Ambassador at the Court of Charles the Second* (1892), 89).
158 *generation*: 'CUFF: Others come hither to procure Conception. / KICK: Ay, Pox, that's not from the Waters, but something else that shall be nameless' (Shadwell 1927, II 107).
165 *With hawk on fist*: this was Rochester's father's disguise, or cover, in his dramatic rescue of Charles II after the defeat at Worcester in 1651 (Clarendon 1707, III 326).
167–9 Rochester's scorn for the cadets' posturing is reflected in the scornful rhymes, 'horse . . . purse . . . arse'.
172 *Bear Garden ape*: the Hope theatre on the Bankside in Southwark reopened in 1664, featuring the blood sports that the Puritans abominated: bull- and bear-baiting, dog- and cock-fights. Pepys found it 'good sport . . . But . . . very rude and nasty' (Pepys, 14 August 1666). Evelyn agreed that it was a 'rude & dirty passetime'. Evelyn also mentions 'the Ape on horse-back' that ended the evening's performance (Evelyn, 16 June 1670).
176 *what thing is man*: cf. 'Lord, what is man that thou of him / tak'st such abundant care?' (Sternhold and Hopkins, *The Whole Book of Psalms* (1703), sig. A3r) (Treglown 1973, 46–7).
180–81 *Thrice happy beasts . . . / Of reason void*: cf. 'Thrice happy then are beasts . . . / They only sleep, and eat, and drink, / They never meditate, nor think' (Thomas Flatman, *Poems and Songs* (1674), 139) (Thormählen 1988, 404n.); *foppery*: except for the outlawed gypsies and the Bear Garden ape, everyone in the poem falls under the speaker's dictum of 'foppery', in the extended sense of self-promoting pretence. Although he is called 'the young gentleman' (l. 175), the Bear Garden ape does not pretend to be a man.
182 *remorse*: in the context the word retains something of its etymological meaning, 'biting back' (David Trotter in Treglown 1982, 126), encapsulating the satyr-speaker's response to what he sees and hears at Tunbridge Wells.

Artemisa to Chloe. A Letter from a Lady in the Town to a Lady in the Country concerning the Loves of the Town (Chloe, In verse by your command I write)

The operative fiction of this satire on love is that of *From Mistress Price* (16), a verse letter written by an inexperienced or nonce-poet. The genre of *Artemisa to Chloe*, however, is not so simple as its prototype: 'an epistle containing a monologue containing a tale containing snatches of discourse' (Sitter 1976, 295). 'Containing . . . containing . . . containing' describes exactly the Chinese-box structure of the poem (Rachel Trickett, in *English Poetry and Prose 1540–1674*, ed. Christopher Ricks (1970), 325):

the most interior narrative of the Chinese box is the tale of Corinna (ll. 189–225) who is ruined by a man of wit, but survives prostitution to become the mistress of a booby squire; her bastard succeeds to the squire's estate when she poisons the squire;

the interior narrative is the monologue of a fine lady (ll. 73–188) who on principle has married 'a diseased, hard-favoured fool' (l. 84) rather than a man of wit;

the frame story is Artemisa's report to Chloe in the country about the latest fashions in 'the Loves of the Town' (ll. 1–264).

Although this model accurately describes the structure of the poem, it does not take into account the importance of Artemisa as narrator and chorus.

Perhaps the structure of the poem is better described as a more complicated version of the original three-cycle structure of *A Satyr against Mankind*:

1st cycle	1–264	*Narrative*: Artemisa, herself disappointed in love (presumably by a man of wit), reports to Chloe in the country that the latest fashion in London is for fine ladies to marry fools, and she provides a distinguished fine lady as an exemplum.
	16–31	*Interruption*: Artemisa interrupts herself to confess that although 'writing's a shame' (l. 25), she can't wait to begin.
2nd cycle	73–188	*Narrative*: Artemisa recounts the fine lady's monologue in which she defends her marriage to a fool on the ground that men of wit demand to know things as they really are whereas fools admire appearances.
	147–68	*Interruption*: Artemisa reflects on the meaning of the fine lady, a 'mixed thing' (l. 148), a woman of wit who chooses to be a fool.
3rd cycle	189–255	*Narrative*: The fine lady recounts the tale of Corinna, ruined by a man of wit, who becomes the mistress of a fool.
	256–64	*Interruption*: Artemisa concludes that the fine lady is still 'Mixed' (l. 257) and promises Chloe more by the next letter.

A subordinate theme of the poem is a paradox: fools make better husbands than men of wit. The fine lady sustains the paradox both in her monologue and in her exemplum of Corinna, but Artemisa thinks she is a fool (l. 151). The main theme, implied in everything Artemisa says, is that the love game has degenerated into a trade (l. 51) entered into for monetary gain. 'This is not the Women's age, let 'em think what they will', Lady Woodvill complains, 'Lewdness is the business now' (Etherege 1927, II 245).

ATTRIBUTION The poem is attributed to Rochester in nine ms. copies (Vienna MS. 14090, ff. 35v–37r; V&A MS. Dyce 43, pp. 61–4; Cambridge MS. Add. 6339, ff. 4r–7v; Bodl. MS. Rawl. Poet. 173, ff. 65v, 132v; Nottingham MS. Portland Pw V 46, pp. 11–14; Harvard MS. Eng. 623F, pp. 1–9; Harvard MS. Eng. 636F, pp. 20–32; Yale MS. Osborn b.105, pp. 45–61; Folger MS. M.b.12, ff. 10v–12v) and three printed copies (Rochester 1680[1], 19–27; Rochester 1691, 65–81; *POAS* 1698, 25–9), representing at least two independent textual traditions. A copy of *A Letter from Artemiza in the Town, to Chloë in the Country* (1679) offered for sale in 1959 is annotated 'By Rochester' (Vieth 1963, 380). Bodl. MS. Don.b.8, p. 490 is annotated 'by the Earl of Rochester, or Mr. Wolseley', but Wolseley, who wrote the preface to Rochester's *Valentinian*, is one of Charles Sackville's 'Most Eminent Ninnies' (*POAS*, Yale, IV 206–7).

DATE 'Probably 1674' (Rochester 1984, 278).

COPY-TEXT *Artemisa to Cloe. A Letter from a Lady in the Town, to a Lady in the Country; Concerning the Loves of the Town*, by a Person of Quality (London: For William Leach, 1679).

EMENDATION OF COPY-TEXT **10** dashed] toss'd **13** wit] War **18** diverts] directs **35** and who] or who **66** obeys] obey **68** for taste] so fast **74** fine] Fair **85** that] your **86** your] the **153** rose] rise **162** a] an **239** a love] alone
The emendation of l. 239 is supplied from *POAS* 1698, 28. The emendations of ll. 68, 85, and 153 are supplied from *A Letter from Artemiza in the Town, to Chloë in the Country*, By a Person of Honour (1679). The remaining emendations are supplied from Rochester 1680[1], 19–27.

ANNOTATION
7 *adventurers for the bays*: cf. 'How vainly men themselves amaze / To win the Palm, the Oke, or Bayes' (Marvell 1927, I 48).
7–8 *adventurers . . . returns*: overseas traders . . . profits.
17 *Bedlam has many mansions*: cf. 'In my father's house are many mansions' (John 14.2).
20 *discreetly*: the net meaning clear of irony is 'self-destructively'.
24 *arrant*: an intensifier 'without opprobrious force' (Rochester 1984, 278).

35 *who . . . together:* cf. 31.2.
39 *ill-bred customs*: cf. 'This ill-bred age' (78.²4).
40 *the most generous passion*: Artemisa's experience in this field (l. 38) suggests that this line be read ironically, articulating Artemisa's suspicion that love may be a totally selfish, self-absorbing, *un*generous passion.
40–42 *Love . . . / The safe director*: a major irony of the poem. Artemisa has lost love (l. 38), Corinna is 'Cozened . . . by love' (l. 191) and degraded, the booby squire is 'faithful in his love' (l. 230) and destroyed.
44 *That cordial drop*: cf. 'The Cordial Drop of Life is Love alone' (Pope 1939–67, IV 245).
46–7 *raise . . . subsidies*: increase the amount . . . of grants.
51 *an arrant trade*: cf. 'dainty trades indeed' (81.53).
52–3 *it . . . that*: love . . . play, i.e. love now employs as many cheats as gambling.
55 *'Tis*: the antecedent is the 'trade' (l. 51) of love.
57 *gypsies*: 'A contemptuous term for a woman, as being cunning, deceitful, fickle' (*OED*) (Rochester 1984, 278). But Artemisa is making another point as well: she observes that women of her class, enjoying all the freedom possible in an ordered society, will nevertheless turn outlaw for the freedom to achieve infamy, which entails the loss of the freedoms enjoyed in an ordered society. Artemisa frames this argument pointedly in an ordered triplet. The choice of infamy is a perverse exercise of free will (357.32n.).
58 *hate . . . infamy*: Dustin Griffin suggests 'hate restraints, even the restraint of avoiding infamy'.
59 *They*: women who do not live for love (l. 50) by 'nature's rules' (l. 60), but who trade in love.

64 *'Tis below wit . . . to admire*: the Horatian commonplace, 'nil admirari' (*Epistles*, I vi 1); cf. 'not to be brought by anything into an impassioned state of mind, or into a state of desire or longing' (Charlton T. Lewis and Charles Short, *A Latin Dictionary* (1962), 40).
72 *that with their ears they see*: i.e. not at all.
83 *had been*: i.e. 'would have been' (Rochester 1980, 92).
96 *let me die*: the identifying speech tag of Melantha, a heroine in Dryden's *Marriage à la Mode* (April 1672?; 1673). 'A Court-Lady' in this play is named Artemis. In the dedication of the play to him Dryden acknowledges that it 'receiv'd amendment' from Rochester, who also 'commended it to the view' of the King (Dryden 1956– , XI 221). Rochester's 'amendments' may have concerned the character of Melantha, whom the fine lady resembles in her affectation (Rochester 1968, 106n.).
98 *Embarrassée*: cf. '*Melantha*: . . . *embarrass* me! what a delicious *French* word' (Dryden 1956– , XI 300).
99 *Indian queen*: *The Indian Queen*, the first rhymed heroic play, by Sir Robert Howard and John Dryden, opened at the Theatre Royal in January 1664. It seems unlikely that the fine lady 'had turned o'er' (l. 162) this play, for neither of the queens, Amexia and Zempoalla, are 'Rude and untaught'.
103–4 *à la mode, / . . . incommode*: cf. 'Un poète à la cour fut jadis à la mode; / Mais des fous aujourd'hui c'est la plus incommode' (Poets used to be in fashion at court, but today they are the most troublesome fools) (Boileau, *Satire* I, 109–10) (Davies 1969, 354).
108–9 *With searching wisdom, fatal to their ease, / They'll still find out why what may, should not please*: cf. 'His wisdom did his happiness destroy, / Aiming to know that world he should enjoy' (73.33–4) (Rochester 1984, 279); *They'll still find out why what may, should not please*: although 'ten low Words' do creep in this one line, the uncertainty in the third and fourth feet – are 'why' and 'may' stressed or unstressed? – the cacophony created by 'why what' and the internal pause between 'may, should' make the line anything but 'dull' (Pope 1937–67, I 278).
115 *The perfect joy of being well deceived*: cf. Ovid, *Amores*, II x (27.47–8); 'O yet happiest if ye . . . know to know no more' (Milton 1931–8, II i 134); '*Happiness . . . is a perpetual Possession of being well deceived*' (Swift, 1939–68, I 108).
122 *Bold . . . before a fool's dull sight*: cf. 332.136n.
155–7 *the very top / . . . of folly we attain / By curious search*: cf. 'The most ingenious way of becoming foolish is by a system' (Anthony Ashley Cooper, 3rd Earl of Shaftesbury, *Characteristics* (1711), ed. John M. Robertson, 2 vols. (1900), I 189).
166–7 *good qualities . . . blest / . . . so distinguished*: 'the tone of irony' in these phrases has been noted (David Sheehan, *Tennessee Studies in Literature* 25 (1980), 77).
183 *Foster*: Biographical Dictionary, s.v. Foster.
183–4 *an Irish lord . . . City cokes*: types of booby squire whom Corinna entraps.
194 *knew*: cf. 'Adam knew Eve his wife; and she conceived' (Genesis 4.1).
206 *In some dark hole*: cf. 'Into some dirty hole' (35.162). *Qu.*: Is this Corinna the Corinna of *A Ramble in St. James's Park*? And if so, is the speaker of *A Ramble in St. James's Park* the 'man of wit' who ruined Corinna 'and went away' (ll. 198–200)?
209 *Easter term*: one of the four times during the year (from seventeen days after Easter to the day after Ascension Day) when the law courts are in session; *new gown*: cf. 'I came up, Madam, as we Country-Gentlewomen use, at an *Easter*-Term, to the destruction of Tarts and Cheese-cakes, to see a New Play, buy a new Gown, take a Turn in the Park, and so down agen to sleep with my Fore-fathers' (Dryden 1956– , IX 214). Dryden adapted this play, *Sir Martin Mar-all* (15 August 1667; 1668),

'purposely' for James Nokes (Biographical Dictionary), who created the role of Sir Martin Mar-all. Sir Martin, 'who is always committing Blunders to the Prejudice of his own Interest' (Cibber 1740, 86) may be the prototype of the booby squire (ll. 210–51).
210–18 another of Ezra Pound's 'exhibits'. Pound observes that whereas Butler, Pope, and Crabbe are dated, 'Rochester is London, 1914 . . . his eye lights on the eternal silliness, persisting after the problem of leisure has been solved' (Pound 1934, 161).
213 *country*: 'a district . . . often applied to a county' (*OED*). 'My young master's . . . great family' rules the county by generous provision of 'strong ale and beef' at quarter sessions and general elections.
236–7 *complains, / Rails . . . maintains*: 'Corinna is the subject' (Rochester 1984, 281).
247 *poison him*: 'a conscious or unconscious daydream of disposing of her [the fine lady's] husband permanently rather than for an afternoon' (Sitter 1976, 296).
248 *in her . . . arms*: when *Artemisa to Chloe* is scored as an opera, this will be the climactic scene. On stage left of a divided stage in a dumb show the booby squire's lady and his children are turned away from the door by a servant in night dress. The squire's lady sinks to the stoop in exhaustion. As it begins to snow she rouses herself to gather the children to her and cover them with her cloak. In a simultaneous action on stage right in a second-floor bedroom the booby squire is discovered in bed with Corinna. He is beginning to feel the effects of poison that Corinna has put into his wine at dinner but rouses himself to sing a passionate aria proclaiming eternal love for Corinna and dies in her arms. She gets up and covers the body with the bed sheet.
261 *such stories I will tell*: cf. 'I dare almost promise to entertain you with a thousand bagatelles every week' (Dryden to Rochester, summer 1673, Rochester *Letters* 1980, 91).
261–4 *tell / . . . swell, / . . . hell; / . . . Farewell*: after 'a virtuoso display of poetic technique' (Howard Weinbrot, *Studies in the Literary Imagination* 5 (1972), 35) including half lines, half rhymes, single and double rhymes, end-stopped couplets, run-on couplets, and twelve triplets, Rochester ends with a unique, resounding quatrain.

Timon. A Satyr (What, Timon, does old age begin t'approach)

The *repas ridicule* motif, 'originally, no doubt, a borrowing from the Hellenistic mime' (Love 1972, 158), has a long history which includes Plato's *Symposium*, Horace's *Satire* II viii, Lucian's *A Feast of Lapithae*, Trimalchio's feast in the *Satyricon* of Petronius, Mathurin Regnier's *Satire* X, Boileau's *Satire* III, as well as Hogarth's *A Midnight Modern Conversation*, and the pie-throwing sequences in Mack Sennett comedies. For *Timon. A Satyr* Rochester borrows the framework of Boileau's *Satire* III, but fills it in with very different material. Dryden describes the method perfectly:

> The third way [Rochester had experimented with literal translation and paraphrase, 323, 324] is that of imitation, where the translator (if he now has not lost that name) assumes the liberty, not only to vary from the words and sense, but to forsake them both as he sees occasion; and taking only some general hints from the original, to run divisions on the ground-work, as he pleases (Dryden 1882–93, XII 16).

The speaker is certainly not Shakespeare's Timon, who offers his fig tree to his 'deere Countrymen' for hanging themselves and whose epitaph boasts, 'Heere lye I Timon, who alive, all living man did hate' (*Timon of Athens* (*c.* 1606; 1623), V iv 38, 72). Rochester's Timon complains in a minor key, like Boileau's 'P', who is René

Bruslart, seigneur du Broussin, the inventor of sauce Robert (Nicolas Boileau-Despreaux, *Satires, Epîtres, Art poetique*, ed. Jean-Pierre Collinet (1985), 293).

Nor is the speaker Rochester. 'Rochester, as a . . . peer, would hardly have been seized in the street, addressed in the familiar form of the second person, and dragged off to dinner by a down-at-heel ex-colonel whom he has never met before' (Love 1972, 161). The speaker is a middle-aged debauchee and gambler (ll. 1–4) who may differ from his host and the other guests only in that he sees them (and himself) as they are. Their vulgarity is matched by his bad taste in ridiculing a man whose hospitality he accepts (l. 12) (Treglown 1982, 77). Like the speaker in *Tunbridge Wells*, he is another satyr-figure, 'querulous, foul-mouthed and dyspeptic' (Love 1972, 153).

Of the other guests we are told only that they are 'brave fellows' and that they 'write' (ll. 37–9). The form of this literary banquet is supplied by Boileau: the successive courses of the dinner and the deipnosophy afterwards. All the good details, the host's wife, the carrots, Cullen's bushel cunt (Plate 5), are supplied by Rochester.

ATTRIBUTION The poem is attributed to Rochester in Harvard MS. 623F, pp. 52–7 and the copy-text, representing two independent textual traditions. The poem is also attributed to Sir Charles Sedley in two ms. copies (Harvard MS. Eng. 636F, pp. 228–36; Yale MS. Osborn b.105, pp. 227–38) representing a single textual tradition, and to Buckingham in George Villiers, Duke of Buckingham, *Miscellaneous Works* (1704), [1]53–63. The claims of the rival poets are carefully scrutinized and rejected in Vieth 1963, 281–92.

DATE April–May 1674? (352.152n.).

COPY-TEXT Rochester 1680^3, 105–10.

EMENDATION OF COPY-TEXT **Title** *Timon. A Satyr*] *Satyr* **16** Shadwell's] *S-------* **29–30**] om. **77** Mosely] *M----* **88** up] om. **90** beer] Bear **93** Blunt] *B---* **94** cunt] *C*--t **101** The King] om. **113** Orrery] *O-----* **122** Etherege] *E--------* **126** Huff] *H---* Settle] *S----* **138** *Viz.*] (*Videl.*) **154** When] If **177** beer-glass] Bear Glass

The emendation of ll. 90 and 177 is supplied from Edinburgh MS. DC.1.3, pp. 56–7. The conjectural emendation of line 101 is supplied by Harold Love (*Bibliographical Society of Australia and New Zealand Bulletin* 6 (1982), 133). The title and the remaining emendations and omissions are supplied from Leeds MS. Brotherton Lt. 54, pp. 92–100 (Rochester 1984, 188–90).

ANNOTATION

1 *A*: Auteur in Boileau, *Satire* III. If the parallel with Boileau were enforced, ll. 1–4 would be spoken by Rochester.

6 *th'Mall*: a walk bordered by trees in St James's Park; cf. 'Ibam forte Via Sacra, sicut meus est mos / nescio quid meditans nugarum, totus in illis. / accurrit quidam notus mihi nomine tantum, / arreptaque manu' (Horace, *Satire*, I ix 1–4) (I was strolling at random along the Via Sacra musing the way I do on some trifle or other and wholly intent thereon, when up runs a man I knew only by name and seizes my hand) (Rochester 1982, 92).

13–32 these lines have no counterpart in Boileau.

15 *the praise of pious queens*: may be the title of a moralizing broadside.

16 *Shadwell's unassisted . . . scenes*: even before *Epsom Wells* was performed, it was charged that 'the best part' (Shadwell 1927, II 278) had been written by Sir Charles

Sedley. Despite Shadwell's repeated denials, the charge found its way into *Mac Flecknoe* (1676; 1682) (Dryden 1956– , II 58).
35–6 *Huff, / Kickum*: almost a spoonerism for 'Cuff and Kick' (48.153).
39 *They will . . . fight*: introducing suspense into the narrative.
40 *tam Marte quam Mercurio*: on the verso of the title-page of *The Steel Glas. A Satyre* (1576) (Wood 1813–20, I 435–6), George Gascoigne included a portrait of himself in armour with this motto. Walter Raleigh wrote commendatory verses for this volume and after Gascoigne's death the motto was 'assumed by, or appropriated to' Raleigh himself (*Biographia Britannica* 1747–66, V 3467).
41 *I saw my error . . . too late*: cf. 'trop tard, reconnaissant ma faute' (seeing my mistake too late) (Boileau, *Satire* III, 37).
42–67 these lines have no counterpart in Boileau.
52 *blear eyes*: the substitution of a spondee for the iamb in the third foot, 'her OLD BLEAR EYES', 'mimes the [hostess's] effort' to ingratiate herself with her unexpected guest (Treglown 1982, 80).
54–5 (*in despite of time*) / *Preserved the affectation of her prime*: Oldham incorporates these lines into his imitation of Horace, *Odes*, IV 13 (Oldham 1987, 339).
57 *the French king's success*: France and England declared war on the United Provinces in April 1672. In May the French army under the personal command of Louis XIV crossed the Rhine at Tolhuys and occupied three of the seven provinces. Louis XIV established his headquarters at Utrecht on 20/30 June (*London Gazette*, 20 June 1672) and was only prevented from marching into Amsterdam when William of Orange ordered the polders to be flooded (*A Narrative of the Progress of His Most Christian Majesties Armies against the Dutch* (1672)). The campaign of 1673 began with the successful reduction of Maastricht (336.11n.), which had been bypassed in 1672. 'The *French* Army go on Conquering and get all', Buckingham complained to the House of Lords in January 1674, 'and we get nothing' (Buckingham, *Miscellaneous Works* (1704), ^{2}3).
59 *two women*: Louise-Françoise de la Vallière (1644–1710) was a maid of honour to Henrietta Anne, Duchess of Orléans, when she became mistress of Louis XIV in 1661. Françoise-Athenais de Rochechouart (1641–1707) married the marquis de Montespan in 1663 and in July 1667 became a mistress of Louis XIV.
73 *champagne*: the copy-text spelling, 'Champoon', may indicate how the word was pronounced.
73–4 *French kickshaws . . . / Ragouts and fricassees*: cf. 'CLODPATE: I . . . spend not scurvy French kick-shaws, but much Ale, and Beef, and Mutton, the Manufactures of the Country . . . I hate *French* Fricasies and Ragousts' (*Epsom Wells* (December 1672; 1673), Shadwell 1927, II 112, 151).
78 *The coachman . . . ridden*: this ironic reversal (Plate 13) is number 15 of Aretino's postures (*I Modi* 1988, 86).
80 *tool*: dildo; *countess*: Elizabeth, Countess of Percy (Biographical Dictionary, s.v. Montagu).
84 *good cheer*: cf. a citizen's idea of a banquet, 'two puddings' (Pope 1939–67, III ii 119).
88 *Instead of ice*: cf. 'Point de glace, bon Dieu! dans le fort de l'été!' (No ice? Good God! In the middle of summer?) (Boileau, *Satire* III, 83).
91–2 *table . . . so large*: Boileau's diners were crowded (Boileau, *Satire* III, 53–4); *six old Italians*: where the host and hostess and five guests sat, there was room at the table for more than six Romans to *recline* (Rochester 1982, 93).
93 *Blunt*: unidentified.
95–110 these lines have no counterpart in Boileau.

13 Posture 15, an engraving by Marcantonio Raimondi after a drawing by Giulio Romano.

105 *virtuous league*: marriage or a discreet affair(?).
108 *taste their former parts*: one critic finds it impossible to determine whether the effect of the *double entendre* is 'malicious ridicule or amused sympathy' (Love 1972, 163), but the affect of the thirty-odd lines describing the hostess, as powerful as that of *A Song of a Young Lady. To her Ancient Lover* (71–2), seems incompatible with 'malicious ridicule'.
109 *the best in Christendom*: i.e. 'the best cunts in Christendom' (30.2) (Rochester 1984, 276).
111 *ourselves*: Timon includes himself as object of satire, or 'acknowledg[es] the incompleteness of his isolation' (Treglown 1982, 83).
112 *regulate . . . the state*: cf. 'Chacun a . . . réformé l'Etat' (everyone . . . remakes the state) (Boileau, *Satire* III, 162–4). The zeugma, 'regulate the stage, and . . . state', is Rochester's invention.
114 *Mustapha and Zanger die*: they commit suicide in Act V of Orrery's *The Tragedy of Mustapha*, 'perhaps composed in half an hour' (100.97) and produced at Lincoln's Inn Fields on 3 April 1665.

117–18 Halfwit misquotes ll. 269–70 of Orrery's *The Black Prince*, which opened at the Bridges Street theatre on 19 October 1667: 'And which is worse, if worse than this can be, / She for it ne'er excus'd her self to me'. It was said to be 'the worst play of my Lord Or[r]ery's' (Pepys, 23 October 1667).
119 *There's fine poetry*: cf. 'C'est là ce qu'on appelle un ouvrage achevé' (That's what you call a finished work) (Boileau, *Satire* III, 195).
120 *So little on the sense the rhymes impose*: applied to Orrery the line may mean, Even in rhyme Orrery's verse remains prosy/prosaic. Applied to Rochester it may mean, Even in rhyme Rochester's verse retains colloquial word order and cadence; cf. '[Rochester] is the first poet in English to write satires . . . which, however artful their . . . rhymes, sound like someone talking' (Treglown 1982, 84).
125 *two . . . plays without one plot*: Etherege's *The Comical Revenge; or, Love in a Tub* (March 1664) and *She wou'd if she Cou'd* (February 1668) are the plays. The 'design' of the latter was found to be 'mighty insipid' (Pepys, 6 February 1668), but both plays have conventional comic plots.
126 *Settle, and Morocco*: Elkanah Settle's *The Empress of Morocco*, rivalling Dryden's heroic dramas, had two performances at court before the public opening at Dorset Garden on 3 July 1673. Rochester wrote a prologue for the second performance at court (36).
128–30 Huff misquotes *The Empress of Morocco*, II i 10, 61–2: 'Their lofty Bulks the foaming Billows bear . . . / *Saphee* and *Salli*, *Mugadore*, *Oran*, / The fam'd *Arzille*, *Alcazer*, *Tituan*'. Settle had a way with place-names like John Milton: 'Close sailing from *Bengala*, or the Isles / Of *Ternate* and *Tidore*' (*Paradise Lost* (1667, 1674), II 638–9).
132 *for Crowne declared*: Rochester began to patronize John Crowne in 1671. Crowne dedicated to Rochester his second play, *The History of Charles the Eighth of France* (November 1671; 1672) with engaging modesty: 'I have not the Honour of much acquaintance with your Lordship . . . I have seen in some little sketches of your Pen excellent Masteries . . . and . . . I have been entertained . . . with the wit, which your Lordship sprinkles . . . in your ordinary converse' (sig. a1v).
133 *the very wits of France*: including Gaultier de Coste, seigneur de la Calprenède, *Cassandra, the Fam'd Romance*, trans. Sir Charles Cotterell (1652); Madeleine de Scudéry, *Artamenes; or, The Grand Cyrus, An Excellent New Romance*, trans. F. G. (1653–5); *Clelia. An Excellent New Romance*, trans. John Davies and C. Haven (1655–6).
134 *Pandion*: Crowne's first publication was a prose romance modelled on Sidney's *The Countesse of Pembrokes Arcadia* (1590) and entitled *Pandion and Amphigeneia, or, The History of the Coy Lady of Thessalia* (1665).
138–40 Kickum quotes (correctly) *The History of Charles the Eighth of France* (1672), II i 85–7.
144 *The Indian Emperour*: Dryden's fourth play, a sequel to *The Indian Queen* (January 1664; 1665) with Sir Robert Howard, opened at the Bridges Street theatre in April 1665.
145–6 the lines quoted (correctly) by Kickum are spoken by stout Cortez in *The Indian Emperour*, I i 3–4; Walter Scott also found them 'ludicrous' (Dryden 1882–93, II 319).
150 *laureate*: Charles II appointed Dryden poet laureate and historiographer royal on 18 August 1670.
152 *Souches*: for some weeks after 9 April 1674 it was expected in London that Ludwig Ratuit von Souches (1608–82), commander of the Imperial Army on the Rhine, would engage Turenne at the head of the French army. This expectation was

dashed when the Imperial Army was diverted into Flanders (*London Gazette*, 8 June 1674) (Harold F. Brooks, *N&Q* 174 (May 1938), 384–5).
159–60 *courage . . . / 'Tis a short pride*: cf. '[No] Virtue . . . can we name, / But what will grow on Pride' (Pope 1939–67, III i 78).
168–9 *at t'other's head let fly / A greasy plate*: cf. 'Lui jette pour défi son assiette au visage' (He hurls his plate in his face as a challenge) (Boileau, *Satire* III, 214).
174 *Their rage once over, they begin to treat*: cf. 'Et, leur première ardeur passant en un moment, / On a parlé de paix et d'accommodement' (Their anger was soon dispersed and they began to talk of peace and accommodation) (Boileau, *Satire* III, 227–8).

Upon his Leaving his Mistress ('Tis not that I am weary grown)

'Donne seems to have invented the pentameter ababccc stanza . . . in "The Good-morrow" and . . . "Loves Deitie"' (Ernest Häublein, *The Stanza* (1978), 28) that Rochester cuts down to an unusual tetrameter stanza rhyming $A^4B^4A^4B^4C^4C^4C^4$, of which these verses are the only example in his work. As well as Donne's stanza form, Rochester may have recalled phrases in Donne's other works.

The unsettling effect (341) in this poem is created by the ambiguity of the speaker's tone of voice (Treglown 1976, 555) wavering between heartbreak and savage sarcasm.

ATTRIBUTION The poem is attributed to Rochester in Harvard MS. 636F, pp. 61–2, Rochester 1680^2, 54–5, *Poems by Several Hands, and on Several Occasions Collected by N. Tate* (1685), 8, and Rochester 1691, 49–50. But the four copies appear to represent the same textual tradition, so the attribution stands unproven. Some parallels to other works of Rochester occur at ll. 11 and 17–18.

COPY-TEXT Rochester 1680^2, 54–5.

ANNOTATION
1–2 *'Tis not that I am weary grown / Of being yours*: cf. 'Sweetest love, I do not goe, / For weariness of thee' (Donne 1912, I 18) (Fredelle Bruser, *UTQ* 15 (1945–6), 391–2).
11 *one happy man*: cf. 'Shall women . . . / Be bound to one man' (Donne 1912, I 83); 'please one man' (101.113).
13 *like nature*: cf. 'By nature, which gave it, this liberty / Thou lov'st' (ibid.).
14 *universal influence*: 'As yet to none could he peculiar prove, / But like an universal Influence . . . / To all the Sex he did his heart dispence' (Davenant, *Gondibert: An Heroick Poem* (1651), 11) (Treglown 1976, 556).
15 *seed-receiving earth*: Donne's mistress is also 'a plow-land' where he 'casts all his seed corne there, / And yet allowes his ground more corne should beare' (Donne, 1912, I 83).
17–18 *no showers unwelcome . . . womb retains 'em all*: cf. 'When your lewd cunt came spewing home / Drenched with the seed of half the town' (34.113–14).

A Pastoral Dialogue between Alexis and Strephon (There sighs not on the plain)

In this exercise in counterpoint the predictable stanza form, $A^4B^3A^4A^4B^3$, is played off against an unpredictable pattern of speech prefixes. All of Alexis's speeches begin with the first line of the stanza, but Strephon breaks in twice in the fifth line and once in the third line. If this difference establishes Strephon as the dominant character, the expectation is overturned in the last speech of each character.

Another variant of the five-line stanza form, $A^4B^4A^4B^4B^4$, with double rhyme in the B lines, occurs in the *Ninth Song* of Sidney's *Astrophel and Stella* (1591) in the same pastoral mode:

> Why (alas) then doth she sweare
> That she loveth me so deerly;
> Seeing me so long to beare
> Coales of love that burne so cleerly,
> And yet leave me hopelesse meerly.
> (Sidney 1912–26, II 297) (312–13)

ATTRIBUTION The verses are attributed to Rochester in the copy-text and in Rochester 1691, 10–15. Since it does not appear that the two witnesses represent independent textual traditions, the attribution stands unproven. But thirty-seven of the thirty-nine poems in Rochester 1691 are included in Rochester 1968 and Rochester 1984 (the other two are by Lady Rochester and Sir Carr Scrope). In some still to be determined fashion, Rochester 1691, edited by Thomas Rymer, is authoritative. And this supposition increases the probability that *A Pastoral Dialogue between Alexis and Strephon* is by Rochester.

DATE The place and date of composition supplied in the copy-text, 'At the Bath, 1674', remain unconfirmed. Rochester may have visited Bath in June 1674 (Rochester *Letters* 1980, 66n.).

COPY-TEXT *A Pastoral Dialogue between Alexis and Strephon, Written by the Right Honourable, the Late Earl of Rochester, at the Bath, 1674*, London: 1683.

EMENDATION OF THE COPY-TEXT **25** add] adds **59** make] makes
Both emendations are supplied from Rochester 1691, 10–15.

ANNOTATION
59 *dull life*: i.e. without love; cf. 'dull men' (325.15n.).
63 *the*: the scansion requires a slight stress.
69 *expire*: cf. 'die with pleasure' (10.16). 'There are few lyrics of [Rochester's] . . . which don't suggest getting into bed' (Treglown 1982, 89).

A Dialogue between Strephon and Daphne (Prithee now, fond fool, give o'er)

This is another exercise in heptasyllabic couplets (cf. 312) with phrases seeming to recall the *Ninth Song* of *Astrophel and Stella* (1591) in the same metre, e.g. 'Faining love, somewhat to please me; / Knowing, if she should display / All her hate, death soone would seaze me' (Sidney 1912–26, II 298).

ATTRIBUTION Since the attribution to Rochester in the copy-text, the only surviving witness to the text, is not confirmed by external evidence, it stands unproven. The imperfect rhymes (ll. 33–4, cf. 9.5–7, 13–15; 12.21–2; 67.49–50, cf. 73.50–51, 75.139–40), the mockery of pastoral, the sexual innuendo (l. 42), and the surprising reversal in the last couplet, may suggest Rochester's style to some readers.

COPY-TEXT Rochester 1691, 3–9.

ANNOTATION

31 *change*: cf. 'to be / *Constant*, in *Nature* were *Inconstancy*' (Cowley, *The Mistress* (1656), 19–20) (Rochester 1984, 231).

33–40 Since it has not always been understood (R. N. Parkinson, *Archiv für das Studium der Neueren Sprache und Literaturen* 207 (August 1970), 142), the tenor of this meteorological metaphor may be noted; it is love-making, from inflammatory foreplay to 'quiet' afterglow.

38 *Like meeting thunder we embrace*: because it is the only iambic tetrameter line in the last sixty-four lines of the poem and because of its imperfect rhyme, this line calls appropriate attention to itself as the climax of the sound effects of the poem and of the love-making within the metaphor.

50 *sincere*: the imperfect rhyme may call into question the sincerity of Daphne's successor; cf. ll. 55–6.

51 *Gentle, innocent, and free*: 'What Strephon means . . . is "promiscuous"' (Treglown 1980, 22).

68 *false*: critics wonder whether Daphne is lying (Righter 1968, 63; Treglown 1980, 22), raising the further possibility that the poem is a version of the Cretan Liar paradox.

71–2 *discovers* . . . *lovers*: the unique double rhyme points the moral of the fable, which is promptly annulled by the rest of the poem in which Strephon's deceit is so carefully balanced against Daphne's deceit that there is nothing to choose between them.

The Fall (How blest was the created state)

Basic to the mishaps of love (324) is the anxiety of lovers, the fear of malfunction, against which Adam and Eve were secured in 'the created state'. The irony is one of which Milton would not have disapproved: by an act of disobedience to God, Adam and Eve forfeited the obedience of their own bodies. For purposes of the poem Rochester may have assumed something that he did not believe. 'He could not apprehend', he told Burnet, 'how there should be any corruption in the Nature of Man, or a Lapse derived from *Adam*' (Burnet 1680, 72). This fact may switch the tone of the poem from tragi-comic to straight comic.

ATTRIBUTION The poem is attributed to Rochester in Harvard MS. 636F, pp. 67–8, the copy-text, and Rochester 1691, 39–40, but the evidence that the ms. copy constitutes an independent textual tradition is equivocal. Internal evidence of subject matter, style, imagery, and tone creates a strong probability that Rochester wrote the poem.

COPY-TEXT Rochester 1680², 70–71.

ANNOTATION

1–2 *the created state / Of man and woman*: Rochester alludes to unfallen sexuality (Plate 7), celebrated in Book IV of *Paradise Lost* (1667, 1674), 'Whatever Hypocrites austerely talk' (IV 744). But Milton says nothing about 'desire' or 'pleasure' until *after* the Fall (IX 1013, 1022) and of course never anything about 'members'.

8 *wish*: Marvell's wish was 'To live in Paradise alone' (Marvell 1927, I 49).

13–14 *duty* . . . / *The nobler tribute*: cf. 'Returning thee the tribute of my dutie' (Samuel Daniel, *Delia* (1592), sig. B1r) (Thormählen 1988, 406n.); *a*: the copy-text reads 'my', but the indefinite article needed to complete the parallel, 'a heart . . . a frailer part', survives in three manuscripts: Leeds MS. Brotherton Lt.54, p. 130; Nottingham MS. Portland Pw V 40, pp. 64–5, and Royal Library, Stockholm MS. Vu.69, p. 175.

The Mistress (An age in her embraces passed)

This striking poem embodying such 'fantastic fancies' (l.29) as value time (ll. 1–2n.) and probative pain (l. 32n.) may have been for Rochester an exercise in assonance and alliteration: 'age . . . embraces . . . day . . . life . . . light' (ll. 1–3), 'no more . . . soul . . . mournfully . . . move' (ll. 9–10), 'wiser . . . despise . . . shades . . . souls' (ll. 13–15), and so on.

Since Rochester made a love song out of Quarles's hymns (304), it is not surprising that a hymn was made out of this love song: 'A thousand Ages in thy Sight / Are like an Evening gone' (Isaac Watts, *The Psalms of David Imitated* (1719), 230) (Vivian de S. Pinto, *N&Q* 205 (June 1960), 225). Rochester's verses, in common ballad metre, can be sung to the familiar broadside tunes, 'Chloris, full of harmless thoughts' and 'Young Phaon' (Simpson 1968, 105–7, 811–12), as well as to the tune of 'Oh God our help in ages past'.

ATTRIBUTION Since it is not confirmed by external evidence, the attribution to Rochester in the copy-text (and copies derived from it) must stand unproven. Internal evidence of subject matter, style, imagery, sound effects, and tone makes the attribution highly probable.

COPY-TEXT Rochester 1691, 25–7.

ANNOTATION
1–2 *An age in her embraces . . . / Would seem a winter's day*: Rochester may recall these lines in *The Mistress* about the opposite effect of love: '*Hours* of late as long as *Days* endure, / And very *Minutes*, *Hours* are grown' (Cowley 1905, 93), but the concept of value time, as expounded by E. M. Forster, is not unfamiliar: 'there seems something else in life besides time, something which may conveniently be called "value", something which is measured not by minutes or hours, but by intensity' (*Aspects of the Novel* (1927), 28). Sterne's novels are constructed on this principle: 'a colloquy of five minutes, in such a situation, is worth one of as many ages, with your faces turned towards the street' (Sterne 1928, 24); *a winter's day*: cf. 'lovers . . . get a winter-seeming summers night' (Donne 1912, I 39).
5 *But oh, how slowly minutes roll*: the pause after 'oh' and the assonance, 'oh . . . slow . . . roll', make the sound imitate the sense.
7 *love . . . is my soul*: cf. '*Love* which is . . . *Soul* of Me' (Cowley 1905, 140).
12 *living tomb*: cf. 'in this [flesh] our living Tombe' (Donne 1912, I 258).
15 *shades of souls*: an impossibility; being immaterial, souls cast no shadows.
15–16 *On shades of souls and heaven knows what: / Short ages live in graves*: David Farley-Hills's proposed punctuation, 'On "Shades of Souls", and "Heav'n knows what / Short Ages live in Graves"' (Farley-Hills 1978, 87), is attractive, particularly since it relegates 'Short ages live in graves' to incoherent raving and relieves the reader of the necessity of trying to make sense of Rochester's epigram. Two paraphrases have been offered: 'Perhaps: "The brevity of man's lifespan leads him to dwell upon his mortality"; or, "the brief lives of men are given eternal life in the grave"' (Rochester 1982, 73), but neither of these addresses the *lover's* predicament. Time seems short in his mistress's embrace but very long in the intervals between

embraces. Compared with the interminable length of time between embraces, the time spent in the grave (eternity) seems short: 'Short ages live in graves'.
26 *Love raised to an extreme*: cf. 'the extremities of . . . Love' (Cowley 1905, 66).
32 *pain can ne'er deceive*: cf. Dostoyevsky's Underground Man who argues that if a man invariably chooses pleasure, he is an automaton, programmed for pleasure, 'a kind of piano key'. Only by choosing pain can a man 'confirm to himself . . . that men are still men, and not piano keys' (*Notes from Underground*, trans. Mirra Ginsburg (1974), 26, 34).

A Song (Absent from thee I languish still)

The most striking feature of these verses in long ballad metre, $A^4B^4A^4B^4$, is similarity to the diction and sound effects of *The Mistress* (68): 'Absent . . . languish . . . fantastic . . . prove . . . torments . . . unblest' (ll. 1, 6, 7, 14), cf. 'absent . . . languishes . . . Fantastic . . . tormenting . . . Prove . . . blest' (68.²6, 8, 70.29, 33, 35, 36). They are another exercise in assonance and alliteration: 'Absent . . . languish . . . ask . . . straying . . . plainly . . . day' (ll. 1–3), 'torments . . . try . . . tears' (ll. 7–8), 'wearied . . . world . . . woe' (l. 9).

ATTRIBUTION Since it is not confirmed by external evidence, the attribution to Rochester in the copy-text (and copies derived from it) must stand unproven. Internal evidence makes the attribution highly probable.

COPY-TEXT Rochester 1691, 28–9.

ANNOTATION
6–7 *prove / The torments*: cf. 'pain' (357.32n.).
7–8 *try / That tears*: i.e. 'undergo for tearing'; *That*: the antecedent is 'mind' (l. 6).
9 *When wearied with a world of woe*: 'certainly the worst line in Rochester' (Farley-Hills 1978, 80); cf. Tennyson, *Despair* (*The Nineteenth Century* 10 (November 1881), 631): 'were worlds of woe'.
15 *Faithless*: the most important word in the stanza is emphasized (1) by the substitution of a trochee for an iamb, (2) by alliteration, 'fall . . . Faithless . . . false . . . unforgiven' (ll. 14–15), and (3) by internal rhyme, '*Lest* . . . un*blest* . . . Faith*less* to . . . *rest*' (ll. 13–16).
16 *my everlasting rest*: cf. 'here / Will I set up my everlasting rest' (*Romeo and Juliet*, V iii 109–10).

A Song of a Young Lady. To her Ancient Lover (Ancient person, for whom I)

One approach to this poem is from the negative example of some iambic pentameter verses by Bishop Henry King (1592–1669). King's *Paradox. That it is best for a Young Maid to marry an Old Man* (1644; 1657) mobilizes witty and far-fetched arguments to support the paradox that it is better for a young woman to marry a man of fifty-two (*The Poems of Henry King*, ed. Margaret Crum (1965), 180–82).

Rochester imagines a young woman who has already committed herself to a man who is older but not yet 'Ancient': 'Long be it ere thou grow old', the girl says (Wilcoxon 1979, 147). By speaking in the person of the young woman, Rochester is able to avoid the judgemental tone of the paradox and to go beyond paradox to the amoral realm of low comedy 'that neither apportions blame nor gives approval' (David Farley-Hills, *The Benevolence of Laughter* (1974), 138; Edith Kern, *The Absolute Comic* (1980), 75).

The arrangement of the heptasyllabic couplets in stanzas of increasing length reduces the 'Song' element of the title but provides the vehicle for a submerged metaphor in the poem, as Vieth hints (*Tennessee Studies in Literature* 25 (1980), 48).

ATTRIBUTION Since the attribution to Rochester in the copy-text (and copies derived from it) is not confirmed by external evidence, it stands unproven. But internal evidence of style, imagery, sound effects, and ironic tone – 'nobler part' (l. 15) for sometime 'worst part' (29.62) – creates a high degree of probability that Rochester wrote the verses.

COPY-TEXT Rochester 1691, 32–3.

EMENDATION OF COPY-TEXT 10 heat] Heart 18 his] their
Both conjectural emendations are Vieth's (Rochester 1968, 89–90).

ANNOTATION
18 *From . . . ice . . . released*: the girl's 'art' restores 'nature' as May restores January every year; art and nature coalesce.

A Satyr against Mankind (Were I (who to my cost already am))

There is some point in retaining the old spelling 'Satyr' in the title of this poem. If it is a satyr speaking, then a creature half-man and half-animal is saying that he would rather be all animal. The urgent reasons that he gives for his choice constitute the argument of the poem. The conclusion of the argument, that the difference between the ideal man and the average man is greater than that between man and animal, or that most men are inferior to animals, is more pointed if spoken by a satyr. 'The bolder the better', as Swift said of paradoxes. 'But the Wit lies in maintaining them' (Swift 1939–68, II 101).

Another reason to retain the old spelling is to remind ourselves that the speaker of the poem is no more the Earl of Rochester (Davies 1969, 350–51) than he is Nicolas Boileau-Despréaux, whose *Satire* VIII (1668) is very distantly imitated in these verses. He is a personated figure, 'querulous, foul-mouthed, and dyspeptic', like the satyr-speaker in *Tunbridge Wells* (Love 1972, 153). Diogenes (362.90n.), or Diogenes who had read George Boas's *The Happy Beast in French Thought of the Seventeenth Century* (1933), could very well stand in for him.

Since the 'non-structure' of the poem has been posited (Peter Thorpe, *PLL* 5 (1969), 241–2), it may not hurt to lay out the structure in a simple diagram. It consists of four cycles of argument and interruption. The arguments, averaging forty-four lines apiece, alternate with interruptions of remarkably decreasing length, the first by a clerical adversary (as in Boileau, *Satire* VIII) but the second, third and fourth by the speaker himself. It is an argument to which the rebuttal fades away like the Cheshire Cat or Northrop Frye's retreating parental eiron. The disappearing rebuttal is the counterpart of the tumescent stanzas in *A Song of a Young Lady. To her Ancient Lover* (above). Here is the diagram:

1st cycle	1–45	*Argument*: If he could choose, the speaker would be an animal. Animal senses are better than human reason. Reason misleads, wit endangers man.
	46–71	*Interruption*: A clerical adversary attacks wit but defends reason. Reason justifies revelation, terminates in certainty.

2nd cycle	72–111	*Argument*: Reason causes pride, terminates in nonsense. Right reason governs behaviour, terminates in happiness.
	112–22	*Interruption*: Speaker abandons attack on reason but not on man, for animal senses function better than reason.
3rd cycle	123–73	*Argument*: Animal morally superior to man. Man's virtue derives from fear. Self-preservation requires dishonesty, knavery, cowardice.
	174–8	*Interruption*: Speaker recapitulates his argument.
4th cycle	179–223	*Argument*: If one honest courtier, one humble priest could be found, speaker would choose to be a man.
	224–5	*Interruption*: But 'God-like' (l. 220) man differs from average man more than average man differs from animal.

On 24 February 1675 the poem suffered an actual interruption when Edward Stillingfleet preached a sermon at court on the text of Hebrews 3.13: 'Lest any of you be hardened through deceitfulness of sin'. Stillingfleet was one of Charles II's chaplains in ordinary, who had to wait until the Revolution to be elevated to a bishopric. It was a daring sermon, repeatedly chiding the King for setting a bad example and railing at 'men of sense' (l. 197):

> and because it is impossible to defend their extravagant courses by *Reason*, the only way left for them is to make *Satyrical invectives* against *Reason* [Stillingfleet must have read the poem in one of the ms. copies, like Bodl. MS. Add. B.106, that have the word 'Reason' in the title] . . . and yet they pretend to shew it in arguing against it: but it is pitty such had not their wish, to have been Beasts rather than man . . . But how hard are such men put to defend their vices, that cannot do it without trampling under foot the most noble persecutions [pursuits] of their own nature!
>
> (Stillingfleet 1675, 33)

Rochester's reply to the argument of Stillingfleet's sermon is the fourth cycle of the poem: if there were an honest courtier or churchman, it would be better to be a man, but there is no honest courtier or churchman. Therefore it is better to be an animal. Thus the paradox (ll. 115–16) is sustained. Lines 191–209 of the poem constitute Rochester's reply to Stillingfleet's 'obstreperous, saucy eloquence' (l. 196).

Samuel Johnson is responsible for the red herring of 'originality' in *A Satyr against Mankind*: 'Rochester can only claim what remains when all Boileau's part is taken away' (Johnson 1779–81, IV ⁴15). When Boileau's part, carefully noted below, is taken away, Rochester's poem stands up like the proverbial jelly turned out of the mould (Crocker 1937, 57).

ATTRIBUTION The attribution to Rochester first made in a letter from John Verney (HMC *Seventh Report*, 467) is confirmed by Anthony à Wood (Wood 1813–20, III 1229). The poem is also attributed to Rochester in twenty ms. and three printed copies (Rochester 1984, 281–2), representing at least two independent textual traditions.

DATE Lines 1–173 are dated 'Anno. 74' in Bodl. MS. Tanner 306, f. 414r. Lines 179–225 were presumably added to the poem after 24 February 1675, when Edward Stillingfleet attacked the poem in a sermon at court, and before 23 March 1676, the date of John Verney's letter.

COPY-TEXTS Lines 1–173, *A Satyr against Mankind* [London: 1675?] (Wing R1759); ll. 174–225, Rochester 1680[1], 12–13.

EMENDATION OF COPY-TEXTS **4** case] sort **8** The] His **12** in] of **13** nature,] mature **16** climbs] thinks **18** Tumbling] Stumbling **22** hope] hopes escaping] skipping **23** dazzled] Dazeling **26** Lead] Leads make] makes **34** that] what **35** his vain] all his **58** ferments] foments **71** grounds] ground **74** Stillingfleet's replies] *Sibbs* Soliloquies **80** puzzling] pushing **81** myst'ries and] mysteries **83** Those] The **88** this] the power] poor **92** modern, cloistered] many modern **103** vigour] vogue, and **115** degree] own Degree **119** his] the **120** Meres] man **125** most gen'rous are] are most Generous **136** Most humanly] inhumanly **139** and] or **143** actions] passions **153** this] his **167** less a] lesser **195** makes preaching a pretence] om.
The emendations of ll. 18, 22, 23, 34, 81, 136, 139, 143, and 153 are supplied from the text quoted in Blount 1680, 81, 152, 227–8. The emendation of l. 120 is supplied from Rochester 1691, 96. The omission in l. 195 is supplied from Rochester 1707 (Bragge), [1]1–4). The remaining emendations are supplied from Rochester 1680[1], 6–13.

ANNOTATION
1–34, 76–7, 80–97 are quoted in Blount 1680, 227–8.
3 *spirit*: cf. 'For Spirits when they please / Can either Sex assume, or both ... in what shape they choose' (Milton, 1931–8, II 23); *share*: a possible pun similar to part/privy part; the *os pubis* was called the share bone, and the share was the groin (*OED*, s.v. **Share**, *sb.*[2]).
5 *bear*: cf. '*Bears* are *better* / Then *Synod-men*' (Butler 1967, 97).
6 *anything but that vain animal*: cf. 'Make me anything but a man' (Menander, *Frag.* 23) (John F. Moore, *PMLA* 58 (June 1943), 399).
7 *so proud of being rational*: cf. 'An ill dream, or a cloudy day, has power to change this wretched creature, who is so proud of a reasonable soul' (Dryden, Dedication of *Aureng-Zebe* (17 November 1675; 1676) (Dryden 1882–93, V 199).
9 *sixth*: the sixth sense in this context is not 'a supposed intuitive faculty' (*OED*), but reason itself. Hobbes is certain that reason is *not* a sense: 'Reason is not as Sense ... borne with us ... but attayned by Industry' (Hobbes 1935, 25).
10 *certain instinct*: cf. 'Reason raise o'er Instinct as you can, / In this 'tis God directs, in that 'tis Man' (Pope, 1939–67, II i 101).
12–14 *Reason, an ignis fatuus ... wandering ways it takes*: cf. 'Metaphors, and senselesse and ambiguous words, are like *ignes fatui*; and reasoning upon them, is wandering amongst innumerable absurdities' (Hobbes 1935, 26).
15 *fenny ... thorny*: is Rochester parodying Milton's 'craggy ... shaggy ... mossy ... mazy' pastoral vocabulary (Milton 1931–8, II i 48, 126; 114, 201, 158, II ii 281; II i 115, II ii 266)?
18–19 *from thought to thought*: cf. 'Mais l'Homme sans arrest, dans sa course insensée / Voltige incessament de pensée en pensée' (Boileau, *Satire* VIII, 35–6) (But sillier Man, in his mistaken way ... / His restless mind rolls from thought to thought) (Oldham 1987, 163); cf. 'Sinking from thought to thought' (Pope, 1939–67, V 278); *falls headlong down / Into ... boundless sea*: cf. 'c'est la voye par où il s'est precipitée à la damnation eternelle' (the way whereby man hath headlong cast himselfe downe into eternall damnation) Montaigne, *The Essays*, trans. John Florio (1603), 288; cf. 'Hurld headlong ... down / To bottomless perdition' (Milton 1931–8, II i 10).
25–8 *Old Age and Experience ... make him understand, / That all his life he has been in the wrong*: Goethe quotes 'jenem schrecklichen Texte' (those frightful words)

in *Aus meinem Leben: Dichtung und Wahrheit* (1811–33), III xiii; Defoe quotes l. 28 only in the *Review*, 12 December 1704.

29 *Huddled in dirt*: cf. 'lodged here in the dirt and filth of the World' (Montaigne 1700, II 190); *engine*: a commonplace of contemporary medical theory, cf. We are 'forced therefore to consider the body of Man, not only as an Engine of curious and admirable workmanship . . . But also as a Machine' (Thomas Coxe, *A Discourse, wherein the Interest of the Patient in Reference to Physick and Physicians is soberly Debated* (1669), 276).

33 *wisdom did his happiness destroy*: cf. 'Knowing too much long since lost Paradise' (Suckling, 1971, I 37) (Thormählen 1988, 402); 'happiest if ye seek / No happier state, and know to know no more' (Milton, 1931–8, II i 134).

34 *that world he should enjoy*: cf. 'enjoy / . . . this happie state' (ibid., II i 162).

39 *threatening doubt*: fear (l. 45) that the joke is on them.

43 *escape*: i.e. when the joke is not on them (this time). Sir Carr Scrope may allude to these lines in *In Defense of Satire* (1677): 'Each knave or fool that's conscious of a crime, / Though he 'scapes now, looks for't another time' (*POAS*, Yale, I 368).

49 *Against . . . wit*: cf. 'these men . . . who turn all things into Burlesque and ridicule . . . are too witty . . . to embrace the principles of Christianity' (Thomas Smith, *A Sermon of the Credibility of the Mysteries of the Christian Religion* (1675, 10).

50–71 The adversary's argument is blunted by a series of imperfect rhymes: 'care . . . severe, heaven . . . given, soaring pierce . . . universe, there . . . fear'.

56 *grand indiscretion*: the speaker's attack on reason (ll. 8–30).

61 *everlasting soul*: Rochester 'thought it more likely that the Soul began anew' in the procreation of each person (Burnet 1680, 65); cf. 303.[1]3n.

62–3 *maker . . . from himself . . . did the image take*: cf. 'Soul that spiritual Image wherein the Divine likeness doth shine' (Nathaniel Ingelo, *Bentivolio and Urania* (1660), 238).

64–5 *in shining reason dressed / To dignify . . . above beast*: cf. 'not prone / And Brute as other Creatures, but endu'd / With Sanctitie of Reason' (Milton 1931–8, II i 229).

66–7 *Reason . . . beyond material sense*: cf. 'elevated beyond things of corporeal sense, [the mind] is brought to a converse and familiarity with heavenly notions' (Simon Patrick, *The Parable of the Pilgrim* (1664), 153) (Griffin 1973, 193).

67–9 *take a flight beyond material sense, / . . . pierce / The flaming limits of the universe*: cf. 'N'est-ce pas l'Homme enfin, dont l'art audacieux / Dans le tour d'un compass a mesuré les Cieux, / Dont la vaste science embrassant toutes choses, / A foüillé la nature, en a percé les causes' (Isn't it Man, whose reckless art, boxing the compass, has surveyed the heavens, whose learning without limits has explored Nature and penetrated into her first causes) (Boileau, *Satire* VIII, 165–8) (Rochester 1982, 108); *flaming limits of the universe*: cf. 'flammantia moenia mundi' (the flaming outworks of the world) (Lucretius, *De rerum natura*, I 73) (Rochester 1926, 356). The irony of having the clerical adversary quote 'the pagan and atheistic Lucretius' has not been lost (Griffin 1973, 192).

71 *true grounds of hope*: cf. 'That Immortality which lay hid in the dark guesses of Humanity, is here [in the Bible] brought to light, and all doubts concerning the Portion of Good men are resolved' (Nathaniel Ingelo, *Bentivolio and Urania* (1660), 214.

72–97 The speaker turns the tables on the adversary by arguing that it is not wit but 'glorious man' (l. 60) and 'shining reason' (l. 64) that is at fault (David Trotter, in Treglown 1982, 130).

73 *Ingelo*: Nathaniel Ingelo's *Bentivolio and Urania* (1660) is a prose romance in four

books. There is no pricking on the plain, however, for Bentivolio (Good Will) and Urania (Heavenly Light) are brother and sister. Included in the work is both an utopia, Theoprepia (The Divine State), and a dystopia, Polistherion (City of the Beasts). In the former, the topics of casual conversation include 'The *Prudence* and *Fidelity* of *Vigilant Magistrates*, the *chearful Submissions* of *Loyall Subjects*, the *wise Deportment* of *Loving Husbands*, the *modest Observance* of *Obedient Wives*, the *indulgent Affections* of *Carefull Parents*, the *ingenuous Gratitude* of *Dutifull Children*, the *discreet Commands* of *Gentle Masters*, and the *ready Performances* of *Willing Servants*' (234).

74 *Patrick's Pilgrim*: Simon Patrick's *The Parable of the Pilgrim* (1665) begins with a vision of the heavenly city and concludes with the heavenly city itself, 'all built of . . . pretious stones' (83–4, 455). Along the way apple trees 'bow themselves to kiss the Pilgrims hands' (458); *Stillingfleet's replies*: '*Sibbs* Soliloquies' is presumably what Rochester wrote in 1674, and 'Stillingfleet's replies' is the emendation that he made after Stillingfleet's attack on the poem in the sermon preached at court on 24 February 1675. Stillingfleet had published three works with the word 'answer' or 'reply' in the title (Wing S5556, S5559, S5630), the most recent of which, *An Answer to Mr. Cressy's Epistle Apologetical*, was licensed for publication on 25 November 1674 (*T.C.*, I 189) (Kristoffer F. Paulson, *PQ* 50 (1971), 657–63).

72–93 The attack on reason is punctuated by 'the repeated use of the contemptuous demonstrative', 'this' (Griffin 1973, 220).

75 *reason*: cf. 'the *Inward Light*, which is more properly called *Reason* . . . doth make us Capable of Converse with God' (Ingelo, *Bentivolio and Urania*, 2nd ed. (1669), [2]177).

80–81 *doubt . . . finds them out*: cf. 'Is busy in finding *Scruples* out, / To languish in eternal *Doubt*' (Butler 1928, 38); *myst'ries*: the adversary uses 'mysteries' in the sense of 'religious truth known only from divine revelation' (*OED*); the speaker's 'mysteries' are verbal: paradoxes, Cretan Liars, non-referential abstractions ('a sense / Of something far more deeply interfused'), '*Accidents of Bread in Cheese*', oxymorons, quiddities, and the like.

86 *ointments*: cf. 'Witches . . . being carried through the Air, for which strange passage, they prepare their bodies with I know not what kind of oyntment; but I suppose it is made of the same ingredients, as that was, which turned *Lucian* into an Ass' (John Wagstaffe, *The Question of Witchcraft Debated* (1669), 31).

90 *philosopher*: Diogenes the Cynic (*c.* 412–323 B.C.) called Plato's lectures a waste of time. The tub story is in Diogenes Laertius, *Lives of Eminent Philosophers*, VI 23.

94–5 *action*: cf. 'il n'y a de réalité que dans l'action . . . il n'y a pas d'amour autre que celui qui se construit . . . un homme n'est rien d'autre qu'une série d'entreprises, qu'il est la somme' (there is no reality except in action . . . no love apart from acts of love . . . a man is no other than a series of undertakings of which he is the sum) (Jean-Paul Sartre, *L'Existentialisme est un humanisme* (1946), 55–8).

96 *happiness*: cf. 'Felicity is a continuall progresse of the desire, from one object to another; the attaining of the former, being still but the way to the later' (Hobbes 1935, 62; 'We hold these truths to be self-evident, that all men . . . are endowed by their Creator with certain unalienable rights, that among these are life, liberty and the pursuit of happiness' (*The Declaration of Independence*, 4 July 1776).

99 *right reason*: cf. 'right Reason constituted by Nature' (Hobbes 1935, 22); 'I alwaies love to keep a little *right reason* in the house' (Eachard, 1672, 90–91).

100 *reason which distinguishes by sense*: nihil in intellectu quod non prius in sensu; cf. 'there is no conception in a mans mind, which hath not at first . . . been begotten upon the organs of Sense' (Hobbes 1935, 7).

102 *bounds desires with a reforming will*: in Hobbes's conception will is not the power of choice. Desires are bound by will only because will is 'the last Appetite, or Aversion' before action or avoidance (Hobbes 1935, 36). It is pointed out that 'This is behaviorism, and . . . that Rochester's . . . argument moves in another direction' (Reba Wilcoxon, *ECS* 8 (1974/5), 196).
109 *"What's o'clock?"*: cf. men 'that have no *Science*, are in better . . . condition with their naturall Prudence; than men, that by mis-reasoning, or by trusting them that reason wrong, fall upon false and absurd generall rules' (Hobbes 1935, 26). John Crowne may allude to these lines in *The Countrey Wit* (1675), 22: 'RAMBLE: The order of Nature . . . is to follow my appetite: am I to eat at Noon, because it is Noon, or because I am a hungry?' (Rochester 1984, 284).
115–16 *beasts . . . / As wise . . . and better*: elaboration of the familiar paradox that animals are intellectually and morally superior to man is the second major argument in Montaigne's 'Apology for Raimond de Sebond' (Montaigne 1700, II 182–250). One critic has observed that 'There is scarcely an idea . . . in [*A Satyr against Mankind*] that is not present in Montaigne' (Crocker 1937, 73).
120 *Meres*: 'man', the reading of the copy-text, may reflect a compositor's fear of *scandalum magnatum*, for Sir Thomas Meres (Biographical Dictionary) was a prominent Whig politician.
122 *Jowler . . . wiser*: cf. 'Well might *an Antient Polish Bard* Decree, / *Jouler the Hound* a Wiser Beast than he [Sir Thomas Meres]' (Defoe, *The Dyet of Poland* (1705) (*POAS*, Yale, VII 114).
122–3 'the center [of the poem] is located physically in the blank space between lines 122 and 123' (David M. Vieth, *Language and Style* 5 (1972), 134).
125 *principles*: cf. 'The argument of orthodox morality is that man's principles restrain the excesses of his fallen nature. But in the *Satyr* those elements that would be identified as excesses of [fallen] nature (treachery, self-interest, and "wantonness" [l. 138]) are treated as principles' (Charles A. Knight, *MLR* 65 (1970), 258).
129–58 Quoted in Blount 1680, 152.
129–38 *beasts on each other prey, / . . . by necessity, they kill for food: / . . . they hunt / Nature's allowance . . . / But man . . . his fellow's life betrays, / . . . through . . . wantonness*: cf. 'L'Homme seul, l'Homme seul en sa fureur extrême / Met un brutal honneur à s'égorger soi-même' (Man alone in the extremity of his rage makes it a point of honour to cut throats) (Boileau, *Satire* VIII, 151–2); cf. 'When Beasts each other chase and then devour, / 'Tis Natures Law, necessity, / Which makes them hunt for food, & not for pow'r: / Men for Dominion, Art's chief vanity, / Contrive to make men die; / Whose blood through wantonness they spil' (Sir William Davenant, *The Cruelty of the Spaniards in Peru* (1658), 22) (Treglown 1976, 557); cf. Shadwell, *The History of Timon of Athens, the Man-Hater* (*c.* January 1678; 1678) (Shadwell 1927, III 232) (K. E. Robinson, *N&Q* 218 (May 1973), 177); Defoe paraphrases these lines in *Serious Reflections during the Life and Surprising Adventures of Robinson Crusoe* (1720), 122–3, and William Empson writes his *Reflections from Rochester* around them (*Collected Poems* (1955), 54–5).
137–8 *With voluntary pains works his distress, / Not through necessity but wantonness*: Dryden turns these lines back on Rochester's *An Allusion to Horace*: 'what can be urg'd in their defence, who not having the Vocation of Poverty to scribble, out of mere wantonness take pains to make themselves ridiculous' (Dryden 1956– , XIII 14) (Paul Hammond, *N&Q* 233 (1988), 171).
140 *fear*: in Hobbes's state of nature there is 'no account of Time; no Arts; no Letters; no Society; and which is worst of all, continuall feare . . . therefore . . . [man]

armes himselfe . . . [and] Force and Fraud, are . . . the two Cardinall vertues' (Hobbes 1935, 84, 85). The speaker has discovered that Hobbes's 'warre of every man against every man' persists into historic time (Griffin 1973, 237); in a brilliant society of arts and letters it has simply gone underground. Hobbes derives the *libido dominandi* from 'a generall inclination of all mankind, a perpetuall and restlesse desire of Power' (Hobbes 1935, 83, 63). Rochester derives it from fear. On the principle of Occam's Razor, Rochester's explanation is more elegant.
143 *fear . . . whence his best actions came*: cf. 'iura inventa metu iniusti' (justice was born of the fear of injustice) (Horace, *Satires*, I iii 111).
155–8 quoted in John Dunton's *Athenian Sport* (1707), 265; Defoe rewrites l. 158, 'That all Men wou'd be Tyrants if they cou'd' (*The History of the Kentish Petition* (1701), 23) and then quotes it twice in the *Review* (6 September 1705, 9 April 1709) and thrice in *Jure Divino: A Satyr* (1706) (Introduction, p. 1, IV 4; V 18).
160 *knaves . . . in their own defence*: it has been said that the speaker urges men to be knaves (Griffin 1973, 244), but it seems that he only observes that knavery is necessary to survive in 'The rabble world' (l. 223) of seventeeth-century London.
162–3 *Amongst known cheats to play upon the square, / You'll be undone*: cf. 'gaming with a Sharper; if you cannot Cheat as well as he, you are certainly undone' (Swift 1939–68, III 37).
162–5 *Amongst known cheats . . . / The knaves will all agree to call you knave*: Defoe twice quotes these lines, apparently from memory, in the *Review* (17 March 1709, 23 October 1711). In addition he quotes l. 165 three times in the *Review* (13 March 1705, 7 April 1709 (Edinburgh), 13 May 1710). Lines 164–5 are quoted in Blount 1680, 81 (Manning 1986, 39).
173 *Who's a knave of the first rate*: quoted in Marvell's *Mr. Smirke or The Divine in Mode* (1676), 16, 'probably [published] in June [1676]' (Pierre Legouis, *Andrew Marvell: Poet, Puritan, Patriot*, 2nd ed. (1968), 202).
174 *All this with indignation*: cf. 'All this with indignation spoke' (Waller, 1893, 88).
177 *False freedoms*: including the 'freedom' of the powerful to exploit the powerless (?).
179–219 These lines constitute one periodic sentence of the form 'If . . . if . . . then': If there is an honest courtier, if there is an honest churchman, then I'll recant my paradox. The structure of the sentence is obscured because the 'If there is an honest churchman' clause is cast in the form of a question, 'Is there an honest churchman?'
179–80 *if . . . there be / . . . yet unknown to me*: cf 'Faith in a woman (if at least there be / Faith in a woman unreveal'd to me)' (Giovanni Battista Guarini, *Il Pastor Fido*, trans. Sir Richard Fanshawe (1647), 27); *in* COURT *so* JUST *a* MAN . . . / *In* COURT *a* JUST *man* YET: the Ovidian 'turn', as Dryden called it, creates an effect like syncopation.
182 *ruin*: his most intimate advisers, beginning with Lady Castlemaine who told him he 'must rule by an Army' (Pepys, 29 July 1667), were urging ruinous policies upon the King; cf. 312.19n.
188 *raise . . . his family*: as soon as Charles replaced the Cabal with Thomas Osborne, whom he appointed lord treasurer in June 1673 and created Earl of Danby in June 1674, Danby 'layes about him and provides for his family . . . It's wonderfull to see his good fortune in the marriage of his Children and settling his family in order; And many are of the opinion that when that is donne he will stop this Career' (*Essex Papers* 1890, 258, 260).
193 *blown up . . . prelatic pride*: cf. 'The aspirings that he [Rochester] had observed at Court, of some of the Clergy' (Burnet 1680, 120–21).

195–206 The prototypical churchman is guilty of all seven deadly sins: envy (l. 195), wrath (l. 197), avarice, pride, sloth, gluttony (l. 203), lechery (ll. 205–6).
210 *bishop*: 'possibly Thomas Barlow' (*Seventeenth Century English Poetry*, ed. John T. Shawcross *et al.* (1969), 608), consecrated Bishop of Lincoln in June 1675 at the age of sixty-nine. His skill in 'Casuistical Divinity' 'always leant to the side of his own self-interest' (*DNB*, I 1145). A better argument might be made for Gilbert Sheldon, Archbishop of Canterbury: (Biographical Dictionary).
219 *Mysterious truths*: in the adversary's sense of the word 'mysteries' (362.80–81n.), especially those in the Book of Revelation (?).
220–21 *If upon earth there dwell such God-like men, / I'll here recant my paradox*: cf. 'O, if the World had but a dozen Arbuthnots in it I would burn my Travells' (*The Correspondence of Swift*, ed. Harold Williams, 5 vols. (1963–5), III 104); *my paradox*: ll. 115–16).
223 *their laws*: as opposed to the 'rules' (l. 101) of right reason.
225 *Man differs more from man than man from beast*: cf. 'il y'a plus de distance de tel à tel homme qu'il n'y a de tel homme à tel beste' (there is more difference betwixt such and such a Man, than there is betwixt such a Man and such a Beast) (Montaigne 1700, I 439) (Crocker 1937, 71), i.e. average beast is superior to average man, maintaining the paradox (ll. 115–16); cf. 'a man hath no preeminence above a beast' (Ecclesiastes 3.19); 'when a Creature pretending to Reason, could be capable of such Enormities, he [the Master Houyhnhnm] dreaded lest the Corruption of that Faculty might be worse than Brutality itself' (Swift 1937–68, XI 232).

Plain Dealing's Downfall (Long time Plain Dealing in the haughty town)

It is tempting to connect these verses with Wycherley's last play, *The Plain Dealer* (December 1676; 1677), particularly since John Dennis records that Rochester and his friends 'by their loud approbation of it, gave it both a sudden and a lasting reputation' (Dennis 1939–43, II 277). But *The Plain Dealer* does *not* dramatize the proverb on which Rochester's poem is based. What is certain is that the proverb was current: 'Plain dealing is a jewel but they that use it die beggars' (Tilley P382) is quoted both in Shadwell's *Epsom Wells* (2 December 1672; 1673) and Wycherley's *The Country Wife* (January 1675; 1675) (Wycherley 1979, 319).

ATTRIBUTION Since the poem is attributed to Rochester only in the copy-text and in *Poems on Several Occasions. By the R. H. the E. of R.* (1701), 48–9, derived from it, the attribution stands unproven.

COPY-TEXT Rochester 1685, 54.

EMENDATION OF COPY-TEXT 2 in a thread-bare] in thread-bare 15 Whilst] Whil's
Both emendations are supplied from *Poems on Several Occasions. By the R. H. the E. of R.* (1701), 48–9.

ANNOTATION
11 *trouble him no more*: cf. 'he from within shall answer and say, Trouble me not: the door is now shut' (Luke 11.7).

What vain, unnecessary things are men

This untitled fragment provides further evidence of Rochester's compositorial practice (393). It was left unfinished in the midst of revision: the first draft is in ink, but ll. 8–10, 29–30, 33–4, and 53–4 are cancelled in pencil, and the three words of l. 55 are written in pencil (Rochester 1984, 195).

The fragment further breaks down into two pieces: in ll. 1–34 the speaker, a woman, complains that actresses have stolen the eligible men; in ll. 35–55 the same speaker petitions the actresses to make restitution. The paradox of the first line of the fragment is not sustained. Instead, the speaker explores one mishap of love (324) from a woman's point of view: the introduction of actresses on the Restoration stage: 'To theatres . . . you are brought' (l. 47). The fragment is a sustained lucubration on the theme: a good man nowadays is hard to find.

ATTRIBUTION The sole witness to the text is a copy in Rochester's hand with revisions in Rochester's hand.

COPY-TEXT Nottingham MS. Portland Pw V 31, ff. 9r–10r.

EMENDATION OF COPY-TEXT 14 by] de 28 give] gave whore] — 52 atheists] Atheist
Emendations of ll. 28 and 52 are those of David M. Vieth (Rochester 1968, 103). The conjectural emendation of l. 14 is defended in a footnote below.

ANNOTATION
5–7 *gave . . . crave . . . have*: the dissonant bump created by the imperfect rhyme emphasizes the sexual sense of 'have'. *OED* cites 'She's neither fish nor flesh; a man knowes not where to have her' (*1 Henry IV* (1598), III iii 133).
8–10 *the . . . playhouse . . . / To chaffer*: cf. 'The Playhouse is a kind of Market-place; / One chaffers for a Voice, another for a Face' (Dryden, Epilogue to John Bancroft's *Henry the Second, King of England* (8 November 1692; 1693); Dryden 1882–93, X 414); *women coursers*: cf. 'I am no Bawd, nor Cheater, nor a Courser / Of broken-winded women' (Beaumont and Fletcher 1905–10, V 303).
13 *Huff*: one of the vulgar guests in *Timon* (57.61–2).
14 *by*: the copy-text reading 'de' can be 'a dialectal (Kentish), foreign, or infantile representation of The' (*OED*), but 'the God' makes no sense in the context.
23–30 The lines constitute an elaborate metaphor: as my lady's frown drives away her Petrarchan lover and as 'th'insulting wife' (l. 27) drives her husband into the arms of his whore, so 'tyrannies to commonwealths convert' (l. 30). While it may be true that tyranny in marriage yields to the commonwealth of whoredom, in public affairs the opposite was held to be true: 'Tyrannies . . . spring naturally out of Popular Governments' (Sir William Temple, *Miscellanea: the First Part* (1680), 49).
24 *ends of plays*: in which boys get girls, and vice versa.
27–9 *th'insulting wife*: the domineering wife proverbially wears the breeches (Tilley B645), but in this case the hen-pecked husband gives the breeches to his whore, who wears them with 'gentler art' than the wife; *it*: probably 'mastery' (understood).
34 *please themselves*: cf. 'candle, carrot, or thumb' (42.74).
35 *kind ladies of the town*: in general, mock genteel for whores, but in the present context, actresses.
36–9 *men . . . / Poor broken properties that cannot serve*: cf. 'youth . . . / Too rotten to consummate the intrigue' (58.104–6); *properties*: 'any article (often an imitation) used as . . . a stage accessory' (*OED*).
46 *Rollo . . . Hart*: John Fletcher's *The Bloody Brother* (*c.* 1616; 1639) was one of the first Jacobean tragedies to be revived after the Restoration (14 August 1660) and was frequently played by the King's Company. The fratricidal brother, Rollo, Duke of

Normandy, was played by Charles Hart (Biographical Dictionary). The fashionable women addressed in the poem could be assumed to know that Hart was an early lover of Nell Gwyn (whom he brought on the stage in 1665) and that Lady Castlemaine was 'mightily in love' with him (*BDAA*, VI 458; Pepys, 7 April 1668).
47 *you*: 'ladies of the town'/ actresses (l. 35).
49 *practise*: cf. 'Practis'd to Lisp, and hang the Head aside' (Pope 1939–67, II 183).
52 *idolators and atheists*: 'the beastly men' (l. 33) are idolators because they worship actresses, and atheists because they do *not* worship Love (l. 48).
54 *miracles*: cf. 'the pleasure he [Rochester] found in ... calling the doing of Miracles, *the shewing of a trick*' (Burnet 1680, 87).

Consideratus, Considerandus (What pleasures can the gaudy world afford?)

Iambic pentameter is 'the metre of moral reproof', Ezra Pound says. 'It came handy or natural to Pope in a misborn world. Rochester, who had less moral urge, uses it better, mostly because he is used to singing' (Pound 1934, 146). In this exercise in iambic pentameter couplets Rochester presents a character that Samuel Butler did not write, the character of Il Considerato, the considerate man, in the original sense of the word 'considerate', 'thoughtful, deliberate, prudent' (*OED*). In Butler's practice the characters are described, whereas the character of Il Considerato, like that of his distant cousin Il Penseroso, is revealed by what he says. What he says makes him sound very much like a proto-Defoe:

> Thoughtfull without Anxiety,
> And Griev'd without Despair,
> Chearfull, but without gayety,
> And Cautious without fear.
> (*RES*, n.s. 36 (1985), 351)

ATTRIBUTION The poem is attributed to Rochester only in the copy-text and *Poems on Several Occasions. By the R. H. the E. of R.* (1701), 58–9, derived from it. Hence the attribution stands unproven. Internal evidence of phraseology and rhyme words, however, make a good case for Rochester.

COPY-TEXT Rochester 1685, 66–7.

ANNOTATION
Title *Consideratus, Considerandus*: a thoughtful man who ought to be thought about.
6 *earth's spacious round*: cf. 'spacious world' (74.91).
11–12 *blood ... withstood*: cf. 'blood ... good' (64.43–4), 'blood ... stood' (26.23–4).
13–14 *fear ... care*: cf. 'there ... fear' (74.70–71), 'tear [rend] ... fear' (75.139–40), 'fear ... where' (39.5–6).
14 *sleep-disturbing*: cf. 'fury-foaming' (27.34), 'cold-complexioned' (87.29).
15 *No beam ... not a ray*: in a remarkable example of biographical fallacy (384.102n.), Vivian de S. Pinto assumes that *Consideratus, Considerandus* is 'clearly connected with Rochester's religious experience of June 1680' (*MLR* 65 (1970), 602). The parallel he claims is between this line and a phrase of Burnet's (Pinto 1962, 220–21): '*the words* [of Isaiah 53] *had an authority which did shoot like Raies or Beams in his* [Rochester's] *Mind*' (Burnet 1680, 141). But this commonplace simile of Burnet's affords no evidence of the poem's date of composition.
22 *fatal'st*: cf. 'peremptoriest' (30.19).

25–6 *in garments poor*: cf. 'in thread-bare gown' (78.[1]2); *appears* ... *wears*: cf. 'appear ... bear' (86.41–2, l.11–12).
27–9 *most* ... *lost* ... *coast*: cf. 'boast ... lost ... most (9.13–17), 'host ... boast ... lost' (58.95–7).
28 [*Virtue*] ... *Urged to be gone*: cf. 'Hence loathed Melancholy (Milton 1931–8, I i 34); 'Hence hated Vertue ... Begone' (Oldham 1987, 58).
39 *on Indians glass for gems intrude*: cf. 'with Indians we / Get gold and jewels' (20.43–4).

Scene i. Mr Dainty's Chamber (J'ai l'amour dans le cœur et la rage dans les os)

ATTRIBUTION The unique copy of this fragment, in Rochester's hand with corrections in Rochester's hand, is the copy-text.

DATE 1674–5 (?). First published in Pinto 1935, 125–6.

COPY-TEXT Nottingham MS. Portland Pw V 31, f. 11.

ANNOTATION
18 *posset*: Mistress Quickly makes a posset for Master Doctor Caius, hot milk laced with liquor and spices (*The Merry Wives of Windsor*, I iv 8).

Mistress Knight's Advice to the Duchess of Cleveland in Distress for a Prick (Quoth the Duchess of Cleveland to councillor Knight)

Like *The Submission* (11), these verses in anapaestic quatrains can be sung to the tune of *Packington's Pound* (Simpson 1966, 564).

ATTRIBUTION The poem is attributed to Rochester in Harvard MS. Eng. 636F, p. 277 and the copy-text, apparently representing two independent textual traditions.

DATE If the last line of the poem refers to the defection of Jermyn and Churchill in 1675, the poem is likely to have been written in that year.

COPY-TEXT Rochester 1680^2, 59.

EMENDATION OF COPY-TEXT **Title** *Mistress Knight's Advice to the Duchess of Cleveland in Distress for a Prick*] *Song* 1 councillor] Mrs. 2 knew I] but 6 Where] There 9 Aye] Ah 11 I'd] I had
The title and the emended readings are preserved in Harvard MS. Eng. 636F, p. 277 (Rochester 1984, 172).

ANNOTATION
4 *not coy*: The Duchess's diversion with a footman is recounted in *The Last Instructions to a Painter* (*c.* August–November 1667; 1689) (Marvell 1927, I 143); Edinburgh MS. La.II.89, f. 229 adds a stanza written after 11 December 1702:

> For footboyes and porters have gotten by Rote
> That Jack* swyved the dutches and had a lac'd coate
> Nay persones of honnor to report doe not stick
> To say Churchill Imbrodred his Coate with his pricke.
>
> *John Churchill after D of Marlboro
> (Rochester 1984, 172)

5 *Sodom*: red-light districts, such as Dirty Lane and Lutenor's Lane at the upper end of Drury Lane, Whetstone's Park between Lincoln's Inn Fields and High Holborn,

and Salisbury Court between Fleet Street and Dorset Stairs, the site of the new Duke's theatre (Dryden 1956– , VIII 60; Butler 1967, 373; *Domestic Intelligence*, 10 July 1679).

7 *open your case*: cf. 'MRS. MARWOOD [to Lady Wishfort]: To . . . have your Case open'd by an old fumbling Leacher in a Quoif' (Congreve 1967, 467).

12 *abused*: perhaps by Jermyn's marriage on 17 April 1675 to Judith Poley, 'a conceited country wench' (Hamilton 1930, 323), and by Churchill's infatuation with fifteen-year-old Sarah Jennings late in the same year (Sir Winston Churchill, *Marlborough, his Life and Times*, 4 vols. (1933–8), I 117). Another meaning of 'abused' is suggested by '[Cleveland] swore she was undone with Keeping: / That C[*hurchil*]*l*, G[*ermy*]*n*, had so drain'd her, / She could not live on the Remainder' (*POAS* 1697–1707, I 144).

Out of mere love and arrant devotion

These verses appear to maintain the paradox that whoredom is better than marriage. But the 'galloping' (l. 2) anapaests make it difficult to take the argument seriously. And confining the argument within the 'narrow room' of a Petrarchan sonnet (of which the octave and sestet are clearly marked) may suggest a different conclusion to some readers.

ATTRIBUTION Since the attribution to Rochester is made only in the copy-text, it stands unproven. Internal evidence includes the following: (1) there are two other poems by Rochester on similar paradoxical themes, *Song* (Love a woman? You're an ass) (37) and 'What vain, unnecessary things are men!' (78); (2) the word 'arrant' (l. 1) occurs five times in Rochester's verse, always in the specialized sense of 'thorough, notorious, downright' (Rochester 1984, 312); (3) the imperfect rhyme 'noble . . . trouble' (ll. 9–10) recurs in *An Epistolary Essay from M. G. to O. B.*: 'alone . . . none' (207.52–3).

DATE Before 15 February 1675, when an answer to the poem was included in *Mock Songs and Joking Poems* (1675), 134, advertised for sale on this date (*T.C.*, I 197). The poem was first published in Rochester 1968, 159.

COPY-TEXT B.L. MS. Add. 23722, f. 51v.

EMENDATION OF COPY-TEXT 6 peep] Peeps
The emendation was first made in Rochester 1968, 159.

ANNOTATION

2 *you*: probably not the reader but a friend contemplating marriage.

7 *brick without stubble or straw*: cf. 'And Pharaoh commanded . . . the taskmasters of the people . . . saying, Ye shall no more give the people straw to make brick . . . let them go and gather straw for themselves . . . So the people were scattered abroad . . . to gather stubble instead of straw' (Exodus 5.6–12).

9–10 *noble . . . trouble*: the imperfect rhyme calls attention to the shaky argument that aside from the risk of disease, relations with whores are trouble-free.

14 *marriage*: stretching out 'MAR-ri-age' to its full trisyllabic length to conform to the 'galloping' metre emphasizes the interminable length of marriages in a society in which divorce was almost unobtainable; *none can*: the other witnesses to the text, Edinburgh MS. DC.1.3, p. 67 and Leeds MS. Brotherton Lt.54, p. 133, read 'the Damned do', which could be authoritative. But editorial tampering is suspected. The

image is not that of an afterlife in Hell but of the unendurable Hell on earth that is marriage.

Epilogue to Love in the Dark, *as it was spoken by Mr Haines* (As charms are nonsense, nonsense seems a charm)

This poem is a skirmish in the civil war between the King's Servants and the Duke's Company. Both companies had new playhouses. The new theatre of the Duke's Company at Dorset Garden, which opened on 9 November 1671, had facilities for staging multimedia spectaculars that Thomas Betterton had observed at the Salles des Machines in the Tuileries. Although probably designed by Sir Christopher Wren, the new theatre of the King's Servants in Convent Garden, Drury Lane, which opened on 26 March 1674, included no innovations.

Rochester's poem is the Epilogue to Sir Francis Fane's comedy *Love in the Dark*, which opened at Drury Lane on 10 May 1674, and of which there is no record of another performance. Rochester directs his attack against two of Thomas Shadwell's semi-operas, *The Tempest* (30 April 1674; 1674) – 'not any succeeding Opera got more Money' – and *Psyche* (27 February 1675; 1675), the scenery of which cost more than £800 (Downes 1987, 74, 75). This was the first production of *The Tempest* in which Ariel actually appears to fly.

Rochester flatters the audience at Drury Lane as 'men of wit' (l. 60) who applaud Michael Mohun's intelligent and natural style of acting and who deplore the 'nonsense' (l. 1) of Thomas Betterton's extravaganzas at Dorset Garden.

ATTRIBUTION Sir Francis Fane fails to mention the *Epilogue* in his dedication of *Love in the Dark* to Rochester, and the attribution of the *Epilogue* to Rochester in Rochester 1691, 130–33 is not confirmed by external evidence. Internal evidence, however, makes a case for Rochester.

DATE After the revival of *Catiline his Conspiracy* (8 March 1675) and before the opening of *Love in the Dark* (10 May 1675).

COPY-TEXT Sir Francis Fane, *Love in the Dark, or The Man of Business. A Comedy* (1675) [95–6].

ANNOTATION

1 *charms are nonsense*: in 1675 this was a statement that not even a scientist could bring himself to make categorically: 'for the most part all charms . . . are inefficacious, fallacious, superstitious and groundless . . . [but] they do sometimes either efficiently or accidentally produce real effects . . . words and rhythms fitly joined and composed, being pronounced do put the atomes of the air into such a site, notion, figure, and contexture, that may at a distance operate upon the subject for which they are so fitted, and produce such effects, as they were composed and intended for' (John Webster, *The Displaying of Supposed Witchcraft* (1677), 329, 343).

1–2 *nonsense . . . does disarm*: cf. 'true No-meaning puzzles more than Wit' (Pope 1939–67, III ii 57).

3 *scenes*: painted sets and movable scenery were still an innovation on the London stage. Scenes designed by John Webb for Sir William Davenant's *The Siege of Rhodes* (28 June 1661) are 'the first that e're were Introduc'd in *England*' (Downes 1987, 50–51); *double audience*: John Fletcher's *The Faithful Shepherdess* (13 June 1663) was said to be 'a most simple thing . . . yet much thronged after and often shown . . . only for the Scenes sake' (Pepys, 13 June 1663).

4 *smiths in satin*: the Cyclopes who, as Act III of Shadwell's *Psyche* opens, are seen in the Palace of Cupid 'at work at a Forge, forging great Vases of Silver'. They dance, 'hammering the Vases upon Anvils', and then present a song (Shadwell 1927, II 306).
6 *wit's the monster*: Shadwell concedes in his dedication of *Psyche* that 'I may want Wit to write a Play' (Shadwell 1927, II 278).
11 *in their tails a wire*: which enabled puppets representing the actors to appear to fly.
12 *They fly through clouds of clouts and showers of fire*: cf. the stage direction for the opening scene of Shadwell's *The Tempest* (30 April 1674): 'the Scene . . . represents a thick Cloudy Sky . . . and a Tempestuous Sea in perpetual Agitation. This Tempest (supposed to be rais'd by Magick) has many dreadful Objects in it, as several Spirits in horrid shapes flying down amongst the sailers, then rising and crossing in the Air. And when the Ship is sinking, the whole House is darken'd, and a shower of Fire falls upon 'em' (Shadwell 1927, II 199).
13 *losing loadum*: any card game in which the player taking the fewest tricks, scoring the fewest points, or holding the lowest cards wins the pot (*OED*, s.v. Loadum). In modern high-low poker the play for the low hand is 'a kind of losing loadum'; cf. 'to converse with *Scandal*, is to play at *Losing Loadum*; you must lose a good Name to him, before you can win it for your self' (Congreve 1967, 226).
16 *awkward actors*: although a consummate actor – 'the best actor in the world' (Pepys, 4 November 1661) – Thomas Betterton stuck his left hand between his coat and waistcoat and declaimed his lines in a demi-chant. Lines 16–27 imply that Rochester favoured a more natural style of acting with true 'accent' and appropriate 'action' (ll. 23–4).
17 Here and in l. 37 Rochester's Virgilian hemistichs may mock Shadwell's blank verse or chopped-up prose: 'ALONZO: Even here I will put off my hope, and keep it no longer / For my Flatterers: he is drown'd whom thus we / Stray to find. / I'm faint with hunger, and must despair / Of food' (Shadwell 1927, II 230).
21 *one*: probably James Nokes (Biographical Dictionary), who specialized in 'Fops of all sorts' (*BDAA*, XI 42; Montague Summers, *The Restoration Theatre* (1934), 313, 334).
26 *an ape's mock face*: in May 1670 when the court went to Dover to meet Charles II's sister, Henrietta Anne, Duchess of Orléans, the entertainment included a performance by the Duke's Company of John Caryll's *Sir Salamon Single; or The Cautious Coxcomb*. In the costume of a French fop Nokes 'lookt . . . like a Drest up Ape' (Downes 1987, 64).
28 *Thorough-paced*: this is a rare example of modernization spoiling the cadence of the verse. In the copy-text 'Thorough-paced' is 'Through-paced', a spondee, an acceptable substitute for an iamb.
30–31 *the age / Of the great wonder of our English stage*: in 1675 Michael Mohun (Biographical Dictionary) was about fifty-five; 'in all his Parts, he was most Accurate and Correct' (Downes 1987, 42).
32–3 *nature . . . / bid Shakespeare write*: Rochester deplores Otway's preference for 'rapture before nature' (205.^{2}3).
35 *his foot*: Mohun evidently suffered from gout.
36 *the Traitor or Volpone*: Mohun played the title role in revivals of James Shirley's *The Traitor* (October 1674) and Jonson's *Volpone* (January 1665). Pepys called the latter 'a most excellent play – the best I think I ever saw' (Pepys, 14 January 1665).
38 *Cethegus . . . Cassius*: Mohun played Cethegus in Jonson's *Catiline His Conspiracy* (8 March 1675) and Cassius in *Julius Caesar* (January 1672).

40 *monsters*: '*Caliban* [and] *Sycorax* his Sister, Two Monsters of the Isle' (Shadwell 1927, II 197); *Merry Andrew's dances*: a pun on Saint André, the French choreographer and dancer (Biographical Dictionary) and Merry-Andrew, a clown who 'entertains . . . by means of antics and buffoonery' (*OED*).
45 *patched*: Shadwell's *The Tempest* (30 April 1674) was a double patch: an adaptation of Davenant and Dryden's adaptation of Shakespeare. Shadwell boasted that he patched up Molière and Corneille's *Psyche* 'in five weeks' (Shadwell 1927, II 279).
47 *hector you*: 'His Majesty has also been pleased to Order the Recorder of London to examine the disorder and disturbance on Tuesday last at the Dukes Theatre by some persons in drink, to proceed against them according to the law for Ryot' (Folger MS. Newdigate Newsletter, 21 March 1674).
48 *Covent Garden men*: the audience at the new Theatre Royal in Covent Garden, Drury Lane, the 'thundering blades' (l. 50) and 'men of wit' (l. 60) of the court side of town as opposed to the more bourgeois audience at Dorset Garden, which was not *in* the City but just outside Ludgate at the foot of Salisbury Court.
52 *muzzled boys and tearing fellows*: the finale to Shadwell's *The Tempest* opens with Amphitrite's song, 'My Lord: Great *Neptune*, for my sake'. Then a chorus of thirty Tritons is silenced by Neptune: 'Great Nephew *Aeolus* . . . / Muzzle your roaring Boys' (Shadwell 1927, II 266, 269).
56 *goddess of each field and grove*: the first scene of Shadwell's *Psyche* (27 February 1675) includes Pan's song in recitative, 'Great *Psyche*, Goddess of each Field and Grove' (Shadwell 1927, II 285).

The Maimed Debauchee (As some brave admiral, in former war)

The genre of this poem poses a difficulty. It may be supposed to be satire, of the mock-heroic sub-variety, written in heroic quatrains. Thomas Rymer calls it Rochester's '*Gondibert*' (Rochester 1691, sig. A6r), implying satire on 'heroic attitudes and phrases' (Rochester 1984, 286). But where the object of the satire should be, there is only an absence. Can Rochester have expected 'statesmanlike' (l. 45) to suggest the privy council in general (the nominal head of the government) or the Duke of York, Lauderdale, and Danby in particular, who were said in September 1674 to '*governe all*' (*Essex Papers* 1890, 258)? 'Safe from action' (l. 46), York and Lauderdale were urging the King to follow the dangerous policy of dismissing Parliament and governing by decree in the manner of Louis XIV (and with subventions from Louis XIV). But Danby, the actual head of the government, opposed this policy (Browning 1951, I 166). Rochester indeed may have thought that all three of them were 'good for nothing' (l. 48), but there is no evidence that York, Lauderdale, and Danby are the tenor of a metaphor in ll. 45–8. Nor is there any evidence that York is the 'brave admiral . . . / Deprived' (ll. 1–2) of his command of the Royal Navy by the Test Act of March 1673.

But if the poem is not a political satire, perhaps it is a social satire on

> . . . old men . . .
> Who envy pleasure which they cannot taste,
> And good for nothing would be wise at last
> 198.14–16),

or a moral fable in which wisdom and virtue force themselves upon an elder statesman of debauchery by means of impotence and disease. Or a *jeu d'esprit* based on an extended metaphor juxtaposing Cupid's wars and real warfare. Or a reverie induced by the famous lines of Lucretius: 'Sweet it is, when on the great sea the winds are buffeting the waters, to gaze from land on another's great struggles . . . Sweet it is to behold great contests of war . . . when you have no part in the danger' (*De rerum natura*, II 1–6), reflecting the Epicurean compulsion to seek pleasure and avoid pain.

The nature of the speaker of the poem is defined by the title. The difficulty here is to separate the fictional character of the speaker from the historical character of the poet, for parallels are evident:

Burnet 1680	*The Maimed Debauchee*
Excesses (11)	debauch (15)
for five years . . . continually Drunk (12)	fleets of glasses (19)
broke the firm constitution of his Health (12)	honourable scars (21)
he had no remorse for his past Actions (36)	Past joys have more than paid what I endure (24)

'Biographical information about the poet', the critics say, 'will not make the poem better' (Cleanth Brooks and Robert Penn Warren, *Understanding Poetry*, 3rd ed. (1960), 207), but this may not always be true. Biographical irony, or the insider effect, is an important factor in the success of *The Maimed Debauchee*. If the poem were known to be written by Aphra Behn, it would lose the excitement generated by the close correspondence between details of Rochester's life recounted by Burnet and fragments of the imagined speaker's life recounted in the poem. So in this case 'biographical information about the poet' seems to make the poem better. For the reader who knows the details in Burnet's biography, *The Maimed Debauchee* is a better poem. Perhaps a better way of putting this would be to say that 'biographical information about the poet' may ameliorate the reader's response.

But to infer from the poem alone that Rochester was poxed would involve one in the biographical fallacy (384.102n.). The clergyman who preached Rochester's funeral sermon on 9 August 1680 seems particularly subject to this error. 'He was so diligent and industrious,' Parsons says, converting the fictional life of the maimed debauchee into historical fact, 'framing Arguments for Sin, making Proselytes to it, and writing Panegyricks upon Vice' (Parsons 1680, 9). The fact remains that the maimed debauchee is *not* John Wilmot, 2nd Earl of Rochester; he is a fictional character, like Falstaff. An unsympathetic contemporary called him

> A Wretch when old Diseases did so bite,
> That he writ Bawdry sure in spight,
> To ruin and disgrace it quite.
> (Otway 1932, II 411).

Rochester wrote *The Maimed Debauchee*, Otway says, to give 'Bawdry' a bad name. And this may be the clue needed to identify the speaker. Like Falstaff he is the Vice of medieval drama. David M. Vieth's suggestion that *The Maimed Debauchee* might be entitled *In Praise of Debauchery* (Vieth and Griffin 1988, 20) comes into play here. The poem stands on its head the *Nichomachean Ethics*. What the Vice is saying and will continue to say is that excess is better than Aristotelian *mediocritas*. Blake says it 'leads to the palace of wisdom' (Blake 1957, 150). Rochester may not be so sure, for he does not conceal the price tag: 'pox ... pains ... scars ... impotence'. For the thoughtful reader the poem may even stand as a cautionary tale: 'be wise' (l. 48), make love, not war.

ATTRIBUTION The poem is attributed to Rochester in eight ms. copies (B.L. Add. MS. 23722, f. 52; Kent County Archives MS. U269.F24; Bodl. MS. Rawl. poet. 81, f. 22r; Bodl. MS. Eng. poet. e.4, pp. 187–8; Bodl. MS. Don.b.8, pp. 409–11; Bodl. MS. Don. f.29, ff. 24v, 23v; Edinburgh MS. DC.1.3, pp. 77–8; National Library of Wales MS. Ottley Papers, uncatalogued) and the copy-text, representing at least two independent textual traditions.

COPY-TEXT Rochester 1680[1], 32–4.

EMENDATION OF COPY-TEXT 15 Forced] Drov'n 17 least] last 18 they] you 25 any youth] hopeful *Youths* 26 his ... inviter] their ... Inviters 30 bold night] *Nights* brisk 40 fucked] used 43 him] them 44 he's] the're 46 action] danger
All the emendations except that in l. 18 are supplied from Royal Library, Stockholm MS. Vu.69, pp. 47–50. The unique reading 'they' in l. 18 is preserved in Harvard MS. 636F, pp. 1–3 (Rochester 1984, 204); all other witnesses read 'you', for which there is no grammatical antecedent. No one has been addressed, not even the reader. 'They' may refer to the debauchees in the debauch imagined by the speaker (ll. 15–20).

DATE B.L. MS. Add. 23722, f. 52 dates the poem 1675 (Rochester 1968, 286).

ANNOTATION
Title *Maimed*: 'Mutilated, crippled, injured' (*OED* cites Bacon's *Essayes* (1625), 184: 'Hospitals for Maimed Soldiers'); cf. 190.243.
1–24 The poem begins, like Donne's *A Valediction: forbidding Mourning* (1633) and Marvell's *An Horatian Ode upon Cromwell's Return from Ireland* (1681), with an extended epic simile.
1 *admiral*: Rochester served under two in the second Dutch War (1665–7), Sir Thomas Teddeman (?–1668) in the Bergen raid of August 1665 and Sir Edward Spragge (?–1673) in the Four Days' Battle of June 1666. Spragge, 'a merry man', sang catches with Pepys at Starkey's, admired Pepys's pretty neighbour, the widow Hollworthy, and left three illegitimate children upon his death in August 1673 (Pepys, 11 January 1666, 15 February 1666, 1 April 1667; Leneve 1873, 196).
1–12 cf. Lucretius, *De rerum natura*, II 1–6, quoted in the headnote (373).
9 *From his fierce eyes flashes of rage he throws*: cf. 'the anger came harder upon him [Achilles] / and his eyes glittered terribly under his lids,' (Homer, *The Iliad*, trans. Richmond Lattimore (1951), 392).
14 *wine's unlucky chance*: cirrhosis of the liver (?). The speaker is 'imagining future incapacities, not describing present ones' (Claude Rawson, *TLS*, 29 March 1985, 335).
18 *they*: 'new-listed soldiers' (l. 23).
27 *Vice*: 'Depravity ... Personified' (*OED*); cf. 'that reverend Vice, that grey Iniquitie' (*1 Henry IV*, II iv 499).
28 *counsel*: cf. 'HARCOURT [to Horner]. ... an old maim'd General, when unfit for action is fittest for Counsel' (Wycherley 1979, 288). *The Country Wife* opened at Drury Lane on or about 12 January 1675.
33–4 *tell of whores attacked (their lords at home)*, / *Bawds' quarters beaten up and fortress won*: cf. 'Tell of towns stormed, and armies overrun, / And mighty kingdoms by your

conduct won' (Waller 1893, 145) (Warren L. Chernaik, *The Poetry of Limitation: A Study of Edmund Waller* (1968), 198).

42 *incline*: 'some cold-complexioned sot' (l. 29) understood.

47 *Sheltered in impotence*: the paradox has been noted (Stuart Silverman, *Enlightenment Essays* 3 (1972), 210); *you*: 'hypocrite lecteur!' (T. S. Eliot, *Collected Poems* (1930), 72).

48 *good for nothing else*: Rochester may be mocking Edward Stillingfleet, who imagines the sinner's conscience telling him '*There is old Age coming, and when you will be good for nothing else, then will be time enough to grow wise and to repent*' (Stillingfleet 1675, 36; cf. 359; *be wise*: Pinto cites La Rochefoucauld, 'Les Vieillards aiment à donner de bons preceptes pour se consoler de n'estre plus en estat de donner de mauvais exemples' (No longer able to set bad examples, old men console themselves by professing good precepts) (*Reflexions ou sentences et maximes morales* (1665), 52) (Rochester 1953, 185), but the maimed debauchee professes bad precepts.

A Very Heroical Epistle from My Lord All-Pride to Doll-Common
(Madam, If you're deceived, it is not by my cheat)

This is the second in a linked group of four poems. The first is Etherege's *Ephelia to Bajazet* (How far are they deceived who hope in vain) in which an unidentified Ephelia reproaches the Earl of Mulgrave *qua* Bajazet for defaulting in love. The third and fourth are Rochester's *On Poet Ninny* (Crushed by that just contempt his follies bring) and *My Lord All-Pride* (Bursting with pride the loathed impostume swells). The four poems occur in this order in four manuscripts (Royal Library, Stockholm MS. Vu.69, pp. 119–30; Edinburgh MS. DC.1.3, pp. 22–4; Yale MS. Osborn b.54, pp. 1180–84; Huntington MS. Ellesmere 8736, f. 1) and in Rochester 1680[3], 138–45 (Vieth 1963, 99, 337–41).

'Heroical Epistle', a sub-genre of Ovid's invention (Dryden 1882–93, XII 14), is the vehicle for the satire in this poem. Ovid's *Heroides* are twenty-one verse epistles from legendary heroes and heroines, most of them (I–XV) to defaulting lovers; Briseis to Achilles, Dido to Aeneas, Sappho to Phaon, etc., with long reaches of unrelieved whining. Ezra Pound may have had the *Heroides* in mind when he noted that 'The Jewel Stairs' Grievance' is 'especially prized because she utters no direct reproach' (*Personae* (1926), 132). *Heroides* XVI–XXI are three exchanges of letters between estranged lovers: Paris to Helen, Helen to Paris, etc., and these exchanges may have suggested to Rochester and Etherege the Ephelia to Mulgrave, Mulgrave to Ephelia exchange. In any case the originality consists in domesticating this 'Very Heroical' genre, of which Tasso, Randolph, Lovelace, and Carew cranked out exemplary types (Etherege 1963, 82), to the purposes of satire.

ATTRIBUTION The poem is attributed to Rochester in Bodl. MS. Don.b.8, pp. 602–3 and in Rochester 1680[3], 140–42, representing two independent textual traditions. The attribution to Sir Carr Scrope made in Edinburgh MS. DC.1.3, p. 23 is a mistake (Vieth 1963, 346–7).

DATE After 4 July 1675 (376.53n.).

COPY-TEXT *A very Heroicall Epistle from my Lord All-Pride to Dol-Common* (1679) (Wing R1761B).

EMENDATION OF COPY-TEXT 1 Madam] om. 42 the pain] thy pain
The emendations are supplied from Rochester 1680[3], 140–42.

ANNOTATION

Title *Lord All-Pride*: Bajazet and Lord All-Pride seem to have been equally current as Mulgrave's nicknames. But since Marlowe's *Tamburlaine* (1590) was not revived during the Restoration, Etherege may have borrowed the name from Racine's *Bajazet* (1672) (Etherege 1963, 80–81); *Doll-Common*: the name of Cheater's whore in Ben Jonson's *The Alchemist* (1610). The historical Doll Common is Katherine Corey of the King's Company, who played the role in the revival of *The Alchemist* in December 1660 or December 1661 and regularly thereafter (*London Stage* I 44; Downes 1982, 15). She was arrested when she took off Lady Elizabeth Hervey in the character of Sempronia, an ageing courtesan (Pepys, 15 January 1669).

1 *Madam, If you're deceived, it is not by my cheat*: this line answers the rejected mistress's complaint: 'How far are they deceived who hope in vain / A lasting lease of joys from love t'obtain' (*Ephelia to Bajazet*, Etherege 1963, 9).

4 *above a day*: cf. 'dull to love above a day' (54.199).

7 *In my dear self I centre everything*: cf. 'In him I centered all my hopes of bliss' (*Ephelia to Bajazet*, ibid.); cf. Dryden's dedication to Mulgrave of *Aureng-Zebe* (17 November 1673; 1676): 'True greatness, if it be anywhere on earth, is in private virtue; removed from the notion of pomp and vanity, confined to a contemplation of itself, and centring on itself' (Dryden 1882–93, V 194). George deF. Lord wonders where Dryden's tongue was when he wrote these lines (*POAS*, Yale, I 345).

17 *'tis as natural to change as love*: cf. 'Since 'tis nature's law to change, / Constancy alone is strange' (66.31–2) (Griffin 1973, 60).

21 *blazing star*: cf. 'the Star by which I steered' (*Ephelia to Bajazet*, Etherege 1963, 10). In April 1674 Mulgrave was elected a Fellow of the Order of the Garter, the insignia of which includes a bejewelled star. But the primary reference is to Mulgrave's insistence that he is a 'blazing star' (comet) and the brilliant centre of admiration (*OED*), not the fixed star that the rejected mistress imagines; *visits and away*: cf. 'a man of wit, / Who found 'twas dull to love above a day, / Made his ill-natured jest, and went away' (54.198–200).

22 *fatal*: comets appearing in December 1665 and March 1666 were followed by plague and fire in London.

23 *some great lady dies*: predictions that persons of great quality, 'especially Women', will die within the month are the stock-in-trade of astrology (Richard Saunders, *Apollo Anglicanus* (1676), sig. B2r; William Lilly, *Merlini Anglici Ephemeris: Or, Astrological Judgments for the Year 1677* (1677), sig. B3r). Adding 'great ladies' gives a further meaning to 'die'.

24 *The boasted favour*: cf. 'to you I brought / My virgin innocence' (*Ephelia to Bajazet*, Etherege 1963, 10).

25 *changing*: glossed 'making change', i.e. getting 'money of another kind (e.g. foreign or smaller coin) in exchange for money of some defined kind' (*OED*) (Rochester 1968, 114; Rochester 1984, 297), but Lord All-Pride may have in mind the proverb, Fair exchange is no robbery (Tilley C228).

37–8 *underneath the shade / Of golden canopies supinely laid*: cf. 'Underneath this Myrtle shade, / On flowry beds supinely laid' (Cowley 1905, 56).

45–6 *marks out the dame / Thou fanciest most to quench thy present flame*: cf. 'some brave Turk . . . beckons to the willing dame, / Preferred to quench his present flame' (Waller 1893, 87–8) (John Hayman, *N&Q* 213 (October 1968), 380–81).

53 *injured kinsman*: on 4 July 1675 Captain Percy Kirke challenged Mulgrave 'for haveing debauch'd & abus'd his sister', Mall Kirke, one of the maids of honour, even though 'shee herself does not accuse him . . . of getting the child . . . in which

adventure the Earl of Moulgrave had the ill luck to receive a wound in his shoulder . . . this or something else has caus'd a 1000 storys to be rais'd about the father of the child' (Sir Richard Bulstrode, *The Bulstrode Papers* (1897), 304–5).

54 *midnight ambushes*: in September 1674 when Mulgrave won the favour of Mall Kirke, she was also mistress to the Duke of York and the Duke of Monmouth. As Captain of the Horse Guards, Monmouth, 'being jealous of Lord Moulgrave's courting his newest mistress', ordered Mall's lodgings in Whitehall to be watched. Mulgrave was arrested and confined to the guardhouse like a common trespasser (HMC *Rutland MSS*., II 27).

56 *Damocles*: invited to occupy the seat of power of Dionysius, the tyrant of Syracuse (*c*. 432–367 B.C.), Damocles notices a sword hanging over his neck by a single horse hair (Cicero, *Tusculan Disputations*, V xxi 61–2).

To all Gentlemen, Ladies, and Others, whether of City, Town, or Country, Alexander Bendo wisheth all Health and Prosperity

In one of his guises Volpone gains access to the inaccessible Celia as Scoto Mantuano, the celebrated mountebank (Jonson 1923–52, V 56). Two of 'the merry gang' at court, the Duke of Buckingham and Sir Charles Sedley, are said to have played the same game (Barbara Everett in Treglown 1982, 2). So there is nothing inherently improbable in the tradition that when Rochester in a moment of drunken confusion handed the King *On King Charles*, 'he was banished from the Court and set up as a Mountebank on Tower Hill' (328), 'laughing at . . . his . . . Enimies; who thought they had exil'd him into France' (Rochester 1961, 26). 'Access' indeed was the name of the game: if a modest lady in the crowd 'had any such [birthmarks] about her, where without blushing she could not well declare them: why the Religious Doctor Bendo would not, for all the world, so much as desire to see it, Yet for fear he should lose a Generous Patient, or the Lady her longing to know the meaning of her Private Mark: she was to leave a token with the Doctor and appoint an hour when his Wife was to bring it, as a Credential that she came on that Errand, upon which she was immediately to be admitted into the Bed Chamber, to View and report the matter'. Then in 'the habit of a grave Matron' Rochester 'did [the lady's] business Effectually' (Rochester 1961, 26–7).

'Being under an unlucky Accident, which obliged him to keep out of the way', Burnet says, 'He disguised himself, so that his nearest Friends could not have known him, and set up in *Tower-street* for an Italian *Mountebank*, where he had a Stage, and practised Physick for some Weeks' (Burnet 1680, 27). By impersonating Hans Buling, a Dutch mountebank practising in London, Rochester even found a role for his monkey. 'His first operations, which did not extend beyond the neighbourhood, were not particularly remarkable. But his reputation very soon spread to the other end of the town, and it was not long before the serving-maids at Court began visiting him, and the abigails of women of quality who, owing to the marvels which they reported of the German doctor, were presently followed by one or two of their mistresses' (Hamilton 1930, 258).

ATTRIBUTION Thomas Alcock was one of Rochester's 'Operators' in the Tower Hill 'laboratory', 'stirring an old boyling kettle, of Soote and Urine, tinged with a little Asafetida and all the nasty Ingredients that would render the smell more unsavoury' while the hawkers made the streets ring dispensing Dr Bendo's printed bills. But in 1687 when Lady Anne Baynton, Rochester's eldest daughter, asked

Alcock to see one, all that remained was an 'almost obliterated' copy that Alcock kept 'for a Relique' (Rochester 1961, 27–8, 30–31). This he transcribed, producing Nottingham MS. 1489, but no copy of the original handbill has survived. It is attributed to Rochester, however, in both the 'perfect' and the 'imperfect' textual traditions (below).

DATE Unencumbered by evidence Hans-Joachim Zimmerman can assign publication of Dr Bendo's Bill to 'summer 1675' (*Functions of Literature: Essays presented to Erwin Wolff on his 60th Birthday*, ed. Ulrich Broich *et al.* (1984), 159). But this date is not inconsistent with the internal or external evidence. 'These secrets I gathered in my travels . . . in France and Italy', Dr Bendo discloses, 'where I have spent my time ever since I was fifteen years old to this my nine and twentieth year' (ll. 195–8). It is not unlikely that Rochester, when he was fifteen, may have visited the University of Montpellier, where the court physician, Sir Alexander Fraser, and Alexander Bendo received their doctor's degrees. And it is certain that Rochester entered upon his 'nine and twentieth year' on 10 April 1675.

On 25 June of that year Rochester smashed the King's chronometer. Some weeks later he incurred the 'more than ordinary indignation' of the King's new *maîtresse en titre*, the Duchess of Portsmouth (Rochester *Letters* 1980, 106). So 'summer 1675' may be the best guess for the printing of Dr Bendo's Bill.

COPY-TEXT Rochester 1709 (Curll), ^{2}1–15. The preface to the copy-text boasts of acquiring 'a perfect Copy of my Lord Rochester's Mountebank Bill', of which the earlier editions omitted 'several Words which alter the Sense' as well as 'one large entire Paragraph'. The evidence of collation confirms this boast.

The text of Dr Bendo's Bill in Rochester 1691, 138–54 omits the loquacious 'I say' (l. 4), substitutes a feeble participle, 'backing' for 'backed with' (ll. 6-7), omits the necessary preposition 'by' (l. 8), reads 'purpose' for 'propose' (l. 12), and so forth throughout the work. Of 'one large entire Paragraph' (ll. 144–61) Rochester 1691 retains only an incomplete sentence, beginning 'Likewise Barrenness', followed by the clause in parentheses (ll. 145–9), and run into the next paragraph, 'Cures of this kind . . . (l. 162), without punctuation.

Two editions of Dr Bendo's Bill must have been hawked in the streets: the 'perfect' edition reproduced in Rochester 1709 (Curll) and the imperfect edition transcribed by Thomas Alcock on 1 January 1687 and reprinted in Rochester 1691. The relations between these witnesses are shown in the following stemma:

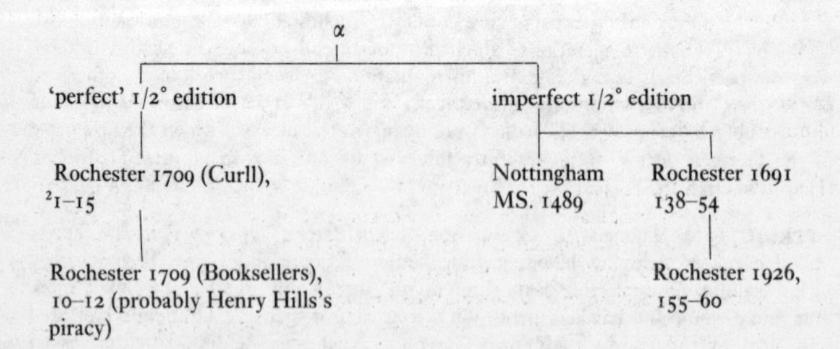

EMENDATION OF COPY-TEXT **72** astrologer] Astroger **92** arrant] errant **201** that] om.
The emendation of l. 92 is preserved in Rochester 1691, 145. The others are editorial.

ANNOTATION
10 *Galenic*: Claudius Galenus (*c.* 130–200? A.D.) was the most celebrated medical writer of the classical era. His practice was based on physical rather than chemical medicine.
30–31 *I . . . have . . . courted these arts*: cf. 'I have beene at my book' (Jonson 1925–52, V 55).
42 *Qui alterum incusat probri, ipsum se intueri oportet*: Plautus, *Truculentus*, I ii 160. The text is corrupt but the meaning is clear: He who finds fault with others better be faultless himself.
50 *the counterfeit's . . . original*: Dr Alexander Bendo has two originals, Dr Alexander Fraser, one of 'the grand doctors of the court' (ll. 128–9), for his given name and medical specialties (urology and gynaecology), and Dr Hans Buling, one of 'the lesser quacks and mountebanks' (ll. 129–30), for his appearance (Plate 11).
87 *deluded, and pleased*: cf. the 'joy of being well deceived' (52.115).
101 *dangerous remedies*: cf. 'new poisons' (302.35n.).
112–15 *nay . . . humours . . . malignant*: cf. 'No, no . . . malignant humours' (Jonson 1925–52, V 52).
137 *Aretine's* Dialogues: the divine Aretino's *Dialogo* is the second part of *Cappricciosi e piacevoli Ragionamenti* (1534), partly translated into English as *The Crafty Whore: or, the Mistery and Iniquity of Bawdy Houses laid open* (1658).
139–40 *fits of the mother*: hysteria, cf. 'Oh how this Mother swels up toward my heart!' (*King Lear*, II iv 56).
185 *rare secrets*: cf. 'rare, and unknowne secrets' (Jonson 1925–52, V 54).
189–92 *when God . . . bestowed on man the power of strength and wisdom . . . it seemed but requisite that* [*woman*] *should be indued likewise . . . with some quality that might beget in him admiration of her*: cf. 'For contemplation hee and valour formd, / For softness she and sweet attractive Grace' (Milton 1931–8, II i 117).
197 *this my nine and twentieth year*: Rochester entered his twenty-ninth year on 10 April 1675.
210–11 *preserve your teeth white . . . as pearls . . . fastening them that are loose*: cf. 'seats your teeth . . . makes them white, as ivory' (Jonson 1925–52, V 57).

An Allusion to Horace. The 10th Satire of the 1st Book (Well sir, 'tis granted I said Dryden's rhymes)

In this poem Rochester invents the imitation as a new vehicle for satire. 'This mode of imitation', Johnson says,

> in which the ancients are familiarised, by adapting their sentiments to modern topicks, by making Horace say of Shakespeare what he originally said of Ennius, and accommodating his satires on Pantolabus and Nomentanus to the flatterers and prodigals of our own time, was first practised in the reign of Charles the Second by Oldham and Rochester.
>
> (Johnson 1779–81, VII 184)

Johnson as usual is right: Cowley calls his 'libertine way of rendering foreign Authors ... *Translating*, or *Imitating*' (Cowley 1905, 156), but Cowley's renderings are not imitations in Johnson's definition; neither are Sir John Denham's, despite his sanction of 'New names, new dressings, and the modern cast' in translation (*The Poetical Works of Sir John Denham*, ed. Theodore H. Banks, Jr. (1928), 144). But Johnson's definition of the sub-genre only repeats what Oldham says in the 'Advertisement' to his volume of imitations published in 1681 and dedicated to the memory of the 'incomparable' Rochester. Oldham undertakes to put

> *Horace* into a more modern dress, than hitherto he has appear'd in, that is, by making him speak as if he were living and writing now. I therefore resolv'd to alter the Scene from *Rome* to *London*, and to make use of *English* names of Men, Places, and Customs.
>
> (Oldham 1987, 87)

Grafting the scion of satire on to the stock of 'imitation' proved to be unusually fruitful. Oldham's *An Imitation of Horace. Book I, Satyr IX* (1681); Swift's *Toland's Invitation to Dismal ... Imitated from Horace, Epist. 5, Lib. 1* (1712), *Part of the Seventh Epistle of the First Book of Horace Imitated* (1713), and *Horace, Lib. 2. Sat. 6. Part of it Imitated* (1714); Pope's *Imitations of Horace* (1733–8); Johnson's *London: A Poem in Imitation of the Third Satire of Juvenal* (1738), and *The Vanity of Human Wishes. The Tenth Satire of Juvenal. Imitated* (1749) are products of Rochester's invention.

A poem that puts Dryden in the position of Shadwell in *MacFlecknoe* (1676; 1682) may make trouble for readers today. The trouble is caused partly by the fact that when *An Allusion to Horace* was written (in the summer of 1675), the works for which Dryden is chiefly prized today had not been written. Most of what Dryden had written were rhymed heroic dramas that were enormously popular but which Buckingham had turned into laughingstock in *The Rehearsal* (December 1671; 1672). As a comic dramatist Dryden was not as successful as Etherege, Wycherley, or even, alas, Shadwell. His non-dramatic works included the embarrassing *Heroic Stanzas consecrated to the Glorious Memory of his Most Serene and Renown'd Highness Oliver, Late Lord Protector* (1659). His more successful works, *Astraea Redux. A Poem on the Happy Restoration & Return of His Sacred Majesty Charles the Second* (1660) and *Annus Mirabilis: The Year of Wonders, 1666, An Historical Poem* (1667), are marred by vestiges of the degenerate metaphysical style that was Dryden's first poetic idiom.

Furthermore, as poet laureate and a public figure Dryden was not popular. His latest biographer acknowledges that 'he was ... proud of his poetic "fancy", impatient with his critics, likely to undervalue his predecessors, eager to invent dramatic devices that would be new and surprising, and not entirely at ease when dealing with those who outranked him' (cf. 376.7n.) (Winn 1987, 231).

In a way Dryden brought this poem on himself. In his 'Defence of an Epilogue' to *The Conquest of Granada* (December 1670; 1672), Dryden defended his adverse criticism of Ben Jonson by the classical precedent of Horace's adverse criticism of Lucilius in *Satire* I x. An imitation of *Satire* I x requires Rochester to find a contemporary equivalent of Lucilius, whose Ilissus runs muddy (*Satire* I x 50), and what better figure could Rochester find than Dryden, the Sisyphean fabricator of turgid rhymed heroic dramas? 'I ... am a sufficient theatre to myself of ridiculous actions', Dryden confesses (Dryden 1882–93, V 195). Dryden had presumptuously assumed the role of Horace in his 'Defence of an Epilogue' (Dryden 1882–93, IV

226), but Rochester demotes him to the role of Lucilius and then takes every advantage of Horace's text to ridicule his victim (Moskovit 1968, 452–3).

And Dryden may be only a stalking horse for the primary target of the satire, the Restoration theatre audience. Pseudo-St Evremond, Benjamin Bragge's hack, explains that Rochester's 'Pique to *Dryden*' arose because Dryden 'deserv'd not that Applause for his Tragedies, which the mad unthinking Audience gave them' (Rochester 1707 (Bragge), sig. b7v).

ATTRIBUTION The poem is attributed to Rochester in seven ms. copies (B.L. MS. Add. 18220, ff. 121r–123r; Bodl. MS. Add. B.106, ff. 5r–6v; Cambridge MS. Add. 6339, ff. 13r–15r; Harvard MS. Eng. 623F, pp. 28–32; Harvard MS. Eng. 636F, pp. 40–46; Yale MS. Osborn b.54, pp. 974–7; Illinois MS. 30 Je 45 Stonehill, pp. 209–12) and two printed copies (the copy-text and Rochester 1707 (Bragge), [1]18–25), representing at least two textual traditions; cf. Vieth 1963, 389.

DATE No literary work published later than September 1675 is mentioned in the poem (John H. Wilson, *RES* 15 (1939), 299).

COPY-TEXT Rochester 1680[1], 40–44.

EMENDATION OF COPY-TEXT **14** assembling] assembled **29** morosest] *Moros* **62** springs] spring
The emendations are preserved in Yale MS. Osborn b.54, pp. 974–7.

ANNOTATION

1 *rhymes*: by attacking Dryden's rhymed heroic drama, Rochester is also teasing Charles II, whose taste was partly formed by watching Corneille and Molière at the court of Louis XIV. 'The favour which heroic plays . . . found upon our theatres', Dryden says, 'has been wholly derived to them from the countenance and approbation they have received at court' (Dryden 1882–93, II 285).

2 *stol'n*: 'for Comedy, he [Dryden] is for the most part beholding to French Romances and Plays, not only for his Plots, but even a great part of his Language; tho' at the same time, he has the confidence to prevaricate, if not flatly deny the Accusation, and equivocally to vindicate himself; as in the Preface to [*An Evening's Love; or,*] *the Mock Astrologer*: where he mentions Thomas Corneille's *le Feint Astrologue* because 'twas translated, and the Theft prov'd upon him; but never says One word of Molière's *Depit amoureux*, from whence the greatest part of *Wild-blood* and *Jacinta*, (which he owns are the chiefest parts of the Play) are stollen' (Langbaine 1691, 131).

3 *foolish patron*: the primary reference is to John Sheffield, Earl of Mulgrave, Rochester's *bête noir*, to whom Dryden dedicated *Aureng-Zebe* (17 November 1675; 1676), but Rochester includes himself in the satire for he had been Dryden's patron in 1671–3.

4 *blindly*: cf. 'Ben Jonson is to be admired for many excellencies . . . but . . . I do not admire him blindly' (Dryden 1882–93, III 243).

7 *paper*: i.e. paper of verses (Rochester 1982, 97). 'Horace is referring back to what he had written about Lucilius in *Satire* I iv' (Rochester 1984, 288).

9 *loose*: cf. 'I am sensible . . . of the scandal I have given by my loose writings' (Dryden 1882–93, XI 231).

11 *Crowne's tedious scenes*: John Crowne's *The History of Charles the Eighth of France* (November 1671; 1672) is called 'a dull Rhiming Play' in the Epilogue (sig. L3v).

13 *false judgement*: cf. 'I . . . am often vex'd to hear the people laugh, and clap . . .

where I intended them no jest; while they let pass the better things, without taking notice of them' (Dryden 1882–93, III 240).
13–14 *audience / Of clapping fools*: Dryden flatters his audience, attributing to 'the wit and conversation of the present age . . . the advantage which we have above' Shakespeare, Jonson, and Fletcher (Dryden 1882–93, IV 242–3). Rochester does not flatter the Restoration theatre audience, calling them 'the rabble' (ll. 17, 120) and 'the vile rout' (l. 102) (Moskovit 1968, 453).
15 *thronged playhouse crack*: cf. 'Rochester . . . was sensible, that [Dryden] deserv'd not that Applause for his Tragedies, which the mad unthinking Audience gave them' (Pseudo-St Evremond, Rochester 1707 (Bragge), sig. b7v).
17 *divert the rabble*: cf. 'he that debases himself to think of nothing but pleasing the Rabble, loses the dignity of a Poet, and becomes as little as a Jugler, or a Rope-Dancer' (Shadwell 1927, I 100).
18 *blundering*: cf. Settle's 'blundering hobling Verse' (*Notes and Observations on the Empress of Morocco* (1674), Dryden 1956– , XVII 89; 'a blund'ring kind of Melody' (ibid., II 74).
19 *puzzling Otway*: 'must refer to Otway's clumsy first play, *Alcibiades* (acted 22 September 1675), not to his highly successful second effort, *Don Carlos* (acted 8 June 1676)' (Vieth 1963, 158).
20 *due proportions*: cf. 'In all true Wit a due proportion's found, / To the just Rules of heighth and distance bound' (Shadwell 1927, II 291).
35–6 *Flatman . . . rides a jaded muse*: whereas Cowley's '*Pindarique Pegasus*' is 'an unruly, and a *hard-Mouth'd Horse*, / Fierce, and unbroken yet' (Cowley 1905, 183); *whipped with*: at this uncertainty in the iambic cadence – is it 'WHIPPED with' or 'WHIPPED WITH'? – Flatman's Rosinante stumbles.
37–8 *Scipio fret and rave, / . . . Hannibal . . . whining*: P. Cornelius Scipio Africanus the Younger frets and raves very little in *Sophonisba. or Hannibal's Overthrow* (April 1675; 1676) (Lee 1954, I 103) and even for this Lee has a precedent in Livy XXVI xlix–l. But he had only poetic licence for a lovesick Hannibal (Lee 1954, I 87, 100, 106, etc.).
43 *hasty Shadwell*: Shadwell boasts that he wrote *The Miser* (January 1672?; 1672) in less than a month, *Psyche* (February 1675; 1675) in five weeks, and the last two acts of *The Libertine* (June 1675; 1676) in four days (Shadwell 1927, II 16, 279; III 21); *slow Wycherley*: Rochester's 'friends . . . ought never to forgive him for commending them perpetually the wrong way, and sometimes by contraries' (Dryden 1882–93, V 337); 'Lord Rochester's character of Wycherley is quite wrong. He was far from being slow in general, and in particular, wrote the *Plain Dealer* in three weeks' (Spence 1966, I 37). 'The lyes in these Libels', Rochester tells Burnet, 'came often in as Ornaments that could not be spared without spoiling the Beauty of the *Poem*' (Burnet 1680, 26), or in this case the beauty of the contrast, 'hasty Shadwell and slow Wycherley'.
45 *force of nature*: cf. 'Trust Nature, do not labour to be dull' (Dryden 1956– , II 58).
54 *Waller . . . for the bays designed*: John Dennis recalls Rochester's habit of 'repeating on every Occasion, the Verses of *Waller*, for whom that noble Lord had a very particular Esteem' (Dennis 1939–43, II 248) (Rochester 1984, 288).
58 *conquerors or . . . kings*: Waller and Dryden both wrote panegyrics to Cromwell and to Charles II (Rochester 1984, 289).
59 *For . . . satires . . . Buckhurst*: Buckhurst's reputation for satire was based on *To Mr. Edward Howard on his Incomparable Incomprehensible Poem called The British Princes* (1669), one phrase of which, 'a strange alacrity in sinking' (Dorset 1979, 8), is the seed of luxuriant flowers in Pope.

60 *The best good man with the worst-natured muse*: cf. 'Never was so much ill nature in a pen as in his [Lord Dorset's], joined with so much good nature as was in himself' (Burnet 1724–34, I 264). Dryden, however, in his *Discourse concerning the Original and Progress of Satire* (1693), which he dedicated to Dorset, took 'strong exception' to this line, calling it 'an insolent, sparing, and invidious panegyric' (Dryden 1882–93, XIII 5; Farley-Hills, 1978, 221). It is doubtful that Dorset was pleased by this attack on his dead friend.
65–6 *impart / The loosest wishes*: Defoe, who wrote 'Some Account of the Life of Sir Charles Sedley' appended to Samuel Briscoe's edition of Sedley's works in 1722, found 'nothing indecent or obscene' in all that Sedley wrote (*The Works of the Honourable Sir Charles Sedley, Bart.*, 2 vols. (1722), I ¹8).
71–3 *Dryden . . . would be sharp*: cf. 'the snobbish delight with which Dryden reveals his social intimacy . . . with the circle now known as the Court Wits' (William J. Cameron, in Love 1972, 282–3).
74 *he'd cry, 'Cunt'*: 'At *Windsor*, in the company of several persons of Quality, Sir *G*[*eorge*] *E*[*therege*] being present . . . When ask'd how they should spend the Afternoon . . . *Let's Bugger one another now by G–d* . . . was [Dryden's] smart reply' (Shadwell 1927, V 253).
75 *dry . . . bob*: Drybob, a character in Shadwell's *The Humourists* (December 1670; 1671) who 'makes it his business to speak fine things', is a caricature of Dryden (Michael W. Alssid, *SEL* 7 (1967), 396–7; Winn 1987, 222–4).
76 *Poet Squab*: '*The Name given him* [Dryden] *by the Earl of Rochester*' (Shadwell 1927, V 254). 'Squab' refers primarily to Dryden's short, dumpy figure, like that of a fat pigeon, but in the context of dry bob (copulation without ejaculation) the term may imply sexual inexperience; a squab is also a newly-hatched chick.
77 *praise*: cf. Horace 'Praised *Lucilius* where he deserv'd it; *Pagina laudatur eâdem*' (Horace, *Satire* I x 4) (Dryden 1956– , XI 322, 527).
79–80 *Nor dare I . . . tear / That laurel which he best deserves to wear*: the sincerity of Rochester's praise of Dryden seems guaranteed by the sincerity of Horace's praise of Lucilius (*Satire* I x 48–9) that these lines translate literally; *deserves*: because his 'talent . . . can divert the rabble and the court' (ll. 16–17).
81–4 *Jonson dull; / Fletcher . . . uncorrect . . . Shakespeare . . . / Stiff and affected*: cf. '*Jonson* did Mechanique humour show, / When men were dull . . . *Fletcher* . . . neither understood correct Plotting, nor that which they call *the Decorum of the Stage* . . . *Shakespear* . . . writes in many places, below the dullest Writer of ours, or of any precedent Age . . . He is many times flat, insipid; his Comick wit degenerating into clenches, his serious swelling into Bombast' (Dryden 1956– , XI 201, 206, 212–13, XVII 55). Dryden did not, however, call Shakespeare 'Stiff and affected' (Winn 1987, 287).
84–6 *to his own . . . / Allowing all the justness . . . to these denied*: Rochester departs from his text here: Lucilius does not appropriate to himself the deficiencies he finds in Accius and Ennius: 'non ridet versus Enni gravitate minores, / cum de se loquitur non ut maiore reprensis?' (Does not Lucilius laugh at the verses of Ennius as lacking in dignity, though he speaks of himself as no greater than those he has blamed?) (Horace, *Satire* I x 54–5) (Moskovit 1968, 452).
85 *pride*: 'Rochester's . . . emphasis on Dryden's pride, uses language taken from Dryden's recent criticism of himself' (Winn 1987, 287), e.g. 'Our author [Dryden] . . . spite of all his pride' (Dryden 1882–93, V 201).
93 *Five hundred verses every morning*: cf. 'in hora saepe ducentos / . . . versus dictabat' (Lucilius would often dictate two hundred verses in a morning) (Horace, *Satire* I iv 9–10).

96 *Mustapha*: cf. 351.114n.; *The English Princess*: presumably a slip of the pen for the failed epic of Dryden's brother-in-law, Edward Howard's *The British Princes: an Heroick Poem* (1668) (*DNB*, X 12; *Restoration Verse*, ed. Harold Love (1968), 299).
97 *composed in half an hour*: cf. 'This Poem [*Tyrannick Love, or The Royal Martyr* (1670)] . . . was contrived and written in seven weeks', 'this play [*Amboyna, or The Cruelties of the Dutch to the English Merchants* (1673)] . . . being contrived and written in a month' (Dryden 1956– , X 111; Dryden 1882–93, V 8); cf. 382.43n.
102 *Scorn all applause the vile rout can bestow*: substitution of a spondee for an iamb in the fourth foot, 'Scorn ALL ap-PLAUSE the VILE ROUT CAN be-STOW', gives this line unusual emphasis, directing the reader to what may be the primary target of the satire, the Restoration theatre audience. The biographical fallacy (Ellis 1951, 1006–8) misleads readers into supposing that this line is 'the haughty snobbery of the Restoration aristocrat who despises *hoi poloi*' (Farley-Hills 1978, 203); it is in fact a critical commonplace (384.120n.).
111 *Betty Morris*: '*Buckhurst*'s whore' (*The Gentleman's Magazine*, May 1780, 218); cf. 53.184.
116 *squints*: cf. 'His [Scrope's] squinting looks' (Buckingham, *A Familiar Epistle to Mr. Julian, Secretary to the Muses* (1677, 57) (*POAS* Yale, I 398).
117 *censures*: none of Scrope's 'censures' of Rochester prior to 1676 are known.
120 *I loathe the rabble*: cf. 'Odi profanum vulgus et arceo' (I hate and shun the ungodly mob) (Horace, *Odes*, III i 1) (Rochester 1984, 290). What may be in the back of Rochester's mind is his belief (in Dryden's words) that 'The Court . . . is the best and surest judge of writing' (Dryden 1956– , XVII 4).
123–4 *And some few more . . . / Approve my sense*: the elitism is Horace's: 'paucorum hominum et mentis bene sanae' (a few friends and plain good sense) (*Satire* I ix 44). Defoe adapts these lines to his own purposes: 'Lord *Rochester* Answered a foolish Ignorant Censurer of his Works:

> If *Sackvill*, *Savil*, *Buckhurst*, *Wytcherly*,
> And some few more, whom I omit to Name,
> Approve my sense, I count your Censure FAME.'
> (*Mercator*, 28 November–1 December 1713)

Dialogue (When to the King I bid good morrow)

This adaptation of a broadside ballad to the purposes of satire can be sung to the tune of 'When first I bid my love good-morrow' (*Roxburghe Ballads*, III 526).

ATTRIBUTION Since the verses are attributed to Rochester only in four ms. copies (Vienna MS. 14090, f. 20r; B.L. MS. Harl. 6914, f. 2v; V&A MS. Dyce 43, p. 26; Bodl. MS. Firth c.15, pp. 25–6) representing the same textual tradition, the attribution remains unproven. The poem was first attributed to Rochester in 1952 (Wilson 1952, 188) and first published by David M. Vieth (Rochester 1958, 129).

DATE December 1675 or shortly thereafter (385.15n.).

COPY-TEXT Yale MS. Osborn b.105, p. 396.

ANNOTATION
1–4 *When to the King . . . kiss mine arse*: cf. 'When first I bid my love good-morrow, / With tear in eye and hand on breast, / My heart was even drown'd in sorrow, / And I, poor soul! was much opprest' (*Roxburghe Ballads*, III 526).
2 *hand*: cf. 329.32n.

7–8 *small . . . / And great*: cf. 'the Lord will bless them all: / Yea, he will bless them every one, / the great and also small' (Sternhold and Hopkins, *The Whole Book of Psalms, Collected into English Metre* (1703), sig. C9v). In the context 'small' means both 'small in size' – Nelly was 'low in stature' (B.L. MS. Burney IV.105*) – and 'inferior in rank' as in the expression 'great and small' (*OED*).
13 *faith's defender*: part of the style of the English monarchs: Dei Gratia of England, Scotland, France and Ireland King, Defender of the Faith. The latter phrase was bestowed by Leo X on Henry VIII for his treatise, *Assertio Septem Sacramentorum* in defence of Roman Catholicism against Luther, and answered by Luther (Chamberlayne 1669, 107).
15 *new pretender*: the Duchess Mazarin was first seen at court on 8 December 1675 (*POAS*, Yale, I 279).
16 *politique*: Gramont's '*politique*' was dedicated to never losing at cards, dice, or cock-fights (Hamilton 1930, 104, 305–6).

Valentinian: A Tragedy (Great is the honour which our Emperor)

Flavius Placidus Valentinianus (419–455 A.D.) was the grandson of the Byzantine emperor Theodosius the Great. At the age of six he was proclaimed Roman emperor, the third of that name. When he assumed the imperial power in 437 A.D. upon reaching his majority, he was found to be interested neither in politics nor war. Flavius Aëtius, his *magister militum*, fought his battles and received his ambassadors. But urged by Pope Leo I, Valentinian found time amid games and debauchery to issue the famous Novel XVII of 444 A.D. giving the bishop of Rome supremacy over the provincial bishops.

Gibbon disposes of Valentinian III in a paragraph:

> Petronius Maximus, a wealthy senator of the Anician family, who had been twice consul, was possessed of a chaste and beautiful wife: her obstinate resistance served only to irritate the desires of Valentinian, and he resolved to accomplish them either by stratagem or force. Deep gaming was one of the vices of the court; the emperor, who, by chance or contrivance, had gained from Maximus a considerable sum, uncourteously exacted his ring as a security for the debt, and sent it by a trusty messenger to his wife, with an order in her husband's name that she should immediately attend the empress Eudoxia. The unsuspecting wife of Maximus was conveyed in her litter to the Imperial palace; the emissaries of her impatient lover conducted her to a remote and silent bed-chamber; and Valentinian violated, without remorse, the laws of hospitality. Her tears . . . excited Maximus to a just revenge; the desire of revenge was stimulated by ambition; and he might reasonably aspire, by the free suffrage of the Roman senate, to the throne of a detested and despicable rival. Valentinian, who supposed that every human breast was devoid like his own of friendship and gratitude, had imprudently admitted among his guards several domestics and followers of Aëtius. Two of these, of barbarian race, were persuaded to execute a sacred and honourable duty by punishing with death the assassin of their patron; and their intrepid courage did not long expect a favourable moment. Whilst Valentinian amused himself in the field of Mars with the spectacle of some military sports, they suddenly rushed upon him with drawn weapons . . . and stabbed the emperor to the heart, without

the least opposition from his numerous train, who seemed to rejoice in the tyrant's death. Such was the fate of Valentinian.

(*The History of the Decline and Fall of the Roman Empire* (1776–88), III 431–2)

This is the story that John Fletcher dramatizes in *The Tragedy of Valentinian* (*c.* 1610–14; 1647) and that Rochester adapts for the Restoration stage. Fletcher's play, which should have been called *The Tragedies of Valentinian and Maximus*, is a typical Jacobean revenge tragedy. The rape of Lucina occurs at the end of the second act but the play struggles on for another three acts in a chain reaction to the violation: Maximus causes Æcius's suicide (IV iv), poisons Valentinian (V iii), forces Valentinian's widow, Eudoxia, to marry him (V vi), and is poisoned by Eudoxia (V viii) in turn.

Of the twenty-two scenes in Fletcher's play, Rochester appropriates three almost verbatim (II i, IV i, and V iii), seven more with substantial additions (I i, II ii, III ii, IV ii–iii, V ii, iv), and adds four scenes of his own (III i, iii; V i, v).

In many of these changes Rochester anticipates Dryden's *Heads of an Answer to Rymer* (1677; 1711), which domesticates Aristotle's theory of tragedy to English practice. In adapting Fletcher's play Rochester shifts the *object* of imitation from plot to character-*plus*-'thoughts' (as Dryden prescribes). He makes the characters lovers: 'we are not touched with the sufferings of any sort of men so much as lovers', Dryden says. And he shifts the *effect* of imitation from *katharsis* to poetic justice (as Dryden also prescribes: 'the suffering of innocence and punishment of the offender is of the nature of English [but not of Greek] tragedy') (Dryden 1882–93, XV 382, 390). Dryden supposes that if Aristotle had known Shakespeare, he would have changed his theory in these ways.

Rochester may also have intended to change the title of Fletcher's play to put the emphasis squarely on 'the suffering of innocence'. The two manuscript copies of Rochester's play are entitled 'The Rape of Lucina'. But when the play was produced at court in February 1684 and published the next year, the title was *Valentinian: A Tragedy*. Many of Rochester's additions to Fletcher, notably I i 163–338, IV ii 195–231, and V v, move the play closer to Dryden's concept of tragedy and away from Aristotle's. Rochester also writes in Dryden's idiom of overstatement. The new speeches that he writes for Valentinian and Lucina cannot have been intended to represent the speech of historic figures (*De arte poetica*, 1451b); they are operatic arias, or trumpet improvisations by Roy Eldredge.

ATTRIBUTION The text of *Valentinian* exists only in one tradition:

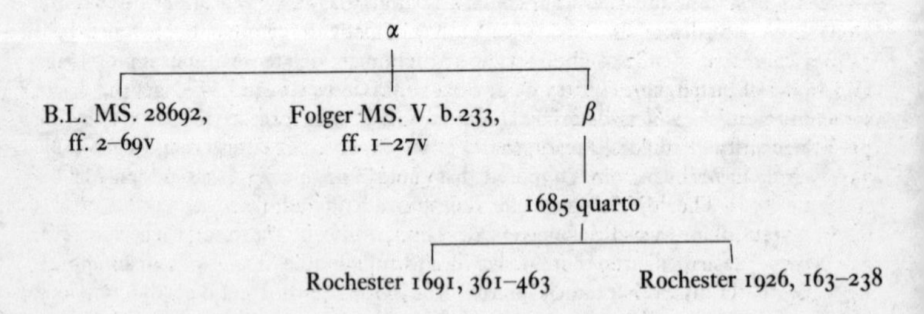

where α represents Rochester's holograph manuscript and β the prompt copy from which the 1685 quarto was set up. But the attribution of the play to Rochester is confirmed by two of his friends, Robert Wolseley and Aphra Behn, who wrote the Preface and the first Prologue for the 1685 quarto.

DATE The 'cast in the extant MSS [Richard Hart, William Wintershall, and Rebecca Marshall in the parts played by Cardell Goodman, Edward Kynaston, and Elizabeth Barry in the 1684 production] implies performance or intended performance by the King's Company *c.* 1675–76' (Downes 1987, 83n.).

COPY-TEXT *Valentinian: A Tragedy. As 'tis Alter'd by the late Earl of Rochester, and Acted at the Theatre-Royal* (1685). Whereas there appear to be two 1685 editions of this work, one 'Printed for Timothy Goodwin' and another 'Printed for Henry Herringman, and are to be sold by Jos. Knight, and Fr. Saunders', the evidence of collation shows that the apparent two are in fact one edition.

EMENDATION OF THE COPY-TEXT **I i 16** his] the **36** fool] fowl **40** traitors, bawds, and wenches] Whores and Bawds and Traitors **43** ragged] rugged **55** those] these **60–63** whilst gods . . . our honours] om. **71** fellows] followers **72** or] And **73** this Emperor] the Emperor **83** For goodness sake] om. **223–4** Each man . . . but I] om. **269** need . . . succours] needs . . . succour **275** look] hope **295–8** None in . . . their turn] om. **414** on] near **421** those] these **423** loving] loading **II i 12** too] to **14** smoky] smoaking **15** blessed] blooming **64** for't] for Her **85** But] om. **98** this is] these are **99** unto] to **100** rarely] om. **125** Madam] om. **140** Runs] Run **171** this] the **173** gelded] hang'd **II ii 18** to her] and to her **64** for] a **66** Let me perish] om. **67** But] Well **69** pleased] us'd **70** ashes] Death **80** sect] Sex **82** fat or] om. **109** Well] om. what's thought] What's to be thought **112** purchase] purpose **119** right] Rights **120** has] hath **122** True to . . . all temptation] om. **135** to] of **147** whips and jails] Jayls and Whips **158** Which adds this flaming . . . fire] A Virtue that adds . . . Flames **III i 25** *Lycias*] *Marcellina* **64** *Here begins the dance of satyrs, which is to represent a frightful dream to Lucina*] Here begins the Masque which is to represent a frightful dream to Lucina MS. *Dance of Satyrs* 1685 4° **65–90** Now to . . . haste away] om. **67** Chylax] Proculus MS. **III ii 8** sir] om. **11** Besides] om. **13–14** For by . . . receive us] om. **16** Then] That **25** VALENTINIAN. Hah?] MAXIMUS. Hah. **III iii 16** honour] Honours **21** desire] Desires **32** on fire] a-fire **57** fills] fits **66** in] with **74** pleases] please **83** Methought] Methoughts **145** assent] consent **IV i 10** true-hearted] true **17** One stroke] om. **65–6** And like . . . do sometimes] om. **69** slave drinks] Slaves drink **70** this too, that] 'em too **71–3** the charity . . . tailors, nurses] om. **79–81** To give . . . and roots] om. **79** a hail to] an MS. om. 1685 4° **89** hold] find **IV ii 14** suddenly] sudden **19** They'd] They'l **31** the] that **36** here] om. **60–65** You think . . . heard you] om. **79** find] finds **83** those] these **120** deserve] desire **129** much-loved lord unto] lov'd Lord to **155** warming] warning **IV iii 14** thorough] through **27** it 'tis] it is **28** o'th'] of our **30** 's] om. **40–43** I'll melt . . . watch 'em] om. **45** Ay] om. **101–6** Those fires . . . to you] om. **127** hold] do **135** his] the **153–4** They have . . . thankful for't] om. **159–63** Must not . . . sad fortune] om. **164** prize] price

185 'T has] Thus **203** one 'mongst] among **207** Long] A long **208** As] And as **222** But a short year] om. so long] om. **223** with grief] om. **226** becoming] coming **231** wrong] Wrongs **292** no] not **293** would to god you were] that thou wert **372** 'gainst] on **377–9** Base notion ... th' dogs'] om. **393** as we see her] om. V i **4** might] may **31** is some] is there some V ii **12** weight] weights wood] Wooll **45** I have ... for ye] om. **58** sin] Sins **92** of this Æcius] of *Æcius* **120** would] will **125** kiss] kill **153** name and dignity of Caesar sacred] sacred Name and Dignity of *Caesar* V iii **13** hit] om. **20** lives too] Lives **31** be traitor] be a Traitor V iv **7** out] om. **8** adventure] Adventures **61** wet] om. **115** promised us] promised **118** and] om. **128** killed] kill **137** wert] art **196** To] om. **197** Of] om. **200** honours] hours **204** planed] plain'd **212** yet] and **216** what] all that V v **77** And pacify ... dear boy] om. **162** for] in **164** and] or **179** thou art] she was **253** start] part
The emendation of II i 173 and II ii 80 is preserved in Fletcher's text. Emendations of I i 36, IV iii 14, and V ii 153 are preserved in Rochester 1691, 370, 424, and 445. Conjectural emendations by the present editor are offered at I i 72, III i 64 (stage direction), III i 79, III ii 25, IV i 79, IV iii 27, V ii 12 (weight), V iv 196, V iv 197, and V iv 204. The remaining emendations are preserved in B.L. MS. 28692, ff. 2–69.

ANNOTATION

I i follows Fletcher's I iii but adds I i 1–27, 163–338, 468–78.

I i 26 *provinces fall*: Valentinian III lost Carthage (Libya) (Procopius, *De bello Vandalico*, III iii).

I i 128 *the Bruti*: instigated by the murder of his father and brother by Tarquinius Superbus and the rape of Lucretia by Sextus Tarquinius, Lucius Junius Brutus aroused the Romans to expel the Tarquin dynasty. Marcus Junius Brutus with much less instigation (or none at all) assassinated Julius Caesar in 44 B.C.

I i 144 *Roman glory ... languishes*: the time of the action of the play, 455 A.D., approaches the moment when the Huns and Ostrogoths, who now constituted almost all of the Roman army, set aside the last Roman emperor, Romulus Augustus, on 4 September 476 A.D.

I i 170 *sacrifice and prayers*: cf. 'sacrifice ... prayers' (*A Scene of Sir Robert Howard's Play*, 187.134–5).

I i 192–3 *honour ... other merit*: cf. 'He that loses his honesty has nothing else to lose' (Tilley H539).

I i 199 *destructive thunder*: cf. 'thunder ... kills' (*A Scene of Sir Robert Howard's Play*, 191.267).

I i 222 *by the gods*: actually by his grandfather, Theodosius the Great, in 425 A.D.

I i 258 *a low myrtle in the humble vale*: cf. 'A Lilly of the valley ... in the humble grass' (Blake 1957, 127).

I i 278 *north winds drive the torrent*: cf. 'torrents drive ... / North winds' (*A Scene of Sir Robert Howard's Play*, 190.223–4).

I i 318–25 *Go call your wives to council ... / And if you prove successful bawds, be great*: 'I must quote Ronsard', Nemours says in Nathaniel Lee's *The Princess of Cleves*, I ii 63 (*c.* December 1682; 1689) (Downes 1987, 80), but the lines he quotes are these (Graham Greene, *TLS*, 2 November 1935, 697).

I i 353 *Empress*: this and IV iii 313 are the only references in the play to the spectacularly beautiful Licinia Eudoxia, Valentinian's first cousin, whom he married in 437 A.D., and who is the only major character left alive at the end of Fletcher's *Valentinian*.

I i 380 *Nero*: Roman emperor 54–68 A.D. He re-enacted the burning of Troy by setting fire to Rome, which he celebrated in song to the accompaniment, not of a fiddle, but of a lyre.
I i 424 *Julius or Germanicus*: the conquest of Gaul by Julius Caesar is recorded by himself. The conquest of Germany by Germanicus, the nephew of Tiberius, is recorded by Tacitus.
I i 445 *service*: Aetius's most celebrated victory was that over Attila the Hun near Châlons in 451 A.D.
I i 456 *slings, and arrows*: cf. 'Slings and Arrowes' (*Hamlet*, III i 58).
II i follows Fletcher's I ii, cutting nine lines and adding none.
II i 30 *And*: if, were I.
II i 81 *Numa*: Numa Pompilius followed Romulus among the legendary kings of Rome.
II i 82 *Octavius*: the emperor Augustus (63 B.C.–14 A.D.) was born Gaius Octavius and called Octavian until he was granted the title Augustus in 27 B.C.
II i 116–19 *devils . . . heaven*: neither Fletcher nor Rochester seems to have decided whether Lucina was pagan or Christian; besides 'angels' and 'grace' (IV iii 91, 239) she repeatedly invokes 'the gods' (I i 201; IV iii 64).
II ii follows Fletcher's I i but adds II ii 114–88.
II ii 23 *two*: i.e. two hundred.
II ii 29 *they to try*: their constancy to be tried; *twice as many*: i.e. twice as many as two hundred (121.23).
II ii 30 *Under*: for less than; i.e. to procure 400 for less than £1,000.
II ii 47 *as much spleen as doves have*: i.e. none: 'Doves have no gall' (Tilley D574).
II ii 91 *pointed to a Lucrece*: Lucina's gesture (in the picture gallery) creates suspense, for Lucrece committed suicide after her rape by Sextus Tarquinius (Livy, I 57–9).
II ii 102–3 *A young man should not dare to read / His moral books*: cf. 'young men, whom Aristotle thought / Unfit to heare Morall Philosophie' (Shakespeare, *Troilus and Cressida*, II ii 166–7); what Aristotle says is 'a young man is not a proper hearer of lectures in political science' (*Ethica Nicomachea*, 1095a).
II ii 107 *it*: being bawdy.
II ii 112 *nets*: cf. 'You dance in a net and think nobody sees you' (Tilley N130).
II ii 122 *the budget*: the beggar's bag for scraps.
II ii 180 *worth a thousand women's nicenesses*: cf. 'a sweet soft page of mine / Does the trick worth forty wenches' (37.15–16). One of Rochester's pages was Jean Baptiste Bellefasse/fesse (*The Rochester–Savile Letters 1671–1680*, ed. John Harold Wilson (1941), 113).
III i is entirely Rochester's.
III i-ii B.L. MS. 28692 calls for a masque between III i and III ii. The text of 'A Mask made at the Request of the late Earl of Rochester, for the Tragedy of *Valentinian*' is included in Nahum Tate's *Poems by Several Hands, and on Several Occasions* (1685), 17–32. It has been attributed to Sir Francis Fane and to Nahum Tate (*DNB*, VI 1037; Giles Jacob, *Poetical Register*, 2 vols. (1719–20), I 321). In the acting version of the play it was (presumably) replaced by a dance of satyrs.
III ii follows Fletcher's II i, but it is heavily rewritten and the interruption by Balbus is added (III ii 44–56).
III ii 1 *set*: in a dice game like craps Valentinian has a hot hand and won't let the other players quit. He insists that they set, or offer, bets that he can cover.

III ii 61–2 *which end of the lady, / Her nose?*: Rochester grafts a Shakespearean joke (*Antony and Cleopatra*, I ii 63) on to Fletcher's simple question, 'But how for her?' (II i).
III iii is entirely Rochester's except III iii 1–4 from Fletcher's II ii 1–4.
III iii 50 *rules . . . affected*: cf. 'Affected rules of honour' (23.12).
III iii 82–3 *Debates . . . betwixt the pow'rs above / And those below*: in 'A Mask made at the Request of the late Earl of Rochester, for the Tragedy of *Valentinian*' (III i–ii above), the debate is between Mercury (who sides with Valentinian) and Venus (who sides with Lucina). Venus invokes Pluto to settle the argument. Pluto rules that 'Women were made . . . to be ravished' (28), whereupon Mercury decrees that 'Great *Valentinian* shall enjoy his Love' (32). Pluto orders his satyrs 'to prepare the willing Fall, / And in soft Dreams preach Honour's Funeral. *Enter Satyrs, and Dance*' (32).
III iii 90–92 *When . . . I came distressed, / . . . Why would you not protect by these your streams*: cf. '"fer, pater," inquit "opem. Si flumina numen habetis"' ('Oh help,' she [Daphne] cried, 'in this extremest need, / If water gods are deities indeed') (Ovid, *Metamorphoses*, I 545; Dryden 1882–93, XII 92).
III iii 91 *absence*: Maximus's absence; *seeking peace and rest*: cf. 'Wrapped in security and rest' (34.130).
III iii 102–3 *when I would have fled, / My limbs benumbed or dead*: cf. 'vix prece finita torpor gravis occupat artus' (when her feet she [Daphne] found / Benumbed with cold, and fastened to the ground) (Ovid, *Metamorphoses*, I 548; Dryden 1882–93, XII 92).
III iii 185 *his orders in his hand*: cf. 'Mounted to the cabin with his orders in his hand' ('Casey Jones', *The Viking Book of Folk Ballads*, ed. Albert B. Friedman (1956), 310).
III iii 213 *sacrifice . . . glory to . . . love*: the distinguishing dilemma of heroic drama exists here (ironically and mistakenly) only in Lucina's mind. So far from having to sacrifice glory to love, Maximus and Lucina are victims of a scam.
IV i follows Fletcher's II iii almost word for word, cutting half-a-dozen lines and adding none.
IV i 17 *One stroke*: Æcius proposes trial by combat limited to a single blow of the broadsword.
IV i 75–7 *pikes to ploughshares . . . / swords . . . / To . . . pruning-knives*: cf. 'beat their swords into plowshares, and their spears into pruninghooks' (Isaiah 2.4).
IV ii follows Fletcher II iv but writes Lycias into the scene, adds IV ii 8–10, 25–31, 36–66, 74–9, 81–2, 84–103, 195–231, and rewrites IV ii 104–31, 158–95.
IV ii 41 *the first*: the superstition that the first person greeted shall be transformed (*Motif-Index* D526).
IV ii 48–9 *owned / By Maximus*: Chylax, one of Valentinian's 'noble Panders', pretends (with heavy sarcasm) to be 'the worthy friend' (IV ii 118) of Maximus.
IV ii 84–103 For Fletcher's two songs, 'Now the lusty Spring is seen' and 'Hear ye Ladies that despise' (II iv), Rochester substitutes his own equally suggestive song, 'Injurious charmer of my vanquished heart', which Lucina does not understand (144.114–15).
IV ii 92 *that*: anyone who (?).
IV ii 93 *With*: on some (?); *therein*: the syntax is obscure but the antecedent of 'therein' seems not to be 'heart' (l. 92), but 'that' (l. 92): i.e. in anyone who would, on some vain pretence, terminate a love affair, falsehood might lie. The text may be corrupt.
IV ii 95 *die*: suicide, the last resort of the rejected lover.

IV ii 103 *expire*: the double meaning of 'expire' (354.69n.) finally clarifies the dramatic situation. The poem turns out to be an unusual *carpe diem* exhortation: 'let . . . hearts be joined' (143.100) at the *end* of the affair; cf. 'one other gawdy night' (*Antony and Cleopatra* (1606–7); 1623), III xiii 183). The song does not quite fit the dramatic situation in the play.
IV ii 215 *shrieks*: listening to the shrieks of a woman being raped is tabu (*Motif-Index* C885.2).
IV iii follows Fletcher's III i but adds IV iii 1–23, 333–81, 383–6, 396–411.
IV iii 315 *one that truly lives*: refers back to Maximus's wish that Æcius were dead and thus unable to prevent Maximus's revenge on Valentinian (156.293).
IV iii 333–81 Reasoning high on foreordination (like the fallen angels) Maximus comes to the conclusion that evil is coexistent with deity (158.368), the Manichaean heresy against which Valentinian III issued Novel XVIII in June 446. Rochester signals the importance of these lines by casting them in cinquains rhyming $A^5 B^5 A^5 B^5 B^5$.
IV iii 346 *The last of men*: cf. 'the last of men' (25.[1]2).
V i is entirely Rochester's.
V ii follows Fletcher's III iv but adds V ii 74–138, 140–61.
V ii 4 *angel . . . devils*: even though he was raised in the palace of Theodosius the Great and in the viceregal court at Ravenna, Valentinian's 'religion was questionable', Gibbon says (III 431–2). He seems to have been more interested in haruspication and astrology than angels and devils.
V ii 48 *Messalina . . . Laïs*: Messalina Valeria (d. 48 A.D.), wife of the emperor Tiberius, prostituted herself in the streets. She is celebrated in Juvenal, *Satire* VI. Laïs (*c.* 340 B.C.) was an expensive prostitute with a sense of humour who became the mistress of Alcibiades.
V ii 82 *Tisiphone*: one of the Furies who punish the wicked in Tartarus. Her attributes include a whip, snaky hair, and snaky bracelets.
V ii 148 *the late discourse*: at I i 337–467.
V iii follows Fletcher's IV iii almost word for word but brings on Aretus after IV iii 19 to overhear the rest of the scene.
V iv follows Fletcher's IV iv but adds V iv 1–4, 89–95.
V iv 92 *Subura*: a district of imperial Rome between the Viminal and Esquiline hills.
V iv 185–230 If Rochester had undertaken the final recension of the text that Wolseley says he intended (1685 4°, sig. A2r), he might have cut the over-sufficient dying words of Pontius along with the following 136 lines of Fletcher's IV iv, which he did cut.
V v is entirely Rochester's.
V v 15–22 For Fletcher's song, 'Care-charming sleep, thou easer of all woes' (V ii), Rochester substitutes the last two stanzas of 'Give me leave to rail at you' (16.[1]9–16).
V v 132 *cut off thy right hand*: the full form of this piece of folklore (*Motif-Index* Q451.1.6) is preserved in Procopius, *De bello Vandalico*, III iv 28: 'he . . . cut off his own right hand with the other'.
V v 167–8 *Tarquin . . . Lucrece*: see I i 128n.
V v 175 *Brutus' vengeance*: see I i 128n.
V v 208 *solid pains*: 'pain can ne'er deceive' (70.32).
V v 227 *striving for the way . . . murdered him*: cf. 'the old man wanted to thrust me out of the way . . . I killed them all' (Sophocles, *Oedipus Tyrannos*, trans. David Grene, 805–13).
V v 270 *Search heav'n for blessings*: cf. 'search heaven' (74.70).

Here's Monmouth the witty and Lauderdale the pretty

ATTRIBUTION The verses are attributed to Rochester in three ms. copies (B.L. MS. Add. 29921, f. 3v; B.L. MS. Harl. 7316, f. 18r; Chetham MS. Mun. A.4.14, f. 64v), in Hearne's diary (*Reliquiae Hearnianae*, I 119), and in the copy-text, representing at least two independent textual traditions.

DATE The copy in Yale MS. Osborn b.54, p. 873 is dated 1676.

COPY-TEXT *The Agreeable Companion; or, An Universal Medley of Wit and Good-Humour* (1745), 341.

ANNOTATION

1 *Monmouth the witty*: Monmouth's most famous attempt at wit may have occurred in January 1680: to the King's command that he return to The Hague, Monmouth replied, 'If His Majesty pleased to send over the Duchess of Portsmouth, Duke of Lauderdale and Lord Sunderland, which would be as useful to him, he would go in the same yacht' (HMC *Ormonde MSS.*, n.s. IV 575). But the King was not amused and Monmouth's career as rebel was launched.

2 *Fraser*: like Dr Sir Alexander Fraser, Dr Alexander Bendo, Rochester's *alter ego*, graduated M.D. from the University of Montpellier and specialized 'in bringing quick relief to poor girls, from all the maladies and accidents, which might have been induced by an excess of loving-kindness towards their neighbours, or by an immoderate regard for their own entertainment' (Hamilton 1930, 258).

3 *the Duke for a jest*: the Duke of York was 'renown'd / For Pox and Popery' (Rochester 1709 (Booksellers), ²10).

4 *the King for a grand politician*: cf. 398.2n.

A Scene of Sir Robert Howard's Play, written by the Earl of Rochester (Lead faster on! Why creep you thus to fight?)

The title of Sir Robert's play is preserved in Dryden's letter of 3 September 1697:

> After my return to town [he writes to his sons in Rome] I intend to alter a play of Sir Robert Howard's written long since, and lately put by him into my hands: 'tis called *The Conquest of China by the Tartars.* It will cost me six weeks study, with the probable benefit of an hundred pounds.

But two or three months later Dryden put aside the play to work on a second edition of his translation of Virgil (Dryden 1882–93, XVIII, 133–4, 138), and Howard's play was neither produced nor printed.

ATTRIBUTION Attribution of the scene to Rochester made in the title of the two surviving ms. copies is confirmed in Sir Robert Howard's letter to Rochester thanking him for 'the sceen you are pleased to write' (Rochester *Letters* 1980, 116).

DATE Shortly before 7 April 1676, the inferred date of Sir Robert's letter to Rochester (Treglown, *RES*, n.s. 30 (1979), 434–6).

COPY-TEXT B. L. MS. 28692, ff. 70–75. Folger MS. V.b.233 (unfoliated) may be a copy of the British Library text, but it is much more likely that the two manuscripts are collateral descendants of the archetype. The Folger manuscript has been 'corrected' by another hand of no authority.

EMENDATION OF COPY-TEXT **109** pays for thee] pays thee **144** sue] shue **153** proof] profe **248** ye] the **265** arms] Arme

The readings adopted in ll. 144, 153, and 265 are preserved in Folger MS. V.b.233. Those in ll. 109 and 248 are conjectural.

ANNOTATION
28 *conquests of her eyes*: cf. 'conquering eyes' (8.²7).
82 *general of the field*: acting field marshal, the rank above general.
122 *greensickness of her mind*: cf. 'Vertue's no more in Woman-kind / But the greensicknesse of the mind' (John Cleveland, *The Poems*, ed. Brian Morris *et al.* (1967), 55).
236 *Cutting my . . . way*: cf. 'Cutting my way through a wall of living flesh, dragging a canoe behind me' (W. C. Fields, *My Little Chickadee* (1940)).
267 *thunder*: i.e. thunderbolts, 'formerly . . . believed to be the destructive agent in a lightning-flash' (*OED*).

Song (How happy, Cloris, were they free)

The survival of three versions of the same poem may help to dispel the myth, promoted by Alexander Pope, that Rochester was a 'holiday writer' who diverted himself 'now and then' with poetry (Spence 1966, I 201); cf. 365.

ATTRIBUTION The first version of the poem is attributed to Rochester in Rochester 1680², 68–9 and Rochester 1685, 58–9, derived from it. The attribution is presumably confirmed by a copy of the second version in Rochester's hand with corrections in Rochester's hand (Nottingham MS. Portland Pw V 31, f. 1).

DATE OF COMPOSITION If ll. 9–10 refer to Sir Fopling Flutter, as seems likely, the first version of the poem must have been written after 11 March 1676 when *The Man of Mode; or Sir Fopling Flutter* opened at Dorset Garden (393.10n.).

COPY-TEXT Rochester 1680², 68–9.

ANNOTATION
3 *formal*: the word may suggest that Cloris is not really jealous but feels that she ought to register jealousy; 'how can you entertain a jealousy', Rochester asks Elizabeth Barry (Rochester *Letters* 1980, 148).
10 *flutters*: the most egregious fop to burst upon the London scene 'piping hot from *Paris*' was Sir Fopling Flutter, the title role created by William Smith in *The Man of Mode; or Sir Fopling Flutter*, written by Rochester's friend, George Etherege, and with Rochester's mistress, Elizabeth Barry, playing Mrs Loveit, which opened at Dorset Garden on 11 March 1676 (*London Stage*, I 243; Downes 1987, 76–7).
19 *pleasure*: cf. I never 'thought it an abuse, / While you had pleasure for excuse' (34.123–4).
19–20 *did you love your pleasure less, / You were not fit for me*: 'possibly alluding to Lovelace's famous song [*To Lucasta, Going to the Wars*]: "I could not love thee, dear, so much / Loved I not honour more"' (Rochester 1968, 83).
23–4 *lusty . . . grapes . . . lusty*: cf. 'Stain'd with bloud of lusty Grapes, / In a thousand lusty shapes' (John Fletcher, *The Tragedy of Valentinian* (1610–14?), V viii) (Rochester 1984, 249).

Song (How perfect, Cloris, and how free)

ATTRIBUTION The only witness to the text is the copy-text, in Rochester's hand with corrections in Rochester's hand, but the attribution to Rochester of the first and third versions of the poem is confirmed by external evidence.

DATE 11 March–12 June 1676?

COPY-TEXT Nottingham MS. Portland Pw V 31, f. 1.

EMENDATION OF COPY-TEXT Title *Song*] om. 18 flutters] flutter
27 your] you
The title and emendations are supplied from Rochester 1680², 68–9.

Song (Such perfect bliss, fair Cloris, we)

The critical reader will decide for himself which of these three versions of the song is the best. The answer is given below.

ATTRIBUTION The third version of this song is attributed to Rochester in two copies representing the same textual tradition: Harvard MS. 636F, p. 8 and Rochester 1691, 36–8. The attribution is presumably confirmed by a copy of the second version of the song in Rochester's hand with corrections in Rochester's hand (Nottingham MS. Portland w V 31, f. 1).

DATE Before 12 June 1676 when the copy-text was licensed for publication.

COPY-TEXT *A New Collection of the Choicest Songs. Now in Esteem in Town or Court* (1676), sig. A4 (Wing N597).

EMENDATION OF COPY-TEXT Title *Song*] *Against Jealousie*
15 liquor] ------ 29–32] om.
The title is supplied from Rochester 1680², 68–9. The omissions are supplied from Harvard MS. 636F, p. 8, where the poem is entitled *To A Lady, in A Letter*.

ANNOTATION
13 *that*: the missing *modifié* is uncertain: ability/gullet/'devouring cunt' (34.119).

Leave this gaudy, gilded stage

Ben Jonson's *Ode to Himself* (Come leave the lothed stage) addresses the 'vulgar censure' of his play *The New Inne* (1629; 1631) (Jonson 1925–52, VI 492–4). Rochester's poem addresses a third person, presumably an actress (Rochester 1968, 85). Besides the first line, Rochester borrows only the mock-Pindaric form of Jonson's poem.

Jonson's poem 'initiated a chain of responses by Randolph, Carew, "I.C.", and other poets, none of which approaches the independence of Rochester's proposal of a sexual alternative ("love's theatre, the bed") where Jonson resigned himself to the Alcaic lute' (Treglown 1973, 43).

ATTRIBUTION The only copy of this poem survives in Rochester's hand and corrected in Rochester's hand. It was first published in Pinto 1935, 120.

COPY-TEXT Nottingham MS. Portland Pw V 31, f. 4r.

EMENDATION OF COPY-TEXT 9 the] this

Against Constancy (Tell me no more of constancy)

This argument in standard ballad metre for sexual promiscuity was set to music by an anonymous composer *c.* 1678–82 (Macdonald Emslie, *TLS*, 26 February 1954, 137). It was added to the Rochester canon by David M. Vieth (*TLS*, 6 November 1953, 716).

ATTRIBUTION The attribution to Rochester in Bodl. MS. Don.b.8, p. 561 is not confirmed by external evidence. The compiler of this manuscript, Sir William Haward, Knt., was a gentleman in ordinary of the privy chamber to Charles II and *ex officio* an acquaintance of Rochester (Sir Edward Bysshe, *A Visitation of the County of Surrey*, ed. Sir St George J. Armytage (1910), 58). So the combination of circumstantial evidence and internal evidence of style, imagery, and tone may create a high degree of probability that Rochester wrote these verses.

DATE Before 12 June 1676, when the copy-text was licensed for publication.

COPY-TEXT *A New Collection of the Choicest Songs. Now in Esteem in Town or Court* (1676), sig. A7r (Wing N597).

EMENDATION OF COPY-TEXT 3 cold] old 5 on] or
The emendations are the readings of both ms. copies: B.L. MS. 29396, f. 107v and Bodl. MS. Don.b.8, p. 561 (Rochester 1984, 166).

ANNOTATION
1 *Tell me no more*: six other seventeenth-century poems begin with this formula (Treglown 1973, 43); *constancy*: cf. 'tedious, trading constancy' (67.56).
7 *higher to advance*: in the *gradus ad Cytheram* (311.16n.).
20 *for worms*: 'to worms' is the reading of both the ms. copies, but J. L. Mackie argues for the more difficult reading of the copy-text: 'the poet is speaking of exchanging one mistress *for* another, and the appropriate antithesis to this is the notice of Fate exchanging [the poet] *for* worms, as if at some stage Fate should get tired of [the poet] and prefer worms instead. The notion of changing one thing *into* another is not strictly appropriate here' (*TLS*, 19 February 1954, 121).

To the Postboy (Son of a whore, God damn you, can you tell)

This is another report from the Maimed Debauchee (87), not in the person of the Vice, but in the person of the Ancient Mariner (396.15n.), compelled for penance to tell the tale of the 'hellish thing' that he had done. '"To the Postboy" is a low-style equivalent of Horace's confessional satires, in which he honestly acknowledges his own moral shortcomings, thus enhancing the . . . authenticity of the satires' (Raman Selden, *English Verse Satire 1590–1765* (1978, 97); cf. 381.3n.

ATTRIBUTION The poem is attributed to Rochester in nine ms. copies (Vienna MS. 14090, f. 128; B.L. MS. Harl. 6914, f. 21; V&A MS. Dyce 43, p. 241; Bodl. MS. Firth c.15, p. 15; Nottingham MS. Portland Pw V 42, pp. 20–21; Princeton MS. Taylor 2, p. 8; Princeton MS. Taylor 3, p. 254; Ohio MS. p. 16; Illinois MS. [The Commonplace book. Poems], f. 16v) representing at least two independent textual traditions. J. H. Wilson's surmise that the 'Buffoon Conceit' in Sir Carr Scrope's *In Defense of Satire* (*POAS*, Yale, I 367) is *To the Postboy* (*MLN* 56 (1941), 373) provides further evidence.

DATE Shortly after Captain Downs's death on 27 June 1676 (396.10n.).

COPY-TEXT B.L. MS. Harl. 6914, f. 21.

ANNOTATION
1 *Son of a whore, God damn you*: cf. 'he [Rochester] could not speak with any warmth, without repeated Oaths, which, upon any sort of provocation, came almost naturally from him' (Burnet 1680, 152).

1–2 *can you tell / . . . the readiest way to Hell*: cf. 'can as eas'ly tell / How many yards and inches 'tis to hell' (Suckling 1971, I 68).
4 *Furies*: with whips of scorpions Tisiphone, Megara, and Alecto executed the vengeance of the classical gods; cf. 391.82n.
5 *Sodom's walls*: defending a door against sexual aggressors, with the embattled constable of Epsom in the role of Lot, is common to the story of Sodom (Genesis 19) and the brawl at Epsom (396.10n.).
6–7 *or the college of Rome's cardinals. / Witness*: under the weight of the collective sexual expertise of the seventy-odd cardinals in the Sacred College, the iambic metre breaks down completely; *heroic scars*: cf. 'honourable scars' (87.21).
9 *fled*: it was said that in the Epsom brawl Rochester 'first ingaged & first fled and abjectly hid himselfe' (Marvell 1927, II 322).
10 *left my life's defender dead*: 'one of the strangest acts of contrition on record' (Vieth 1963, 201). 'Mr. [i.e. Captain] Downs is dead. The Ld. Rochester doth abscond, and soe doth [George] Etheridge, and Capt. Bridges who ocasioned the riot Sunday sennight [18 June 1676]. They were tossing some fidlers in a blanket [cf. 'in *Epsom* Blankets tost' (Dryden 1956–   , II 55) (Vieth 1963, 143n.)] for refusing to play, and a barber, upon the noise, going to see what the matter, they seized upon him, and, to free himself from them, he offered to carry them to the handsomest woman in Epsom, and directed them to the constables house, who demanding what they came for, they told him a whore, and, he refusing to let them in, they broke open his doores and broke his head, and beate him very severely. At last, he made his escape, called his watch, and Etheridge made a submissive oration to them and soe far appeased them that the constable dismissed his watch. But presently after, the Ld. Rochester drew upon the constable, Mr. Downs, to prevent his pass, seized on him, the constable cryed out murther, and, the watch returning, one came behind Mr. Downs and with a sprittle staff cleft his scull. The Ld. Rochester and the rest run away, and Downs, having noe sword, snatched up a sticke and striking at them, they run him into the side with a half pike, and so bruised his arme that he wase never able to stirr it after' (Hatton Correspondence, I 133–4). Downs died on 27 June 1676 (HMC *Seventh Report*, 467).
14 *blasphemed . . . God*: in Seneca's *Troas,* Act 2. Chorus (39) (?); *libelled kings*: in *On King Charles* (30) (?).
15 *ne'er stir*: the speaker's repetition of this injunction (l. 7) may indicate that the postboy is anxious to get away from this not-so-ancient mariner.

On the Supposed Author of a Late Poem in Defence of Satire (To rack and torture thy unmeaning brain)

Sir Carr Scrope's 'censures' of Rochester's verse provoked a reply in *An Allusion to Horace* (101.115–17). Sir Carr shot back *In Defence of Satire*, an imitation of Horace's *Satire* I iv in which he defends his practice but warns his readers to beware of an unnamed man who

> To fatal midnight frolics can betray
> His brave companion and then run away,
> Leaving him to be murdered in the street,
> Then put it off with some buffoon conceit,

i.e. *To the Postboy* (Vieth 1963, 201). Having already confessed his guilt in *To the*

Postboy, Rochester may have resented this attack sufficiently to justify the *ad hominem* lampoon that is the present poem. 'To make a *Satyre* without Resentments', he told Burnet, 'was as if a man would in cold blood cut mens throats who had never offended him' (Burnet 1680, 26). Swift, who knew better, determined that '*Anger and Fury, though they add Strength to the* Sinews *of the* Body, *yet are found to relax those of the* Mind, *and to render all its Efforts feeble and impotent*' (Swift 1939–68, I 140).

ATTRIBUTION The poem is attributed to Rochester in four ms. copies (Edinburgh MS. DC.1.3, p. 13; Harvard MS. Eng. 623F, pp. 37–8; Harvard MS. Eng. 636F, pp. 51–3; Yale MS. Osborn b.54, pp. 1021–4) and the copy-text, representing two independent textual traditions.

DATE 'Probably summer 1676' (Rochester 1984, 298).

COPY-TEXT Rochester 1680[1], 49–50.

ANNOTATION
6 *God made one on man when he made thee*: cf. 'Nature has done the business of lampoon' (43.29).
11 *A lump . . . shapeless . . . born*: cf. 'born a shapeless Lump' (Dryden 1956– , II 10).
15 The chiastic sound effect, *l*ove's thy *b*usiness, *b*eauty thy de*l*ight', recurs in Dryden and Pope. [numbered above the letters: 1 2 3 3 2 1]
21 *an ugly beau garçon*: cf. Mulgrave 'thinks himself a beau garçon' (Scrope, *In Defence of Satire*, *POAS*, Yale, I 369). Nell Gwyn calls Scrope an ugly beau garçon in a letter of June 1678 (Wilson 1952, 288).
27–8 *proved, / . . . beloved*: the imperfect rhymes here and in ll. 21–2 make these the most prominent couplets in the poem, both of them emphasizing Scrope's unattractiveness to women or women's unattractiveness to him. In either case Scrope died unmarried and the baronetcy became extinct.
31 *scarce half brave*: Scrope's younger brother John was killed by the 'Bully Knight', Sir Thomas Armstrong, in a fight over an actress, Susanna Uphill, on 28 August 1675 (HMC *Seventh Report*, 465; Hatton Correspondence, I 121; Langbaine 1691, 460). Scrope responded in *In Defence of Satire* by calling Armstrong a Bessus, the cowardly braggart in Beaumont and Fletcher's *A King and No King* (1619) (*POAS*, Yale, I 369). 'His brother murder'd', Buckingham observes, 'yet still his pen's his sword' (*POAS*, Yale, I 391).
33–4 *not . . . anything . . . but an ass*: Scrope's parting shot is an epigram:

> Rail on, poor feeble scribbler, speak of me
> In as ill terms as the world speaks of thee.
> Sit swelling in thy hole like a vex'd toad,
> And all thy pox and malice spit abroad.
> Thou canst blast no man's name by thy ill word:
> Thy pen is full as harmless as thy sword.
> (*POAS*, Yale, I 373)

Pope alludes to Scrope's lines in *An Epistle to Dr. Arbuthnot* (1734) (Pope 1939–67, IV 118–19) (James A. Means, *N&Q* 228 (February 1983), 34).

God bless our good and gracious King

'According to one source, these famous verses were "*Posted on* White-Hall-Gate". The antiquary Thomas Hearne describes them as "the lord Rochester's verses upon the king, on occasion of his majestie's saying, he would leave every one to his liberty in talking, when himself was in company, and would not take what was said at all amiss" [*Reliquiae Hearnianae*, I 119–20]. Still another account relates that "King Cha: praiseing the Translation of the Psalmes, Lord Rochester said Ile show you presently [i.e. right away] how they run"' [B.L. MS. Harl. 6914, f. 8v] (Rochester 1968, 134). Given Rochester's interest in '*the Sternholdian* Strain' (18, 344.176n.), the last account not only seems most likely but also recalls Johnson's parody of Thomas Percy's ballad in similar circumstances (James Boswell, *The Life of Samuel Johnson, LL.D.*, ed. G. Birkbeck Hill and L. F. Powell, 6 vols. (1934–50), II 136n.). Rochester's epigram sounds like a parody of Sternhold and Hopkins's version of Psalm XIX:

> The fear of God is excellent
> and doth endure forever:
> The judgments of the Lord are true,
> and righteous altogether.
> (*The Whole Book of Psalms, Collected into English Metre* (1703), [sig. A5v])

In his reply to *An Allusion to Horace*, Dryden predictably calls Rochester 'this legitimate son of Sternhold' (Dryden 1882–93, V 336).

ATTRIBUTION The epigram is attributed to Rochester in the copy-text, in Princeton MS. M.a.104, p. 39, Princeton MS. V.a.308, f. 108v, *Reliquiae Hearnianae*, I 119–20, and in Rochester 1707 (Bragge),[4]135, representing three independent textual traditions.

COPY-TEXT B.L. MS. Harl. 6914, f. 8v.

ANNOTATION
2 *Whose promise none relies on*: cf. 'those princes have accomplished most who paid little heed to keeping their promises . . . Thus a prudent prince cannot and should not keep his word when to do so would go against his interest' (Machiavelli 1977, 49–50).

Love and Life (All my past life is mine no more)

These verses in a five-line version of common ballad metre, $A^4B^3A^4A^4B^3$, like *Fair Cloris in a pigsty lay* (22), versify the *Leviathan*:

> The *Present* onely has a being in Nature; things *Past* have a being in the Memory onely, but things *to come* have no being at all; the *Future* being but a fiction of the mind, applying the sequels of actions Past, to the actions that are Present.
> (Hobbes 1935, 11) (Treglown 1973, 44)

They were set to music by Henry Bowman in 1677 and by Pietro Reggio in 1680.

ATTRIBUTION The poem is attributed to Rochester in two ms. copies (Bodl. MS. Add. B.106, f. 45; Harvard MS. Eng. 636F, pp. 246–7) and three printed copies (*Songs set by Pietro Reggio* (1680), 36; Rochester 1680[2], 69–70; and Rochester 1691, 41–2), representing at least two independent textual traditions.

COPY-TEXT Henry Bowman, *Songs, for 1, 2, & 3 Voyces to the Thorow-Bass,* 2nd ed., Oxford (1679), 9 (Wing B3887).

EMENDATION OF COPY-TEXT Title *Love and Life, a Song*] om. 11 not of inconstancy] no more of Constancy 14 livelong] long liv'd
The title and the two emendations are supplied from Rochester 1680², 69–70.

ANNOTATION
4–5 *images . . . kept in store / By memory*: cf. 'This *decaying sense* . . . wee call *Imagination* . . . But when we would express the *decay*, and signifie that the Sense is fading, old, and past, it is called *Memory*' (Hobbes 1935, 4); *alone*: the imperfect (fading) rhyme, 'are gone . . . alone', calls attention to fading memory.
14 *This livelong minute*: the phrase is much discussed. Tillotson glosses it 'the whole length of this minute', which seems clear and distinct (*Eighteenth-Century English Literature*, ed. Geoffrey Tillotson *et al.* (1969), 38). But Walker finds the phrase 'more paradoxical than this' (Rochester 1984, 251) and cites Treglown: '"This livelong minute" beguilingly echoes Christian descriptions of heaven, like Cowley's "Nothing is there *To Come*, and nothing *Past*, / But an *Eternal Now* does always last"' (Cowley 1905, 251) (Treglown 1973, 44). Perhaps the joke lies in applying 'livelong' ('An emotional intensive of *long*, used of periods of time. Chiefly in *the livelong day*, [*the livelong*] *night*' (*OED*)) to the short period of a minute, with a possible sidelong glance at 'the lucky minute' (21.²23).

Upon Carey Fraser (Her father gave her dildoes six)

ATTRIBUTION The attribution to Rochester in the unique witness to the text is unconfirmed by external evidence.

DATE The verses are dated 1677 in the copy-text and were first published in Vieth 1963, 237.

COPY-TEXT Yale MS. Osborn b.54, p. 1094.

EMENDATION OF COPY-TEXT Title *Upon Carey Fraser*] Upon Betty Frazer 1677

ANNOTATION
3 *She loves nought but living pricks*: cf. 'To the Duke I will go, / I have no more need for Signior Dildo' (40.²7–8).

The Epilogue to Circe (Some few from wit have this true maxim got)

Sir William Davenant, who 'seemd contented enough to be thought [Shakespeare's] son' (Aubrey 1898, I 204), was poet laureate and first patentee of the Duke's Company. When he died in April 1668, his widow, Dame Mary Davenant, inherited the proprietorship of the company, which was then playing in the theatre at Lincoln's Inn Fields. Her eldest son, Charles Davenant (1656–1714), while still an undergraduate at Balliol College, Oxford, took advantage of the opportunity to write and produce an opera, *Circe*, for which John Banister wrote the music, Dryden the Prologue, and Rochester the Epilogue (possibly because Elizabeth Barry was in the cast). It is exactly the kind of play that Rochester ridicules in his *Epilogue to Love in the Dark* (91–4), but despite his evident misgivings, the opera, which opened at the new Dorset Garden theatre on 12 May 1677 (Downes 1987, 68n., 77n.), was a popular success and the printed book required two editions.

ATTRIBUTION Although the attribution to Rochester in the copy-text (and in Rochester 1691, 128–9 which was set up from it) is not confirmed by external evidence, there is no reason to doubt it.

DATE Shortly before 12 May 1677.

COPY-TEXT Charles Davenant, *Circe, a Tragedy* (1677), [59].

ANNOTATION
4–5 *critics . . . agree / To loathe each play*: cf. 'All *Fools* have still an Itching to deride' (Pope 1939–67, I 243).
16 *And good for nothing would be wise at last*: cf. 'And being good for nothing else, be wise' (89.48). When a sound like 'laced' is expected, the imperfect rhyme 'last' heightens the scorn for dull critics who learn too late that ''tis . . . better to be pleased than not' (l. 2).
21 *beauty on his side*: cf. 'beauty, your allies and friends' (36.24).

The Mock Song (I swive as well as others do)

In this parody of Sir Carr Scrope's song, 'I cannot change as others do', Rochester takes up the foul-mouthed satyr's persona of *Tunbridge Wells* (341). But in mocking Scrope's gentle Petrarchan lyric with its tricky reduplicated refrain, Rochester is also mocking himself. The ugly hyperbolic imagery of *The Mock Song* distances Rochester from his own early work in the same genre and style, 'Insulting beauty you misspend' (8) and 'While on those lovely looks I gaze' (9), for example.

ATTRIBUTION Although the attribution to Rochester in the copy-text is not confirmed by external evidence, the fact of the Rochester–Scrope quarrel (Vieth 1963, 231–8) and the internal evidence of style and tone give the attribution a high degree of probability.

DATE Before 5 August 1677 (Vieth 1963, 236; Rochester 1984, 295; Oldham 1987, 260).

COPY-TEXT Rochester 1680^2, 75.

ANNOTATION
2 *deformed*: Scrope seems not to have been deformed, but he was small (one of his nicknames was Tom Thumb), he suffered from facial dermatitis : 'Such carbuncles his fiery Face confess / As no *Hungarian* water can redress' (*Roxburghe Ballads*, IV 571), and he may have been homosexual (397.27–8n.).
3 *true*: cf. 'a knight [John Sheffield, Earl of Mulgrave, Knight of the Garter] made love to her [Carey Fraser], / He wore a star and garter blue; / He got the better of Sir Carr, / Although his love was not so true' (B.L. MS. Add. 34362, f. 118) (Wilson 1976, 240).
9–10 *larded o'er / With darts*: Phillis is smitten with so many of Cupid's darts that she looks like a roast larded with strips of bacon inserted with a larding needle (Wilcoxon 1979, 142), also called a larding prick.
11–12 *in every pore / A . . . standing prick*: cf. 'and spend at every pore' (28.16). Dryden may allude to this image in his translation of Juvenal VI, 68–70, 'If his new bride prove not an arrant whore, / In head, and tail, and every other pore' (Dryden 1882–93, XIII 157) (Rochester 1982, 84).

On Mistress Willis (Against the charms our ballocks have)

The news in June 1677 was that Thomas Colepeper, Baron Colepeper of Thoresby, had returned from Paris with his mistress. She was Sue Willis, 'whom he carry'd thither to buy whatsoever pleased her there and this nation could not afford' (*Savile Correspondence*, 62).

ATTRIBUTION The poem is attributed to Rochester in Harvard MS. Eng. 636F, pp. 68–9 and two printed copies (the copy-text and Rochester 1718, 69–70), all belonging to the same textual tradition. Internal evidence, however, establishes a high degree of probability that Rochester wrote the verses.

COPY-TEXT Rochester 1680², 73–4.

EMENDATION OF COPY-TEXT Title *On Mistress Willis*] *Song* 4 Willis] *Phillis* 18 though] and
The emendations are supplied from Royal Library, Stockholm MS. Vu. 69, pp. 157–8.

ANNOTATION
10–12 *beautiful, / . . . pert and dull*: the dissonance created by the imperfect rhyme calls attention to Willis's oxymoronic ugly beauty and dull mirth; cf. 196.21.

Song (By all love's soft yet mighty powers)

The Phillis in foul linen of this nasty song may have an historic counterpart: Rochester 'us'd the body of one Nell Browne of Woodstock, who, tho' she look'd pretty well when clean, yet she was a very nasty, ordinary, silly Creature' (Hearne 1884–1918, IX 79). The verses can be sung to the rollicking tune of 'Young Phaon', which John Banister Sr. wrote for a song in Charles Davenant's *Circe* (12 May 1677; 1677) (Simpson 1966, 811).

ATTRIBUTION The attribution to Rochester in Harvard MS. 636F, pp. 69–70 and the copy-text, representing a single textual tradition, is not confirmed by external evidence, but internal evidence of style and tone creates a high degree of probability that Rochester wrote the song.

COPY-TEXT Rochester 1680², 72.

EMENDATION OF COPY-TEXT 13 wise] kind
The emendation is supplied from Harvard MS. 636F, pp. 69–70.

ANNOTATION
5 *be clean*: cf. 'Fair *Decency*, celestial Maid, / Descend from Heav'n to Beauty's Aid; / Though Beauty may beget Desire, / 'Tis thou must fan the Lover's Fire' (Swift 1937, 590).
14–16 *sinning; / . . . linen*: the imperfect rhyme provides an appropriately cacophonous close to the poem.

On Poet Ninny (Crushed by that just contempt his follies bring)

The original Ninny is the character who represents Edward Howard in Shadwell's first play, *The Sullen Lovers* (May 1668; 1668). Ninny is 'A conceited Poet, always troubling men with impertinent Discourses of Poetry, and the repetition of his own Verses' (Shadwell 1927, I 14). Here he is Sir Carr Scrope (Vieth 1963, 327–49).

ATTRIBUTION The attribution to Rochester in the copy-text is not confirmed by external evidence unless Vieth's argument that *On Poet Ninny* is 'his [Rochester's] verses on Sir Car. Scroope at large' mentioned in John Verney's letter of 25 April

1678 (Vieth 1963, 348–9) proves to be true. Internal evidence (l. 9n., l. 17n.) makes a good case for Rochester (and not for Mulgrave as implied in Edinburgh MS. DC.1.3, p. 24).

DATE 'early in 1678'? (Vieth 1963, 349).

COPY-TEXT Rochester 1680[3], 143–4.

EMENDATION OF COPY-TEXT 19 modish] Modest
The emendation is supplied in Yale MS. Osborn b.105, pp. 348–9.

ANNOTATION
2 *the vermin fain would sting*: cf. 'this Bug . . . that stinks and stings' (Pope 1939–67, IV 118).
3 *satire . . . so softly bite*: possibly an allusion to the last line of Buckhurst's 'To Mr. Edward Howard, on his Incomparable, Incomprehensible Poem called The British Princes' (1669), 'Did ever libel yet so sharply bite?' (Dorset 1979, 9) (Rochester 1968, 141); cf. Shadwell's 'inoffensive Satyrs' (Dryden 1956– , II 59); 'satire . . . without pain' (James Thomson, *Winter* (1730), 676–7).
4 *gentle George*: Etherege's sobriquet occurs earlier in *A Session of the Poets* (November–December 1676) which has been attributed to Rochester (*POAS*, Yale, I 353).
9 *hopeless love*: cf. 'none . . . endure to be beloved' (197.27–8).
14 *reverse of Nokes*: Nokes created the role of Ninny in *The Sullen Lovers*. The contrast may be between Sir Carr's finical 'capering' (l. 12) and Nokes's 'shuffling Shamble in his Gait, with so contented an Ignorance in his Aspect, and an aukward Absurdity in his Gesture' (Cibber 1740, 87).
17 *hideous sight*: cf. 'hideous to the sight' (196.[2]14; 400.2n.); 'this hideous sight' (Buckingham, *A Familiar Epistle to Mr. Julian, Secretary to the Muses* (1677; 1705), *POAS*, Yale, I 389).
18 *the Melancholy Knight*: after Don Quixote loses his teeth, Sancho Panza calls him 'the Knight of the *Ilfavourd face*' (Cervantes, *The History of the Valorous and Wittie Knight-Errant, Don Quixote*, trans. Thomas Shelton (1612), 160); cf. 'A Knight . . . / From Don Quixote descended' (*POAS*, Yale, I 389).
23 *face of farce joined to a head romancy*: a generic monstrosity, like a funny tragedy; cf. 402.3n.
27–8 *The worst . . . no more / Than what thy very friends have said*: the couplet derives its force from Scrope's self-righteous insistence that he says nothing 'in [his] rhymes . . . / That . . . hurts his friend', while Rochester notoriously deserts his friend (*POAS*, Yale, I 367, 368). Rochester retorts that what Scrope says about his friends is irrelevant, for they have deserted him.

Upon Nothing (Nothing, thou elder brother even to Shade)

Maintaining the *ex nihilo omnis fit* paradox was a popular rhetorical exercise in the late Renaissance. Samuel Johnson supposes that Rochester's poem had its origins in Jean Passerat's Latin poem *Nihil* (1587) and Johann von Wowern's *Dies Æstiva, sive De Umbra Paegnion* (1636). But a crude broadside ballad in black letter, *Much A-do, about Nothing* (1660) (Plate 12) (Manning 1986, 479–80) may have supplied Rochester with the paradox on which his satire is based, the verse form, and even some of the phraseology:

Fire, Air, Earth and Water, Beast, Birds, Fish and Men,
Did start out of Nothing.

Johnson is right, however, in supposing that Rochester's '*Nothing* must be considered as having not only a negative but a kind of positive signification' (Johnson 1779–81, IV 411). The poem constructs a positive genealogy of Nothing:

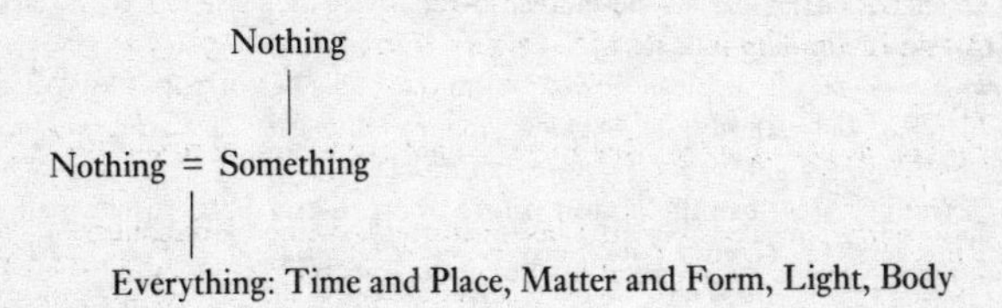

Nothing, of course, is androgynous. The Something that is 'Severed' from Nothing (l. 8) is female and their incestuous union produces Everything, an arrangement that exactly replicates the genealogy of Satan, Sin, and Death in *Paradise Lost* (Milton 1931–8, II i 61–9).

The shape of the poem is a Cartesian vortex. It begins with 'Emptiness' (l. 11), gives a new meaning to the Big Bang theory (ll. 5–6), works through the great abstractions of Being and Not-being (l. 31), swirls around in Time and Place until it focuses on 'sacred monarchs' at the council board 'With persons thought, at best, for nothing fit' (ll. 38–9), and concludes in triviality, 'British policy . . . Kings' promises, whores' vows' (ll. 46, 50), a notable political satire grafted on to the nihil paradox in the metrical form of a broadside ballad.

Like its ballad prototype, *Upon Nothing*, in anapaestic tetrameter triplets, can be sung to the tune of 'Which nobody can deny', a short form of 'Greensleeves' (Simpson 1966, 274). The poem was so popular that two pirated editions were published in 1679 and the title was tacked on to other broadside ballads even when it was totally irrelevant, as in *Of Bow-Church and Steeple, Burnt, An. 1666. Rebuilt, 1679. Or A Second Poem upon Nothing* [no imprint]. Pope's imitation of *Upon Nothing* is entitled *On Silence* (Pope 1939–67, VI 17–19).

ATTRIBUTION Besides eleven ms. copies (B.L. MS. Add. 4457, f. 43; B.L. MS. Add. 30162, ff. 1v–2v; Bodl. MS. Don.b.8, pp. 654–5; Bodl. MS. Add. B.106, ff. 19v–20v; Bodl. MS. Sancroft 53, p. 68; Bodl. MS. Rawl. poet. 173, f. 151v; Cambridge MS. Add. 6339, ff. 12r–13r; Harvard MS. Eng. 623F, pp. 10–11; Harvard MS. Eng. 636F, pp. 55–8; Yale MS. Osborn b.52/2, pp. 173–4; Yale MS. Osborn fb. 142, pp. 25–6) and two printed copies (the copy-text and Rochester 1680[1], 51–4). Anthony à Wood and Joseph Addison also attribute the poem to Rochester (Wood 1813–20, III 1230; *Spectator*, 19 February 1712). The attribution to Rochester and Buckingham (*The Works of His Grace, George Villiers, Late Duke of Buckingham*, 3rd ed., 2 vols. (1715), I 149), has been ignored.

DATE Before 14 May 1678 (Rochester 1968, 206–7).

COPY-TEXT *Upon Nothing A Poem* [no imprint] ['Light' edition] (Wing R1761).

EMENDATION OF COPY-TEXT 1 even] *Eve* 12 Snatched] Snatch

24 the] thy 30 dull] blind 32 And] Of 36 least unsafe] least, tho safe
41 coffers] Courts from] frō the 45 like thee] om. 50 Kings'] Court
they] I 51 swiftly] Swift, Fly in thee ever] severs in the
The emendation of l. 24 is supplied from Yale MS. Osborn c.160, f. 95r. The remaining emendations are from Rochester 1680[1], 51–4.

ANNOTATION

1 *Shade*: elemental darkness (Genesis 1.2); cf. '*Nothing* . . . is elder then darknesse' (Donne, *Essayes in Divinity* (1651), 35).
2 *the world was made*: cf. 'It pleased God . . . to . . . make of nothing, the World' (*The Humble Advice of the Assembly of Divines, Now by Authority of Parliament sitting at Westminster, concerning part of a Confession of Faith* (1646), 10).
6 *all proceeded*: cf. 'Here lies the inmost centre of creation, / From whence all inward forms and life proceed' (Henry More, *Psychozoia Platonica: or A Platonicall Song of the Soul* (1642),[1]17); *united what*: to make more obvious the pun on the pronominal use of 'what' and 'twat', the female pudendum (*OED*), Dunton prints 'the great united – *WHAT*?' (*Athenian Sport* (1707), 354); cf. 'In Prayse of a Twatt, By a faire Ladys Command' (Yale MS. Osborn f.b.66, f. 6).
7–9 *all, / . . . must . . . fall*: in Rochester's version of entropy, Nothing is 'fixed' (l. 3) but everything is in a state of flux tending toward dissolution into Nothing.
13–14 *Matter . . . / By Form assisted*: 'In Aristotelian and scholastic use: [matter is] That component of the essence of any thing . . . which has bare existence, but which requires the addition of a particular "form" to constitute the thing . . . as determinately existent' (*OED*, s.v. **Matter** *sb.*II, 6).
22 *mysteries*: cf. 73.67–9.
24 *truth*: one of Joseph Glanvill's 'Principles of Reason . . . that God hath implanted in our Souls . . . [is] *That nothing hath no attributes*' (*Logou Threskeia: Or, A Seasonable Recommendation, and Defence of Reason, in the Affair of Religion* (1670), 6–7).
27 *to be* [*nothing*]: cf. 'to be Nothing, is so deep a curse, and high degree of punishment, that Hell and the prisoners there, not only have it not, but cannot wish so great a loss to themselves, nor such a frustration of Gods purposes' (Donne, *Essayes in Divinity* (1651), 61).
33–6 *designs of state, / . . . least unsafe*: cf. *The Maimed Debauchee* headnote, 372.
41 *princes' coffers*: Harold Love cites the stop on the Exchequer in January 1672 (Rochester 1984, 262), but the reference may be to later crises. In November 1677 when Louis XIV stopped the subsidies to Charles II for keeping England neutral in the wars on the Continent, Charles wept (Hutton 1989, 346).
45 *furs, and gowns*: worn by holders of civil, legal, parliamentary, or academic office (*OED*, s.v. **Gown**).
46 *French truth*: cf. 'Punic faith: . . . faithlessness' (*OED*, s.v. **Faith** 11b), treachery; *Dutch prowess*: cf. 'Dutch courage: bravery induced by drinking' (*OED* s.v. **Courage** *sb.* 4d).
50 *to thee they bend*: cf. 'Towards him [Satan] they bend' (Milton 1931–8, II i 55).

My Lord All-Pride (Bursting with pride the loathed impostume swells)

This is the fourth in a linked group of four poems on John Sheffield, Earl of Mulgrave, and Sir Carr Scrope (375). Like *On Poet Ninny* it is straight lampoon in the person of a foul-mouthed satyr.

ATTRIBUTION The attribution to Rochester in Rochester 1680[3], 144–5 is not confirmed by external evidence (but see l. 16n.). Internal evidence of phrasing and tone (ll. 7–8n., 12n., 16n.) makes a good case for Rochester and none at all for Sir Carr Scrope to whom the verses are attributed in Edinburgh MS. DC.1.3, p. 24 (Vieth 1963, 348–50).

DATE '?1679' (Rochester 1984, 299) .

COPY-TEXT *A Very Heroical Epistle from my Lord All-Pride to Dol-Common* (1679) (Wing R1761B).

EMENDATION OF COPY-TEXT Title *My Lord All-Pride*] *Epigram upon my Lord All-Pride* 1 impostume] Imposture 3 'tis] is
The emendations are supplied from Rochester 1680[3], 144–5.

ANNOTATION
3–4 *writes / With as much force to nature as he fights*: i.e. writing verse and fighting duels are equally foreign to Lord All-Pride's nature.
7–8 *weak / . . . rake*: a common rhyme in Rochester's verse (12.21–2, 66.33–4, 89.1–2, 91.55–6).
12 *gruntling*: cf. 'murmuring gruntlings' (22.3).
16 *looby mien*: in *Rochester's Ghost* (*c.* 1682) Rochester's spirit comes back from Hell to impeach those 'old Associates' who 'justly merit Hell' (*POAS*, 1697–1707, II 128–31). One of these is Mulgrave, 'With Nose cock't up, and . . . slouching Looby Mien'. Putting this phrase from *My Lord All-Pride* into the mouth of Rochester's ghost seems to imply that the anonymous poet thought that *My Lord All-Pride* 'was written by Rochester' (Vieth 1963, 350).
19 *takes up arms*: Like Rochester, Mulgrave volunteered for service in the second Dutch War and saw action at Lowestoft (June 1665). In June 1667 he was commissioned captain but unsuccessfully opposed Monmouth for captaincy of the King's Own Troop of Horse Guards. He volunteered again for service in the third Dutch War and saw action at Solebay (May 1672). In January 1673 he was promoted colonel and his Old Holland regiment served one campaign on the Continent under Turenne (Dalton 1960, I 76, 136, 163).
22 *Harlequin*: 'in English pantomime a mute character supposed to be invisible to the clown and pantaloon; he has many attributes of the clown (his rival in the affections of Columbine) with the addition of mischievous intrigue; he usually wears particoloured bespangled tights and a visor, and carries a light "bat" of lath as a magic wand' (*OED*, citing Joseph Addison, *Remarks on Several Parts of Italy, &c.* (1705), 101: 'Harlequin's Part [in the *commedia dell'arte*] is made up of Blunders and Absurdities').
23 *fair*: Bartholomew Fair opened in Smithfield market on St Bartholomew's Eve (23 August) and lasted two weeks. Originally an important cloth fair, it had evolved into a carnival, with puppet shows, performing monkeys, clockwork figures, rope dancers, and freak shows. Pepys called it 'nasty' and 'dirty' but never failed to attend (Pepys, 31 August 1661).
25 *elephant*: 'at Bartholomew fair. Saw Elephant wave colours, shoot a gun, bend and kneel, carry a castle and a man, etc.' (*The Diary of Robert Hooke*, ed. Henry W. Robinson *et al.* (1935), 423) (Rochester 1968, 143).
30 *Knight o'th' Burning Pestle*: the original Knight of the Burning Pestle is Ralph, a grocer's apprentice who appropriates the role of Grocer Errant in Francis Beaumont's comedy, *The Knight of the Burning Pestle* (1607?; 1613). Rochester gives the phrase a phallic twist and a suggestion of venereal disease – 'Pestle' was probably pronounced

'pizl' (Rochester 1984, 300). Lord All-Pride and his 'famous disease' survived to make sport for readers of Defoe's *The Dyet of Poland* (1705) (*POAS*, Yale, VII 119).

The Earl of Rochester's Answer to a Paper of Verses sent him by L[ady] B[etty] Felton and taken out of the Translation of Ovid's Epistles, 1680
(What strange surprise to meet such words as these)

An edition of Ovid's *Heroides* was one of Jacob Tonson's first publishing ventures. He collected translations by a dozen poets, hired Dryden to write a Preface, and advertised *Ovid's Epistles, Translated by Several Hands* for sale on 6 February 1680. Lady Betty Felton's 'Paper of Verses . . . taken out of the Translations of Ovid's Epistle's' is unfortunately lost, but some idea of its content may be gained from the following:

> There had lately been published Ovid's *Epistles*, translated by the wits of the Court; she [Frances Jennings] set to work composing the epistle of a forlorn shepherdess, addressed to the perfidious [Henry] Jermyn. As her model she took the letter of Adriadne to Theseus, and began by reproducing word for word the complaints of that offended lover to the cruel deceiver by whom she was abandoned.
>
> (Hamilton 1930, 322; cf. 375)

ATTRIBUTION The attribution to Rochester in the unique witness to the text is unconfirmed by external evidence. Internal evidence of style, including the 'rough syntax' of the verse (Rochester 1968, 149; Fabricant 1969, 703) and the tone may make a good case for Rochester.

DATE Shortly after 6 February 1680 (Dryden 1956– , I 323).

COPY-TEXT *A Collection of Poems by Several Hands* (1693), 126–7 (Wing C5174).

EMENDATION OF COPY-TEXT 6 far] for
The conjectural emendation is proposed by Patrick Lyons (Rochester 1984, 307); cf. 75.116.

ANNOTATION
1 *such words*: cf. 'Oft have I thirsted for a pois'nous draught, / As oft a death from some kind Ponyard sought; / Oft round that neck a silken Twine I cast, / Which once thy dear perfidious Arms embrac'd. / By death I'le heal my present Infamy, / But stay to choose the speediest way to dye' ('Phillis to Demophoon', *Ovid's Epistles, Translated by Several Hands* (1680), 96).
8 *sword and pen*: two of Ovid's heroines, Dido and Canace, write with sword in hand (ibid., 8, 227); *pen . . . unfit* [for women]: cf. writing verse 'dangerous' [for women] (49.1–4).
11 *Approve of fights*: cf. 'Windows demolished, watches overcome' (89.35).
12 *slain . . . revive*: cf. 'She smil'd to see the doughty Hero slain, / But at her Smile, the Beau reviv'd again' (Pope 1939–67, II 201).

To form a plot

It is suggested that 'Possibly Rochester thought he was attacked as "Lord Lampoon and Monsieur Song" in Otway's poem *The Poet's Complaint of his Muse*, which was published on or about 22 January 1679/80' (Rochester 1968, 148). But Lord Lampoon and Monsieur Song sound like two people. Montague Summers identifies Monsieur Song as Thomas Durfey, who was known as 'Sing-Song Durfey' and wrote '7953 Songs, 2250 Ballads, and 1956 Catches' (Otway 1926, III 310; *POAS*, Yale, VI 143). It is hard to imagine that Rochester would resent being called Lord Lampoon who introduces Otway's muse at court, for Rochester had already done that (Otway 1926, I 75–6). So presumably the epigram *To form a plot* records Rochester's response not to *The Poet's Complaint to his Muse* but to Otway's 'almost sacrilegious misuse of Plutarch' (Vieth 1963, 221) in *The History and Fall of Caius Marius* (*c.* October 1679; 1680) in which Elizabeth Barry created the role of Lavinia.

There is no evidence that the epigram is a fragment, as Vieth supposes (Vieth, 1963, 225).

ATTRIBUTION The unique witness to the text of the epigram is the copy-text in Rochester's hand.

DATE During the rehearsals for or the first run of Otway's *The History and Fall of Caius Marius*, *c.* October 1679 (*London Stage*, I 281–2).

COPY-TEXT Nottingham MS. Portland Pw V 31, f. 8r.

ANNOTATION

1 *form a plot*: Otway forms the plot of *The History and Fall of Caius Marius* by grafting Shakespeare's *Romeo and Juliet* on to Plutarch's *Life of Caius Marius.*

2 *blustering*: this may allude to Otway's challenging Elkanah Settle to a duel. Believing that Settle had written *A Session of the Poets* (Since the sons of the Muses grow num'rous and loud) in which Otway is called 'The scum of a playhouse' (*POAS*, Yale, I 355), 'Mr. O. a Man of the Sword, as well as the Pen . . . immediately call'd him to an account, and required the satisfaction of a Gentleman from him', which Settle declined to provide (*A Character of the True Blue Protestant Poet: or, The Pretended Author of the Character of a Popish Successor* (1682), 2) (Roswell G. Ham, *Otway and Lee* (1931), 108–11).

2–3 *rhyme . . . line*: Rochester supplies a sample of Otway's 'rough, unruly' verse in which assonance is frequently substituted for rhyme; *Gives Plutarch . . . the lie*: Otway gives Plutarch the lie by inventing a daughter, Lavinia, for Caecilius Metellus, Marius's mortal enemy, and involving her in a fatal marriage with Marius Junior. Then he stirs in lines from *Julius Caesar*, *Richard II*, *Richard III*, and *Titus Andronicus*, with allusions to English politics in 1678–9, concluding with an unequivocal message to Charles II: 'Oh! what an excellent Master is an Army, / To teach Rebellious Cities Manners!' and an equally unequivocal warning to Shaftesbury: 'Be warn'd by me, ye Great ones, how y'embroil / Your Country's Peace, and dip your Hands in Slaughter' (Otway 1932, I 503, 518).

4 *rapture before nature*: In Shakespeare's *Romeo and Juliet* Juliet kisses the dead Romeo and speaks two and a half lines. In *The History and Fall of Caius Marius* Lavinia (played by Elizabeth Barry) kisses the dead Marius Junior and raves on for ten lines, concluding 'Oh! I could rend these walls with Lamentation, / Tear up the Dead from their corrupted Graves, / And dawb the face of Earth with her own Bowels' (Otway 1932, I 516).

5 *turned his own imager*: the narrator of *The Poet's Complaint of his Muse* (1680) describes himself as a kind of proto-Wordsworth, 'A wandring bard, whose Muse was crazy grown' (Otway 1932, II 405).

An Epistolary Essay from M.G. to O.B. upon their Mutual Poems (Dear friend, I hear this town doth so abound)

As he did in *A Very Heroical Epistle from My Lord All-Pride* (89), Rochester again takes on the persona of Mulgrave ('M.G.'), this time to reply to the attack on himself in ll. 230–69 of *An Essay upon Satire*, of which Rochester read a ms. copy on 21 November 1679. 'The author is apparently Mr. [Dryden]', Rochester writes to Henry Savile, 'his patron my [Lord Mulgrave], having a panegyric in the midst [ll. 194–209]' (Rochester *Letters* 1980, 232–3; *POAS*, Yale, I 410–11). In *An Epistolary Essay from M.G. to O.B. upon their Mutual Poems* Rochester casts Mulgrave in the role of impresario of O.B.'s (Dryden's) verses, 'through me / . . . [readers] are partakers of your poetry' (ll. 7–8).

It is now agreed, however, that *An Essay upon Satire* (12 September–21 November 1679; 1680) (Wing E3299) is 'pretty clearly the unassisted work of Mulgrave, who stated in 1682 that Dryden had been "praised and punish'd for another's Rimes"', and was '"intirely innocent of the whole matter"' (Winn 1987, 328; Macdonald 1939, 217–18). But if Rochester thought Dryden wrote *An Essay upon Satire*, why did he blame Mulgrave (Rochester 1984, 293)? Perhaps he changed his mind. Perhaps he became better informed. Perhaps he decided that there was nothing of Dryden in the poem, no alien Dryden 'To lard with wit' Mulgrave's 'feebly laborious' verses (Dryden 1956– , II 58; Johnson 1779–81, V [3]16). Considering that Dryden's reply to *An Allusion to Horace* in the Preface to *All for Love* (December 1677; 1678) magisterially dismisses Rochester as a trifler and his poem as 'ignorant and vile' (Dryden 1882–93, V 332–8), it is difficult to gauge the degree of irony with which ll. 10–11 and 38–43 are to be read.

Despite the salutation 'Dear friend', *An Epistolary Essay from M.G. to O.B. upon their Mutual Poems* is a generic monster, like Sir Carr Scrope (402.23n.). It is neither a letter nor an essay, but a dramatic monologue with an *adversarius* (presumably Dryden) who twice interrupts (208.81, 87).

ATTRIBUTION The poem is attributed to Rochester in five ms. copies (Royal Library, Stockholm MS. Vu.69, pp. 71–6; Leeds MS. Brotherton Lt.54, pp. 108–12; Nottingham MS. Portland Pw V 40, pp. 1–4; Harvard MS. Eng. 636F, pp. 4–8; Yale MS. Osborn b.105, pp. 1–7), and the copy-text, representing at least two independent textual traditions.

DATE Shortly after 21 November 1679 (Rochester *Letters* 1980, 232–3).

COPY-TEXT Rochester 1680[1], 3–6.

EMENDATION OF COPY-TEXT 5 spleen] spleens 6 brow] Brows
40 excrement] Excrements 41 Runs in a costive and] Flows in a harsh
75 should] cou'd could] shou'd 81 thereby] hereby 84 of] on
The emendations are preserved in Harvard MS. Eng. 636F, pp. 4–8.

ANNOTATION
3 *what*: presumably Mulgrave's *An Essay upon Satire* (12 September–21 November 1679).
11 *The British Prince*: Edward Howard's *The British Princes* (1668) became a byword for bad poetry (Rochester 1968, 144n.).
13 *Nor . . . hope to be admired*: in his Dedication of *Aureng-Zebe* (November 1675; 1676) to Mulgrave, Dryden, with an indeterminate degree of irony, says, 'Your

lordship is not of that nature, which either seeks a commendation or wants it . . . How much more great and manly in your lordship, is your contempt of popular applause' (Dryden 1882–93, V 190–91).

15 *T'avoid . . . all sort of self-denial*: cf. ''tis my maxim to avoid all pain' (90.13) cf. 357.32n.

16–17 *lead . . . tread*: in the context of Mulgrave boldly setting off down the path of 'desire and fancy', the flat-footed rhyme recalls Mulgrave's 'splay-foot' (204.15).

19 *To my dear self a pleasure I beget*: cf. 'In my dear self I centre everything' (89.7). Again with indeterminate irony Dryden remarks to Mulgrave that 'True greatness . . . is in a private virtue . . . centring on itself' (Dryden 1882–93, V 194).

38 *you write better than I do*: although he contradicts himself (ll. 77–8), it is not out of character for Mulgrave to acknowledge Dryden's superiority. In *An Essay upon Poetry* (1682), 10, he shows Dryden 'Crown'd by *Mac-Fleckno* with immortal Bays'.

41 *insipid*: cf. 'His verses are often insipid' (Johnson 1779–81, V 320).

45 *sublime*: in the dramatic context of the poem Mulgrave means 'Standing high above others by reason of nobility or grandeur of nature or character' (*OED*, A. *adj.* 5), 'the best' (l. 78). Rochester almost certainly means 'haughty, proud' (*OED*, A. *adj.* 3), 'My Lord All-Pride'; cf. 'Rochester's poetry studiously *avoids* the sublime' (Farley-Hills 1978, 130).

49 *as none e'er writ before*: cf. '*that*'s new' (60.141); Durfey 'scorn'd to borrow from the Wits of yore; / But ever writ, as none e'er writ before' (Pope 1939–67, VI 101) (Vieth, *N&Q* 211 (1966), 457). Rochester is an 'ancient'.

52–3 *alone . . . none*: the imperfect rhyme calling attention to 'none' raises the suspicion that this may in fact be Mulgrave's portion of wit.

60–64 *providence . . . / In wit alone . . . magnificent*: contradicting l. 29.

67 *due division*: cf. 'Right understanding is the most equally divided thing in the World; for every one beleevs himself so well stor'd with it, that even those who in all other things are the hardest to be pleas'd, seldom desire more of it then they have' (René Descartes, *A Discourse of a Method* (1649), 2) (Vieth 1963, 126n.).

90 *false as common fame*: cf. 'the publick . . . is to pass the last sentence upon literary claims' (Johnson, *The Rambler*, 5 June 1750).

97 *this* –: 'implying a gesture such as snapping the finger' (Rochester 1968, 147).

100 *idle rumour*: the structure comes full circle (ll. 1–4).

Index of Titles and First Lines

Absent from thee I languish still, 70
Advice, The, 19
After death nothing is, and nothing, death, 39
Against Constancy, 195
Against the charms our ballocks have, 199
All my past life is mine no more, 197
All things submit themselves to your command, 19
Allusion to Horace, An. The 10th Satire of the 1st Book, 98
An age in her embraces passed, 68
Ancient person, for whom I, 71
And after singing Psalm the 12th, 17
Another Song in Imitation of Sir John Eaton's Songs, 10
Artemisa to Chloe. A Letter from a Lady in the Town to a Lady in the Country concerning the Loves of the Town, 49
As charms are nonsense, nonsense seems a charm, 85
As Chloris full of harmless thought, 21
As some brave admiral, in former war, 87
At five this morn when Phoebus raised his head, 43
At last you'll force me to confess, 10

Bursting with pride the loathed impostume swells, 204
By all love's soft yet mighty powers, 200
By Heavens, 'twas bravely done, 18

Celia, the faithful servant you disown, 13
Chloe, In verse by your command I write, 49
Consideratus, Considerandus, 81
Could I but make my wishes insolent, 24
Crushed by that just contempt his follies bring, 200
Custom does often reason overrule, 5

Dear friend, I hear this town doth so abound, 206
Dialogue, 101
Dialogue between Strephan and Daphne, A, 65

Earl of Rochester's Answer to a Paper of Verses sent him by L[ady] B[etty] Felton and taken out of the Translations of Ovid's Epistles, *1680, The*, 205
Epigram, 39
Epilogue to Circe, *The*, 198
Epilogue to Love in the Dark, *as it was spoken by Mr Haines*, 85

Epistolary Essay from M.G. to O.B. upon their Mutual Poems, An, 206

Fair Cloris in a pigsty lay, 22
Fall, The, 68
Fling this useless book away, 12
From Mistress Price, Maid of Honour to Her Majesty, who sent [Lord Chesterfield] a Pair of Italian Gloves, 16

Give me leave to rail at you, 15
God bless our good and gracious King, 197
Gods by night of nature must possess, The, 26
Great is the honour which our Emperor, 102
Great mother of Aeneas and of love, 25
Grecian Kindness, 39

Her father gave her dildoes six, 198
Here's a health to Kate, our sovereign's mate, 13
Here's Monmouth the witty and Lauderdale the pretty, 184
How blest was the created state, 68
How happy, Cloris, were they free, 191
How perfect, Cloris, and how free, 192

I am by fate slave to your will, 17
I could love thee till I die, 20
I, John Roberts, writ this same, 17
I swive as well as others do, 199
If Rome can pardon sins, as Romans hold, 8
Imperfect Enjoyment, The, 28
Impia blasphemi sileant convitia vulgi, 1
Impromptu on Louis XIV, 18
In Obitum Serenissimae Mariae Principis Arausionensis, 1
In the isle of Great Britain long since famous grown, 30
Insulting beauty, you misspend, 8

J'ai l'amour dans le cœur et la rage dans les os, 82

Lead faster on! Why creep you thus to fight, 184
Leave this gaudy, gilded stage, 194
Long time Plain Dealing in the haughty town, 78
Lorraine you stole; by fraud you got Burgundy, 18
Love a woman? You're an ass, 37
Love and Life, 197
Love bade me hope, and I obeyed, 11

Madam, If you're deceived, it is not by my cheat, 89
Maimed Debauchee, The, 87
Mistress, The, 68
Mistress Knight's Advice to the Duchess of Cleveland in Distress for a Prick, 83
Mock Song, The, 199
Much wine had passed with grave discourse, 31

My dear mistress has a heart, 9
My Lord All-Pride, 204
My Lord Rochester attempting to Kiss the Duchess of Cleveland as she was stepping out of her Chariot at Whitehall Gate, she threw him on his Back, and before he rose he spoke the following Lines, 18
My Lord, These are the gloves that I did mention, 16

Naked she lay, clasped in my longing arms, 28
Nothing, thou elder brother even to Shade, 201

O Love! how cold and slow to take my part, 26
Oh, that I could by any chemic art, 4
On King Charles, 30
On Mistress Willis, 199
On Poet Ninny, 200
On Rome's Pardons, 8
On the Supposed Author of a Late Poem in Defence of Satire, 196
Out of mere love and arrant devotion, 83

Pastoral Dialogue between Alexis and Strephon, A, 62
Phillis, be gentler, I advise, 23
Plain Dealing's Downfall, 78
Platonic Lady, The, 20
Poet, whoe'er thou art, I say God damn thee, 39
Prithee now, fond fool, give o'er, 65

Quoth the Duchess of Cleveland to councillor Knight, 83

Ramble in St James's Park, A, 31
Respite, great Queen, your just and hasty fears, 3
Rhyme to Lisbon, 13
Rochester Extempore, 17
Rodomontade on his Cruel Mistress, A, 18

Sab: lost, 25
Satire, 35
Satyr against Mankind, A 72
Scene of Sir Robert Howard's Play, written by the Earl of Rochester, A, 184
Scene i. Mr Dainty's Chamber, 82
Second Prologue at Court to The Empress of Morocco *Spoken by the Lady Elizabeth Howard, The*, 36
Seek not to know a woman, for she's worse, 18
Seneca's Troas, *Act 2. Chorus*, 39
She yields, she yields, pale Envy said amen, 25
Signior Dildo, 40
Some few from wit have this true maxim got, 198
Son of a whore, God damn you, can you tell, 195
Song, A (Absent from thee I languish still), 70
Song (As Cloris full of harmless thought), 21
Song (At last you'll force me to confess), 10

Song (By all love's soft yet mighty powers), 200
Song (Give me leave to rail at you), 15
Song (How happy, Cloris, were they free), 191
Song (How perfect, Cloris, and how free), 192
Song, A (Insulting beauty, you misspend), 8
Song (Love a woman? You're an ass), 37
Song, A (My dear mistress has a heart), 9
Song of a Young Lady. To her Ancient Lover, A, 71
Song (Phillis, be gentler, I advise), 23
Song (Such perfect bliss, fair Cloris, we), 193
Song to Cloris, 22
Song (While on those lovely looks I gaze), 9
Spoken Extempore to a Country Clerk after having heard him Sing Psalms, 18
Sternhold and Hopkins had great qualms, 18
Submission, The, 11
Such perfect bliss, fair Cloris, we, 193

Tell me no more of constancy, 195
The utmost grace the Greeks could show, 39
There sighs not on the plain, 62
Timon. A Satyr, 56
'Tis not that I am weary grown, 61
To all Gentlemen, Ladies, and Others, whether of City, Town, or Country, Alexander Bendo wisheth all Health and Prosperity, 91
To Celia, 13
To Corinna, 23
To form a plot, 205
To Her Sacred Majesty, the Queen Mother, on the Death of Mary, Princess of Orange, 3
To his Mistress, 6
To his more than Meritorious Wife, 17
To his Sacred Majesty, 1
To Love, 26
To rack and torture thy unmeaning brain, 196
To the Postboy, 195
To this moment a rebel I throw down my arms, 11
Too late, alas, I must confess, 10
Too long the wise Commons have been in debate, 35
Tunbridge Wells, 43
'Twas a dispute 'twixt heaven and earth, 5
Two fragments, 5

Under King Charles II's Picture, 17
Upon Carey Fraser, 198
Upon his Drinking a Bowl, 38
Upon his Leaving his Mistress, 61
Upon Nothing, 201

Valentinian. A Tragedy, 102
Verses put into a Lady's Prayer-book, 12

Very Heroical Epistle from My Lord All-Pride to Doll-Common, A, 89
Virtue's triumphant shrine, who dost engage, 1
Vulcan, contrive me such a cup, 38

Well sir, 'tis granted I said Dryden's rhymes, 98
Were I (who to my cost already am), 72
What cruel pains Corinna takes, 23
What pleasures can the gaudy world afford, 81
What strange surprise to meet such words as these, 205
What, Timon, does old age begin t'approach, 56
What vain, unnecessary things are men, 78
When to the King I bid good morrow, 101
Whereas this famous metropolis of England . . ., 91
While on those lovely looks I gaze, 9
Why dost thou shade thy lovely face? oh, why, 6
Wish, The, 4
Wit has of late took up a trick t'appear, 36
Wit like tierce claret, when't begins to pall, 5
Woman's Honour, 11

You ladies all of merry England, 40

Index of Proper Names

(*Page references to the Biographical Dictionary are in* **bold type**.)

Adderbury, 316
Addison, Joseph, 403, 405
Aëtius, Flavius, 385
Albemarle, Elizabeth Cavendish, Duchess of, 336
Albemarle, George Monck, Duke of, 299, 301
Albertoni, Paluzzi degli, 340
Alcibiades, 391
Alcock, Thomas, 377–9
All Souls College, 298
Alssid, Michael W., 383
Amsterdam, 350
Anjou, Philippe, Duc d'. *See* Orléans, Philippe, Duc d'
Aretino, Pietro, 331, 379
Aristotle, 386, 389
Armstrong, Sir Thomas, 397
Armytage, Sir St George J., 395
Arrowsmith, William, 326
Attila the Hun, 389
Aubrey, John, 327, 343, 399
Augustus, 389

Bachrens, E., 319
Bacon, Francis, 374
Balfour, Andrew, 328
Balliol College, 399
Bancroft, John, 366
Banister, John, 399, 401
Banks, Theodore H., Jr., 380
Banqueting House, 301
Banstead Downs, 331–2
Barlow, Thomas, Bishop of Lincoln, 365
Barnardi, James, **225**, 339
Barry, Elizabeth, 332, 387, 393, 399, 407
Bartholomew Fair, 405
Barton, Anne, 303
Bateson, F.W., 309
Bath, 301, 354
Baynton, Lady Anne, 377–8
Beaumont, Francis, 366, 397, 405
Becke, Betty, 330
Beesley, Alfred, 316
Behn, Aphra, 306, 320, 325, 373, 387
Belleau, Remy, 327
Bellefasse, Jean Baptiste, 389
Bendo, Alexander, 377–9, 392
Bergen, 374
Bergholt, 340
Berkshire, Thomas Howard, Earl of, 340
Berman, Ronald, 330
Betterton, Thomas, **225**, 370, 371
Blackheath, 299, 333, 336
Blake, William, 373, 388
Blount, Charles, 324, 337, 360, 363, 364
Boas, George, 358
Boileau-Despreaux, Nicolas, 334, 347, 349, 350, 351, 352, 353, 358, 359, 360, 361, 363
Bovey, Sir Ralph, 50, **226**
Bowers, Fredson, xv
Bowman, Henry, 398
Boyle, Roger. *See* Orrery, Roger Boyle, Earl of
Bragge, Benjamin, 304, 316, 360, 381, 382, 398
Brest, 301
Bretby Park, 314
Bridges, Captain, 396
Bridges Street Theatre, 352
Briscoe, Samuel, 383
Broich, Ulrich, 378
Brooks, Cleanth, 373
Brooks, Harold F., 317, 353
Broussin, René Bruslart, seigneur du, 348–9
Brown, Thomas, 310, 317

Browne, Nell, 401
Browne, William, 318
Browning, Andrew, 372
Brudenell, Anne Maria. *See* Shrewsbury, Anne Maria Brudenell, Countess of
Bruser, Fredelle, 353
Brutus, Lucius Junius, 388
Brutus, Marcus Junius, 388
Buckhurst, Charles Sackville, Lord. *See* Dorset, Charles Sackville, Earl of Middlesex and
Buckingham, George Villiers, Duke of, **227**, 340, 349, 350, 377, 380, 384, 397, 402, 403
Buling, Hans, 377, 379
Bulstrode, Sir Richard, 377
Burnet, Gilbert, xiii, xiv, 324, 328, 332, 338, 355, 361, 364, 367, 373, 377, 382, 383, 395, 397
Burns, Robert, 315
Busby, Richard, 99, **229**
Butler, Samuel, **229**, 336, 348, 360, 362, 367
Bysshe, Sir Edward, 395

Cademan, Philip, 340
Caesar, Julius, 388, 389
Cairns, Francis, 325
Calprenède, Gaultier de Coste, seigneur de la, 352
Cameron, William J., 341, 383
Canterbury, 343
Carew, Thomas, 375, 394
Carisbroke Castle, 301
Carthage, 388
Carwell. *See* Portsmouth, Louise de Kéroualle, Duchess of
Caryll, John, 371
Castlemaine, Lady, 364, 367. *See* Cleveland, Barbara Villiers, Duchess of
Castlemaine, Roger Palmer, Earl of, 329
Catherine of Bragança, **229**, 311, 340, 341
Cavendish, Elizabeth. *See* Albemarle, Elizabeth Cavendish, Duchess of
Cervantes, Miguel de, 402
Châlons, 389
Chamberlayne, Edward, 307, 335, 340, 385
Charleroi, 316
Charles I, 299, 301
Charles II, xiii–xiv, 298, 299, 307, 311, 312, 314, 318, 328–9, 331, 332–4, 338–9, 341, 344, 347, 352, 359, 364, 371, 377, 378, 379, 381, 382, 404, 407
Chaucer, Geoffrey, 305, 338
Chernaik, Warren L., 375
Chesterfield, Philip Stanhope, 2nd Earl of, **230**, 314
Child, Francis J., 339
Christie, W. D., 339
Churchill, John, **231**, 368, 369
Churchill, Sir Winston, 369
Cibber, Colley, 331, 332, 348, 402
Cicero, 377
Clanbrassil, Lady Alice Moore, Countess of, **231**
Clarendon, Edward Hyde, Earl of, **232**, 300, 311, 328, 344
Clement VII, 331
Clement X, 340
Cleveland, Barbara Villiers, Duchess of, **233**, 315–16, 368–9
Cleveland, John, 393
Colepeper, Thomas. *See* Thoresby, Thomas Colepeper, Baron Colepeper of
Collinet, Jean-Pierre, 349
Cominges, Gaston Jean Baptiste, comte de, 344
Congreve, William, 313, 325–6, 332, 369, 371
Coote, Lady Jane and Lady Dorothy, 35, **234**
Corey, Katherine, 376
Corneille, Pierre, 372, 381
Corneille, Thomas, 381
Cotterell, Sir Charles, 352
Cotton, Charles, 310
Covent Garden, 370, 372
Coventry, Sir William, 333
Cowley, Abraham, **234**, 319, 326, 355, 356, 357, 380, 382, 399
Coxe, Thomas, 361
Crabbe, George, 348
Crashaw, Richard, 311
Crocker, S.F., 359, 363, 365
Cromwell, Oliver, 299, 382
Crowne, John, xiv, **235**, 352, 363, 381

Crum, Margaret, 357
Cullen, Elizabeth Trentham, Viscountess, 59, **237**
Cully, Sir Nicholas, 341
Curll, E., 302, 317, 326, 378–9

Dalton, Charles, 405
Danby, Thomas Osborne, Earl of, 364, 372
Daniel, Samuel, 355
Davenant, Charles, 399, 400, 401
Davenant, Dame Mary, 399
Davenant, Sir William, 319, 353, 363, 370, 372, 399
Davies, John, 352
Davies, Paul C., 327, 347, 358
Dayrell, Sir Francis, **237**, 342
Dearmer, Percy, 315
Defoe, Daniel, 321, 327, 361, 363, 364, 367, 383, 384, 406
de Hesse, Charlotte, 249
Denham, Sir John, 380
Dennis, John, 365, 382
Derbyshire, 314
Derwentwater, Edward Radclyffe, 2nd Earl of, 306
Descartes, René, 409
Dirty Lane, 368
Donne, John, 303, 353, 356, 374, 404
Dorset, Charles Sackville, Earl of Middlesex and, **226**, 317, 331, 339, 346, 382–3, 402
Dorset Garden Theatre, 352, 369, 370, 372, 393, 399
Dorset Stairs, 369
Dostoyevsky, Fyodor Mikhaylovich, 357
Douai, 316
Dover, 299, 371
Downes, John, 370, 371, 376, 387, 388, 393, 399
Downs, Captain, 395, 396
Doyle, Charles C., 326
Drury Lane, 368, 370, 372, 374
Dryden, John, **237**, 302, 303, 312, 313, 320, 323, 324, 325, 326, 334, 336, 337, 338, 343, 347, 348, 350, 352, 363, 366, 372, 375, 376, 379–84, 386, 390, 392, 396, 397, 398, 399, 400, 402, 406, 408–9
Dunton, John, 364, 404
Durfey, Thomas, 407, 409

Eachard, John, 362
East Suffolk, 340
Eaton, Sir John, 307–8
Edinburgh, 364
Edwards, A.S.G., 316
Eldredge, Roy, 386
Eliot, T.S., 375
Elizabeth, Princess, 301, 302
Ellis, Clement, 342
Ellis, Frank H., 384
Empson, William, 363
Emslie, Macdonald, 394
Epsom, 396
Esquiline Hills, 391
Este, Maria Beatrice d'. *See* Mary of Modena
Estremadura, Portugal, 311
Etherege, Sir George, **238**, 307, 320, 325, 327, 342, 352, 375, 376, 380, 383, 393, 396
Eudoxia, Licinia, 388
Euripides, 338
Evelyn, John, 312, 336, 339, 344
Everett, Barbara, 306, 377
Exeter, 301

Fabricant, Carole, 302, 328, 406
Fairfax, Thomas, 3rd Baron, 299
Falkland, Lucius Cary, 2nd Viscount, 58, **239**
Falmouth, 301
Falmouth, Mary Bagot, Countess of, 41, **239**
Fane, Sir Francis, 299, 370, 389
Fanshawe, Sir Richard, 364
Farley-Hills, David, 326, 332, 356, 357, 383, 384, 409
Felton, Lady Betty, 406
Fenton, Elijah, 337
Fields, W.C., 393
Fisher, Nicholas, 314
Flanders, 353
Flatman, Thomas, **240**, 344
Fleet Street, 369
Fletcher, John, 366, 370, 382, 386, 388, 389, 390, 391, 393, 397
Florence, 331
Florio, John, 360

Forster, E.M., 356
Foster, **240**, 347
Fox, 35, **240**
France, 301, 333, 340, 378
Fraser, Sir Alexander, **240**, 300, 378, 392
Fraser, Carey, **241**, 399
Freke, John, 298
Fribble, Dorothy, 341
Friedman, Albert B., 390
Frye, Northrop, 358

Galenus, Claudius, 379
Garth, Samuel, 320
Gascoigne, George, 350
Gaul, 389
Germanicus, 389
Germany, 389
Ghent, 300
Gibbon, Edward, 385
Ginsburg, Mirra, 357
Glanvill, John, 320
Glanvill, Joseph, 404
Gloucester, Henry, Duke of, 301, 302
Godolphin, Sidney, 101, **241**
Goethe, Johann Wolfgang von, 360–61
Goodman, Cardell, 387
Goodwin, Timothy, 387
Gramont, Philibert de Gramont, comte de, **242**, 385
Gray, Thomas, 312
Greene, Graham, 388
Greenwich, 299
Gregg, W.W., xv
Grene, David, 391
Gresham College, 312
Griffin, Dustin, 332, 346, 361, 362, 364, 373, 376
Guarini, Giovanni Battista, 364
Gwyn, Nell, **243**, 329, 367, 397

Hague, The, 392
Haines, Joseph, 85, **244**
Haley, K.H.D., 328
Halifax, Sir George Savile, Marquis of, 329
Ham, Roswell G., 407
Hamilton, Antony, xiii, xiv, 369, 377, 385, 392, 406
Hammond, Paul, 337, 363
Harris, Brice, 317, 339
Harris, Henry, **245**, 340
Hart, Charles, **246**, 367
Hart, James, 320
Hart, Richard, 387
Harvey, William, 302
Hastings, Theophilus. *See* Huntingdon, Theophilus Hastings, Earl of
Häublein, Ernest, 353
Haven, C., 352
Haward, Sir William, 337, 395
Hayman, John, 376
Hayward, John, 305, 306, 319
Head, Richard, 341
Hearne, Thomas, 397–8, 401
Henrietta Anne, Princess. *See* Orléans, Henrietta Anne, Duchess of
Henrietta Maria, Queen Consort of Charles I, 300–302
Henry VIII, 331, 385
Herbert, George, 309
Herbert of Cherbury, Edward Herbert, Lord, 319
Herrick, Robert, 321
Herringman, Henry, 387
Hervey, Lady Elizabeth, 376
High Holborn, 368
Hill, G. Birkbeck, 398
Hindmarsh, J., 306
Hobbes, Thomas, 338, 360, 362–4, 398, 399
Hogarth, William, 348
Hohenheim, Philippus Aureolus Theophrastus Bombastus von, 302
Hollworthy, widow, 374
Homer, 374
Hood, Paul, 300
Hooke, Robert, 312
Hope Theatre, 344
Hopkins, John, 315, 316–17, 344, 385, 398
Horace, 348, 349, 350, 364, 379–81, 383–4, 396
Howard, Anne, 340
Howard, Dorothy, 340
Howard, Edward, **246**, 384, 401, 402, 408
Howard, Lady Elizabeth, **247**, 334, 340, 406
Howard, Henry. *See* Norfolk, Henry Howard, Earl of

Howard, Sir Robert, **248**, 313, 341, 342, 343, 347, 352, 392
Howard, Thomas. *See* Berkshire, Thomas Howard, Earl of
Howard, William, 340
Huns, 388
Huntingdon, Theophilus Hastings, Earl of, 330, 333
Hutton, Ronald, 404
Hyde, Ann. *See* York, Anne Hyde, Duchess of
Hyde, Edward. *See* Clarendon, Edward Hyde, Earl of

Ingelo, Nathaniel, 361, 362
Ireland, 333, 334
Italy, 331, 378

Jacob, Giles, 389
James, son of Zebedee, 331
James II. *See* York, James, Duke of
Jenkins, William, 340
Jennings, Frances, 406
Jennings, Sarah, 369
Jermyn, Henry, **249**, 368, 369, 406
Johnson, Samuel, 359, 379–80, 398, 402–3, 408, 409
Jonson, Ben, 303, 317, 319, 341, 371, 376, 377, 379, 380, 381, 382, 394
Jordan, Robert, 342
Jusserand, J.J., 344

Kent, 299
Kern, Edith, 357
Kéroualle, Louise-Renée de. *See* Portsmouth, Louise de Kéroualle, Duchess of
Kickum, 352
Kijkduin, 335
Killigrew, Thomas, xix, **249**, 340
King, Bishop Henry, 319, 357
Kirke, Mall, **250**, 376, 377
Kirke, Percy, 376
Knight, Charles A., 363
Knight, Jos., 387
Knight, Mary, 102, **250**
Kynaston, Edward, 387

Laertius, Diogenes, 362
Langbaine, Gerard, 336, 381, 397
Lansdowne, George Granville, Lord, 310
La Rochefoucauld, François de, 375
Lattimore, Richmond, 321, 374
Lauderdale, John Maitland, 2nd Earl of, **351**, 312, 372, 392
Lawner, Lynne, 331
Leach, William, 346
Lee, Nathaniel, **252**, 306, 336, 337, 382, 388
Legouis, Pierre, 364
Leneve, Peter, 374
Leo I, 385
Leo X, 385
Lewis, Charlton T., 347
Libya, 388
Lille, 316
Lilly, William, 376
Lincoln College, 300
Lincoln's Inn Fields, 336, 351, 368, 399
Lisbon, 311
Livy, 389
Locke, John, 298, 299
Locke, Matthew, 334
London, 299, 301, 302, 327, 332, 335, 337, 339, 340, 341, 342, 346, 352, 354, 360, 364, 376, 377, 393
Long, Jane, 102, **253**
Lord, George deF., 376
Lorraine, 316
Louis XIV, 301, 316, 329, 336, 340, 350, 372, 381, 404
Louvre, 301
Love, Harold, 330, 341, 348, 349, 351, 358, 384, 404
Lovelace, Richard, 375, 393
Lowestoft, 405
Lucian, 348
Lucilius, 380, 381, 383
Lucina, 390
Lucretia, 388, 389
Lucretius, 337, 338, 361, 373, 374
Ludgate, 372
Lutenor's Lane, 368
Luther, Martin, 385
Lyons, Patrick, 406

Maastricht, 335, 336, 350
Macdonald, Hugh, 408
Machiavelli, Niccolò, 398

Mackie, J.L., 395
Madan, Falconer, 299, 300
Maitland, John. *See* Lauderdale, John Maitland, 2nd Earl of
Malet, Elizabeth. *See* Rochester, Elizabeth Malet, Countess of
Malherbe, François de, 309, 311
Manning, Gillian, 324, 364, 402
Marlowe, Christopher, 319, 325, 327, 376
Marshall, Rebecca, 387
Martz, Louis L., 328
Marvell, Andrew, 300, 318, 327, 328, 342, 343, 346, 355, 364, 368, 374, 396
Mary, Princess Royal of England and Princess of Orange, 300–302
Mary of Modena (Maria Beatrice d'Este), **255**, 338–9
Maximus, Petronius, 385, 390, 391
Mazarin, Hortense Mancini, Duchess of, **253**, 385
Means, James A., 397
Menander, 360
Meres, Sir Thomas, **254**, 333, 363
Merton College, 298, 300, 317
Messalina Valeria, 332, 391
Milton, John, 301, 322, 347, 352, 355, 360, 361, 368, 379, 403, 404
Miner, Earl, 341
Modena, Laura Martinozzi, Duchess of, **255**
Mohun, Michael, **255**, 370, 371
Molière, 372, 381
Monck, George. *See* Albemarle, George Monck, Duke of
Monmouth, Ann Scott, Duchess of Buccleuch and, 334
Monmouth, James Scott, Duke of, **256**, 335, 336, 377, 392, 405
Montagu, Lady Elizabeth, **258**, 340, 350
Montague, Walter, 318
Montaigne, Michel, seigneur de, 360, 361, 363, 365
Montespan, Françoise-Athenais de Rochechouart, Marquise de, 350
Montpellier, University of, 378, 392
Moore, John F., 360
More, Henry, 404
Morris, Betty, **259**, 384
Morris, Brian, 393
Moseley, Mother, 58, **259**
Moskovit, Leonard A., 381, 382, 383
Mountagu, Edward. *See* Sandwich, Edward Mountagu, Earl of
Mulgrave, John Sheffield, Earl of, **259**, 334, 375, 376–7, 381, 400, 402, 404, 405, 408–9
Murphy, John A., 322

Naylour, Mrs Samuel, 317
Needham, Francis, 299, 303, 322
Netherlands, 336
Nokes, James, **259**, 342, 348, 371, 402
Norfolk, Henry Howard, Earl of, 334
Northumberland, Elizabeth Wriothesley, Countess of. *See* Montagu, Lady Elizabeth
Novak, Maximillian E., xvii
Nussbaum, Felicity, 320

Ober, William B., 326
Octavius, Gaius (Octavian). *See* Augustus
Ogg, David, 316, 333
Oldham, John, xiv, 318, 327, 350, 360, 368, 379–80, 400
O'Neill, John H., 326, 327
Orléans, Princess Henrietta Anne, Duchess of, 301, 302, 350, 371
Orléans, Philippe, Duc d', 301
Orrery, Roger Boyle, Earl of, **260**, 351, 352
Osborne, Thomas. *See* Danby, Thomas Osborne, Earl of
Ostrogoths, 388
Otway, Thomas, **261**, 371, 373, 382, 406–7
Ovid, 305, 312, 314, 320, 322, 324–5, 326, 327, 328, 347, 375, 390, 406
Oxford, 301, 328, 399
Oxfordshire, 300

Palmer, Roger. *See* Castlemaine, Roger Palmer, Earl of
Paracelsus, 302
Paris, 400
Parker, Samuel, **262**, 341, 342, 343
Parkinson, R.N., 355
Parsons, Robert, xiv, 321, 373
Pasch, Thomas K., 330

Passerat, Jean, 402
Patrick, Simon, 361, 362
Patterson, John D., 331, 335
Paulson, Kristoffer F., 331, 332, 362
Paulson, Ronald, 328
Pepys, Samuel, 300, 301, 302, 312, 313, 329, 330, 331, 333, 341, 344, 352, 364, 367, 370, 371, 374, 376, 405
Percy, Elizabeth, Countess of, 350
Percy, Thomas, 398
Petronius, 318–19, 326, 348
Phillips, Ambrose, 298
Pinto, Vivian de S., 305, 306, 308, 323, 328, 356, 367, 368, 375, 394
Plato, 348, 362
Plautus, 379
Plutarch, 407
Poley, Judith, 369
Pompilius, Numa, 389
Pope, Alexander, 303, 312, 325, 326, 341, 346, 347, 348, 350, 353, 360, 367, 370, 380, 382, 393, 397, 400, 402, 403, 406, 409
Pordage, Samuel, **263**, 336, 337
Porter, George, 102, **264**
Portman, Sir William, 298
Portsmouth, 301, 302, 311
Portsmouth, Louise Renée de Penancoët de Kéroualle, Duchess of, **264**, 328, 378, 392
Portugal, 311
Pound, Ezra, xiv, 348, 367, 375
Powell, L.F., 398
Praz, Mario, 305
Price, Goditha, xiv
Price, Henrietta Maria, **265**, 314
Privy Garden, 340
Procopius, 388
Pseudo-St Evremond, 381, 382

Quaintance, Richard E., 325–6
Quarles, Francis, 304, 305, 320, 356

Racine, Jean, 376
Radcliffe, Alexander, **265**, 322
Radclyffe, Edward. *See* Derwentwater, Edward Radclyffe, 2nd Earl of
Raimondi, Marcantonio, 331, 351
Raleigh, Walter, 350
Randolph, Thomas, 375, 394
Ravenna, 391
Rawlins, Giles, 340
Rawson, Claude, 338, 374
Reggio, Pietro, 398
Regnier, Mathurin, 348
Reynel, Carew, 329
Rhine, River, 350, 352
Ricks, Christopher, xvii, 344
Righter, Anne, 304, 355
Robertson, John M., 347
Robertson, William, 338
Robinson, Henry W., 405
Robinson, K.E., 363
Rochester, Elizabeth Malet, Countess of, 305, 306, 313, 354
Rochester, Henry Wilmot, 1st Earl of, **266**, 300, 344
Romano, Giulio, 331, 351
Rome, 305, 331, 385, 389, 391
Romulus, 389
Romulus Augustus, 388
Ronsard, Pierre de, 335
Root, Robert L., 343
Rosidore, Count, xxi, 336
Rowzee, Lodwick, 342, 343
Ruyter, Michael de, 335
Rymer, Thomas, 354, 372

Sackville, Charles. *See* Dorset, Charles Sackville, Earl of Middlesex and
St Albans, Henry Jermyn, Earl of, **267**, 340
St André, **268**, 372
St James's Park, 330–31, 349
Salisbury Court, 369, 372
Salles des Machines, 370
Sanderson, Bridget Tyrrell, Lady, 32, **268**
Sandwich, Edward Mountagu, Earl of, 330
Sandys, Lady Lucy Hamilton, **268**, 341
Santiago de Compostela, 331
Sartre, Jean-Paul, 362
Saunders, Fr., 387
Saunders, Richard, 376
Savile, Sir George. *See* Halifax, Sir George Savile, Marquis of
Savile, Henry, **269**, 329, 340, 342, 408
Schomberg, Frederick Herman, 333
Scott, Ann. *See* Monmouth, Ann Scott, Duchess of Buccleuch and

Scott, James. *See* Monmouth, James Scott, Duke of
Scott, Walter, 352
Scrope, Sir Carr, **269**, 320, 354, 361, 375, 384, 395, 396–7, 400, 401–2, 404–5, 408
Scudéry, Madeleine de, 352
Sedley, Sir Charles, **270**, 312, 322, 349, 350, 377, 383
Selden, Raman, 395
Seneca, Lucius Annaeus, 337–8
Sennett, Mack, 348
Settle, Elkanah, **271**, 334, 336, 352, 382, 407
Shadwell, Thomas, **272**, 323, 343–4, 349–50, 363, 365, 370, 371, 372, 380, 382, 383, 401, 402
Shaftesbury, Anthony Ashley Cooper, 1st Earl of, 333, 407
Shaftesbury, Anthony Ashley Cooper, 3rd Earl of, 347
Shakespeare, William, 320, 326, 332, 343, 348, 372, 379, 382, 383, 386, 389, 399, 407
Shawcross, John T., 365
Sheehan, David, 347
Sheffield, John. *See* Mulgrave, John Sheffield, Earl of
Sheldon, Sir Edward, 340
Sheldon, Frances, 340
Sheldon, Gilbert, Archbishop of Canterbury, **273**, 311, 365
Sheldonian Theatre, 299
Shelton, Thomas, 402
Sheppard, Sir Fleetwood, **274**, 310, 327, 339
Shirley, James, 371
Short, Charles, 347
Shrewsbury, Anne Maria Brudenell, Countess of, **275**, 340
Shrewsbury, Francis Talbot, 11th Earl of, 340
Sidney, Sir Philip, 312–13, 352, 354
Silverman, Stuart, 375
Simpson, Claude M., 307, 309, 311, 320, 326, 333, 339, 356, 368, 401, 403
Sitter, John E., 344, 348
Smith, Thomas, 361
Smith, William, 393
Smithfield, 405
Socrates, 311
Solebay, 335, 405
Sophocles, 391
Souches, Ludwig Ratuit von, 352
South, Robert, 298
Southborough, 342
Southesk, Lady Anne Hamilton, Countess of, **275**
Southwark, 344
Southwold Bay, 335
Spanish Netherlands, 316
Spelsbury, 300
Spence, Joseph, 382, 393
Spenser, Edmund, 327
Spragge, Sir Edward, 374
Staggins, Nicholas, 320
Stanhope, Philip. *See* Chesterfield, Philip Stanhope, 2nd Earl of
Starkey's, 374
Steinman, George, 314
Stephen College, 305
Sterne, Laurence, xvi, 325, 326, 336, 356
Sternhold, Thomas, 315, 316–17, 344, 385, 398
Stillingfleet, Edward, 359, 360, 362, 375
Stinchcomb Hill, 299
Stone Gallery, 340
Subura, 391
Suckling, Sir John, **276**, 319, 361, 396
Suffolk, 335
Suffolk, Barbara Villiers, Countess of, **277**
Summers, Montague, 371, 407
Sunderland, Robert Spencer, 2nd Earl of, 392
Surrey, 331
Sutton, Sir Edward, **277**, 331
Swift, Jonathan, 336, 340, 343, 347, 358, 364, 365, 380, 397, 401

Tacitus, Cornelius, 389
Talbot, Francis. *See* Shrewsbury, Francis Talbot, 11th Earl of
Tanselle, G. Thomas, xv
Tarquinius, Sextus, 388, 389
Tarquinius Superbus, 388
Tasso, Torquato, 375
Tate, Nahum, 389
Teddeman, Sir Thomas, 374
Temple, Philippa, 340
Temple, Sir William, 366

Tennyson, Alfred, 357
Thacker, Godfrey, 330, 333
Thames, River, 331
Theatre Royal, 347, 372
Theodosius the Great, 385, 388, 391
Thompson, Paul V., 340
Thomson, James, 402
Thoresby, Thomas Colepeper, Baron Colepeper of, 400–401
Thormählen, Marianne, 344, 355, 361
Thorpe, James, 302
Thorpe, Peter, 358
Tiberius, 389, 391
Tibullus, Albius, 326, 327
Tilley, Morris P., 315, 318, 332, 342, 365, 366, 376, 389
Tillotson, Geoffrey, 399
Tolhuys, 350
Tonson, Jacob, 306, 406
Tower Hill, 377
Treglown, Jeremy, 306, 307, 309, 311, 318, 320, 321, 322, 326, 339, 342, 344, 349, 350, 351, 352, 353, 354, 355, 361, 363, 377, 392, 394, 395, 398, 399
Trickett, Rachel, 344
Trotter, David, 342, 344, 361
Troy, 338, 389
Tuileries, 370
Tunbridge Wells, 341–4
Turenne, Henri de la Tour d'Auvergne, Vicomte de, 335, 352, 405

Uphill, Susanna, 397
Utrecht, 350

Valentinianus, Flavius Placidus, 385–91
Vallière, Louise-Françoise de la, 350
Venice, 331
Verney, John, 359, 401–2
Versailles, 316
Vieth, David M., 303, 305, 306, 307, 308, 314, 315, 317, 332, 341, 346, 358, 363, 366, 373, 375, 381, 382, 384, 394, 396, 399, 400, 401, 402, 405, 407, 409
Villiers, Barbara. *See* Cleveland, Barbara Villiers, Duchess of
Villiers, Barbara. *See* Suffolk, Barbara Villiers, Countess of
Villiers, George. *See* Buckingham, George Villiers, Duke of
Viminal Hills, 391
Virgil, 326, 392

Wadham College, 300, 337
Wagstaffe, John, 362
Walker, Keith, 305, 306, 307, 308, 314, 319
Waller, Edmund, 278, 326, 331, 341, 364, 375
Warren, Robert Penn, 373
Watts, Isaac, 356
Webb, John, 370
Webster, John, 370
Weinbrot, Howard, 348
West, David, 325
Whetstone's Park, 368
Whitehall Palace, 301, 328, 377
Whitehall, Robert, 298–9, 300
Wilcoxon, Reba, 357, 363, 400
William of Orange, 350
Williams, Aubrey, 328
Williams, Harold, 365
Willis, Susan, 279, 400–401
Wilmot, Henry. *See* Rochester, Henry Wilmot, 1st Earl of
Wilson, John H., 309–10, 340, 381, 384, 389, 395, 397, 400
Windsor Castle, 336
Wing, Donald, 360, 362, 394, 408
Winn, James A., 380, 383, 408
Wintershall, William, 387
Wolseley, Robert, 387, 391
Wood, Anthony à, 298, 300, 350, 359, 403
Woodstock, 401
Worcester, 299
Wordsworth, William, 407
Wowern, Johann von, 402
Wren, Sir Christopher, 370
Wriothesley, Elizabeth. *See* Montagu, Lady Elizabeth
Wyatt, Sir Thomas, 325
Wycherley, William, 280, 331, 365, 374, 380, 382

Yarmouth, 336
Yarrow, Joseph, 311
York, Anne Hyde, Duchess of, 340, 341
York, James, Duke of, 301, 329, 333, 335, 336, 338, 339, 340, 341, 372, 377, 392

Zeeland, 336
Zimansky, Curt A., 335
Zimmerman, Hans-Joachim, 378